TAD WILLIAMS
HAS ALSO WRITTEN

Tailchaser's Song

MEMORY, SORROW AND THORN
The Dragonbone Chair (Book One)

Stone
OF FAREWELL

The Nornfells

RIMMERSGARD

YIQANUC

The FROSTMARCH

The Wealdhelm

HERNYSTIR

ALDHEORTE

Hayholt (Asu'a)

ERKYNLAND

HIGH THRITHING

N

MEADOW THRITHING

Warinsten

PERDRUIN

LAKE THRITHING

NABBAN

W   E

S

Osten Ard

The WRAN

STONE
OF FAREWELL

TAD WILLIAMS

BOOK TWO OF
Memory, Sorrow and Thorn

DAW BOOKS, INC.
DONALD A. WOLLHEIM, PUBLISHER

New York

DAW Book Collectors No. 824.

Quality Printing and Binding by:
R.R. Donnelley & Sons Company
1009 Sloan Street
Crawfordsville, IN 47933 U.S.A.

ISBN 0-88677-435-7

This series is dedicated to my mother, Barbara Jean Evans, who taught to me a deep affection for Toad Hall, the Hundred Aker Woods, the Shire, and many other hidden places and countries beyond the fields we know. She also induced in me a lifelong desire to make my own discoveries, and to share them with others. I wish to share these books with her.

Author's Note

. . . Of all the many changing things
In dreary dancing past us whirled,
To the cracked tune that Chronos sings,
Words alone are certain good.
Where are now the warring kings,
Word be-mockers?—By the Rood,
Where are now the warring kings?
An idle word is now their glory,
By the stammering schoolboy said,
Reading some entangled story:
The kings of the old time are dead;
The wandering earth herself may be
Only a sudden flaming word,
In clanging space a moment heard,
Troubling the endless reverie.

—WILLIAM BUTLER YEATS
  (from *The Song of the Happy Shepherd*)

I am indebted to Eva Cumming, Nancy Deming-Williams, Paul Hudspeth, Peter Stampfel, and Doug Werner, who all had a hand in the cultivation of this book. Their insightful comments and suggestions have taken root—in some instances, putting forth rather surprising blossoms. Also, and as usual, special thanks go to my brave editors, Betsy Wollheim and Sheila Gilbert, who have labored mightily through both storm and drought.

(By the way, all the above mentioned are just the kind of folk I want at my side if I'm ever ambushed by Norns. This might be construed as a somewhat dubious honor, but 'tis mine own to bestow.)

NOTE: There is a cast of characters, a glossary of terms, and a guide to pronunciation at the back of this volume.

Synopsis of
The Dragonbone Chair

For eons the Hayholt belonged to the immortal Sithi, but they had fled the great castle before the onslaught of Mankind. Men have long ruled this greatest of strongholds, and the rest of Osten Ard as well. *Prester John*, High King of all the nations of men, is its most recent master; after an early life of triumph and glory, he has presided over decades of peace from his skeletal throne, the Dragonbone Chair.

Simon, an awkward fourteen year old, is one of the Hayholt's scullions. His parents are dead, his only real family the chamber maids and their stern mistress, *Rachel the Dragon*. When Simon can escape his kitchen-work he steals away to the cluttered chambers of *Doctor Morgenes*, the castle's eccentric scholar. When the old man invites Simon to be his apprentice, the youth is overjoyed—until he discovers that Morgenes prefers teaching reading and writing to magic.

Soon ancient King John will die, so *Elias*, the older of his two sons, prepares to take the throne. *Josua*, Elias' somber brother, nicknamed Lackhand because of a disfiguring wound, argues harshly with the king-to-be about *Pryrates*, the ill-reputed priest who is one of Elias' closest advisers. The brothers' feud is a cloud of foreboding over castle and country.

Elias' reign as king starts well, but a drought comes and plague strikes several of the nations of Osten Ard. Soon outlaws roam the roads and people begin to vanish from isolated villages. The order of things is breaking down, and the king's subjects are losing confidence in his rule, but nothing seems to bother the monarch or his friends. As rumblings of discontent begin to be heard throughout the kingdom, Elias' brother Josua disappears—to plot rebellion, some say.

Elias' misrule upsets many, including *Duke Isgrimnur* of Rimmersgard and *Count Eolair*, an emissary from the western country of Hernystir. Even King Elias' own daughter *Miriamele* is uneasy, especially about the scarlet-robed Pryrates, her father's trusted adviser.

Meanwhile Simon is muddling along as Morgenes' helper. The two become fast friends despite Simon's mooncalf nature and the doctor's refusal to teach him anything resembling magic. During one of his meanderings through the secret byways of the labyrinthine Hayholt, Simon discovers a secret passage and is almost captured there by Pryrates. Eluding the priest, he enters a hidden underground chamber and finds Josua, who is being held captive for use in some terrible ritual planned by Pryrates. Simon fetches Doctor Morgenes and the two of them free Josua and take him to the doctor's chambers, where Josua is sent to freedom down a tunnel that leads beneath the ancient castle. Then, as Morgenes is sending off messenger birds bearing news of what has happened to mysterious friends, Pryrates and the king's guard come to arrest the doctor and Simon. Morgenes is killed fighting Pryrates, but his sacrifice allows Simon to escape into the tunnel.

Half-maddened, Simon makes his way through the midnight corridors beneath the castle, which contain the ruins of the old Sithi palace. He surfaces in the graveyard beyond the town wall, then is lured by the light of a bonfire. He witnesses a weird scene: Pryrates and King Elias engaged in a ritual with black-robed, white-faced creatures. The pale things give Elias a strange gray sword of disturbing power, named *Sorrow*. Simon flees.

Life in the wilderness on the edge of the great forest Aldheorte is miserable, and weeks later Simon is nearly dead from hunger and exhaustion, but still far away from his destination, Josua's northern keep at Naglimund. Going to a forest cot to beg, he finds a strange being caught in a trap—one of the Sithi, a race thought to be mythical, or at least long-vanished. The cotsman returns, but before he can kill the helpless Sitha, Simon strikes him down. The Sitha, once freed, stops only long enough to fire a white arrow at Simon, then disappears. A new voice tells Simon to take the white arrow, that it is a Sithi gift.

The dwarfish newcomer is a troll named *Binabik*, who rides a great gray wolf. He tells Simon he was only passing by, but now he will accompany the boy to Naglimund. Simon and Binabik endure many adventures and strange events on the way to Naglimund: they come to realize that they have fallen afoul of a threat greater than merely a king and his counselor deprived of their prisoner. At last, when they find themselves pursued by unearthly white hounds who wear the brand of Stormspike, a mountain of evil reputation in the far north, they are forced to head for the shelter of *Geloë*'s forest house, taking with them a pair of travelers they have rescued from the hounds. Geloë, a blunt-spoken forest woman with a reputation as a witch, confers with them and agrees that somehow the ancient Norns, embittered relatives of the Sithi, have become embroiled in the fate of Prester John's kingdom.

Pursuers human and otherwise threaten them on their journey to Naglimund. After Binabik is shot with an arrow, Simon and one of the rescued travelers, a servant girl, must struggle on through the forest. They are attacked by a shaggy giant and saved only by the appearance of Josua's hunting party.

The prince brings them to Naglimund, where Binabik's wounds are cared for, and where it is confirmed that Simon has stumbled into a terrifying swirl of events. Elias is coming soon to besiege Josua's castle. Simon's serving-girl companion was Princess Miriamele traveling in disguise, fleeing her father, whom she fears has gone mad under Pryrates' influence. From all over the north and elsewhere, frightened people are flocking to Naglimund and Josua, their last protection against a mad king.

Then, as the prince and others discuss the coming battle, a strange old Rimmersman named *Jarnauga* appears in the council's meeting hall. He is a member of the *League of the Scroll*, a circle of scholars and initiates of which Morgenes and Binabik's master were both part, and he brings more grim news. Their enemy, he says, is not just Elias: the king is receiving aid from *Ineluki the Storm King*, who had once been a prince of the Sithi—but who has been dead for five centuries, and whose bodiless spirit now rules the Norns of Stormspike Mountain, pale relatives of the banished Sithi.

It was the terrible magic of the gray sword Sorrow that caused Ineluki's death—that, and mankind's attack on the Sithi. The League of the Scroll believes that Sorrow has been given to Elias as the first step in some incomprehensible plan of revenge, a plan that will bring the earth beneath the heel of the undead Storm King. The only hope comes from a prophetic poem that seems to suggest that "three swords" might help turn back Ineluki's powerful magic.

One of the swords is the Storm King's Sorrow, already in the hands of their enemy, King Elias. Another is the Rimmersgard blade *Minneyar*, which was also once at the Hayholt, but whose whereabouts are now unknown. The third is *Thorn*, black sword of King John's greatest knight, *Sir Camaris*. Jarnauga and others think they have traced it to a location in the frozen north. On this slim hope, Josua sends Binabik, Simon, and several soldiers off in search of Thorn, even as Naglimund prepares for siege.

Others are affected by the growing crisis. Princess Miriamele, frustrated by her uncle Josua's attempts to protect her, escapes Naglimund in disguise, accompanied by the mysterious monk *Cadrach*. She hopes to make her way to southern Nabban and plead with her relatives there to aid Josua. Old Duke Isgrimnur, at Josua's urging, disguises his own very recognizable features and follows after to rescue her. *Tiamak*, a swamp-dweller Wrannaman scholar, receives a strange message from his old mentor Morgenes that tells of bad times coming and hints that Tiamak has a part to play. *Maegwin*, daughter of the king of Hernystir, watches helplessly as her own family and country are drawn into a whirlpool of war by the treachery of High King Elias.

Simon and Binabik and their company are ambushed by *Ingen Jegger*, huntsman of Stormspike, and his servants. They are saved only by the reappearance of the Sitha *Jiriki*, whom Simon had saved from the cotsman's trap. When he learns of their quest, Jiriki decides to accompany them to Urmsheim mountain, legendary abode of one of the great dragons, in search of Thorn.

By the time Simon and the others reach the mountain, King Elias has brought his besieging army to Josua's castle at Naglimund, and though the first attacks are repulsed, the defenders suffer great losses. At last Elias' forces seem to retreat and give up the siege, but before the stronghold's inhabitants can celebrate, a weird storm appears on the northern horizon, bearing down on Naglimund. The storm is the cloak under which Ineluki's own horrifying army of Norns and giants travels, and when the *Red Hand*, the Storm King's chief servants, throw down Naglimund's gates, a terrible slaughter begins. Josua and a few others manage to flee the ruin of the castle. Before escaping into the great forest, Prince Josua curses Elias for his conscienceless bargain with the Storm King and swears that he will take their father's crown back.

Simon and his companions climb Urmsheim, coming through great dangers to discover the Uduntree, a titanic frozen waterfall. There they find Thorn in a tomblike cave. Before they can take the sword and make their escape, Ingen Jegger appears once more and attacks with his troop of soldiers. The battle awakens *Igjarjuk*, the white dragon, who has been slumbering for years beneath the ice. Many on both sides are killed. Simon alone is left standing, trapped on the edge of a cliff; as the ice-worm bears down upon him, he lifts Thorn and swings it. The dragon's scalding black blood spurts over him as he is struck senseless.

Simon awakens in a cave on the troll mountain of Yiqanuc. Jiriki and *Haestan*, an Erkynlandish soldier, nurse him to health. Thorn has been rescued from Urmsheim, but Binabik is being held prisoner by his own people, along with *Sludig* the Rimmersman, under sentence of death. Simon himself has been scarred by the dragon's blood and a wide swath of his hair has turned white. Jiriki names him "Snowlock" and tells Simon that, for good or for evil, he has been irrevocably marked.

Foreword

The wind sawed across the empty battlements, yowling like a thousand condemned souls crying for mercy. Brother Hengfisk, despite the bitter cold that had sucked the air from his once-strong lungs and withered and peeled the skin of his face and hands, took a certain grim pleasure in the sound.

Yes, that is what they will all sound like, all the sinful multitude who scoffed at the message of Mother Church—including, unfortunately, the less rigorous of his Hoderundian brothers. *How they will cry out before God's just wrath, begging for mercy, when it is far, far too late. . . .*

He caught his knee a wicked blow on a stone lying tumbled from a wall, and pitched forward into the snow with a crack-lipped squeal. The monk sat whimpering for a moment, but the painful bite of tears freezing on his cheek forced him back onto his feet. He hobbled forward once more.

The main road that climbed through Naglimund-town toward the castle was full of drifting snow. The houses and shops on either side had nearly disappeared beneath a smothering blanket of deadly white, but even those buildings not yet covered were as deserted as the shells of long-dead animals. There was nothing on the road but Hengfisk and the snow.

As the wind changed direction, the whistling of the fluted battlements at the top of the hill rose in pitch. The monk squinted his bulging eyes up at the walls, then lowered his head. He trudged on through the gray afternoon, the crunch of his footsteps a near-silent drumbeat accompanying the skirling wind.

It is no wonder the townspeople have fled to the keep, he thought, shivering. All around him gaped the black idiot-mouths of roofs and walls staved in by the weight of snow. But inside the castle, under the protection of stone and great timbers, there they must be safe. Fires would be burning, and red, cheerful faces—sinners' faces, he reminded himself scornfully: damned, heedless sinners' faces—would gather around him and marvel that he had walked all this way through the freakish storm.

It is Yuven-month, is it not? Had his memory suffered so, that he could not remember the month?

But of course it was. Two full moons ago it had been spring—a little cold, perhaps, but that was nothing to a Rimmersman like Hengfisk, reared in the chill of the north. No, that was the freakish thing, of course, that it should be so deadly cold, the ice and snow flying, in Yuven—the first month of summer.

Hadn't Brother Langrian refused to leave the abbey, and after all Hengfisk had done to nurse him back to health? *"It's more than foul weather, Brother,"* Langrian had said. *"It's a curse on God's entire creation. It's the Day of Weighing-Out come in our lifetimes."*

Ah, that was well enough for Langrian. If he wanted to stay in the burned wrack of Saint Hoderund's abbey, eating berries and such from the forest— and how much fruit would there be anyway, in such unseasonable cold? —then he could do as he pleased. Brother Hengfisk was no fool. Naglimund was the place to go. Old Bishop Anodis would welcome Hengfisk. The bishop would admire the monk's clever eye for what he had seen, the stories that Hengfisk could tell of what had happened at the abbey, the unseasonable weather. The Naglimunders would welcome him in, feed him, ask him questions, let him sit before their warm fire. . . .

But they must know about the cold, mustn't they? Hengfisk thought dully as he pulled his ice-crackling robe closer about him. He was in the very shadow of the wall now. The white world he had known for so many days and weeks seemed to have come to an ending, a precipice that vanished into stony nothingness. *That is, they must know about the snow and all. That's why they've all left the town and moved into the keep. It's the damnable, demon-cursed weather that's keeping the sentries off the walls, isn't it? Isn't it!?*

He stood and surveyed with mad interest the pile of snow-mantled rubbish that had been Naglimund's greater gate. The huge pillars and massive stones were charred black beneath the drifts. The hole in the sagging wall stood large enough to hold twenty Hengfisks standing abreast, shoulder to bony, trembling shoulder.

Look how they've let things go. Oh, they'll shriek when their judgment comes, shriek and shriek with never a chance to make amends. Everything has been let go—the gate, the town, the weather.

Somebody must be scourged for such negligence. Doubtless Bishop Anodis had his hands full trying to keep such an unruly flock in line. Hengfisk would be only too happy to help that fine old man minister to such slackers. First, a fire and some warm food. Then, a little monasterial discipline. Things would soon be brought to rights. . . .

Hengfisk stepped carefully through the splintered posts and white-covered stones.

The thing of it was, the monk slowly realized, in a way it was quite . . . beautiful. Beyond the gate, all things were covered in a delicate tracery of ice, like lacy veils of spiderweb. The sinking sun embellished the frosted towers and ice-crusted walls and courtyards with rivulets of pale fire.

The cry of the wind was somewhat less here within the battlements. Hengfisk stood for a long while, abashed by the unexpected quiet. As the weak sun slid behind the walls, the ice darkened. Deep violet shadows welled up in the corners of the courtyard, stretching laterally across the faces of the ruined towers. The wind softened to a feline hiss, and the pop-eyed monk lowered his head in numb recognition.

Deserted. Naglimund was empty, with not a single soul left behind to greet a snow-bewildered wanderer. He had walked leagues through the storm-ridden white waste to reach a place that was as dead and dumb as stone.

But, he wondered suddenly, *if that is so . . . then what are those blue lights that flicker in the windows of the towers?*

And what were these figures who approached him across the shambles of the courtyard, moving as gracefully over the icy stones as blowing thistledown?

His heart raced. At first, as he saw their beautiful, cold faces and pale hair, Hengfisk thought them angels. Then, as he saw the fell light in their black eyes, and their smiles, he turned, stumbling, and tried to run.

The Norns caught him effortlessly, then carried him back with them into the depths of the desolated castle, beneath the shadowed, ice-mantled towers and the ceaselessly flickering lights. And when Naglimund's new masters whispered to him in their secretive, musical voices, his screams for a while overtopped even the howling wind.

PART ONE

Storm's Eye

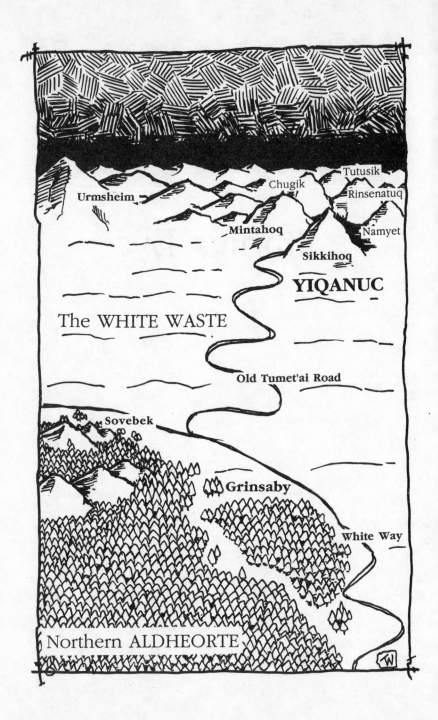

Tutusik

Chugik

Rinsenatuq

Urmsheim

Namyet

Mintahoq

Sikkihoq

YIQANUC

The WHITE WASTE

Old Tumet'ai Road

Sovebek

Grinsaby

White Way

Northern ALDHEORTE

1

The Music of High Places

Even in the cave, where the crackling fire sent gray fingers of smoke up to the hole in the stony roof, and red light played across the wall carvings of twining serpents and tusked, staring-eyed beasts, the cold still gnawed at Simon's bones. As he floated in and out of fevered sleep, through curtained daylight and chill night, he felt as though gray ice grew inside him, stiffening his limbs and filling him with frost. He wondered if he would ever be warm again.

Fleeing the chill Yiqanuc cave and his sickened body, he wandered the Road of Dreams, slipping helplessly from one fantasy to the next. Many times he thought he had returned to the Hayholt, to his castle home as it once had been, but would never be again: a place of sun-warmed lawns, of shadowed nooks and hiding-holes—the greatest house of all, full of bustle and color and music. He walked again in the Hedge Garden, and the wind that sang outside the cave in which he slept sang in his dreams as well, blowing gently through the leaves and shaking the delicate hedges.

In one strange dream he seemed to travel back to Doctor Morgenes' chamber. The doctor's study was now at the top of a tall tower, with clouds swimming past the high-arched windows. The old man hovered fretfully over a large, open book. There was something frightening about the doctor's single-mindedness and silence. Simon did not seem to exist at all for Morgenes; instead, the old man stared intently at the crude drawing of three swords that stretched across the splayed pages.

Simon moved to the windowsill. The wind sighed, though he could feel no breeze. He looked down to the courtyard below. Staring up at him with wide, solemn eyes was a child, a small, dark-haired girl. She lifted a hand in the air, as if in greeting, then suddenly was gone.

The tower and Morgenes' cluttered chamber began to melt away beneath Simon's feet like a receding tide. Last to vanish was the old man himself. Even as he slowly faded, like a shadow in growing light, Morgenes still did not lift his eyes to Simon's; instead, his gnarled hands busily traced the pages of his book, as though restlessly looking for answers. Simon called out to him, but all the world had turned gray and cold, full of swirling mists and the tatters of other dreams. . . .

He awakened, as he had so many times since Urmsheim, to find the cave night-darkened, and to see Haestan and Jiriki bedded down near the rune-scrawled stone wall. The Erkynlander was curled sleeping in his cloak, beard on breastbone. The Sitha stared at something cupped in the palm of his long-fingered hand. Jiriki seemed deeply absorbed. His eyes gleamed faintly, as though whatever he held reflected the last embers of the fire. Simon tried to say something—he was hungry for warmth and voices—but sleep was tugging at him again.

The wind is so loud . . .

It moaned in the mountain passes outside, as it did around the tower tops of the Hayholt . . . as it had across the battlements of Naglimund.

So sad . . . the wind is sad . . .

Soon he was asleep once more. The cave was quiet but for faint breathing and the lonely music of high places.

It was only a hole, but it made a very sufficient prison. It plunged twenty cubits down into the stone heart of Mintahoq Mountain, as wide as two men or four trolls lying head to foot. The sides were polished like the finest sculptor's marble, so that even a spider would have been hard-pressed to find a foothold. The bottom was as dark and cold and damp as any dungeon.

Though the moon ranged above the snowy spires of Mintahoq's neighbors, only a fine spray of moonlight reached down to the bottom of the pit, where it touched but did not illuminate two unmoving shapes. For a long while since moonrise it had been this way: the pale moon-disk— Sedda, as the trolls called her—the only moving thing in all the night world, crossing slowly through the black fields of the sky.

Now something stirred at the mouth of the pit. A small figure leaned over, squinting down into the thick shadows.

"*Binabik . . .*" the crouching shape called at last in the guttural tongue of the troll folk. "*Binabik, do you hear me?*"

If one of the shadows at the bottom moved, it made no sound in doing so. At last the figure at the top of the stone well spoke again.

"*Nine times nine days, Binabik, your spear stood before my cave, and I waited for you.*"

The words were spoken in a ritual chant, but the voice wavered unsteadily, pausing for a moment before continuing. "*I waited and I called out your name in the Place of Echoes. Nothing came back to me but my own voice. Why did you not return and take up your spear again?*"

Still there was no reply.

"Binabik? Why do you not answer? Surely you owe me that, do you not?"

The larger of the two shapes at the bottom of the pit stirred. Pale blue eyes caught a thin stripe of moongleam.

"What is that trollish yammering? It's bad enough you throw a man down a hole who's never done you harm, but must you come shouting your nonsense-talk at him when he's trying to sleep?"

The crouching shape froze for a moment like a startled deer splashed by lantern-glare, then disappeared into the night.

"Good." The Rimmersman Sludig curled himself up once more in his damp cloak. "I do not know what that troll was saying to you, Binabik, but I do not think much of your people, that they come to mock at you—and me, too, although I am not surprised that they hate my kind."

The troll beside him said nothing, only stared at the Rimmersman with dark, troubled eyes. After a while, Sludig rolled over again, shivering, and tried to sleep.

"But Jiriki, you can't go!" Simon was perched at the edge of his pallet, wrapped in his blanket against the insinuating chill. He gritted his teeth against a wave of light-headedness; he had not been off his back often in the five days since he had awakened.

"I must," the Sitha said, eyes downcast as though he could not meet Simon's imploring stare. "I have already sent Sijandi and Ki'ushapo ahead, but it is my own presence that is demanded. I shall not leave for a day or two, Seoman, but that is the utmost length I can put off my duty."

"You have to help me free Binabik!" Simon lifted his feet off the cold stone floor back onto the bed. "You said the trolls trust you. Make them set Binabik free. Then we'll all go together."

Jiriki let out a thin whistle of air between his lips. "It is not so simple, young Seoman," he said, almost impatiently. "I have no right or power to make the Qanuc do anything. Also, I have other responsibilities and duties you cannot understand. I only stayed as long as I have because I wanted to see you on your feet once more. My uncle Khendraja'aro has long since returned to Jao é-Tinukai'i, and my duties to my house and my kin compel me to follow."

"Compel you? But you're a prince!"

The Sitha shook his head. "That word is not the same in our speech as in yours, Seoman. I am of the reigning house, but I order no one and rule no one. Neither am I ruled, fortunately—except in certain things and at certain times. My parents have declared that this is such a time." Simon thought he could almost detect a touch of anger in Jiriki's voice. "Never fear, though. You and Haestan are not prisoners. The Qanuc honor you. They will let you leave when you wish."

"But I won't leave without Binabik." Simon twisted his cloak between his fists. "And Sludig, too."

A small dark figure appeared in the doorway and coughed politely. Jiriki looked over his shoulder, then nodded his head. The old Qanuc woman stepped forward and set a steaming pot down at Jiriki's feet, then quickly pulled three bowls out of her tentlike sheepskin coat, arranging them in a semicircle. Though her diminutive fingers worked nimbly, and her seamed, round-cheeked face was expressionless, Simon saw a glimmer of fear in her eyes as they rose briefly to meet his. When she had finished, she backed quickly out of the cave, disappearing under the door flap as silently as she had appeared.

What is she afraid of? Simon wondered. *Jiriki? But Binabik said the Qanuc and Sithi have always gotten along—more or less.*

He suddenly thought of himself: twice as tall as a troll, red-haired, hairy-faced with his first man's beard—skinny as a switch, too, but since he was wrapped in blankets the old Qanuc woman couldn't know that. What difference could the people of Yiqanuc see between himself and a hated Rimmersman? Hadn't Sludig's people warred on the troll folk for centuries?

"Will you have some, Seoman?" Jiriki asked, pouring out steaming liquid from the pot. "They have provided you with a bowl."

Simon reached out a hand. "Is it more soup?"

"It is *aka*, as the Qanuc call it—or as you would say, tea."

"Tea!" He took the bowl eagerly. Judith, Kitchen Mistress of the Hayholt, had been very fond of tea. She would sit down at the end of a long day's work to nurse a great hot mug full of the stuff, the kitchen filling with the vapors of steeped southern island herbs. When she was in a good mood, she would let Simon have some, too. Usires, how he missed his home!

"I never thought . . ." he began, and took a great long swallow, only to spit it out a moment later in a fit of coughing. "What is it?" he choked. "That's not tea!"

Jiriki might have been smiling, but since he had his bowl up to his mouth, sipping slowly, it was impossible to tell. "Certainly it is," the Sitha replied. "The Qanuc people use different herbs than you Sudhoda'ya, of course. How could it be otherwise, when they have so little trade with your kind?"

Simon wiped his mouth, grimacing. "But it's salty!" He took a sniff of the bowl and made another face.

The Sitha nodded and sipped again. "They put salt in it, yes—and butter as well."

"Butter!"

"Marvelous are the ways of all Mezumiiru's grandchildren," Jiriki intoned solemnly, ". . . endless is their variety."

Simon set the bowl down in disgust. "Butter. Usires help me, what a miserable adventure."

Jiriki calmly finished his tea. The mention of Mezumiiru reminded Simon again of his troll friend, who one night in the forest had sung a song about the Moon-woman. His mood turned sour once more.

"But what *are* we going to do for Binabik?" Simon asked. "Anything?"

Jiriki lifted calm, catlike eyes. "We will have a chance to speak on his behalf tomorrow. I have not yet discovered his crime. Few Qanuc speak any language but their own—your companion is a rare troll indeed—and I am not very accomplished in theirs. Neither do they like to share their thoughts with outsiders."

"What's happening tomorrow?" Simon asked, sinking back into his bed again. His head was pounding. Why should he still feel so weak?

"There is a . . . court, I suppose. Where the Qanuc rulers hear and decide."

"And we are going to speak for Binabik?"

"No, Seoman, not as such," Jiriki said gently. For a moment a strange look flitted across his spare features. "We are going because you met the Dragon of the Mountain . . . and lived. The lords of the Qanuc wish to see you. I do not doubt that your friend's crimes will also be addressed, there before the whole of his people. Now take rest, for you will have need of it."

Jiriki stood and stretched his slender limbs, moving his head in his disconcertingly alien way, amber eyes fixed on nothing. Simon felt a shudder travel the length of his own body, followed by a powerful weariness.

The dragon! he thought groggily, halfway between wonderment and horror. *He* had seen a dragon! He, Simon the scullion, despised muckabout and mooncalf, had swung a sword at a dragon and lived—even after its scalding blood had splashed him! Like in a story!

He looked at blackly gleaming Thorn, which lay partly covered against the wall, waiting like a beautiful, deadly serpent. Even Jiriki seemed unwilling to handle it, or even discuss it; the Sitha had calmly deflected all of Simon's questions as to what magic might run like blood through Camaris' strange sword. Simon's chilled fingers crept up his jaw to the still-painful scar running down his face. How had a mere scullion like himself ever dared to lift such a potent thing?

Closing his eyes, he felt the huge and uncaring world spin ever so slowly beneath him. He heard Jiriki pad across the cave toward the doorway, and a faint *swish* as the Sitha slid past the flap and out, then sleep tugged him down.

Simon dreamed. The face of the small, dark-haired girl swam before him once more. It was a child's face, but the solemn eyes were old and deep as a well in a deserted churchyard. She seemed to want to tell him something. Her mouth worked soundlessly, but as she slipped away through the murky waters of sleep, he thought for a moment he heard her voice.

He awoke the next morning to find Haestan standing over him. The guardsman's teeth were bared in a grim smile and his beard sparkled with melting snow.

"Time y'were up, Simon-lad. Many doin's this day, many doin's."

It took some time, but even though he felt quite feeble, he managed to dress himself. Haestan helped him with his boots, which he had not worn since waking up in Yiqanuc. They seemed stiff as wood on his feet, and the fabric of his garments scraped against his strangely sensitive skin, but he felt better for being up and dressed. He walked gingerly across the length of the cave a few times, beginning to feel like a two-legged animal once more.

"Where's Jiriki?" Simon asked as he pulled his cloak around his shoulders.

"That one's gone ahead. But ha' no worry 'bout goin' t' meetin'. I could carry ye, stickly thing that y'are."

"I was carried here," Simon said, and heard an unexpected coldness creeping into his voice, "but that doesn't mean I'll have to be carried always."

The husky Erkynlander chortled, taking no offense. "I'm as happy if y'walk, lad. These trolls make paths narrow enough, I've no great wish t'carry anyone."

Simon had to wait a moment just inside the cave-mouth to adjust to the glare leaking through the raised door-flap. When he stepped outside, the reflective brilliance of the snow, even on an overcast morning, was almost too much for him.

They stood on a wide stone porch that extended almost twenty cubits out from the cave. It stretched away to the right and left on either side, running along the face of the mountain. Simon could see the smoking mouths of other caves all along its length, until it bent back out of sight around the curve of Mintahoq's belly. There were similar wide trackways on the slope above, row upon row up the mountain's face. Ladders dangled down from higher caves, and where the irregularities of the slope made the joining of the paths impossible, many of the different porches were connected across empty space by swaying bridges that seemed made of little more than leather thongs. Even as Simon stared, he saw the tiny, fur-coated shapes of Qanuc children skittering across these slender spans, gamboling blithely as squirrels, though a fall would mean certain death. It made Simon's stomach churn to watch them, so he swung around to face outward once more.

Before him lay the great valley of Yiqanuc; beyond, Mintahoq's stony neighbors loomed out of the misted depths, towering up into the gray, snow-flecked sky. Tiny black holes dotted the far peaks; minuscule shapes, barely discernible across the dark valley, bustled along the twining paths between them.

Three trolls, slouching in wrought-hide saddles, came riding down the track on their shaggy rams. Simon stepped forward out of their way, moving slowly across the porch until he was within a few feet of the edge. Looking down, he felt a momentary surge of the vertigo he had felt on Urmsheim. The mountain's base, bewhiskered here and there by twisted evergreens, fell away below, crisscrossed by more ladder-hung porches like the one on which he stood. He noticed a sudden silence and turned to look for Haestan.

The three ram-riders had stopped in the middle of the wide pathway, gazing at Simon in slack-mouthed wonderment. The guardsman, nearly hidden in the shadow of the cave-mouth on their far side, gave him a mocking salute over the heads of the trolls.

Two of the riders had sparse beards on their chins. All wore necklaces of thick ivory beads over their heavy coats and carried ornately carved spears with hooked bottoms, like shepherd's crooks, which they used to guide their spiral-horned steeds. They were all larger than Binabik: Simon's few days in Yiqanuc had taught him that Binabik was one of the smallest adults of his people. These trolls also seemed more primitive and dangerous than his friend, well-armed and fierce-faced, threatening despite their small stature.

Simon stared at the trolls. The trolls stared at Simon.

"They've all heard of ye, Simon," Haestan boomed; the three riders looked up, startled by his loud voice, "—but no one's hardly seen ye yet."

The trolls looked the tall guardsman up and down in alarm, then clucked at their mounts and rode on hurriedly, disappearing around the mountain face. "Gave them some gossip," Haestan chuckled.

"Binabik told me about his home," Simon said, "but it was hard to understand what he was saying. Things are never quite what you think they're going to be, are they?"

"Only th' good Lord Usires knows all answers," Haestan nodded. "Now, if y'would see y'r small friend, we'd best move on. Walk careful now—and not so close t'edge, there."

They made their way slowly down the looping path, which alternately narrowed and widened as it traversed the mountainside. The sun was high overhead, but hidden in a nest of soot-colored clouds, and a biting wind swooped along Mintahoq's face. The mountaintop above was white-blanketed in ice, like the high peaks across the valley, but at this lower height the snow had fallen more patchily. Some wide drifts lay across the path, and others nestled among the cave mouths, but dry rock and exposed soil were also all around. Simon had no idea if such snow was normal for the first days of Tiyagar-month in Yiqanuc, but he did know that he was mightily sick of sleet and cold. Every flake that swooped into his eye felt like an insult; the scarred flesh of his cheek and jaw ached terribly.

Now that they had left what seemed like the populous section of the mountain, there were not many troll folk to be seen. Dark shapes peered out of the smoke of some of the cave-mouths, and two more groups of riders passed by heading in the same direction, slowing to stare, then bustling along as hastily as had the first troop.

The pair passed a gaggle of children playing in a snowdrift. The young trolls, barely taller than Simon's knee, were bundled up in heavy fur jackets and leggings; they looked like little round hedgehogs. Their eyes grew wide as Simon and Haestan trudged past, and their high-pitched chatter was stilled, but they did not run or show any sign of fear. Simon liked that. He smiled gently, mindful of his pained cheek, and waved to them.

When a loop of the path led them far out toward the northward side of the mountain, they found themselves in an area where the noise of Mintahoq's inhabitants disappeared entirely and they were alone with the voice of wind and fluttering snow.

"Don't like this bit m'self," Haesten said.

"What's that?" Simon pointed up the slope. On a stone porch far above stood a strange egg-shaped structure made of carefully ordered blocks of snow. It gleamed faintly, pink-tinged by the slanting sun. A row of silent trolls stood before it, spears clutched in their mittened hands, their faces harsh in their hoods.

"Don't point, lad," Haestan said, gently pulling at Simon's arm. Had a few of the guards shifted their gazes downward? "It be somethin' important, y'r friend Jiriki said. Called 'Ice House.' Th' little folk be all worked up over it right this moment. Don't know why—don't want t'know, either."

"Ice House?" Simon stared. "Does someone live there?"

Haestan shook his head. "Jiriki didna say."

Simon looked to Haestan speculatively. "Have you talked with Jiriki much since you've been here? I mean, since I wasn't around for you to talk to?"

"Oh, aye," Haestan said, then paused. "Not much, in truth. Always seems like . . . like he's thinkin' on something' grand, d'ye see? Somethin' important. But he's nice enough, in's way. Not like a person, quite, but not a bad'un." Haestan thought a bit more. "He's not like I thought magic-fellow 'd be. Talks plain, Jiriki does." Haestan smiled. "Does think well on ye, he does. Way he talks, un'd think he owed ye money." He chuckled in his beard.

It was a long, wearying walk for someone as weak as Simon: first up, then down, back and forth over the face of the mountain. Although Haestan put a steadying hand under his elbow each time he sagged, Simon had begun to wonder if he could go any farther when they trudged around an outcropping that pushed out into the path like a stone in a river and found themselves standing before the wide entranceway of the great cavern of Yiqanuc.

The vast hole, at least fifty paces from edge to edge, gaped in the face of Mintahoq like a mouth poised to pronounce a solemn judgment. Just inside stood a row of huge, weathered statues: round-bellied, humanlike figures, gray and yellow as rotted teeth, stoop-shouldered beneath the burden of the entranceway roof. Their smooth heads were crowned with ram's horns, and great tusks pushed out between their lips. So worn were they by centuries of harsh weather that their faces were all but featureless. This gave them, to Simon's startled eye, not a look of antiquity, but rather of unformed newness—as if they were even now creating themselves out of the primordial stone.

"*Chidsik Ub Lingit,*" a voice said beside him, "—the House of the Ancestor."

Simon jumped a little and turned in surprise, but it was not Haestan who had spoken. Jiriki stood beside him, staring up at the blind stone faces.

"How long have you been standing there?" Simon was shamed to have been so startled. He turned his head back to the entranceway. Who could guess that the tiny trolls would carve such giant door-wardens?

"I came out to meet you," Jiriki said. "Greetings, Haestan."

The guardsman grunted and nodded his head. Simon wondered again what had passed between the Erkynlander and the Sitha during the long days of his illness. There were times when Simon found it very hard to converse with veiled and roundabout Prince Jiriki. How might it be for a straightforward soldier like Haestan, who had not been trained, as Simon had, on the maddening circularities of Doctor Morgenes?

"Is this where the king of the trolls lives?" he asked aloud.

"And the queen of the trolls, as well," Jiriki nodded. "Although they are not really called a king and queen in the Qanuc language. It would be closer to say the Herder and Huntress."

"Kings, queens, princes, and none of them are what they are called," Simon grumbled. He was tired and sore and cold. "Why is the cave so big?"

The Sitha laughed quietly. His pale lavender hair fluttered in the sharp wind. "Because if the cave were smaller, young Seoman, they would doubtless have found another place to be their House of the Ancestor instead. Now we should go inside—and not only so that you can escape the cold."

Jiriki led them between two of the centermost statues, toward flickering yellow light. As they passed between pillarlike legs, Simon looked up to the eyeless faces beyond the polished bulges of the statues' great stone bellies. He was reminded again of the philosophies of Doctor Morgenes.

The Doctor used to say that no one ever knows what will come to them—"don't build on expectation," he said that all the time. Who would ever have thought someday I would see such things as this, have such adventures? No one knows what will come to them. . . .

He felt a twinge of pain along his face, then a needle of cold in his gut. The Doctor, as was so often the case, had spoken nothing but the truth.

Inside, the great cavern was full of trolls and dense with the sweetly sour odors of oil and fat. A thousand yellow lights blazed.

All around the craggy, high-ceilinged stone room, in wall-niches and in the very floor, pools of oil bloomed with fire. Hundreds of such lamps, each with its floating wick like a slender white worm, gave the cavern a light that far outshone the gray day outside. Hide-jacketed Qanuc filled the room, an ocean of black-haired heads. Small children sat pickaback, like seagulls floating placidly atop the waves.

At the room's center an island of rock protruded above the sea of troll folk. There, on a raised stone platform hewn from the very stuff of the cavern floor, two smallish figures sat in a pool of fire.

It was not exactly a pool of pure flame, Simon saw a moment later, but a slender moat cut into the gray rock all the way around, filled with the same burning oil that fueled the lamps. The two figures at the center of the ring of flames reclined side by side in a sort of hammock of ornately-figured hide bounded by thongs to a frame of ivory. The pair nested unmoving in the mound of white and reddish furs. Their eyes were bright in their round, placid faces.

"She is Nunuuika and he is Uammannaq," Jiriki said quietly, "—they are the masters of the Qanuc . . ."

Even as he spoke, one of the two small figures gestured briefly with a hooked staff. The vast, packed horde of troll folk drew back to either side, pressing themselves even closer together, forming an aisle that stretched from the stone platform to the place where Simon and his companions stood. Several hundred small, expectant faces turned toward them. There was much whispering. Simon stared down the open length of cavern floor, abashed.

"Seems clear enough," Haestan growled, giving him a soft shove. "Go on, then, lad."

"All of us," Jiriki said. He made one of his oddly-articulated gestures to indicate that Simon should lead the way.

Both the echoing whispers and the scent of cured hides seemed to increase as Simon made his way toward the king and queen . . .

—Or the Herdsman and Huntress, he reminded himself. *Or whatever.*

The air in the cavern suddenly seemed stiflingly thick. As he struggled to get a deep breath he stumbled and would have fallen had not Haestan caught at the back of his cloak. When he reached the dais he stood for a moment staring at the floor, struggling with dizziness, before looking up to the figures on the platform. The lamplight glared into his eyes. He felt angry, although he didn't know at whom. Hadn't he more or less just gotten out of bed today for the first time? What did they expect? That he would leap right out and slay some dragons?

The startling thing about Uammannaq and Nunuuika, he decided, was that they looked so much alike, as though they were twins. Not that it wasn't instantly obvious which was which: Uammannaq, on Simon's left, had a thin beard that hung from his chin, knotted with red and blue thongs into a long braid. His hair was braided as well, held in intricate loops upon his head with combs of black, shiny stone. As he worried at his beard gently with small, thick fingers, his other hand held his staff of office, a thick, heavily carved ram-rider's spear with a crook at one end.

His wife—if that was the way things worked in Yiqanuc—held a straight spear, a slender, deadly wand with a stone point sharpened to translucency. She wore her long black hair high on her head, held in place with many combs of carved ivory. Her eyes, gleaming behind slanting lids in a plump face, were flat and bright as polished stone. Simon had never had a woman look at him in quite that cold and arrogant way. He remembered that she was called Huntress, and felt out of his depth. By contrast, Uammannaq seemed far less threatening. The Herder's heavy face seemed to sag in loose lines of drowsiness, but there was still a canny edge to his glance.

After the brief moment of mutual inspection, Uammannaq's face creased in a wide yellow grin, his eyes nearly disappearing in a cheerful squint. He lifted his two palms toward the companions, then pressed his small hands together and said something in guttural Qanuc.

"He says you are welcome to Chidsik Ub Lingit and to Yiqanuc, the mountains of the trolls," Jiriki translated. Before he could say more, Nunuuika spoke up. Her words seemed more measured than Uammannaq's, but were no more intelligible to Simon. Jiriki listened to her carefully.

"The Huntress also extends her greetings. She says you are quite tall, but unless she is very mistaken in her knowledge of the Utku people, you seem young for a dragon-slayer, despite the white in your hair. *Utku* is the troll word for lowlanders," he added quietly.

Simon looked at the two royal personages for a moment. "Tell them that I'm pleased to have their welcome, or whatever should be said. And please tell them that I didn't slay the dragon—likely only wounded it—and that I did it to protect my friends, just as Binabik of Yiqanuc did for me many other times."

When he finished the long sentence he was momentarily out of breath, bringing a rush of dizziness. The Herder and Huntress, who had been watching curiously as he spoke—both had frowned slightly at the mention of Binabik's name—now turned expectantly to Jiriki.

The Sitha paused for a moment, considering, then rattled off a long stream of thick trollish speech. Uammannaq nodded his head in a puzzled way. Nunuuika listened impassively. When Jiriki had finished, she glanced briefly at her consort, then spoke again.

Judging by her translated reply, she might not have heard Binabik's name at all. She complimented Simon on his bravery, saying that the Qanuc had long held the mountain Urmsheim—*Yijarjuk*, she called it—as a place to be avoided at all costs. Now, she said, perhaps it was time to explore the western mountains again, since the dragon, even if it had survived, had most likely disappeared into the lower depths to nurse its wounds.

Uammannaq seemed impatient with Nunuuika's speech. As soon as Jiriki finished relaying her words the Herder responded with some of his own, saying that now was hardly the time for such adventures, after the terrible winter just passed, and with the evil *Croohokuq*—the Rimmersmen—so malevolently active. He hastened to add that of course Simon and his companions, the other lowlander and the esteemed Jiriki, should stay as long as they wished, as honored guests, and that if there was anything he or Nunuuika could grant them to ease their stay, they had only to ask.

Even before Jiriki finished converting these works to the Westerling speech, Simon was shifting his weight from one foot to the other, anxious to respond.

"Yes," he told Jiriki, "there *is* something they can do. They can free Binabik and Sludig, our companions. Free our friends, if you would do us a favor!" he said loudly, turning to the fur-swaddled pair before him, who regarded him with incomprehension. His raised voice caused some of the trolls crowded around the stone platform to murmur uneasily. Simon dizzily wondered if he had gone too far, but for the moment was beyond caring.

"Seoman," Jiriki said, "I promised myself that I would not mistranslate or interfere in your speech with the lords of Yiqanuc, but I ask you now as a favor to me, do not ask this of them. Please."

"Why not?"

"Please. As a favor. I will explain later; I ask you to trust me."

Simon's angry words spilled out before he could control them. "You want me to desert my friend as a favor to you? Haven't I already saved your life? Didn't I get the White Arrow from you? Who owes the favors here?"

Even as he said it he was sorry, fearing that an unbreachable barrier had suddenly grown between himself and the Sitha prince. Jiriki's eyes burned into his. The audience began to fidget nervously and mutter among themselves, sensing something amiss.

The Sitha dropped his gaze. "I am ashamed, Seoman. I ask too much of you."

Now Simon felt himself sinking like a stone into a muddy pool. Too fast! It was too much to think about. All he wanted was to lie down and not know anything.

"No, Jiriki," he blurted out, "I'm ashamed. I'm ashamed of what I said. I'm an idiot. Ask the two of them if I can speak to them tomorrow. I feel sick." Suddenly the dizziness was horribly real; he felt the whole cavern tilt. The light of the oil lamps wavered as though in a stiff wind. Simon's knees buckled and Haestan caught his arms, holding him up.

Jiriki turned quickly to Uammannaq and Nunuuika. A rumble of fascinated consternation ran through the trollish throng. Was the red-crested, storklike lowlander dead? Perhaps such long thin legs were *not* capable of bearing weight for long, as some had suggested. But then, why were the other two lowlanders still standing upright? Many heads were shaken in puzzlement, many whispered guesses exchanged.

"*Nunuuika, keenest of eye, and Uammannaq, surest of rein: the boy is still sick and very weak.*" Jiriki spoke quietly. The multitude, cheated by his soft speech, leaned forward. "*I ask a boon, on the primeval friendship of our people.*"

The Huntress inclined her head, smiling slightly. "*Speak, Elder Brother,*" she said.

"*I have no right to interfere in your justice, and will not. I do ask that the judgment of Binabik of Mintahoq not go forward until his companions—including the boy Seoman—have a chance to speak in his behalf. And that the same be granted also for the Rimmersman, Sludig. This I ask of you in the name of the Moon-woman, our shared root.*" Jiriki bowed slightly, using only his upper body. There was no suggestion of subservience.

Uammannaq tapped the shaft of his spear with his fingers. He looked to the Huntress, his expression troubled. At last he nodded. "*We cannot refuse this, Elder Brother. So shall it be. Two days, then, when the boy is stronger—but even if this strange young man had brought us Igjarjuk's toothy head in a saddlebag, that would not change what must be. Binabik, apprentice of the Singing Man, has committed a terrible crime.*"

"*So I have been told,*" Jiriki replied. "*But the brave hearts of the Qanuc were not the only thing that gained them the esteem of the Sithi. We loved the kindness of trolls as well.*"

Nunuuika touched the combs in her hair, her gaze hard. "*Kind hearts must never overthrow just law, Prince Jiriki, or all Sedda's spawn—Sithi as well as mortals—will return naked to the snows. Binabik shall have his judgment.*"

Prince Jiriki nodded and made another brief bow before turning away. Haestan half-carried the stumbling Simon as they walked back across the cavern, down the gauntlet of curious trolls, back out into the cold wind.

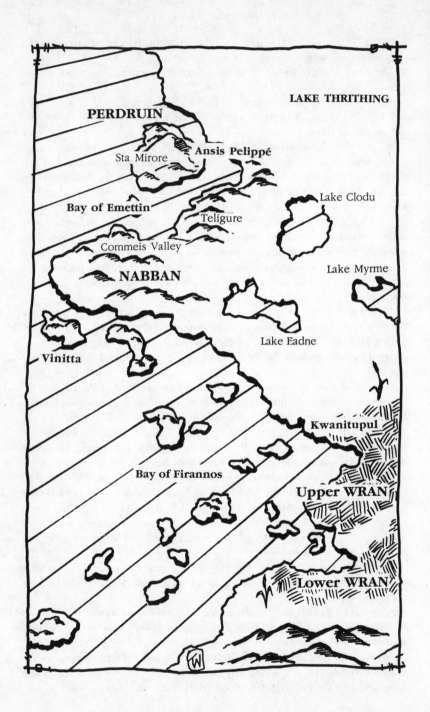

LAKE THRITHING

PERDRUIN

Sta Mirore Ansis Pelippé

Lake Clodu

Bay of Emettin

Teligure

Commeis Valley

NABBAN

Lake Myrme

Lake Eadne

Vinitta

Kwanitupul

Upper WRAN

Bay of Firannos

Lower WRAN

2

Masks and Shadows

The Fire popped and spat as snowflakes drifted down into the flames to boil away in an instant. The surrounding trees were still striped with orange, but the campfire had burned down almost to embers. Beyond this fragile barrier of firelight, mist and cold and dark waited patiently.

Deornoth held his hands closer to the embers and tried to ignore the vast living presence of Aldheorte Forest all around, the twining branches that blotted the stars overhead, the fog-shrouded trunks swaying somberly in the cold, steady wind. Josua sat across from him, facing away from the flames toward the unfriendly darkness; the prince's angled face, red-washed by rippling firelight, was contorted in a silent grimace. Deornoth's heart went out to his prince, but it was too difficult to look at him just now. He turned his eyes away, kneading his chilled fingers as though he could rub away all suffering—his, his master's, and that of the rest of their pitiful, lamed flock.

Someone moaned nearby, but Deornoth did not look up. Many in their party were suffering, and some—the little handmaiden with the terrible throat wound, and Helmfest, one of the Lord Constable's men, gut-bitten by those unholy creatures—he doubted would live through the night.

Their troubles had not ended when they had escaped the destruction of Josua's castle at Naglimund. Even as the prince's party had staggered down the last broken steps of the Stile, they had been set on. Mere yards from the outer stand of Aldheorte, the ground had erupted around them and the false, storm-carried night had rung with chirping cries.

There had been diggers everywhere—*Bukken*, as young Isorn called them, shouting the name hysterically as he lay about him with his sword. Even in his fear the duke's son had killed many, but Isorn had also taken a dozen shallow wounds from the diggers' sharp teeth and crude, jagged knives. That was something else to worry about: in the forest, even small wounds were likely to fester.

Deornoth shifted uneasily. Those small shapes had clung to his own arm like rats. In his choking fear, he had almost cut his hand loose from his body to get the chittering things off. Even now, the thought made him squirm. He rubbed at his fingers, remembering.

Josua's beleaguered company had finally escaped, hacking free long enough to make a dash for the forest. Strangely, the forbidding trees seemed to provide a sort of sanctuary. The swarming diggers, far too numerous to have been defeated, did not follow.

Is there some power in the forest that prevented them? Deornoth wondered. *Or more likely, does something live here more fearsome even than they are?*

Fleeing, they had left behind five torn things that had once been human beings. The prince's troop of survivors now numbered perhaps a dozen— and judging by the tortuous, gasping breaths of the soldier Helmfest, who lay wrapped in his cloak near the fire, they would be fewer than that soon.

Lady Vorzheva was dabbing the blood away from Helmfest's ghost-pale cheek. She had the distant, distracted look of a madman Deornoth had once seen, who had sat in the Naglimund-town square pouring water from one bowl to another for hours at a time, back and forth, never spilling a drop. Tending this living dead man was just as useless a thing to do, Deornoth felt sure, and it showed in Vorzheva's dark eyes.

Prince Josua had been paying no greater heed to Vorzheva than to anyone else in the battered company. Despite the terror and weariness she shared with the rest of the survivors, it was obvious that she was also furiously angry about his inattention. Deornoth had long been a witness to Josua and Vorzheva's stormy relationship, but was never quite sure how he felt about it. Sometimes he resented the Thrithings-woman as a distraction, a hindrance to his prince's duties; at other moments he found himself pitying Vorzheva, whose sincere passions often outstripped her patience. Josua could be maddeningly careful and deliberate, and even at the best of times tended toward melancholy. Deornoth guessed that the prince would be a very difficult man for a woman to love and live with.

The old jester Towser and Sangfugol the harper were talking dispirit-edly nearby. The jester's wine sack lay empty and flattened on the ground beside them; it was the only wine any of the survivors would see for a while. Towser had drained it dry himself in just a few gulps, occasioning more than a few sharp words from his fellows. His rheumy eye had blinked angrily as he drank, like an old rooster warning away a henyard interloper.

The only ones engaged in useful activity at this moment were the Duchess Gutrun, Isgrimnur's wife, and Father Strangyeard, the archivist of Naglimund. Gutrun had slit the front and back of her heavy brocade skirt and was now sewing the open pieces together, making something like a pair of breeches for herself, the better to travel through Aldheorte's clinging brush. Strangyeard, recognizing the good sense of this idea, was sawing away at the front of his own gray robe with Deornoth's dulled knife.

The brooding Rimmersman Einskaldir sat near Father Strangyeard; between them lay a quiet shape, a dark bump below the wash of firelight. That was the little handmaiden whose name Deornoth could not remember. She had fled with them from the residence, and had cried quietly all the long way up and down the Stile.

Cried, that is, until the diggers had reached her. They had clung to her throat like terriers to a boar, even after their bodies had been sheared loose by the blades of her would-be rescuers. Now she cried no longer. She was very, very still, holding precariously to life.

Deornoth felt a shudder of trapped horror surge up within him. Merciful Usires, what had they done to deserve such dreadful retribution? Of what abominable sin were they guilty, to be punished by the harrowing of Naglimund?

He fought down the panic that he knew showed plainly on his face, then looked around. No one was watching him, thank Usires: no one had seen his shameful fear. Such conduct was not fitting, after all. Deornoth was a knight. He was proud that he had felt his prince's gauntlet upon his head, had heard the pronouncement of service. He only wished for the clean terror of battle with human enemies—not tiny, squealing diggers, or the stone-faced, fish-white Norns who had destroyed Josua's castle. How could you battle creatures out of childhood bogey-tales?

It must be the Day of Weighing-Out come at last. That was the only explanation. These might be living things they fought—they bled and died, and could demons be said to do so?—but they were forces of Darkness, nevertheless. The final days had come in truth.

Oddly, the idea made Deornoth feel a little stronger. Was this not, after all, a knight's true calling, to defend his lord and land against enemies spiritual as well as corporeal? Hadn't the priest said so before Deornoth's vigil of investiture? He forced his fearful thoughts back into their proper track. He had long prided himself on his calm face, his slow and measured anger; for just that reason, he had always felt very comfortable with the reserved manners of his prince. How could Josua lead, except by the mastery of his own person?

Thinking of Josua, Deornoth stole another look at him and felt worry come surging back. It seemed that the prince's armor of patience was at last breaking apart, wracked by forces no man should bear. As his liege man watched, Josua stared out into the windy darkness, lips working as he spoke soundlessly to himself, brow wrinkled in pained concentration.

The watching became too difficult. "Prince Josua," Deornoth called softly. The prince finished his silent speech, but did not turn his eyes to the young knight. Deornoth tried again. "Josua?"

"Yes, Deornoth?" he replied at last.

"My lord," the knight began, then realized he had nothing to say. "My lord, my good lord . . ."

As Deornoth bit at his lower lip, hoping inspiration might strike his weary thoughts, Josua suddenly sat forward, eyes fixed where moments before they had aimlessly roved, staring at the dark beyond the fire-reddened breakfront of the forest.

"What is it?" Deornoth asked, alarmed. Isorn, who had been slumbering behind him, roused with an incoherent cry at the sound of his friend's voice. Deornoth fumbled for his sword, pulling it free from the scabbard, half-standing as he did so.

"Be silent." Josua raised his arm.

A thrill of dread swept through the camp. For stretching seconds there was nothing, then the rest heard it, too: something breaking clumsily through the undergrowth just beyond the ring of light.

"Those creatures!" Vorzheva's voice rose up out of a whisper into a wavering cry. Josua turned and grasped her arm tightly. He gave her a single harsh shake.

"*Quiet,* for the love of God!"

The sound of branches breaking came nearer. Now Isorn and the soldiers were on their feet, too, hands clutching fearfully at sword-hilts. Some of the rest of the company were quietly weeping and praying.

Josua hissed: "No forest dweller would go so noisily . . ." His anxiousness was poorly hidden. He pulled Naidel out of the sheath. "It walks two-legged . . ."

"*Help me . . .*" called a voice out of the dark. The night seemed to grow deeper still, as though the blackness might roll over them and obliterate their feeble campfire.

A moment later something pushed through into the ring of trees. It flung its arms up before its eyes as the firelight beat upon it.

"God save us, God save us!" Towser cried hoarsely.

"Look, it is a man," Isorn gasped. "Aedon, he is covered in blood!"

The wounded man lurched another two steps toward the fire, then slid jerkily to his knees, pushing forward a face nearly black with dried blood, but for the eyes that stared unseeingly toward the circle of startled people.

"Help me," he moaned again. His voice was slow and thick, almost unrecognizable as a man speaking the Westerling tongue.

"What is this madness, Lady?" Towser groaned. The old jester was tugging at Duchess Gutrun's sleeve as might a child. "Tell me, what is this curse that has been put on us?"

"I think I know this man!" Deornoth gasped, and a moment later felt the freezing fear drop away; he sprang forward to grab the trembling man's elbow and ease him closer to the fire. The newcomer was draped in tattered rags. A fringe of twisted rings, all that remained of a mail shirt, hung about his neck on a collar of blackened leather. "It is the pikeman who came with us as a guard," Deornoth told Josua. "When you met your brother in the tent before the walls."

The prince nodded slowly. His gaze was intent, his expression momentarily unfathomable. "Ostrael . . ." Josua murmured. "Was that not his name?" The prince stared at the blood-spattered young pikeman for a long instant, then his eyes brimmed with tears and he turned away.

"Here, you poor, wretched fellow, here . . ." Father Strangyeard reached forward with a skin of water. They had scarcely more of that than they had of wine, but no one said a word. The water filled Ostrael's open mouth and overflowed, streaming down his chin. He could not seem to swallow.

"The . . . diggers had him," Deornoth said. "I am sure I saw him caught by them, back at Naglimund." He felt the pikeman's shoulder quiver beneath his touch, heard the man's breath whistling in and out. "Aedon, how he must have suffered."

Ostrael's eyes turned up to his, yellow and glazed even in the dim light. The mouth opened again in the dark-crusted face. "Help . . ." The voice was painfully slow, as though each heavy word were being hoisted up his throat to his mouth before tumbling out into the air. "It . . . hurts me," he wheezed. "Hollow."

"God's Tree, what can possibly be done for him?" Isorn groaned. "We are all hurting."

Ostrael's mouth gaped. He stared up with blind eyes.

"We can bandage his wounds." Isorn's mother Gutrun was recovering her considerable poise. "We can get him a cloak. If he lives until the morning, we can do more then."

Josua had turned back to look at the young pikeman again. "The duchess is right, as usual. Father Strangyeard, see if you can find a cloak. Perhaps one of the less injured can spare theirs . . ."

"No!" Einskaldir growled. "I do not like this!"

A confused silence fell on the gathering.

"Surely you do not begrudge . . ." Deornoth began, then gasped as Einskaldir leaped past him and seized the panting Ostrael by the shoulders, throwing him roughly to the ground. Einskaldir squatted on the young pikeman's chest. The bearded Rimmersman's long knife appeared from nowhere to lie against Ostrael's blood-smeared neck like a glinting smile.

"Einskaldir!" Josua's face was pale. "What is this madness?"

The Rimmersman looked over his shoulder, a strange grin slashing his bearded face. "This is no true man! I do not care where you think you have seen him before!"

Deornoth reached a hand toward Einskaldir, but drew it back quickly when the Rimmersman's knife whickered past his outstretched fingers.

"Fools! Look!" Einskaldir pointed with his hilt toward the fire.

Ostrael's bare foot lay among the embers at the edge of the firepit. The flesh was being consumed, blackening and smoking, yet the pikeman himself lay almost placidly beneath Einskaldir, his lungs fluting as he forced breath in and out.

There was a moment of silence. A smothering, bone-chilling fog seemed to settle over the clearing. The moment had become as horribly strange yet inalterable as a nightmare. Fleeing the ruin of Naglimund, they might have wandered into the trackless lands of madness.

"Perhaps his wounds . . ." Isorn began.

"Idiot! He feels no fire," Einskaldir snarled. "And he has a slash in his throat that would kill any man. *Look! See!*" He forced back Ostrael's head until those gathered around could see the ragged, fluttering edges of the wound, which stretched from one angle of his jaw to the other. Father Strangyeard, who had been leaning close, made a choking noise and turned away.

"Tell me he is not some ghost . . ." the Rimmersman continued, then was almost thrown to the ground as the body of the pikeman began to thrash beneath him. "Hold him down!" Einskaldir shouted, trying to keep his face away from Ostrael's head, which whipped from side to side, the teeth snapping shut on empty air.

Deornoth dove forward and clutched at one of the slender arms; it was cold and hard as stone, but still horribly flexible. Isorn, Strangyeard, and Josua were also struggling to find handholds on the wriggling, lunging form. The half-darkness was rich with panicky curses. When Sangfugol came forward and wrapped himself around the last unprisoned foot, hanging on with both arms, the body became quiescent for a moment. Deornoth could still feel the muscles moving beneath the skin, tightening and relaxing, mustering strength for another try. Air hissed in and out of the pikeman's distended, idiot-mouth.

Ostrael's head craned out on his uplifted neck, his blackened face swinging to look at each of them in turn. Then, with terrifying suddenness, the staring eyes seemed to blacken and fall inward. A moment later, wavering crimson fire blossomed in the empty pits and the labored breathing stopped. Somebody shrieked, a thin cry that quickly fell away into choking silence.

Like the clammy, crushing grip of a titan hand, loathing and raw dread reached out and enfolded the entire camp as the prisoner spoke.

"*So,*" it said. Nothing human was left in its tones, only the dreadful, icy inflection of empty spaces; the voice droned and blew like a black, unfenced wind. "*This would have been much the easier way . . . but a swift death that comes in sleep is denied to you, now.*"

Deornoth felt his own heart speeding like a snared rabbit's, speeding until he thought it might leap from his breast. He felt the strength flowing out of his fingers, even as they clutched at the body that had once been Ostrael Firsfram's son. Through the tattered shirt he could feel flesh chill as a headstone but nevertheless trembling with awful vitality.

"What are you!?" Josua said, struggling to keep his voice even. "And what have you done to this poor man?"

The thing chuckled, almost pleasantly, but for the awful emptiness of its voice. *"I did nothing to this creature. It was already dead, of course, or nearly so—it was not hard to find dead mortals in the ruins of your freehold, prince of rubble."*

Somebody's fingernails were cutting into the skin of Deornoth's arm, but the ruined face gripped his gaze like a candle gleaming at the end of a long, black tunnel.

"Who are you?" Josua demanded.

"I am one of the masters of your castle . . . and of your ultimate death," the thing replied with poisonous gravity. *"I owe no mortal answers. If not for the bearded one's keen eye, your throats would have all been quietly slit tonight, saving us much time and trouble. When your fleeing spirits go squealing at last into the endless Between from which we ourselves escaped, it will be by our doing. We are the Red Hand, knights of the Storm King—and He is the master of all!"*

With a hiss from the ruptured throat, the body abruptly doubled over like a hinge, struggling with the horrifying strength of a scorched snake. Deornoth felt his hold slipping away. As the fire was kicked up into fluttering sparks, he heard Vorzheva sobbing somewhere nearby. Others were filling the night with frightened cries. He was sliding off; Isorn's weight was being pushed down on top of him. Deornoth heard the terrified shouts of his fellows intertwine with his own hysterical prayer for strength . . .

Suddenly the thrashing became weaker. The body beneath him continued to flail from side to side for long moments, like a dying eel, then finally stopped.

"What. . . ?" he was able to force out at last.

Einskaldir, gasping for breath, pointed to the ground with his elbow, still maintaining a tight grip on the unmoving body. Severed by Einskaldir's sharp knife, Ostrael's head had rolled an arm's length away, almost out of the firelight. Even as the company stared, the dead lips pulled back in a snarl. The crimson light was extinguished; the sockets were only empty wells. A thin whisper of sound passed the broken mouth, forced out on a last puff of breath.

". . . No escape . . . Norns will find . . . No . . ." It fell silent.

"By the Archangel . . ." Hoarse with terror, Towser the jester broke the stillness.

Josua took a shaky breath. "We must give the demon's victim an Aedonite burial." The prince's voice was firm, but it clearly took a heroic effort of will to make it so. He turned to look at Vorzheva, who was wide-eyed and slack-mouthed with shock. "And then we must flee. They are indeed pursuing us." Josua turned and caught Deornoth's eye, staring. "An Aedonite burial," he repeated.

"First," Einskaldir panted, blood welling in a long scratch on his face, "I cut the arms and legs off, too." He bent to the task, lifting his hand axe. The others turned away.

The forest night crept in closer still.

Old Gealsgiath walked slowly along the wet, pitching deck of his ship toward the two hooded and cloaked figures huddling at the starboard rail. They turned as he approached, but did not remove their hands from the railing.

"Be-damned-to-Hell stinking weather!" the captain shouted above the moaning of the wind. The hooded figures said nothing. "Men are going down to sleep in kilpa-beds on the Great Green tonight," Old Gealsgiath added in a conversational roar. His thick Hernystiri burr carried even above the flapping and creaking of the sails. "This be drowning weather, sure enough."

The heavier of the two figures pushed back his hood, eyes squinting in his pink face as the rain lashed at him.

"Are we in danger?" Brother Cadrach shouted.

Gealsgiath laughed, his brown face wrinkling. The sound of his mirth was sucked away by the wind. "Only if you plan to go in for swimming. We're already near the shelter of Ansis Pelippé and harbor-mouth."

Cadrach turned to stare out into the swirling twilight, which was dense with rain and fog. "We're almost there?" he shouted, turning back.

The captain lifted a hooked finger to gesture at a deeper smear of darkness off the starboard bow. "The big black spot there, that's Perdruin's mountain—'Streawé's Steeple,' as some do call it. We'll be slipping past the harbor-gate before full dark. Unless the winds play tricksy. Brynioch-cursed strange weather for Yuven-month."

Cadrach's small companion snuck a look at the shadow of Perdruin in the gray mist, then lowered his head again.

"Anyhap, Father," Gealsgiath shouted above the elements, "we dock tonight, and remain two days. I take it you'll be leaving us, since y'paid fare only this far. P'raps you'd like to come down dockside and join me for a drink of something—unless your faith forbids it." The captain smirked. Anyone who spent time in taverns knew that Aedonite monks were no strangers to the pleasures of strong drink.

Brother Cadrach stared for a moment at the heaving sails, then turned his odd, somewhat cold gaze onto the seafarer. A smile creased his round face. "Thank you, captain, but no. The boy and I will remain on board for a bit after we dock. He's not feeling well and I'm in no hurry to rush him out. We'll have far to walk before we reach the abbey, much of it uphill." The small figure reached up and tugged meaningfully at Cadrach's elbow, but the monk paid him no attention.

Gealsgiath shrugged and pulled his shapeless cloth hat farther down on his head. "You know best, Father. You paid your way and did your work aboard—although I would say your lad did the heartiest share of it. You can leave anytime afore we hoist sail for Crannhyr." He turned with a wave of his knob-knuckled hand and started back along the slippery boards, calling: "—but if the lad ain't feeling well, I'd get him below soon!"

"We were just taking some air!" Cadrach bellowed after him. "We'll go ashore tomorrow morning, most likely! Thanks to you, good captain!"

As Old Gealsgiath stumped away, fading into the rain and mist, Cadrach's companion turned and confronted the monk.

"Why are we going to stay on board?" Miriamele demanded, anger plainly displayed on her pretty, sharp-featured face. "I want to get off this ship! Every hour is important!" The rain had soaked even through her thick hood, plastering her black-dyed hair across her forehead in sodden spikes.

"Hush, milady, hush." This time Brother Cadrach's smile seemed a touch more genuine. "Of course we're going off—nearly as soon as we've touched the dock, don't you worry."

Miriamele was angry. "Then why did you tell him. . . ?"

"Because sailors talk, and I'll wager none of them talk louder or longer than our captain. There was no way for keeping him quiet, Saint Muirfath knows. If we'd given him money to keep silent, he'd just get drunk faster and be talking sooner. This way, if anyone's listening for news of us, they'll at least think we're aboard the ship still. Maybe they'll sit and watch for us to come off until it sets out again, back to Hernystir. Meanwhile, we'll be quietly ashore in Ansis Pelippé." Cadrach clucked his tongue in satisfaction.

"Oh." Miriamele considered silently for a moment. She had underestimated the monk again. Cadrach had been sober since they had boarded Gealsgiath's ship in Abaingeat. Small wonder, since the voyage had made him violently ill several times. But there was a shrewd brain behind that plump face. She wondered again—and not for the last time, she felt sure—what Cadrach was really thinking.

"I'm sorry," she said at last. "That was a good idea. Do you really think somebody is looking for us?"

"We would be fools to suppose otherwise, my lady." The monk took her elbow and headed back toward the limited shelter of the lower deck.

When at last she saw Perdruin, it was as if a great ship had risen out of the unquiet ocean, coming suddenly upon their small, frail craft. One moment it was a deeper blackness off the bow; in the next, as though a final curtain of obscuring mist had been drawn away, it loomed overhead like the prow of a mighty vessel.

A thousand lights gleamed through the fog, small as fireflies, making the great rock sparkle in the night. As Gealsgiath's cargo-hauler glided in through the harbor passages, the island continued to rise above them, its mountainous back a wedge of darkness pushing ever upward, blocking out even the mist-cloaked sky.

Cadrach had chosen to remain below decks. Miriamele was quite satisfied with the arrangement. She stood at the railing, listening to the sailors shouting and laughing in the lantern-pricked darkness as they furled the sails. Voices rose in ragged song, only to end abruptly in curses and more laughter.

The wind was gentler here, in the lee of the harborside buildings. Miriamele felt a strange warmth climb up her back and into her neck, and knew without thinking what it signified: she was happy. She was free and going where she chose to go; that had not been true for as long as she could remember.

She had not set foot on Perdruin since she had been a small girl, but she still felt, in a way, as if she were returning home. Her mother Hylissa had brought her here when Miriamele had been very young, as part of a visit to Hylissa's sister, the Duchess Nessalanta in Nabban. They had stopped in Ansis Pelippé to pay a courtesy call on Count Streáwe. Miriamele remembered little of the visit—she had been very young—except a kind old man who had given her a tangerine, and a high-walled garden with a tiled walkway. Miriamele had chased a long-tailed, beautiful bird while her mother drank wine and laughed and talked with other grown people.

The kind old man must have been the count, she decided. It was certainly a wealthy man's garden they had visited, a carefully-tended paradise hidden in a castle courtyard. There had been flowering trees and beautiful silver and golden fish floating in a pond set right into the path. . . .

The harbor wind gained strength, tugging at her cloak. The railing was cold beneath her fingers, so she tucked her hands under her arms.

It had been not long after the visit to Ansis Pelippé that her mother had gone on another journey, this time without Miriamele. Uncle Josua had taken Hylissa to join Miriamele's father Elias, who was in the field with his army. That had been the journey which had crippled Josua, and from which Hylissa had never returned. Elias, almost mute with grief, too full of anger to speak of death, would only tell his little daughter that her mother could never come back. In her child's mind, Miriamele had pictured her mother captive in a walled garden somewhere, a lovely garden like the one they had visited on Perdruin, a beautiful place that Hylissa could never leave, even to visit the daughter who missed her so. . . .

That daughter lay awake many nights, long after her handmaidens had tucked her into bed, staring up into the darkness and plotting to rescue her lost mother from a flowering prison threaded by endless, tiled paths. . . .

Nothing had been right since then. It was as though her father had drunk of some slow poison when her mother had died, some terrible venom that had festered within, turning him into stone.

Where was he? What was High King Elias doing at this moment?

Miriamele looked up at the shadowy, mountainous island and felt her moment of joy swept away as the wind might snatch a kerchief from her hand. Even now, her father was laying siege to Naglimund, venting his terrible rage on the walls of Josua's keep. Isgrimnur, old Towser, all of them were fighting for their lives even as she floated in past the harbor lights, riding the ocean's dark, smooth back.

And the kitchen boy Simon, with his red hair and his awkward, well-meaning ways, his unconcealed concerns and confusions—she felt a pang of sorrow as she thought of him. He and the little troll had gone into the trackless north, perhaps gone forever.

She straightened up. Thinking of her former companions had reminded her of her duty. She was posing as a monk's acolyte—and a sick one at that. She should be below decks. The ship would be docking soon.

Miriamele smiled bitterly. So many impostures. She was free now of her father's court, but she was still posing. As a sad child in Nabban and Meremund, she had often pretended happiness. The lie had been better than answering the well-meaning but unanswerable questions. As her father had retreated from her she had pretended not to care, even though she had felt that she was being eaten away from within.

Where was God, the younger Miriamele had wondered; where was He when love was slowly hardening into indifference and care becoming duty? Where was God when her father Elias begged Heaven for answers, his daughter listening breathlessly in the shadows outside his chamber?

Perhaps He believed my lies, she thought bitterly as she walked down the rain-slicked wooden steps onto the lower deck. *Perhaps He wanted to believe them, so He could get on with more important things.*

The city on the hillside was bright-lit and the rainy night was full of masked revelers. It was Midsummer Festival in Ansis Pelippé: despite the unseasonable weather, the narrow, winding streets were riotous with merrymakers.

Miriamele stepped back as a half-dozen men dressed as chained apes were led past, clanking and staggering. Seeing her standing in the shadowy doorway of one of the shuttered houses, a drunken actor turned, his false fur matted with rainwater, and paused as if to say something to her. Instead, the ape-man belched, smiled apologetically through the mouth hole of his skewed mask, then returned his sorrowful gaze to the uneven cobblestones before him.

As the apes tumbled away, Cadrach reappeared suddenly at her side.

"Where have you been?" she demanded. "You have been gone nearly an hour."

"Not so long, lady, surely." Cadrach shook his head. "I have been finding out certain things that will be useful. Very useful." He looked around. "Ah, but it's a riotous night, is it not?"

Miriamele tugged Cadrach out into the street once more. "You'd never know there was war in the north and people dying," she said disapprovingly. "You wouldn't know that Nabban may soon be at war, too, and Nabban's just across the bay."

"Of course not, my lady," Cadrach huffed, matching his shorter strides to hers as best he could. "It is the way of the Perdruinese *not* to know such things. That is how they remain so cheerfully uninvolved in most conflicts, managing to arm and supply both the eventual victor and the eventual vanquished—*and* turn a neat profit." He grinned and wiped water from his eyes. "Now there's something your Perdruin-folk would be going to war about: protecting their profit."

"Well, I'm surprised no one's invaded this place." The princess wasn't sure why the heedlessness of Ansis Pelippé's citizens should nettle her so, but she was nevertheless feeling exceedingly nettlesome.

"Invade? And muddy the waterhole from which all drink?" Cadrach seemed astonished. "My dear Miriamele . . . your pardon, my dear *Malachias*—I must remember, since we will soon be moving in circles where your true name is not unfamiliar—my dear Malachias, you have much to learn about the world." He paused for a moment as another gang of costumed folk swirled by, engaged in a loud, drunken argument about the words to some song. "There," the monk said, gesturing after them, "there is an example of why that which you say will never come to pass. Were you hearing that little debate?"

Miriamele pulled her hood lower against the slanting rain. "Some of it," she replied. "What does it matter?"

"It is not the subject of the argument that matters, but the method. They were all Perdruinese, unless my ear for accents has gone wrong from all that ocean roar—yet they were arguing in the Westerling tongue."

"So?"

"Ah," Cadrach squinted his eyes as if looking for something down the crowded, lantern-lit street, but continued speaking all the while. "You and I are speaking Westerling, but except for your Erkynlandish fellow-countrymen—and not even all of them—no one else speaks it among their own people. Rimmersmen in Elvritshalla use Rimmerspakk; we Hernystiri speak our own tongue when in Crannhyr or Hernysadharc. Only the Perdruinese have adopted your grandfather King John's universal language, and to them it is now truly their first language."

Miriamele stopped in the middle of the slickened roadway, letting the press of celebrants eddy around her. A thousand oil lamps raised a false dawn above the housetops. "I'm tired and hungry, Brother Cadrach, and I don't understand what you are getting at."

"Simply this. The Perdruinese are what they are because they strive to please—or, put more clearly, they know which way the wind is blowing and they run that direction, so the wind is always at their backs. If we Hernystir-folk were a conquering people, the merchants and sailors of Perdruin would be practicing their Hernystiri. 'If a king wants apples,' as the Nabbanai say, 'Perdruin plants orchards.' Any other nation would be foolish to attack such a compliant friend and helpful ally."

"Then you are saying that the souls of these Perdruin-folk are for sale?" Miriamele demanded. "That they have no loyalty to any but the strong?"

Cadrach smiled. "That has the ring of disdain, my lady, but it seems an accurate summing up, yes."

"Then they're no better than—" she looked around carefully, fighting down anger, "—no better than whores!"

The monk's weathered face took on a cool, distant cast; his smile was now a mere formality. "Not everyone can stand up and be a hero, Princess," he said quietly. "Some prefer to surrender to the inevitable and salve their consciences with the gift of survival."

Miriamele thought about the obvious truth of what Cadrach had said as they walked on, but could not understand why it made her so unutterably sad.

The cobbled paths of Ansis Pelippé not only wound tortuously, in many places they climbed in gouged stone steps up the very face of the hill, then spiraled back down, doubling and redoubling, crossing each other at odd angles like a basket of serpents. On either side the houses stood shoulder to shoulder, most with windows shadowed like the closed eyes of sleepers, some ablaze with light and music. The foundations of the houses tilted upward from the streets, each structure clinging precariously to the hillside so that their upper stories seemed to lean over the constricted roads. As her hunger and fatigue began to make her giddy, Miriamele felt at times that she was back beneath the close-stooping trees of Aldheorte Forest.

Perdruin was a cluster of hills surrounding Sta Mirore, the central mountain. Their lumpy backs rose up almost directly from the island's rocky verges, looking over the Bay of Emettin. Perdruin's silhouette thus resembled a mother pig and her feeding young. There was little flat land anywhere, except in the saddles where high hills shouldered together, so the villages and towns of Perdruin clung to the faces of these hills like gulls' nests. Even Ansis Pellipé, the great seaport and the seat of Count Streáwe's house, was built on the steep slopes of a promontory that the residents called Harborstone. In many places the citizens of Ansis Pellipé could stand on one of the capital's hill-hugging streets and wave to their neighbors on the thoroughfare below.

*   *   *

"I must eat something," Miriamele said at last, breathing heavily. They stood at a turnout of one of the looping streets, a place where they could look down between two buildings to the lights of the foggy harbor below. The dull moon hung in the clouded sky like a chip of bone.

"I am also ready to stop, Malachias," panted Cadrach.

"How far is this abbey?"

"There is no abbey, or at least we are not going to such a place."

"But you told the captain . . . oh." Miriamele shook her head, feeling the damp heaviness of her hood and cloak. "Of course. So, then, where are we going?"

Cadrach stared at the moon and laughed quietly. "Wherever we wish, my friend. I do think there is a tavern of some repute at the top of this street: I must confess I was leading us in that general direction. Certainly not because I enjoy climbing these *goirach* hills."

"A tavern? Why not a hostel, so we can find a bed after we eat?"

"Because, begging your pardon, it is not eating that I am thinking about. I have been aboard that abominable ship longer than I care to think. I will take my rest after I have indulged my thirst." Cadrach wiped his hand across his mouth and grinned. Miriamele did not much like the look in his eyes.

"But there was a tavern every cubit down below . . ." she began.

"Exactly. Taverns full of drunken tale-passers and minders of others' business. I cannot be taking my well-deserved rest in such a place." He turned his back on the moon and began stumping away up the road. "Come, Malachias. It is only a little farther, I am sure."

It seemed that during Midsummer Festival there was no such thing as an uncrowded tavern, but at least the drinkers in *The Red Dolphin* were not cheek to cheek, as they were in the dockside inns, only elbow to elbow. Miriamele gratefully slid down onto a bench set against the far wall and let the wash of conversation and song flow over her. Cadrach, after putting down his sack and walking stick, moved off to find himself a mug of Traveler's Reward. He returned after only a moment.

"Good Malachias, I had forgotten how nearly beggared I am from paying our sea passage. Do you have a cintis-piece or two I might employ in the removal of thirst?"

Miriamele dug in her purse and produced a palm full of coppers. "Get me some bread and cheese," she said, pouring the coins into the monk's outstretched hand.

As she sat wishing she could take off her wet cloak to celebrate being out of the rain, another group of costumed celebrants banged in through the door, shaking water from their finery and calling for beer. One of the loudest wore a mask shaped like a red-tongued hound. As he thumped his fist on a table, his right eye lit on Miriamele for a moment and seemed to pause. She felt a rush of fear, suddenly remembering another hound mask, and flaming arrows slashing through the forest shadows. But this dog quickly turned back to his fellows, making a jest and throwing his head back in laughter, his cloth ears swinging.

Miriamele pushed her hand against her chest as if to slow down her speeding heart.

I must keep this hood on, she told herself. *It's a festival night, so who will look twice? Better that than someone recognizing my face—however unlikely that might seem.*

Cadrach was gone a surprisingly long time. Miriamele was just starting to feel restive, wondering if she should go and look for him, when he returned with a jar of ale in each hand. A half-loaf of bread and an end of cheese were prisoned between the jars.

"A man could die of thirst a-waiting for beer, tonight," the monk said.

Miriamele ate greedily, then took a long swallow of the ale, which was bitter and dark in her mouth. The rest of the jar she left for Cadrach, who did not protest.

When the last crumbs were licked from her fingers and she was pondering whether she was hungry enough to eat a pigeon pie, a shadow fell across the bench she and the monk shared.

The raw-boned face of Death stared down at them from a black cowl.

Miriamele gasped and Cadrach sputtered ale on his gray robe, but the stranger in the skull mask did not move.

"A very pretty joke, friend," Cadrach said angrily, "and merry midsummer to you, too." He swiped at the front of his garments.

The mouth did not move. The flat, unexcited voice issued from behind the bared teeth. *"You come with me."*

Miriamele felt the skin on the back of her neck crawl. Her recently-consumed meal felt very heavy in her stomach.

Cadrach squinted. She could see tension in his neck and fingers. "And who might you be, mummer? Were you truly Brother Death, I would expect you clad in finer clothing." The monk pointed a slightly trembling finger at the tattered black cloak the figure wore.

"Stand up and come with me," the apparition said. "I have a knife. If you shout, things will be very bad for you."

Brother Cadrach looked at Miriamele and grimaced. They rose, the princess on wobbly knees. Death gestured for them to walk ahead, through the press of tavern guests.

Miriamele was entertaining disconnected thoughts of making a bolt for freedom when two other figures slipped discreetly out of the crowd near the doorway. One wore a blue mask and the stylized garb of a sailor; the other was dressed as a rustic peasant in an oversized hat. The somber eyes of the newcomers belied their gaudy costumes.

With the sailor and peasant on either side, Cadrach and Miriamele followed black-cloaked Death out into the street. Before they had gone three dozen paces, the little caravan turned into an alley and down a flight of stairs to the next street below. Miriamele slipped for a moment on one of the rainwashed stone steps and felt a thrill of horror as her skull-faced captor reached out a hand to steady her. The touch was fleeting and she could not draw away without falling down, so she suffered it silently. A moment later they were off the stairway, then quickly into another alleyway, up a ramp, and around a corner.

Even with the faint moon overhead and the cries of late revelers echoing from the tavern above and the harbor district below, Miriamele quickly lost any sense of where she was. They traveled down tiny back streets like a string of skulking cats, ducking in and out of hidden courtyards and vine-shrouded walkways. From time to time they heard the murmur of voices from a darkened house, and once the sound of a woman crying.

At last they reached an arched gateway in a tall stone wall. Death produced a key from his pocket and opened the lock. They stepped through into an overgrown courtyard roofed with leaning willow trees, from whose trailing branches rainwater dripped patiently onto the cracked stone cobbles. The leader turned to the others, gestured briefly with his key, then indicated that Miriamele and Cadrach should walk ahead of him toward a shadowed doorway.

"We have come with you so far, man," the monk said, whispering as if he, too, were a conspirator. "But there is no benefit to us in walking into an ambush. Why should we not fight you here and die beneath open sky, if we must be dying?"

Death leaned forward without a word. Cadrach started back, but the skull-masked man only leaned past him and knocked on the door with black-gloved knuckles, then pushed it inward. It swung open silently on oiled hinges.

A dim, warm light burned inside the portal. Miriamele stepped past the monk and through the doorway. Cadrach followed a moment later, muttering to himself. Skull-face came last of all and pushed the door shut behind him.

It was a small sitting room, lit only by a fire in the grate and one candle burning in a dish beside a decanter of wine on the table top. The walls were covered with heavy velvet tapestries, their designs distinguishable in the firelight only as swirls of color. Behind the table, in a high backed chair, sat a figure fully as strange as any of their escorts: a tall man in a russet-brown cloak, wearing the sharp-featured mask of a fox.

The fox leaned forward, indicating two chairs with a graceful sweep of his velvet-gloved fingers.

"Sit down." His voice was thin but melodious. "Sit down, Princess Miriamele. I would rise, but my crippled legs do not permit it."

"This is madness," Cadrach blustered, but kept an eye on the skull-faced specter at his shoulder. "You have made a mistake, sir—this is a boy you address, my acolyte . . ."

"Please." The fox gestured amiably for silence. "It is time to doff our masks. Is that not how Midsummer Night always ends?"

He lifted the fox face away, revealing a shock of white hair and a face seamed with age. As his unmasked eyes glittered in the fireglow, a smile quirked his wrinkled lips.

"Now that you know who I am . . ." he began, but Cadrach interrupted him.

"We do not know you, sir, and you have mistaken us!"

The old man laughed dryly. "Oh, come. You and I may not have met before, my dear fellow, but the princess and I are old friends. As a matter of fact, she was my guest, once—long, long ago."

"You are . . . Count Streáwe?" Miriamele breathed.

"Indeed," the count nodded. His shadow loomed on the wall behind him. He leaned forward, clasping her wet hand in his velvet-sheathed claw. "Perdruin's master. And, beginning the moment you two touched foot on the rock over which I rule, your master as well."

3

Oath-Breaker

Later in the day of his meeting with the Herder and Huntress, when the sun was high in the sky, Simon felt strong enough to go outside and sit on the rocky porch before his cave. He wrapped a corner of his blanket about his shoulders and tucked the remainder of the heavy wool beneath him as a cushion against the mountain's stony skin. But for the royal couch in Chidsik ub Lingit, there seemed to be nothing like a chair in all of Yiqanuc.

The herders had long since led their sheep out of the protected valleys where they slept, taking them down-mountain in search of fodder. Jiriki had told him that the spring shoots on which the animals usually fed had been all but destroyed by the clinging winter. Simon watched one of the flocks milling on a slope far below him, tiny as ants. A faint clacking sound wafted up to him, the rams butting horns as they contested for mastery of the herd.

The troll women, their black-haired babies strapped to their backs in pouches of finely stitched hide, had taken up slender spears and gone out hunting, stalking marmots and other animals whose meat could help to eke out the mutton. Binabik had often said that the sheep were the Qanuc people's true wealth, that they ate only such members of their flocks as were good for nothing else, the old and the barren.

Marmots, coneys, and other such small game were not the only reason the troll women carried spears. One of the furs ostentatiously wrapped around Nunuuika had been that of a snow leopard, dagger-sharp claws still gleaming. Remembering the Huntress' fierce eyes, Simon had little doubt that Nunuuika had brought down that prize herself.

The women were not alone in facing danger; the task of the herdsmen was just as perilous, since there were many large predators that had to be kept from the precious sheep. Binabik had once told him that the wolves and leopards, although a threat, were scarcely comparable to the huge snow bears, the biggest of them heavy as two dozen trolls. Many a Qanuc herder, Binabik had said, met a swift and unpleasant end beneath the claws and teeth of a white bear.

Simon repressed a reflexive tremor of unease at this thought. Hadn't he stood before the dragon Igjarjuk, grander and deadlier by far than any ordinary animal?

He sat as late morning passed into afternoon, watching the life of Mintahoq as it lay spread before him, as simultaneously hectic yet organized as a beehive. The elders, their years of hunting and herding past, gossiped from porch to porch or crouched in the sun, carving bone and horn, cutting and sewing cured hide into all manner of things. Children too big to be carried off to the hunt by their mothers played games up and down the mountain under the old folks' bemused supervision, shinnying up the slender ladders or swinging and tumbling on the swaying thong bridges, heedless of the fatal distances that stretched beneath them. Simon found it more than a little difficult to watch these dangerous amusements, but through all the long afternoon not a single troll child came to harm. Though the details were alien and unfamiliar, he could sense the order here. The measured beat of life seemed as strong and stable as the mountain itself.

That night Simon dreamed once more of the great wheel.

This time, as in a cruel parody of the passion of Usires the Son of God, Simon was bound helplessly to the wheel, a limb at each quarter of the heavy rim. It turned him not only topside-down, as Lord Usires had suffered upon the Tree, but spun him around and around in an earthless void of black sky. The stars' bleak radiance blurred before him like the tails of comets. Something else—some shadowy, icy thing whose laugh was the empty buzzing of flies—danced just beyond his sight, mocking him.

He called out, as he often did in such terrible dreams, but no sound came forth. He struggled, but his limbs were without strength. Where was God, who the priests said saw every act? Why should He leave Simon in the grasp of such dreadful darknesses?

Something seemed to form slowly out of the pale, attenuated stars; his heart filled with awful anticipation. But what emerged from the spinning void was not the expected red-eyed horror, but a small, solemn face: the little dark-haired girl he had seen in other dreams.

She opened her mouth. The madly revolving sky seemed to slow.

She spoke his name.

It came to him as down a long corridor, and he realized he had seen her somewhere. He knew that face—but who . . . where. . . ?

"Simon," she said again, somehow clearer now. Her voice was filled with urgency. But something else was reaching out for him, too—something closer to hand. Something quite near . . .

He awoke.

⋆   ⋆   ⋆

Someone was looking for him. Simon sat up on his pallet, breathless, alert for any sound. But for the endless sighing of the mountain winds and the faint snoring of Haestan, wrapped in his heavy cloak near the coals of the evening's fire, the cavern was still.

Jiriki was absent. Could the Sitha have called to him from outside the cave? Or was it only the residue of dream? Simon shivered and considered pulling the fur coverlet back over his head once more. His breath was a dim cloud in the ember-light.

No, somebody was waiting outside. He did not know how he knew, but he was sure: he felt tuned like a harp string, trembling. The night seemed tight-stretched.

What if someone *did* wait for him? Perhaps it was someone—some *thing*—from which it would be better to hide?

Such thoughts made little difference. He had gotten it into his head that he must go out. Now the need tugged at him, impossible to ignore.

My cheek aches terribly, anyway, he told himself. *I won't be able to fall asleep for a long while.*

He snaked his breeches out from under the sleeping-cloak where they stayed warm in the bitter Yiqanuc night, wrestling them on as silently as he could, then pulled his boots onto his cold feet. He briefly debated putting on his mail shirt, but the thought of its chilly rings, rather than any surety of safety, decided him against it. He furled the cloak around him, stilting quietly past sleeping Haestan and out under the door-skin into the cold.

The stars over high Mintahoq were mercilessly clear. As Simon stared up, amazed, he felt their distance, the impossible vastness of the night sky. The moon, not quite full, hovered low over distant peaks. Bathed in its diffident light, the snow on the heights gleamed, but all else lay sunken in shadow.

Even as he turned his eyes down and took a few steps to the right, away from the cave-mouth, he was stopped short by a low growl. A strange silhouette loomed on the pathway before him, moonbrushed at the edges, black at the core. The deep rumble came again. Eyes flared green as they caught the moonlight.

Simon's breath snagged in his throat for a moment, until he remembered.

"Qantaqa?" he said quietly.

The growl changed into a curious whine. The wolf tipped its head.

"Qantaqa? Is it you?" He tried to think of some of Binabik's troll speech, but could summon nothing. "Are you hurt?" He silently cursed himself. He had not once thought of the wolf since he had been brought down from the dragon's mountain, although she had been a companion—and, in a way, a friend.

Selfish! he chided himself.

With Binabik imprisoned, who knew what Qantaqa had done? Her friend and master had been taken from her, just as Doctor Morgenes had been taken from Simon. The night seemed suddenly colder and emptier, full of the world's heedless cruelty.

"Qantaqa? Are you hungry?" He took a step toward her and the wolf shied back. She growled again, but it sounded more like excitement than anger. She took a few prancing steps, the shimmer of her gray coat almost invisible, then growled again before bounding away. Simon followed her.

It occurred to him as he went, stepping carefully on the wet stone pathways, that he was doing a foolish thing. The twisting roadways of high Mintahoq were no place for a midnight walk, especially without a torch. Even the native trolls knew better: the cave-mouths were lightless and silent, the paths empty. It was as if he had wakened from one dream to enter another, this shadowy pilgrimage beneath the distant and uncaring moon.

Qantaqa seemed to know where she was going. When Simon lagged too far behind she trotted back, stopping just out of reach until he caught up, her hot breath pluming the air. As soon as he drew within an arm's length she was off again. Thus, like a spirit of the afterworld, she led him away from the fires of his own kind.

It was only when they had walked for some time, traveling well around the curve of the mountain from the sleeping-cave, that Qantaqa bounded all the way back to Simon. She did not pull up short this time. Her great frame struck him so suddenly that even though she had merely bumped against him, he fell back onto his seat. She stood over him for a moment, her face buried in his neck, cold nose rooting ticklingly near his ear. Simon reached up to scratch her ears and felt her tremble even through her thick fur. A moment later, as if her need for comfort had been satisfied, she leaped away again and stood whining quietly until he rose, rubbing his tailbone, and followed.

It seemed that Qantaqa had led him halfway around Mintahoq. She stood now at the edge of a great blackness, yipping in excitement. Simon walked forward cautiously, feeling the raw stone face of the mountain with his right hand as he went. Qantaqa paced in seeming impatience.

The wolf was standing at the rim of a great pit, which burrowed away from the side of the path into the very mountain. The moon, sailing low in the sky like an overloaded carrack, could only silver the stone around the hole's mouth. Qantaqa barked again with barely contained enthusiasm.

To Simon's staggering surprise, a voice echoed thinly from below.

"Go away, wolf! Even sleep is taken from me, Aedon curse it!"

Simon threw himself to the cold gravel and crawled forward on elbows and knees, stopping at last with his head hanging over blind nothingness.

"Who's there?" he cried. His words reverberated as though they journeyed a great distance. "Sludig?"

There was a pause.

"Simon? Is that you who calls?"

"Yes! Yes, it's me! Qantaqa brought me! Is Binabik with you? Binabik! It's me, Simon!"

A silent moment passed, then Sludig spoke again. Now Simon could hear the strain in the Rimmersman's voice. "The troll will not speak. He is here, but he will not speak to me, to Jiriki when he came, to anyone."

"Is he sick? Binabik, it's Simon! Why don't you answer me?"

"He is sick in his heart, I think," Sludig said. "He looks as he always did—thinner, perhaps, but so I am, too—but he acts like one already dead." There was a scraping noise as Sludig, or someone, moved in the depths. "Jiriki says they will kill us," the Rimmersman said a moment later, his voice flat with resignation. "The Sitha spoke for us—not with heat or anger, as far as I could tell, but he spoke for us all the same. He said the troll people did not agree with his arguments and were determined to have their justice." He laughed bitterly. "Some justice, to kill a man who never did them harm, and kill one of their own as well, both of whom have suffered much for the good of all folk—even the trolls. Einskaldir was right. But for this silent fellow beside me, they are all hell-wights."

Simon sat up, holding his head in his hands. The wind blew uncaringly about the heights. Helplessness spread through him.

"Binabik!" he cried, leaning over once more. "Qantaqa waits for you! Sludig suffers at your side! No one can help if you don't help yourself! Why won't you speak to me?!"

Only Sludig answered. "It's no good, I tell you. His eyes are closed. He does not hear you, will not speak at all."

Simon slapped his hand against the rock and cursed. He felt tears start in his eyes.

"I will help you, Sludig," he said at last. "I do not know how, but I will." He sat up. Qantaqa nosed him and whimpered. "Can I bring you something? Food? Water?"

Sludig laughed dully. "No. They feed us, although not to bursting. I would ask for wine, but I do not know when they come for me. I will not go with my head foggy from drink. Only pray for me, please. And for the troll, too."

"I will do more than that, Sludig, I swear." He stood up.

"You were very brave on the mountain, Simon," Sludig called quietly. "I am glad that I knew you."

The stars glittered coldly above the pit as Simon walked away, fighting to stand straight and cry no more.

★   ★   ★

He walked a while beneath the moon, lost in the swirl of his distracted thoughts, before he realized that he was again following Qantaqa. The wolf, who had paced anxiously beside the edge of the pit while Simon talked to Sludig, now trotted purposefully along the path before him. She did not allow him a chance to catch up as she had on their outward journey, and he was hard pressed to keep to her pace.

The moonlight was just bright enough for Simon to see where he was going, the trail just wide enough to allow for recovery from the occasional misstep. Still, he was feeling decidedly weak. He wondered more than once whether he should just sit down and wait until dawn came, when someone would find him and return him safely to his cave, but Qantaqa trotted on, full of lupine determination. Feeling that he owed her a sort of loyalty, Simon did his best to follow.

He soon noted with more than a little alarm that they seemed to be climbing above the main trail, angling up Mintahoq's face along a steeper, narrower pathway. As the wolf led him ever upward, and as they cut across more than a few horizontal paths, the air began to seem thinner. Simon knew he had not climbed so far, that the sensation was due instead to his own flagging wind, but he nevertheless felt himself to be passing out of the realms of safety into the upper heights. The stars seemed very close.

He wondered for a moment if those cold stars might somehow be the airless peaks of other, incredibly distant mountains, vast bodies lost in darkness, snow-capped heads gleaming with reflected moonlight. But no, that was foolishness. Where could they be standing, that they would not be visible in daylight beneath the bright sun?

In truth, the air might have been no scarcer, but the cold was certainly growing, undeniable and intrusive despite his heavy cloak. Shivering, he decided he should turn around and make his way back down to the main roadway, no matter what moonlight pastime Qantaqa found so enticing. A moment later, he was surprised to find himself stepping up off the path and following the wolf onto a narrow shelf in the mountainside.

The rocky porch, dotted with patches of dimly gleaming snow, stood before a large, black crevice. Qantaqa jogged forward and stopped before it, sniffing. She turned to regard Simon, her shaggy head tipped at an angle, then barked once inquiringly and slipped into blackness. Simon decided there must be a cave hidden in the shadows. He was wondering whether he should follow her—letting a wolf lead him on a foolish hike along the mountainside was one thing, but letting her lead him into a lightless cavern in the middle of the night was another thing entirely—when a trio of small dark shapes appeared out of the blackness of the cliff face before him, startling Simon so badly that he almost stepped backward off the stone porch.

Diggers! he thought wildly, scrabbling on the barren ground for some weapon. One of the shapes stepped forward, raising a slender spear toward him as if in warning. It was a troll, of course—they were quite a bit larger than the subterranean Bukken, when calmly examined—but still he was frightened. These Qanuc were small but well-armed; Simon was a stranger wandering about at night, perhaps in some sacred place.

The nearest troll pushed back a fur-ringed hood. Pallid moonlight shone on the face of a young woman. Simon could see little of her features but the whites of her eyes, but he was sure her expression was fierce and dangerous. Her two companions moved up beside her, muttering in what seemed like angry voices. He took a step backward down the pathway, feeling carefully for a safe foothold.

"I'm sorry. I'm just going," he said, realizing even as he spoke that they could not understand him. Simon cursed himself for not having Binabik or Jiriki teach him some words of troll speech. Always regretting, always too late! Would he be a mooncalf forever? He was tired of the position. Let someone else take it on.

"I'm just going," he repeated. "I was following the wolf. Following . . . the . . . wolf." He spoke slowly, trying to make his voice sound friendly despite his tightened throat. One misunderstanding and he might be plucking one of those wicked-looking spears out of his midsection.

The troll woman watched him. She said something to one of her companions. The one addressed took a few steps toward the shadowed cave-mouth. Qantaqa growled menacingly from somewhere within the echoing depths and the troll quickly scuttled away again.

Simon took another step back down the path. The trolls watched him in silence, their small dark forms poised and watchful, but they made no move to hinder him. He turned his back on them slowly and helped himself down the trail, picking his way among the silvered rocks. After a moment the three trolls, Qantaqa, and the mysterious cave were all out of sight behind him.

He made his way downslope alone in dreaming moonlight. Halfway back to the main trail he had to stop and sit, elbows on trembling knees. He knew that his exhaustion and even his fear would eventually recede, but he could imagine no cure for such loneliness.

"I am truly sorry, Seoman, but there is nothing to be done. Last night Reniku, the star we call Summer-Lantern, appeared above the horizon at sundown. I have stayed too long. I can remain no longer."

Jiriki sat cross-legged atop a rock on the cave's vast porch, staring down into the mist-carpeted valley. Unlike Simon and Haestan, he wore no heavy clothing. The wind plucked at the sleeves of his glossy shirt.

"But what will we do about Binabik and Sludig?" Simon flung a stone

into the depths, half-hoping it would wound some fog-hidden troll below.
"They'll be killed if you don't do something!"

"There is nothing I could do, in any circumstance," Jiriki said quietly.
"The Qanuc have a right to their justice. I cannot honorably interfere."

"Honor? Hang honor, Binabik won't even speak! How can he defend
himself?"

The Sitha sighed, but his hawkish face remained impassive. "Perhaps
there is no defense. Perhaps Binabik knows he has wronged his people."

Haestan snorted his disgust. "We dunna even know th' little man's
crime."

"Oath-breaking, I am told," Jiriki said mildly. He turned to Simon. "I
must go, Seoman. The news of the Norn Queen's Huntsman attacking the
Zida'ya has upset my people very much. They wish me home. There is
much to discuss." Jiriki brushed a strand of hair from his eye. "Also,
when my kinsman An'nai died and was buried on Urmsheim, a responsibility fell upon me. His name must now be entered with full ceremony in
the Book of Year-Dancing. I, of all my people, can least shirk that
responsibility. It was, after all, Jiriki i-Sa'onserei and no other who brought
him to the place of his death—and it was much to do with me and my
willfulness that he went." The Sitha's voice hardened as he clenched his
brown fingers into a fist. "Do you not see? I cannot turn my back on
An'nai's sacrifice."

Simon was desperate. "I don't know anything about your Dancing
Book—but you said that we would be allowed to speak for Binabik! They
told you so!"

Jiriki cocked his head. "Yes. The Herder and Huntress so agreed."

"Well, how will we be able to do that if you are gone? We can't speak
the troll-tongue and they can't understand ours."

Simon thought he saw a look of bewilderment flit briefly across the
Sitha's imperturbable face, but it passed so swiftly he was not sure. Jiriki's
flake-gold eyes caught and held his gaze. They stared at each other for
long moments.

"You are right, Seoman," Jiriki said slowly. "Honor and heritage have
pincered me before, but never quite so neatly." He dropped his head
down and stared at his hands, then slowly lifted his eyes to the gray sky.
"An'nai and my family must forgive me. *J'asu pra-peroihin!* The Book of
Year-Dancing must then record my disgrace." He took a deep breath. "I
will stay while Binabik of Yiqanuc has his day at court."

Simon should have exulted, but instead felt only hollowness. Even to a
mortal, the Sitha prince's unhappiness was profoundly apparent: Jiriki was
making some terrible sacrifice that Simon could not understand. But what
else could be done? They were all caught here on this high rock beyond
the known world, all prisoners—at least of circumstance. They were
ignorant heroes, friends to oath-breakers . . .

A chill dashed up Simon's backbone. "Jiriki!" he gasped, waving his hands as if to clear a way for the sudden inspiration.

Would it work? Even if it did, would it help?

"Jiriki," he said again, more quietly this time, "I believe I have thought of something that will let you do what you need to and help Binabik and Sludig, too."

Haestan, hearing the tightness in Simon's voice, put down the stick he had been carving and leaned forward. Jiriki raised an expectant eyebrow.

"You will only need to do one thing," Simon said. "You must go with me to see the king and queen—the Herder and the Huntress."

After they had spoken to Nunuuika and Uammanaq, gaining the pair's grudging acceptance of their proposal, Simon and Jiriki walked back in mountain twilight from the House of the Ancestor. The Sitha wore a faint smile.

"You continue to surprise me, young Seoman. This is a bold stroke. I have no idea if it will help your friend, but it is a beginning, nevertheless."

"They would never have agreed if you hadn't asked, Jiriki. Thank you."

The Sitha made a complicated gesture with his long fingers. "There is still a brittle respect between the Zida'ya and some of the Sunset Children—chiefly the Hernystiri and the Qanuc. Five desolate centuries cannot so easily overwhelm the millennia of grace. Still, things have changed. You mortals—Lingit's children, as the trolls say—are in ascendancy. It is not my people's world any longer." His hand reached out, touching lightly on Simon's arm as they walked. "There is also a bond between you and me, Seoman. I have not forgotten that."

Simon, trudging along at the side of an immortal, could think of no reply.

"I ask only that you understand this: my kin and I are now very few. I owe you my life—twice, in fact, to my great distress—but my obligations to my people greatly outweigh even the value of my own continued existence. There are some things that cannot be wished away, young mortal. I hope for Binabik's and Sludig's survival, of course . . . but I am Zida'ya. I must take back the story of what happened on the dragon-mountain: the treachery of Utuk'ku's minions and the passing of An'nai."

He stopped suddenly and turned to face Simon. In the violet-tinged evening shadows, with his hair blowing, he seemed a spirit of the wild mountains. For a moment, Simon perceived Jiriki's immense age in his eyes, and felt he could almost grasp that great ungraspable: the vast duration of the prince's race, the years of their history like grains of sand on a beach.

"Things are not so easily ended, Seoman," Jiriki said slowly, "even by my leaving. It is a very unmagical wisdom that tells me we shall meet again. The debts of the Zida'ya run deep and dark. They carry with them the stuff of myth. I owe you such a debt." Jiriki again flexed his fingers in a peculiar sign, then reached into his thin shirt and produced a flat, circular object.

"You have seen this before, Seoman," he said. "It is my mirror—a scale of the Greater Worm, as its legend has it."

Simon took it from the Sitha's outstretched palm, marveling at its surprising lightness. The carved frame was cool beneath his fingers. Once this mirror had shown him an image of Miriamele; another time, Jiriki had produced the forest-city of Enki-e-Shao'saye from its depths. Now, only Simon's own somber reflection stared back, murky in the half-light.

"I give it to you. It is has been a talisman of my family's since Jenjiyana of the Nightingales tended fragrant gardens in the shade of Sení Anzi'in. Away from me, it will no longer be anything but a looking glass." Jiriki raised his hand. "No, that is not quite true. If you must speak with me, or have need of me—*true need*—tell the mirror. I will hear and know." Jiriki pointed a stern finger at the speechless Simon. "But do not think to summon me in a puff of smoke, as in one of your folk's goblin stories. I have no such magical powers. I cannot even promise you I will be able to come. But if I hear of your need, I will do what is in my power to help. The Zida'ya are not totally without friends, even in this bold young world of mortals."

Simon's mouth worked for a moment. "Thank you," he said at last. The small gray glass suddenly seemed a thing of great weight indeed. "Thank you."

Jiriki smiled, showing a stripe of white teeth. Again he seemed what he was among his own folk—a youth. "And you have your ring, as well." He gestured at Simon's other hand, to the thin gold band with its fish-shaped sign. "Talk of goblin stories, Seoman! The White Arrow, the black sword, a golden ring, *and* a Sithi seeing-glass—you are so weighted down with significant booty that you will clank when you walk!" The prince laughed, a trill of hissing music.

Simon stared at the ring, saved for him from the wrack of the doctor's chambers, sent on to Binabik as one of Morgenes' final acts. Grimy with the oil of the gloves Simon had been wearing, it sat unflatteringly on a dirt-blackened finger.

"I still don't know what the writing inside means," he said. On a whim, he twisted it off and handed it to the Sitha. "Binabik couldn't read it either, except for something about dragons and death." He had a sudden thought. "Does it help the person wearing it to slay dragons?" It was an oddly depressing idea, especially since he didn't think he'd actually managed to slay the ice-worm. Had it only been a magical spell after all? As he recovered his strength, he found himself more and more proud of his bravery in the face of the terrible Igjarjuk.

"Whatever happened on Urmsheim was between you and ancient Hidohebhi's child, Seoman. There was no magic." Jiriki's smile had disappeared. He shook his head solemnly, passing the ring back. "But I cannot tell you more about the ring. If the wise man Morgenes did not provide for your understanding when he sent it to you, then I will not presume to tell. I have perhaps already burdened you unfairly during our short acquaintance. Even the bravest mortals grow sick with too much truth."

"You can read what it says?"

"Yes. It is written in one of the languages of the Zida'ya—although, interestingly for a mortal trinket, one of the more obscure. I will tell you this, however. If I understand its meaning, it does not concern you now in any direct fashion, and knowing what it said would not help you in any palpable way."

"And that's all you'll tell me?"

"For now. Perhaps if we meet again, I will have more understanding of why it was given to you." The Sitha's face was troubled. "Good fortune to you, Seoman. You are an odd boy—even for a mortal. . . ."

At that moment they heard Haestan's shout and saw the Erkynlander striding up the path toward them, waving something. He had caught a snow hare. The fire, he called happily, was ready for cooking.

Even with a stomach comfortably full of broiled meat and herbs, it took Simon a long time to fall asleep that night. As he lay on his pallet looking up at the flickering red shadows on the cave ceiling, his mind tumbled with all that had happened, the maddening tale in which he had been caught up.

I'm in a sort of story, just like Jiriki said. A story like Shem used to tell—or is it History, like Doctor Morgenes used to teach me. . . ? But no one ever explained how terrible it is to be in the middle of a tale and not to know the ending. . . .

He slipped away at last, awakening with a start some time later. Haestan, as always, was snorting and sighing in his beard, deep in slumber. There was no sign of Jiriki. Somehow, the cavern's curious emptiness told Simon that the Sitha was truly gone, headed down the mountain to return to his home.

Stung by loneliness, even with the guardsman grumbling stuporously away nearby, he found himself crying. He did so quietly, ashamed at this failure of manhood, but he could no more stop the flow of tears than lift great Mintahoq on his back.

Simon and Haestan came to Chidsik ub Lingit at the time Jiriki had told them—an hour after dawn. The cold had worsened. The ladders and thong bridges swayed in the cold wind, unused. Mintahoq's stone byways had become even more treacherous than usual, covered in many places by a thin skin of ice.

As the two outsiders pressed their way in through a horde of chattering trolls, Simon leaned heavily on Haestan's fur-cloaked elbow. He had not slept well after the Sitha had gone, his dreams shot through with the shadows of swords and the compelling but inexplicable presence of the small, dark-eyed girl.

The troll folk around them were done up as if for a festival, many in shiny necklaces of carved tusk and bone, the women with their black hair bound up in combs made from the skulls of birds and fish. Men and women both passed skins of some highland liquor back and forth, laughing and gesturing as they drank. Haestan watched this procedure gloomily.

"I talked one of 'em into givin' me sip o' that," the guardsman said. "Tasted like horse piss, did. What I wouldna give for drop o' red Perdruin."

At the center of the room, just within the moat of unlit oil, Simon and Haestan found four intricately-worked bone stools with seats of stretched hide, which stood facing the empty dais. Since the milling trolls had made themselves comfortable all around, but had left the seats empty, the interlopers guessed that two of the stools were theirs. No sooner had they seated themselves than the Yiqanuc folk gathered around them stood up. A strange noise rose, echoing from the cavern walls—a sonorous, humming chant. Incomprehensible Qanuc words, like castoff spars floating on an uneasy sea, bobbed to the surface and then slipped back beneath the steady moaning. It was a strange and disturbing sound.

For a moment Simon thought the chanting had something to do with his and Haestan's entrance, but the dark eyes of the assembled trolls were focused on a door in the far cavern wall.

Through this door at last came not the masters of Yiqanuc, as Simon had expected, but a figure even more exotic than the folk who surrounded him. The newcomer was a troll, or at least of troll size. His small, muscular body was oiled so that it gleamed in the lamplight. He wore a fringed skirt of hide and his face was hidden behind a mask made from a ram's skull which had been decoratively carved and gouged until the bone was scarcely more than a filigree, a white basket around the black eye holes. Two enormous, curving horns that had been hollowed to near transparency stood out over his shoulders. A mantel of white and yellow feathers and a necklace of curved black claws swung beneath the bony mask.

Simon could not tell if this man was a priest, a dancer, or simply a herald for the royal couple. When he stamped his gleaming foot the crowd roared happily. When he touched the tips of his horns, then raised his palms to the sky, the troll folk gasped and quickly resumed their chanting. For long moments the man capered across the raised dais, as intent on his work as any solemn craftsman. At last he paused as though listening. The murmuring of the crowd stopped. Four more figures appeared in the doorway—three of troll size, one towering over the rest.

Binabik and Sludig were brought forward. One troll guard stood on each side, the heads of their sharp spears remaining at all times near the prisoners' backbones. Simon wanted to stand and shout, but Haestan's broad hand fell on his arm, holding him down on his stool.

"Quiet, lad. They be comin' this way. Wait for 'em t'get here. We make no show for this rabble."

Both the troll and the fair-haired Rimmersman were considerably thinner than when Simon had last seen them. Sludig's bushy-bearded face was pink and peeling, as though he had been too much in the sun. Binabik was paler than he had been, his once-brown skin now the color of porridge; his eyes seemed sunken, surrounded by shadows.

The pair walked slowly, the troll head down, Sludig looking defiantly around the room until he saw Simon and Haestan, to whom he offered a grim smile. As they stepped over the moat into the inner circle, the Rimmersman reached out and patted Simon's shoulder, then grunted in pain as one of the guards following close behind pricked his arm with a spear point.

"Had I but a sword," Sludig murmured, stepping forward and gingerly seating himself on one of the stools. Binabik took the seat at the far end. He had not yet raised his eyes to meet those of his companions.

"Take more than swords, friend," Haestan whispered. "They be small, but stern—an' look at th'Usires-cursed numbers of 'em!"

"Binabik!" said Simon urgently, leaning across Sludig. "Binabik! We've come to speak for you!"

The troll looked up. For a moment it seemed he might say something, but his dark eyes were distant. He gave the slightest, gentlest shake of his head, then returned his gaze to the cavern floor. Simon felt rage burning inside him. Binabik must fight for his life! He was sitting like old Rim the plow-horse, waiting for the killing blow to fall.

The growing buzz of excited voices was abruptly stilled. Another trio of figures appeared in the doorway, moving slowly forward: Nunuuika the Huntress and Uammannaq the Herder, in full ceremonial trappings of fur and ivory and polished stones. Another troll followed them on silent, soft-booted feet—a young woman, her large eyes expressionless, her mouth set in a firm line. Her shuttered stare flicked across the line of stools, then away. The man with the ram horns danced before the threesome until they reached the dais and ascended to their divan of hides and fur robes. The unfamiliar troll woman sat just before the royal pair, one step below the top. The capering herald—or whatever he was: Simon still could not decide—thrust a taper into one of the wall lamps, then touched it to the ring of oil, which caught with a blazing huff. Flames raced around the circle, trailing black smoke. A moment later the smoke dissipated upward into the shadowy reaches of the cavern ceiling. Simon and the others were surrounded by a ring of fire.

The Herder leaned forward, lifting his crooked spear, and waved it at Binabik and Sludig. As he spoke the crowd chanted again, just a few words before they fell silent, but Uammannaq kept speaking. His wife and the young female looked on. The Huntress' eyes seemed to Simon piercingly unsympathetic. The attitude of the other was harder to discern.

The speech went on for some time. Simon was just beginning to wonder if the lords of Yiqanuc had broken their promise to Jiriki when the Herder broke off, waving his spear at Binabik, then gesturing angrily to Binabik's companions. Simon looked at Haestan, who raised his eyebrow as if to say: *wait and see.*

"This is a strange thing, Simon."

It was Binabik who spoke, his eyes still fixed on the ground before him. His voice seemed to Simon as fine a thing to hear as birdsong or rain upon the roof. Simon knew he was beaming like a fool, but for the moment he did not care.

"It seems," Binabik continued, his voice scratchy from disuse, "that you and Haestan are guests of my masters, and that I must render these proceedings into a speech you can understand, since no one else here speaks both tongues."

"We canna' speak for you if canna' be understood," Haestan said softly.

"We'll help you, Binabik," Simon said emphatically, "but your silence will help nobody."

"This, as I said, is a strangeness," Binabik rasped. "I am condemned for dishonor, yet for honor's sake I must translate my wrongs for outsiders, since they are honored guests." A hint of a grim smile played at the corners of his mouth. "Esteemed guest, dragon-slayer, meddler in other people's affairs—somehow I am sensing your hand in this, Simon." He squinted for a moment, then extended a stubby finger as if to touch Simon's face. "You wear a brave scar, friend."

"What have you done, Binabik? Or what do they think you've done?"

The little man's smile evaporated. "I have broken my oath."

Nunuuika said something sharp. Binabik looked up and nodded. "The Huntress says I have had time enough to explain. Now my crimes must be dragged out into the light for inspecting."

With Binabik rendering the proceedings into the Westerling tongue, everything seemed to happen much more quickly. Sometimes it seemed he repeated what was spoken word for word, other times long speeches would be dispatched in a quick summation. Although Binabik seemed to regain a little of his familiar energy as he went about the business of translating, there was no mistaking the perilousness of his situation.

"Binabik, apprentice to the Singing Man, great Ookequk, you are held as an oath-breaker." Uammannaq the Herder leaned forward, twisting his thin beard fretfully, as though he found the proceedings upsetting. "Do you deny this?"

There was a long silence after Binabik finished translating the Herder's question. After a moment, he turned from his friends to face the lords of Yiqanuc. "I have no denial," he said at last. "I will offer the full truth, though, if you will be hearing it, Sharpest of Eye and Surest of Rein."

Nunuuika leaned back on her cushions. "There will be time for that." She turned to her husband. "He does not deny it."

"So," Uammannaq responded heavily, "Binabik is charged. You, *Croohok*," he swiveled his round head toward Sludig, "are accused of being of an outlaw race who have attacked and injured our people since time out of mind. That you are a Rimmersman no one can deny, so your charge remains as spoken."

As the Herder's words were translated, Sludig began an angry retort, but Binabik raised a hand to silence him. Surprisingly, Sludig complied.

"There can be no real justice between old enemies, it seems," the northerner murmured to Simon. His fierce glare became an unhappy frown. "Still, there are trollkind who have had less chance at the hands of my kinsmen than I have here."

"Let those who have reason to accuse now speak," Uammannaq said.

A certain expectant stillness filled the cavern. The herald stepped forward, his necklaces rattling and shivering. From the eyes of his ram skull he looked at Binabik with undisguised contempt, then lifted his hand and spoke in a thick, harsh voice.

"Qangolik the Spirit Caller says that the Singing Man Ookekuq did not appear at the Ice House on the Winter Lastday, as has been the law of our people since Sedda gave us these mountains," Binabik translated. His own voice had taken on some of the unpleasant tone of his accuser's. "Qangolik says that Binabik, the Singing Man's apprentice, also did not come to the Ice House."

Simon could almost feel the hatred flowing between his friend and the masked troll. There seemed little doubt that there was some rivalry or dispute of long standing between the two.

The Spirit Caller continued. "Since Ookequk's apprentice did not come to his duty—to sing the Rite of Quickening—the Ice House still has not melted. Because the Ice House is unmelted, Winter will not leave Yiqanuc. Through his treachery, Binabik has doomed his people to a bitter season. The summer will not come and many will die.

"Qangolik calls him oath-breaker."

There was a rush of angry talk through the cavern. The Spirit Caller had already squatted down once more before Binabik finished putting his words into Westerling.

Nunuuika looked about with ritual deliberateness. "Does anyone else here accuse Binbinaqegabenik?"

The unknown young woman, whom Simon had nearly forgotten in the furor of Qangolik's words, got up slowly from her seat on the topmost step. Her eyes were demurely lowered and her voice was quiet. She spoke for only a few brief moments.

Binabik did not immediately explain her words, though they set off a great rustle of whispering among the gathered trolls. He wore an expression Simon had never seen before on his friend's face: complete and utter unhappiness. Binabik stared at the young woman with grim fixedness, as though he watched some terrible event that it was nevertheless his duty to remember and later report in detail.

Just when Simon thought Binabik had been silenced again, this time perhaps forever, the troll spoke—flatly, chronicling the receipt of an old and now insignificant wound.

"Sisqinanamook, youngest daughter of Nunuuika the Huntress and Uammannaq the Herder, also accuses Binabik of Mintahoq. Though he placed his spear before her door, when nine times nine days had passed and the appointed day of marriage came, he was gone. Neither did he send any word or explanation. When he returned to our mountains, he came not to the home of his people, but traveled with Croohok and Utku to the shunned peak Yijarjuk. He has brought shame on the House of the Ancestor and on his once-betrothed.

"Sisqinanamook calls him oath-breaker."

Thunderstruck, Simon stared at Binabik's dejected face as the troll droned his translation. Marriage! All the while Simon and the little man had been fighting their way to Naglimund and making their way across the White Waste, Binabik's people had been waiting for him to fulfill his marriage oath. And he had been betrothed to a child of the Herder and Huntress! He had never given the slightest hint!

Simon looked more closely at Binabik's accuser. Sisqinanamook, although as small to Simon's eye as all of her folk, seemed actually a little taller than Binabik. Her glossy black hair was plaited on either side of her face, the two braids joining beneath her chin into one wide plait interlaced with a sky-blue ribbon. She wore little jewelry, especially when compared with her formidable mother, the Huntress. A single deep blue gem sparkled on her forehead, held in place by a slender black leather thong.

She had a flush of color in her brown cheeks. Although her gaze was clouded as though by anger or fright, Simon thought he sensed a strong-willed, defiant tilt to her jaw, a sharpness to her eye—not her mother Nunuuika's blade-edged glance, but the look of someone who made up her own mind. For a moment, Simon felt he could see her as one of her own would—not a gentle, pliant beauty, but a comely and clever young woman whose admiration would not be easy to win.

He abruptly realized that this was the one who had stood before Qantaqa's cave last night—the one who had menaced him with her spear! Something indefinable in the angle of her face told him so. Remembering, he knew she was a huntress after all, just like her mother.

Poor Binabik! Her admiration might not be easy to gain, but Simon's friend *had* won her over, or so it seemed. However, the wit and determination that Binabik must have so admired was now bent against him.

"I have no disagreement with Sisqinanamook, daughter of the Line of the Moon," Binabik finally replied. "That she ever accepted the spear of so unworthy a one as the Singing Man's apprentice was to me astonishing."

Sisqinanamook curled a lip at this speech, as if in disgust, but Simon did not think her contempt seemed altogether convincing.

"Great is my shame," Binabik continued. "Nine times nine nights, in truth, my spear stood before her door. I did not come to be married when those nights were through. There is no word I can speak that will be mending the hurt, or be making less of my fault. A choice there was to be made, as is the way of things once the Walk of Manhood or Womanhood has been walked. I was in a strange land and my master was dead. I made my choosing; had I the same to decide once more, I say with regret, I would make this same choosing again."

The crowd was still buzzing with shock and perturbation as Binabik finished interpreting what he had said for his companions. As he finished, he turned back to the young woman standing before him and said something to her, quietly and rapidly, calling her "Sisqi" instead of her full name. She swung her face away quickly, as if she could not stand to look at him. He did not translate his last speech, but sadly turned back to her mother and father.

"And what," Nunuuika asked scornfully, "might you have had to decide about? What choice could have turned you into an oath-breaker— you, who had already climbed far beyond the snows to which you were accustomed, whose betrothal-spear had been chosen by one high above you?"

"My master Ookequk made a promise to Doctor Morgenes of the Hayholt, a very wise man of Erkynland. With my master dead, I felt it was my place to keep his promise."

Uammannaq leaned forward, his beard wagging with surprise and anger. "You thought a promise to a lowlander more important than wedding a child of the House of the Ancestor—or the bringing of summer? Truly, Binabik, those who said you had learned madness at fat Ookequk's knee were right! You turned your back on your people for . . . for *Utku?*"

Binabik shook his head helplessly. "It was more than that, Uammannaq, Herder of the Qanuc. My master had fears of grave danger, not just to Yiqanuc but to all the world below the mountains as well. Ookequk feared a winter coming far worse than any we have experienced, one that would leave the Ice House hard-frozen for a thousand black years. And it was far more than only evil weather that Ookequk foresaw. Morgenes, the old man in Erkynland, shared his fears. It was because of these dangers that the promise seemed important. Because of this, too—because I believe my master's worries are justified—I would again break my oath if I had no other choice."

Sisqinanamook had returned her gaze to Binabik once more. Simon hoped to see a softening of her expression, but her mouth was still clenched in a firm, bitter line. Her mother Nunuuika slapped a palm on the butt of her spear.

"This is no argument at all!" the Huntress exclaimed. "Not at all. If I feared loose snow in the upper passes, should I then never leave my cave, letting my children starve? This is as much as saying that your people and the mountain home that gave you nurture mean nothing to you. You are worse than a drunkard, who at least says 'I should not drink,' but falls again into bad ways by weakness. *You* stand before us, bold as a robber of others' saddlebags, and say: 'I will do it again. My oath means nothing.' " She shook her spear in rage. The gathered assembly hissed its agreement. "You should be put to death immediately. If your madness infects others, the wind will howl in our empty caves before a generation passes."

Even as Binabik finished his dull rendering of this last, Simon stood up, shaking with anger. His face ached where the scar had been burned across his cheek, and every throb brought back the memory of Binabik clinging to the frost-worm's back, shouting for Simon to run, to save himself while the troll fought on alone.

"No!" Simon cried furiously, surprising even Haestan and Sludig, who had been listening dumbfoundedly to every strange detail of the exchange. "No!" Simon steadied himself with his stool. His head was whirling. Binabik, dutifully, turned to his masters and his betrothed and began explaining the red-haired lowlander's words.

"You don't understand what is happening," Simon began, "or what Binabik has done. Here in these mountains, the world is far away—but there *is* danger that can reach you. In the castle where I lived once, it seemed to me that evil was only something talked about by the priests, and that even they did not truly believe in it. Now I know better. There are dangers all around us and they are growing stronger every day! Don't you see? Binabik and I have been chased, chased by this evil all through the great forest and across the snows below these mountains. It followed us even to the dragon-mountain!"

Simon stopped for a moment, dizzied, breathing swiftly. He felt as though he held some squirming thing that was wriggling out of his grip.

What can I say? I must sound like a madman. Look, Binabik tells them what

I've said and they stare at me as though I'm barking like a dog! I will get Binabik killed for certain!

Simon groaned quietly and began again, trying to marshal his nearly unmanageable thoughts. "We are all in danger. A terrible power is in the north—I mean, no, we're in the north now . . ." He hung his head and tried to think for a moment. "To the north, but also to the west of here. There's a huge mountain of ice. The Storm King lives there—but he's not alive. Ineluki is his name. Have you heard of him? Ineluki? He is *terrible!*"

He leaned forward, his balance abruptly uncertain, and goggled at the alarmed faces of Herder and Huntress and their daughter Sisqinanamook.

"He is terrible . . ." he said again, staring straight into the troll maiden's dark eyes.

Binabik called her Sisqi, he thought disjointedly. *He must have loved her . . .*

Something seemed to grab his mind and shake it, as a hound shakes a rat. Suddenly he was tumbling forward, down a long, spinning shaft. The dark eyes of Sisqinanamook deepened and grew, then changed. A moment later, the troll woman was gone, her parents, Simon's friends, and all of Chidsik ub Lingit vanished with her. But the eyes remained, transmuted now into another grave stare that slowly filled his field of vision. These brown eyes belonged to one of his own kind—the child who had haunted his dreams . . . a child he finally recognized.

Leleth, he thought. *The little girl we left in the house in the forest, because her wounds were so awful. The girl we left with . . .*

"Simon," she said, her voice reverberating oddly in his head, *"this is my last opportunity. My house will soon fall and I will flee into the forest—but first there is something I must tell you."*

Simon had never heard the girl Leleth speak. The reedy tones seemed fitting for a child her age—but something about the voice was wrong: it was too solemn, too articulate and heavy with self-knowledge. The pace and the phrasing sounded like a grown woman's, like . . .

"Geloë?" he said. Although he did not think he actually spoke, he heard his voice echo out through some empty place.

"Yes. I have no time left. I could not have reached you, but the child Leleth has abilities . . . she is like a burning-glass through which I can narrow my will. She is a strange child, Simon." Indeed, the nearly expressionless child's face that spoke the words did seem somehow different than that of any other mortal child. There was something in the eyes that saw through him, beyond him, as though he himself were insubstantial as mist.

"Where are you?"

"In my house, but not long. My fences have been thrown down and my lake is full of dark things. The powers at my door are too strong. Rather than stand against such gale winds, I will flee to fight another day.

"What I have to tell you is this: Naglimund is fallen. Elias has won the day—but the real victor is He of whom we both know, the dark one in the north. Josua, however, is alive."

Simon felt a chilly twist of fear in his stomach. *"And Miriamele?"*

"She who was Marya—and also Malachias? I know only that she is gone from Naglimund: more than that, friendly eyes and ears cannot tell me. Now I must say something else: you must remember it and think of it, since Binabik of Yiqanuc has closed himself to me. You must go to the Stone of Farewell. That is the only place of safety from the growing storm—safety for a little while, anyway. Go to the Stone of Farewell."

"What? Where is this stone?" Naglimund fallen? Simon felt despair settle into his heart. Then all was truly lost. *"Where is the stone, Geloë?"*

Without warning a black wave crashed through him, sudden as a blow from a giant hand. The little girl's face disappeared, leaving only a gray void. Geloë's parting words floated in his head.

"It is the only place of safety . . . Flee! . . . the storm is coming . . ."

The gray slid away, like waves receding down a beach.

He found himself staring into the shimmering, transparent yellow light of a pool of blazing oil. He was on his knees in the cavern of Chidsik ub Lingit. Haestan's fearful face was bent close to his.

"What devils ye, lad?" the guardsman asked, supporting Simon's heavy head with a shoulder as he helped him up onto a stool. Simon felt as though his body were made of rags and green twigs.

"Geloë said . . . she said a storm . . . and the Stone of Farewell. We must go to the Stone of Fare . . ." Simon trailed off, looking up to see Binabik kneeling before the dais. "What's Binabik doing?" he asked.

"Waitin' th' word," Haestan said gruffly. "When y'fell swoonin', he said would fight no longer. Spoke t'king an' queen some while, now he be waitin'."

"But that's not right!" Simon tried to rise, but his legs buckled beneath him. His head hummed like an iron pot struck by a hammer. "Not . . . right."

" 'Tis th' will o' God," Haestan murmured unhappily.

Uammannaq turned from a whispered colloquy with his wife to stare at the kneeling Binabik. He said something in the guttural Qanuc-tongue that sent a windy moan through the spectators. The Herder lifted his hands to his face, slowly covering his eyes in a stylized gesture. The Huntress solemnly repeated the gesture. Simon felt a chill descend, heavier and bleaker even than winter's cold. He knew beyond doubt that his friend had been given a judgment of death.

4

A Bowl
of Calamint Tea

Sunlight filtered through the swollen clouds, falling mutedly on a
great party of horses and armored men riding up Main Row toward the
Hayholt. The light of their bright banners was dulled by uneven shadow,
and the click of the horse's hooves died in the muddy road, as though the
brave army rode silently along the bottom of the ocean. Many of the
soldiers held their eyes downcast. Others peered out from the shadow of
their helms like men who feared to be recognized.

Not all appeared so dismayed. Earl Fengbald, soon to be a duke, rode at
the head of the king's party beneath Elias' green and sable dragon-banner
and his own silver falcon. Fengbald's long black hair spilled down his
back, held only by a scarlet band knotted around his temples. He smiled
and waved a gauntleted fist in the air, eliciting cheers from the several
hundred spectators lining the roadway.

Riding close behind, Guthwulf of Utanyeat restrained a scowl. He, too,
held an earl's title—and supposedly the king's favor—but he knew beyond
doubt that the siege of Naglimund had changed everything.

He had always envisioned the day when his old comrade Elias would
reign as king and Guthwulf would stand at his side. Well, Elias *was* king
now, but somehow the rest of the story had gone wrong. Only a fat-
headed young idiot like Fengbald could be either too ignorant to notice
. . . or too ambitious to let it bother him.

Guthwulf had shorn his graying hair close to his head before the siege
had started. Now his helmet fit loosely. Even though he was a strong man
still in the prime of his health, he felt almost as though he were shrinking
away inside of his armor, becoming smaller and smaller.

Was he the only one uneasy, he wondered? Perhaps he had grown soft
and womanish in his too many years away from the field of battle.

But that could not be true. It was true that during the siege a fortnight
ago his heart had beaten very swiftly, but that had been the racing pulse of
exhilaration, not of fear. He had laughed as his enemies had swept down

upon him. He had broken a man's back with a single blow of his longsword, and taken blows in turn without losing his seat, handling his mount as well as he had twenty years ago—better, if anything. No, he had not grown soft. Not that way.

He also knew that he was not the only soul who felt a gnawing disquietude. Though crowds stood by cheering, most of them were young bravos and drunkards from the town. A goodly number of the windows facing Erchester's Main Row were shuttered; more than a few others showed only a stripe of darkness, out of which peered those citizens who did not care to come down and cheer the king.

Guthwulf turned his head to look for Elias, then experienced an unsettling chill when he discovered the king was already staring at him—a rapt, green stare. Almost against his will, Guthwulf nodded his head. The king stiffly returned the gesture, then looked sourly out on the welcoming folk of Erchester. Elias, feeling the pains of some undisclosed but minor illness, had only left his tented wagon to climb atop his black charger a furlong or so before their arrival at the city gate. Nevertheless, he was riding well, concealing any discomfort he might feel. The king was thinner than he had been in some years; the firm line of his jaw could be seen quite plainly. Except for his pale skin—not as obvious in the blotchy afternoon light as it sometimes was—and the distracted glare of his eyes, Elias looked slender and strong, as befitted a warrior king returning in triumph from a successful siege.

Guthwulf stole a worried glance at the double-guarded gray sword bumping in its scabbard against the king's hip. Cursed thing! How he wished that Elias would throw the damned blade down a well. There was something wrong about it, Guthwulf knew that beyond question. Some among the crowd obviously felt the uneasiness the blade engendered as well, but only Guthwulf had been in Sorrow's presence often enough to recognize the true source of their distress.

And the sword was not the only thing troubling the people of Erchester. Just as the mounted king of the afternoon had been a sick man in a wagon at mid-morning, so also had the breaking of Naglimund been something less than a glorious victory over a usurping brother. Guthwulf knew that even far from the scene, the citizens of Erchester and the Hayholt had come to hear something about the odd, terrible fate of Josua's castle and people. Even if they had not, the faintly sickened expressions and bowed posture of what should be an exulting, victorious army proclaimed that all was not as it should be.

It was more than shame, Guthwulf thought, and it was more than just feeling unmanned—for him as well as for the soldiers. It was fear they felt and could not quite hide. Was the king mad? Had he brought evil down on them all? God did not fear a fight, the earl knew, or a little blood—in such ink were His intentions written, a philosopher had once said. But, Usires curse it, this was different, was it not?

He sneaked another look at the king, his stomach churning. Elias was listening closely to his counselor, red-robed Pryrates. The priest's hairless head bobbed near the king's ear like a skin-covered egg.

Guthwulf had considered killing Pryrates, but had decided it might only make things worse, like killing the houndkeeper when the dogs waited at one's throat. Pryrates might be the only one left who could control the king—unless, as the Earl of Utanyeat sometimes felt sure, it was the meddling priest himself who was leading Elias down the road to perdition. Who could know, God damn them all? Who could know?

Perhaps in response to something Pryrates said, Elias bared his teeth in a smile as he looked over the sparseness of the cheering throng. It was not, Guthwulf saw, the expression of a happy man.

"I am very angry. My patience is strained by this ingratitude."

The king had taken to his throne, his father John's great Dragonbone Chair.

"Your monarch returns from war, bringing news of a great victory, and all that greets him is a paltry rabble." Elias curled his lip, staring at Father Helfcene, a slightly-built priest who was also the chancellor of the mighty Hayholt. Helfcene kneeled at the king's feet, the top of his bald head facing the throne like a pitifully inadequate shield. "Why was there no welcome for me?"

"But there was, my Lord, there was," the chancellor stuttered. "Did I not meet you at the Nearulagh Gate with all your household who remained at the Hayholt? We are thrilled to have Your Majesty back in good health, awed by your triumph in the north!"

"My cringing bondsmen of Erchester did not appear to be either very thrilled or awed." Elias reached for his cup. Ever-vigilant Pryrates handed it to him, careful not to slosh the dark liquid over the rim. The king took a long draught and made a face at its bitterness. "Guthwulf, did you feel that the king's subjects showed him proper fealty?"

The earl took a deep breath before speaking slowly. "Perhaps they were . . . perhaps they had heard rumors . . ."

"Rumors? Of what? Did we or did we not throw down my treacherous brother's keep at Naglimund?"

"Of course, my king," Guthwulf felt himself far out on a slender branch. Elias' sea-green eyes stared at him, as insanely curious as an owl's. "Of course," the earl repeated, "but our . . . allies . . . were bound to cause rumor."

Elias turned to Pryrates. The king's pale brow was furrowed, as though he were genuinely puzzled. "We have acquired mighty friends, have we not, Pryrates?"

The priest nodded silkily. "Mighty friends, Majesty."

"And yet they have served our will, have they not? They have done what we wished done?"

"To the exact length of your intent, King Elias." Pryrates snuck a glance at Guthwulf. "They have done your will."

"Well, then." Elias turned, satisfied, and regarded Father Helfcene once more. "Your king has gone away to war and has destroyed his enemies, returning with the allegiance of a kingdom older even than the long-gone Imperium of Nabban." His voice wavered dangerously. "Why do my subjects skulk like whipped dogs?"

"They are ignorant peasants, sire," Helfcene said. A drop of sweat hung on his nose.

"I think that someone here has been stirring up trouble in my absence," Elias said with frightful deliberation. "I would like to know who has been spreading tales. Do you hear me, Helfcene? I must find out who thinks they know the good of Osten Ard better than does her High King. Go now, and when I see you next, have something to tell me." He pulled at the skin of his face, angrily. "Some of these be-damned, stay-at-home nobles need to see the shadow of the gibbet, I think. That may remind them who rules this land."

The bead of sweat finally fell free of Helfcene's nose, spattering on the tile floor. The chancellor nodded briskly and several other drops, strangely numerous on a cool afternoon, leaped from his face.

"Of course, my Lord. It is good, so good, to have you back once more." He rose to a half crouch, bowed again, then turned and walked quickly from the throne room.

The thump of the great door closing echoed up amidst the the ceiling beams and serried banners. Elias leaned back against the vast spreading cage of yellowed bones, rubbing at his eye sockets with the backs of his powerful hands.

"Guthwulf, come here," he said, voice muffled. The Earl of Utanyeat stepped forward, feeling a strange but compelling urge to flee the room. Pryrates hovered at Elias' elbow, his face smooth and emotionless as marble.

Even as Guthwulf reached the Dragonbone Chair, Elias dropped his hands to his lap. The blue circles beneath his eyes made it seem as though the king's gaze had pulled back farther into his head. For a moment it almost seemed to the earl that the king was peering out of some dark hole, some trap into which he had fallen.

"You must protect me from treachery, Guthwulf." A ragged fringe of desperation sounded in Elias' words. "I am vulnerable now, but there are great things coming. This land will see a Golden Age such as the philosophers and priests have only dreamed of—but I must survive. I *must* survive, or all will be ruined. All will be ashes." Elias leaned forward, grasping Guthwulf's callused hand with fingers cold as fish tails.

"You must help me, Guthwulf." A powerful note ran through his straining voice. For a moment, the earl heard his companion of many battles and many taverns the way he remembered him, which only made the king's words all the more painful. "Fengbald and Godwig and the rest are fools," Elias said. "Helfcene is a frightened rabbit. You are the only one in all the world I can trust—besides Pryrates here, that is. You are the only ones whose loyalty to me is complete."

The king slumped back and covered his eyes again, clenching his teeth as though in pain. He waved Guthwulf's dismissal. The earl looked up to Pryrates, but the red priest only shook his head and turned to refill Elias' goblet.

As he pushed open the door of the chamber and walked out into the lamplit hallway, Guthwulf felt a heavy stone of fear settle in his gut. Slowly, he began to consider the unthinkable.

Miriamele pulled away, freeing her hand from Count Streáwe's grasp. She took a sudden step backward and fell into a chair that the man in the skull mask had slid up behind her. For a moment she only sat, trapped.

"How did you know it was me?" she asked at last. "That I was coming here?"

The count chuckled, extending a crabbed finger to tap the fox mask he had discarded. "The strong rely on strength," he said. "The not-so-strong must be clever and quick."

"You haven't answered my question."

Streáwe raised an eyebrow. "Oh?" He turned to his skull-faced helper. "You may go, Lenti. Wait with your men outside."

"It's raining," Lenti said mournfully, bone-white face bobbing, eyes peering from the black sockets.

"Then wait upstairs, fool!" the count said testily. "I will ring the bell when I need you."

Lenti sketched a bow, then darted a glance at Miriamele and went out.

"Ah, that one," Streáwe sighed, "he is like a child sometimes. But still, he does what he is told. That is more than I can say for many of those who serve me." The count pushed the decanter of wine toward Brother Cadrach, who sniffed at it suspiciously, obviously torn. "Oh, drink it," the count snapped. "Do you think I would go to all this trouble to drag you across Ansis Pelippé and then poison you in one of my own residences? If I had wished you dead, you would have been facedown in the harbor before you reached the end of the gangplank."

"That doesn't make me any easier," Miriamele said, beginning to feel like herself again—and more than a little angry. "If your intentions are honorable, Count, then why were we brought here by the threat of knives?"

"Did Lenti tell you he had a knife?" Streáwe asked.

"He certainly did," Miriamele responded tartly. "Do you mean that he doesn't?"

The old man chortled. "Blessed Elysia, of course he does! Dozens of the things, all shapes, all lengths, some sharpened on both sides, some forked into a double blade—Lenti has more knives than you have teeth." Streáwe chuckled again. "No, it's just that I keep telling him not to announce it constantly. All around the town they call him Lenti 'Avi Stetto.' " Streáwe stopped laughing for a moment, wheezing slightly.

Miriamele turned to Cadrach for explanation, but the monk was absorbed in a goblet of the count's wine, which he had apparently decided was safe.

"What does . . . 'Avi Stetto' . . . mean?" she finally asked.

"It's Perdruinese for 'I have a knife.' " Streáwe shook his head fondly. "He does know how to use his toys, though, that one does. . . ."

"How *did* you know about us, sir?" Cadrach asked, wiping his lips with the back of his hand.

"And what are you going to do to us?" Miriamele demanded.

"As to the first," Streáwe said, "as I told you, the weak must have their ways. My Perdruin is not a country whose might makes others tremble, so we must instead have very good spies. Every port in Osten Ard is an open market of knowledge, and all of the best brokers belong to me. I knew you had left Naglimund before you reached the River Greenwade; I have had people taking note of your progress ever since." He picked a reddish fruit out of a bowl on the table top and began peeling it with trembling fingers. "As to the second," he said, "well, that *is* a pretty question."

He was struggling with the fruit's tough rind. Miriamele, feeling a sudden and unexpected sympathy for the old count, reached out and gently took it from him.

"Let me do it," she said.

Streáwe raised an eyebrow, surprised. "Thank you, my dear. Very kind. So, then, the question of what I should do with you. Well, now, I must admit that when I first got word of your . . . temporarily detached state . . . it occurred to me that there might be more than a few who would pay for word of your whereabouts. Then, later, when it became clear you would be changing ship here in Ansis Pelippé, I realized that those who would find value in mere tidings might be willing to pay even *more* for an actual princess. Your father or uncle, for instance."

Furious, Miriamele dropped the fruit into the bowl, half-peeled. "You would sell me to my enemies!?"

"Now, now, my dear," the count said soothingly, "whoever said anything about that? And who are you calling an enemy, in any case? Your father the king? Your fond uncle Josua? We are not talking of handing you over to Nascadu slave-merchants for a few coppers. Besides," he hastily added, "that alternative is now closed in any case."

"What do you mean?"

"I mean I am not going to sell you to anyone," Streáwe said. "Please, do not worry about that."

Miriamele picked up the fruit again. Now *her* hand was trembling. "What is going to happen to us?"

"Perhaps the count will be forced to go locking us up in his deep, dark wine cellars, for our own protection," Cadrach said, gazing with fondness at the near-empty decanter. He seemed utterly and splendid drunk. "Ah, now wouldn't *that* be a terrible fate!"

She turned away from him in disgust. "So?" she asked Streáwe.

The old man took the slippery fruit from her hand and bit it carefully. "Tell me one thing," he said. "Do you go to Nabban?"

Miriamele hesitated, wrestling with her thoughts. "Yes," she answered at last. "Yes, I do."

"Why?"

"And why should I tell you? You have not harmed us, but you have not yet proved yourself a friend, either."

Streáwe stared at her. A smile slowly spread across the lower part of his face. His eyes, red-rimmed, retained their hard edge. "Ah, I like a young woman who knows what she knows," he said. "Osten Ard is full to brim with sentiment and imprecise understanding—it is not sin, you know, but foolish sentiment that sets the angels to moaning in despair. But you, Miriamele, even when you were a small child you had the look of someone who would do something in this world." He pulled the decanter away from Cadrach and refilled his own goblet. The monk looked after it comically, like a dog whose bone had been stolen.

"I said no one would sell you," Count Streáwe said at last. "Well, that is not quite true—no, do not glare so, mistress! Wait until you have heard all I have to say. I have a . . . friend, I suppose you would say, although we are not personally close. He is a religious man, but he moves in other circles as well—the best kind of friend I could ask for, since his knowledge is wide and his influence great. The only problem is, he is a man of rather irritating moral rectitude. Still, he has given help to Perdruin and to me many times, and—to put it simply—I owe him more than a few favors.

"Now, I am not the only one who knew of your departure from Naglimund. This man, also, the religious fellow, had it through his own private sources . . . ."

"He, too?" Miriamele demanded. She turned to Cadrach in anger. "What, did you send out a crier to trumpet the news?!"

"Not a word passed my lips, m'lady," the monk said slurringly. Did she fancy that he was not as drunk as he pretended to be?

"Please, Princess." Streáwe raised a shaking hand. "As I said, this friend is an influential man. Even those around him do not guess the breadth of his influence. His network of information, although smaller than mine, is of a depth and scope that often makes me shake my head in amazement.

"What I have been saying, though, is this. When my friend sent word to me—we each have a little flock of trained birds who carry our letters back and forth—he told me about you. This was a thing I already knew. He, however, did not know of my plans for you—those plans I spoke of earlier."

"Selling me, you mean."

Streáwe coughed apologetically. For a moment it became a real cough. When he had regained his breath, he continued. "And, as I have said, I owe this man several favors. So when he asked me to prevent you going on to Nabban, I really had no choice . . ."

"He asked you *what?*" Miriamele could not believe her ears. Would she never escape the meddling and interference of others?

"He does not want you to go to Nabban. It is not the right time."

"Not the right time? Who is this 'he,' and what right. . . ?"

"He? He is a good man—one of the few of whom the term can be used. I do not have much respect for the type, myself. The 'right,' he says, is the saving of your life. Or at least your freedom."

The princess felt her hair sticking to her forehead. The room was warm and humid, and the baffling, irritating old man across the table was smiling again, happy as a child who has learned a new trick.

"You are going to keep me here?" she said slowly. "You are going to imprison me and so protect my freedom?"

Count Streáwe reached a hand to his side and tugged at a dark rope that hung nearly invisible before a rumpled wall hanging. Somewhere in the building above a bell tolled faintly. "I am afraid that is true, my dear," he said. "I must hold you until my friend sends to say otherwise. A debt is a debt and a favor must be repaid." There was a sound of booted feet on the doorstep outside. "It truly is to your advantage, Princess, although you may not know it yet."

"I'll be the judge of that," Miriamele snarled. "How could you? Don't you know that there is a war brewing? That I am carrying important news to Duke Leobardis?" She *had* to reach the duke, to convince him to join with Josua. Otherwise, her father would destroy Naglimund and his madness would never cease.

The count cackled. "Ah, but my child, horses travel so much more slowly than do birds—even birds who carry the weight of heavy tidings. You see, Leobardis and his army left for the north nearly a month ago. If you had not passed so swiftly, skulkingly, and secretively through the towns of Hernystir, had you but spoken with a few people, you would have known."

As Miriamele slumped in her chair, dumbstruck, the count rapped his knuckles loudly on the table. The door swung open and Lenti and his two henchmen, still wearing their costumes, came into the room. Lenti had taken off his Death mask; his sullen eyes peered out of a face that was pinker, but not a great deal livelier, than the one he had doffed.

"Make them comfortable, Lenti," Streáwe said. "Then, lock the door behind you and come back to help me into my litter."

As the nodding Cadrach was rousted from his chair, Miriamele turned on the count. "How could you do this?" she sputtered. "I had always remembered you fondly—you and your treacherous garden!"

"Ah, the garden," Streáwe said. "Yes, you would like to see that again, wouldn't you? Don't be angry, Princess. We will talk more—I have much to tell you. I am charmed to see you again. To think that pale, shy Hylissa should have birthed such a fierce child!"

As Lenti and the others hustled them out into the rain, Miriamele caught a last glimpse of Streáwe. The count was staring at the gate, his white-haired head nodding slowly up and down.

They brought her to a tall house full of dusty hangings and ancient, creaking chairs. Streáwe's castle, perched on a spur of Sta Mirore, was empty but for a handful of silent servants and a few nervous-looking messengers who crept in and out like stoats through a fence hole.

Miriamele had her own room. It might have been pretty once, long, long ago. Now the faded tapestries showed only dim ghosts of people and places, and the straw of her mattress was so old and brittle and dry that it whispered in her ears all night.

She dressed every morning with the help of a heavy-faced woman who smiled tightly and spoke very little. Cadrach was being kept somewhere else, so she had no one to talk with during the long days and little to do except read an old Book of the Aedon whose illuminations had faded until the cavorting animals were mere outlines, as though carved in crystal.

From the moment she was brought to Streáwe's house, Miriamele schemed, dreaming of ways she might get free, but for all its air of stuffy disuse, the count's decaying palace was harder to escape than the Hayholt's deepest, dankest cells. The front hallway door of the wing in which she was housed was kept firmly locked. The rooms along the passageway were similarly barred. The woman who dressed her and the other servants were brought in and out by a broad-boned and serious-looking warder. Of all the potential routes of escape, only the door at the other end of the long hallway was ever left open. Beyond this door lay Streáwe's walled garden, and that was where Miriamele spent most of her days.

The garden was smaller than she remembered, but that was not surprising: she had been very young when she had seen it last. It seemed older, too, as if the bright flowers and greenery had grown a bit weary.

Banks of red and yellow roses lined the garden, but they were being gradually supplanted by exuberantly snaking vines whose beautiful bell-shaped flowers shone the color of blood, and whose cloying scent mingled with a myriad of other sweet, sad odors. Columbine clung to the walls and door-frames, its spurred blossoms dotting the twilight like softly-glowing stars. Here and there streaks of even wilder colors flashed among the tree branches and flowering shrubs—the tails of shrill-voiced, onyx-eyed birds from the Southern Islands.

The top of the high-walled garden was open to the sky. Her first morning in the garden Miriamele tried to climb the wall, but quickly discovered that the stone was too smooth for fingerholds, the vines too flimsy to offer support. As if to remind her of the proximity of freedom, tiny hill birds frequently spiraled down through this sky-window, hopping from branch to branch until something startled them and they leaped away into the air once more. Occasionally a gull, swept far in from the sea, flapped down to pace and preen before the more colorful denizens of the garden, keeping an urchin's eye open all the while for scraps from Miriamele's meals. But even with the unfenced sky churning with clouds just a short distance away, the brilliantly-plumed island birds stayed where they were, squawking resentfully in the green shadows.

Some evenings Streáwe joined her in the garden, carried in by sullen Lenti and propped in a high-backed chair, the count's useless, withered legs covered with a figured lap robe. Unhappy in her captivity, Miriamele deliberately made little response when he tried to amuse her with funny stories or sailors' gossip and rumors from the port. Still, she found she could not truly hate the old man, either.

As the futility of trying to escape became clear to her, and as the passing days wore away the edge of her bitterness, she came to find an unexpected comfort in sitting in the garden while late afternoon turned to evening. At the end of each day, as the sky overhead turned slowly from blue to pewter to black and the candles burned down in their sconces, Miriamele mended garments she had torn on her journey south. While the night birds sang their first hesitant notes, she drank calamint tea and pretended not to listen to the old count's stories. When the sun had gone down, she put on her riding cloak. It had been an uncommonly cold Yuven-month, and even in the sheltered garden the nights were brisk.

When Miriamele had been prisoned for nearly a week in Streáwe's castle, he came to her sadly and told her of the death of her uncle Duke Leobardis in combat before the walls of Naglimund. The duke's eldest son Benigaris—a cousin that she had never much cared for—had returned to rule Nabban from the throne of the Sancellan Mahistrevis. With help, Miriamele presumed, from his mother Nessalanta, another relative who had never been one of Miriamele's favorites. The news upset her: Leobardis has been a kind man. Also, his death meant Nabban had quit the field, leaving Josua without allies.

Three days later, as the evening of the first day of Tiyagar-month came on, Streáwe poured her a bowl of tea with his own trembling hand and told her that Naglimund had fallen. Rumor said there had been great slaughter, that few had survived.

He held her awkwardly in his dry-stick arms as she sobbed.

The light was waning. The patches of sky that showed through the dark embroidery of leaves were the unwholesome blue of bruised flesh.

Deornoth stumbled on an unseen root and Sangfugol and Isorn crashed to the ground beside him, Isorn losing his grip on the harper's arm as he fell. Sangfugol rolled to a halt and lay groaning. The bandage around his calf, strips of thin cloth from one of the ladies' underskirts, reddened with fresh blood.

"Oh, the poor man," Vorzheva said, limping forward. She squatted, spreading out the skirt of her tattered dress, then took Sangfugol's hand. The harper's eyes were fixed in an agonized stare on the tree limbs overhead.

"My lord, we must stop," Deornoth said. "It is growing too dark to see."

Josua turned slowly. The prince's thin hair was disarranged, his face distracted. "We should walk until full dark, Deornoth. Every moment of remaining light is precious."

Deornoth swallowed. It made him feel almost ill to contradict his liege lord. "We *must* make a secure place for the night, my prince. It will be hard to do that after dark. And the wounded are even more at risk if we continue to travel."

Josua looked down at Sangfugol, his expression distant. Deornoth did not like the change he was seeing in his prince. Josua had always been quiet, and many thought him strange, but still he had been a decisive leader—even in the last terrible weeks before Naglimund fell. Now he appeared unwilling to do anything, in small matters as well as large.

"Very well," the prince said at last. "If you think so, Deornoth."

"I beg pardon, but might we not move just a little farther up this . . . this defile?" Father Strangyeard asked. "It is only another few steps, and it seems safer than making camp in the bottom of a gulley—doesn't it?" He looked expectantly at Josua, but the prince only grunted. After a moment, the archivist turned to Deornoth. "Do you think?"

Deornoth looked around at the ragged party, at the white, frightened eyes in the dirt-streaked faces. "That is a good idea, Father," he said. "We shall do that."

They made a tiny fire in a hastily-dug pit surrounded with stones, more for light than anything else. Heat would have been most welcome—with nightfall, the forest air was turning bitterly cold—but they could not risk so much of a display. There was nothing to eat, in any case. Their pace had been far too hurried for any hunting.

Together, Father Strangyeard and Duchess Gutrun were cleaning Sangfugol's wound and rewinding the bandage. The white and black feathered arrow, which had knocked the harper down late yesterday afternoon, seemed to have struck the bone. Despite the care taken with its removal, not all the arrowhead had come out. When Sangfugol could talk, he complained that the feeling in his leg was nearly gone; at the moment, he was in shallow, uneasy sleep. Vorzheva stood nearby, looking on sorrowfully. She had been pointedly shunning Josua, who did not seem much bothered.

Deornoth silently cursed his thin cloak. *If I had only known we would be tramping the open woods*, he lamented, *I would have brought my fur-hooded riding cloak.* He smiled grimly at his own thoughts and suddenly laughed aloud, a short bark of amusement that caught the attention of Einskaldir, squatting nearby.

"What's funny?" the Rimmersman asked, frowning as he worked his hand-axe up and down a small whetstone. He held it up, testing the blade with his callused thumb, then laid it back against the stone once more.

"Nothing, really. I was just thinking about how stupid we've been—how unprepared."

"Waste of time, crying," Einskaldir growled, his eyes never leaving the blade as he lifted it to the red firelight. "Fight and live, fight and die, God waits for all."

"It's not that." Deornoth stopped for a moment and considered. What had begun as an idle thought had grown into something more; suddenly, he was afraid to lose his grip on it. "We have been pushed and pulled," he said slowly, "driven and drawn. We have been chased for three days since we escaped Naglimund, with barely a moment free from fear."

"What is to fear?" Einskaldir said gruffly, tugging at his dark beard. "If they catch us, they will kill us. There are worse things than to die."

"But that's just it!" Deornoth said. His heart was pounding. "That's just the point!" He leaned over, realizing that he had raised his voice almost to a shout. Einskaldir had stopped scraping his axe-blade to stare. "That is what I wonder," Deornoth said more quietly. "Why haven't they killed us?"

Einskaldir looked at him, then grunted. "They tried."

"No." Deornoth was suddenly sure. "The diggers . . . the Bukken as your people call them . . . *they* tried. The Norns haven't."

"You are mad, Erkynlander," Einskaldir said in disgust. Deornoth bit back a retort and crawled around the fire pit toward Josua.

"My prince, I need to speak with you."

Josua did not answer, again in one of his faraway moods. He sat, staring at Towser. The old jester slept with his back against a tree, bald head bobbing on his chest. Deornoth did not see anything particularly interesting about the old man's slumber, so he interposed himself between the prince and the object of his attention. Josua's face was almost invisible, but enough of a glow escaped the fire pit that Deornoth thought he saw Josua's eyebrow lift in mild surprise.

"Yes, Deornoth?"

"My prince, your people need you. Why are you so strange?"

"My people are very few now, aren't they?"

"They are your people still—and they need you all the more, since our danger is so great."

Deornoth heard Josua take a breath, as if in surprise or in preparation for some angry remark. Instead, when the prince spoke, his voice was calm. "We are in bad times, Deornoth. Everyone faces them in their own way. Was this what you wished to discuss with me?"

"Not all, my lord." Deornoth crept a little closer, until he sat within arm's reach of the prince. "What do the Norns want, Prince Josua?"

Josua chuckled ruefully. "I should think that was obvious enough. To kill us."

"Then why have they not done so?"

There was a moment of silence. "What do you mean?"

"Just what I asked. Why have they not killed us? They have had many opportunities."

"We have been fleeing them for . . ."

Deornoth impetuously grasped Josua's arm. The prince was very thin. "My lord, do you believe that the Norns—the Storm King's minions who destroyed Naglimund—could not catch a dozen hungry and wounded men and women?"

He felt Josua's arm grown taut. "And that signifies. . . ?"

"I don't know!" Deornoth let go of the prince and picked up a stick from the ground, nervously plucking at the bark with his fingernails. "But I can't believe they couldn't have brought us to bay if they had wanted to."

"Usires on the Tree," Josua breathed. "I am ashamed you have had to take the responsibility that is rightfully mine, Deornoth. You are right. It makes no sense."

"Perhaps there is something more important than our deaths," Deornoth said, thinking. "If they want us dead, why did they not surround us? If a walking corpse could be upon us almost before we knew, why not the Norns?"

Josua pondered for a moment. "Perhaps they fear *us*." Again the prince was silent. "Call the others," he said finally. "This is too grave to keep between the two of us."

When the rest were gathered, huddling around the small fire, Deornoth looked over their numbers and shook his head. Josua, himself, Einskaldir and Isorn, Towser—groggy from sleep—and Duchess Gutrun; with Strangyeard now finding a place, and Vorzheva tending Sangfugol, they were all accounted for. Only nine left—could that be? They had buried Helmfest and the young handmaiden two days ago. Gamwold, an older guardsman with a gray mustache, had died from a long fall in the attack that felled Sangfugol. They had not been able to retrieve Gamwold's body, let alone bury him. Unwillingly, they had left him lying on a ledge of the open ridge, surrendered to the attentions of wind and rain.

Nine left, he thought, *Josua is right—it is a small kingdom, indeed.*

The prince had finished explaining. Strangyeard spoke up hesitantly.

"I hate even to say this," he began, "but . . . but perhaps they are only toying with us, as . . . as does a cat with a rat it has cornered."

"What a horrible thought!" Gutrun said. "But they are heathen, so anything is possible."

"They are more than heathen, Duchess," Josua said, "they are immortal. They have lived, many of them, since before Usires Aedon walked the hills of Nabban."

"They can die," Einskaldir said. "I know."

"But they are terrible," Isorn said. His wide frame shuddered. "Now I know that they are the ones who came out of the north when we were held captive in Elvritshalla. Their very shadows are cold—like a wind from *Huelheim*, the land of death."

"Just a moment," Josua said. "You have reminded me of something. Isorn, you said once that when you were captive, some of your fellows were tortured."

"Yes. I will never forget."

"Who did it?"

"The Black Rimmersmen, the ones who live in the shadow of Stormspike. They were Skali of Kaldskryke's allies—although, as I think I told you, Prince Josua, I don't believe Skali's men got what they bargained for. In the end, they were almost as terrified as we prisoners."

"But it was the Black Rimmersmen who tortured you. What about the Norns?"

Isorn thought for a moment, his broad face pensive. "No . . ." he said slowly, "I don't believe the Norns had anything to do with it. They were just black shadows in hooded cloaks, passing back and forth to Elvritshalla. They seemed to take little notice of anything—although we did not see them much, for which I was very grateful."

"So," said Josua, "it does not seem that the Norns are interested in torture."

"It does not seem to bother them much," Einskaldir growled. "And Naglimund showed that they do not love us."

"Still, I somehow do not think they would follow us all the way through Aldheorte Forest just for enjoyment." The prince frowned, thinking. "I find it hard to think of why they might fear us, straggling lot that we are. What else could they want?"

"To put us in cages," Towser said grumpily, rubbing his sore legs. The long day's walking had been harder on him than on anyone else except Sangfugol. "To make us dance for them."

"Quiet, old man," Einskaldir snarled.

"Do not order him," Isorn said, giving Einskaldir a purposeful look—a difficult thing to do in near-darkness.

"I think Towser is right," Strangyeard said in his quiet, apologetic way.

"What do you mean?" Josua asked.

The archive-master cleared his throat. "It seems to make sense," he began, "—not that they want us to dance, I mean." He tried to smile. "But the putting us in cages. They may want to capture us."

Deornoth was excited. "I think Strangyeard has it! They did not kill us when they might have. They must want us taken alive."

"Or want *some* of us alive," Josua said carefully. "Perhaps that is why they used the corpse of that poor young pikeman—to get safely among us and then spirit one or more of us away."

"No," Deornoth's excitement suddenly dissipated, "for why didn't they surround us then, when they had the chance? I asked myself that earlier and I still cannot answer."

"If they wanted to . . . to capture one of our number," Strangyeard offered, "perhaps they were afraid that one would be killed in a struggle."

"If so," Duchess Gutrun said, "it is surely not me they are after. I am scarcely of any use, even to myself. They are after Prince Josua." She made the sign of the Tree over her breast.

"Of course," Isorn said, putting his big arm around his mother's shoulder. "Elias sent them to capture Josua. He wants you alive, my lord."

Josua looked uncomfortable. "Perhaps. But why are they shooting arrows at us now?" He pointed to where Sangfugol lay, Vorzheva holding the harper's head as she gave him a drink of water. "It seems that there is even greater danger of accidentally killing their target, now that we are on the move."

No one could answer this. They sat uncomfortably for some long while, listening to the sounds of the damp night.

"Hold a moment," Deornoth said. "We are confusing ourselves, I think. When have we been attacked by them?"

"Early in the morning after the night that . . . that the young pikeman came to our fire," Isorn said.

"And was anyone hurt?"

"No," Isorn said, thinking back. "But we were lucky to escape. Many of the arrows missed by very little."

"One of 'em took my hat off!" Towser said querulously. "My best hat! Lost!"

"Pity it wasn't your best head," Einskaldir snapped.

"But the Norns are very good archers," Deornoth continued, ignoring the Rimmersman and the old jester. "And when has anyone else been shot?"

"Yesterday!" Isorn said, shaking his head. "You should know. Gamwold dead, Sangfugol badly wounded."

"But Gamwold wasn't shot."

Everyone turned to look at Josua. There was a sudden power in the prince's voice that sent a thrill up Deornoth's back.

"Gamwold fell," the prince said. "All of our party who've been killed except for Gamwold died from our battles with the diggers. Deornoth has it aright! The Norns have been chasing us for three days—three full days— and have fired upon us many times. Sangfugol is the only one who has been hit."

The prince stood up, his face disappearing from the fireglow. The others could hear him pacing. "But why? Why did they risk an arrow then? We were doing something that frightened them. Doing something—" He stopped. "Or going somewhere . . ."

"What do you mean, Prince Josua?" Isorn asked.

"We were turning east—toward the heart of the forest."

"That's true!" Deornoth said, thinking back. "We had been going south since we came down the Stile from Naglimund. That was the first time we tried to turn east, in toward the deeper part of the forest. Then, when the harper was shot and Gamwold fell, we retreated back down the hill and kept walking south along Aldheorte's outskirts thereafter."

"We are being herded," Josua said slowly. "Like ignorant animals."

"But that is because we tried to do something that worried them," Deornoth pointed out. "They are trying to keep us from going east."

"And we still do not really know what for," Isorn said. "Herded toward capture?"

"More likely to slaughter," Einskaldir said. "They just want to do the killing at home. Have a feast. Invite guests."

Josua actually smiled as he sat down, the fire catching a quick gleam of teeth.

"I have decided," he said, "to decline their invitation."

An hour or two before dawn, Father Strangyeard came and tapped Deornoth on the shoulder. Deornoth had heard the archive-master crawling about in the darkness, but the touch of a hand on his shoulder still made him start.

"Only me, Sir Deornoth," Strangyeard said hastily. "It is my turn to take watch."

"That's not necessary. I don't think I will sleep, anyway."

"Well, then, perhaps we can . . . can share the watch. If my talk will not irritate you."

Deornoth smiled to himself. "Not at all, Father. And you need not call me 'Sir.' It is nice to have a calm hour or so—we have had precious little calm lately."

"It is just as well, I suppose, that I am not left to stand guard alone." Strangyeard said. "My sight is not good, you know—and that is in my one remaining eye." He chuckled apologetically. "There is nothing more frightening than to see the words in my beloved books growing fainter every day."

"Nothing more frightening?" Deornoth asked gently.

"Nothing." Strangyeard was firm. "Oh, not that I do not fear other things, but death, just for example—well, my Lord will take me when He knows it is time. But to spend my last years in darkness, unable to see the writings that are my work on this earth . . ." The archivist broke off, embarrassed. "I am sorry, Deornoth, I am babbling of trivialities. It is this hour of the night. At home in Naglimund, I often wake at this time, just before the sun comes up . . ." The priest paused again. Both men thought silently of what had happened to the place where they had lived.

"When we are safe, Strangyeard," Deornoth began suddenly, "if you cannot read, I will come and read to you. My eyes are not as quick as yours, nor my mind, but I am stubborn as an unfed horse. I will grow better with practice. I will read to you."

The archivist sighed, then was quiet. "That is too kind," he said a moment later. "But you will have more important things to do when we are safe again and Josua sits the high throne of Osten Ard—matters far graver than reading to an old book-shifter."

"No. No, I do not think so."

They sat for a long while and listened to the wind.

"So we will . . . will strike out toward the east today?" Strangyeard asked.

"Yes. And I think the Norns will not be happy about such a plan. I fear that more of us will be wounded or killed. But we must seize our destiny with both hands. Prince Josua recognizes that, thank the Good God."

Strangyeard sighed. "Do you know, I have been thinking. I feel quite . . . quite ridiculous saying it, but . . ." He trailed into silence.

"What?"

"Perhaps it is not Josua they seek to capture. Perhaps it is . . . me."

"Father Strangyeard!" Deornoth was quite surprised. "Why would that be?"

The priest bobbed his head, ashamed. "I know it seems foolish, but I must mention it. You see, I am the one who had studied Morgenes' manuscript telling of the Three Great Swords—and I am the one carrying it now." He tapped the pocket of his voluminous robe. "With Jarnauga, I searched and studied, trying to divine the whereabouts of Fingil's sword Minneyar. Now that he is dead—well, I hate to sound as if I were shouting my own importance, but . . ." He held out something small that swung from a chain, just visible in the growing light. "He gave me his Scroll, the badge of his League. Perhaps that has made me dangerous to the rest of the party. Maybe if I surrendered, they would let the rest of you go?"

Deornoth laughed. "If it is you they wish kept alive, Father, then we are lucky to have you among us, else we would have already been flushed and slaughtered like doves. Don't go anywhere."

Strangyeard seemed uncertain. "If you say so, Deornoth . . ."

"I do. Not to mention that we need your wits more than anything else we have—except for the prince himself."

The archivist smiled shyly. "That is very kind."

"Of course," Deornoth said, and felt his mood souring, "if we are to survive the coming day, we will need more than wits. It will take a great deal of luck as well."

After sitting with the archivist for a while longer, Deornoth decided to find himself a more comfortable spot to snatch an hour of sleep before dawn came. He nudged Strangyeard, whose head had sunk to his chest.

"I'll let you finish out, Father."

"Mmmm. . . ? Oh! Yes, Sir Deornoth." The priest nodded vigorously, demonstrating his alertness. "Certainly. You go and sleep."

"The sun will be up soon, Father."

"Just so." Strangyeard smiled.

Deornoth went only a few dozen paces before settling on a level patch of ground in the lee of a fallen tree. A bitter wind ranged across the forest floor as though hunting for warm bodies. Deornoth wrapped his cloak tightly around himself and tried to find a comfortable position. After a long, chilly interval, he decided that there was scant chance he would ever fall asleep. Grumbling quietly, so as not to wake the others who were sleeping nearby, he rose to his feet and rebuckled his sword belt, then headed back toward Father Strangyeard's sentry post.

"It's me, Father," he said quietly, as he stepped out of the trees into the small clearing. He stopped, astonished. A startlingly white face looked up, black eyes narrowing. Strangyeard was slumped in the arms of this dark-clad attacker, sleeping or senseless. A knife blade like the thorn of a great ebony rose lay against the priest's exposed neck.

Even as Deornoth threw himself forward, he saw two more pallid, slit-eyed faces in the night-shadows and called them by their old name. *"White Foxes!"* he shouted. *"The Norns! We are attacked!"*

Bellowing, he struck the pale-skinned thing and grappled it with his arms. They toppled, the archivist tangled with them, so that for a moment Deornoth was lost in a welter of flailing limbs. He felt the thing reach out for him, its thin limbs full of slithery strength. Hands grasped at his face and pushed back his chin to expose his neck. Deornoth flung out his fist, which landed on something hard as bone. He was rewarded by a hissing cry of pain. Now he could hear crashing and shouting in the trees all around. He wondered dimly whether it meant more foes, or that his friends were awake at last.

Sword! he thought. *Where's my sword?*

But it was caught in the scabbard, twisted around on his belt. The moonlight seemed to burst into brilliance. The white face rose before him once more, lips skinned back, teeth bared like a drowning cur. The eyes that locked with his were as coldly inhuman as sea-stones. Deornoth fumbled for his dagger. The Norn grasped at his throat with one hand; its other hand, a pale blur, lifted free.

He has a knife! Curiously, Deornoth felt as though he were floating on a wide river, carried forward on a slow and generous current, but at the same moment panicky thoughts flew around his head like grassflies. *Damn me, I forgot his knife!*

He stared for another endless instant at the Norn before him, at the thin, otherworldly features, the white spiderweb hair matted across the brow, the faint lips drawn tight against the red gums. Then Deornoth swung his head forward, smashing his forehead into the cadaverous face. Before he had even felt the first shock, he threw himself forward again into yet another red impact. A great shadow mushroomed inside him. The shrieks and night wind faded to a muted and diminishing hum and the moon was drenched with clinging darkness.

When he could think again, he looked up to see Einskaldir, who seemed to be swimming toward him, arms windmilling, his war-axe a shimmering smear. The Rimmersman's mouth was open as though he shouted, but Deornoth heard no sound. Josua came just behind. Deornoth's two companions flung themselves against another pair of shadowy figures. Blades whirled and glinted, slicing the darkness with stripes of reflected moonlight. Deornoth wanted to stand and help them, but a weight lay upon him, some amorphous, unshakable burden. He struggled, wondering where his strength had gone, until the burden fell away at last and left him exposed to the rasping wind.

Josua and Einskaldir were still moving before him, their faces weird masks in the blue night. Other two-legged shapes were beginning to appear from the forest shadows, but Deornoth could not tell if they were friends or foes. His sight seemed to be obscured—something was in his eyes, something that stung. He moved his hands questingly over his face. It was wet and sticky. His fingers, when he held them up to catch the light, were black with blood.

A long, damp tunnel led down through the hillside. A narrow, torchlit staircase ran through it, half a thousand mossy, centuried steps that snaked down through the very heart of Sta Mirore, from Count Streáwe's great house to a small, hidden dock. Miriamele guessed that the tunnel had been the salvation of many an earlier nobleman, forced to flee his stately quarters by night when the peasantry became unexpectedly frisky or turned disputatious about the rights of the privileged.

After the end of a foot-wearying journey under the watchful eyes of Lenti and another of the count's closed-faced servants, Miriamele and Cadrach found themselves standing on a stone landing beneath an overhanging arch of cliff, the slate-colored harbor waters spread before them like a disheveled carpet. Just below, a small rowboat bobbed at the end of its painter.

A few moments later Streáwe himself arrived by another path, carried down the winding cliff roads in his carved and becurtained litter by four brawny men wearing sailors' garb. The old count wore a heavy cloak and muffler against the night fog. Miriamele thought that the sallow light of dawn made him look ancient.

"So," he said, waving for his bearers to lower him to the stone platform, "our time together is at an end." He smiled ruefully. "I feel a deep regret at letting you go—not least because the Victor of Naglimund, your beloved father Elias, would pay much for your safe return." He shook his head and coughed. "Still, I am a honorable man, and an obligation unpaid is a ghost unshriven, as we say here in Perdruin. Say hello to my friend when you meet him. Extend my regards."

"You haven't told us who this 'friend' is," Miriamele said tightly. "The one to whom we are being given."

Streáwe waved his hand dismissively. "If he wishes you to know his true name, he will tell you himself."

"And you will be setting us across to Nabban on the open sea in this tiny little *isgbahta*," Cadrach growled, "—this fishing boat?"

"It is scarcely a stone's throw," the count said. "And you will have Lenti and Alespo along to protect you from kilpa and such." He indicated the two servants with a wave of his trembling hand. Lenti was chewing sullenly at something. "You don't think I would let you go alone, do you?" Streáwe smiled. "How could I ever be sure you would reach my friend and resolve my debt?"

He waved for his servants to lift the litter. Miriamele and Cadrach were herded into the pitching boat, squeezed side by side into the tiny bow.

"Do not think unkindly of me, Miriamele and Padreic, I beg you," Streáwe called as his servants wrestled him back up the slippery stairs. "My little island must maintain a delicate balance, a very delicate balance. Sometimes the adjustments seem cruel." He pulled the curtain closed before him.

The one whom Streáwe had called Alespo untied the rope and Lenti reached out with his oar to push the little wooden boat away from the dock. As they drifted slowly away from the light of the dockside lanterns, Miriamele felt her heart sinking. They were going to Nabban, a place that now held little hope for her. Cadrach, her only ally, had been sullenly quiet since they had been reunited—and what name had Streáwe called him? Where had she heard that before? Now she herself was being sent to some unknown friend of Count Streáwe's, a pawn in some sort of strange business arrangement. And everyone, from the local nobles to the humblest peasant, seemed to know her affairs better than she did herself. What else could go wrong?

Miriamele let out a sigh of grief and frustration.

Lenti, seated across from her, stiffened. "Don't try anything, now," he growled. "I have a knife."

5

Singing Man's House

Simon slapped a hand against the cold stone wall of the cave and felt a strange satisfaction at the pain. "Bleeding Usires!" he swore. "Bleeding Usires, Usires bleeding on the Tree!" He raised an arm to strike the wall again, but instead dropped it to his side and dug furiously at his breeches-leg with his fingernails.

"Calm y'rself, boy," Haestan said. "Was naught we c'do."

"I won't let them kill him!" He turned to Haestan imploringly. "And Geloë said we must go to the Stone of Farewell. I don't even know where that is!"

Haestan shook his head unhappily. "Whatever this stone may be. I've not understood ye right since fell down and struck y'r head this afternoon. Y've been talkin' moon-mad. But about th' troll an' Rimmersman—what can we do?"

"I don't know!" Simon barked. He put out his aching hand to lean against the wall. The night wind keened beyond the door-flap. "Free them," he said at last. "Free them both—Binabik and Sludig." The tears he had felt himself holding back were gone. He suddenly felt cold-minded and full of strength.

Haestan started to reply, then checked himself. He looked at the youth's trembling fists and the livid scar striping his cheek. "How, then?" he asked quietly. "Two 'gainst a mountain?"

Simon stared furiously. "There must be a way!"

"Th'only rope trolls took with Binabik's pack. Down a deep hole they are, lad. With guards 'round."

After a long moment, Simon turned and slid down to sit on the cave floor, pushing away the sheepskin rug to bring himself as close as possible to the unforgiving rock.

"We can't just let them die, Haestan. We can't. Binabik said his people would throw them from the cliffs. How can they be such . . . such demons!?"

Haestan squatted and poked the coals with his knife. "I've no under-standing of heathens and suchlike," the bearded guardsman said. "They be tricksy folk. Why should they prison them and give us freedom—an' leave our weapons besides?"

"Because we've got no rope," Simon said bitterly, and shivered. He was finally beginning to feel the cold. "Besides, even if we killed the guards, what good would it do us? They'd throw *us* down the mountain as well, and no one would ever take Thorn back to Josua." He thought. "Perhaps we could steal some rope?"

Haestan looked doubtful. "In darkness, in a strange place? Like as not we'd just rouse guards an' get spear-stabbed."

"Damnation and sin! We must do *something,* Haestan! Are we cowards? We can't just stand by." A sharp wind stabbed in past the door curtain. He hugged his arms tight around his chest. "At the very least, I'm going to have that Herder's rotten little head off. Then they can kill me, too, and I won't care."

The guardsman smiled sadly. "Ah, boy, y'r talkin' stupid. Said y'rself someone must take that black sword t'Prince Josua." He indicated cloth-wrapped Thorn lying beside the cavern wall. "If the sword be not taken t'prince, Ethelbearn and Grimmric died for naught. That'd be cruel shame. Too many hopes, slender 'uns though may be, rest on yon blade." Haestan chuckled. " 'Sides, lad, d'ye think they'd spare one if th' other killed their king? Y'r bound t'get me killed, too." Haestan poked at the fire again. "No, no, ye be green yet an' don't understand th' world. Ye've not been in war, lad, like me—not seen what I have. Didn't I see two of my fellows die just since we left Naglimund? The Good God saves his justice and such for th' Day of Weighin' Out. 'Til then, we have t'look t'ourselves." He leaned forward as he began to warm to the topic. "Each 'un must do his best, but things can't always be made right, Simon . . ."

He stopped abruptly, staring at the doorway. Seeing the look of surprise on the soldier's round face, Simon turned swiftly. A figure had stepped past the flap of hide.

"Th' troll girl," Haestan breathed softly, as though she might startle and bolt like a fawn. Sisqinanamook's eyes were wide with apprehension, but Simon also saw determination in the set of her jaw. He thought she looked readier to fight than to flee.

"Do you come to gloat?" he asked angrily.

Sisqinanamook steadfastly returned his stare. "Help me," she said at last.

"Elysia, Mother of God," Haestan gasped, "she can talk!"

The troll maiden shied back at the guardsman's outburst, but held her ground. Simon clambered up onto his knees before her. Kneeling, he was still taller than Binabik's once-betrothed.

"*Can* you speak our tongue?"

She looked at him for a moment as if puzzled, then made a sign with crossed fingers. "Little," she said. "Little talk. Binabik teach."

"I should have guessed," Simon said. "Binabik has been trying to pound things into *my* head as long as I've known him."

Haestan snorted. Simon gestured for Sisqinanamook to enter. She slithered away from the door-flap, crouching near the cave's entrance with her back against the wall. A snow serpent carved in relief upon the stone coiled about her head like a saint's halo.

"Why should we help you?" Simon said. "And help you do what?"

She stared at him uncomprehendingly. He repeated himself more slowly. "Help Binbinaqegabenik," she replied at last. "Help me, help Binabik."

"Help Binabik?" Haestan hissed in surprise. "Why, y'r what's got him in trouble!"

"How?" Simon asked. "Help Binabik how?"

"Go away," Sisqinanamook replied. "Binabik go away Mintahoq." She reached under her thick hide jacket. For a moment Simon feared some kind of trick—had she understood enough of what they had been saying to know they were discussing a rescue?—but when her small hand appeared again it bore a coil of slender gray rope. "Help Binabik," she repeated. "You help, I help."

"Merciful Aedon," said Simon.

They quickly gathered up all their belongings, throwing them into two packs with little concern for order. When they were finished and had donned their fur-lined cloaks, Simon went to the corner of the room where the black sword Thorn lay—the object, as Haestan had said, of many hopes, fruitless or otherwise. In the dim firelight it was only a sword-shaped hole in the furs that cradled it. Simon pressed its cold surface with his fingers, remembering how it had felt when he raised it before the onrushing Igjarjuk. For a moment it seemed to grow warm beneath his hand.

Someone touched him on the shoulder.

"No, no kill," Sisqinanamook said. She pointed frowningly at the sword, then tugged gently at his arm. Simon wrapped his hand around Thorn's cord-wrapped hilt and hefted: it was too heavy to lift without using both arms. As he struggled upright, he turned to the troll maiden.

"I'm not bringing it to kill anybody. This is the reason we went to the dragon-mountain. No kill."

She stared at him, then nodded.

"Let me carry it, lad," Haestan said. "I'm rested."

Simon bit back a sullen retort and let him take the sword. It seemed no lighter in the burly guardsman's hands, but no heavier either. Haestan reached over his head and carefully eased Thorn's black length down through a pair of thick loops on the back of his pack.

It's not my sword, Simon reminded himself. *I knew that already. And Haestan's right to take it—I'm too weak.* He felt his thoughts wandering. *It doesn't belong to anyone. It belonged to Sir Camaris once, but he's dead. Seems almost to have a spirit of its own . . .*

Well, if Thorn wanted to leave this God-cursed mountain, it would have to go down with them.

They extinguished the fire and went silently out past the door-flap. The chill night air made Simon's head throb. He stopped in the doorway.

"Haestan," he whispered, "you must promise me something."

"What's that, lad?"

"I don't feel very . . . strong. It's going to be a long walk to wherever we're going. In the snow, too. So if anything happens to me . . ." he hesitated for a moment, "if anything happens to me, please bury me someplace warm." He shivered. "I'm tired of being cold."

For a moment Simon had the embarrassing idea that Haestan might cry. The guardsman's bearded face screwed up in a strange grimace as he leaned in to look closely at Simon. A moment later he grinned, although the smile seemed a bit forced, and wrapped one of his bearlike arms around Simon's quaking shoulders. "Here now, lad, no way t'talk," he whispered. "It'll be long march, an' cold, too, that's sure—but not as bad as y'think. We'll all make it through." Haestan snuck a look at Sisqinanamook, who was staring impatiently at them from the porch outside the cavern. "Jiriki left us horses," he hissed into Simon's ear, "at mountain-bottom, stabled in cave. Told me where. So dunna fear, lad, dunna fear. If we but knew where 'tis we go—why, we'd be halfway there!"

They pushed out onto the stone track, squinting their eyes against a fierce wind that scraped the face of Mintahoq like a razor. The mists had blown away. A cat's-eye sliver of yellow moon glared down on the mountain and shadow-blanketed valley. Staggering under their heavy loads, they turned to follow the one small shadow that was Sisqinanamook.

It was a long, silent trek around the edge of Mintahoq, stumbling through the buffeting wind. After a few hundred paces Simon already felt his steps slowing. How would he ever climb all the way down the mountain? And why couldn't he shake off this cursed weakness?

At last the troll maiden gestured them to a halt, then directed them into a crevice, off the pathway and back into the shadows. It was a tight squeeze because of their bulky packs, but with the help of Sisqinanamook's small hands they managed to slide in. A moment later she was gone. They stood, pinioned, and watched their breath fill the mouth of the crevice, glittering in the moonlight.

"What d'ye think she's about?" Haestan whispered at last.

"I don't know." Simon was happy just to lean against the stone. Out of the wind, he suddenly felt flushed and dizzy. The White Arrow given to him by Jiriki was digging at his spine through the heavy cloth of his pack.

"We be coney-catched, an' no mistake . . ." Haestan began, but the sound of voices on the path silenced him. As the voices grew louder, Simon caught his breath and held it.

A triumvirate of trolls stumped down the trail past the crevice, dragging the butts of their sharp spears carelessly along the stone, talking in their low, grumbling tongue. All three carried shields of stretched hide. One had a ram's horn dangling from his belt; Simon had no doubt that a call from that instrument would bring well-armed trolls tumbling out of the caves all around like ants from a shaken nest.

The horn-bearer said something and the group paused just before the hiding spot. Simon struggled to hold his breath and felt his head whirl. A moment later the trolls burst into a fizz of quiet laughter as the story was completed, then continued their march back around the face of the mountain. In a few moments their quiet chatter had dwindled away.

Simon and Haestan waited a long while before peering out of the opening in the rock. The moon-painted path stretched on either side, untenanted. Haestan wriggled out of the narrow entrance, then helped Simon to emerge.

The moon had slipped past the mouth of the pit, plunging the prisoners back into near-complete darkness. Sludig was breathing quietly but not sleeping. Binabik lay on his back, short legs outstretched, staring up at the wheeling stars as the wind gusted noisily across the opening of their prison.

A head appeared at the rim of the pit. A moment later, a coil of rope hissed down from above to smack onto the stone. Binabik stiffened but did not stir, staring intently at the shadowy silhouette above.

"What?" Sludig growled in the darkness. "Do they not even wait until dawn in this barbaric place? Must they kill us at midnight to hide their deed from the sun? Still God will know." He reached out and gave the rope a tug. "Why should we climb? Let us sit here. Maybe they will send a few guards down to get us." The Rimmersman chuckled unpleasantly. "Then I will break some necks. At the least, they will have to spear us in our hole like bears."

"*Qinkipa's Eyes!*" a voice hissed in the troll language. Binabik sat upright. "*Grab the rope, you fool!*"

"*Sisqi?*" Binabik gasped. "*What are you doing?*"

"*Something I will never forgive myself for—as I also would not forgive myself if I left it undone. Now be silent and climb!*"

Binabik pulled gingerly at the rope. "*But how can you hold it? There is nothing to tie it to and the edge is slippery.*"

"Who are you talking to?" Sludig asked, disconcerted by the Qanuc speech.

"I have brought allies," Sisqinanamook called softly. "Climb! The guards will return when Sedda touches on Sikkihoq's peak!"

Binabik, after explaining swiftly, sent Sludig up the line. The Rimmersman, weakened by imprisonment, made his slow way to the top and disappeared over the rim into darkness, but Binabik did not follow.

Sisqi appeared once more at the rim. "Hurry, before I regret my stupidity! Climb!"

"I cannot. I will not run from the justice of my people." Binabik sat down.

"Are you mad? What do you mean? The guards will be back very soon!" Sisqi could not keep the fear from her voice. "You will get your lowlander friends killed with this foolish trick."

"No, Sisqi, take them. Help them get away. You will have my gratitude. You already do."

She bounced up and down, shiveringly anxious. "Ah, Binabik, you are a curse to me! First you humiliate me before our people, now you talk madness from the bottom of a hole! Come out! Come out!"

"I will not break another oath."

Sisqinanamook stared up at the moon. "Qinkipa Snow Maiden save me. Binbinaqegabenik, why are you so stubborn! Would you die to prove that you are right!?"

Astonishingly Binabik began to laugh. "Would you save my life just to prove me wrong?"

Two more heads appeared at the edge of the hole. "Damnation, troll," Sludig growled, "why do you wait? Are you hurt?" The Rimmersman dropped to his knees as though to scramble back down the rope.

"No!" Binabik cried in the Westerling tongue. "Do not be waiting for me. Sisqinanamook can take you to a place of safeness where you can begin your trip down-mountain. You can be beyond the Yiqanuc boundaries by sunrise."

"What is keeping you here?" Sludig asked, amazed.

"I am condemned by my people," Binabik said. "I broke my oath. I will not break it for a second time."

Sludig muttered in confusion and anger.

The dark figure beside him leaned out. "Binabik," he said. "It's me, Simon. We have to go. We have to find the Stone of Farewell. Geloë said so. We have to take Thorn there."

The troll laughed again, but hollowly. "And without me, no going, no Stone of Farewell?"

"Yes!" Simon's desperation was clear. Time was running short. "We don't know where it is! Geloë said you must take us there! Naglimund has fallen. We may be Josua's only hope—and *your* people's only hope!"

Binabik sat in silence at the bottom of the pit, thinking. At last he reached out to grasp the dangling rope and began to make his way up the sheer wall. When he reached the top, he stumbled over into Simon's fierce embrace. Sludig thumped the little man on the shoulder, a comradely blow that nearly toppled Binabik back into the pit. Haestan stood by, breath steaming in his beard, thick hands now hurriedly coiling the rope up from below.

Binabik pulled away from Simon. "You are not looking very well, friend. Your wounds are troubling you." He sighed. "Ah, this is cruel. I cannot be leaving you to the mercies of my folk, but I have no wishes to break another oath. I do not know what I should do." He turned toward the fourth figure. *"So,"* he said in troll speech, *"you have rescued me—or at least my companions. Why have you changed your mind?"*

Sisqinanamook eyed him, her arms wrapped tightly around herself. *"I am not certain I have,"* she replied. *"I heard what this strange one with the white streak said,"* she indicated Simon, watching in bewildered silence. *"It had the ring of truth—that is, I believed there truly **was** something you thought more important even than our pledge."* She glowered. *"I am not a lovesick fool who will forgive you anything, but neither am I a vengeful demon. You are free. Now go."*

Binabik moved uneasily. *"This thing that kept me from you,"* he said, *"it is not only important to me, but to everybody. A terrible danger is coming. There is only slim hope of resistance, but even that hope must be nurtured."* He lowered his eyes for a moment, then raised them and boldly met her gaze. *"My love for you is as strong as the mountain's rocky bones. It has been so since I first saw you on your Walk of Womanhood, lovely and graceful as a snow otter beneath the stars of Chugik Mountain. But even for that love I could not stand by and see the whole world blighted by unending black winter."* He took her jacketed arm. *"Now tell me this: what will **you** do, Sisqi? You sent the guards away, then the prisoners escaped. You might just as well mark your name-rune in the snow."*

"That will be between me and my father and mother," she said angrily, pulling free of his grasp. *"I have done what you wanted. You are free. Why do you waste that freedom trying to convince me of your innocence? Why do you throw Chugik up to me? Go!"*

Sludig did not speak the language, but he understood Sisqi's gestures. "If she wants us to leave, Binabik, then she speaks rightly! Aedon! We must be swift."

Binabik waved a hand. "Go, I soon will catch you." His friends did not move as he turned again to face his once-intended. *"I will stay,"* he said. *"Sludig is innocent, and it is a great kindness that you have helped him, but I will stay and honor my people's will. I have done a good share already in the struggle against the Storm King . . ."* he glanced toward the west, where the moon had entered a murk of inky clouds, *". . . and others can now carry my load. Come, let you and I go lead the guards a chase so my friends can make their escape."*

A look of fear animated Sisqi's round face. *"Curse you, Binbinaqegabenik, will you go now?! I do not wish to see you killed!"* Angry tears stood in her eyes. *"There, are you pleased!? I still feel for you, although you have torn my heart into pieces!"*

Binabik stepped toward her and caught at her arms again, pulling her close. *"Then come with me!"* he said, his voice suddenly full of wild possibility. *"I will not be separated from you again. Run away and come with me, and my oath be broken and damned! You can see the world—even in these dark days, there are things beyond our mountains that would fill you with wonder!"*

Sisqi pulled away, turning her back. She seemed to be weeping.

After a long moment, Binabik turned to the others. "Whatever will be happening," he said in Westerling speech, his face lit with a strange, unstable smile, "—stay or go, flee or fight—it is first to my master's cave we must go."

"Why?" asked Simon.

"We have not my casting-bones or other things. They have likely been thrown into the cave that I shared with Ookequk my master, since my people would not dare to go destroying things that were the Singing Man's. But even more of importance, unless I am looking into the scrolls, little chance there will be that I can find your Stone of Farewell."

"Then move, troll," Haestan growled. "I dunna know how y'r ladyfriend lured guards away, but no doubt they'll be back."

"You are correct." Binabik beckoned to Simon. "Come, Simon-friend, we must be running again. Such, it is seeming, is the nature of our companionship." He gestured to the troll maiden. She came without a word, leading the way up the path.

They followed the main trail back, but after only a few dozen ells Sisqi suddenly stepped off the track, taking them onto a trail so narrow that it would have been hard to see even in daylight, a slender defile that traversed the broad side of Mintahoq at a sharp upward angle. It was little more than a gouge running between the rocks, and though there were handholds aplenty, progress was cruelly slow in the near-total darkness. Simon's booted shin struck painfully on many stones.

The track led upward, cutting across the grain of two more spirals of the main track, then angled sharply back, still climbing. Pale Sedda was sliding across the sky toward the dark bulk of one of Mintahoq's neighbors, making Simon wonder how they would see at all when the moon had vanished for good. He slipped, waving his arms until he regained his balance, and promptly remembered that they were all clambering up a narrow track on the face of a very dark mountain. Clutching at a handhold, Simon stood in place and closed his eyes, bringing an instant of true blackness as he listened to Haestan's laboring breath behind him. He still felt the weakness that had troubled him all through Yiqanuc. It would be sweet to lie down and sleep, but it was a fruitless hope. After a moment he made the sign of the Tree and started forward again.

At last they reached level ground, a flat porch before a small cave that was set back in a deep crevice in the mountainside; Simon thought that there was something familiar to the moonlight and the shapes of the stones. Just as he realized that Qantaqa had once led him through the darkness to this very place, a gray-white shape leaped from the mouth of the cave.

"*Sosa*, Qantaqa!" Binabik called quietly; a second later he was bowled over by an avalanche of fur. His companions stood by awkwardly for a moment as he was laved by the wolf's steaming tongue. "*Muqang*, friend," the troll gasped at last, "—that's enough! I am sure that you have been bravely guarding Ookequk's house." He struggled to his feet as Qantaqa backed away, her entire body aquiver with delight. "I am more in danger from the greetings of friends than the spears of enemies," Binabik grinned. "We must hurry to the cave. Sedda is hastening west."

He went in standing up, Sisqi after him. Simon and the others had to stoop through the low doorway. Qantaqa, determined not to be left outside, made a jarring rush past Simon's and Haestan's legs, nearly tripping them.

They stood for a moment in a darkness thick with Qantaqa's musky scent and a host of other, stranger odors. Binabik struck sparks from a flint until a small flower of yellow fire appeared and was quickly set to growing on the end of an oil-soaked torch.

The Singing Man's cave was a quite singular place. In contrast to the low door, the curving roof stretched high overhead, up into shadows the torch could not dispel. Like a beehive, the walls were riddled with a thousand alcoves that seemed to have been gouged into the very rock of the cavern. Each niche held something. One contained only the dried remains of a single small flower, others were crammed with sticks and bones and covered pots. But most were filled with rolled skins, more than a few stuffed so full that some of the rolls dangled halfway from the niche, like the imploring hands of beggars.

Qantaqa's week-long residence had left its mark. In the middle of the floor, close to the wide fire pit, were the remains of what once had been a complex circular picture made entirely from small colored stones. The wolf had apparently used this for scratching her back, since the design bore the distinct marks of having been rolled upon. All that remained was part of the rune-wrapped border and an edge of some white thing beneath a sky filled with twirling red stars.

Numerous other objects showed traces of Qantaqa's attention as well. She had pulled a great pile of robes into the cave's far corner and poked the garments into a suitable wolf-nest. Beside this bed lay several much-chewed articles, including the remains of a few of the rolled skins—the fragments crawling with writing unfamiliar to Simon—and Binabik's walking stick.

"I could have wished you were finding something else for chewing, Qantaqa," the troll said, frowning as he picked it up. The wolf tipped her head to one side and whined uneasily, then padded over to Sisqi, who was looking into some of the alcoves, and who distractedly pushed the wolf's large head away. Qantaqa flopped down on the floor and began disconsolately scratching herself. Binabik held his stick up to the torch's light. The toothmarks were not deep.

"Chewing more for comfort of Binabik-smell than any other thing," the troll smiled. "Fortunately."

"What is it you seek?" Sludig said urgently. "We must be going while darkness holds."

"Yes, you speak correctly," Binabik said, sliding his stick in beneath his belt. "Come, Simon, help me as we make a quick searching."

With Haestan and Sludig joining in, Simon pulled down scrolls from the niches that Binabik himself could not reach. They were made of thin-pounded hide, so thoroughly greased that they were slimy to the touch; the runes that covered them were burned directly into the hide, as though with a hot poker. Simon handed one after another to Binabik, who perused each quickly before tossing it onto one of several growing piles.

Looking around at the great rocky honeycomb and all the scrolls, Simon marveled at what an arduous job it must have been to create such a library—and it was just that, he realized, as much as Father Strangyeard's archive at Naglimund or Morgenes' workshop full of heavy volumes, even though these books were furls of hide, scribed with fire instead of ink.

At last Binabik had a pile of a dozen or so that seemed to interest him. These he spread flat and rolled together into one heavy bundle, then dropped the whole mass into his sack, which he had found near the cave's entrance.

"Now we can go?" Sludig asked. Haestan was rubbing his hands together, trying to keep them warm. He had taken off his clumsy gloves to help with the scrolls.

"As soon as we are putting these back into the holes." The troll indicated the large pile of discarded skins.

"Are ye mad?" Haestan said heatedly. "Why waste precious time doin' such?"

"Because these are rare, precious things," Binabik said calmly, "and if we are leaving them here on cold ground, they will be soon ruined. 'He who is not bringing in his flock at night gives away free mutton'—that is what we Qanuc say. It will be taking a moment, only."

"S'Bloody Tree," Haestan swore. "Lend me help, Simon-lad," he grunted, stooping to the pile, "else we'll be here 'til dawn-time."

Binabik directed Simon in the filling of some of the empty upper niches. Sludig watched impatiently for a moment before joining the effort. Sisqi had been quietly rummaging through the alcoves until she had amassed her own pile of rolled skins, which she had then rolled up and slipped under her hide jacket, but now she suddenly turned and called in rapid Qanuc. Binabik pushed past a wad of tangled furs to stand at her side.

She held out a scroll tied shut with a black leather thong. The cord was wrapped not only around the middle of the roll of skin, but around both ends as well. Binabik took it from her, touching two fingers to his forehead in a gesture of seeming reverence.

"This is Ookekuq's knot," he said quietly to Simon. "There is no doubting of that."

"This is Ookekuq's cave, too, isn't it?" Simon said, puzzled. "Why is a knot surprising?"

"Because this knot tells it is something of importance." Binabik explained. "It is also something I have not seen before—something that was hidden from me, or that my master was making just before we left on the journey where he died. And this knot, I am thinking, was only used for things of great power, messages and spells that were for certain eyes only." He again ran his fingers over the knot, his brow wrinkled in thought. Sisqi stared at the scroll, her eyes bright.

"Well, that's last of th'damnable things," Haestan said. "If that be somethin' y'want, little man, bring it with. We've no more time for wastin'."

Binabik hesitated for a moment, caressing the knot gently while he looked once more around the cavern, then slipped the knotted scroll into his sleeve. "Time it is," he agreed. He gestured the others to the cavern doorway ahead of him, extinguishing the torch in a depression in the stone floor as he followed them out.

The rest of the troll's companions had stopped, huddled before the cave like a herd of wind-rattled sheep. Sedda, the moon, had at last vanished in the west behind Sikkihoq, but the night was suddenly full of light.

A large troop of trolls was moving toward them. Faces grim in their hoods, spears and firebrands in their hands, they had fanned out around Ookequk's cave and now held the path on both sides. Even in force, the trolls were so quiet that Simon could hear the burning hiss of their torches before the sound of a single footfall reached him.

"Chukku's Stones," Binabik said bleakly. Sisqi dropped back to take his arm, her eyes wide in the torchlight, her mouth set in a grim line.

Uammannaq the Herder and Nunuuika the Huntress guided their rams forward. They both wore belted robes and boots. Their black hair flowed loose, as though they had dressed hurriedly. As Binabik stepped forward to meet them, armed trolls moved in behind him, hemming his companions in a thicket of spears. Sisqinanamook stepped out of the encirclement to join him, standing at his side with her chin lifted defiantly. Uammannaq avoided his daughter's eyes, staring down instead at Binabik.

"*So, Binbinaqegabenik,*" he said, "*you will not stand and face the justice of your people? I had thought more of you than that, however low your birth.*"

"*My friends are innocent,*" Binabik replied. "*I held your daughter as hostage until the Rimmersman Sludig had made it to safety with the others.*"

Nunuuika rode forward until her mount stood shoulder to shoulder with her husband's. "*Please credit us with some wisdom, Binabik, even though we are not either of us as clever as your master was. Who sent the guards away?*" She peered down at Sisqi. The Huntress' face was cold, but showed a trace of harsh pride. "*Daughter, I thought you were a fool when you determined to marry this wizardling. Now—well, I will say at least that you are a loyal fool,*" She turned to Binabik. "*Because you have recharmed my daughter, do not think you will escape your sentence. The Ice House is unmelted. Winter has killed the Spring. The Rite of Quickening went unperformed—and instead you return to us with childish tales. Now you are back hatching devil-tricks in your master's cave that your pet wolf has guarded for you.*" Nunuuika was in the grip of a rising fury. "*You have been judged, oath-breaker. You will go to the ice cliffs of Ogohak Chasm and you will be thrown over!*"

"*Daughter, go back to our home,*" Uammannaq growled. "*You have done great wrong.*"

"*No!*" Sisqi's cry caused a stir among the watching trolls. "*I have listened to my heart, yes, but listened to what wisdom I have gained as well. The wolf has kept us from Ookequk's house—but that has not been to Binbiniqegabenik's benefit.*" She pulled the thong-tied scroll from Binabik's sleeves and thrust it forward. "*This I found there. None of us thought to see what Ookequk had left behind.*"

"*Only a fool hurries to rummage in the effects of a Singing Man,*" Uammannaq said, but his expression had subtly changed.

"*But Sisqi,*" Binabik said, nonplussed, "*we do not know what the scroll contains! It could be a spell of great peril, or . . .*"

"*I have a good idea,*" Sisqi said grimly. "*Do you see whose knot this is?*" she asked, handing the scroll to her mother.

The Huntress looked at it briefly and made a dismissive gesture as she handed it to her husband. "*It is Ookequk's knot, yes . . .*"

"*And you know what kind of knot as well, Mother,*" Sisqi turned to her father. "*Has it been opened?*"

Uammannaq frowned. "*No . . .*"

"*Good. Father, open it and read it, please.*"

"*Now?*"

"*If not now, when? After the one to whom I am pledged has been executed?*" Sisqi's breath hung in the air after her angry rejoinder. Uammannaq carefully picked the knot and removed the black thong, then slowly unrolled the sheet of hide, beckoning for one of the torch-bearers to move nearer.

"Binabik," Simon shouted from behind a circle of spear-heads, "what is happening?"

"Stay, all of you, and do nothing for a moment," Binabik called to him in Westerling. "I will tell you all when I can."

"Know this," Uammannaq read,

> *". . . That I am Ookequk, Singing Man of Mintahoq, of Chugik, Tutusik. Rinsenatuq, Sikkihoq and Namyet, and all other mountains of Yiqanuc."*

The Herder read slowly, with long, squint-eyed pauses as he puzzled out the sense of the blackened runes.

> *"I go on a long journey, and in such times that I cannot know I will come back. So, I lay my death-song on this hide, that it can be my voice when I am gone."*

"Clever, clever, Sisqi," Binabik said quietly as her father's voice droned, *"it is you who should have been Ookequk's student, not me! How could you know!?"* She waved a hand to quiet him. *"I am a daughter of Chidsik ub Lingit, where all the petitions for judgment come from all the mountains. Do you think I would not recognize the knot used on a death testament?"*

> *"I must warn those who remain after me,"*

Uammannaq continued with Ookequk's words,

> *". . . That I have seen the coming of a great cold darkness, the like of which my people have never seen. It is a dreadful winter that will come from the shadow of Vihyuyaq, the mountain of the immortal Cloud Children. It will blast the lands of Yiqanuc like a black wind from the Lands of the Dead, cracking the very stone of our mountains in cruel fingers . . ."*

As the Herder read these words, several of the listening trolls cried out, hoarse voices echoing down the night-shrouded mountainside. Others swayed, so that the torchlight flickered.

> *"My student, Binbinaqegabenik, I will bring with me on my journey. In the time that remains I will instruct him in the small things and long stories that may help our people in this foul time. There are other ones beyond Yiqanuc who have prepared lamps against this coming darkness. I go to add my light to theirs, small as it may shine against the storm that threatens. If I cannot return, young Binbinaqegabenik will come in my stead. I ask you to honor him as you would me, for he is eager in his learning. One day he may grow to be a greater Singing Man than I.*

"Now I end my death song. I give my farewell to mountain and sky. It has been good to be alive. It has been good to be one of the Children of Lingit, and to live my life on the beautiful mountain Mintahoq."

Uammannaq lowered the scroll, blinking. A low wail bubbled up among the watchers in response to the Singing Man Ookekuq's final song.

"He did not have enough time," Binabik murmured. Tears welled in his eyes. *"He was taken away too quickly and told me nothing—or at least not enough. Oh, Ookequk, how we will miss you! How could you have left your people with no wall between them and the Storm King but an untrained weanling like Binabik!"* He dropped to his knees and touched his forehead to the snow.

An awkward silence fell, pierced only by the lamenting wind.

"Bring the lowlanders," Nunuuika said to the spearmen, then turned a stiff, painful glance on her daughter. *"We will all go to the House of the Ancestor. There is much to think about."*

Simon awakened slowly, and stared at the inconstant shadows on the craggy ceiling of Chidsik ub Lingit for a long time while he tried to remember where he was. He felt a little better now, more clearheaded, but the scar on his cheek stung like fire.

He sat up. Sludig and Haestan were leaning against the wall a short distance away, sharing a skin of some drink and a muttered conversation. Simon untangled himself from his cloak and looked around for Binabik. His friend was near the center of the room, squatting before the Herder and Huntress as if in supplication. For a moment Simon was fearful, but others squatted there too, Sisqinanamook among them. As he listened to the rise and fall of guttural voices, he decided it seemed more a council than a judgment. Other small groups of trolls were discernible here and there in the deep shadows, crouched in little circles throughout the vast stone room. A few scattered lamps burned like bright stars in a sky full of thunderheads.

Simon curled up again, wriggling to find a smooth place on the floor. How terribly strange, to be in this place! Would he ever have a home again, a place where he would wake up every morning in the same bed, unsurprised to find himself there?

He drifted slowly back into half-sleep, into a dream of cold mountain passes and red eyes.

"Simon-friend!" It was Binabik, gently shaking him. The troll looked drawn, the circles under his eyes visible even in the half-light, but he was smiling. "It is time for waking."

"Binabik," Simon said groggily, "what is happening?"

"I have brought for you a bowl of tea and some tidings. It appears I am no longer bound for an unfortunate plunging," the troll grinned. "No longer are Sludig and myself to be thrown into Ogohak Chasm."

"But that's wonderful!" Simon gasped. He felt his heart ache inside him, a fierce wrench of released tension. He leaped to embrace the small man and his sudden lunge toppled the troll. The tea puddled on the stone.

"You have been too long in the company of Qantaqa," Binabik laughed, extricating himself. He looked pleased. "You have gained her liking for the giving of exuberant greetings."

Other heads in the room turned to watch this strange spectacle. Many Qanuc tongues muttered in amazement at the mad and lanky lowlander who hugged trolls as if he were a clansman. Simon saw the stares and ducked his head in embarrassment. "What have they said?" he asked. "Can we go?"

"Put with simpleness: yes, we can go." Binabik sat down beside him. He was carrying his bone walking stick, recovered from Ookequk's cave. He proceeded to examine it as he spoke, frowning at the numerous toothmarks Qantaqa had added. "But much there is to be decided. Ookequk's scroll has convinced the Herder and Huntress on the truth of my tellings."

"But what is there to decide?"

"Many things. If I go with you to take Thorn back to Josua, then my people are again without a Singing Man. But I am thinking I *must* accompany you. If Naglimund has fallen truly, then we should be following the words of Geloë. She may be the last one of great wisdom that remains. Besides, it is seeming more certain that our only hope is in the getting of the other two swords, Minneyar and Sorrow. Not for nothing should your gallantry on the dragon-mountain be."

Binabik gestured at Thorn, which stood against the wall near where Haestan and Sludig sat. "If the Storm King's rising is unchecked," he said, "then no use there will be my staying on Mintahoq, since none of the craft Ookequk taught me will keep away the winter we fear." The little man made a broad gesture. "So, 'when the snowslide takes your house,' as we troll folk say, 'do not stay to hunt for potshards.' I have told my people they should be moving down-mountain, to the spring hunting grounds— even though there will be no spring there, and small hunting."

He stood, tugging down the hem of his thick jacket. "I wanted you to know that there was no danger now to Sludig and myself." He smirked. "A bad joke. We are all, it is obvious, in terrible danger. But the danger is not from my own people any longer." He laid a small hand on Simon's shoulder. "Sleep again, if you can. We will likely leave at dawn. I will go and speak to Haestan and Sludig, then there is much planning still ahead this night." He turned and walked across the cave. Simon watched his small form pass in and out of the shadows.

A great deal of planning has been done already, he thought grumpily, *and I have not been invited to much of it. Someone always has a plan, and I always wind up walking along while someone else decides where to go. I feel like a wagon—an old, falling-apart wagon at that. When do I get to decide things for myself?*

He thought about this as he waited for sleep.

As it turned out, the sun had risen high in the gray sky before the final arrangements were finished—a span of time Simon was more than happy to spend sleeping.

Simon, his companions, and a large number of trolls trooped out onto the byways of Mintahoq, following the Herder and Huntress in the strangest parade Simon had ever seen. As they wound in and out through Mintahoq's most populous sections, hundreds of trolls stopped on the swinging bridges or came dashing out of their caves to watch the company pass, standing amazed beneath the swirling smokes of their cooking fires. Many clambered down the thong ladders and joined the procession.

Much of the journey was uphill, and the vast crowd strung out along the narrow track made the going slow. It seemed quite a long while before they made their way around to the northern face. As they trudged on, Simon found himself slipping into a kind of numbed dreaminess. Snow flurried in the gray void beyond the pathway; Yiqanuc's other peaks stood up along the valley's far side like teeth.

The march stopped at last on a long stone porch atop a promontory that stood out above the northern part of Yiqanuc's valley. Another path hugged the mountainside below them, then the rock walls of Mintahoq fell sharply away, down into white obscurity touched with patches of bright sunsplash. Staring down, Simon was stuck by a memory of dream, of a dim white tower lapped by flames. He turned away from the unsettling view to find the rocky ledge on which he stood dominated by the tall, egg-shaped snow-building he had seen his first day out of the cave. Closer this time, he could clearly see the marvelous care with which the triangular blocks of snow had been cut and fitted together, the bold carvings that seemed to slice down into the blocks themselves, so that the Ice House was as multifaceted as a cut diamond, its walls alive with hidden interior angles, prisms that reflected cyan and pink.

The row of armed trolls who guarded the Ice House stood respectfully to one side as Nunuuika and Uammanaq moved past them to stand between the pillars of tight-packed snow that framed the door. Simon could see nothing of the Ice House's interior but a blue-gray hole beyond the doorway. Binabik and Sisqi took places on the icy step below, mittened hands clasped. Qangolik the Spirit Caller clambered up beside them.

Though Qangolik's face was hidden by his ram-skull mask, Simon thought the muscular troll seemed rather subdued. The Spirit Caller, who had pranced like a courting bird before the judgment in Chidsik ub Lingit, now slumped like a weary harvest hand.

As the Herder lifted his crook-spear and spoke, Binabik translated for his lowlander companions.

'Strange days are upon us.'' Uammannaq's eyes were deep-shadowed. "We have known that something was wrong. We live too closely with the mountain, which is of the bones of the earth, not to sense the unease in the lands around us. The Ice House is still here. It has not melted." The wind rose, whistling, as if to underscore his words. "Winter will not leave. At first we blamed Binabik. The Singing Man or his apprentice has always sung the Rite of Quickening; Summer has always come. But now we are told that it is not failure to perform the Rite that keeps Summer hidden. Strange days. Things are different." He shook his head heavily, his beard wagging.

"We must break with tradition," Nunuuika the Huntress added. "The word of the wise should be law to those of less wisdom. Ookequk has spoken as if he were here among us. Now we know more of the thing that we feared, but could not name. My husband speaks truly: strange days are upon us. Tradition served us, but now it shackles us. Thus, Huntress and Herder declare that Binbinaqegabenik is free from his punishment. We would be fools to kill one who has been striving to protect us from the storm of which Ookequk spoke. We would be worse than fools, it is now clear, to kill the only one who knew Ookequk's heart."

Nunuuika paused, waiting for Binabik to complete his reinterpretation, then continued, passing her hand across her forehead in some ritual gesture. "The Rimmersman Sludig is an even stranger problem. He is no Qanuc, so he was not guilty of oath-breaking, as we declared Binabik. But he is of an enemy people, and if the tales of our farthest-ranging hunters are true, Rimmersmen in the east have grown even more savage than before. However, Binabik assures us that this Sludig is different, that he fights the same fight as Ookequk. We are not sure, but in these days of madness we cannot say it is not so. Thus, Sludig is also declared freed from punishment and may leave Yiqanuc as he wishes—the first Croohok so pardoned since the Battle of Huhinka Valley in my great-grandmother's day, when the snows ran red with blood. We call on the spirits of high places, pale Sedda and Qinkipa of the Snows, Morag Eyeless, bold Chukku, and all the rest, to protect the people if our judgment is faulty."

When the Huntress had finished, Uammannaq stood beside her and made a broad gesture, as though to break something in two and cast it away. The watching trolls chanted one sharp syllable, then lapsed into excited whispering.

Simon turned and clasped Sludig's hand. The northerner smiled tightly, jaw set behind his yellow beard. "The little people speak rightly," he said. "Strange times indeed."

Uammannaq raised his hand to still the murmur of conversation. "The lowlanders shall now leave. Binbinaqegabenik, who if he returns will be our next Singing Man, may go with them to take this strange, magical object—" he pointed to Thorn, which Haestan held propped on the ground before him, "—to the lowlanders, who he says can use it to frighten away the winter.

"We shall send with them a party of hunters, led by our daughter Sisqinanamook, who shall be their escort until they leave the lands of the Qanuc. The hunters will then go to the spring city by Blue Mud Lake and prepare for the coming of the rest of our clans." Uammannaq made a gesture and one of the other trolls stepped forward with a skin bag that had been covered nearly completely in delicate tracings of colored embroidery. "We have gifts we wish to give you."

Binabik brought his friends forward. The Huntress presented Simon with a sheath of supple hide, the leather subtly tooled and studded with stone beads the color of a spring moon. The Herder then gave him a knife to put in it, a beautiful pale blade made from a single piece of bone. The handle was wrought with smoothed carvings of birds.

"A magical lowlander sword is very good for fighting snow-worms," Nunuuika told him, "but a humble Qanuc knife is easier to hide and easier to use in close quarters."

Simon thanked them politely and stepped aside. Haestan was given a capacious drinking skin decorated with ribbons and stitchery, filled to the stopper with Qanuc liquor. The guardsman, who had drunk enough of the sour stuff during the previous evening to finally develop a bit of taste for it, bowed, mumbled some words of gratitude, then withdrew.

Sludig, who had come to Yiqanuc as a prisoner but was now leaving more or less as a guest, received a spear with a viciously sharp head hewn from shiny black stone. The haft was uncarved, since it had been hurriedly constructed—the trolls did not use spears of a length that would have been appropriate—but it was nicely balanced and could double as a walking stave.

"We hope you also appreciate the gift of your life," Uammannaq said, "and will remember that the justice of the Qanuc is stern but not cruel."

Sludig amazed them by dropping quickly to a knee. "I will remember," was all he said.

"Binbinaqegabenik," Nunuuika began, "you have already received the greatest gift it is in our capacity to bestow. If she will still have you, we renew our permission for you to marry our youngest daughter. When the Rite of Quickening can be performed next year, you will be joined."

Binabik and Sisqi clasped hands and bowed on the step before the

Herder and Huntress as words of blessing were said. The ram-faced Spirit Caller came forward. He chanted and sang as he daubed their foreheads with oil, but with what Simon thought was a very dissatisfied air. When Qangolik finished and stalked grumpily back down the steps of the Ice House, the betrothal had been reinstated.

The Huntress and Herder said a brief personal farewell to the company, Binabik interpreting. Though she smiled and touched his hand with her small, strong fingers, Nunuiika still seemed cold and hard as stone to Simon, sharp and dangerous as her own spearhead. He had to force himself to smile back and retreat slowly when she had finished.

Qantaqa was waiting for them, curled in a nest of snow outside of Chidsik ub Lingit. The noon sun had disappeared behind a spreading fog; the wind set Simon's teeth to chattering.

"Down the mountain we must now go, friend," Binabik said to him. "I am wishing you and Haestan and Sludig were not so large, but there are no rams strong enough for your riding. It will make our going slower than I would wish."

"But where are we going?" Simon asked. "Where *is* this Stone of Farewell?"

"All things in their season," the troll replied. "I will look at my scrolls when we stop tonight, but we should leave now as soon as we can. The mountain passes will be treacherous. I smell more snow upon the wind."

"More snow," Simon repeated, shouldering his pack. More snow.

6

The Nameless Dead

"... *So Drukhi found her,*"

Maegwin sang,

> "*Beloved Nenais'u, wind-footed dancer,*
> *Stretched on the green grass, as silent as stone.*
> *Her dark eyes sky-watching,*
> *Only her shining blood gave him answer,*
> *Her head lay uncradled, her black hair undone.*"

Maegwin drew her hand over her eyes, shielding them from the sting-ing wind, then leaned forward to rearrange the flowers on her father's cairn. Already the wind had scattered the violets across the stones; only a few dried petals remained on Gwythinn's grave nearby. Where had the treacherous summer gone? And when would the flowers bloom again, so she could tend her loved ones' resting places as they deserved?

As the wind rattled the skeletal birch trees, she sang again.

> "*Long time he held her,*
> *Through gray-shadowed evening, beneath shamefaced night,*
> *Matching the hours she had lain there alone.*
> *His bright eyes unblinking,*
> *Drukhi sang songs of the East's timeless light.*
> *He whispered to her they would wait for the sun.*

> "*Dawn, golden-handed,*
> *Caressed but could not warm the nightingale's child.*
> *Nenais'u's swift spirit had fled unhomed.*
> *Close Drukhi clutched her,*
> *His voice echoed out through woods and through wild.*
> *Where two hearts had sounded now beat only one ...*"

She broke off, wondering absently if she had once known the rest of the words. She remembered her nurse singing it to her when she was young, a sad song about the Sithi-folk—"The Peaceful Ones," as her ancestors had named them. Maegwin did not know the legend behind it. She doubted her old nurse had known, either. It was only that, a sad song from happier times, from her childhood in the Taig . . . before her father and brother died.

She stood, brushing the dirt from the knees of her black skirt, and scattered a few last withered flowers among the slender spears of grass pushing up from Gwythinn's cairn. As she turned back up the path, clasping her cloak tight against the gnawing wind, she wondered once more why she should not join her brother and father Lluth here in peace on the mountainside. What did life hold for her?

She knew what Eolair would say. The Count of Nad Mullach would tell her that her people had no one else but Maegwin to inspire and guide them. "Hope," Eolair often said, in that quiet but fox-clever way of his, "is like the belly-strap on a king's saddle—a slender thing, but if it snaps the world turns topside-down."

Thinking of the count, she felt a rare flash of anger. What could *he* know—what could anyone know about death who was as alive as Eolair, to whom life seemed a gift from the gods? How could he understand the dreadful weight of waking up each day, knowing that the ones she loved most were gone, that her people were uprooted and friendless, doomed to a slow, humiliating extinction? What gift of the gods was worth the gray burden of pain, the unceasing rut of bleak thoughts?

Eolair of Nad Mullach came to her often these days, speaking to her as he would to a child. Once, long ago, Maegwin had fallen in love with him, but she had never been so foolish as to believe he might feel for her in turn. Tall as a man, clumsy and blunt in her words, far more like a farmer's daughter than a princess—who could ever love Maegwin? But now that she and her bewildered young stepmother Inahwen were all that remained of Lluth ubh-Llythinn's house, now Eolair was concerned.

Not out of any base motives, though. She laughed out loud and did not like the sound of it. Oh, gods, base motives? Not honorable Count Eolair. That was the thing she hated in him more than anything else: his unrelenting kindness and honor. She was sick to death of pity.

Besides, even if—impossibly—he *could* have thought of profiting at such a time, how would joining his fate to hers benefit him in any case? Maegwin was the last daughter of a broken house, the ruler of a shattered nation. The Hernystiri had become wild creatures living in the woodlands of the Grianspog Mountains, driven back to their primeval caves by the whirlwind of destruction brought down on them by High King Elias and his Rimmersman tool, Skali of Kaldskryke.

So perhaps Eolair was right. Perhaps she did owe her life to her people. She was the last of Lluth's blood—a thin tie to a happier past, but the only such link that the survivors of Hernysadharc retained. She would live, then—but whoever would have thought that merely living could become a burdensome duty!

As Maegwin made her way along the steep trail, something wet touched her face. She looked up. A host of tiny spots swarmed against the leaden sky. Another bit of wetness flecked her.

Snow. The realization made her cold heart even colder. *Snow in midsummer, in Tiyagar-month. Brynioch of the Skies and all the other gods have truly turned their backs on the Hernystiri.*

A single sentry, a boy of perhaps ten summers with a red and dripping nose, greeted her as she entered the camp. A few fur-wrapped children played on the mossy rocks before the cavern, trying to catch the now fast-falling snowflakes on their tongues. They scrambled back, wide-eyed, as she walked past with her black skirts swirling in the wind.

They know the princess is mad, she thought sourly. *Anyone would. The princess talks to herself, but to no one else for days at a time. The princess speaks of nothing but death. Of course the princess is mad.*

She thought it might be good to smile for the fearful-looking children, but as she looked down at their dirty faces and their tattered rags of clothing, she decided that such an effort might frighten them further. Instead, Maegwin hurried past into the cave.

Am I *mad?* she wondered suddenly. *Is this crushing weight what madness feels like? These heavy thoughts that make my head feel like the arms of a drowning swimmer, struggling, failing. . . ?*

The wide cavern was largely empty. Old Craobhan, recovering slowly from wounds received in the futile defense of Hernysadharc, lay by the banked fire talking quietly to Arnoran, who had been one of her father Lluth's favorite harpers. They looked up as she approached. She could see them both studying her, trying to divine her mood. As Arnoran began to rise, she waved him back down.

"It's snowing," she said.

Craobhan shrugged. The ancient knight was nearly bald but for a few wisps of white hair, his scalp a puzzle of delicate blue veins. "Not good, Lady. That's not good. We've little livestock, but we're close-quartered in these few caves as it is, and that's with most of us outside during the day."

"More crowding." Arnoran shook his head. He was not nearly as old as Craobhan, but was even more frail. "More angry folk."

"Do you know 'The Leavetaking Stone'?" Maegwin asked the harper suddenly. "It's an old song about the Sithi, about someone named Nenais'u dying."

"I think I knew it once, long ago," Arnoran said, squinting his eyes as he stared into the fire and tried to think. "It is a very old song—very, very old."

"You don't have to sing the words," Maegwin said. She settled cross-legged beside him, her skirt tight as a drumhead between her knees. "Just play the melody for me."

Arnoran scrabbled for his harp, then played a few tentative notes. "I'm not sure I remember how to . . ."

"It doesn't matter. Try." She wished she could think of something to say that would bring a smile to their faces, even for a moment. Did her people deserve to see her always in mourning? "It will be good," she said at last, "to think of other times."

Arnoran nodded and plucked briefly at his strings, eyes closed, his quarry easiest sought in darkness. He finally began a delicate air, full of strange notes that quavered just on the edge of dissonance without ever crossing over. As he played, Maegwin, too, shut her eyes. She could once again hear the voice of her nurse from long ago, telling her the story of Drukhi and Nenais'u—what strange names they had in old ballads!—telling of their love and tragic deaths, their warring families.

The music went on for a long while. Maegwin's thought swirled with images of the distant and not-so-distant past. She could see pallid Drukhi bent in grief, swearing vengeance—but he wore her brother Gwythinn's anguished face. And Nenais'u, sprawled lifeless on the greensward: was that not Maegwin herself?

Arnoran had stopped. Maegwin opened her eyes, not knowing how long the music had been silent.

"When Drukhi died avenging his wife," she said as if continuing an earlier conversation, "his family could not live with Nenais'u's family anymore."

Arnoran and Craobhan exchanged glances. She ignored them and went on.

"I remember the story now. My nurse used to sing the song to me. Drukhi's family fled away from their enemies, went far away to live apart." After a pause, she turned to look at Craobhan. "When will Eolair and the others return from their expedition?"

The old man counted on his fingers. "They should be back by the new moon, in a little less than a fortnight."

Maegwin stood up. "Some of these caverns run deep into the mountain's heart," she said. "Is that not true?"

"There were always deep places in the Grianspog," Craobhan nodded slowly, trying to understand her. "And some were delved even deeper, for mining."

"Then we will start exploring tomorrow at dawn. By the time the count and his men come back, we will be ready to move."

"Move?" Craobhan squinted, surprised. "Move where, Lady Maegwin?"

"Farther into the mountains," she said. "It came to me as Arnoran sang. We Hernystiri are like Drukhi's family in the song: we cannot live here anymore." She rubbed her hands together, trying to ward off the chill of the cavern. "King Elias has destroyed his brother Josua. Now there is nothing and no one left to drive Skali away."

"But my lady!" Arnoran said, startled into interrupting her. "Still there is
Eolair, and with him many other brave Hernystirmen remaining . . ."

"—There is no one to drive Skali away," she continued harshly, "and
the Thane of Kaldskryke will doubtless find Hernystir's meadows a more
hospitable home in this freezing summer than his own lands in Rimmersgard.
If we stay here, we shall be trapped eventually, slaughtered before our caves
like rabbits." Her voice grew stronger. "But if we go deeper, they will
never find us. Then Hernystir will survive, far away from the madness of
Elias and Skali and the rest!"

Old Craobhan looked up at her worriedly. She knew he was wondering
what everyone else wondered: had Maegwin been unbalanced by her
losses—by all their losses?

Perhaps I have, she thought, *but not in this. In this, I am sure I am right.*

"But, Lady Maegwin," the old counselor said, "how will we eat? What
will we do for cloth, for grain. . . ?"

"You said it yourself," she responded. "The mountains are shot through
with tunnels. If we learn and explore them, we can live deep in stone and
be safe from Skali, yet come out wherever we wish—to hunt, to gather
stores, even to raid Kaldskryke's own camps if we choose!"

"But . . . but . . ." The old man turned to Arnoran, but the harper
could offer no support. "But what will your mother Inahwen think of
such a plan?" he said at last.

Maegwin snorted in contempt. "My *step*mother spends her days sitting
with the other women, complaining about how hungry she is. Inahwen is
less use than a child."

"Then what will Eolair think? What of the brave count?"

Maegwin stared at Craobhan's shaking hands, his rheumy old eyes. For
a moment she felt sorry for him, but that did not quell her anger. "What
the Count of Nad Mullach thinks, he may tell us—but remember,
Craobhan: he does not command me. He has taken the oath to my father's
house. Eolair will do what *I* say!"

She walked away, leaving the two men whispering beside the fire. The
biting chill outside the cave could not cool her heated face, even though
she stood in the snowy wind for a long time.

Earl Guthwulf of Utanyeat awakened to hear the Hayholt's midnight
bell, high above in Green Angel Tower, shuddering into silence.

Guthwulf closed his eyes, waiting for sleep to return, but slumber was
elusive. Picture after picture appeared before his shuttered gaze, images
of battles and tournaments, the dry repetitions of court etiquette, the
chaos of the hunt. Foremost in every scene was King Elias' face—the flash
of panicky relief, quickly hidden, that had greeted Guthwulf as he broke

through a ring of attackers to rescue his friend during the Thrithings wars; the blank, black stare with which Elias received confirmation of his wife Hylissa's death; and most disturbing of all, the secretive, gleeful, yet at the same moment shamefaced stare that the king now wore whenever he and Guthwulf met.

The earl sat up, cursing. Sleep had fled and would not return soon.

He did not light the lamp, but dressed in darkness, relying on the sprinkle of starlight from the narrow window to help him step over his manservant, who lay dozing on the floor at the foot of Guthwulf's bed. He pulled a cloak over his nightshirt and donned a pair of slippers, then made his way out into the corridor. Addled with such foolish, troubled thoughts, he decided he might as well walk for an hour.

The halls of the Hayholt were empty, with not a guard or servant in sight. Here and there torches burned fitfully in their wall sconces, consumed almost to the socket. The halls were untenanted, but still faint murmurs swept through the darkened passageways—voice of sentries on the walls, the earl decided, rendered bodiless and spectral by distance.

Guthwulf shivered. *What I need is a woman*, he thought. *A warm body in the bed, a prattling voice to silence when I wish and to fill the quiet when I let. This monkish living would unman anyone.*

He turned and strode down the hall, heading for the servant's quarters. There was a saucy, curly-headed chambermaid who wouldn't say no—hadn't she told him her intended had died at Bullback Hill, that she was all alone?

*If that one is in mourning—hah! Then I **will** become a monk!*

The great door to the servant's quarters was locked. Guthwulf snarled and tugged, but the bolt was shot on the inner side. He contemplated banging on the heavy oak with his fist until someone came to open it—someone who would swiftly feel Utanyeat's wrath—but decided against it. Something about Hayholt's silent corridors made him unwilling to attract attention. Besides, he told himself, the curly-haired wench was not worth the beating down of doors.

He stepped away, rubbing his bristled chin, and saw something pale moving at the turning of the hall, near the edge of his vision. He whirled, startled, but found nothing there. He walked a few steps and leaned around the corner. The hall beyond was also empty. A breathless whisper drifted along the passageway—a woman's low voice, muttering as if in pain. Guthwulf turned on his heel and stalked back toward his chamber.

Night tricks, he grumbled to himself. *Doors locked, corridors empty—the whole damnable, Bleeding Usires castle might as well be deserted!*

He stopped, suddenly, looking around. What hallway was this? He did not recognize the polished tiles, the oddly-shaped banners hanging shadowed on the dark wall. Unless he had made a wrong turning and lost his way, this should be the chapel's walking-hall. He retraced his way back to the forking of the hall and turned, taking the other route. Now, although this new corridor was featureless but for a few window-slits, he was sure he had found his way once more.

He grabbed at the base of one of the windows and pulled himself up, hanging by his strong arms. Outside would be either the front or side of the chapel courtyard. . . .

Startled, Guthwulf let go and slid the short distance back to the ground. His knees buckled, dropping him to the floor. He rolled quickly to his feet, heart pounding, and reached for the window slit to haul himself up again.

It was the chapel courtyard, sunk in deep night, just as it should be.

But what then had he seen the first time? There had been white walls and the forest of looming spires that he had first taken for trees, then recognized in an instant later as towers—a forest of slim minarets, ivory needles that caught the moonlight and glowed as if full-charged with it! The Hayholt had no such towers!

But there! Again the evidence of his eyes confirmed that all was right and usual. There was the courtyard, the chapel door and awning, the shrubs standing beside the pathways like drowsy sheep. Beyond, he could just make out the moonbathed silhouette of Green Angel Tower—a solitary sky-pointing finger where a moment before he had seen a dozen hands raised in supplication.

He dropped to his feet and leaned against the cold stone. Then what had he seen that first time? Night tricks? No, this was more! This was sickness, or madness . . . or witchcraft!

After a moment he collected himself. *Steady, you fool.* He stood up, shaking his head. *These aren't the fruits of madness, but of too much pondering, too much womanish worry. My sire used to sit up at night staring wide-eyed at the fire and claimed he saw ghosts there. Still, he was fit enough in his head when he died, and lived a full seventy summers. No, it is all this thought about the king that is preying on me. Black witchcraft may be all around us—God knows, I'm last to argue against it after what I've seen this cursed year—but not here in the Hayholt.*

Guthwulf knew the castle had belonged to the Fair Folk once, many hundreds of years ago, but now it was so wound about with spells and charms against them that surely there was no other spot on earth in which they were less welcome.

No, he thought, *it is the way the king has changed that fills my mind with strange thoughts: how Elias shifts from moment to moment, from lunatic anger to childish worry.*

He walked to the door at the end of the hallway and out into the courtyard. Everything was as he had last seen it. A solitary light burned in one of the windows across the garden, in the king's private rooms.

Elias is awake. He pondered this for a moment. *He has not slept well since Josua first began plotting against him.*

Guthwulf strode across the courtyard toward the king's residence, the unseasonable breeze frisking about his bare ankles. He would talk to his old friend Elias, here in the empty hours of night when men told the truth. He would demand to know about Pryrates and about the horrible army Elias has summoned, the host that had come down on Naglimund like a plague of white locusts. Guthwulf and the king had been comrades in arms too long for the earl to allow their friendship to fall apart like rusting armor. Tonight they would talk. Guthwulf would find out just what dire troubles caused his old comrade to act so strangely. It would be their first chance in a year to speak without Pryrates hovering close by, watching with those black ferret's eyes, listening to every word.

The courtyard doorway was locked, but the great key Elias had given him on his succession to the throne still hung on a cord around Guthwulf's neck. His soldier's practicality had not allowed him to take it off, even though it had been many months since Elias had called on him to undertake a secret mission.

The locks had not been changed. The heavy door swung inward without a sound; Guthwulf was grateful for that, although he did not know why. As he mounted the stairs toward the king's residence, he was astonished to find not even a single guard in place before the inner door. Was Elias so sure of his power that he did not even fear assassination? Surely that did not accord with his behavior since he had returned from the siege of Naglimund?

At the top of the stairs Guthwulf heard muffled voices. Suddenly full of misgivings, he leaned forward, placing his ear near the keyhole.

He frowned. *I should've known*, he thought sourly. *I would recognize Pryrates' jackal-barking anywhere. Curse the unnatural bastard, can he give the king no peace?*

As he debated whether he should knock, he heard the king's low murmur. A third voice froze Guthwulf's hand in midair, knuckles poised before the doorframe.

This last voice was high-pitched and sweet, but there was something alien in its tone, something inhuman in its music. It acted on his senses like a plunge in cold water, bringing up the hair on the back of his arms and setting a shiver into his breath. He thought he recognized the words "sword" and "mountains" before the numbing fear overcame him. He stepped back from the door so quickly he almost tumbled down the stairs.

Have those hell-things come here? he wondered. He wiped his sweating palms on his nightshirt and retreated a step down from the landing. *What devil's work is this? Has Elias lost his mind? His soul?*

The voices rose in volume, then the door squeaked as someone lifted the inside bolt. All thought of confronting Elias gone, the Earl of Utanyeat knew only that he did not want to be found listening at the keyhole—did not want to meet the thing that spoke so strangely. He looked around distractedly for a place to hide, but the staircase was narrow. He vaulted down the steps in a rush, but had only just reached the outer door when he heard footsteps on the landing above. Guthwulf ducked into the alcove beneath the stairway, pushing himself back into the shadows as the steps creaked. Two figures, one more distinct than the other, paused in the doorway.

"The king is pleased with this news," Pryrates was saying. The darker shape beside him said nothing. A smear of white face gleamed in the depths of its dark hood. Pryrates stepped through the door, his scarlet garments showing deep violet-blue in the moonlight as he pivoted his bald head this way and that, looking carefully. A shadow followed him out into the garden.

Anger suddenly rose inside Guthwulf, overwhelming even his unreasoning fear. That the master of Utanyeat should cower under stairs—and from something that the cursed priest treated as companionably as a country uncle!

"Pryrates!" Guthwulf cried, stepping out from beneath the stairway. "I would have a word with you . . ."

The earl's slippered feet crunched to a halt on the gravel. The priest stood before him, alone in the middle of the path. The wind sighed in the hedges, but there was no other sound, no other movement but the faint rippling of leaves.

"Earl Guthwulf," Pryrates said, wrinkling his hairless brow in apparent surprise, "what are you doing out here? And at such an hour." He looked Guthwulf's costume up and down. "Have you had trouble sleeping?"

"Yes . . . no . . . damn you, priest, that's not important! I was just on my way to see the king!"

Pryrates nodded. "Ah. Well, I've just left His Majesty. He's just taken his sleeping draught, so whatever you desire to speak of should wait until morning."

Guthwulf looked up at the mocking moon, then around the courtyard. It was empty but for the two of them. He felt dizzy, betrayed by his own senses. "You were alone with the king?" he asked at last.

The priest stared at him for a moment. "But for his new cupbearer, yes. And a few body-servants in the outer rooms. Why?"

The earl felt the last bit of ground sliding from beneath his feet. "Cupbearer? That is, I just wanted to know . . . I thought . . ." Guthwulf struggled to regain his poise. "There's no guard posted on that door." He pointed.

"With such a doughty warrior as yourself stalking the gardens," Pryrates smiled, "there is scarce need for one—but you are correct. I will speak to the chief constable about it. Now, if you'll excuse me, my lord, I must go to my narrow bed. I have had a long, wearying day of statecraft. Good night."

With a swirl of his robe, the priest turned and walked away, vanishing in a cluster of shadows at the far side of the courtyard.

The traveler's spirit came back to him as he rode through the endless snows, but his name did not. He could not remember how he came to be riding the horse, or if the beast was his. Neither did he know where he had been, or what had happened to cause the dreadful pain that ran through his body, twisting and crippling his limbs. He knew only that he must ride on toward a spot behind the horizon, following a curved seam of stars that burned in the northwestern skies at night. He could not remember what place he would find there.

He stopped only seldom for sleep: the ride itself was a kind of waking dream, a long white tunnel of wind and ice that seemed never-ending. Ghosts attended him, a vast crowd of homeless dead walking at his stirrups. Some of these were of his own making—or so it seemed from the reproach written on their pale faces—others were the importuning spirits for whom he had killed. But none of them held any power over him now. Without his name, he was as much a phantom as were they.

So they traveled together, the unnamed man and the nameless dead: a lone rider and a whispering, insubstantial horde that accompanied him like foam carried on before an ocean wave.

Each time the sun died and the star-crescent bloomed in the shimmering northwest sky, he made a slash with his knife in the leather of his saddle. Sometimes when the sun vanished, the wind filled the dark sky with sleet and the stars did not appear. Still, he marked his saddle. Seeing the pale weals in the oil-darkened leather reassured him, proved that something could change in this eternal sameness of mountains and stones and snowy plain, and suggested that he was not merely crawling in a pointless circle like a blind insect on the rim of a cup. The only other measure of time's passage was his hunger, which now shouted above even the most terrible of his other pains. And that, too, was a queer comfort. To starve was to live. Dead, he might find himself condemned to join the throng of whispering shades that surrounded him, doomed to flitter and sigh in this lifeless waste forever. While he lived, there was at least a faint, cold hope—although what it was that he might hope for he could not quite recall.

There were eleven slashes on the saddle when his horse died. One moment they were striding forward, breasting a drift of new snow; the next moment his mount sank slowly to its knees, quivering, then toppled over, a silent spray of white thrown up all around. After a while he pulled himself free, his pain a voice as distant as the stars he followed. He clambered to his feet and began, unsteadily, to walk.

Two more suns rose and fell as he trudged on. Even his ghosts disappeared at last, scrubbed away by the howling snows. He thought the weather might be getting colder, but could not remember for certain what cold was.

When the next sun climbed, it was into a freezing, slate-gray sky. The wind had subsided and the swirling snows had dropped back down into feathery drifts. Before him, looming jagged and severe as a shark's tooth against the horizon, stood the mountain. A grim crown of iron-gray clouds hung about its shadowed peak, fed by smokes and steam that issued from cracks along its icy flanks. Seeing it, he fell forward onto his knees and uttered a silent prayer of thanks. He still did not know his name, but he knew that this was what he sought.

When another darkness and light had passed, he found himself nearing the mountain's shadow, walking in a land of icy hills and dark dales. Mortal men and women lived here, pale-haired, suspicious-eyed, huddling in clan-houses made of muddied stone and heavy black beams. He did not pass through their bleak villages, though he thought them dimly familiar. When the inhabitants hailed him and approached, coming no closer than superstition allowed, he ignored them and stumbled on.

Another day of painful trudging carried him beyond the dwellings of the pale-haired folk. Here the mountain blocked the sky so that even the sun seemed small and remote, and a kind of perpetual evening covered the land. Sometimes staggering, sometimes crawling, he climbed the steps of the old, old road through the hills at the mountain's foot, through the silvery, frost-veiled ruins of a long-dead city. Pillars like broken bones pushed up through the snowy crust. Arches like the long-vacant eyes of skulls loomed against the mountain's shadowed ridges.

His strength was fading at last, so near to his goal. The crumbling, icy road ended at a great gate in the face of the mountain, a gate taller than a tower, made of chalcedony quartz, shining alabaster, and witchwood, hung on hinges of black granite and graven with strange shapes and stranger runes. It was before this gate that he stopped, the last dregs of life leaking from his tortured frame. As the final blackness began to descend on him, the mighty gate opened. A flock of white figures came forth, beautiful as ice in the sun, terrible as winter. They had watched him come. They had witnessed his every failing step across the white wilderness. Now, their unfathomable curiosity somehow satisfied, they brought him at last into the fastness of the mountain.

The nameless traveler awakened in a great pillared chamber within the mountain's blue-lit heart. Smoke and vapor from the titan well at the chamber's center rose to mix with the snow that flurried beneath the impossibly high ceiling. For a long while he could only lie staring up at the swirling clouds. When he could move his eyes further, he saw before him a great throne of black rock, covered all over with a patina of frost. Upon this seat was a white-robed figure whose silver mask glowed like an azure flame, reflecting the light that spilled from the great well. He was suddenly filled with exaltation, but also with horrible, horrible shame.

"Mistress," he cried as remembrance came flooding back, "destroy me, mistress! Destroy me, for I have failed you!"

The silver mask tilted toward him. A wordless chant arose in the shadows of the chamber, where eyes glittered down at him from a crowd of watchers, as if the ghosts that had accompanied him through the waste had come now to judge him and witness his undoing.

"Be silent," said Utuk'ku. Her terrible voice seized him with invisible hands, laying a spell of chill that reached down into his very heart, making him stone. "I will find out what I wish to know."

After his dreadful wounds and his hideous journey across the snows, his pain had become so general that he had forgotten there was any other kind of sensation. He had worn his torment as unheedingly as he had his namelessness, but that had been pain only of the body. Now he was reminded—as were most who visited Stormspike—that there were agonies that far outstripped any corporeal injuries, and suffering that was unmitigated by the possibility of death's release.

Utuk'ku, the mountain's mistress, was old beyond comprehension and had learned many things. She could, perhaps, have gained the knowledge she sought from him without inflicting terrible torture. If such mercy was possible, she chose not to exercise it.

He screamed and screamed. The great chamber echoed.

The icy thoughts of the Queen of the Norns crept through him, wrenching at his very being with cold, heedless claws. It was an agony beyond anything, beyond fear, or imagination. She emptied him, and he was a helpless witness. All that had happened, all his experiences, leaped from him, his inmost thoughts and private self ripped out and exhibited; it felt as though she had slit him open like a fish and pulled free his struggling soul.

He saw again the pursuit up Urmsheim Mountain, his quarry's discovery of the sword they had sought, his own battle with the mortals and Sithi. He witnessed once more the coming of the snow-dragon and his own terrible wounding, how he had been crushed and bloodied, buried beneath blocks of centuried ice. Then, as if he observed a stranger, he watched a dying creature struggling across the snows toward Stormspike, a nameless wretch who had lost his quarry, lost his company, and had even lost the hound-helm that marked him as the first mortal ever to be Queen's Huntsman. At last, the spectacle of his shame faded.

Utuk'ku nodded again, her silver mask seeming to stare into the tumult of fogs above the Well of the Breathing Harp. "It is not for you to say whether or not you have failed me, mortal," she said at last. "But know this: I am not unpleased. I have learned many useful things today. The world still spins, but it spins toward us."

She raised a hand. The chant swelled in the shadows of the chamber. Something vast seemed to move in the depths of the Well, setting the vapors to dancing. "I give you back your name, Ingen Jegger," Utuk'ku said.

"You are still the Queen's Hunter." From her lap she lifted a new helm of gleaming white shaped like the head of a questing hound, eyes and lolling tongued worked in some scarlet gem, the serried teeth daggers of ivory in the gaping jaw. *"And this time I will give to you a quarry such as no mortal has ever hunted!"*

A billow of radiance leaped in the Well of the Harp, splashing the high pillars; a roar as of thunder rang through the chamber, so deep it seemed to set the underpinnings of the mountain itself to shaking. Ingen Jegger felt his spirit surge. He made a thousand silent promises to his wonderful mistress.

"But first you must sleep deeply and be healed," the silver mask said, *"for you have crossed farther into the realms of death than mortals may usually go and yet return. You will be made stronger, for your coming task will be a hard one."*

The light abruptly vanished, as though a dark cloud had rolled over him.

The forest was still deep in night. After the shouting, the silence seemed to ring in Deornoth's ears as burly Einskaldir helped him to his feet.

"Usires on the Tree, look there," the Rimmersman said, panting. Still stunned, Deornoth looked around, wondering what he had done that would make Einskaldir stare so strangely.

"Josua," the Rimmersman called, "come here!"

The prince slid Naidel back into its sheath and stepped forward. Deornoth could see the other members of the company pressing in.

"For once they have not just struck and melted away," Josua said grimly. "Deornoth, are you well?"

The knight shook his head, still confused. "My head hurts," he said. What were they all looking at?

"It . . . it had a knife to my throat," Father Strangyeard said, wonderingly. "Sir Deornoth saved me."

Josua bent toward Deornoth, but surprised him by continuing downward until he crouched on one knee. "Aedon save us," the prince said softly.

Deornoth looked down at last. On the ground by his feet was the crumpled, black-garbed form of the Norn with whom he had struggled. The moonlight played over the corpselike face, spatters of blood in dark relief against the white skin. A wickedly slender knife was still clutched in the Norn's pallid hand.

"My God!" Deornoth said, and swayed.

Josua leaned nearer to the body. "You struck a strong blow, old friend," he said, then his eyes widened and he sprang up. Naidel whicked out of its scabbard once more.

"He moved," Josua said, striving to keep his voice level. "The Norn is alive."

"Not long," Einskaldir said, raising his axe. Josua's hand shot out, so that Naidel lay between the Rimmersman and his intended victim.

"No." Josua motioned the others back. "It would be foolish to kill him."

"It tried to kill us!" Isorn hissed. The duke's son had just returned, bearing a torch he had lit with his flint-stone. "Think of what they did to Naglimund."

"I do not speak of mercy," Josua said, dropping the tip of his sword to rest on the Norn's pale throat. "I speak of the chance to question a prisoner."

As if from the pricking of his flesh, the Norn stirred. Several in the company gasped.

"You are too close, Josua!" Vorzheva cried. "Step away!"

The prince turned a cold look on her but did not move. He lowered Naidel's point a little, pushing it against the prisoner's breastbone. The Norn's eyes fluttered open as he sucked a great rasp of breath past his blooded lips.

"*Ai, Nakkiga,*" the Norn said hoarsely, flexing his spidery fingers, "*o'do 'tke stazho. . . .*"

"But he's heathen, Prince Josua," Isorn said. "He can't speak a human tongue."

Josua said nothing, but prodded again. The Norn's eyes caught the torchlight, throwing back a strange violet reflection. The slitted gaze slid up the blade of the sword balanced on his slender chest until it settled at last on the prince.

"I speak," the Norn said slowly. "I speak your tongue." His voice was high and cold, brittle as a glass flute. "Soon it will be spoken only by the dead." The creature sat up and swiveled his head, looking carefully all around him. The prince's sword followed each movement. The Norn seemed jointed in strange places, his motions fluid where a mortal's would be awkward, but elsewhere full of unexpected hitches. Several of those watching started away, frightened that the stranger was strong enough to move without show of pain, despite the bleeding ruin that had been his nose and the marks he bore of numerous other wounds.

"Gutrun, Vorzheva . . ." Josua spoke without looking away from the prisoner. Beneath the web of drying blood, the Norn's face seemed to glow like a moon. "You, too, Strangyeard," the prince said. "The harper and Towser are alone. Go see to them and start a fire. Then make ready to depart. There is no use in our trying to hide now."

"There never was, mortal man," said the thing on the ground.

Vorzheva visibly bit back a response to Josua's command. The two women turned away. Father Strangyeard followed after them, making the sign of the Tree and clucking worriedly.

"Now, hell-wight, speak. Why do you follow us?" Though his tone was harsh, Deornoth thought he saw a sort of fascination on the prince's face.

"I will tell you nothing." The thin lips parted in a smirk. "Pitiful, short-lived things. Are you not yet used to dying with your questions unanswered?"

Infuriated, Deornoth stepped forward and kicked at the thing's side with his booted foot. The Norm grimaced, but showed no other sign of pain. "You are a devil-spawn, and devils are masters of lies," Deornoth snarled. His head hurt fiercely, and the sight of this grinning, bony creature was almost too much to bear. He remembered them swarming through Naglimund like maggots and felt his gorge rising.

"Deornoth . . ." Josua said warningly, then addressed the prisoner once more. "If you are so mighty, why do your fellows not slay us and be done with it? Why waste your time on ones so much lower than you?"

"We will not wait much longer, never fear." The Norn's taunting voice took on a note of satisfaction. "You have caught me, but my fellows discovered all that we need to know. You may as well offer up your death-prayers to that little man-on-a-stick that you worship, for nothing will stop us now."

Now it was Einskaldir who moved with a growl toward the Norn. "Dog! Blaspheming dog!"

"Silence," Josua snapped. "He does it purposefully." Deornoth laid a cautious hand on Einskaldir's muscled arm. One did not grab heedlessly at the Rimmersman, who had a cold but swift temper. "Now," Josua said, "what do you mean, 'discovered what you need to know'? What might that be? Speak, or I shall let Einskaldir have you."

The Norn laughed, the sound of wind in dry leaves, but Deornoth thought he had seen a change in the purple eyes when Josua spoke. It seemed the prince had struck close to some delicate spot. "Kill me, then—swiftly or slowly," the prisoner taunted. "I will say no more. Your time—the time of all mortals, shifty and annoying as insects—is nearly over. Kill me. The Lightless Ones will sing of me in the lowest halls of Nakkiga. My children will remember my name with pride."

"Children?" Isorn's surprise was clear in his voice. The prisoner turned a look of icy contempt onto the blond northerner, but did not speak.

"But why?" Josua demanded. "Why should you ally yourself with mortals? And what threat are we to you, far up in your northern home? What does your Storm King gain from this madness?"

The Norn only stared.

"Speak, damn your pale soul to hell!"

Nothing.

Josua sighed. "Then what do we do with him?" he murmured, almost to himself.

"This!" Einskaldir stepped away from Deornoth's restraining arm and lifted his axe. The Norn stared up at him for a silent heartbeat, angled face like a blood-smeared mask of ivory, before the Rimmersman brought the hand-axe around, shearing through the skull and smashing the prisoner back against the earth. The Norn's thin frame began to writhe, doubling over, straightening, then snapping forward once more as though he were hinged in the middle. A fine mist of blood sprayed from his head. The death-throes were as horribly monotonous as the contortions of a smashed cricket. After several moments, Deornoth had to turn away.

"*Curse you, Einskaldir,*" Josua said at last, voice ragged with rage. "*How dare you? I did not tell you to do that!*"

"And if I didn't, then what?" Einskaldir said. "Take him with us? Wake up with that grinning corpse-face over yours some night?" He seemed a little less sure than he sounded, but his words were stiff with anger.

"By the Good God, Rimmersman, can you never wait before you strike? If you have no respect for me, what of your Master Isgrimnur, who bade you obey me?" The prince leaned forward until his agonized face was only a hand's breadth from Einskaldir's bristling dark beard. The prince held Einskaldir's eye, as though trying to see something hidden. Neither man spoke.

Staring at his prince's profile, at Josua's moon-painted face so full of fierceness and sorrow, Deornoth was reminded of a painting of Sir Camaris riding to the first Battle of the Thrithings. King John's greatest knight had worn just such a look, proud and desperate as a starving hawk. Deornoth shook his head, trying to clear the shadows away. What a night of madness this had become!

Einskaldir turned aside first. "It was a monster," he grumbled. "Now it is dead. Two of its fellows are wounded and driven away. I will go clean the fairy blood from my sword."

"First you will bury the body," Josua said, "Isorn, help Einskaldir. Search the Norn's clothing for anything that might tell us more. God help us, we know so little."

"Bury it?" Isorn was respectful but dubious.

"Let us not give away anything that might save us—including information." Josua sounded tired of talking. "If the Norn's fellows do not find the body, they may not know he is dead. They may wonder what he is telling us."

Isorn nodded without much conviction and bent to the unpleasant task. Josua turned and took Deornoth by the arm.

"Come," the prince said. "We must talk."

They walked a little way from the clearing, staying within hearing of the campsite. The shards of night sky visible through the thick trees had gone dark blue, beginning to warm to dawn. A solitary bird whistled.

"Einskaldir means well, Prince Josua," Deornoth said, breaking the stillness between the two men. "He is fiery, impatient—but not a traitor."

Josua turned to him in surprise. "Heaven save us, Deornoth, do you think I do not know? Why do you think I said so little? But Einskaldir acted rashly—I would have wished to hear more from the Norn, though the end would have to have been the same. I hate cold-blooded killing, but what *would* we have done with the murderous creature? Still, Einskaldir considers me too much a thinker to be a good warrior." His laugh was melancholy. "He is probably correct." The prince raised his hand to still Deornoth's response. "But that is not why I wanted to speak alone. Einskaldir is my affair. No, I wanted to hear your thoughts on the Norn's words."

"Which, Highness?"

Josua sighed. "He said that his fellows had found what they wanted. Or learned what they wished to know. What could that mean?"

Deornoth shrugged. "My skull is still rattling, Prince Josua."

"But you said yourself that there must be a reason that they haven't killed us." The prince sat down on the mossy trunk of a toppled tree, motioning the knight to join him. The bowl of sky was turning lavender overhead. "They send a walking dead man to come among us; they shoot arrows but don't kill us, to prevent us from turning east—and now they send a few of their creatures to sneak into our camp like thieves. What do they want?"

No answer would come, no matter how hard Deornoth thought. He could not shake his memory free from the Norn's mocking smile. But there had been another look, too, that momentary glimmer of unease . . .

"They fear . . ." Deornoth said, feeling the idea very close, ". . . they fear . . ."

"The *swords*," Josua hissed. "Of course! What else would they fear?"

"But we have no magical sword," Deornoth said.

"Perhaps they do not know that," Josua said. "Perhaps that is one of the virtues of Thorn and Minneyar—that they are invisible to the Norns' magic." He slapped at his thigh. "Of course! They must be, or the Storm King would have found them and destroyed them! How else could weapons deadly to him still exist!?"

"But why have they tried to prevent our going east?"

The prince shrugged. "Who can say? We must think on this more, but I believe it is the answer. They fear we already have one or both of the swords and they are afraid to come against us until they know."

Deornoth felt his heart sinking. "But you heard what the creature said. They know now."

Josua's smile faded. "True. Or at least they must be fairly sure. Still, it is a piece of knowledge that might still work in our favor, somehow. *Somehow.*" He stood. "But they are no longer afraid to approach us. We must travel even more swiftly. Come."

Wondering how a company so injured and dispirited could make any greater haste, Deornoth followed the prince back through the dawn light to camp.

7

Spreading Fires

The seagulls wheeling in the gray morning sky balefully echoed the creaking of the oarlocks. The rhythmic squeak, squeak, squeak of the oars was like an insistent finger digging at her side. Miriamele felt her anger building. At last, she turned on Cadrach in a fury.

"You . . . you *traitor!*" she spat.

The monk goggled at her, his round face growing pale with alarm.

"What?" Cadrach looked as though he would have liked to move away, and quickly, but they were cramped together in the rowboat's narrow stern. Lenti, Streáwe's sullen servitor, watched them in irritation from the rowing bench where he and the other servant pulled languidly at the handles. "My lady . . ." Cadrach began, "I don't . . ."

His feeble denials only made her angrier. "Do you think I'm a fool?" she snarled. "I am slow to realize, but if I think long enough, I get there. The count called you *Padreic*—and he's not the first to call you by that name!"

"A confusion, lady. The other was a dying man, if you remember—maddened by pain, his life leaking out on the Inniscrich . . ."

"You *swine!* And I suppose it's a coincidence that Streáwe knew I had left the castle—practically before I knew I was going myself? You have had a fine time, haven't you? Pulling both ends of the rope, that's what you've been doing, isn't it? First you took Vorzheva's gold to escort me, then you've taken mine while we were on the road, borrowing for a jug of wine here, cadging a meal there . . ."

"I am only a poor man of God, my lady," tried Cadrach gamely.

"Be quiet, you . . . you treacherous drunkard! And you took gold from Count Streáwe, too, didn't you? You let him know I was coming—I wondered why you kept sneaking away when we were first in Ansis Pellipé. And while I was prisoner, where were you? Run of the castle? Suppers with the count?" She was so upset she could hardly speak. "And . . . and you probably also passed the word on to whoever it is I'm being sent to now, didn't you? *Didn't you!* How can you wear religious robes? Why doesn't God just . . . just kill you for your blasphemy? Why don't you just burst into flames on the spot?" She stopped, choking on angry tears, and tried to catch her breath.

"Here now," Lenti said ominously, his single eyebrow creasing downward toward his nose, "stop all this shouting. And don't you try any tricks!"

"Shut your mouth!" Miriamele told him.

Cadrach thought he saw his chance. "That's right, sirrah, don't you get to insulting the lady. By Saint Muirfath, I can't believe . . ."

The monk never got to finish his sentence. With an inarticulate shout of rage, Miriamele leaned into him and pushed hard. Cadrach huffed out a surprised breath, waved his arms briefly trying to keep his balance, then toppled into the Bay of Emettin's green waves.

"Are you mad?" Lenti roared, dropping his oar and leaping upright. Cadrach disappeared under a wash of jade water.

Miriamele stood to shout after him. The boat rocked, dropping Lenti back down into his seat; one of his blades slipped from his hands, diving into the bay like a silvery fish. "You faithless rogue!" she screamed at the monk, who was not currently in view. *"Damn you to hell!"*

Cadrach broke the surface, spewing a great plume of salty water. "I'll drown!" he gurgled. "Drown! Help me!" He slid back under.

"So drown, you traitor!" Miriamele shouted, then shrieked as Lenti grabbed her arm and dragged her down onto her seat, twisting it cruelly in the process.

"Mad bitch!" he shouted.

"Let him die," she panted, struggling to pull free. "What do you care?"

He reached out and slapped her on the side of the head, bringing fresh tears to her eyes. "Master said carry two to Nabban-side, you mad bitch. Show up with one, that's the end of me."

Meanwhile, Cadrach had bobbed up spluttering once more, thrashing and making noises that indeed sounded as though they came from a drowning man. Streáwe's other servant, wide-eyed, had continued to pull at his oar, so that by lucky accident the little boat was now coming about, turning toward where Cadrach splashed and shouted.

The monk saw them coming, panic in his bulging eyes. He began to strain toward them, but his untutored movements dipped him forward so that his head sank beneath the waves once more. A moment later he was up again, the look of panic on his face even more raw.

"Help!" he screeched breathlessly, flinging his arms about in a paroxysm of horror. "Something's. . . ! *Something's in here. . . !*"

"Aedon and the saints!" Lenti snarled, leaning over the side, fighting to keep his own balance. "What now, sharks?"

Miriamele huddled sobbing in the bow, uncaring. Lenti snatched up the tie-rope and flung it toward the monk. Cadrach did not see it at first as he beat wildly against the water, but in a few moments his arm had become tangled in one of the coils.

"Grab it, you fool!" Lenti shouted. "Grab hold!"

At last the monk did, grasping the rope with both hands. He was hauled through the water toward the boat, legs kicking like a frog's. When Lenti had pulled him close enough, the other servant let go of his oar and leaned forward to help. After a couple of failed attempts and a great deal of cursing they managed to heave his sodden weight up over the wale. The rowboat pitched. Cadrach lay in the bottom, choking and vomiting bay water.

"Take your cloak and dry him off," Lenti told Miriamele as the monk subsided at last into hoarse breathing. "If he goes and dies, I'll have you swimming all the way to shore."

She grudgingly complied.

The brown and sable hills of Nabban's northeastern coast rose steadily before them. The sun was climbing toward noon, burnishing the surface of the bay with a fierce, coppery glare. The two men rowed, the boat rocked back and forth, and the oarlocks creaked and creaked and creaked.

Miriamele was still furious, but it had become a flat, hopeless anger. The eruption was over, the fires burning down to ashen coals.

How could I have been so foolish? she wondered. *I trusted him—worse, I was even beginning to like him! I enjoyed his company, half-drunken though it usually was.*

Only a few moments before, as she had shifted position on the bench, she had heard something clinking in the pocket of Cadrach's robe. When removed, this proved to be a purse embossed with the seal of Count Streáwe, half full of silver quinis-pieces and a pair of gold Imperators. This indisputable proof of the monk's treachery momentarily brought back her rage. She considered pushing him back overboard, suffering Lenti's punishment if necessary, but after a little deliberation she decided that she was no longer angry enough to kill him. In fact, Miriamele was a little surprised that her earlier fury had burned as hotly as it had.

She looked down at the monk, who lay curled in exhausted, fitful sleep, his head propped on the bench beside her. Cadrach's mouth was open, his breath coming in little gasps as though even in his dreams he battled for air. His pink face was becoming even pinker. Miriamele lifted her hand and peered upward at the sun through shielding fingers. It had been a cold summer, but here in the middle of the water the sun beat down mercilessly.

Without thinking about it too much, she took her threadbare cloak and draped it over Cadrach's forehead, shading his face. Lenti, watching silently from the rowing bench, scowled and shook his head. In the bay beyond his shoulder, Miriamele saw something smooth break the water, then slip sinuously back into the deeps.

For a while she watched the gulls and pelicans whirling through the air, returning to the coastal rocks to land with a great back-flapping of wings. The gulls' cold cries reminded her of Meremund, her childhood home on the coast of Erkynland.

I could stand on the southern wall there and watch the rivermen pushing up and down the Gleniwent. From the western wall I could see the ocean. I was a princess, trapped by my position, yet I had every thing I wanted. Now look at me.

She snorted in disgust, occasioning another unpleasant stare from Lenti.

Now I'm free to adventure, she thought, *and I'm more a prisoner than ever. I go about in disguise, yet thanks to this traitorous monk, I am better-announced than I ever was at court. People I hardly know deliver me from hand to hand like a favorite trinket. And Meremund is lost to me forever, unless . . .*

The wind ruffled her shorn hair. She felt quite hollow.

Unless what? Unless my father changes? He will never change. He has destroyed Uncle Josua—killed Josua! Why should he ever turn back? Nothing will ever be as it was. The only hope of things getting better died with Naglimund. All their plans, the old Rimmersman Jarnauga's legends, the talk of magical swords . . . and all the people who lived there—gone. So what is left? Unless Father changes or dies, I will be a fugitive forever.

But he will never change. And if he dies—what is left of me, I'll die, too.

Staring out at the Bay of Emettin's metallic sheen, she thought about her father as he once had been, remembering the time when she had been three years of age and he had first lifted her onto a horse. Miriamele could picture that moment as clearly as if it had been only days ago instead of her whole life. Elias had grinned with pride as she clung, terrified, to what seemed a monster's back. She had not fallen, and she had stopped crying as soon as he swung her back down.

How can one person, even a king, let such ugliness loose on the land as my father has? He loved me, once. Perhaps he still does—but he has poisoned my life. Now he seeks to poison all the world.

The waves slapped as the rocks drew nearer, gold-capped by the late morning sun.

Lenti and the other servitor unshipped the oars, using them to guide the boat between the craggy rocks that thrust up on every side. As they came close to the shore and the water became more translucent, Miriamele again saw something break the surface close by. There was a brief shimmer of glossy gray before it vanished with a splash, then reappeared a moment later on the far side of the boat, a long stone's throw away.

Lenti saw her staring and turned to look over his shoulder. What he saw brought a look of fear to his stolid face. After a muttered exchange, he and his companion redoubled their efforts, hurrying the boat in toward shore.

"What is it," the princess asked, "a shark?"

Lenti did not look up. "Kilpa," he snapped, rowing hard.

Miriamele stared, but now saw only low waves breaking into spray against the rocks. "Kilpa in the Bay of Emettin?" she said incredulously. "Kilpa never come in so far! They are deep-sea dwellers."

"Not nowadays," Lenti growled. "Been deviling ships all along the coast. Any fool knows so. Now be quiet!" He panted, pulling at the oars. Disquieted, Miriamele continued to stare. Nothing else disturbed the bay's placid surface.

When the keel rasped on sand, Lenti and the other rower leaped out and quickly dragged the boat up onto the beach. Together they lifted Cadrach out and dumped him unceremoniously onto the ground, where he lay, quietly moaning. Miriamele was left to shift for herself. She waded the half-dozen steps with her monk's robe held high.

A man in a priest's black cassock was picking his way down to the beach by the steep cliff path. He reached the bottom and came striding across the sand toward them.

"I suppose this is the slave trader I am to be delivered to?" Miriamele said in her frostiest tone as she squinted at the approaching figure. Lenti and his companion, staring nervously at the bay, did not reply.

"Ho, there!" the black-robed man called. His voice was loud and cheerful above the sea's somnolent roar.

Miriamele looked at him, then looked again, astonished. She took a couple of steps toward the newcomer. "Father Dinivan?" she asked haltingly. "Could it be you?"

"Princess Miriamele!" he said happily. "Here you are. I am so glad." His wide, homely smile made him look like a young boy, but the curly hair around his shaven scalp was touched with gray. He dropped briefly to a knee before rising to look her over carefully. "I wouldn't have known you from much farther away than this. I was *told* you were traveling as a boy—quite effective. And you've turned your hair black."

Miriamele's mind was awhirl, but a great burden seemed abruptly lifted from her spirit. Of all those who had visited her father's households in Meremund and the Hayholt, Dinivan had been one of the few who had been a real friend, giving her truth where others offered only flattery, bringing her both outland gossip and good advice. Father Dinivan was chief secretary to Lector Ranessin, the master of Mother Church, but he had always been so humble and forthcoming that Miriamele often had to remind herself of the exalted position he held.

"But . . . what are you doing here?" she said at last. "Have you come to . . . to what? To save me from the slave traders?"

Dinivan laughed. "I *am* the slave trader, my lady." He tried to compose a more serious expression, but had little luck. " 'Slave traders'—Blessed Usires, what did old Streáwe tell you? Well, time for that later." He turned to Miriamele's captors. "You two. Here is your master's seal." He held up a parchment with an "S" mark in red wax at the bottom. "You may go back and give the count my thanks."

Lenti inspected the seal in a cursory way. He looked worried.

"Well?" said the priest impatiently. "Is anything wrong?"

"There's kilpa out there," Lenti declared mournfully.

"There are kilpa *everywhere* in these evil times," Dinivan said, then smiled charitably. "But it is midday, and you are two strong men. I think you have little to fear. Are you armed?"

Streáwe's servant drew himself up to his full height and stared imperiously at the priest. "I have a knife," he said sternly.

"*Ohé, vo stetto,*" his companion echoed in Perdruinese.

"Well, I'm sure you'll have no problems," Dinivan said reassuringly. "The protection of the Aedon be on you." He made a desultory sign of the Tree in their general direction before turning his back on them to address Miriamele once more. "Let us go. We shall stay here tonight, but then we must hurry. It is a good two days journey or more to the Sancellan Aedonitis, where Lector Ranessin is anxious to hear your news."

"The lector?" she said, astonished. "What does he have to do with this?"

Dinivan waved a placating hand, looking down on Cadrach, who lay on his side, face shrouded in his sodden hood. "We will talk about this and many other things soon. It appears that Streáwe told you even less than I told him—not that I am surprised. He is a clever old jackal." The priest's eyes narrowed. "What's wrong with your companion—he is your companion, am I right? Streáwe said there was a monk traveling with you."

"He almost drowned," Miriamele said flatly. "I pushed him overboard."

One of Dinivan's thick eyebrows shot up. "You did? The poor man! Well, then your Aedonite duty is to help get him on his feet—unless you fellows would like to lend a hand?" He turned back to the two servants, who were wading gingerly back to the boat.

"Can't," was Lenti's sullen reply. "Got to get back before night. Before dark."

"I thought as much. Oh, well, Usires gives us burdens out of His love." Dinivan bent, catching Cadrach under the armpits. Dinivan's robe tightened across his broad, muscular back as he wrestled the monk into a sitting position. "Come now, Princess," he said, then stopped as the monk groaned. The priest stared at Cadrach's face. An unrecognizable expression crept onto Dinivan's thick features.

"It's . . . it's Padreic," he said quietly.

"*You, too?!*" Miriamele exploded. "What has this idiot been doing? Did he send a crier to every town between Nascadu and Warinsten?"

Dinivan was still staring, as if quite dumbfounded. "What?"

"Streáwe knew him also—it was Cadrach here who sold me out to the count! So he told *you* of my leaving Naglimund as well?"

"No, princess, no." The priest shook his head. "This is the first I knew about him being with you. I haven't seen him for years." Reflectively, he made the sign of the Tree. "Truth to tell, I thought he was dead."

"Usires in His suffering!" Miriamele swore. "Will someone tell me what this is all about?!"

"'We must get to shelter—and privacy. The beacon tower on the cliff top is ours tonight." He pointed to a stone spire on the headland west of where they stood. "But it will be no festival game getting him there if he cannot walk."

"I'll make him walk," Miriamele promised grimly. Together they bent to hoist mumbling Cadrach onto his feet.

The tower was smaller than it looked from the beach, a squat pile of masonry with a wooden hoarding cobbled around the uppermost story. The door was tight-swollen by the ocean air, but Dinivan wrenched it open and they entered, supporting the monk between them. The circular room was empty but for a rough-hewn table and chair and a ragged carpet that had been rolled and tied, then left to lie at the base of the stone staircase. Sea air swirled through the unshuttered window. Cadrach, who had not spoken during the walk up the cliff path, staggered a few paces away from the door and sank down onto the wooden floor, laying his head on the carpet and falling quickly back into sleep.

"He is exhausted, poor man," Dinivan said. He took a lamp from the table and lit it from another already burning, then stopped to look carefully at the monk. "He has changed, but perhaps some of it is the result of his mishap."

"He was in the water a long time," Miriamele said, a little guiltily.

"Ah, well, then." Dinivan stood up. "We shall leave him to sleep and go upstairs. There is much to talk about. Have you eaten?"

"Not since last night." Miriamele was suddenly ravenous. "I need water, too."

"All shall be yours," Dinivan smiled. "Go on up. I am going to get your companion out of these wet clothes, then I will join you."

The room upstairs was better furnished, with a cot, two chairs, and a large chest that stood against the wall. A door, swinging gently, led out onto the hoarding. On top of the chest sat a plate covered with a kerchief. Miriamele lifted the cloth to reveal cheese, fruit, and three round loaves of brown bread.

"The grapes grown over the hill in Teligure are really splendid," the priest said from the doorway. "Help yourself."

Miriamele fell to without having to be invited again. She took a whole loaf and a lump of cheese, then pulled loose a large bunch of grapes and retired to one of the chairs. Pleased, Dinivan watched her eat for a moment, then disappeared down the stairs. He returned shortly with a sloshing pitcher.

"The well is nearly empty, but the water is good," he said. "Well, where should we begin? You have heard about Naglimund by now, haven't you?"

Miriamele nodded, her mouth full.

"Something you may not know. Josua and some others escaped."

In her excitement she choked on a crust of bread. Dinivan helped hold the pitcher so she could drink.

"Who went with him?" she asked when she could speak. "Duke Isgrimnur? Vorzheva?"

Dinivan shook his head. "I do not know. There was terrible destruction and few survived. All the north is thick-shot with rumors. It is hard to sift truth from them, but Josua's escape is certain."

"How did you find out?"

"I'm afraid there are some things I may not say—not yet, anyway, Princess. Please believe that it is for the best. The Lector Ranessin commands me, and I am sworn to him—but there are some things I don't even tell His Sacredness." He grinned. "Which is as it should be. A great man's secretary must exercise discretion everywhere, even with the great man himself."

"But why did you have Count Streáwe send me to you?"

"I did not know how informed you were. I heard that you were bound for the Sancellan Mahistrevis to speak to your uncle, Duke Leobardis. I could not let you go there. You know that Leobardis is dead?"

"Streáwe told me." She got up and took a peach from the plate. After a moment's consideration, she broke off another hunk of cheese.

"But did you know Leobardis died by treachery? By the hand of his own son?"

"Benigaris?" She was astonished. "But has he not taken the duke's place? Haven't the nobles resisted?"

"His treachery is not common knowledge, but there are whispers of it everywhere. And his mother Nessalanta is his strongest supporter—although I am sure that she at least suspects what her son did."

"But if you know, why don't you do something!? Why hasn't the lector done anything?"

Dinivan bowed his head, a look of pain on his face. "Because that is one of the things I haven't told him. I am sure he has heard the rumors, however."

Miriamele put her plate on the bed. "Elysia, Mother of God! Why haven't you told him, Dinivan?"

"Because I cannot prove it, nor can I reveal the source of my information. And there is nothing he could do without proof, my lady, except to upset an already strained situation. There are other grave problems in Nabban, Princess."

"Please." She waved her hand impatiently. "Here I sit in a monk's robe, wearing my hair like a boy, and everyone is my enemy but you—or so it seems. Call me Miriamele. And tell me what is happening in Nabban."

"I will tell you a little, but most should wait. I have not entirely ignored my secretarial duties: my master the lector would like you to come to see him in the Sancellan Aedonitis and we will have plenty of time to talk as we ride." He shook his head. "It is enough to say that people are unhappy, that the doom-criers who once were scorned in the streets of Nabban are suddenly the subject of great attention. Mother Church is under siege." He bent forward, staring at his large hands as he searched for words. "The people feel a shadow over them. Although they cannot name it, still it darkens their world. Leobardis' death—and your uncle was much-beloved, Miriamele—has shaken his subjects, but it is rumor that truly frightens them: rumor of things worse than war in the north, worse than any contending of princes."

Dinivan stood and pulled the door all the way open to let in the breeze. The sea below was flat and glossy. "The doom-shouters say that a force is arising to cast down Holy Usires Aedon and the kings of men. In the public squares they cry that all must prepare to bow to a new sovereign, the rightful master of Osten Ard."

He came back and stood over Miriamele. Now she could see the signs of deep worry on his face. "In some dark places a name is even being whispered—the name of this coming scourge. They whisper of the Storm King."

Miriamele let out her breath in a great sigh. Even the staring sun of noon could not disperse the shadows that seemed to come crowding into the tower room.

"They spoke of these things at Naglimund," Miriamele said later, as they stood outside on the walkway looking out over the water. "The old man at Naglimund, Jarnauga, seemed to think the end of the world was coming, too. But I did not hear everything." She turned to look at Dinivan, fierce grief upon her slender face. "They kept things from me because I'm a girl. That's not right—I'm smarter than most of the men I know!"

Dinivan did not smile. "I've no doubt of that, Miriamele. In fact, I think you should seek a greater challenge than merely being wiser than men."

"But I left Naglimund to do something," she continued unhappily. "Hah! That was smart, wasn't it? I thought I'd bring Leobardis in on my uncle's side, but he already was. And then he was killed, so what good did it do Josua anyway?" She trooped a little way around the tower until she looked out on the spine of the cliff and the backslope that fell away into a green valley. Rolling hills stretched beyond, brushed with rippling light as the wind moved among the grasses. She tried to imagine the end of the world and could not do so. "How do you know Cadrach?" she asked at last.

"Cadrach is a name I never heard until you mentioned it," he replied. "I knew him as Padreic, long years ago."

"How many years ago could that be?" Miriamele smiled. "You're not that old."

The priest shook his head. "I have a young face, I suppose, but actually I am nearing forty years—not much younger than your Uncle Josua."

She scowled. "All right, many years ago. Where did you know him?"

"Here and elsewhere. We were members of the same . . . order, I suppose you would say. But something happened to Padreic. He fell away from us, and when I later heard tell of him the stories were not good. It seemed that he had descended into very bad ways."

"I'll say." Miriamele made a face.

Dinivan looked at her curiously. "And how did you happen to give him this unexpected—and no doubt undesired—bath?"

She told him about their trip together, about Cadrach's suspected small treacheries and her confirmation of his larger one. When she had finished, Dinivan led her inside again, where Miriamele found her hunger had returned.

"He has not done right by you, Miriamele, but has not, I think, done entirely wrong either. There may be hope for him—and not merely the ultimate hope of salvation, which we all share. I mean that he may move away from his criminal and drunkard ways." Dinivan walked a few steps down from the top of the staircase, leaning over to look at Cadrach. Now wrapped in a coarse blanket, the monk still slept, arms flung out as though he had only this moment been dragged from the perilous waves. His wet clothes were hanging in the low rafters.

Dinivan returned to the room. "If he were beyond hope, why would he have remained with you after he had received his silver from Streáwe?"

"So he could sell me to someone else," she responded bitterly. "My father, my aunt, Naraxi child-merchants—who knows?"

"Perhaps," said the lector's secretary, "but I do not think so. I think he has conceived a feeling of responsibility to you—although that responsibility does not prevent him from profiting where he thinks you will be unharmed, as with the master of Perdruin. But unless the Padreic I know is totally gone, vanished beyond any retrieval, I think he would not harm you, nor would he willingly let harm come to you."

"Small chance," Miriamele said grimly. "I will trust him again when stars shine at noontime, but no sooner."

Dinivan looked at her closely, then sketched the sign of the Tree in the air. "We must be careful of such pronouncements in these strange days, my lady." A grin came back to his face. "However, this talk of shining stars reminds me—we have a job to do. When I arranged to use this place to meet you, I promised the tower-keeper that we would light the beacon tonight. The mariners who ply the coastline expect it to be there, warning them away from the rocks so they can go east to the harbor at Bacea-sá-Repra. I should do it now, before it starts to get dark. Do you want to come along?" He clattered down the stairs and returned with the lamp.

Miriamele nodded, following him out onto the hoarding. "I was at Wentmouth once when they lit the Hayefur there," she said. "It was huge!"

"Far bigger than our modest candle," Dinivan agreed. "Be careful as you climb here. This is an old ladder."

The tower's topmost room was little more than a place to hold the beacon, a very large oil lamp squatting in the middle of the floor. There was a smoke-hole overhead in the tower's roof and a fence of metal screens around the wick to slow the wind. A large curved metal shield hung on the inside wall behind the lamp, facing out toward the sea.

"What does this do?" she asked, running a finger over the shield's highly polished surface.

"Helps the light travel farther," Dinivan said. "You see how it is curved away from the flame, like a cup? That collects the lamplight and flings it out through the window—more or less. Padreic could explain it better."

"You mean Cadrach?" Miriamele asked, puzzled.

"Well, once he could have, anyway. He was very clever about mechanical things when I knew him—pulleys and levers and such. He studied a great deal about Natural Philosophy, before he . . . changed." Dinivan lifted the hand lamp to the large wick and held it there. "The Aedon only knows how much oil this great thing must burn," he said. After some moments it caught and the flame rose. The shield on the wall did make it brighter, even though failing sunlight still streamed in through the wide windows.

"There are snuffers hanging on the wall," Dinivan said, pointing at a pair of long staves, each with a metal cup on one end. "We must remember to put it out in the morning."

When they had returned to the second floor, Dinivan suggested they look in on Cadrach. Trailing after, Miriamele turned and went back for the pitcher of water and some grapes. There was really no sense starving him to death.

The monk was up, sitting on the lone chair, staring out through the window at the twilit, slate-blue bay. He was withdrawn, and at first did not respond to Miriamele's offer of food, but at last took a drink of water. After a moment he accepted the grapes as well.

"Padreic," Dinivan said, leaning close, "do you not remember me? I am Dinivan. We were friends once."

"I recognize you, Dinivan," Cadrach said at last. His hoarse voice echoed strangely in the small round room. "But Padreic ec-Crannhyr is long dead. There is only Cadrach now." The monk avoided Miriamele's eyes.

Dinivan watched him intently. "Have you no wish to speak?" he asked. "There is nothing you can have done that would make me think badly of you."

Cadrach looked up, a smirk on his round face, his gray eyes full of pain. "Oh, is that true? Nothing so foul I might have done that Mother Church and . . . and our other friends . . . would not take me back?" He laughed bitterly and waved his hand in disgust. "You lie, brother Dinivan. There are crimes beyond forgiveness, and a special place prepared for their perpetrators." Angry, he turned away and would not speak any more.

Outside the waves murmured as they struck the rocky coast and fell back, hushed voices that seemed to welcome the settling night.

Tiamak watched Older Mogahib, Roahog the Potter, and the other elders climb into the rocking flatboat. Their faces were grave, as befitted the ceremonial occasion. The ritual feather necklaces drooped in the damp heat.

Mogahib stood uneasily in the stern of the boat and turned to look back. "Do not fail us, Tiamak son of Tugumak," he croaked. The ancient one frowned and impatiently brushed the leaves of his headdress out of his eyes. "Tell the drylanders that the Wrannamen are not their slaves. Your people have given you their greatest trust." Older Mogahib was helped to sit down by one of his great-nephews. The overloaded boat wallowed away down the watercourse.

Tiamak made a sour face and looked down at the Summoning Stick they had given him, its surface knobby with carvings. The Wrannamen were upset because Benigaris, the new master of Nabban, had demanded greater tithes of grain and jewels, as well as young sons from the houses of the Wran to come and serve on the holdings of Nabbanai nobles. The elders wanted Tiamak to go and speak for them, to protest this further meddling by the drylanders in the lives of the Wrannamen.

So yet another responsibility was now laid on Tiamak's slender shoulders. Had any of his people ever said one respectful word to him about his learning? No, they treated him as little more than a madman, someone who had turned his back on the Wran and his people to follow the ways of the drylanders—until they needed someone to write or speak to the Nabbanai or Perdruinese in their own tongue. Then, it was: "Tiamak, do your duty."

He spat from the porch of his house and watched the green water ripple below. He pulled up his ladder and left it lying in a heap instead of neatly rolled as was usual. He was feeling very bitter.

*   *   *

One good thing would come of this, he decided later while waiting for his water pot to boil. If he went to Nabban, as his tribesmen insisted, he would be able to visit his wise friend who lived there and find out if anything more could be discovered about Doctor Morgenes' strange note. He had been fretting over it for weeks, yet felt no closer to a solution. His messenger birds to fat Ookequk in Yiqanuc had returned, their messages unopened. That was troubling. The birds he had sent to Doctor Morgenes had returned as well, but that, although disappointing, was less worrisome than Ookequk's silence, since Morgenes had said in his last note that he might not be able to communicate for some while. Neither had his messages been answered by the witch woman who lived in Aldheorte Forest, or by his friend in Nabban. Tiamak had only sent those last birds out a few weeks ago, however, so they still might reply.

But if I am traveling to Nabban, he realized, *I will not see any replies for two months or more.*

In fact, now that he thought of it, what would he do with his birds? He didn't have nearly enough seed to keep them penned for the entire time he would be gone, and he certainly couldn't take them all with him. He would have to turn them loose to fend for themselves, hoping that they would stay close to his little house in the banyan tree so he could recapture them when he returned. And if they flew away and did not come back, what would he do? He would have to train more, that was all.

Tiamak's sigh was subsumed in the hiss of steam escaping from beneath the pot lid. As he dropped in the yellowroot to steep, the little scholar tried to remember the prayer for a safe journey that one should make to He Who Always Steps on Sand, but could only think of the Showing-the-Hiding-Places-of-Fish prayer, which was not really appropriate. He sighed again. Even though he didn't quite believe in his people's gods anymore, it never hurt to pray—but one really ought to say the right prayer.

As long as he was pondering such things, what would he do with that damnable parchment Morgenes talked about in his letter—or seemed to talk about, for how could the old doctor know that Tiamak had it? Should he take it with him and risk losing it? But he had to, if he was going to show it to his friend in Nabban and ask his advice.

So many problems. They seemed to be crowding his head like black-flies, buzzing and buzzing. He had to think it all through clearly—especially if he was to leave in the morning for Nabban. He had to look at each piece of this puzzle.

First Morgenes' message, which he had read and reread dozens of times in the four moons or so since he had received it. He took it from the top of the wooden chest and smoothed it, leaving smudges with his yellowroot-stained hands. He knew the contents by heart.

Doctor Morgenes wrote of his fears that *". . . the time of the Conqueror Star"* was surely upon them—whatever that might mean—and that Tiamak's help would be needed *". . . if certain dreadful things which—it is said—are hinted at in the infamous lost book of the priest Nisses . . ."* were to be avoided. But what things? *"The infamous lost book . . ."*—that was Nisses' *Du Svardenvyrd*, as any scholar knew.

Tiamak reached down into the chest and removed a leaf-wrapped bundle, unrolling it to remove his prized parchment, which he spread on the floor beside Morgenes' letter. This parchment page, which Tiamak had stumbled on by luck at the market in Kwanitupul, was of much higher quality than anything he himself could afford. The rusty brown ink formed the northern runes of Rimmersgard, but the language itself was the archaic Nabbanai of five centuries gone.

> *". . . Bringe from Nuanni's Rocke Garden*
> *The Man who tho' Blinded canne See*
> *Discover the Blayde that delivers The Rose*
> *At the foote of the Rimmer's greate Tree*
> *Find the Call whose lowde Claime*
> *Speakes the Call-bearer's name*
> *In a Shippe on the Shallowest Sea—*
> *—When Blayde, Call, and Man*
> *Come to Prince's right Hande*
> *Then the Prisoned shall once more go Free . . ."*

Below this incomprehensible poem was printed the name *"NISSES."*

So what was Tiamak to think? Morgenes could not know that Tiamak had discovered a page of the near-mythical book—the Wrannaman hadn't told a soul—yet still the doctor had said that Tiamak would have important work to do, something to do with *Du Svardenvyrd*!

His inquiries to Morgenes and the others had gone unanswered. Now he must go to Nabban to plead his people's cause to the drylanders, yet he still did not know what it could all mean.

Tiamak poured the tea out of the pan into his third-favorite bowl—he had dropped and broken his second-favorite bowl that morning, when Older Mogahib and the others had started braying beneath his window. He cupped the warm bowl in his slender fingers and blew across the top. "Hot day, hot tea," his mother had always said. Today was certainly hot. The air was so still and oppressive that he almost felt he could leap off his porch and swim through it. Hot weather alone did not make him unhappy, since he was always less hungry when the heat was fierce, but nevertheless there was something disconcerting about the air today, as though the Wran were a smoldering bar of tin on the world-anvil, with a great hammer trembling above it, ready to smash down and change everything.

That morning Roahog the Potter, taking a moment to gossip while

Older Mogahib was helped up the ladder, had said that a colony of ghants was building a new nest just a couple of furlongs down the watercourse from Village Grove. Ghants had never come so close to a human settlement before, and although Roahog had chuckled about how the Wrannamen would soon put the nest to fire, the story nevertheless left Tiamak unsettled, as if some undefined but recognized law had been violated.

As the slow, sweltering afternoon wore on toward evening, Tiamak kept trying to think about the demands of the Duke of Nabban, and about Morgenes' letter, but visions of the nest-building ghants pushed in—their brownish-gray jaws clicking industriously, their mad little black eyes glittering—and try as he might, he could not rid himself of the ridiculous notion that somehow all these things were related.

It is the heat, he told himself. *If only I had a cool jug of fern beer, these wild ideas would disappear.*

But he did not even have enough yellowroot to make another cup of tea, let alone any fern beer. His heart was troubled and there was nothing in the wide, hot Wrán that would give him peace.

Tiamak rose with the first light of dawn. By the time he had cooked and eaten a rice-flour biscuit and drunk a little water, the swamp was already becoming unpleasantly warm. He grimaced as he began his packing. This was a day to go splashing and swimming in one of the safe ponds, not set out on a journey.

There was actually little to pack. He selected a spare breechclout and a robe and pair of sandals to wear in Nabban—there was no reason to reinforce the unfortunate opinion of his people's backwardness held by most Nabbanai. He had no use on this trip, however, for his stretched-bark writing board, his wooden chest, or most of his other meager lot of possessions. His precious books and scrolls he dared not take, since there was a better than average chance he would wind up in the water a few times before he reached the cities of the drylanders.

He had decided he must take the Nisses parchment, so he wrapped it in a second layer of leaves and bundled the whole into an oiled skin bag given to him by Doctor Morgenes when Tiamak had lived in Perdruin. He put the bag, the Summoning Stick, and his clothes into his flat-bottomed boat, along with his third-best bowl, a handful of cooking implements, and a throwing-sling with a folded leaf full of round stones. He hung his knife and his coin-pouch on his belt. Then, having stalled as long as he could, he climbed up the banyan tree to the top of the house to set his birds free.

As he climbed across the thatched roof he could hear the drowsy, muffled speech of the birds within their small cottage. He had put the remaining seed in his fourth-best—and last—bowl, setting it out on the windowsill below. They would at least stay near the house for a while after his departure.

He poked his hand into the little bark-roofed box and delicately removed one of his pigeons, a pretty white-and-gray named So-fast, then tossed her up into the air. She fanned her wings briskly, settling at last on a limb above his head. Unsettled by this unusual behavior, she hooted quietly, questioningly. Tiamak knew the grief of a father whose daughter must be sent to strangers. But he had to remove the birds, and the door to their house, which only opened inward, had to be fastened shut. Otherwise, these birds or their absent kindred would enter and be trapped. With no Tiamak to rescue them, they would soon starve.

Feeling very unhappy, he carefully removed Red-eye, Crab-foot, and Honey-lover. Soon there was a disapproving chorus perched above him. Alerted that something unusual was happening, the birds still inside had fled skittishly to the back of the little house, so that Tiamak had to strain to reach them. As he tried to grasp one of these last recalcitrants, his hands brushed against a small, cold bundle of feathers that lay just out of sight in the shadows at the far end.

Suddenly full of worry, he closed his hand around the object and lifted it out. It was one of his birds, he saw immediately, and it was dead. Eyes wide, he examined it closely. It was Ink-daub, one of the pigeons he had dispatched to Nabban several days ago. Ink-daub had apparently been injured by some animal: many of his feathers were missing and he was spotted with dried blood. Tiamak was sure the bird hadn't been there yesterday, so he must have arrived during the night, flying with his last strength despite his wounds, reaching his home only to die.

Tiamak found the world swimming before his eyes as the tears came. Poor Ink-daub. He was a fine bird, one of the fastest fliers. He had been very brave, too. Everywhere on the bird's body that Tiamak looked, blood showed beneath the tattered feathers. Poor, brave Ink-daub.

A slender strip of parchment was curled around the pigeon's twiglike ankle. Tiamak placed the silent bundle aside for a moment and coaxed out the last two birds, then wedged the small door closed with a notched stick. With Ink-daub's body curled in a gentle hand, Tiamak climbed down to the window and into the house. He set down the pigeon's body and carefully removed the parchment, spreading it out on the floor between his fingertips, squinting at the tiny characters. The message was from his wise friend in Nabban, whose hand Tiamak recognized even in bird-writing, but was inexplicably unsigned.

The time has come,

it read,

and you are sorely needed. Morgenes cannot ask you, but I ask for him. Go to Kwanitupul, stay at the inn we have spoken of, and wait there until I can

tell you more. Go there immediately and do not stray. More than lives may
depend on you.

At the bottom was scribbled a drawing of a feather in a circle—the symbol of the League of the Scroll.

Tiamak sat dumbstruck, staring at the message. He read it two more times, hoping it would miraculously say something different, but the words remained unchanged. Go to Kwanitupul! But the elders had ordered him to Nabban! There was no one else in his tribe who could speak the drylander languages well enough to serve as an emissary. And what would he tell his tribesmen—that some drylander they didn't know had told him to go wait for instructions at Kwanitupul, that this was reason enough to turn his back on his people's wishes? What did the League of the Scroll mean to Wrannamen? A circle of drylander scholars who talked of old books and older events? His people would never understand.

But how could he ignore the gravity of the summons? His friend in Nabban had been explicit—had even said that this was what Morgenes wanted him to do. Without Morgenes, Tiamak would never have survived his year in Perdruin, let alone gained the wonderful fellowship to which the doctor had introduced him. How could he not do this one thing—this, the only favor Morgenes had ever asked of him?

The hot air was pushing in at the windows like a hungry beast. Tiamak folded the note and slipped it into his sheath. He must attend to Ink-daub. Then he would think. Perhaps it would be cooler as evening drew closer. Surely he could wait one more day before leaving, wherever he was to go? Surely?

Tiamak wrapped the bird's small body in oil palm leaves, then wound it in a length of thin cord. He stilted through the shallows to a sandbar behind his house, where he set the bundle of leaves on a rock and surrounded it with bark and precious strips of old parchment. After uttering a prayer for Ink-daub's spirit to She Who Waits to Take All Back, he used his flint and steel to set the tiny pyre aflame.

As the smoke coiled upward, Tiamak reflected that there was something to be said for the old ways after all. If nothing else, they provided something to do at a time when the mind was weary and hurting. For a moment, he was even able to push aside the troubling thoughts of duty, feeling instead a strange sort of peace as he watched Ink-daub's smoke take flight, rising slowly into the feverish gray sky.

Soon, though, the smoke was gone and the ashes were scattered across the green water.

When Miriamele and her two companions came down off the hill path onto the North Coast Road, Cadrach jogged his mount ahead, putting several lengths between himself and Dinivan and the princess. The morning sun was at their backs. The horses Dinivan had brought trotted along with heads waving, nostrils wide to catch the scents on the early breeze.

"Ho, Padreic!" Dinivan shouted, but the monk did not reply. His round shoulders bounced up and down. His hood was lowered as if he hung his head in thought. "Very well, then—*Cadrach,*" the priest called, "why do you not ride with us?"

Cadrach, a graceful horseman despite his bulk and short legs, reined up. When the other two had nearly caught him, he turned.

"It is a problem with names, brother," he said, showing his teeth in an angry smile. "You call me by one that belongs to a dead man. The princess, well now, she's given me a new one—"traitor"—and baptized me with it in Emettin Bay to seal the bargain. So you see, don't you, it would be all too confusing, this—one might say—*multiplicity* of names." With an ironic bow of the head, he dug his heels into his horse's ribs and forged ahead, slowing again to match their pace when he had extended his lead to a dozen ells or so.

"He is very bitter," Dinivan said as he watched Cadrach's hunched shoulders.

"What does *he* have to be bitter about?" Miriamele demanded.

The priest shook his head. "God knows."

Coming from a priest, she decided, it was hard to tell exactly what that phrase might signify.

Nabban's North Coast Road meandered along between the ridge of hills and Emettin Bay, sometimes jogging inland so that the hills' tan flanks rose on the right, blocking all view of the water. Farther on, the hills fell away again for a short time and the rocky coastline appeared once more. As the trio approached Teligure, the road began to fill with other traffic: farm wains shedding streams of loose hay, foot peddlers carrying their wares hung on poles, small troops of local guardsmen marching officiously from one place to another. Many travelers, seeing the golden Tree that hung on Dinivan's black-robed chest and the monkish robes of his companions, bowed their heads or made the Tree-sign across their breasts. Beggars ran alongside the priest's horse, crying: "Father, Father! Aedon's mercy, Father!" If they seemed truly crippled in some way, Dinivan reached into his robes and produced a cintis-piece, which he tossed down to them. Miriamele noticed that few of the beggars, no matter how hobbled or deformed, ever let the coin strike the ground.

They stopped at midday in Teligure itself, a sprawling market town set in the lap of the hills, where they refreshed themselves with fruit and hard bread bought from stalls in the town square. Here, in the crush of commerce, three religious travelers drew little notice.

*   *   *

Miriamele was basking in the bright sun, hood pushed back so that she could feel the warmth on her forehead. All around her echoed the cries of the hawkers and the outraged shrieks of swindled buyers. Cadrach and Dinivan stood nearby, the priest bargaining with a seller of boiled eggs while his sullen companion eyed a wine-merchant's booth next door. Miriamele realized with some surprise that she felt happy.

Just like that? she chided herself, but the sun felt too nice for self-vilification. She had been fed, had ridden all morning free as the wind, and nobody around was paying the slightest attention to her. At the same time, she felt strangely protected.

She thought suddenly of the kitchen boy Simon and her contented mood expanded to touch the memory of him as well. He had a nice smile, Simon had—not practiced, like one of her father's courtiers. Father Dinivan had a good smile, too, but it never looked surprised at itself, as Simon's almost always did.

In a strange way, she realized, the days spent traveling to Naglimund with Simon and Binabik the troll had been some of the best of her life. She laughed at herself, at such a ridiculous notion, and stretched as luxuriously as a cat on a windowsill. They had faced terror and death, had been chased by the terrible hunter Ingen and his hounds, and had nearly been killed by a Hunë, a murderous, shaggy giant. But still she had felt very free. Pretending to be a servant, she had felt more herself than ever before. Simon and Binabik talked to *her*—not to her title, not to her father's power or their own hopes for reward or advancement.

She missed them both. She felt a sharp and sudden pang thinking of the little troll and poor, gawky, red-thatched Simon wandering in the snowy wilderness. In the frustration of her imprisonment in Perdruin she had almost forgotten them—where were they? Were they in danger? Were they even alive?

A shadow fell across her face. She flinched, startled.

"I don't think I can keep our friend out of the wine-stalls much longer," Dinivan said. "Nor am I sure I have a right to. We should take to the road again. Were you sleeping?"

"No." Miriamele pulled her hood forward and stood up. "Just thinking."

Duke Isgrimnur sat wheezing before the fire, thinking seriously about breaking something or hitting someone. His feet hurt, his face had itched like sin ever since he had shaved off his beard—and what kind of be-damned madman was he to have agreed to that?!—and he was not one whit closer to finding Princess Miriamele than he had been when he left Naglimund. All that was bad enough, but now things had gotten even worse.

Isgrimnur had felt sure he was narrowing the gap. When he had followed Miriamele's trail to Perdruin, and confirmed with the old tosspot Gealsgiath that the captain had left her and the criminal monk Cadrach here in Ansis Pellipé, the duke had been certain it was only a matter of time. Even hobbled by his monk's disguise, Isgrimnur knew Ansis Pellipé well, and could find his way through most of its seedier neighborhoods. Soon, he had felt sure, he would have her in hand and could take her back to her uncle Josua at Naglimund, where she would be safe from her father Elias' doubtful charities.

Then the twin blows had fallen. The first had been slower in effect, the culmination of many fruitless hours and a small fortune in pointless bribes: it had gradually become clear to Isgrimnur that Miriamele and her escort had disappeared from Ansis Pelippé, as completely as if they had sprouted wings and flown away. Not a single smuggler, cutpurse, or tavern harlot had seen them since Midsummer's Eve. She and Cadrach were a hard pair to miss—two monks traveling together, one fat, one young and slender—but they had vanished. Not a single boatman had seen them carried away, or even heard of them inquiring after passage at the docks. Gone!

The second blow, falling on top of his personal failure, struck Isgrimnur like a great stone. He had not been on Perdruin a fortnight before the wharfside taverns were alive with stories of the fall of Naglimund. The sailors repeated the rumors cheerfully, talking of the slaughter Elias' mysterious second army had wreaked on the castle's inhabitants as if reveling in the twists and turns of an old fireside tale.

Oh, my Gutrun, Isgrimnur had prayed, his innards knotted with fear and rage, *Usires protect you from harm. Let you come out safe again, wife, and I will build a cathedral to Him with my bare hands. And Isorn, my brave son, and Josua and all the rest . . .*

He had cried that first night, in a dark alley by himself, where no one would see the huge monk sobbing, where for at least a little while he need not falsify. He was frightened in a way he had never quite been before.

How could it have happened so swiftly? he wondered. *That damnable castle was built to last out a ten-year siege! Was it treachery from within?*

And how, even if his family had been saved by some miracle and he could find them again, how would he ever get back his lands that Skali Sharp-nose had stolen with the High King's help? With Josua broken, with Leobardis and Lluth dead, there was none who could stand in Elias' way.

Still, he must find Miriamele. He could at least discover her, rescue her from the traitor Cadrach and take her somewhere safe. That one piece of misery still remained which he could prevent Elias from accomplishing.

So, defeated, he had come at last to *The Hat and Plover,* an inn of the lowest sort, which was just what his aching spirit craved. His sixth jug of sour beer sat at his side, as yet untouched. Isgrimnur brooded.

*   *   *

He might have dozed, for he had been walking the long waterfront all day and was very tired. The man who stood before him might have been there for some time. Isgrimnur did not like his look.

"What are you staring at?" he growled.

The stranger's eyebrows came together over his eyes. His lantern jaw was set in a contemptuous smirk. He was tall and dressed in black, but the Duke of Elvritshalla did not find him nearly as impressive as the stranger obviously felt himself to be.

"Are you the monk who has been asking questions all over the city?" the stranger demanded.

"Go away," Isgrimnur replied. He reached to take a draught of beer. It made him feel a little more alert, so he took another swallow.

"Are you the one who has been asking about the other monks?" the stranger began again. "About the tall and short ones?"

"I might be. Who are you, and what business do you have with me?" Isgrimnur grunted, wiping the back of his hand across his mouth. His head hurt.

"My name is Lenti," the stranger said. "My master wishes to speak with you."

"And who is your master?"

"Never mind. Come. We will go now."

Isgrimnur belched. "I do not wish to go meet any nameless masters. He can come to me if he wishes. Now go away."

Lenti bent forward, his eyes keenly fixed on Isgrimnur's. There were pimples on his chin.

"You will come now, fat old man, if you don't want to be hurt," he whispered fiercely. *"I have a knife."*

Isgrimnur's hamhock fist struck him right where his eyebrows met. Lenti pitched backward and dropped bonelessly, as though he had been struck with a slaughtering-hammer. A few of the other tavern-goers laughed before turning back to their various unpleasant conversations.

After a while the duke leaned forward, pouring a stream of beer onto his black-clad victim's face. "Get up, man, get up. I have decided I will go with you and meet your master." Isgrimnur grinned wickedly as Lenti spluttered foam. "I was feeling poorly before, but by Aedon's Holy Hand, I suddenly feel a great deal better!"

Teligure disappeared behind the three riders. They continued west on the Coast Road, following its winding course through a handful of compact towns. The work of bringing in the hay was going forward at full speed on the hillsides and in the valley below, haycocks rising all over the fields like the heads of wakened sleepers. Miriamele listened to the chanting voices of the field-masters and the joking cries of the women as they waded out into the tawny pastures with bottles and wallets containing the workers' mid-afternoon meals. It seemed a happy, simple life, and she said as much to Dinivan.

"If you think working each day from before sunup to dark, breaking your back in the fields is happy and simple work, then you are right," he answered, narrowing his eyes against the sun. "But there is little rest, and when the year is bad, little food. And," he said, smiling wickedly, "most of your crop goes out as tithes to the baron. But that seems to be what God intended. Certainly, honest labor is better than a life of beggary or theft—in the eyes of Mother Church, anyway, if not in the eyes of some beggars and most thieves."

"Father Dinivan!" exclaimed Miriamele, a little shocked. "That sounds . . . I don't know . . . heretical, I suppose."

The priest laughed. "God the Highest gifted me with a heretical nature, my lady, so if He regrets his gift, he will soon gather me back to His bosom again and make all right. But my old teachers would agree with you. I was frequently told that my questions were the devil's tongue speaking in my head. Lector Ranessin, when he offered me the position of his secretary, told my teachers: 'Better the devil's tongue to argue and question than a silent tongue and an empty head.' Some of the Church's more proper priests find Ranessin a difficult master." Here Dinivan frowned. "But they know nothing. He is the best man on earth."

During the long afternoon Cadrach allowed the distance between himself and his companions to diminish gradually, until at last they were riding nearly side-by-side once more. This concession did not loosen his lips, however; although he seemed to be listening to Miriamele's questions and Dinivan's stories of the land through which they passed, he did not in any way join the conversation.

The cloud-strewn sky had turned orange and the sun was streaming into their eyes as they approached the walled town of Granis Sacrana, the spot Dinivan had chosen for them to spend the night. The town sat on a bluff overlooking the Coast Road. The hills all around, sunset brushed, were tangled with grape vines.

To the travelers' surprise, a squad of guardsmen sat mounted at the broad gate questioning those who sought entrance. They were not local-levied troops, but armored men wearing the gold kingfisher of the royal Benidrivine House. When Dinivan gave their names—choosing Cadrach's by default and offering "Malachias" on the princess' behalf—they were told that they must ride on and harbor elsewhere that night.

"And why should such a thing be?" Dinivan demanded.

The sheepish guardsman could only stubbornly repeat his order.

"Then let me speak to your sergeant."

The sergeant, when produced, echoed his subordinate's words.

"But why, man?" the priest asked hotly. "By whose orders? Is there plague here, or something like?"

"Something like indeed," the sergeant said, scratching his long nose in a worried manner. "It's by the orders of Duke Benigaris himself, or so I take it to be. I have his seal on it."

"And I bear the seal of the Lector Ranessin," Dinivan said, producing a ring from his pocket and waggling its blood-red ruby beneath the startled sergeant's nose. "Know that we are on the holy business of the Sancellan Aedonitis. Is there plague, or what? If there is no dangerous air or diseased water, we will stay here tonight."

The troop-sergeant took off his helmet and squinted at Dinivan's signet ring. When he looked up, his thick face was still troubled.

"As I said, Your Eminence," he begun unhappily, "it's like a plague. It's those madmen, those Fire Dancers."

"What are Fire Dancers?" Miriamele asked, remembering to imitate a boy's gruff tones.

"Doom-criers," Dinivan said grimly.

"If that were all," the sergeant said, spreading his hands helplessly. He was a large man, broad-shouldered and thick-legged, but he looked quite undone. "They're mad, the lot of them. Duke Benigaris has commanded that we . . . well, keep a watch over them. We are not to interfere, but I thought that at least we could keep more strangers from coming in . . ." He trailed off, looking uneasily at Dinivan's ring.

"We are not strangers, and as the lector's secretary I am in little danger of falling under the sway of these people's exhortations," Dinivan said sternly. "So let us in, that we may find shelter for the night. We have ridden long. We are tired."

"Very well, Your Eminence," the sergeant said, waving for his troops to unblock the gates. "But I take no responsibility . . ."

"We all take responsibility in this life, every one of us," the priest responded seriously, then softened his expression. "But our Lord Usires understands about difficult burdens." He made the sign of the Tree as they rode in past the sergeant's jostling men-at-arms.

"That soldier seemed very upset," Miriamele said as they clattered up the central row. Many houses were shuttered, but pale faces peeped from doorways, watching the travelers. For a town the size of Granis Sacrana, the streets were surprisingly empty. Small groups of soldiers rode back and forth from the gates, but only a few other folk hurried along the dusty street, darting uneasy glances at Miriamele and her companions before dropping their eyes and hustling on.

"The troop-sergeant is not the only one," Dinivan answered as they rode along in the shadows of the tall houses and shops. "Fear sweeps through all Nabban like a plague these days."

"Fear goes where it is invited," Cadrach said quietly, but turned away from their questioning looks.

When they reached the marketplace in the center of town they discovered why Granis Sacrana's streets were so preternaturally empty. A crowd stood half a dozen deep around the town square, whispering and laughing. Although the final glimmers of afternoon still warmed the horizon, the torches had been lit in their sconces all around the square, throwing quivering shadows into the dark places between houses and illuminating the white robes of the Fire Dancers, who swayed and shouted in the middle of the commons.

"There must be a hundred of them or more!" Miriamele said in surprise. Dinivan wore a scowling, worried face. Some in the watching crowd were shouting derisively or throwing stones and refuse at the capering dancers, but others stared intently, even fearfully, as if at some animal upon which they feared to turn their backs.

"Too late for repentance!" one of the robed ones screeched, bounding away from his fellows to bob up and down like a jumping jack before the front row of spectators. The crowd eddied away from him as if fearful of some contagion. "Too late," he shouted. His face, that of a young man with his first beard, split in a grin of glee. "Too late! The dreams told us! The master's coming!"

Another of the white-clad figures climbed onto a stone in the center of the commons, waving to silence fellow dancers. The watchers murmured as this one threw back a capacious hood, revealing the yellow-haired head of a woman. She would have been very pretty, but for her staring eyes, white-rimmed in the torchlight, and her huge, ghastly smile.

"The fire is coming!" she cried. The other dancers capered and shouted, then quieted. A few in the surrounding crowd called out insults, but quickly fell silent as she turned her burning eyes upon them. "Do not fear you will be left out," she said, and in the sudden quiet her voice carried clearly. "The fires are coming for everyone—the fires and the ice that will bring the Great Change. The master will spare no one who has not prepared for him."

"You blaspheme against our true Ransomer, demon-lover!" Dinivan abruptly shouted, standing in his stirrups. His voice was powerful. "You tell these people lies!"

A few in the crowd repeated his words and their murmuring began to grow. The woman in white turned and made a sign to some of the robed ones near her. Several had been kneeling at the stone below her feet, as if in prayer; one of them now rose and walked across the courtyard as she stood staring imperiously outward, her mad eyes fixed on the lowering twilit sky. He returned a moment later with a torch from one of the sconces, which she took and raised above her head.

"What is Usires Aedon," she screamed, "but a little wooden man on a little wooden tree? What are any of the kings and queens of men but apes raised far above their station? The master will throw down all that stands before him and his majesty shall rise above all the oceans and lands of Osten Ard! The Storm King comes! He brings with him ice to freeze the heart, deafening thunder—and cleansing fire!''

She threw the brand down at her feet. A fierce sheet of flame leaped up around the rock. Some of the other dancers shrieked as their robes caught fire. The crowd pushed back with a shout of surprise as a wall of heat pushed out at them.

"Elysia, Mother of God!" Dinivan's voice was full of horror.

"So it shall be!" the woman shouted, even as the flames ran up her robe into her hair, crowning her with fire and smoke. She was still smiling, a lost, damned smile. "He speaks in dreams! Doom is coming!" The blaze mounted, obscuring her, but her last words rang out over and over. *"The master is coming! The master is coming. . . !"*

Miriamele leaned over her horse's neck, fighting to keep from being sick. Dinivan rode forward a short way before dismounting to try and help some of those who had been knocked down and trampled in the crowd's retreat. The princess straightened up, gasping for breath.

Blind to her presence, Cadrach stared at the charnel scene before them. His face, scarlet in the leaping light, was suffused with an unhappy but hungering look—as though an important, terrible thing had come to pass, a thing feared for so long that the waiting had become even worse than the fear.

8

On Sikkihoq's Back

"**Where** are we going, Binabik?" Simon leaned in, moving his reddened hands nearer the fire. His gloves steamed on a fir trunk nearby.

Binabik looked up from the scroll he and Sisqi were studying. "For now, it is down the mountains. After that, we will be needing guidance. Now let me continue to look for such guidance, please."

Simon resisted the unmanly urge to stick out his tongue, but the troll's rebuff did not really bother him very much. He was in a good mood.

Simon's strength was returning. He had felt a little more fit each of the two days of hard journeying that had brought them down across Mintahoq, chief mountain of the Trollfells. Now they had left Mintahoq altogether and had crossed over to the flank of her sister-peak Sikkihoq. Tonight, for the first time, Simon had not wanted simply to fall asleep when the party had stopped to make camp. Instead, he had helped find a scanty supply of deadwood to build the fire, then dug snow out of the shallow cave where they would spend the night. It was good to feel himself again. The scar on his cheek pained him, but it was a quiet ache. More than anything else, it helped him to remember.

The dragon's blood had changed him, he realized. Not in a magical way, like in one of Shem Horsegroom's old stories—he couldn't understand the speech of animals, or see a hundred leagues. Well, that was not quite true. When the snow had stopped for a moment today, the white valleys of the Waste had leaped into clarity, seeming as near as the folds in a blanket, but stretching all the way to the dark blur of faraway Aldheorte Forest. For a moment, standing quiet as a statue despite the wind biting his neck and face, he had felt as though he *did* possess magical vision. As in the days when he climbed Green Angel Tower to see all Erkynland spread below him like a carpet, he had felt as if he could reach out a hand and so change the world.

But moments like that were not what the dragon had brought him. Pondering as he waited for his damp gloves to dry, he looked to Binabik and Sisqi, saw the way they touched even when they did not touch, the long conversations that passed between the two of them in the shortest of glances. Simon realized that he felt and saw things differently than he had before Urmsheim. People and events seemed more clearly connected, each part of a much larger puzzle—just as Binabik and Sisqi were. They cared deeply for each other, but at the same time their world of two interlocked with many other worlds: with Simon's own, with their people's, with Prince Josua's, and Geloë's . . . It was really quite startling, Simon thought, how everything was part of something else! But though the world was vast beyond comprehension, still every mote of life in it fought for its own continued existence. And each mote *mattered*.

That was what the dragon's blood had taught him, in some way. He was not great; he was, in fact, very small. At the same moment, though, he was important, just as any point of light in a dark sky might be the star that led a mariner to safety, or the star watched by a lonely child during a sleepless night. . . .

Simon shook his head, then blew on his chill hands. His ideas were getting away from him, cavorting like mice in an unlocked pantry. He felt the gloves again, but they were not yet dried. He tucked his hands into his armpits and inched a little nearer the fire.

"Are you of great sureness that Geloë said 'Stone of Farewell,' Simon?" Binabik asked. "I have been reading Ookequk's scrolls for two nights and no luck am I having."

"'I told you everything she said." Simon looked out beyond the lip of the cavern, where the tethered rams huddled, bumping together like an ambulatory snowdrift. "I could not forget. She spoke through the little girl we saved, Leleth, and she said: *'Go to the Stone of Farewell. That is the only place of safety from the growing storm—safety for a little while, anyway.'* "

Binabik pursed his lips, frustrated. He spoke a few quick words of Qanuc to Sisqi, who nodded solemnly. "I have no doubt of you, Simon. We have seen too much together. And I cannot be doubting Geloë, who is the wisest one I know. It is a problem of my poor understanding." He waved a small hand at the flattened hide before him. "Perhaps I did not bring the correct works."

"You think too much, little man," Sludig called from the other side of the cavern. "Haestan and I are showing your friends how to play 'Conqueror.' It works nearly as well with your troll throwing-stones as with real dice. Come, play, take your mind off these things for a while."

Binabik looked up and smiled, giving Sludig a wave of his hand. "Why do you not join them in this play, Simon?" he asked. "Surely it would be more interesting than watching my confusion."

"I'm thinking, too," Simon said. "I've been thinking about Urmsheim. About Igjarjuk and what happened."

"It was not as you were when young imagining it to be, hmmm?"

Binabik said, absorbed in the perusal of his scroll once more. "Things are not always as old songs tell them to be—especially when it is concerning dragons. But you, Simon, acted as bravely as any Sir Camaris or Tallistro."

Simon felt a pleasant flush. "I don't know. It didn't seem like bravery. I mean, what else could I have done? But that isn't what I was thinking about. I was thinking about the dragon's blood. It did more than this to me." He indicated his cheek and the white stripe that now ran through his hair. Binabik did not look up to see his gesture, but Sisqi did. She smiled shyly, her dark, upturned eyes fixed on him as though on a friendly but possibly dangerous animal; a moment later, the troll maiden rose and walked away. "It made me think differently about things," Simon continued, watching her go. "The whole time you were in that hole, a prisoner, I was thinking and dreaming."

"And what did you think?" Binabik asked.

"It's hard to say. About the world and how old it is. About how small I am. Even the Storm King is small, in a way."

Binabik inspected Simon's face. The troll's brown eyes were serious. "Yes, he is perhaps small beneath the stars, Simon—as a mountain is small in comparing to the whole world. But a mountain is bigger than we, and if it falls on us, we will still be very dead in a very big hole."

Simon fluttered his hand impatiently. "I know, I know. I'm not saying that I'm not afraid. It's just . . . it's hard to say." He struggled for the proper words. "It's like the dragon's blood taught me another language, another way to see things when I think. How can you explain another language to someone?"

Binabik started to reply, then stopped, staring just over Simon's shoulder. Alarmed, Simon turned, but nothing was there but the oblique stone of the cavern and a patch of gray, white-flecked sky.

"What's wrong? Are you ill, Binabik?

"I have it," the troll said simply. "I knew there was something of familiarity in it. But it was a confusion of language. They are translating differently, you see." He bounced up onto his feet and trotted over to his bag. A few of his fellow trolls looked up. One started to say something, but broke off, deterred by Binabik's fixed expression. A few moments later the little man returned with an armful of new scrolls.

"What's going on?" Simon asked.

"It was language—the difference between tongues. You said: Stone of Farewell."

"That's what Geloë told me," he answered defensively.

"Of course. But Ookequk's scrolls are not in the language you and I are now speaking. Some are copied from original Nabbanai, some are in Qanuc-tongue, and some few in the original speech of the Sithi. I was looking for 'Stone of Farewell,' but in Sithi language, it would be named 'Leavetaking Stone'—a small difference, but one that makes much differentness in the finding of it. Now wait."

He began to read swiftly through the scrolls, his lips moving as he followed the movement of his stubby finger from one line to another. Sisqi returned, bearing two bowls of soup. One she sat beside Binabik, who was too preoccupied to do more than nod his thanks. The other bowl she offered to Simon. Not knowing what else to do, he bowed his head as he took it.

"Thank you," he said, wondering if he should call her by name.

Sisqinanamook started to say something in reply, then stopped as if she could not remember the appropriate words. For a moment she and Simon stared at each other, an inclination toward friendship hindered by their inability to converse. At last, Sisqi bowed in return, then snuggled in next to Binabik, asking him a quiet question.

"*Chash,*" he replied, "that is correct," then went silent again, searching. "Ho ho!" he cried at last, thumping his palm on his hide-suited leg. "This is the answer. We have found it!"

"What?" Simon leaned in. The scroll was covered with strange marks, little drawings like the feet of birds and the tracks of snails. Binabik was pointing at one symbol, a square with rounded corners, full of dots and slashes.

"*Sesuad'ra,*" the little man breathed, stretching the word out as if examining fine cloth. "*Sesuad'ra*—Leavetaking Stone. Or, as Geloë spoke it, the Stone of Farewell. A Sithi thing it is, as I guessed."

"But what is it?" Simon stared at the runes, but could not imagine getting meaning from it as he could from Westerling script.

Binabik squinted at the scroll. "It is the place, this is saying, where covenant was broken when the Zida'ya and Hikeda'ya—the Sithi and the Norns—split asunder to be going their separate ways. It is a place of power and of great sorrow."

"But where *is* it? How can we go there if we don't know where it is?"

"It was once being part of Enki-e-Shao'saye, the Summer-City of the Sithi."

"Jiriki told me about that," Simon said, suddenly excited. "He showed it to me in the mirror. The mirror he gave me. Maybe we could find it there!" He fumbled in his pack, searching for Jiriki's gift.

"No need, Simon, no need!" Binabik laughed. "A fool I would truly be—and the poorest apprentice Ookequk could ever be having—if I did not know of Enki-e-Shao'saye. It was one of the Nine Cities, great in beauty and lore."

"Then you know where the Stone of Farewell is?"

"Enki-e-Shao'saye was at the southeast edge of the great forest Aldheorte." Binabik frowned. "So it is not near, obviously. Many weeks of journeying we will have. Where the city was standing is on the far side of the forest from us, above the flat lands of the High Thrithings." His expression brightened. "But we are knowing now our destination. That is good.

Sesuad'ra." He savored the word again reflectively. "I have never seen it, but words of Ookequk come to me. It is a strange and grim place, as legend speaks."

"I wonder why Geloë chose it?" Simon said.

"Perhaps there was no other choosing she could make." Binabik turned his attention to his cold soup.

The rams, understandably enough, did not like to walk with Qantaqa behind them. Even after several days, the smell of the wolf still troubled them deeply, so Binabik continued to ride ahead. Qantaqa picked her way deftly along the steep, narrow trails, the ram-riders following after, talking or singing quietly among themselves, keeping their voices low so as not to wake Makuhkuya, the avalanche goddess. Simon, Haestan, and Sludig trooped along at the rear, trying to stay out of the hoof-ruts and thereby keep the snow from creeping in over the tops of their well-oiled boots.

Where Mintahoq was rounded like an old man bent by years, Sikkihoq was all angles and steep sides. The troll-paths clung to the mountain's back, winding far out to swing around icy columns of rock, then passing out of the sunlight in the mountain's own shadow, following the inside line of a vertical crevice that dropped away beyond the path into mist and snow.

Trudging down the narrow trails hour after hour, constantly wiping the fluttering snow from his eyes, Simon found himself praying they would reach the bottom soon. Returning strength or no, he was not meant for mountain life. The thin air hurt his lungs and made his legs feel heavy and weak as sodden loaves of bread. When he tried to sleep at the end of the day, his muscles were so painfully tight they almost seemed to hum.

The very heights in which they traveled also disturbed him. He had always thought of himself as a fearless climber, but that had been before he left Hayholt for the wide world. Now, Simon found it much easier to keep his eyes fastened to the back of Sludig's brown boots as they lifted and fell than to look elsewhere. When his gaze swung away to the leaning masses of stone above them or the empty depths below, he found it difficult to remember level ground. Somewhere, he reminded himself, there were places where a person could turn and walk in any direction without risking a death-fall. He had lived in such a place, so they must still exist. Somewhere mile after flat mile lay like a deep carpet, waiting for Simon's feet.

They had stopped at a wider place to rest. Simon helped Haestan take off his pack, then watched as the guardsman slumped down onto a snow-dampened stone, breathing so heavily that he soon surrounded himself with a fog of vapors. Haestan slipped his hood off for a moment, then shivered as the high wind struck him. He quickly pulled it back on. Ice crystals glimmered in his dark beard.

"S'cold, lad," he said. "Bitter." He suddenly looked old.

"Do you have a family, Haestan?" Simon asked.

The guardsman paused for a moment as if taken aback, then laughed. "Of sorts. I've a woman, a wife, but no little'uns. First baby died, we've gotten none since. I've not seen her since 'fore winter." He shook his head. "She be safe, though. Gone t'live with folk in Hewenshire— Naglimund be too dangerous, told her. War comin'." He shook his head. "Now if y'r witch woman speaks true, war's over an' Prince Josua lost."

"But Geloë said he escaped," Simon put in hurriedly.

"Aye, that be somethin'."

They sat in silence for a while, listening to the wind among the rocks. Simon looked down at the sword Thorn lying atop Haestan's pack, gleaming blackly, dotted with melting snowflakes. "Is the sword too heavy for you? I could carry it for a while."

Haestan considered him for a moment before grinning. "Y'r welcome to it, Simon-lad. Y'should have sword, what with that first manly beard an' all. Thing is, hard t'say if it be any good *as* a sword, if y'take my meaning."

"I know. I know how it changes." He remembered Thorn in his own hands. At first it had been cold and heavy as an anvil. Then, as he stood poised, balanced on the cliff's edge staring into the dragon's milky blue eyes, it had become light as a birch-staff. The glossy blade had seemed inspirited, as though it breathed. "It's almost like it's alive. Like an animal or something. Is it heavy for you now?"

Haestan shook his head, looking up at the flurrying snow. "No, lad. Seems it wants t'go where we're goin'. Thinks it be goin' home, mayhap."

Simon smiled to hear them both talking about a sword as though it were a dog or a horse. Still, there was an undeniable tension to the thing, like a spider still in a web, or a fish hanging suspended in the cold darkness of a river bottom. He looked at it again. The sword, if it *was* alive, was a wild thing. The blackness of it devoured light, leaving only a thin residue of reflection, sparkling crumbs in a miser's beard. A wild thing, a dark thing.

"It's going where we're going," Simon said, then considered for a moment. "But that's not going to be home. Not my home."

As he lay that night in a narrow cavern which was little more than a nick in Sikkihoq's muscular stone back, Simon dreamed of a tapestry. It was a moving tapestry, hanging on a wall of absolute blackness. In it, as in the religious pictures of the Hayholt's chapel, a great tree stood, arms rising to heaven. This tree was white and smooth as Harcha marble.

Prince Josua hung upon it head down, like Usires Aedon Himself in His suffering.

A shadowy figure stood before Josua, driving nails into him with a great, gray hammer. Josua did not speak or cry out, but his followers all around were moaning. The prince's eyes were wide with patient suffering, like the carved face of Usires that had hung on the wall of Simon's boyhood home in the servant's quarters.

Simon could not bear to see any more. He thrust himself through into the tapestry itself and ran at the shadow-figure. As he ran, he felt a weighty something dangling in his hand. He lifted his arm to swing it, but the murky thing reached up and caught his hand, pulling Simon's weapon away. He had been holding a black hammer. But for its color, it was the twin of the gray.

"Better," the thing said. It hefted the ebony mallet in its other shadowy hand and began once more to drive nails. This time Josua screamed with each blow, screamed and screamed . . .

. . . Simon awakened to find himself shivering in darkness, the raspy breathing of his traveling companions all around him, vying with the wind that moaned as it searched the mountain passes outside the cavern. He wanted to waken Binabik, or Haestan, or Sludig—anybody who could speak to him in his own tongue—but could not find any of them in the dark, and knew even in his fear that he should not startle the others awake.

He lay down once more, listening to the crooning wind. He was afraid to go back to sleep, afraid he would hear those awful screams once more. He strained to see in the darkness so he would know his eyes were open, but there was nothing.

Some time before light returned, exhaustion overmatched his fretting mind and he at last fell asleep. If more dreams troubled him, he did not remember them on awakening.

They were three more days on heart-freezingly narrow trails before they made their way down out of Sikkihoq's heights. On the mountain's shoulders they no longer had to travel single file, so as they came down onto a broad shelf of snow-dotted granite the company stopped to celebrate. It was a rare hour of afternoon sunlight. The light had broken through the cobweb of clouds and the wind for once seemed playful instead of predatory.

Binabik rode Qantaqa ahead to scout the terrain, then turned the wolf loose to hunt. She was gone into a tumble of white-mantled boulders in an instant. Binabik walked back to the rest of the party, a broad smile on his face.

"It is good to be off the cliffs for a time," he said, sitting next to Simon, who had removed his boots and was rubbing blood back into his white toes. "There is little time for thinking of anything else but balancing when one rides on such narrow and endangering trails."

"Or walks on them," Simon said, looking critically at his toes.

"Or walks," Binabik agreed. "I will be returning in a moment." The little man got up and walked across the gently curving stone to where most of the trolls sat in a circle on the ground, passing around a drinking skin. Several of them had taken off their jackets to sit bare-chested in the thin sunlight, brown skins acrawl with tattoos of birds, bears, and sinuous fish. The rams had been unsaddled and turned loose to graze on such scanty fodder as they might find, moss and clumps of scruffy brush that had taken root in rocky crevices. One of the troll men watched over them as shepherd, although his heart did not seem to be in the job. He poked the ground disconsolately with his crook-spear as he watched the skin go around the circle. One of his fellows, pointing and laughing at his misery, at last stumped over and shared the bag with him.

Binabik approached Sisqi, who was sitting with some of the hunting maidens. He bent to say something, then rubbed her face with his own. She laughed, pushing him away, but her cheeks reddened. Watching, Simon felt a faint tremor of jealously at his friend's happiness, but swallowed it down. Someday maybe he, too, would find someone. He thought sadly of Princess Miriamele, who stood far above any scullion. Nonetheless, she was only a girl, like those with whom Simon had bumblingly conversed in the Hayholt in what seemed far-gone days of old. When he and Miriamele had stood side by side at the bridge in Da'ai Chikiza, or before the giant, there had been no difference between them. They had been friends, facing danger together and equally.

But I didn't know then that she was above me. Now I do, and that is the difference. But why? Am I different? Is she? Not truly. And she kissed me! And that was after she was the princess again!

He felt a curious mixture of elation and frustration. Who was to say what was right, anyway? The order of the world seemed to be changing, and where was the law written that a heroic kitchen boy could not stand proudly before a princess—who was at war with her father the king, after all?

A moment of grand daydreaming followed. Simon envisioned himself entering a great city as a hero, riding on the back of a proud horse, the sword Thorn held before him as in a picture of Sir Camaris he had once seen. Somewhere, he knew, Miriamele was watching and admiring. The daydream foundered as he suddenly wondered what city he might enter heroically into. Naglimund, by Geloë's word, had fallen. The Hayholt, Simon's only home, was banned to him utterly. The sword Thorn was no more his than Simon himself was Sir Camaris, the blade's most famous owner—and what was most important, he realized as he stared at his blistered heels, he had no horse at all.

"Here, friend Simon," Binabik said, rousing him out of this doleful reverie, "I have secured you a draught of hunt-wine." He held out a skin bag, smaller than the one being passed around the circle nearby.

"I already drank some," Simon asked, sniffing suspiciously. "It tasted— well, Haestan said it tasted like horse piss and I think he's right."

"Ah. It is seeming that Haestan has changed his mind about kangkang." Binabik chuckled, tilting his head in the direction of the drinking-circle. The Erkynlander and Sludig had joined the trolls; Haestan was even now taking a healthy swallow from the bag. "But this is not kangkang," Binabik said, pressing the bag into Simon's hand. "It is hunt-wine. The men of my folk are not allowed to drink it—except for those, like myself, who are using it sometimes for the purposes of medicine. Our huntresses drink when they must be awake all the night away from our caves. It is good especially for tired and hurting limbs and such."

"I feel fine," Simon said, looking doubtfully at the drinking skin.

"That is not being the point of my giving." Binabik was becoming exasperated. "Be understanding that it is rare for anyone to get this hunt-wine. We sit here now celebrating luck in having come a difficult journey with no losses or woundings. We are celebrating a little sun and hoping for some small luck on the rest of our journey. Also, it is a sort of gift, Simon. Sisqinanamook wished you to have it."

Simon looked up to the troll maiden, who sat in laughing conversation with her fellow huntresses. She smiled and hoisted her spear as if in salute.

"I'm sorry," he said. "I didn't understand." He lifted the bag and took a swig. The sweet, oily fluid slid down his throat. He coughed, but a moment later felt its soothing warmth in his stomach. He took another swallow, then held some in his mouth, trying to decide what the taste reminded him of.

"What's it made from?" he asked.

"Berries from the high meadows of Blue Mud Lake, where my tribesmen will be going. Berries and teeth."

Simon wasn't sure he had heard correctly. "Berries and what?"

"Teeth." Binabik grinned, showing his own yellow ones. "Teeth of the snow bear. Made into a powder, of course. That is for strongness and quietness on the hunt."

"Teeth . . ." Simon, remembering that this was a gift, thought for a moment before saying anything more. There wasn't really anything wrong with teeth—he had a mouthful himself. The hunt-wine did not taste bad at all, and made for a comforting tingle in his belly. He carefully lifted the skin and took a final swallow. "Berries and teeth," he said, handing the bag back. "Very good. How do you say thank you in Qanuc?"

Binabik told him.

"Guyop!" Simon called to Sisqi, who smiled and nodded her head as her companions burst into high-pitched laughter once more, hiding their faces in the fur of their hoods.

For a while Simon and Binabik sat quietly side by side, enjoying the warmth. Simon felt the hunt-wine creeping pleasantly through his veins, so that even the daunting lower slopes of Sikkihoq that still awaited them began to look friendly. The mountain fell away below into a rumpled quilt of snow-covered hills, leveling out at the bottom into the tree-spiked monotony of the Waste.

As he turned to survey the terrain, Simon's attention was caught by Namyet, one of Sikkihoq's sister mountains, which in the momentary clarity of the bright afternoon seemed to loom only a stone's throw away on his left side. Namyet's skirts were creased with long blue vertical shadows. Her white crown sparkled in the sun.

"Do trolls live there, too?" he asked.

Binabik looked up and nodded. "Namyet is also one of the Yiqanuc mountains. Mintahoq, Chugik, Tutusik, Rinsenatuq, Sikkihoq and Namyet, Yamok, and the Huudika—the Gray Sisters—those are the troll-country. Yamok, which means Little Nose, is the place where my parents died. That is her, out beyond Namyet, do you see?" He pointed at a dim angular shape limned by the sun.

"How did they die?"

"In dragon snow, as we call it on the Roof of the World—snow that freezes on its top, then breaks through without warning, jaws closing swiftly. Like a dragon's jaws are closing. As you know."

Simon scuffed at the ground with a stone, then looked up, squinting at the faint outline of Yamok in the east. "Did you cry?"

"With certainty—but in my own secret place. And you . . . but no, you were not knowing your parents, were you?"

"No. Doctor Morgenes told me about them. A little. My father was a fisherman and my mother was a chambermaid."

Binabik smiled. "Poor yet honorable forebears. Who could ask for more, as a place from which to make a starting? Who would be born into the tight restricting of royal blood? Who could think to be finding their true selves when all around are bowing and kneeling?"

Simon thought of Miriamele, and even Binabik's betrothed, Sisqinana-mook, but said nothing.

After a while, the troll stretched and pulled his pack closer. He rummaged in it for a few moments, at last producing a clinking leather bag. "My knuckle bones," he said as he spilled them gently out onto the stone. "We will be seeing if they are now a more truthful guide than at the last questioning." He began humming quietly to himself as he scooped them up in his palms. For long moments he held the handful of bones before him, eyes closed in concentration while he muttered a song. At last he dropped them to the ground. Simon could see no discernible pattern in the jumble.

"*Circle of Stones,*" Binabik said, as calmly as though it were written on the bones' yellowed smoothness. "That is where we are standing, so to speak. It means, I am thinking, a council meeting. We are searching for wisdom, for help in our journeying."

"The bones you ask for help tell you that you're looking for help?" Simon grunted. "That's not much of a trick."

"Silence, foolish lowlander," Binabik said mock-severely. "There is more to the bones than you understand. The reading of them is not so simple." He hummed and cast again. "*Torch at the Cave-Mouth,*" he said, but cast again without pause for explanation. He frowned and sucked his lip as he surveyed the scatter. "*The Black Crevice.* That is the second time only I have ever seen that patterning, and both have been in the time we have been together. It is an ominous throw."

"Explain, please," Simon said. He pulled his boots back on, testing his toes by wiggling.

"The second throwing, *Torch at the Cave-Mouth*, means we must look for an advantage in the place we go—Sesuad'ra, I make that, Geloë's Stone of Farewell. That is not proving we will find luck there, but it is our chance for advantage. *The Black Crevice*, the last throwing, I have told you of before. The third throw is that which should be feared, or that which we need being aware of. *The Black Crevice* is a strange, rare pattern that could mean treachery, or could mean something coming from *elsewhere . . .*" He broke off, staring absently at the littered bones, then swept them back into his bag.

"So what does it all mean?"

"Ah, Simon-friend," the troll sighed, "the bones are not simply answering questions, even at the best of times. At a troubled hour like the one we are living, the understanding becomes more difficult still. I must think long about these throws. I must perhaps sing a song of slight differentness, then cast again. This is the first throwing in a long while that I have not seen *The Shadowed Path*—but I cannot be thinking that our path is any less shadowy. There, you see, is the danger of trying to take simple answers from the bones."

Simon stood up. "I don't understand much of what you're saying, but I wish we *did* have a few simple answers. It would make things much easier."

Binabik smiled as one of his folk approached. "Simple answers to life's questioning. That would be a magic beyond any I have ever been seeing."

The new troll, a stocky, tuft-bearded herder Binabik introduced as Snenneq, threw a distrustful look up at Simon, as though his very height was an affront to civilized behavior. He conversed excitedly with Binabik in Qanuc for a short time, then trudged away. Binabik sprang up and whistled for Qantaqa.

"Snenneq says the rams are acting skittishly," Binabik explained. "He wanted to know where Qantaqa was, if she had been at stalking their mounts." A moment later the wolf's gray form appeared on a crag half a furlong away, head tilted questioningly. "She is down the wind from us," the little man said, shaking his head. "If the rams are restless, it is not Qantaqa's scent that is so making them."

Qantaqa sprang down from the rocky outcropping. A few moments later she was at her master's side, butting his ribs with her large, broad head.

"She herself seems disturbed," Binabik said. He kneeled to scratch the wolf's belly, his arms disappearing into her thick fur up to the shoulder. Qantaqa did indeed seem distracted, standing still only a moment before lifting her snout to the breeze. Her ears flicked like the wings of an alighting bird. She made a low rumbling noise before butting Binabik with her head again. "Ah," he said, "a snow bear, perhaps. This must be a season of hungering for them. We should move to a lower place—we may be in less danger when we are leaving Sikkihoq's heights." He called to Snenneq and the rest of his fellows. They began striking the makeshift camp, resaddling their rams and stowing the drinking skins and food bags.

Sludig and Haestan approached. "Ho, lad," Haestan said to Simon, "back to our boot leather again. Now you know what's like t'be soldier. March, march, march, 'til feet freeze and lungs go limp."

"I never did want to be a foot soldier," Simon said, shouldering his pack.

The friendly weather did not hold. By the time they made camp that night near the edge of the long flat shelf, the stars had disappeared. The company's cookfires were the only light beneath a wild and snow-spread sky.

Dawn lightened the dark horizon to a stony gray that oddly mirrored the granite below their feet. The traveling party made their way carefully down from the shelf and onto another series of narrow trails that wound back and forth across the mountain face in steep switchbacks. By midday they had come to another relatively level place, a long, down-sloping talus hill, a vast refuse heap of boulders and smaller stones left by the passage of some ancient glacier. The footing was treacherous: even the rams had to pick their way carefully, sometimes choosing to leap from one large stone to another rather than walk across the loose rubble. Simon, Haestan, and Sludig followed behind. Their trudging footsteps occasionally freed a fist-sized stone to bound down the slope, eliciting bleats and annoyed stares from the saddled rams. Such terrain was also hard on the knees and ankles. Before they had gone far down the slope, Simon and his companions stopped to wind rags about their boots for support.

Snow fluttered all around, not a heavy fall, but enough to dust the tops of the larger stones with pale powder and fill the crevices between the smaller rocks like mortar. As Simon looked back up the long disordered slope, the upper reaches of Sikkihoq loomed through the mist and squall like a dark shadow in a doorway. He was amazed by how far they had come, but on turning found himself disheartened in equal measure by the length of descent that still remained before they would reach the doubtful comforts of the Waste below.

Haestan saw his expression and offered Simon the beribboned wineskin that had been the trolls' gift to the guardsman. "Two more days t'flat ground, lad," he said, smiling sourly. "Have some."

Simon warmed himself with a swallow of kangkang before passing it along to Sludig. A toothy smile showed briefly in the Rimmersman's yellow beard as he lifted the skin to his mouth. "Good," he said. "It is not the mead I know, or even southern wine, but it is certainly better than nothing."

"God's curse if that don't be truth," Haestan said. He took the skin back, savoring a long swallow before letting the bag drop to his belt once more. Simon thought the guardsman's voice a little furry, and realized that Haestan had been drinking all day. Still, what else did they have to combat the pain in their legs and the monotonous, flurrying snow? Better a little drunkenness to take off the chill than hours of misery.

Simon squinted against the sleet flying into his face. He could see the bobbing shapes of the trolls riding just before them, but beyond he could discern only misty shapes. Somewhere past even the foremost, Binabik and Qantaqa were searching for the best route off the talus slope. The guttural exclamations of the ram-riders ahead drifted back to Simon on the wind, incomprehensible but oddly reassuring.

A stone bounced past his foot and rolled to a halt a few cubits ahead, the sound of its passage obliterated by the song of the wind. Simon wondered what would happen if a truly large stone ever began rolling downhill toward them. Would they even hear it above the clamor of the elements? Or would it be upon them suddenly, like a hand dropping down to crush a fly sunning on a windowsill? He turned anxiously to look back, seeing in his mind's eye a vast, round shape growing larger, a great stone that would crush all in its path.

There was no great stone, but there were shapes moving on the slope above. Caught staring open-mouthed, Simon knew a moment's unsureness as he wondered if some strange snow blindness caused him to see things that could not be real, huge shadows flailing in the uncertain light. Following Simon's backward glance, Sludig opened his eyes wide.

"*Hunën!*" the Rimmersman shouted. "*Vaer Hunën!* There are giants up the slope behind us!" Downslope, invisible in the drifting snows, one of the trolls echoed Sludig's alarm with a harsh cry.

Dim, elongated figures were loping down the rock-strewn hill. Dislodged stones rolled before them, bounding past Simon and his companions as the shouting trolls tried to pull their rams about to face this sudden danger. The advantage of surprise lost, the charging giants bellowed out wordless challenges in voices that seemed deep enough to shake down the very mountain. Several huge figures plunged through the mist, brandishing broad clubs like gnarled tree limbs. The black faces, snarling-mouthed, seemed to float bodilessly in the flurrying snow, but Simon knew the strength in those shaggy white forms. He recognized Death's face in the leathery masks and Death's inescapable clutch in the broad sinews and lashing arms twice as long as any man's.

"*Binabik!*" Simon screamed. "Giants are coming!"

One of the Hunën snatched up a boulder and heaved it down the slope. It struck and spun end over end, bounding downhill like a runaway wagon. Even as a flurry of troll-spears sliced back through the air toward the attackers, the great stone crunched past Simon and smashed into the nearest ranks of the trolls. The shrill, terrified bleating of rams and the howls of their broken and dying riders echoed across the foggy slope. Simon found himself gaping in stunned immobility as a towering shape rose before him, club backflung like the straining arm of a catapult. As the black bar of shadow whistled down, Simon heard someone call his name, then something struck him aside and he was flung on his face among stones and snow.

A moment later he was on his feet, stumbling back through the mist toward the roaring, contorted shapes of conflict. Hunën loomed and then disappeared, huge, grasping shadows that at some moments were almost invisible in the flurrying snow.

Inside Simon's mind a hysterical, terrified voice shouted for him to run away, to hide, but the voice was muffled, as though his head were stuffed with cushioning down. There was blood on his hands, but he did not know whose. He wiped it absently on his shirt front before reaching down to pull his Qanuc knife from its sheath. The roaring was all around now.

A group of trolls had couched their spears and were spurring their rams up the slope. Their bellowing target flailed with a shaggy arm broad as a tree trunk and swept the foremost trolls from their saddles. Men and mounts together soared back down the rise in a bloody tangle, tumbling to a boneless halt at flight's end, but their trailing fellows drove home half a dozen spears, raising a coughing, sputtering roar from the beleaguered giant.

Simon saw Binabik downslope. The troll dismounted Qantaqa, who charged off into the swirling shadows of another skirmish. Binabik was pushing darts into the hollow section of his walking stick—darts with poison-blacked tips, Simon knew—but before Simon could take even a step toward his friend another shape pushed hard against him, then fell to the ground at his feet.

It was Haestan, lying facedown among the stones, the sword Thorn still hanging from his pack. As Simon stared, something howled so loudly it cut through the fuzziness in his ears and mind; he whirled to see Sludig backing toward him down the unstable slope, his long troll-spear jabbing before him as he retreated from a giant whose angry screams rattled the sky. The giant's white belly and arms were dotted with crimson blood-flowers, but Sludig, too, was bloodied: his left arm looked as though it had been dipped into a bowl of red paint.

Simon bent and grasped Haestan's cloak, shaking him, but the guardsman was limp. Grabbing at Thorn's black hilt, Simon pulled it slowly back through the loop on Haestan's pack. It was cold as frost and heavy as a suit of horse-armor. Cursing with anger and terror, he tried with all his strength to lift it, but could not bring the point off the ground. Despite his ever more panicky exertions, he could not even lift the hilt above his waist.

"Usires, where are You!?" he railed, letting the blade fall heavily to the ground like a block of tumbled masonry. "Help me! What *use* is this damnable sword!?" He tried again, praying for God's help, but Thorn lay flat on the ground, beyond his strength.

"Simon!" Sludig shouted breathlessly. "Flee! I . . . cannot. . . !" The giant's shaggy white arm swung out and the Rimmersman stumbled back, just out of reach. He opened his mouth to call to Simon once more, but had to throw himself to one side to avoid a clawing backswipe. Blood flecked the northerner's pale beard and matted his yellow hair. His helmet was gone.

Simon looked around wildly, then spotted a troll-spear lying among the rocks. He caught it up and circled around the giant, whose reddened eyes and wide-flaring nostrils were fixed only on Sludig. The creature's shaggy back loomed before him like a white wall. A moment later, before he even had time to be surprised at himself, Simon was leaping forward over the slippery stones, thrusting the spear as hard as he could into the matted fur. The shock of impact leaped up his arms, rattling his teeth, and for a moment he slumped strengthlessly against the giant's broad back. The Hunë threw its head up in a howl, weaving from side to side as Sludig drove in from the front with his spear. Simon saw the Rimmersman disappear, then saw the beast bend, shuddering, and knock Sludig to the ground.

Coughing blood, the giant stood over Sludig, feeling for its club with one arm, clutching at its red-dripping stomach with the other. With a shout of anger, mad with fury that this horrible thing should strike at his friends even while its own life leaked out, Simon snatched a handful of its pelt in one hand and the wagging spear butt protruding from the giant's back in the other, then dragged himself up onto its back.

Reeking of wet fur and musk and rotting meat, the great, quivering body straightened beneath him. Huge talon-nailed hands came up, smacking sightlessly in search of the insect that had lighted upon it, even as Simon drove his Qanuc dagger to the hilt in the giant's neck, just below the contorted jaw. A moment later he felt himself caught up and flung loose by wrist-wide fingers.

There was a moment of weightlessness; the sky was a cracked swirl of gray and white and dimmest blue. Then Simon struck down.

He was staring at a round stone, just a hand's breadth beyond his nose. He could not feel his extremities, his body limp as boned fish, nor could he hear any sounds but a faint roaring in his ears and thin squeals that might be voices. The stone lay before him, spherical and solid, unmoving. It was a chunk of gray granite, banded with white, which might have lain in this place since Time itself was young. There was nothing special about it. It was only a piece of the earth's bones, rough corners smoothed by eons of wind and water.

Simon could not move, but he could see the immobile, magnificently unimportant stone. He lay staring at it for a long time, feeling nothing but emptiness where his body had been, until the stone itself began to gleam, throwing back the faintest pink sheen of sunset.

They came for him at last when Sedda the moon appeared, her pale face peering down through the mist and twilight. Small, gentle hands lifted him and laid him on a blanket. He swayed gently as they carried him downslope and set him down near a roaring fire. Simon stared up at the moon as she mounted higher in the sky. Binabik came to him and said many soothing things in a quiet voice, but the words seemed nonsense. As others helped bind his wounds and laid cool, water-soaked rags on his head, Binabik crooned strange, circular songs, then gave him a bowl of something warm to drink, holding up Simon's limp head as the sour draught trickled down his throat.

I must be dying, Simon thought. He felt a certain peace in the idea. It seemed as though his soul had left his body already, for he felt very little connection with his own flesh. *I would have liked to have gotten out of the snows, first. I would have liked to have gone home. . . .*

He thought of another stillness such as he now felt: the moment when he had stood before Igjarjuk, the silence that had seemed to envelop the whole world, the timeless time before he had brought the sword down, before the black blood had fountained up.

But this time the sword didn't help me . . . Had he lost some kind of worthiness since he had left Urmsheim? Or was Thorn merely as inconstant as the wind and weather?

Simon remembered a warm summer afternoon back in the Hayholt, when the sunlight had angled down through the high windows of Doctor Morgenes' chambers, making the lazily floating dust gleam like drifting sparks.

"Never make your home in a place," the old man had told him that day.
*"Make a home for yourself inside your own head. You'll find what you need to
furnish it—memory, friends you can trust, love of learning, and other such things.
That way it will go with you wherever you journey . . ."*

Is that what dying is? Simon wondered. *Is it going home? That's not so bad.*

Binabik was singing again, a drowsy sound like rushing water. Simon
let go and drifted.

When he awakened late the next day, he was not immediately certain
that he was still alive. The survivors had moved during the morning and
Simon had been carried, along with the other wounded, to a cave beneath
a leaning rock. On waking, he saw before him only an open hole into the
gray sky. It was the ragged black birds gliding past the cave-mouth that
taught him at last that he was still in the world—the birds, and the pain in
all his limbs.

He lay for a while testing his hurts, bending his joints one by one. He
ached, but movement had come back with the pain. He was sore but
whole.

After a while Binabik came to him again with another drink of his
healing beverage. The troll himself had not escaped without harm, as long
runnels down his cheek and neck attested. Binabik's look was solemn, but
he seemed to give Simon's wounds only a cursory inspection.

"We have received grievous damaging," the troll said. "I wished I had
not to say this, but . . . Haestan is dead."

"Haestan?!" Simon sat up, forgetting his aching muscles for a moment.
"Haestan?" His stomach seemed to sink away inside him.

Binabik nodded his head. "And of my twice-dozen companions, nine
were killed and six more are being badly wounded."

"What happened to Haestan?" He felt a sickening sense of unreality.
How could Haestan be dead? Had they not spoken only a few moments
before . . . before. . . ?" What about Sludig?"

"Sludig was hurt, but not badly. He is out with my tribesmen, cutting
up wood for building of fires. It is important for healing the injured, do
you see? And Haestan . . ." Binabik thumped his chest with the heel of his
hand—a gesture the Qanuc used, Simon had learned, to ward evil. The
troll looked profoundly unhappy. "Haestan was struck to the head by one
of the giant's clubs. I am told that he pushed you away from danger and
was shortly after himself killed."

"Oh, Haestan," Simon groaned. He expected tears to come, but they
did not. His face felt strangely numb, his sorrow somehow weak. He put
his head in his hands. The big guardsman had been so alive, so hearty. It
was wrong that a life could be taken just that swiftly. Doctor Morgenes,
Grimmric and Ethelbearn, An'nai, now Haestan—all dead, all struck down
because they tried to do what was right. Where were those powers that
should protect such innocents?

"And Sisqi?" Simon asked, suddenly remembering the troll maiden. He scanned Binabik's face anxiously, but the troll showed only a distracted smile.

"She has survived, and with only small wounding."

"Can we take Haestan down off the mountain? He wouldn't want to be left here."

Binabik reluctantly shook his head. "We cannot carry his body, Simon. Not on our rams. He was a man of largeness, too much for our mounts. And we still have a dangerous way to go before we are on flat land. He must stay here, but his bones will lie in honor with the bones of my people. He will be with other good and brave warriors. That is, I think, as he would be wishing. Now, you should sleep again—but first there are two who would speak with you."

Binabik stepped back, Sisqi and the herder Snenneq were there, waiting at the cave-mouth. They came forward to stand beside Simon. Binabik's intended spoke to Simon in troll speech. Her dark eyes were grave. Beside her, Snenneq seemed uncomfortable, shuffling from foot to foot.

"Sisqinanamook says she is sorrowful for you in the losing of your friend. She also says you showed rare bravery. Now all have seen the courage that you showed also on the dragon-mountain."

Simon nodded, embarrassed. Snenneq made a throat-clearing noise and began a speech of his own. Simon waited patiently until Binabik could explain.

"Snenneq, herd-chief of Lower Chugik, says he, too, is sorry. Many good lives were lost yesterday. He also wishes to give you something back which you lost."

The herder produced Simon's bone-handled knife, passing it to him with a show of reverence.

"It was taken from the neck of a dead giant," Binabik said quietly. "The gift of the Qanuc has been blooded in defense of Qanuc lives. This means much to my people."

Simon accepted the knife, sliding it back into the decorated sheath on his belt. *"Guyop,"* he said. "Please tell them I am glad to have it back. I'm not quite sure what 'defense of Qanuc lives' means—we all fought the same enemy. But I don't want to think about killing just now."

"Of course." Binabik turned to Sisqi and the herder, speaking briefly. They nodded. Sisqi leaned forward to touch Simon's arm in wordless commiseration, then turned and led awkward Snenneq from the cave.

"Sisqi is leading the others in building the cairns of stone," Binabik said. "And as for you, Simon-friend, there is nothing more to be done by you this day. Sleep."

After tucking the cloak carefully around Simon's shoulders, Binabik disappeared out through the opening of the cavern, stepping carefully around the sleeping forms of the other wounded. Simon watched him go, thinking of Haestan and the rest of the dead. Were they even now traveling the road toward the complete stillness that Simon had glimpsed?

As he fell asleep, he thought he saw his Erkynlandish friend's broad back vanishing down a corridor into white silence. Haestan, Simon thought, did not seem to walk like a man who bore regrets—but then, it was only a dream.

Next day the noon sun pierced the mists, splashing light on Sikkihoq's proud slopes. Simon's pain was less than he had thought it would be. With Sludig's help, he was able to limp down from the cave to the flat shelf of rock where the cairns were being finished. There were ten, nine small and one large, the rocks carefully piled so that no wind or weather would shift them.

Simon saw Haestan's pale face, blood-striped, before Sludig and his troll helpers finished winding the guardsman's cloak about him. Haestan's eyes were shut, but his wounds were such that Simon could not maintain any illusion that his long-time companion only slept. He had been killed by the Storm King's brutal minions, and that was something to be remembered. Haestan had been a simple man. He would appreciate the notion of vengeance.

After Haestan had been laid away and the stones fitted atop his cairn, Binabik's nine tribesmen and tribeswomen were lowered into their own graves, each with some article particular to him or her—or so Binabik explained it to Simon. When this was done and the nine cairns were sealed, Binabik stepped forward. He raised his hand. The other trolls began to chant. There were tears in many eyes, both male and female; one glimmered on Binabik's own cheek. After some time had passed, the chanting came to a halt. Sisqi stepped forward, handing Binabik a torch and a small bag. Binabik sprinkled something from the bag on each grave, then touched the flame to it. A thin coil of smoke rose from each cairn in his wake, quickly shredded by the mountain wind. When he had finished the last, he handed the torch to Sisqi and began to sing a long string of Qanuc words. The melody was like the voice of the wind itself, rising and falling, rising and falling.

Binabik's wind-song came to an end. He took torch and sack and raised a plume of smoke on Haestan's barrow as well.

"Sedda told her children,"

he sang in the Westerling speech,

"Lingit and Yana,
Told them to choose their way
Bird's way or moon's way
'Choose now,' she said.

"Bird's way is egg's way
Death is a door then
Egg-children stay behind
Fathers and mothers go beyond
Do you choose this?

"Moon's way is no-death
Live always under stars
Go through no shadowed doors
Find no new land beyond
Do you choose this?

"Swift-blooded Yana
Pale-haired and laughing-eyed
Said: 'I choose moon's way.
I seek no other doors.
This world is my home.'

"Lingit her brother
Slow-footed, dark-eyed,
Said: 'I'll take bird's way.
Walk under unknown skies
Leave world to my young.'

"We children of Lingit all
Share his gift equally
Pass through the lands of stone
Just once, then we are gone,
Out through the door

"We go to walk beyond
Search for stars in the sky
Hunt the caves past the night
Strange lands and different lights
But do not return."

When he had finished singing, Binabik bowed to Haestan's cairn. "Farewell, brave man. The trolls will remember your name. We will sing of you in Mintahoq a hundred springs from now!" He turned to Simon and

Sludig, who stood by solemnly. "Would you like to be saying something?"

Simon shook his head uncomfortably. "Only . . . God bless you, Haestan. They will sing of you in Erkynland, too, if I have my way."

Sludig stepped forward. "I should say an Aedonite prayer," he said. "Your song was very good, Binabik of Mintahoq, but Haestan was an Aedonite man and must be properly shriven."

"Please," Binabik said. "You have listened to ours."

The Rimmersman took his wooden Tree from beneath his shirt and stood at the head of Haestan's cairn. The smoke continued to waver upward.

> *"Our Lord protect you,"*

Sludig began,

> *"And Usires His only Son lift you up.*
> *May you be carried to the green valleys*
> *Of His domains.*
> *Where the souls of the good and righteous sing from the hilltops,*
> *And angels are in the trees,*
> *Speaking joy with God's own voice.*
>
> *"May the Ransomer protect you*
> *From all evil,*
> *And may your soul find peace everlasting,*
> *And heart's ease beyond compare."*

Sludig laid his Tree atop the stones, then walked back to stand by Simon.

"One last thing let me say," Binabik called out, raising his voice. He spoke the same words in Qanuc and his people listened attentively. "This is the first day in a thousand years that Qanuc and Utku—troll and lowlander—have been fighting at each other's side, have been blooded together and have fallen together. It is the hate and the hating of our enemy that has been bringing this upon us, but if our peoples can stand together for the battle that is coming—a greatest, but perhaps also last, battle—the deaths of all our friends will be even better given than they now are." He turned and repeated the words for his tribesmen. Many of them nodded their heads, pounding their spear butts on the ground. From somewhere up the slope, Qantaqa howled. Her mournful voice echoed all over the mountain.

"Let us not forget them, Simon," Binabik said as the rest of his fellows mounted up. "These, or any of the others who have already died. Let us be taking strength from the gifting of their lives—because if we fail, they will perhaps be seeming the lucky ones. Are you able to walk?"

"For a while," Simon replied. "Sludig will walk with me."

"We will not ride long today, for the afternoon has far advanced," the troll said, squinting up at the white spot of sun. "But all speed is necessary. Half our company, nearly, we have lost in killing five giants. The Storm King's mountains to the west are full of such creatures, and we cannot be knowing there are not more nearby."

"How long before your fellow trolls turn their own way," Sludig asked, "to go to this Blue Mud Lake your master and mistress spoke of?"

"That is another thing for concern," Binabik agreed grimly. "Another day or two days, then we will be three travelers only in the Waste." He turned as a large gray shape appeared at his elbow, panting hugely. Qantaqa nudged him impatiently with her broad nose. "*Four* travelers, if I may be pardoned," he amended, but did not smile.

Simon felt himself empty as they started down Sikkihoq's last reaches, hollowed out, so that if he stood just right the wind might whistle through him. Another friend was gone, and home was only a word.

9

Cold and Curses

The afternoon was failing. Prince Josua's tattered minions were tumbled all together beneath a tangle of willows and cypresses in a moss-carpeted gulley that had once been a riverbed. A slender, muddy trickle ran along in the middle, all that remained of the watercourse. Above them rose a hilly slope whose heights were hidden behind close-crowding trees.

They had hoped to be atop the rise when the sun went down, a defensive position superior to anything they could hope to find in this thick-shrouded valley, but twilight was now imminent and the company's progress had slowed to a crawl.

Either they had guessed correctly, Deornoth reflected, and the Norns were indeed trying to herd them rather than kill them, or else they had been very lucky. Arrows had flown in biting swarms throughout the day. Several had found targets, but none of the wounds had been mortal. Einskaldir had been struck on his helmet, causing a gash above his eye that wept blood all the long afternoon. The back of Isorn's neck had been slashed by another arrow, and Lady Vorzheva had received a long, bloody weal on her forearm.

Surprisingly, Vorzheva had seemed almost unaffected by her injury, binding it with a strip of her tattered skirt and plodding on without a word of complaint. Deornoth had been impressed by this show of courage, but had also wondered if it might not be an indication of dangerous and despairing unconcern. She and Prince Josua were pointedly not speaking with each other. Vorzheva's face turned grim whenever the prince was near.

Josua, Father Strangyeard, and Duchess Gutrun had so far escaped damage. Ever since their fleeing troop had reached the gulley and had taken advantage of its scanty protection to fall down exhausted, they had all been busily engaged in binding of wounds. At the moment, the priest was tending to Towser, who had fallen sick during the march; the other pair were looking after Sangfugol's injuries.

Even if the Norns do not mean to kill us, they obviously intend to stop us,
Deornoth thought, rubbing his aching leg. *Perhaps they no longer care
whether we have one of the Great Swords, or perhaps their spies told them we do
not. But why don't they simply kill us, then? Do they wish to capture Josua?*
Trying to understand the Norns was dizzying. *What should we do, in any
case? Is it better to be shot to pieces and then captured, or to turn and fight to the
death?*

But did they even have a choice? The Norns were mere shadows in the
forest. As long as they had arrows to shoot, the white-faced pursuers
could do as they wished. What could Josua's folk do to force them to
fight?

Fog was forming rapidly on the damp ground, turning the trees and
stones indistinct, as though Josua's people were trapped in some between-
world that straddled life and death. An owl flitted silently overhead like a
gray ghost.

Deornoth struggled to his feet and went to help Strangyeard. The prince
came to join them, watching as the priest swabbed Towser's feverish
brow with his kerchief.

"It is a pity . . ." Strangyeard said without looking up. "A pity, I mean,
that the fog is everywhere, but we still have so little clean water. Even the
ground is wet, but it does us no good."

"If tonight is as damp and cold as the last," Deornoth said, grasping
Towser's hand as the old man fretfully clutched at the kerchief, "we will
be able to wring out our clothes and fill the Kynslagh."

"We must not spend the night here," Josua said. "We must get to high
ground."

Deornoth looked at him carefully. The prince was showing no signs of
his earlier lassitude—in fact, Josua's eyes were bright. He seemed to be
coming back to life just as all around him were dying. "But how, my
prince?" Deornoth asked. "How can we hope to drag our bleeding bodies
up that hill? We do not even know how high it is."

Josua nodded, but said: "Nevertheless, we must climb it before dark.
What little ability to resist that we retain will be useless if they can come
down on us from above."

His fierce face daubed with dried blood, Einskaldir came and crouched
beside them. "If only they *would* come within reach." He dandled his axe
and laughed sourly. "If we show ourselves, they pick us to pieces. They
see better in dark than us."

"We must go up the slope all in a herd," the prince said, "—huddled up
like frightened cattle. Those on the outside will wrap their legs and arms
in whatever thick clothing we have. That way, if they fear to make a fatal
shot, they will be perhaps less likely to let fly into a crowd, where the
missed wounding in the front may take a life in the rear."

Einskaldir grunted. "So we make us an unmissable target—cannot shoot
one without shooting more. Madness!"

Josua turned on him sharply. "You are not answerable for the lives of this company, Einskaldir. I am! If you would fight your own way, then go! If you would remain with us, then be silent and do as I say."

Several among the company who had been talking fell silent, waiting. The Rimmersman stared at Josua for a moment, his eyes blank, his bearded jaw twitching. Then he smiled in grim admiration.

"*Haja*—yes, Prince Josua," was all Einskaldir said.

The prince put a hand on Deornoth's shoulder. "We can do nothing else, even when hope is gone, but struggle on . . ."

"*There is still hope, if you will hear it.*"

Deornoth turned, expecting to find Duchess Gutrun standing by—for it had seemed an older's woman's voice, deep and a little hoarse—but Gutrun was tending the harper Sangfugol and was too far away to have been the source.

"Who speaks?" Josua said, staring away from his companions, out into the forest. He drew his slender sword from its scabbard. Those around him fell silent, sensing his alarm. "I said, who speaks?"

"*I do,*" the voice replied in a matter-of-fact way. The accent was that of one not native to the Westerling speech. "*I did not want to catch you unaware. There is hope, I said. I come as a friend.*"

"Norn tricks!" Einskaldir snarled, hefting his axe as he tilted his head to locate the source of the voice.

Josua raised his hand to hold him back and called: "If you are a friend, then why do you not come forward?"

"*Because I have not finished changing and I do not want to frighten you. Your friends are my friends—Morgenes of the Hayholt, Binabik of Yiqanuc.*"

Deornoth felt the hair stirring on his neck at the invisible being's words. To hear those names here, in the middle of unknown Aldheorte! "Who are you?" he cried.

There was a rustling in the shadowed undergrowth. A strangely-shaped figure stepped toward them through the rising fog. No, Deornoth realized, there were two figures, one large and one small.

"In this part of the world," the taller one said, with what sounded like a touch of amusement in her harsh voice, "I am known as Geloë."

"Valada Geloë!" Josua breathed. "The wise woman. Binabik spoke of you."

"Some say wise, some say witch," she answered. "Binabik is small but polite. Such things we may talk about later, however. Now it grows dark."

She was not tall or particularly large, but there was something in her posture that spoke of strength. Her short-cropped hair was mostly gray, her nose prominent and sharp, with a downward curve. Geloë's most arresting feature was her eyes: wide and heavy-lidded, they caught the dying sun with a peculiar yellow gleam, reminding Deornoth of nothing so much as a hawk or owl. So striking were they that it was some time before he noticed the young girl whose hand she held.

This one was small, perhaps eight or nine years, and pale of face. Her eyes, although an unexceptional shade of dark brown, had much of the curious intensity of the older woman's. But where Geloë's gaze seized attention like an arrow quivering on a drawn string, the little girl looked starkly into nothingness, her stare as objectless as a blind beggar's.

"Leleth and I are here to join you," Geloë said, "—and to lead you if we may, at least for a short while. If you try to climb that hill, some of you will die. None of you will reach the summit."

"What do you know about it?" Isorn demanded. He looked confused. He was not the only one.

"This. The Norns are reluctant to slay you—this is obvious, or a party like yours on foot would not have gotten a tenth this far into the forest. But if you cross that hill, you will have crossed over into territory through which the Hikeda'ya cannot follow. If there are any of you they do not need alive—and surely not all of you are valuable to them, if that is even the reason the Norns have let you get so far—they will take the risk of trying to kill the dispensable ones to frighten the rest off the slopes."

"So what are you telling us, then?" Josua asked, stepping forward. Their eyes locked. "Over this hill safety lies, but we dare not go there? What, should we lay down and die?'

"No," Geloë responded calmly. "I only said you should not climb the hill. There are other ways."

"Fly?" Einskaldir snarled.

"Some do." She smiled as at a quiet joke. "But all you need do is follow us." Taking the girl's hand again, she started off along the edge of the gulley.

"Where are you going?" Deornoth cried, and felt a pang of fear at being left behind as the pair began to fade into the twilit shadows.

"Follow," Geloë called back over her shoulder. "Darkness is growing."

Deornoth turned to stare at the prince, but Josua was already helping Duchess Gutrun onto her feet. As the rest hurried to pick up their meager belongings, Josua walked briskly to where Vorzheva sat and extended his hand. She ignored him and got to her feet, then strode down into the gulley with head held high, like a queen in procession. The others followed limping after her, whispering wearily among themselves.

Geloë stopped to wait for the farthest-trailing stragglers. At her side Leleth disconcertingly stared off into the forest, as if she expected someone.

"Where are we going?" Deornoth asked as he and Isorn rested, scraping the slimy mud of the streambed from their boots. The harper Sangfugol, who could not walk without someone at either shoulder, was sitting on his own for a moment, breathing heavily.

"We are not leaving the forest," the witch woman said, inspecting the bit of purple sky that could be seen through the willow branches. "But we will pass beneath the hill into a part of the old woods once known as *Shisae'ron*. As I said, the Hikeda'ya are not likely to follow us there."

"Pass under the hill? What can that mean?" Isorn demanded.

"We walk in the bed of *Re Suri'eni*, an ancient river," Geloë said. "When I first came here, the forest was a lively country, not the dark tangle it has become. This river was one of many that spanned the great woods, carrying all manner of things and all manner of folk from Da'ai Chikiza to high Asu'a."

"Asu'a?" Deornoth wondered. "Was that not the Sithi name for the Hayholt?"

"Asu'a was more than the Hayholt ever will be," Geloë said sternly, her eyes searching for the last of the wandering line. "Sometimes you men are like lizards, sunning on the stones of a crumbled house, thinking: 'what a nice basking-spot someone built for me.' You stand in the sad mud of what was a wide, beautiful river, where the boats of the Old Ones skimmed and flowers grew."

"This was a fairy river?" Isorn's attention had been wandering. Now, startlement on his broad face, he peered around as though the streambed itself might exhibit signs of treachery.

"Idiot!" Geloë said scornfully. "Yes, it was a 'fairy river.' This entire land was—as you would put it—a fairy *country*. What sort of creatures do you think pursue you?"

"I . . . I knew that," Isorn muttered, abashed. "But I had not thought of it that way. Their arrows and swords were real, that was all I could think of."

"As were the arrows and swords of your ancestors, *Rimmersmannë*, which accounts for some of the bad blood between your folk and theirs. The difference is, though King Fingil's reavers killed many Sithi with their blades of black iron, Fingil and your other ancestors at last aged and died. The Children of the East do not die—at least, not in such a time as you can understand—and neither do they forget old wrongs. If they are old, they are all the more patient for it." She stood up, looking about for Leleth, who had wandered off. "Let us go," she called sharply. "Time to nurse wounds when we have passed through."

"Passed through where?" Deornoth asked. "How? You never told us."

"Nor need I waste my breath now," she said. "We will be there soon."

The light was fading fast and the footing was treacherous, but Geloë was an unflagging guide. She had increased the pace, waiting only long enough for the first stragglers to catch up before pushing on again.

The sky had taken on night's earliest hues when the riverbed bent again. A darker shape suddenly loomed before them, a shadow tall as the trees and blacker than the surrounding obscurity. The walkers stumbled to a halt, those who could summon the breath moaning in weariness.

Geloë took an unlit brand from her bag, handing it to Einskaldir. His sour remark died in his throat as she narrowed her yellow eyes. "Take this and put flint and steel to it," she said. "We will at least need some light where we are going."

A furlong or less from where they stood, the streambed vanished into darkness as it entered a vast hole in the hillside, an arched mouth whose dressed stones had been almost completely engulfed by a clinging blanket of moss.

Einskaldir struck with his axe head; a flint spark jumped, igniting the torch. Its growing yellow light brought forward other stones that shone pale beneath the overgrown frontage. Trees of great size and age had thrust out from the hillside above the arch, pushing aside the facing in their reach toward the sun.

"A tunnel all the way through the hill?" Deornoth gasped.

"The Old Ones were mighty builders," Geloë said, "but never better than when they built around the things earth had already grown, so that city lived together with forest or mountain."

Sangfugol coughed. "It looks . . . an abode of ghosts," he whispered.

Geloë snorted. "Even if so, they are not the dead that you should fear." She seemed about to say something else when there was a hiss and a smack. Suddenly an arrow was shivering in the trunk of a cypress near Einskaldir's head.

"*You who would flee,*" a cold voice called, echoing so that it was impossible to discern its source, "*you must surrender now. We have spared you thus far, but we may not allow you to cross through. We will destroy you all.*"

"Aedon preserve us!" Duchess Gutrun wept, her great courage finally weakening. "Save us, Lord!" She sagged down onto the wet turf.

"It is the torch!" Josua said, coming up quickly. "Put out the torch, Einskaldir."

"No," Geloë said, "you will never find your way in the dark." She raised her voice. "*Hikeda'yei,*" she cried, "do you know who I am?"

"*Yes, we know you, old woman,*" the voice said. "*But whatever respect you might deserve was lost the moment you threw in your lot with these mortals. The world could have spun on, leaving you undisturbed in your solitary house—but you would not let well enough alone. Now you also are unhomed, and must go naked like a crab with no shell. You too can die, old woman.*"

"Douse the torch, Einskaldir," Josua snapped, "we can light another when we have reached shelter."

The Rimmersman stared at the prince for a moment. Darkness had arrived: but for the torch's rippling flame, Josua would never have seen him smile.

"Don't wait too long to follow me," was all Einskaldir said. A moment later he had dashed away down the riverbed toward the great arch, the flame held high over his head. Arrow hissed past his companions as the Rimmersman, now only a leaping spot of light, swerved and dodged.

"Go! Up and run!" Josua cried. "Help the one nearest you. *Run!*"

Someone was shouting in an alien tongue—indeed, the whole forest seemed suddenly alive with noise. Deornoth reached down and caught at Sanfugol's arm, dragging the wounded harper to his feet, and together they plunged through the overhanging greenery after the dwindling spark of Einskaldir's torch.

Branches slapped at their faces and snatched at their eyes with cruel talons. Another shout of pain rang out before them and the shrill cries redoubled. Deornoth turned to look briefly over his shoulder. A swarm of pale shapes were sweeping forward over the misty ground, faces whose pitchy eyes filled him with despair, even from afar.

Something struck the side of Deornoth's head violently, staggering him. He could hear Sangfugol sobbing in pain as the harper tugged at his elbow. For a long moment it seemed to the knight that it would be easier just to lie on the ground.

"Merciful Aedon, give me rest," he heard himself praying, *"in Your arms will I sleep, upon Thy bosom I will take my peace . . ."* but Sangfugol would not stop pulling at him. Dazed, irritated, he stumbled to his feet once more and saw a scatter of stars gleaming through the treetops.

Not enough light to see under the hill, he thought, then noticed he was running again. But running or not, Deornoth thought, he and Sangfugol were moving very slowly: the dark smear on the hillside didn't seem to be getting any closer. He put his head down and watched his feet, dim, shadowy shapes slipping on the muddy streambed.

My head. I've hurt my head again . . .

The next thing Deornoth knew, he had plunged into darkness as abruptly as if someone had thrown a sack over him. He felt more hands take his elbows and help him forward. His head felt curiously light and empty.

"There's the torch, ahead," someone said nearby.

That sounds like Josua's voice, Deornoth decided. *Is he under the sack, too?*

He staggered on a few steps and saw a light glowing. He looked down, trying to make sense of it all. Einskaldir sat on the ground, leaning against a stone wall that rose and curved overhead. The Rimmersman held a torch in his hand. There was blood in his beard.

"Take this," Einskaldir said to no one in particular. "I've got . . . arrow in . . . back. Can't . . . breathe . . ." He sagged slowly forward against Josua's leg. It looked so odd that Deornoth tried to laugh, but couldn't. The empty feeling was spreading. He bent forward to help Einskaldir, but instead found himself down a deep black hole.

"Usires save us, look at Deornoth's head. . . !" someone cried. He didn't recognize the voice, and wondered who it was they were so upset about . . . Then the darkness had returned and it was hard to think. The hole that he had fallen into seemed very deep indeed.

Rachel the Dragon, the Hayholt's Mistress of Chambermaids, lifted her bundle of wet linens higher on her shoulders, trying to find the balance least trying to her aching back. It was useless, of course: there would be no ending to the pain until God the Father gathered her up to Heaven.

Rachel was feeling distinctly un-Dragonlike. The chambermaids who had given her the name long ago, when the force of Rachel's will had been all that stood between the age-old Hayholt and the tides of decay, would have been surprised to see her as she was now—a bent, complaining old woman. She was surprised herself. A chance reflection in a silver serving tray one recent morning had shown her a gaunt-faced harridan with dark-circled eyes. It had been many a long year since she had thought much about her looks, but still, this seemed a shocking transformation.

Had it been only four months since Simon died? It felt like years. That had been the day when she felt things beginning to slip away from her. She had always lorded over the Hayholt's vast household like a tyrant river-captain, but despite her young charges' whispered complaints, the work had always gotten done. Mutinous talk had never bothered Rachel much, in any case: she knew that life was but a long struggle against disorder, and that disorder was the inevitable winner. Rather than leading her to accept the futility of her role, however, this knowledge instead had whipped Rachel on to greater resistance. Her parents' fierce northern Aedonite faith had taught her that the more hopeless the struggle, the more crucial it was to struggle valiantly. But some of the life had leaked out of her when Simon died in the smoking inferno that had been Doctor Morgenes' chambers.

Not that he had been a well-behaved boy—no, far from it. Simon had been willful and disobedient, a woolgatherer and a mooncalf. He had, however, brought a certain irritating liveliness to Rachel's life. She would have even welcomed the sputtering rages into which he provoked her—if only he were still here.

In fact, it was still hard to believe he was dead. Nothing could have survived the firing of the Doctor's quarters—caused when some of Morgenes' devilish potions had caught flame, or so members of the king's Erkynguards had informed her. The fused wreckage and shattered beams made it impossible to suppose anyone in the room could have lived for more than a few moments. But she could not *feel* that he was really dead. She had been almost a mother to the boy, had she not? Raised him—with the help of her chambermaids, of course—since his first hour, when his mother had died in childbirth despite all Doctor Morgenes' attempts to save her. So shouldn't Rachel know if he was truly gone? Shouldn't she feel the final severing of the cord that had bound her to that stupid, addle-pated, gawky boy?

Oh, merciful Rhiap, she thought, *are you crying again, old woman? Your brains have gone soft as sweetmeats.*

Rachel knew of other domestics who had lost actual birth-children and still talked about them as if they were alive, so why should she feel any differently about Simon? It didn't change anything. The boy was undeniably dead, killed by his love for hanging about with that mad alchemist Morgenes, and that was that.

But things had certainly seemed to go wrong since then. A cloud had descended on her beloved Hayholt, a fog of discomfort that crept into every corner. The battle against untidiness and dirt had swung against her, becoming lately a thoroughgoing rout. All this, despite the fact that the castle seemed emptier than it had any time she could remember—at least at night. In daylight, when the clouded sun shone through the high windows and lit the gardens and commons, the Hayholt was still a riot of activity. In fact, with the Thrithings mercenaries and South Islanders now flooding in to replace the soldiers Elias had lost at Naglimund, the castle's environs were noisier than ever. Several of her girls, frightened by the scarred, tattooed Thrithings-men and their rough manners, had left the Hayholt entirely to live with country relatives. To Rachel's disgust and increasing dismay, despite the hordes of hungry mendicants roaming Erchester and camped around the walls of the Hayholt itself, it was almost impossible to replace the departing chambermaids.

But Rachel knew that it was not just the castle's wild new inhabitants that made it hard to find new girls. Crowded with brawling soldiers and disdainful nobles as it was during the light of day, by night the Hayholt seemed as uninhabited as the lich-yard beyond Erchester's walls. Echoes and strange voices floated through the corridors. Footfalls sounded where no one walked. Rachel and her remaining wards now locked themselves in at night. Rachel told them it was to keep out the drunken soldiery, but she and her chambermaids both knew that the carefully-checked door bolt and shared prayers before retiring did not come from fear of anything as easy to name as a besotted Thrithings-man.

Even stranger—although she would never, never admit it to her Blessed-Rhiap-preserve-them charges—Rachel had found herself lost a few times in recent weeks, wandering in corridors she did not recognize. Rachel herself! She who had bestrode this castle as confidently as any ruler for decades, now lost in her own home. This was either madness or the folly of age . . . or some demon's curse.

Rachel thumped down the sack of wet sheets and leaned against a wall. A trio of older priests eddied around her in their passage, talking heatedly in Nabbanai. They gave her no more of a glance than they would a dog dead in the road. She stared after them as she fought to catch her breath. To think that at her age, after all her years of service, she should be carrying around sodden bed linens like the lowliest downstairs maid! But it had to be done. Someone had to carry on the fight.

Yes, things had been going wrong ever since the day Simon died, and did not look to get better soon. She frowned and hoisted her burden once more.

Rachel had finished hanging out the wet bedding. Watching the linen flap in the late-afternoon breeze, she marveled at such cool weather. Tiyagar-month, the middle of summer, and still the days were as cold as early spring. It was certainly better than the deadly drought that had ended last year, but even so, she felt herself longing for the hot days and warm nights that were the yearly summer's-due. Her joints hurt and chill mornings only made the hurting worse. The dampness seemed to slip stealthily into her very bones.

She crossed back across the commons, wondering where her helpers had gotten to. Having a sit-down and a giggling conversation, no doubt, while the Mistress of Chambermaids labored like a yeoman. Rachel was sore, but there was enough strength still in her good right arm to sting a few girls into service!

It was too bad, she reflected as she made her way slowly around the Outer Bailey, that there wasn't somebody who could take a strong hand to this castle. Elias had seemed like the type after blessed old King John had died, but Rachel had been sorely disappointed. The apple, she thought, had fallen quite a bit farther from the tree than anyone could have guessed. But that was no surprise, really. It was just men, was what it was. Swaggering, bragging men—exactly like little boys, when you got down to it, even the grown ones acting no smarter than young mooncalf Simon had been. They didn't know how to deal with things, men didn't, and King Elias was no exception.

Take this madness with his brother. Now, Rachel had never much liked Prince Josua. He was a sight too clever and solemn for her, obviously one who thought himself pretty blessed smart. But to think that he was a traitor—well, that was just foolishness and anyone could tell it! Josua had been too bookish and high-minded for such nonsense, but what had his brother Elias done? Gone dashing off to the north with an army, and through some trick pulled down Josua's castle at Naglimund and slaughtered and burned. And why? Some damned man's pride on King Elias' part. Now a lot of Erkynlandish women were widows, the harvest was going badly, and all the Hayholt and its inhabitants were—Lord Usires pardon for her thinking it, but it was only the truth—going straight to Hell.

The back of the Nearulagh Gate loomed before her, its long shadow painting the walls on either side with darkness. Quarreling birds, kites and ravens, fought over the few remaining scraps of the ten skeletal heads fixed on pikes atop the gate.

Rachel shuddered despite herself as she made the sign of the Tree. This was something else that had changed. Never in all the long years she had kept house for King John had there been such a show of cruelty as Elias had made of these traitors. They had all been beaten and quartered in Battle Square down in Erchester, before a restive and uneasy crowd. Not that any of the executed nobles had been particularly popular—Baron Godwig, especially, was much hated for his ill-rule of Cellodshire—but everyone had sensed the wispiness of the king's accusations. Godwig and the rest had gone to their deaths like men astounded, shaking their heads and protesting their innocence until the cudgels of the Erkynguards had smashed the life out of them. Now their heads had stood above the Nearulagh Gate for a full two weeks while the carrion birds, like clever little sculptors, slowly brought the skulls to the surface. Few of those who passed beneath them stared for long. Most who looked up turned away quickly, as if they had glimpsed something forbidden instead of the abject public lesson the king desired.

Traitors, the king called them, and as traitors they had died. Rachel thought they would be little missed, but still their deaths brought the fog of despair down a bit closer.

As Rachel hurried past with eyes averted, she was almost knocked down by a young squire sloshing through the muddy road leading a horse. After she had scrambled to a position of safety against the outer wall, Rachel turned to see the riders pass.

They were all soldiers—all but one. Where the armored men wore the green tunics of the king's Erkynguard, the other wore a robe of flaming scarlet, a black traveling cloak, and tall black boots.

Pryrates! Rachel stiffened. Where was that devil going with his honor guard of soldiers?

The priest seemed to float above his companions. As the soldiers laughed and talked, Pryrates looked neither right or left, his hairless head rigid as a spearpoint, his black eyes fixed on the gate before him.

Things had truly begun to go wrong when the red priest arrived—as if Pryrates himself had put an evil spell on the Hayholt. Rachel had even wondered for a while if Pryrates, whom she knew had not liked Morgenes, might have burned down the doctor's rooms. Could a man of Mother Church do such a thing? Could he kill innocent people—like her Simon— for a grudge? But the rumors did say that the priest's father was a demon, his mother a witch. Rachel made the sign of the Tree again, watching his proud back as the party ambled past.

Could one man bring evil down on everyone, she wondered? And why?

Just to be doing the devil's work? She looked around carefully, embarrassed, then spat in the mud to ward evil. What did it matter? There was nothing an old woman like her could do, was there?

She watched Pryrates and the company of soldiers ride out through the Nearulagh Gate, then turned and began trudging toward the residences, thinking about curses and cold weather.

The late afternoon sun slanted in through the trees, making the thin leaves glow. The forest mist had finally burned away. A few birds trilled in the treetops. Deornoth, feeling the pain in his head diminishing, stood up.

The wise woman Geloë had nursed Einskaldir's terrible wounds all morning before leaving him at last to the ministrations of Duchess Gutrun and Isorn. The Rimmersman, feverish and raving while Geloë had applied poultices to the arrow-spites in his back and side, now lay quietly. She could not say if he would live.

Geloë had labored the rest of the afternoon on the other members of the company, treating Sangfugol's festering leg wound and the many injuries the rest of the party had suffered as well. Her knowledge of healing herbs was wide and her pockets were well-stuffed with useful things. She seemed certain that all except for the Rimmersman would be quickly improved.

The forest on this side of the hill-tunnel was not much different from that which they had just left, Deornoth thought—at least in looks. The oaks and elders grew close here, too, and the ground was powdery with the remains of long-dead trees, but there was something different in the heart of it, some faint grace or inner liveliness, as if the air were lighter or the sun shone more warmly. Of course, Deornoth realized, it might only be that he and the others in Prince Josua's party had lived another day longer than they had expected.

Geloë was sitting on a log with Prince Josua. Deornoth started to approach, then hesitated, unsure of his welcome. Josua smiled wearily and waved him over.

"Come, Deornoth, sit down. How is your head?"

"Sore, Highness."

"It was a cruel blow," Josua said, nodding.

Geloë looked up and briefly surveyed Deornoth. Earlier she had scanned the bloody wound in Deornoth's scalp where the tree limb had struck him, then pronounced it "not serious."

"Deornoth is my right hand," Josua told her. "It is good that he should hear all this, against the chance anything should happen to me."

Geloë shrugged. "Nothing I will speak of is a secret. At least, not the kind we should keep from each other." She turned for a moment to watch Leleth. The child sat quietly in Vorzheva's lap, but her eyes were fixed on nothing visible, and no words or caresses from Vorzheva could arouse her attention.

"Where do you think to go, Prince Josua?" Geloë said at last. "You have escaped the vengeance of the Norns, at least for a while. Where will you go?"

The prince frowned. "I have not thought of anything but winning our way to safety. I suppose if this—" he waved his hand at the forest clearing, "is a place of refuge against the demons, as you say it is, we should stay here."

The witch woman shook her head. "Of course, we must stay until all are well enough to walk. But then?"

"I have no idea yet." Josua looked at Deornoth, as if hoping for some suggestion. "My brother stands victorious over all the lands of the High King's Ward. I cannot think of who would hide me under peril of Elias' anger." He slapped his left hand against the stump of his right. "All our chances seem to have come to nothing. It was a poor game."

"I did not ask the question innocently," Geloë said, rearranging her seat upon the log. She wore boots as a man did, Deornoth saw, and well-traveled boots at that. "Let me tell you of some important things and you will be better able to see the possibilities. First of all, before Naglimund fell, you sent out a party in search of something, did you not?"

Josua narrowed his eyes. "How could you know?"

Geloë shook her head impatiently. "I told you when we met that I knew both Morgenes and Binabik of Yiqanuc. I also knew Jarnauga of Tungoldyr. We were in communication while he was at your castle and he told me much."

"Poor Jarnauga," Josua said. "He died bravely."

"Many of the wise have died; there are few left," she answered him. "And bravery is by no means the province only of soldiers and nobles. But since the circle of the wise is growing smaller with each such death, it has become more than ever important that we share knowledge among ourselves and with others. So it was that Jarnauga passed on to me all that he did after reaching Naglimund from his home in the north. Ah!" She sat up. "I am reminded of something." She raised her voice. "Father Strangyeard!"

The priest looked up at her call, uncertain. She gestured for him to come and he rose from the harper Sangfugol's side and approached.

"Jarnauga thought highly of you," Geloë said. A smile crossed her weathered features. "Did he give you anything before he left you?"

Strangyeard nodded. He produced a glittering pendant from beneath his cassock. "This," he said quietly.

"I thought so. Well, you and I shall speak of it later, but as a member of the League of the Scroll, you should certainly be part of our councils."

"A member . . ." Strangyeard seemed astonished. "Me? Of the League. . . ?"

Geloë smiled again. "Certainly. Knowing Jarnauga, I'm sure it was a careful choice. But as I said, we shall talk more of this later, you and I." She turned back to the prince and Deornoth. "You see, I know about the search for the Great Swords. I do not know if Binabik and the others have succeeded in their search for Camaris' blade Thorn, but I *can* tell you that as of a day or so ago, the troll and the boy Simon were both still alive."

"Aedon be praised," Josua breathed, "that is good news! Good news in a time that has been short of it. My heart has been heavy for them ever since they set out. Where are they?"

"I believe they are in Yiqanuc among the trolls. It is hard to explain quickly, so I will say only this: my contact with young Simon was brief and did not allow much discussion. Also, I had a message to give to them that was most important."

"And what was that?" Deornoth asked. As pleased as he had been at the witch woman's arrival, he now found himself a little resentful at how she had stolen the initiative away from Prince Josua. It was a foolish and presumptuous worry, but he wanted very much to see the prince leading in the way that Deornoth knew he could.

"The message I gave Simon I will also give to you," Geloë responded, "but there are other things we must speak of first." She turned to Strangyeard. "What have you found of the other two swords?"

The priest cleared his throat. "Well," he began, "we . . . we know altogether too well the whereabouts of Sorrow. King Elias wears it—a gift from the Storm King, if stories we heard are true—and it goes with him everywhere. Thorn, we think, is somewhere in the north; if the troll and the others still live, I suppose there is hope they may find it. The last one, Minneyar, once King Fingil's sword—but dear me, you must have known that, of course—well, Minneyar seems never to have left the Hayholt. So two . . . two . . ."

"Two of the swords are in my brother's hands," Josua finished, "and the third is being sought in the trackless north by a troll and a young boy." He smiled worriedly, shaking his head. "As I said before, it is a poor game."

Geloë fixed him with her fierce yellow eyes and spoke sharply. "But a game, Prince Josua, in which surrender is not an alternative, a game which we must play with the pieces we have drawn. The stakes are very large indeed."

The prince sat up straighter, raising his hand to silence Deornoth's angry response. "Your words are well-spoken, Valada Geloë. This is the only game we can play. We dare not lose. So, is there more you would tell us?"

"Much you know already, or can guess. Hernystir in the west is fallen, King Lluth dead and his people taken to the hills. By treachery, Nabban is now the dukedom of Elias' ally Benigaris. Skali of Kaldskryke rules Rimmersgard in Isgrimnur's stead. Now Naglimund is cast down and the Norns haunt it like ghosts." As she spoke she took her walking stick and drew a map in the dirt before them, marking each place as she spoke of it. "Aldheorte Forest is free, but it is not a place for men to come together in resistance, except perhaps in the last hope, when all else is denied them."

"And what is this, if not the last hope?" Josua said. "This is my kingdom, Geloë, as you see it, all gathered here within a stone's throw. We may hide, but how could we challenge Elias with so few, let alone his ally the Storm King?"

"Ah, now we come to what I said should be saved for later," Geloë answered, "and also where we speak of matters stranger than human wars." Her gnarled brown hands moved quickly, sketching once more on the ground beside her boots. "Why are we safe in this part of the forest? Because it is under the ward of the Sithi, and the Norns dare not attack them. A fragile peace has stood for countless years between the two families. Even the soulless Storm King, I should think, is in no hurry to rouse the remaining Sithi to action."

"They are *families?*" Deornoth asked. Geloë turned her fierce stare upon him.

"Did you not listen to what Jarnauga told you at Naglimund?" she demanded. "What use is there in the wise giving up their lives if those for whom they sacrifice do not listen?"

"Jarnauga told us that Ineluki—the Storm King—was once a prince of the Sithi," Strangyeard said hurriedly, flapping his hands as if to fan away strife. "That we knew."

"The Norns and Sithi were for eons one people," Geloë said. "When they went their separate ways, they divided Osten Ard between them and promised they would not cross over into each other's fields without warrant."

"And what use is this knowledge to we poor mortals?" Deornoth asked.

Geloë waved her hand. "We are safe here because the Norns tread carefully along the borders of the Sithi lands. Also, even in these diminished days there is a power in such places that would make them hesitate in any case." She looked fixedly at Deornoth. "You have felt it, have you not? But the problem is that we ten or eleven are not enough to fight back. We must find some place safe from the Norns, but also a place where the others who resent your brother Elias' misrule can find us. If King Elias tightens his control over Osten Ard, if the Hayholt becomes an unbreachable stronghold, then we will never pry loose the Great Sword we know he has, or the other that he may have. We do not fight sorcery only, but also a war of position and placement."

"What are you saying?" Josua asked, his eyes intent on the witch woman's face.

Geloë pointed at the map with her walking stick. "Out here, beyond the forest to the east, run the meadows of the High Thrithings. There, near the site upon which the ancient city of Enki-e-Shao'saye once stood, along the border between woods and grassland, is the place where Norns and Sithi parted ways forever. It is called Sesuad'ra—the Stone of Farewell."

"And . . . and we would be safe there?" Strangyeard asked, excited.

"For a time," Geloë responded. "It is a place of power, so its heritage may keep us safe from the Storm King's minions for a short while. But that is good enough, for time is what we need most—time to gather those who would fight back against Elias, time to bring our scattered allies together. But most importantly, we need time to solve the mystery of the three Great Swords and find a way to fight the menace of the Storm King."

Josua sat and stared at the line-scratched dirt. "It is a beginning," he said at last. "Against all despair, it is a small flame of hope."

"That is why I came to you," the witch woman said. "And that is why I told the boy Simon to come there when he could, bringing any who were with him."

Father Strangyeard coughed apologetically. "I'm afraid I do not understand, Goodwoman Geloë. How did you speak to the boy? If he is in the distant north, you would not have been able to get here in time. Did you use messenger birds, as Jarnauga often did?"

She shook her head. "No. I spoke to him through the girl, Leleth. It is hard to explain, but she helped make me stronger so I could reach out all the way to Yiqanuc and tell Simon of the Stone of Farewell." She began scratching away her map with the toe of her boot. "Not smart to leave a message showing where we're bound," she said and chuckled hoarsely.

"But could you reach out to speak with anyone this way?" Josua asked keenly.

Geloë shook her head. "I have met Simon and touched him. He was in my house. I do not think I could find and converse with someone I did not already know."

"But my niece Miriamele was at your house, or so I was told," the prince said eagerly. "I have been deeply worried about her. Could you find her for me, speak to her?"

"I have already tried." The witch woman got up, looking again to Leleth. The little girl was walking aimlessly along the rim of the clearing, pale lips moving as though in silent song. "There is something or someone close to Miriamele that prevented my reaching her—a wall of some kind. I had very little strength and my time was short, so I did not try twice."

"Will you try again?" Josua asked.

"Perhaps," she said, turning to look at him once more. "But I must use my strength carefully. There is a long struggle before us." She turned to Father Strangyeard. "Now, priest, come with me. There are things we must speak about. You have been given a responsibility that may prove a heavy burden."

"I know," Strangyeard answered quietly. The two of them moved away, leaving Josua deep in thought. Deornoth watched his prince for some long moments, then wandered back to his cloak.

Towser, lying nearby, was tossing and babbling in the throes of a nightmare. "White faces . . . hands reaching for me, hands . . ." The old man's clawed fingers raked at the air, and for a moment the noise of birdsong was stilled.

". . . So," Josua finished, "there is a gleam of hope. If Valada Geloë thinks we can find sanctuary in this place . . ."

"—And strike a blow at the king," Isorn growled, his pink face scowling.

". . . Yes, and prepare to resume the struggle," Josua continued, "then we must do so. There is nowhere else for us to go, in any case. When all can walk, we will leave the forest and cross the High Thrithings, heading east to the Stone of Farewell."

Vorzheva, pale with anger, opened her mouth as if to say something, but Duchess Gutrun spoke up instead. "Why leave the forest at all, Prince Josua? Why should we go a longer way just to expose ourselves on the plains?"

Geloë, sitting beside the prince, nodded. "You ask a good question. One reason is that we can move twice as quickly across open land and time is precious. Also, we must leave the forest because the same ban that keeps the Norns at a distance serves for us as well. These are Sithi lands. We have come here because we have been driven here in peril of our lives, but to stay long would be to invite their notice. The Sithi do not love mortals."

"But won't the Norns pursue us?"

"I know ways through the forest that will keep us safe until we reach the meadowlands beyond," the witch woman responded. "As to the High Thrithings, I doubt the Norns are already so cocksure that they will cross over in light of day to open country. They are deadly, but still far, far fewer than humans. The Storm King has waited centuries; I think he is patient enough to keep his full power hidden from mortals a little longer. No, it is likely Elias' armies and the Thrithings-men we need to worry about." She turned to Josua. "You know better than I, perhaps. Do the Thrithings-dwellers now serve Elias?"

The prince shook his head. "They are never predictable. Many clans live there and their allegiance even to their own March-thanes is loose. Besides, if we do not venture far from the forest's edge, we may never see another soul. The Thrithings are vast."

As he finished speaking, Vorzheva rose and stalked away, disappearing from the clearing into a stand of birches. Josua watched her go, then a moment later stood, leaving Geloë to answer the questions of those who had not heard her earlier explanation of Sesuad'ra.

Vorzheva was leaning against a birch trunk, angrily peeling away strips of papery bark. Josua paused for a long moment, watching her. Her gown was a tattered rag, torn away to just above her knees. Her underslip had also been shredded for bandages. Like everyone else she was dirty, her thick black hair full of twigs and tangles, her arms and legs crisscrossed with scratches. The arrow-wound on her forearm was wrapped in a soiled and bloody rag.

"Why are you angry?" he asked. His voice was soft.

Vorzheva whirled, eyes wide. "Why am I angry? *Why?* You are a fool!"

"You have avoided me since we were cast out of Naglimund," Josua said, taking a step nearer. "When I lie down beside you, you stiffen like a priest with the stench of sin in his nostrils. Is this the way a lover acts?"

Vorzheva raised her hand as though to slap at him, but he was too far away. *"Love?"* she choked, her accent changing the word into something heavy and painful. "Who are you, saying love to me? I have lost all for you and you say this?" She rubbed at her face with her hand, leaving a dark smear.

"The lives of all are in my hands," the prince said slowly. "And on my soul. Men, women, children, hundreds dead in the ruins of Naglimund. Perhaps I have been distant since the castle fell, but it was because of the darkness of my thoughts, the ghosts who haunt me."

"Since the castle fell, you say," she hissed. "Since the castle fell, you have treated me like a whore. You do not speak to me, you speak to all others but me, then at night you come to touch me and hold me! Do you think you bought me at market like a horse? I came away with you to be free of the plains-lands . . . and to love you. You never treated me well. Now you will drag me back—drag me back and show my shame to everyone!" She burst into angry tears and quickly moved to the other side of the tree, so that the prince could not see her face.

Josua looked puzzled. "What do you mean? Show your shame to whom?"

"To my people, you fool!" Vorzheva cried. Her voice echoed dully through the copse. "To my people!"

"To the Thrithings-people . . ." Josua said slowly. "Of course."

She came around the tree like an angry spirit, eyes bright. "I will not go. You take your little kingdom and walk where you will, but I will not return to my homeland in shame, like . . . like *this!*" She gestured furiously at her raggedness.

Josua smiled sourly. "This is foolish. Look at me, the son of High King

Prester John! I am a scarecrow! What does it matter? I doubt we shall see any of your people, but even if we did, what does it matter? Are you so stiff-necked that you would rather die in the forest than have a few of your wagon-folk see you in tatters?"

"Yes!" she shouted. "Yes! You think I am a fool! You are right! I left my home for you and fled my father's lands. Should I come back to them like a whipped dog? I would die a thousand times before that! Everything else has been taken from me, would you see me crawl, too?" She dropped to the ground, her white knees sinking into the loam. "Then I will beg you. Do not go to the High Thrithings. Or if you do, leave me enough food to live for a while and I will walk to this place through the forest."

"This is madness of the worst sort," Josua growled. "Did you not hear what Geloë said? If the Sithi do not kill you as a trespasser, the Norns will catch you and do worse."

"Then kill me." She reached up to snatch at Naidel, sheathed on Josua's belt. "I will die before I go back to the Thrithings."

Josua grabbed her wrist and pulled her upright. She squirmed in his grip, kicking at his shins with feet clad in muddy, threadbare slippers. "You are a child," he said angrily, then leaned away as her free hand struck at his face. "A child with claws." He pulled her around so her back was to him, then pushed her stumbling ahead of him until they reached a fallen tree. He sat, pulling her down with him so that she was caught in his lap, his arms wrapped around hers, pinioning them at her side.

"If you will act like a willful girl, I will treat you like one," he said through clenched teeth. He swayed backward, avoiding the flailing sweep of her head as she struggled.

"I hate you!" she panted.

"At this moment, I hate you, too," he said, squeezing harder, "—but that may pass."

At last her writhing slowed until she sagged in his arms, exhausted. "You are stronger," she moaned, "but you must sleep sometime. Then I will kill you and kill myself."

Josua, too, was breathing heavily. Vorzheva was not a weak woman and the prince having but one hand did not make the struggle any easier for him. "There are too few of us left for any killing," he muttered. "But I will sit here and hold you until it is time to walk again, if necessary. We *will* go to this Sesuad'ra, and we will all reach there alive if I have any power to make it so."

Vorzheva again tried to pull free, but gave up quickly when it became obvious Josua had not relaxed his grip. She sat quietly for some time, her breathing gradually slowing, the trembling of her limbs abating.

The shadows grew longer. A lone cricket, anticipating the evening, began its creaking recitation. "If you only loved me," she said at last, staring out at the darkening forest, "I would not need to kill anyone."

"I am tired of talking, Lady," the prince said.

Princess Miriamele and her pair of religious companions left the Coast Road in late morning, riding down into the Commeis Valley, the gateway to the city of Nabban. As they followed the steep switchbacks down the face of the hill, Miriamele found it hard to watch the road beneath her horse's hooves. It had been a long time since she had seen the real face of Nabban, her mother's homeland, and the temptation to gawk was very strong. Here the farmlands began to give way to the sprawl of the once-imperial city. The valley floor was crowded with settlements and towns; even the steep Commeian hills were encrusted with houses of whitewashed stone that jutted from the hillsides like teeth.

The smoke of countless fires rose up from the valley floor, a grayish cloud hanging overhead like an awning. Most days, Miriamele knew, the winds from the sea swept the blue sky clear, but today the breezes were absent.

"So many people," she marveled. "And more in the city itself."

"But in some ways," Father Dinivan remarked, "that means little. Erchester is less than a fifth this size, but the Hayholt there is the capital of the known world. Nabban's glory is only a memory—except for Mother Church, of course. Nabban is her city now."

"Is it not interesting, then, how those who slew our Lord Usires now clasp Him to their bosom?" Cadrach said, a little farther down the trail. "One always makes more friends after one is dead."

"I do not understand your meaning, Cadrach," Dinivan said, his homely face solemn, "but it sounds like bitterness rather than insight."

"Does it?" said Cadrach. "I speak of the usefulness of heroes who are not present to speak for themselves." He scowled. "Lord love me, I wish I had some wine." He turned away from Dinivan's questioning glance, offering no further remarks.

The plumes of smoke reminded Miriamele of something. "How many of those Fire Dancers we saw in Teligure are there? Are they in every town?"

Dinivan shook his head. "There are some few that come from every town, I would guess, but they join together and travel from place to place, preaching their vile message. It is not their numbers that should frighten you, but the despair they carry with them like a plague. For every one who joins and follows them to the next town, there are a dozen more who take the message into their secret hearts, losing faith in God."

"People believe in what they see," Cadrach said, eyes suddenly intent on Dinivan. "They hear the Storm King's message and see what the Storm King's hand can inspire. They wait for God to strike down the heretics. But God does nothing."

"That is a lie, Padreic," Dinivan said hotly. "Or Cadrach, or whatever

name you now choose. For choosing is what matters. God allows each
man or woman to choose. He does not compel love.''

The monk snorted as if in disgust, but continued to stare at the priest.
"That He certainly does not."

In a strange way, Miriamele thought, Cadrach seemed to be pleading
with Dinivan, as though trying to show the lector's secretary something
that Dinivan would not recognize.

"God wishes . . ." the priest began.

"But if God does not cajole, and does not force, and does not respond
to challenges from the Storm King or anyone else," Cadrach interrupted,
his voice hoarse with suppressed emotion, "why, *why* do you find it
surprising that people think there is no God, or that He is helpless?"

Dinivan stared for a moment, then shook his head angrily. "That is
why Mother Church exists. To give out God's word, so that people may
decide."

"People believe what they see," Cadrach replied sadly, then dropped
back into silent thought as they plodded slowly down toward the valley
floor.

At midday they reached the crowded Anitullean Road. Streams of
people moved in each direction, eddying around wagons going to and
from market. Miriamele and her companions attracted little attention. By
sundown they had covered a great distance up the valley.

They stopped for the evening in Bellidan, one of the score of towns that
had grown together along the road until it was nearly impossible to tell
where one left off and the next began. They slept at the local priory,
where Dinivan's lectoral signet ring and exalted status made them the
center of a great deal of interest. Miriamele slipped off early to the small
cell provided for her, not wanting to take the chance of her disguise being
compromised. Dinivan explained to the monks that his companion was ill,
then brought her a satisfying meal of barley soup and bread. When she
blew out the candle to sleep, the image of the Fire Dancer was again
before her eyes, the white-robed woman bursting into flame, but here
behind the priory's thick walls it did not seem quite so frightening. It had
been just another unsettling occurrence in an unsettling world.

By late afternoon of the following day they had reached the spot where
the Anitullean Road began to climb upward through the hill passes that
led to Nabban proper. They passed dozens of pilgrims and merchants who
sat exhausted by the roadside, fanning themselves with wide-brimmed
hats. Some had merely stopped to rest and drink water, but several others
were frustrated peddlers whose donkeys had proved reluctant to pull
overloaded wagons up the steep road.

"If we stop before dark," Dinivan said, "we can stay the night in one of the hill towns. Then it would be a short ride into the city in the morning. For some reason, though, I am reluctant to take any longer than necessary. If we ride past nightfall, we can reach the Sancellan Aedonitis before midnight."

Miriamele looked back down the road, then ahead, where it wound out of sight among the dry golden hills. "I wouldn't mind stopping," she said. "I'm more than a little sore."

Dinivan looked worried. "I understand. I am less used to riding than you are, Princess, and my rump is smarting, too." He blushed and laughed. "Your pardon, Lady. But I feel that the sooner we reach the lector, the better."

Miriamele looked to Cadrach to see if he had something to add, but the monk was deep in his own private thoughts, swaying from side to side as his horse plodded uphill. "If you think there is any advantage in it at all," she said at last, "then let us ride the night through if necessary. Truthfully, though, I can't think what I might tell the lector—or that he might tell me—that would be spoiled if it waits another day."

"There are many things changing, Miriamele," Dinivan replied, lowering his voice, though the road in this spot was empty but for a farm-wagon creaking along half a furlong up the road. "In times like these, when all is uncertain and many dangers are still not completely known, a chance for speed not taken is often regretted later. This much wisdom I have. With your permission, I will trust in it."

They rode all through the darkening evening and did not stop when the stars began to appear above the hills. The road wound through the passes and then down, past more towns and settlements, until at last they reached the outskirts of the great city, lit with so many lamps that it outshone the sky.

The streets of Nabban were crowded, even as midnight approached. Torches burned on every corner. Jugglers and dancers performed in pools of flickering light, hoping for a coin or two from drunken passersby. The taverns, their window shutters up on a cool summer night, spilled lantern light and noise out into the cobbled streets.

Miriamele was nodding with weariness as they left the Anitullean Road and followed the track of the Way of the Fountains up the Sancelline Hill. The Sancellan Aedonitis loomed before them. Its famous spire was only a slender thread of gold in the lamplight, but a hundred windows glowed with warm light.

"Someone is always awake in God's house," Dinivan said quietly.

As they climbed through the narrow streets, heading for the great square, Miriamele could see the pale, curving shapes of the Sancellan Mahistrevis' towers just beyond the Sancellan Aedonitis to the west. The ducal castle sat on the rocky promontory at Nabban's outermost point, commanding the sea view as Nabban itself had once commanded the lands of men.

The two Sancellans, Miriamele thought, *one built to rule the body, the other to rule the soul. Well, the Sancellan Mahistrevis has fallen already to that father-murderer Benigaris, but the lector is a godly man—a good one, too, Dinivan says, and Dinivan is no fool. At least there is hope there.*

A seagull keened somewhere in the darkness above. She felt a pang of regret. If her mother had never married Elias, then Miriamele could have grown up and lived here, above the ocean. This would have been her home. She would be coming back to a place she belonged.

But if my mother had never married my father, she thought sleepily, *I wouldn't be me anyway. Stupid girl.*

Their arrival at the doors of the lectoral palace was a confusing blur for Miriamele, who was finding it difficult to stay awake. Several people greeted Dinivan warmly—he seemed to have many friends—and the next thing she knew, she was being shown to a room with a warm, soft bed. She did not bother to take off anything but her boots, crawling beneath the blanket while still wrapped in her hooded cloak. Hushed voices spoke in the corridor outside her room, then a little later she heard the Clavean bell tolling far above her, striking more times than she could count.

She fell asleep to the sound of distant singing.

Father Dinivan woke her in the morning with berries and milk and bread. She ate sitting up in bed while the priest lit the candles and paced back and forth across the windownless room.

"His Sacredness was up early this morning. He was gone before I got to his chambers, out walking somewhere. He often does that when he has something to think about. Just takes to the corridors in his night robe. He doesn't take anyone with him—except me, if I'm around." Dinivan flashed a boyish smile. "This place is nearly as big as the Hayholt. He could be anywhere."

Miriamele dabbed milk from her chin with a flapping sleeve. "Will he see us?"

"Of course. As soon as he comes back, I'm sure. I wonder what he thinks about. Ranessin is a deep man, deep as the sea, and like the sea, it is often difficult to tell what hides beneath a placid surface."

Miriamele shuddered, thinking of the kilpa in the Bay of Emettin. She put her bowl down. "Shall I wear men's clothes?" she asked.

"What?" Dinivan stopped, surprised by her question. "Oh. To meet the lector, you mean. I don't think anyone should know yet that you are here. I would like to say that I trust my fellow priests with my life, and I suppose I do, but I have lived and worked here too long to trust tongues not to wag. I did bring you some cleaner robes." He gestured to a bundle of garments lying on a stool, beside a basin of water that steamed faintly.

"So if you are ready and have finished breaking your fast, let us be off." He stood, waiting expectantly.

Miriamele stared at the clothes for a moment, then back at Father Dinivan, whose face wore a distracted half-frown. "Could you turn around," she asked at last, "so I can change?"

Father Dinivan gaped for a moment, then blushed furiously, much to Miriamele's secret amusement. "Princess, forgive me! How could I be so discourteous? Forgive me, I will leave at once. I will be back for you soon. My apologies. I am thinking of so many other things this morning." He backed out of the room, closing the door carefully behind him.

When he was gone, Miriamele laughed and rose from bed. She shucked the old robes over her head and washed herself, shivering, noting with more interest than dismay how sun-browned her hands and wrists had become. They were like a barge-man's hands, she thought with some satisfaction. How her ladies-in-waiting would wince if they could see her!

The water was warm, but the chamber itself was cold, so when she finished she hurriedly pulled on the clean clothes. Running her hands through her short-cropped hair, she considered washing it, too, but decided against it, thinking of the drafty corridors. The cold reminded her of young Simon, walking somewhere in the chilly north. In an impulsive moment she had given him her favorite blue scarf, a favor that now seemed pitifully inadequate. Still, she had meant it well. It was too thin to keep him warm, but perhaps it would help him remember the frightening journey they had survived together. Perhaps he would take heart.

She found Dinivan in the hall outside, trying his best to look patient. Back in his familiar home, the priest seemed like a war-horse awaiting battle, full of trembling need to go, to do. He took her elbow and led her gently down the corridor.

"Where is Cadrach?" she asked. "Is he going with us to see the lector?"

Dinivan shook his head. "I am not sure of him anymore. I said that I think there is no great harm in him, but I also think he is a man who has given in to many weaknesses. That is sad, because the man he once was would have been valuable counsel indeed. Still, I thought it best to expose him to no temptations. He is having a pleasant meal with some of my brother priests. He will be quietly and discreetly watched."

"What *was* Cadrach?" she asked, craning her head to stare at the ceiling-high tapestries that lined the corridor, scenes of Aedon's Elevation, the Renunciation of Saint Vilderivis, the chastising of Imperator Crexis. She thought of these frozen figures, eyes wide and white-rimmed, and of all the centuries they had hung here while the world spun on. Would her uncle and father someday be the subjects of murals and tapestries, long after she and all she knew were dust?

"Cadrach? He was a holy man, once, and not just in dress." Dinivan appeared to consider for a moment before speaking again. "We will speak

of your companion another time, Princess, if you will pardon my rudeness. Now you might be thinking of what things you would tell the
lector."

"What does he want to know?"

"Everything." Dinivan smiled, the harried edge to his voice softening.
"The lector wishes to know everything about everything. He says it is
because the weight and responsibility of Mother Church are upon his
shoulders and his decisions must be informed ones—but I think that he is
also a very curious fellow." He laughed. "He knows more about book-
keeping than most of the Writing-Priests in the Sancellan chancelry, and I
have heard him talk for hours about milking with a Lakelands farmer."
Dinivan's expression became more serious. "But these are truly grave
times. As I said before, some of my sources of knowledge cannot be
revealed even to the lector, so your words and the witness of your own
eyes will be of great help in telling him things he must know. You need
fear to tell him nothing. Ranessin is a wise man. He knows more of what
spins the world than anyone else I know."

To Miriamele, the walk though the dark corridors of the Sancellan
Aedonitis seemed to take an hour. But for the tapestries and the occasional
flock of priests hurrying by, each corridor seemed identical to the last, so
that before long she was hopelessly lost. The great stone hallways were
also damp and poorly-lit. When they at last reached a large wooden door,
delicately carved with a spreading Tree, she was grateful that their journey
had ended.

Dinivan, about to push the door open, stopped. "We should continue to
exercise caution," he said, leading her to a smaller door a few ells down
the corridor. He pushed this open and they went through into a small
chamber hung with velvet cloth. A fire burned in a brazier against the
wall. The wide table that filled much of the room was scattered with
parchments and heavy books. The priest left Miriamele to warm her hands
before the flames.

"I will return in a moment," he said, pushing aside a curtain in the wall
beside the table. When the curtain fell back, he was gone.

When her fingers were tingling satisfactorily, she left the brazier to
examine some of the parchments lying unrolled on the table. They seemed
quite uninteresting, full of numbers and descriptions of property boundaries. The books were uniformly religious, except for one strange volume
full of woodcuts of strange creatures and unfathomable ceremonies that
lay open atop the rest. As she flipped carefully through the pages, she
found one that had been marked with a ribbon of cloth. It was a crude
illustration of an antlered man with staring eyes and black hands. Terrified
people huddled at the horned one's feet; above his head, a single dazzling
star hung in a black sky. The eyes seemed to stare out of the page and
directly into her own.

Sa Asdridan Condiquilles, she read from the caption below the picture. The Conqueror Star.

A fit of shivering came over her. The picture chilled her in a way that the Sancellan's dank corridors never could. It seemed something she had seen in a nightmare, or a story told her in childhood whose evil she only now recognized. Miriamele hastily restored the book to its original position and moved away, rubbing her fingers up and down her cloak as though she had touched something unclean.

Soft voices were coming from behind the arras through which Dinivan had disappeared. She moved closer, straining to make out the words, but they were too faint. She cautiously pulled the hanging aside to expose a sliver of light from the room beyond.

It seemed to be the lector's audience room, for it was ornate beyond anything she had seen since the entry chamber which she had sleepily traversed the night before. The ceilings were high, painted with hundreds of scenes from the Book of the Aedon. The windows were slices from the gray morning sky. Behind a chair at the room's center hung a great azure banner embroidered with the Pillar and Tree of Mother Church.

Lector Ranessin, a slender man in a tall hat, was sitting on the chair listening to a fat man who wore the tentlike golden robes of an escritor. Dinivan stood to one side, scuffing his foot back and forth impatiently in the deep carpet.

". . . But that is the point, Your Sacredness," the fat one said, his face shiny, his tone beautifully measured. "Of all times to avoid offending the High King . . . well, he is not in the most receptive mood just now. We must think carefully of our lofty position, as well as the welfare of all who look to Mother Church for moderation and good influence." He pulled a small box from his sleeve and popped something into his mouth. His round cheeks flattened briefly as he sucked at it.

"I understand, Velligis," the lector responded, raising his hand with a gentle smile. "Your counsel is always good. I am eternally grateful that God brought us together."

Velligis tilted his round head in a bow of acknowledgment.

"Now, if you will be so good," Ranessin continued, "I really should give some time to poor Dinivan here. He has been riding for days and I am anxious for his news."

The escritor dropped to his knees—not an easy feat for a man his size—and kissed the hem of the lector's blue robe. "If you need me for anything, Your Sacredness, I will be in the chancelry until afternoon." He rose and left the room in a graceful waddle, prying another sugar-sweet from his box.

"Are you truly grateful God brought you together?" Dinivan asked with a smile.

The lector nodded. "Indeed. Velligis is a living reminder to me of why men should not take themselves seriously. He means well, but he is so blessedly pompous."

Dinivan shook his head. "I am willing to believe he means well, but his advice is criminal. If there is ever a time when Mother Church must show herself a living force for good, this is the time."

"I know your feelings, Dinivan," the lector said gently. "But this is not a time in which decisions may be hastily made, lest they be repented later at tragic length. Did you bring the princess?"

Ranessin's secretary nodded. "I'll fetch her. I left her in my workroom." He turned and headed across the Audience Chamber. Miriamele hurriedly dropped the hanging back into place; when Dinivan came through, she was standing before the brazier once more.

"Come with me," he said. "The lector is free now."

When she reached the chair, Miriamele curtseyed, then kissed Ranessin's hem. The old man reached down a surprisingly strong hand and helped her to her feet.

"Please, sit beside me," he said as he gestured for Dinivan to bring her a chair. "On second thought," he told his secretary, "fetch one for yourself as well."

While Dinivan was getting the chairs, Miriamele had her first chance to look at the lector. She had not seen him for over a year, but he seemed little different. His thin gray hair hung down beside his pale, handsome face. His eyes were as alert as a child's, with an air almost of hidden mischief. Miriamele could not help comparing him to Count Streáwe, the lord of Perdruin. Streáwe's lined face had been suffused with cunning. Ranessin looked much more innocent, but Miriamele did not need Dinivan's assurances to believe that a great deal went on behind the lector's gentle exterior.

"Well, my dear princess," Ranessin said when they had seated themselves, "I have not seen you since your grandfather's funeral. My, you have grown—but what odd clothes you wear, my lady." He smiled. "Welcome to God's house. Do you lack for anything?"

"Not in the way of food or drink, Your Sacredness."

Ranessin frowned. "I am not a lover of titles, and mine is particularly awkward upon the tongue. When I was a young man in Stanshire, I never dreamed I would end out my life in far Nabban, being called 'Sacred' and 'Exalted' and never hearing my birth name again."

"Isn't Ranessin your real name?" Miriamele asked.

The lector laughed. "Oh, no. I was born an Erkynlander, hight Oswine. But since Erkynlanders are seldom elevated to such heights, it seemed politic to take a Nabbanai name." He reached out to pat softly at her hand. "Now, speaking of assumed names, Dinivan tells me you have traveled far and seen much since you left your father's house. Will you tell me something of your journeys?"

Dinivan nodded encouragingly, so Miriamele took a deep breath and began to talk.

As the lector listened attentively, she spoke of her father's growing madness and how it had at last driven her from the Hayholt, of the evil counsels of Pryrates, and of the imprisoning of Josua. Brighter sunlight began to creep in through the windows high overhead. Dinivan got up to have someone bring them some food, as the noon hour was fast approaching.

"This is fascinating," the lector said as they waited for his secretary to return. "It confirms many rumors that I have heard." He rubbed his finger along the side of his thin nose. "Lord Usires grant us wisdom. Why can men not be content with what they have?"

Dinivan soon returned, followed by a priest with a heaping salver of cheese and fruit, as well as a posset of mulled wine. Miriamele began again. As she talked and ate, and as Ranessin plied her with gentle yet shrewd questions, she began to feel almost as though she spoke with some kindly old grandfather. She told him of the Norn hounds that had pursued her and the maidservant Leleth, then of their rescue by Simon and Binabik. As she told of the revelations in the house of the witch woman Geloë, and related Jarnauga's dire warnings at Naglimund, Dinivan and the lector exchanged glances.

When she had finished, the lector pushed his tall hat back into place—it had slipped down several times during the course of the audience—and sat back in his chair with a sigh. His bright eyes were sad.

"So much to think about, so many dreadful questions unanswered. Oh, God, You have seen fit to test Your children sternly. I have a premonition of dire evil coming." He turned to Miriamele. "Thank you for your news, Princess. It is none of it happy, but only a fool desires cheerful ignorance and I try not to be a fool. That is my heaviest burden." He pursed his lips in thought. "Well, Dinivan," he said at last, "this lends an even more ominous air to the news I received yesterday."

"What news is that, Sacredness?" Dinivan asked. "We have had little chance to talk since I returned."

The lector took a sip of wine. "Elias is sending Pryrates to see me. His ship arrives tomorrow from the Hayholt. His mission, the message said, is an important one from the High King."

"Pryrates is coming?" Miriamele asked, alarmed. "Does my father know I'm here?"

"No, no, do not fear," the lector said soothingly. He patted her hand again. "It is Mother Church with whom he would trade words. No one knows you are here but Dinivan and myself."

"He's a devil," she said harshly. "Do not trust him."

Ranessin nodded gravely. "Your warning is well taken, Princess

Miriamele, but sometimes it is my duty to speak with devils." He lowered his eyes to stare at his hands, as if hoping to find clutched therein a solution to all problems. When Dinivan took Miriamele out, the lector bid her good-bye courteously, but he seemed wrapped in melancholy.

10

The Mirror

Simon found himself in the grip of a stubborn anger that would not go away. As he and Sludig followed the mounted trolls away down the mountain, away from the solemn piles of stone lying nakedly beneath the sky, he felt a rage seeping through him that muddled all his thoughts, so that he could scarcely think of anything for more than a moment at a time.

He walked stiffly, his body still bruised and sore, his stomach churning with anger. As he walked, he brooded. Haestan was dead. Another friend was dead. There was nothing he could do about it. He couldn't change it. He couldn't even cry over it. That was the most infuriating thing: he could do nothing. *Nothing*.

Sludig, pale-faced and shadow-eyed, did not seem anxious to break the silence. The two lowlanders trudged along side by side down broad, flat sheets of weathered granite and waded through drifts of snow churned into a white froth by rams' hooves.

The foothills seemed to be growing up to meet them. At each bend in the trail the snowy-shouldered hills emerged once more into the travelers' view, each time larger than before. Sikkihoq, in turn, seemed to be stretching away into the sky behind them as they steadily descended, ever taller, as though the mountain had finished its business with these mortals and now returned to the loftier and more congenial company of the sky and clouds.

I won't forget you, Simon warned Sikkihoq as he looked back up the great dagger of stone. He fought the urge to shout it aloud. If he squinted, he thought he could still see the spot where the cairns stood. *I won't forget that my friend is buried on your slopes. I'll never forget.*

Afternoon passed swiftly. They made faster time as the mountain broadened and the paths began to level out, with longer stretches between switchbacks. Simon noticed signs of the mountain's life that he had not seen higher up: a family of white and brown rabbits grazing between patches of snow, jays and squirrels bickering in the stunted, wind-curled trees. This evidence of life on what had seemed a barren and heartless rock should have made him feel better; instead, it served only to fuel his directionless anger. What right to exist did all these small and insignificant things have, when others were dying? He wondered why they should bother, when any moment a hawk or snake or hunter's arrow might snuff out their lives. The thought of life scrabbling pointlessly beneath the shadow of death filled him with an oddly exhilarating disgust.

When evening came, the company chose a gently sloping expanse of stone and brush in which to make camp, sheltered by Sikkihoq's body from the worst of the snow-laden wind. Simon shed his pack and began picking up deadwood for the fire, but stopped to watch the sun slip down behind the mountains to the west—one of which, he knew, was Urmsheim, the dragon-mountain. The horizon was streaked with light, as richly colored as any rose grown in the Hayholt's gardens.

An'nai, Jiriki's Sithi kinsman, who had been killed while fighting for the lives of his companions, was buried there on Urmsheim; the soldier Grimmric, a wiry, quiet man, had been interred beside him. Simon remembered Grimmric whistling as they rode north from Naglimund, a thin trill of sound alternately annoying and reassuring. Now he would be eternally silent. He and An'nai would never see a sunset like the one that painted the sky before Simon, beautiful and meaningless.

Where were they? Heaven? How could Sithi go to heaven when they didn't believe in it—and where *did* they think they went when they died? They were pagans, Simon supposed, which meant they were different— but An'nai had been loyal and brave. More than that, he had been kind to Simon, very kind in his strange Sithi way. How could An'nai not go to heaven? How could heaven be such a stupid place?

The anger, which had abated for a moment, returned. Simon flung one of the sticks he had gathered as hard as he could. It whirled through the air, then struck and cartwheeled down the long stony hill, disappearing at last into the underbrush below.

"Come, Simon," Sludig called from behind him. "We need your wood for the fire. Aren't you hungry now?"

Simon ignored him, staring out at the reddening sky as he ground his teeth in frustration. He felt a hand on his arm and angrily shrugged it off.

"Please, come," the Rimmersman said kindly. "Supper will be ready soon."

"Where is Haestan?" Simon asked through tight lips.

"What do you mean?" Sludig cocked his head. "You know where we left him, Simon."

"No, I mean where is Haestan? The *real* Haestan."

"Ah." Sludig smiled. His beard had grown very thick. "His soul is in heaven, with Usires and the Lord God."

"*No.*" Simon turned to look at the sky again, darkening now with the first mortal blues of night.

"What? Why do you say that?"

"He's not in heaven. There is no heaven. How can there be a heaven, when everyone thinks it's different?"

"You are being foolish." Sludig stared at him for a moment, trying to sense Simon's thought. "Perhaps everyone goes to their own heaven," the soldier said, then placed his hand again on Simon's shoulder. "God knows what He knows. Come and sit down."

"How could God let people die for no reason?" Simon demanded, hugging himself as though trying to keep something inside. "If God can do that, then He is cruel. If He isn't cruel, well . . . well, then, He just can't do anything. Like an old man who sits at the window, but can't go out. He's old and stupid."

"Do not talk against God the Father," Sludig said, his voice chilly. "God will not be mocked by an ungrateful boy. He has given you all the gifts of life . . ."

"It's a lie!" Simon shouted. The soldier's eyes widened in surprise. Heads turned from the campfire, looking to the sudden noise. "It's a lie, a lie! *What* gifts? To crawl around like a bug, here and there, trying to find something to eat, somewhere to sleep—and then without warning something smashes you? What kind of gift is that!? To do the right thing, and . . . and fight against evil, like the Book of the Aedon says—if you do that you get killed! Just like Haestan! Just like Morgenes! The bad ones live on—live on and grow rich and laugh at the good ones! It's a stupid lie!"

"That is terrible, Simon!" Sludig said, his voice also rising. "You speak from madness and grief . . ."

"It's a lie—and you are an idiot to believe it!" Simon yelled, throwing his wood down at Sludig's feet. He turned and ran down the mountain path with a great, grieving pain in his middle that almost took his breath away, following the twisting course until the camp had disappeared from view. Qantaqa's bark wafted after him, faint and percussive as someone clapping in another room.

At last he sank down on a stone beside the path, rubbing his hands back and forth over the worn cloth of his breeches. There was moss growing on the stone, burnt brown by frost and wind, but still somehow vital and alive. He stared at it, wondering why he could not cry and whether he even wanted to.

After some time he heard a clicking noise and looked up to see Qantaqa pacing toward him over the sloping rocks above the path. The wolf's nose hovered low, sniffing close to the stone. She hopped down onto the path, and regarded him quizzically for a moment with her head cocked to one side, then walked past, brushing against his leg. Simon trailed his fingers along the thick pelt of her flank as she went by. Qantaqa continued on down the path, a dim gray shape in the growing darkness.

"Simon-friend." Binabik appeared around the bend in the track. "Qantaqa is off to hunt," he said, watching her disappearing form. "It is hard for a wolf to be walking all day where I ask her. She is a good companion to make such sacrifice for my sake."

When Simon did not respond, the troll came forward and squatted at his side, his walking stick balanced on his knees.

"You are much upset," he said.

Simon took a deep breath, then let it out. "Everything is a lie," he sighed.

Binabik raised an eyebrow. "What is 'everything'? And what is making it a lie?"

"I don't think we can do anything at all. Anything to make things better. We're going to die."

"At some time," the troll nodded.

"We're going to die fighting the Storm King. It's a lie if we say we're not. God's not going to save us, or even help us." Simon picked up a loose stone and flung it across the path, where it went rattling into darkness. "Binabik, I couldn't even pick up Thorn. What good is the sword going to be if we can't even use it? How is a sword—even three Great Swords or whatever they're called—going to kill an enemy like him? Kill someone who's already dead?"

"These are questions that need answering," the little man replied. "I do not know. How do you know that the sword is for killing? And if it is for that, what makes you think any of us is to be the killer?"

Simon chose another rock and threw it. "I don't know anything, either. I'm just a kitchen boy, Binabik." He felt immensely sorry for himself. "I just want to go home." The word caught in his throat.

The troll stood, brushing off his seat. "You are not a boy, Simon. You are a man in all the ways for measuring. A young man, true, but a man—or with great nearness."

Simon shook his head. "It doesn't matter, anyway. I thought . . . I don't know. I thought that it would be like a story. That we would find the sword and it would be a powerful weapon, that we would destroy our enemies and things would be right again. I didn't think any more people would die! How could there be a God who would let good people die, no matter what they do?"

"Another question I cannot be answering." Binabik smiled, but gently, mindful of Simon's pain. "And I cannot be telling you what is right for belief. The truths that became our stories of gods are far away in the past. Even the Sithi, who live for eons, do not know how the world began or what began it—at least not for certain, I am thinking. But *I* can tell you something important . . ."

The troll leaned forward, touching Simon's arm, waiting until his young friend had raised his eyes from the moss once more. "Gods in the heaven or in the stone are distant, and we can guess only at what they intend." He squeezed Simon's forearm. "But you and I, we are living in a time when a god walks the earth once more. He is not a god who intends kindness. Men may fight and die, they may build walls and break stone, but Ineluki has died and come back: that is something no one else has ever been doing, not even your Usires Aedon. Forgive me, because I am not meaning blasphemy, but is not what Ineluki has done a thing like a god can do?" Binabik gave Simon a little shake, staring into his eyes. "He is jealous and terrible, and the world he can make will be a terrible place. We are having a task of great fear and very great difficulty, Simon—it may even be that there is no possibility of succeeding—but it is not a task we can be fleeing."

Simon tore his gaze from Binabik's. "That's what I said. How do you fight a god? We'll be crushed like ants." Another stone went flying out into darkness.

"Perhaps. But if we are not trying, then there is no chance of anything *but* this antlike crushing, so we must try. There is always something beyond even the worst of bad times. We may die, but the dying of some may mean living for others. That is not much to cling to, but it is a true thing in any case."

The troll moved a little way down the path and took a seat on another stone. The sky was darkening swiftly. "Also," Binabik said gravely, "it may or may not be foolishness to pray to the gods, but there is certainly being no wisdom in cursing them."

Simon said nothing. They passed some time in silence. At last Binabik twisted loose the knife end of his walking stick, allowing the bone flute inside the hollow stick to slide free. He blew a few experimental notes, then began to play a slow, melancholy air. The dissonant music, echoing down the mountainside in darkness, seemed to sing with the voice of Simon's own loneliness. He shivered, feeling the wind through his tattered cloak. His dragon-scar stung fiercely.

"Are you still my friend, Binabik?" he said at last.

The troll took the flute from his lips. "To death and beyond, Simon-friend." He began to play once more.

When the flutesong was finished, Binabik whistled for Qantaqa and walked back up the path toward camp. Simon followed him.

The fire had burned low and the wineskin was making the last of many trips around the circle when Simon finally worked up the courage to approach Sludig. The Rimmersman was sharpening the head of his Qanuc spear with a whetstone; he continued for some while as Simon stood before him. At last he looked up.

"Yes?" His voice was gruff.

"I'm sorry, Sludig. I should not have said what I did. You were only being kind."

The Rimmersman stared at him for a moment, a certain cold look in his eyes. At last his expression softened. "You may think as you like, Simon, but do not speak such blasphemy of the One God before me."

"I'm sorry. I'm only a kitchen boy."

"Kitchen boy!" Sludig's laugh was harsh. He looked searchingly into Simon's eyes, then laughed again with better humor. "You really think so, don't you! You're a fool, Simon." He stood up, chuckling and shaking his head. "A kitchen boy! A kitchen boy who swords dragons and slays giants. Look at you! You are taller than I am, and Sludig is not small!"

Simon stared at the Rimmersman, surprised. It was true, of course: he stood half a hand taller than Sludig. "But you're strong!" Simon protested. "You're a grown man."

"As you are fast becoming. And you are stronger than you know. You must see the truth, Simon. You are a boy no more. You cannot act as though you are one still." The Rimmersman contemplated him for a long moment. "As a matter of fact, it is dangerous not to train you better. You have been lucky to survive several bad fights, but luck is fickle. You need sword and spear teaching; I will give them to you. Haestan would have wanted it, and it will give us something to work at on our long trip to your Stone of Farewell."

"Then you forgive me?" Simon was embarrassed by this talk of manhood.

"If I must." The Rimmersman sat down again. "Now go and sleep. We have a long walk again tomorrow, then you and I will drill for some time after we make camp."

Simon felt more than a little resentful about being sent to bed, but did not want to risk another argument. As it was, it had been difficult for him to come back to the campfire and eat with the others. He knew they had all been watching him, wondering if he would have another outburst.

He retreated to the bed he had made of springy branches and leaves and wrapped himself tightly in his cloak. He would be happy to be in a cave, or down off the mountain entirely, where they would not be exposed so nakedly to the wind.

The bright, cold stars seemed to quiver in the sky overhead. Simon stared up at them through unfathomable distances, letting thoughts chase themselves through his head until sleep came at last.

The sound of the trolls singing to their rams woke Simon from a dream. He dimly remembered a little gray cat and a feeling of being trapped by someone or something, but the dream was fading fast. He opened his eyes to the thin morning light, then closed them quickly. He did not want to get up and face the day.

The singing went on, accompanied by the clinking of harnesses. He had seen this ritual so many times since leaving Mintahoq that he could picture it in his head as vividly as if he was watching. The trolls were cinching up the straps and filling the saddlebags, guttural yet high-pitched voices busy with their seemingly endless chant. From time to time they would pause, stroking their mounts, currying the rams' thick fleeces, leaning in close to sing softly and intimately while the sheep blinked their yellow, slotted eyes. Soon it would be time for salty tea and dried meat and quiet, laughing conversation.

Except, of course, there would not be as much laughter today, the third morning since the hillside battle with the giants. Binabik's folk were a cheerful people, but a little bit of the frost lodged in Simon's heart seemed to have touched them, too. A folk that laughed at cold and at dizzying, breakneck falls at every turning of every trail had been chilled by a shadow they could not understand—not that Simon understood much himself.

He had spoken truly to Binabik: somehow, he had thought things would get better once they found the great sword Thorn. The blade's power and strangeness was so palpable it seemed impossible that it would not make a change in the struggle against King Elias and his dark ally. But perhaps the sword by itself was not enough. Perhaps whatever the rhyme had spoken of would not happen until all three swords had been brought together.

Simon groaned. Even worse, perhaps the queer rhyme from Nisses' book meant nothing at all. Didn't people say Nisses was a madman? Even Morgenes had not known what the rhyme truly meant.

> *When frost doth grow on Claves' bell*
> *And Shadows walk upon the road*
> *When water blackens in the Well*
> *Three Swords must come again*
>
> *When Bukken from the Earth do creep*
> *And Hunën from the heights descend*
> *When Nightmare throttles peaceful Sleep*
> *Three Swords must come again*
>
> *To turn the stride of treading Fate*
> *To clear the fogging Mists of Time*
> *If Early shall resist Too Late*
> *Three Swords must come again . . .*

Well, Bukken had certainly crept from the earth, but the memory of the squealing diggers was not one he wanted to pursue. Ever since the night of their attack on Isgrimnur's camp near St. Hoderund's, Simon had never felt the same way about the solid earth beneath his feet. That was the only advantage he could think of to traveling over Sikkihoq's unforgiving stone.

As for the rhyme's mention of giants, with Haestan's death so fresh in his mind that seemed like a cruel joke. The monsters hadn't even needed to descend from the heights, because Simon and his friends had been foolish enough to venture into their mountain territory. But the Hunën *had* left their high refuges, which Simon knew as well as anybody. He and Miriamele—the thought of her brought a sudden yearning—had faced one in Aldheorte Forest, only a week's ride from the very gates of Erchester.

The rest did not make much sense to him, but none of it seemed impossible: Simon did not know who Claves was, or where his bell might be, but it seemed that soon there would be frost everywhere. Even so, what could the three swords do?

I wielded Thorn, he thought. For a moment he felt the power of it once more. *In that instant, I was a great knight . . . wasn't I?*

But had it been Thorn, or had it only been that he had stood up and put fear aside? If he had done the same with a less mighty sword, would he have been any less brave? He would have been dead, of course . . . just like Haestan, just like An'nai, Morgenes, Grimmric . . . but did that matter? Didn't great heroes die? Hadn't Camaris, Thorn's true master, died in the angry seas. . . ?

Simon's thoughts were wandering. He felt himself sliding back toward sleep. He almost let it happen, but he knew it would only be a short while before Binabik or Sludig would be shaking him awake. Last night they had both said he was a man, or nearly so. Just for once he didn't want to be awakened last, a child allowed to sleep while the grown-ups talked.

He opened his eyes, letting the light in, and groaned again. Uncurling himself from the cloak, he picked loose twigs and clusters of pine needles from his clothing, then shook the cloak out before quickly wrapping it around himself once more. Suddenly unwilling to be parted even for a short while from his few miserable possessions, he picked up his pack, which had pillowed his head, and took it with him.

The morning was chilly, a light scatter of snow in the air. Stretching the kinks out of his muscles, he walked slowly to the fire, where Binabik sat talking to Sisqi. The pair were seated side by side before the low, translucent flames, their hands clasped. Thorn lay propped on a tree stump beside them, a dull black bar that reflected no light. From behind, the two trolls looked like children talking earnestly about a game they might play or an interesting hole they might explore, and Simon felt a strong protective urge toward them. A moment later, as he realized they were probably discussing how to keep Binabik's people alive if the winter did not abate, or what they should do if more giants found them, the illusion shredded and blew away. They were not children, and if not for their bravery he would be dead.

Binabik turned and saw him staring. The little man smiled a greeting as he listened intently to Sisqi's rapid Qanuc words. Simon grunted, bending to take the lump of cheese and heel of bread that Binabik pointed out, set on a stone near the fire. He took his meal and went to sit by himself.

The sun, still hidden from view behind Sikkihoq, was not visible. The mountain's shadow lay over the campsite, but the tops of the mountains in the west glowed with the sun's rising light. The White Waste below was sunk in gray dawn-shadow. Simon took a bite of dry bread and chewed as he stared out across the Waste at the distant line of forest which lay on the horizon like dark cream in a milk pail.

Qantaqa, who had been lying at Binabik's side, got up, stretched, and padded silently toward Simon. Her muzzle was red-flecked with the lifeblood of whatever poor animal had surrendered itself for her morning feeding, but the last traces were even now being scoured away by her long pink tongue. She approached Simon briskly, ears up, as if on some clearly-defined errand, but when she arrived she only stood for a moment to let him scratch her, then curled up beside him, exchanging one napping spot for another. Her bulk was such that when it pushed against his leg he was almost forced off his stone seat.

He finished his meal and opened the flap of his pack, rooting for his water bottle. A bright tangle of blue came up with it, wound on the carrying cord.

It was the scarf Miriamele had given him, the one he had worn around his neck on the way up the dragon-mountain. Jiriki had removed it while nursing him back to health, but had thoughtfully stowed it with the rest of Simon's meager belongings. Now it lay in his hands like a stripe of sky; the sight brought the sting of almost-tears to his eyes. Where in the great world was Miriamele? Geloë, in their brief moment of contact, had not known. Where in Osten Ard was the princess wandering? Did she ever think of Simon? And if she did, what did she think?

Probably: Why did I give my nice scarf to a dirty kitchen boy? He enjoyed a brief twinge of self-pity. Well, he was not just any scullion. As Sludig said, he was a kitchen boy who sworded dragons and slew giants. Just at this moment, however, he would rather be a kitchen boy in a nice warm kitchen in the Hayholt and nothing more.

Simon tied Miriamele's scarf about his neck, tucking the ends under the collar of his tattered shirt. He took a swallow of water, then rummaged in the pack again, but could not find what he was looking for. He remembered after a moment that he had put it in his cloak pocket and felt a moment of panic. When would he learn to be more careful? It could have easily fallen out a hundred times. He was happily reassured to feel its outline through the cloth. After some digging, he lifted it out into the morning light.

Jiriki's mirror was icy cold. He buffed it on his sleeve, then held it up, staring at his reflection. His beard had come in more thickly since he had last surveyed himself. The reddish hairs, almost brown in the dim light, were beginning to obscure the line of his jaw—but the same old nose poked out above the beard, and the same blue eyes stared back at him. Becoming a man, it seemed, would not mean becoming anything other than a slightly different type of Simon, which was a faintly saddening thought.

The beard did hide most of his spots, so there was something for which to be grateful. But for a blemish or two on his forehead, he thought he looked like a reasonable approximation of a young man. He tilted the glass, staring at the white streak burned into his reddish locks by the dragon's blood. Did it make him look older? More manly? It was hard to tell. His hair was curling on his shoulders, though. He should ask Sludig or someone to cut it shorter, as many of the king's knights had worn theirs. But why bother? They would probably all be dead at the hands of giants before it grew long enough to get in his way.

He lowered the mirror to his lap, staring down into it as though it were a pool of water. The frame was finally beginning to warm beneath his fingers. What was it Jiriki had told him? That the mirror would be no more than a mere looking glass unless Simon needed him? That was it. Jiriki had said that Simon could talk to him . . . with the mirror? In the mirror? *Through* the mirror? It had not been clear at all, but for a moment Simon very much wanted to call for Jiriki's help. The thought crept over him unbidden, but its claws were not easily dislodged. He would call Jiriki and tell him that they needed help. The Storm King was an enemy that mortals alone could not defeat.

But the Storm King is not here, Simon thought, *and Jiriki knows everything about the situation that he needs to. What would I tell him? That he should come running back to the mountains because a kitchen boy is scared and wants to go home?*

Simon stared into the mirror, remembering when it had shown him Miriamele. The princess had been on a ship, staring out over the railing at cloudy skies, gray and cloudy skies . . .

As he watched his own face in the upturned mirror, it suddenly seemed that he could again see that misty sky, tatters of cloud floating across the mirror's surface obscuring his features. A fog seemed to be drifting past him, and he could no longer separate himself from the image in the looking glass. He wavered dizzily, as though he were falling into the reflection. The noises of the camp diminished and then disappeared as the mist became a solid and featureless curtain of gray. It was all around him, shutting away the light . . .

The gray mist slowly dissolved, like steam escaping from beneath a pot lid, but as it cleared he saw that the face before him was no longer his own. Staring back at him through narrowed eyes was a woman—a beautiful woman who was both old and young at the same time. The lines of her face were shifting, as though she gazed up through rippling water. Her hair was white beneath a circlet of gemlike flowers; her stare burned like molten gold, the eyes bright and reflective as a cat's. She was old, he somehow knew, very old, but there was little about her face that spoke of age, only a tightness in the line of her jaw and mouth, a brittleness to her features as though the skin was stretched close against the bone. Her eyes were glorious with ancient knowledge and imprisoned memory. Her high cheekbones and smooth forehead made her look like a statue . . .

A statue. . . ? His thoughts were a jumble, but Simon knew he had seen a statue that looked like this woman . . . he had seen such a face . . . seen it in . . . in . . .

"Please answer me," she said. *"I come to you a second time. Do not ignore me again! Please forget your ancient grievances, however justified. Ill will has stood too long between our house and that of Ruyan Vé. Now we have a common enemy. I need your help!"*

Her voice was faint in his head, as though it echoed down a long corridor, but even so, she wielded a commanding power—like Valada Geloë's, but in some way deeper, smoother, with none of the witch woman's rough but reassuring edges. This one was as different from Geloë as the forest-woman herself was from Simon.

"I do not have the strength I once wielded," the woman pleaded. *"And what little I have may be needed against the Shadow in the North—and you must know of that shadow. Tinukeda'yei! Children of the Garden, please answer!"* The woman's voice faded on an imploring note. There was a long moment of silence, but if reply was made, Simon did not hear it. Suddenly, the flake-gold eyes seemed to see him for the first time. The musical voice abruptly took on a note of suspicion and concern. *"Who is this? A mortal child?"*

Frozen in alarm, Simon said nothing. The face in the mirror stared, then Simon could feel something reaching out to him through the mist, a force as diffuse but powerful as the sun hidden behind clouds.

"Tell me. Who are you?"

Simon tried to answer, not because he wanted to, but because it was impossible not to try with such compelling words echoing in his head. Something prevented him.

"You are traveling in places not meant for you," the voice said. *"You do not belong here. Who are you?"*

He struggled, but found that something was throttling his responses as surely as fingers on his throat would choke off words. The face before him rippled as a pallid blue light began to shine through it, fraying the image of the beautiful old woman. A wave of cold passed through him that it seemed might turn his very innards to black ice.

A new voice spoke, harsh, chilling.

"Who is he? He is a meddler, Amerasu."

The first face was now entirely gone. A gleam of silver swam upward through the mirror's gray depths. A face appeared, all gleaming metal, expressionless and immobile. He had seen that face on the Dream Road and had felt the same sick dread. He knew the name: Utuk'ku, Queen of the Norns. Try as he might to look away, he could not. He was held in an unshakable grip. Utuk'ku's eyes were invisible in the mask's black depths, but he felt their stare on his face like freezing breath.

"The manchild is a meddler." Each word came sharp and cold as an icicle. *"As are you, granddaughter. And meddlers will not prosper when the Storm King comes . . ."*

The thing in the silver mask laughed. Simon felt hammerblows of frost against his heart. A poisonous cold began climbing inexorably upward, from fingers to hand to arm. Soon it would reach his face, like a deadly kiss from silvery, frost-glittering lips . . .

Simon dropped the mirror, tumbling after it. The ground seemed a league away, the fall endless. Somebody was screaming. *He* was screaming.

Sludig helped Simon to his feet, where he swayed, panting. After a moment he shook off the Rimmersman's hands. He felt wobbly, but wanted to stand on his own. The trolls had gathered around and were muttering among themselves, clearly confused.

"What has happened, Simon?" Binabik asked, pushing his way through to his side. "Are you hurt by something?" Sisqi, still holding Binabik's hand, stared up at the strange lowlander as though trying to read his malady in his eyes.

"I saw faces in Jiriki's mirror," Simon said, shivering uncontrollably. Sisqi held up his cloak, which he took gratefully. "One of them was the Norn Queen. She could see me, too, I think."

Binabik spoke to the other ram-riders, gesturing with his hands. They turned and wandered back to the fire. Stocky Snenneq waved his spear at the sky as though taunting an enemy.

Binabik fixed Simon with his brows. "Tell it to me."

Simon related all that had happened from the moment he first lifted the mirror. As he described the first face Binabik frowned in concentration, but when the recitation was finished the troll only shook his head.

"The Norn Queen we are knowing all too well," Binabik growled. "It was her hunters who arrowed me at Da'ai Chikiza and I have not been forgetting that gift. But thinking of who the other might be, I have unsureness. You say that Utuk'ku called her 'granddaughter'?"

"I think so. And the Norn Queen called her something else, too. A name—but I can't remember it." Some of the details, once spoken aloud, were not so sure in his mind as they had been moments before.

"Then it is someone of one of the ruling houses, Sithi or Norn. If Jiriki were now with us, he would be knowing in an instant who it was and what her words meant. You say she seemed to be at pleading with someone?"

"I think so. But Binabik, Jiriki told me that the mirror was nothing but a mirror now! He said the magic was gone, unless I wanted to call him—and I didn't try to call him! I truly didn't!"

"Calm, Simon, is how you must be. I am having no doubts of what you say. Jiriki himself may have misunderstood the nature of the mirror's powers—or, it is being possible, many things may be changing just since Jiriki has gone from us. In either way, I think it best you are leaving the mirror, or at the least not using it more. That is a suggestion, only—it is your gift to do as you like. Remember, please, it may bring danger for all."

Simon looked at the mirror, which lay facedown on the rock. He picked it up and brushed dust from its surface without looking at it, then slid it into his cloak pocket. "I won't leave it," he said, "because it was a gift. Also, we may need Jiriki someday." He patted it. The frame was still warm. "But I won't use it until then."

Binabik shrugged. "The deciding is yours. Come back to the fire and make yourself warm. Tomorrow we are riding with dawn's appearance."

After an early start, the ragged troop reached Blue Mud Lake in the late afternoon of the following day. Nestled among the foothills of Sikkihoq, the lake was a dark blue mirror, flat as the glass in Simon's pocket, fed by two cataracts that spilled from the icy heights. The noise of their falling was deep and sonorous as the breathing of gods.

As the party crossed through the last pass above the lake and the quiet rumble of the water rose, the trolls reined up their mounts. The wind had abated. The steaming breath of rams and riders hung in the air. Simon could see fear written in every trollish face.

"What's wrong?" he asked nervously, expecting at any moment to hear the bellowing voices of giants.

"I think they had hoped Binabik was wrong," Sludig said. "Perhaps they were hoping to find springtime hidden here."

Simon saw little that was unusual. The sheltering hills were thatched with snow and many of the trees that surrounded the lake were bare of leaf. The evergreens were mantled in white, like cottonwool spears.

Many of the trolls brought the heels of their hands to their chests, as if what they saw spoke more eloquently of trouble than any words of Binabik or his master Ookequk. As they spurred their mounts along the narrow trail, Simon and Sludig trudged forward once more, following the tracks of the rams into the lake valley. Another flurry of snow came sifting down from Sikkihoq.

They made camp at a great cavern on the lake's northwestern banks. The cave was surrounded by well-worn pathways. The massive stone fire pit, nearly brimful with frozen ash, testified to the generations of trolls who had camped there. Soon a huge fire, the biggest they had made since leaving Mintahoq, was burning by the lakeside. As darkness fell and the stars began to kindle, the flames threw wild shadows on the rocky faces of the hills.

Simon was sitting near the fire oiling his boots when Binabik found him. At the troll's bidding, he put the boots back on and took a burning brand from the blaze, then followed Binabik away into the darkness. They walked along the edge of the hillside for a furlong, circling around the lakeshore until they reached another cave, its high entranceway almost hidden behind a stand of spruces. A strange whistling noise came from within. Simon knitted his brows in apprehension, but Binabik only smiled and waved at him to follow, pushing back a low-hanging branch with his walking stick so taller Simon could enter without catching his torch in the trees.

The cavern was thick with the smell of animals, but it was a familiar smell. Simon lifted the brand so the light splashed the farthest depths of the cavern. Six horses looked back, whinnying nervously. The cavern floor was piled high with dried grass.

"Good that is," Binabik said, coming up beside him. "I had been fearing they might have run away, or the food might not have been of sufficiency."

"Are they ours?" Simon asked, approaching slowly. The nearest horse fluttered its lips and danced back a step; Simon held out his hand for it to smell. "I think they are."

"Of course," Binabik chuckled. "We Qanuc are not horse-murderers. My folk put them here for safety when we were all taken up-mountain. We also keep this place for our rams when they are birthing and the weather is cold. From now on, Simon-friend, you need be walking no more."

After stroking the nearest horse, which submitted grudgingly but did not pull away, Simon saw the gray and black spotted mare he had ridden from Naglimund. He moved toward her, wishing he had something to give her.

"Simon," Binabik called, "catch!"

He turned in time to receive something small and hard, which crumbled slightly as he clutched it in his palm.

"Salt," Binabik said. "I brought it from Mintahoq. I have brought one lump for each. The rams have a great fondness for salt and I am guessing your horses will, too."

Simon offered it to the gray-and-black. She took it, her mouth tickling his hand. He stroked her powerful neck, feeling it tremble beneath his fingers. "I don't remember her name," he whispered sadly. "Haestan told me, but I forgot."

Binabik shrugged and began distributing the salt among the other horses.

"It's good to see you again," Simon told the mare. "I'll give you a new name. How about 'Homefinder'?"

Names did not seem to be very important to her. She flicked her tail and nosed Simon's pockets for more salt.

When Simon and Binabik got back to the fire the kangkang was flowing vigorously and the trolls were singing, rocking back and forth before the flames. As they approached, Sisqi detached herself from the group and came to take Binabik's hand, silently laying her hooded head upon his shoulder. From a distance the trolls sounded as though they were having a hilarious time of it, but as Simon drew nearer the expressions on their faces told differently.

"Why do they look so sad, Binabik?"

"We are having a saying on Mintahoq," the little man explained, "—'Mourning is for home.' When we are losing one of our folk on the trail we bury them in that place, but we save our tears until we are safe in our caves once more. Nine of our folk died on Sikkihoq."

"But you said 'mourn at home.' These people are not home yet."

Binabik shook his head, then answered a quiet question from Sisqi before returning his attention to Simon. "These hunters and herders are making ready for the coming of the rest of Yiqanuc's folk. The word is even now flying from one mountain to another: the highlands are not a place of safety and spring is not coming." The little man smiled wearily. "They *are* home, Simon-friend."

Binabik patted Simon's hand, then he and Sisqi veered off toward the fire to join the chorus. The blaze was fed and the flames leaped higher, so that all the lake valley seemed to glow with orange light. The mourning songs of the Qanuc echoed out across the still waters, carrying even above the bitter voice of the wind and the rush of the falls.

Simon went off in search of Sludig. He found the Rimmersman bundled in his cloak a short distance from the fire, sitting on a rock with a skin full of kangkang between his knees. Simon sat down beside him and took a long swallow from the offered wineskin, sucking cold air afterward. He wiped his mouth with his sleeve and handed it back.

"Have I told you of the Skipphavven, Simon?" Sludig asked, staring at the fire and the swaying trolls. "You have not seen beauty until you have seen the maidens who gather mistletoe from the mast of Sotfengsel, Elvrit's buried ship." He took a drink and passed it to Simon. "Ah, sweet God, I hope Skali of Kaldskryke at least has enough Rimmersman pride to tend to the graves of the longships at the Skipphavven. May he rot in hell."

Simon took two more long pulls on the wineskin, hiding the faces he made from Sludig. The kangkang tasted awful, but it warmed him. "Skali is the one who took Duke Isgrimnur's land?" he asked.

Sludig looked over, a little blearily. He had been working at the skin for some time. "He is. Black-hearted, treacherous son of a wolf-bitch and a carrion crow. May he rot in Hell. It is blood feud now." The Rimmersman pulled meditatively at his beard and turned his gaze upward to the stars. "It is blood feud all over the world, these days."

Simon looked up with him and saw an advancing line of dark clouds out of the northwest obscuring the stars along the horizon. For a moment he thought he could see the Storm King's dark hand reaching out, blotting light and warmth. He trembled, pulling his cloak tighter, but the cold did not go away. He reached for the skin again. Sludig was still staring upward.

"We are very small," Simon said between swallows. The kangkang seemed to be flowing in his veins like blood.

"So are the stars, *kundë-mannë*," Sludig murmured. "But they each one burn as bright as they can. Have another drink."

Later—in truth, Simon was not sure exactly how much time had passed, or what had become of Sludig—he found himself seated on a log beside the fire, Sisqi on one side of him, the bearded herder Snenneq on the other. They were all holding hands. Simon reminded himself to be gentle with the small, rough palms folded in his own. All around him the trolls swayed and he swayed with them. They sang, and although he did not understand the words of their song, he added his voice to theirs, listening to the brave roar they all made beneath the night sky, feeling his heart beating in his chest like a drum.

"Do we really have to go today?" Simon asked, struggling to hold the saddle in place while Sludig tightened the belly-strap. The single torch did not throw much light in the darkened cave that served as a stable. Beyond the wall of spruces dawn was unfolding.

"It is seeming a good thought to me," Binabik said, voice muffled, his head hidden by a leather flap as he inspected the saddlebags. "Chukku's Stones! Why am I not waiting until we are outside in the light? Like hunting white weasels in deep snow, this is."

"I would have liked a day to rest," Simon said. In fact, he was not feeling too badly, considering all the Qanuc liquor he had drunk the night before; but for a faint hammering in his temples and a certain weakness in his joints, he was doing fairly well.

"As would I. As also, no doubt, would Sludig . . ." the troll replied. "Ah! *Kikkaksut!* There is something sharp in here!"

"Hold that damned thing!" Sludig growled as the saddle jerked free of Simon's grasp. The horse nickered in irritation and jogged a step to the side before Simon grasped the saddle again.

"But, you are seeing," Binabik continued, "we have no knowledge how long it will take to cross the Waste. If winter is spreading, the sooner this is done will make the better for us. There are others, too, who may be carrying word of us to ears that are not friendly. We are not knowing who survived Urmsheim from the huntsman's troop. They saw Thorn, I am thinking." He patted the sword, which was now wrapped in hides and strapped to the back of Simon's saddle.

The mention of Ingen Jegger made Simon's stomach—already uneasy after a morning meal of dried fish—twist. He did not like to think of the terrible Queen's Huntsman in his snarling-muzzled helm, who had pursued them like an avenging ghost.

Please, God, Simon thought, *let him be dead on the dragon-mountain. We don't need any more enemies, especially one like him.*

"I suppose you're right," he said heavily. "But I don't like it."

"What was it that Haestan used to say?" Sludig asked, straightening up. " 'Now you know what it is like to be a soldier'?"

"That's what he used to say." Simon smiled sadly.

Sisqinanamook and her folk gathered around as Simon and his companions brought out their saddled mounts. The Qanuc men and women seemed torn between the ceremonies of leavetaking and the fascination inspired by the horses, whose legs were longer than the herders and huntresses were tall. The horses shuffled nervously at first as the little people stroked and patted them, but the trolls seemed to have learned more than a little in their generations of sheepherding; the horses soon gentled, pluming the frosty air with their breath as the Qanuc admired them.

At last Sisqi waved for order, then spoke rapidly to Simon and Sludig in the language of the Trollfells. Binabik smiled and said: "Sisqinanamook bids you farewell on behalf of the Mintahoq Qanuc and our Herder and Huntress. She says that the Qanuc people have seen many new things in late days, and though the world is changing for worse, not *all* the changes are being for bad." He nodded to Sisqi and she spoke again, now fixing her eyes on Sludig.

"Good-bye, Rimmersman," Binabik translated. "You are the kindest Croohok she has ever heard about, and none of the folk who stand here are now afraid of you any more. Tell *your* Herder and Huntress—" he grinned, perhaps imagining Duke Isgrimnur answering to either title, "—that the Qanuc are being a brave folk, too, but also a just folk who do not like pointless fighting."

Sludig nodded. "I will."

Sisqi turned her attention to Simon. "And you, Snowlock, do not be afraid. She will tell any of the Qanuc back on Mintahoq who wonder at the story of your dragon-lashing about the bravery she has been able to witness. Any others here will be doing the same." He listened carefully for a moment, then grinned. "She also urges you for being careful of her intended—who is me—and for using your bravery to keep him safe. This she is asking in the name of new friendship."

Simon was touched. "Tell her," he said slowly, "that I will protect her intended—who is also my friend—to death and beyond."

As Binabik relayed his words, Sisqi stared at Simon, her eyes intent and serious. When the troll had finished, Sisqi bowed her head toward them, stiff and prideful. Simon and Sludig did the same. The other Qanuc pressed forward, touching those who were about to leave as though to send something with them. Simon found himself surrounded by small, black-haired heads, and again had to remind himself that the trolls were not children, but mortal men and women who loved and fought and died just as bravely and seriously as any knight of Erkynland. Callused fingers squeezed his hand and many things that sounded kind were said to him in words he could not understand.

Sisqi and Binabik had wandered off from the others, back toward the sleeping cave. When they got there, Sisqi ducked in, emerging a moment later with a long spear in her hands, its shaft busy with carvings.

"Here," she said. *"You will need this where you are going, beloved, and it will be longer than nine times nine days before you return. Take it. I know we will be together once more—if the gods are kind."*

"Even if they are not." Binabik tried to smile, but could not. He took the spear from her and rested it against the facing of the cave. *"When we meet again, may it be granted that it is beneath no shadow. I will hold you in my heart, Sisqi."*

"Hold me against you now," she said quietly, and they stepped forward into each other's arms. *"Blue Mud Lake is cold this year."*

"I will be back . . ." Binabik began.

"No more talk. Our time is short."

Their faces came together, vanishing as their hoods touched each other, and they stood that way for a long time. They were both trembling.

PART TWO

Storm's Hand

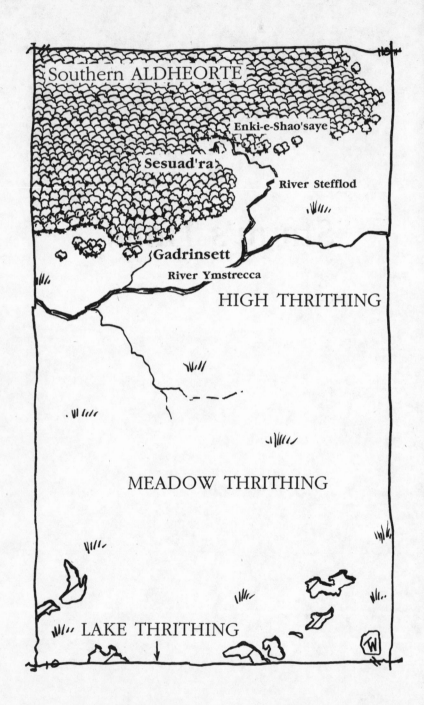

Southern ALDHEORTE

Enki-e-Shao'saye

Sesuad'ra

River Stefflod

Gadrinsett

River Ymstrecca

HIGH THRITHING

MEADOW THRITHING

LAKE THRITHING

11

Bones of the Earth

It was often said that of all the lands of men in Osten Ard, secrets ran deepest in Hernystir. Not that the land itself was hidden, like the fabled Trollfells lurking beyond the icy fence of the White Waste, or the land of the Wrannamen, shrouded in treacherous swamps. The secrets Hernystir kept were hidden in the hearts of its people, or below its sunny meadows, deep in the earth.

Of all mortal men, the Hernystiri once had known and loved the Sithi best. They learned much from them—although the things they had learned were now mentioned only in old ballads. They had also traded with the Sithi, bringing back to their own grassy country articles of workmanship beyond anything the finest smiths and craftsmen of Imperial Nabban could produce. In return, the Hernystirmen offered their immortal allies the fruits of the earth—nightblack malachite, ilenite and bright opal, sapphire, cinnabar, and soft, shiny gold—all painstakingly mined from the thousand tunnels of the Grianspog Mountains.

The Sithi were gone now, vanished absolutely from the earth as far as most men knew or cared. Some of the Hernystiri knew better. It had been centuries since the Fair Ones had fled their castle Asu'a, deserting the last of the Nine Cities accessible to mortal man. Most mortals had forgotten the Sithi entirely, or saw them only through the distorting veil of old stories. But among the Hernystiri, an open-hearted and yet secretive folk, there were still a few who looked at the dark holes that pitted the Grianspog and remembered.

Eolair was not particularly fond of caves. His childhood had been spent upon the grasslands in the meadows of western Hernystir, at the conjoining of the Inniscrich and the Cuimnhe rivers. As Count of Nad Mullach, he had ruled over that territory; later, in service to his king, Lluth ubh-

Llythinn, he had traveled to all the great cities and courts of Osten Ard, carrying out Hernystir's wishes beneath the lights of countless lamps and the skies of every nation.

Thus, although his bravery was questioned by no one, and though his oath to King Lluth meant he would follow Lluth's daughter Maegwin to the fires of perdition if that were his duty, he was not altogether pleased to find himself and his people living deep in the rock of the mighty Grianspog.

"Bagba bite me!" Eolair cursed. A drop of burning pitch had fallen on his sleeve, scorching his arm through the thin cloth in the time it took him to put it out. The torch was guttering and would not last much longer. He considered lighting the second, but that would mean it was time to turn back; he was not ready to do that. He briefly weighed the risks of finding himself stuck without light in an unfamiliar tunnel deep in the bowels of the earth, then cursed again, quietly. If he had not been such a hasty idiot, he might have remembered to bring his flints with him. Eolair did not like making that sort of mistake. Too many errors of such an obvious sort and one's luck would at last run out.

His sleeve extinguished, he turned his attention back to the forking of the tunnel, squinting at the floor in the vain hope of seeing something that would help him decide which way to go. Seeing nothing, he hissed in exasperation.

"*Maegwin!*" he called, and heard his voice go rolling out into darkness, echoing down the tunnels. "My lady, are you there?"

The echoes died. Eolair stood in silence with a dying torch and wondered what to do.

It was painfully evident that Maegwin knew her way about this underground maze far better than he did, so perhaps his concern was misplaced. Surely there were no bears or other animals dwelling this far in the depths, or they would have made themselves apparent by now. The tattered remainder of Hernysadharc's citizens had already spent a fortnight in the mountain deeps, building a new home for an unhomed people among the bones of the earth. But there were other things to fear down here beside wild beasts; Eolair could not so lightly dismiss danger. Strange creatures walked in the heights of the mountains, and there had been mysterious deaths and disappearances all across the face of the land long before Skali of Kaldskryke's army came at King Elias' bidding to put down the rebellious Hernystirmen.

Other, more prosaic dangers might await as well: Maegwin could fall and break a leg, or tumble into an underground river or lake. Or she might overestimate her own knowledge of the caverns and wander lost and lightless until she died from starvation.

There was nothing to do but go on. He would walk a short way farther, but turn to go back before his torch was half-consumed. That way, by the time darkness overcame him he should be within hailing distance of the caverns that now housed the greatest remnant of the Hernystiri nation-in-exile.

Eolair lit his second torch with the smoldering remains of the first, then used the smoking butt of the expired brand to mark the wall at the forking of the tunnels with the signature runes of Nad Mullach. After a moment's consideration he chose the wider of the two ways and started forward.

This tunnel, like the one he had just left, had once been part of the mines that crisscrossed the Grianspog. At this depth within the mountains it knifed through solid rock. A moment's thought brought home the unimaginable labor that must have gone into its making. The cross-timbers that braced it up were broad as the trunks of the greatest trees! Eolair could not help admiring the careful but heroic work of the vanished workmen—his and Maegwin's ancestors—who had burrowed their way through the very stuff of the world to bring beautiful things back to the light.

The old tunnel slanted downward. The bobbing torch shone on strange, dim marks scratched into the walls. These tunnels were long-deserted, but still there seemed an expectant air to them, as though they waited for some imminent return. The sound of Eolair's boots on the stone seemed loud as a god's heartbeat, so that the Count of Nad Mullach could not help but think of Black Cuamh, the master of deep places. The earth-god suddenly seemed very real and very near, here in a darkness the sun had never touched since Time's beginning.

Slowing to look more closely at the shallow carvings, Eolair suddenly realized that many of the curious shapes scratched on the walls were crude pictures of hounds. He nodded as understanding came. Old Criobhan had once told him that the miners of elder days called Black Cuamh "Earthdog," and left him offerings in the farthest tunnels so that he would grant his protection against falling rocks or bad air. These carvings were pictures of Cuamh surrounded by the runes of miner's names, tokens that begged the god's favor. Other offerings implored the help of Cuamh's servants, the deep-delving dwarrows, supernatural beings presumed to grant favors and wealthy ore-veins to lucky miners.

Eolair took the snuffed torch and made his initials again beneath a round-eyed hound.

Master Cuamh, he thought, *if you still watch these tunnels, bring Maegwin and our people through to safety. We are sorely, sorely pressed.*

Maegwin. Now there was a distressing thought. Had she no feeling for her responsibilities? Her father and brother were dead. The late king's wife Inahwen was little older than Maegwin herself and far less capable. Lluth's heritage was in the princess' hands—and what was she doing with it?

Eolair had not objected so much to the idea of moving deeper into the caverns: summer had brought no respite from the cold or from Skali's armies, and the slopes of the Grianspog Mountains were not the kind of place to last out a siege of either sort. The Hernystiri who had survived the war were scattered throughout the farthest wildernesses of Hernystir and the Frostmarch, but a large and important part was here with the shreds of the king's household. This was indeed where the kingdom would endure or fail: it was time to make it a more permanent and defensible home.

What *had* worried Eolair, though, was Maegwin's wild fascination with the depths of the earth, with moving ever deeper into the mountain's heart. For days now, long after the shifting of the camps was finished, Maegwin had been wandering away on unspecified errands, disappearing into remote and unexplored caverns for hours at a stretch, returning at sleeping-time with her face and hands dirty and her eyes full of a preoccupation that looked much like madness. Old Criobhan and the others asked her not to go, but Maegwin only drew herself up and coldly declaimed that they had no right to question Lluth's daughter. If she was needed to lead the people in defense of their new home, she said, or to tend the wounded, or to make decisions of policy, she would be there. The rest of the time was her own. She would use it as she saw fit.

Concerned with her safety, Eolair also asked her where she went, suggesting that she should not go wandering in the depths again without him or some other companions. Maegwin, unmoved, would only speak mysteriously of "help from the gods," and the "tunnels that led back into the days of the Peaceful Ones"—as much as saying that small-minded idiots like the Count of Nad Mullach should not concern themselves with things they could not understand.

Eolair thought she was going mad. He was frightened for Maegwin and her people—and also for himself. The count had watched her long slide. Lluth's mortal injury and the treacherous slaying of her brother Gwythinn had wounded something inside her, but the wound was in a place Eolair could not reach and all his best efforts seemed only to make things worse. He did not know why his attempts to help her in her sorrow should distress her so, but he understood that the king's daughter feared being pitied more than she feared death.

Unable to ease her pain, or his own hurt at the sight of her suffering, he could at least help keep her alive. But how could he do even that when the king's daughter did not want to be saved?

Today had been the worst yet. Maegwin had risen before the first gleam of dawn bled through the chink in the cavern roof, then had taken torches and ropes and a collection of other ominous things before vanishing into the tunnels. She had not returned by the end of the afternoon. After supper, Eolair—tired himself from a day's patrolling through the Circoille Woods—had set out after her. If he did not find her soon, he would return and raise a search party.

*   *   *

For the better part of an hour he followed the meandering tunnels downward, marking his progress on the walls, watching his torch dwindle. He had gone beyond the point where he could pretend to himself he would be able to walk all the way back in light. He was unwilling to give up, but if he waited much longer there would be two lost in the catacombs, and what benefit was that to anybody?

He stopped at last in a place where the way opened out into a rough-hewn chamber, with black tunnel mouths leading away in three more directions. He swore, realizing that the time had come to stop fooling himself. Maegwin could be anywhere; he might even have passed her. He would return to the jibes of the others, the princess back safely an hour before. Eolair smiled grimly and bound up his horsetail of black hair, which had come unbraided as he walked. Jokes would not be so bad. Better to suffer a little humiliation than . . .

A thin voice whispered into the rock chamber, a trace of melody faint as an old memory.

> ". . . His voice echoed out through woods and through wild.
> Where two hearts had sounded now beat only one . . ."

Eolair's heart sped. He walked into the chamber's center and cupped his hands around his mouth.

"Maegwin!" he cried. "Where are you, Lady? Maegwin!"

The walls boomed with echoes. When they had died he listened carefully, but there was no answering cry.

"Maegwin, it is Eolair!" he called. Again he waited for the chorus of shouting voices to quiet. This time the stillness was broken by another tenuous strand of song.

> ". . . Her dark eyes sky-watching,
> Only her shining blood gave him answer,
> Her head lay uncradled, her black hair undone . . ."

He moved his head from side to side, determining at last that the singing seemed loudest from the left-hand opening. He ducked his head through and shouted in surprise as he almost tumbled into blackness. He pushed outward at the craggy walls to steady himself, then bent to pick up the torch he had dropped, but even as he reached down, the flame sizzled and vanished. His hand felt water by the torch's haft and empty space beyond. Dancing before his blinded eyes was the last thing he had seen before the light went out, a crude but discernible image painted on black nothing. He was standing at the top of a rough stone staircase that fell away down the steep tunnel, a parade of steps that seemed to lead to the center of the world.

Blackness. Trapped in absolute darkness. Eolair felt a spasm of fear beginning and choked it off. It had been Maegwin's voice he had heard, he was nearly certain. Of course it had been! Who else would be singing old Hernystiri songs in the deeps of creation!

A quiet, childish fear of something that might hide in the dark and summon its prey with familiar voices struggled inside him. Bagba's Herd, what kind of man was he?

He touched the walls on either side. They were damp. The step below him, when he kneeled to inspect it with his fingers, was sunken in the middle; water had pooled there. At a reasonable distance below it lay another step. His probing foot found another lying a similar length below the second.

"Maegwin?" he called again, but no one was singing.

Stepping down cautiously, keeping his hands above his shoulders so he could grab at the walls, Eolair began to make his way down the coarse-hewn stairway. The last flash of light and the picture it had painted had vanished from his eyes. He strained, but could see only darkness. The noise of dripping water, running steadily from the walls on all sides, was the only sound beside his own scuffling feet.

After many cautiously negotiated steps and a drift of time that could have been hours, the stairway ended. As far as he inched his foot ahead, the ground stayed level. Eolair took a few cautious steps forward, cursing himself once more for not bringing his flints. Who would ever have guessed that this short search for a wandering princess would have turned into a struggle for life? And where was the one who had sung, whether Maegwin or some less friendly cavern-dweller?

The tunnel seemed level. He pushed on slowly, following the pathway's twists with one hand dragging on the wall and the other held before him, probing in blackness. After he had gone a few hundred paces the tunnel turned once more. To his immense relief, he found that here he could actually see something: a faint glow outlined the tunnel's interior, brighter at its turning a dozen ells ahead.

As he came around the corner, he was splashed with a strong light welling up from an opening in the tunnel wall. The stone corridor itself continued on until it bent to the right and he could see no farther, but the hole in the wall now drew all his attention. Apprehension speeding his heart more than a little, Eolair got down on his knees and stared through, starting up again with such surprise that he grazed his head on the stone. A moment later he had dangled his legs through the opening, letting himself slide off the floor of the tunnel down into the hole. He landed, bending his knees to keep from falling over, then slowly stood upright.

He was in a wide cavern whose fluted ceilings, ornate with hanging spikes of stone, seemed to waver in the light from a pair of flickering oil lamps. At the far end of the cavern stood a great door, twice as tall as a man, flush with the very face of the rock. The door joined the stone lintel as closely as if it had grown there, its mighty hinges bolted directly to the wall of the cavern. Sitting against the door in a clutter of ropes and tools was . . .

"*Maegwin!*" he cried, running forward, tripping on the uneven ground. The princess' head rested upon on her knees, unmoving. "Maegwin, are you. . . ?"

She raised her head as he approached. Something in her eyes caught him up short. "Princess. . . ?"

"I was sleeping." She shook her head slowly and ran her hands through her sorrel hair. "Sleeping, and dreaming . . ." Maegwin paused and stared at him. Her face was almost black with dirt; her eyes gleamed eerily. "Who. . . ?" she began, then shook her head again. "Eolair! I was having the oddest dream . . . you were calling me . . ."

He sprang forward, squatting at her side. She seemed to have suffered no injury. He quickly ran his hands through her hair, feeling her head for the mark of a fall.

"What are you doing?" she asked, but did not seem overly concerned. "And what are you doing *here?*"

He leaned away so he could look at her face. "I must ask *you* that question, Lady. What are you doing here? Your people are sick with worry."

She smiled lazily. "I knew I would find it," she said. "I knew it."

"What are you talking about?" Eolair said angrily. "Come, we must go back. Thanks to the gods that you have lamps, otherwise we would be trapped here forever!"

"Do you mean you didn't bring a torch? Foolish Eolair! I have brought many things with me, since it is such a long way back to the upper caverns." She gestured at her scattered tools. "I have some bread, I think. Are you hungry?"

Eolair sat back on his heels, baffled. Was this what happened when someone went irretrievably mad? The princess seemed quite happy, here in a hole far beneath the earth. What had happened to her?

"I ask you again," he said as calmly as he could. "What are you doing here?"

Maegwin laughed. "Exploring. At least at first. It is our only hope, you know. To go deeper, that is. We must always keep going deeper, or our enemies will find us."

Eolair let out a hiss of exasperation. "We have done as you wish already, Princess. The people have taken to the caves, as you directed. Now they wonder where the king's daughter has gone."

"But I also knew I would find this," she said, continuing as if Eolair had not spoken. Her voice dropped to a whisper. "The gods have not deserted us," she said, looking around as though she feared eavesdroppers, "—for they have spoken to me in dreams. They have not deserted us." She pointed at the great door behind them. "And neither have our old allies the Sithi—for that is what we need, do we not, Eolair? Allies?" Her eyes were fearfully bright. "I have thought about this until my head is splitting and I know I am right! Hernystir needs help in this terrible hour—and what better allies than the Sithi, who stood with us once before?! Everyone thinks the Peaceful Ones have disappeared from the earth. But they haven't! I am sure they have only *gone deeper*."

"This is more than I can stand," Eolair said, taking her arm. "This is madness, Lady, and it tears my heart in my chest to see you so. Come. Let us go back."

Maegwin pulled away, eyes bright with anger. "You are the one who speaks madness, Count! Go back?! I have spent more hours than I can count cutting the bolt. I had to sleep for a little when I had finished, but I have done it! It is done, and I am going to go through the door! Do not speak to me of going back!"

Eolair looked up to see that the princess spoke truthfully. The bolt, big as a man's wrist, had been chipped through. A hammer and dented chisel lay nearby.

"What is this door?" he asked suspiciously. "It is part of the old mines, surely."

"I told you," she responded coldly. "It is the door to the past—the door that leads to the Peaceful Ones. To the Sithi." As she faced him, her iron gaze seemed to soften and melt. Another emotion pushed its way to the surface, bringing confusion and longing to Maegwin's face; the Count of Nad Mullach felt a deep, helpless pang of sorrow. "Oh, Eolair," she said, pleading now, "don't you see? We can be safe! Come, help me! Please, Eolair, I know you think I am a fool, a plainfaced horse of a woman, but you loved my father! Please, help me open the door!"

Eolair could not meet her gaze. He turned away to stare up at the great door, tears welling in his eyes. Wretched girl! What could have tormented her so? The death of a father and brother? The loss of a kingdom? Tragedies, all—but others who had suffered the same did not fall into such pitiable notions. The Sithi had been real once, certainly—real as rain and stone. But five long centuries had passed since even a rumor of the Fair Folk had made its way to Hernystir. And the idea that the gods were leading Maegwin to these long-vanished Sithi . . . even Eolair, with his respect for the unknown, could still see that this was clearly the madness of her loss speaking.

He wiped his face with his sleeve. The stone facing around the door was covered with strange, intricate symbols and minutely detailed carvings of faces and figures, mostly worn down by dripping water. It was true that they were constructions of exquisite subtlety, seemingly far above even the most ambitious work of Hernystiri miners. What could this place have been? Some ancient temple, from the earliest days? Had strange rituals been performed here for Black Cuamh, away from the simple shrines of other gods that dotted the face of the land above?

Eolair took a breath and wondered if he was making a foolish decision. "I do not wish to hear you malign yourself untruthfully any longer, Princess, and I do not want to carry you back by force. If I help you open the door," he said slowly, not daring to see the painful look of hope on her face, "will you return with me afterward?"

"Oh, yes, whatever you want!" She was childlike in her eagerness. "I will let you decide, because I know when you see the land where the Sithi still live, you will not want to hurry back to any sooty cavern. Yes!"

"Very well, then. I have your word, Maegwin." He stood up and grasped the handle of the door, giving it a sharp tug. There was no movement at all.

"Eolair," Maegwin said quietly.

He pulled again, harder, until he could feel the cords of his neck standing out, but the door did not budge.

"Count Eolair," Maegwin said.

He gave the door another futile pull, then turned. "What?"

She gestured at the door with a broken-nailed finger. "I sawed the bolt through, but the pieces are still there. Shouldn't we take them out?"

"That would make no difference . . ." he began, then looked more closely. Part of the severed bolt had fallen into the door loop, effectively preventing the door's opening. Eolair hissed, then pushed the pieces out. They fell clinking to the damp stone.

This time, as Eolair pulled, the hinges creaked protestingly. Maegwin came forward, curling her hands around the door handle beside the count's, adding her strength to his. The hinges spoke louder. As he kept up the pressure, he distractedly watched the muscles in her forearms. She was strong, this young woman—but then, she never had been a weak or retiring type. Except around him, where he had often noticed her sharp tongue suddenly blunted.

Straining, Eolair sucked in a chestful of air and could not help noticing Maegwin's scent. Sweaty and covered with dirt, the princess did not smell like a perfumed lady from the court in Nabban, but there was something raw and warm and lively about her that was not unpleasant at all. Eolair shook his head at such musings and redoubled his effort, watching Maegwin's determined face as the noise of the hinges rose to a shriek. The door began to grate open—an inch, then a few inches more, then a foot, protesting loudly all the way. When a cubit of blackness was exposed they stopped, leaning against the heavy timbers to catch their breath.

Maegwin bent and picked up a lamp, then slipped through the opening while Eolair was still gasping.

"Princess!" he called breathlessly, then edged through after her. "Wait!

The air may be bad!" Even as he spoke he realized that the air was fine, if a little heavy. "Just . . ." he began, then stopped short at Maegwin's shoulder. The lamp she held threw light all around.

"I told you!" Her voice was full of satisfied awe. "This is where our friends live!"

"Brynioch of the Skies!" Eolair murmured, stunned.

A great city lay before them, stretched along the bottom of a wide canyon. As they stood at the canyon's edge, gazing down, the vast expanse of buildings seemed to be hewed directly from the mountain's heart, as though the entire city were one seamless, incalculably immense piece of living stone. Every window and door had been cut into solid rock, every tower carved out of pillars of pre-existing stone, pillars that stretched up toward the cavern's ceiling far overhead. But for all its size, the city also looked to be surprisingly close, as though it were in truth only a miniature, made to trick the eye. From where they stood on the top steps of a broad staircase that wound down into the canyon, it seemed they could almost reach out and touch the domed roofs.

"The city of the Peaceful Ones . . ." Maegwin said happily.

If it was a Sithi city, Eolair thought, then its immortal inhabitants must have decided their declining years would be better spent on the sunny surface, for this spread of delicately hewn and shaded stone was empty—or so it certainly seemed. Shaken by the discovery of such an uncanny place, the count found himself fervently hoping that it was indeed as deserted as it looked.

The small cell was cold. Duke Isgrimnur snorted miserably, rubbing his hands together.

Mother Church would do better to take a few of those damned offerings and use them to heat her greatest house, he thought. *The tapestries and gold candlesticks are all well and good—but how can anyone admire them when he's freezing to death?*

He had stayed long in the common room the night before, sitting quietly before the great fireplace as he listened to the stories of other traveling monks, most of whom had come to the Sancellan Aedonitis on some sort of business with the lectoral establishment. When friendly questions were directed toward him, Isgrimnur had replied tersely and infrequently, knowing that here—among others of the same guild, so to speak—the danger of his masquerade being detected was greatest.

Now, as he sat listening to the Clavean bell tolling for morning prayer, he felt himself strongly inclined to go back to the common room again. The risk of exposure was great, but how else could be help to uncover the news he so urgently sought?

If only that damnable Count Streáwe spoke straightly. Why should he bring me all the way across Ansis Pelippé just to tell me Miriamele was at the Sancellan Aedonitis? How could he know that? And why should he tell **me,** *about whom he knew only that I was asking questions about two monks, an old one and a young?*

Isgrimnur considered briefly the possibility that Streáwe had known who he was, and worse, that the count had set him to some kind of wild chase on purpose, when Miriamele was in reality nowhere near the lector's palace. But if that was the case, why should Perdruin's master speak to him personally? They had sat there, the count and monkishly-disguised Isgrimnur, drinking wine in the count's own sitting room. *Did* Streáwe know who he was? What did the man have to gain by sending Isgrimnur to the Sancellan Aedonitis?

Trying to puzzle out Count Streáwe's game made Isgrimnur's head ache. What choice did he have, anyway, but to take the count's word at its face value? He had been at a complete dead end, combing the alleyways of Perdruin's greatest city for word of the princess and the monk Cadrach with little result. So here he was, a mendicant monk taking a little charity in Mother Church's bosom, hoping to find out if Streáwe was correct.

He stamped his feet. The soles of his boots were worn thin and the chill seemed to crawl up through the dank stone floors right into the bottoms of his feet. This was foolishness, this hiding in his cell; it would not help him in his quest. He must get out and mix with the Sancellan's swarming throngs. Besides, when he sat too long by himself, the faces of his wife Gutrun and his children came to him, filling him with despair and helpless rage. He remembered the joy when Isorn had come back to him out of captivity, the bursting pride, the exhilaration of fear defeated. Would he live to have another such reunion with them all? God grant that he would. It was his fondest hope, but one that seemed so tenuous that, like a spider web, to handle it unnecessarily might spell its ruin.

But in any case, hope alone was not a fit diet for a knight—even an old one like the duke, with his best days behind him. There was also duty. Now that Naglimund was fallen and Isgrimnur's folk were all scattered God knew where, the only duty he had left was to Miriamele, and to Prince Josua who had sent him after her. Indeed, he was grateful there was something left for him to do.

Isgrimnur stood in the hallway stroking his chin. Praise Usires, the beard stubble was not too pronounced. He had not been able to force himself to shave this morning. The bowl of water had been nearly frozen, and even after several weeks of traveling as a monk he was still not reconciled to running a sharp blade over his face every day. He had worn a beard since his first year as a man. He mourned it now the way he would have a missing hand or foot.

The duke was trying to decide which direction might lead him back

toward the common room—and toward its blazing fire—when he felt a
hand on his arm. He turned quickly, startled, and found himself surrounded by a trio of priests. The one who had touched him, an old man
with a harelip, smiled.

"Did I not see you in the room last night, brother?" he asked. He spoke
the Westerling tongue carefully, hampered by a strong Nabbanai accent.
"You have just come from the north, no? Come and join us for the
morning meal. Are you hungry?"

Isgrimnur shrugged and nodded.

"Good." The old man patted his arm. "I am Brother Septes. These are
Rovalles and Neylin, two others of my order," He indicated the younger
monks. "You will join us, yes?"

"Thank you." Isgrimnur smiled uncertainly, wondering if there was
some monkish etiquette known only to initiates. "God bless you," he
added.

"And you," Septes said, taking Isgrimnur's large arm with his thin
fingers, leading him up the corridor. The other two monks fell in behind,
talking quietly.

"Have you seen the Elysia Chapel yet?" the old man asked.

Isgrimnur shook his head. "I only arrived last night."

"It is beautiful. Beautiful. Our abbey is near Lake Myrme, to the east,
but I try to come here once a year. I always bring a few of the younger
ones with me, to show them the glory that God has built for us here."

Isgrimnur nodded piously. They walked on in silence for a while, their
path joining that of other monks and priests who converged from crisscrossing hallways onto the main thoroughfare, blending together like
shoals of drab fish, being drawn as though by a current toward the dining
hall.

The mass migration slowed at the hall's wide doors. As Isgrimnur and
his new companions joined the pressing throng, Septes asked the duke a
question. Isgrimnur could not hear above the clamor of voices, so the old
man stood on tiptoe to speak into his ear.

"I said, how are things in the north?" Septes almost shouted. "We have
heard terrible stories. Famine, wolves, deadly blizzards."

Isgrimnur nodded, frowning. "Things are very bad," he called back. As
he spoke, he and the others were propelled through the door like a stopper
from the neck of a bottle, and found themselves milling inside the dining
hall entrance. The roar of conversation seemed enough to shake the
roofbeams.

"I thought it was custom to have silence at mealtimes!" Isgrimnur
shouted. Septes' young followers, like the duke, stared goggle-eyed at the
scores of tables that stretched end to end across the wide room. There
were some dozen or so rows, and each table in each row was crowded
with the hunched backs of cassocked men, their tonsured heads a profu-

sion of pink spots, like the fingernails of some hundred-handed ogre. Each man seemed to be engaged in loud conversation with his neighbors, some waving their spoons for attention. The sound was as vast as the ocean that surrounded Nabban.

Septes laughed, the sound subsumed in the greater roaring. He stood on tiptoe again. "It is silent in our abbey at home and in many others—as no doubt it is in your Rimmersgard monasteries, yes? But here at the Sancellan Aedonitis are those who are doing God's business: they must speak and listen just like merchants."

"Speculating on the price of souls?" Isgrimnur grinned sourly, but the old man did not hear him.

"If you prefer silence," Septes shouted, "you should go down to the archives. The priests there are silent as the tomb and a whisper sounds like a thunderclap. Come! Bread and soup can be got over there, where that door is, then you will tell me more about what happens in the north, yes?"

Isgrimnur tried not to watch the old man eat, but it was difficult. Because of his harelip, Septes dribbled soup constantly, and soon had a little river of it running down the front of his robe.

"I am sorry," the old man said at last, mumbling at a crust of bread; he did not seem to have many teeth, either. "I have not asked your name. What are you called?"

"Isbeorn," the duke said. It was his father's name and fairly common.

"Ah, Isbeorn. Well, I am Septes . . . but I told you that, no? Tell us more of what happens in the north. That is another reason I come to Nabban—for news we do not get in the Lakelands."

Isgrimnur told him something of what had happened north of the Frostmarch, of the killing storms and evil times. Choking down his bitterness, he told of Skali of Kaldskryke's usurpation of his own power in Elvritshalla and the devastation and kinslaying that had resulted.

"We had heard that Duke Isgrimnur was proved a traitor to the High King," Septes said, mopping the last of the soup from his bowl with a rind of bread. "Travelers told us that Elias found out the duke was in league with the king's brother Josua to take the throne."

"That's a lie!" Isgrimnur said angrily, smacking his hand on the table so that young Neylin's bowl almost overtipped. Heads turned on all sides.

Septes raised an eyebrow. "Forgive us," he said, "for we only speak of rumors we have heard. Perhaps we have touched on a painful subject. Was Isgrimnur a patron of your order?"

"Duke Isgrimnur is an honest man," the duke said, cursing himself for letting his temper get the best of him. "I hate to hear him slandered."

"Of course," Septes spoke as soothingly as he could while still being heard above the ruckus. "But we have heard other stories from the north as well, very frightening, yes? Rovalles, tell him what the traveler told to you."

Young Rovalles started to speak, but broke into a fit of coughing as he choked on a crust. Neylin, the other acolyte, pounded him on the back until he got his breath, then continued pounding, perhaps a little overexcited at being in Nabban for the first time.

"A man we meet when we are coming here," Rovalles said when Neylin had been restrained, "he is from Hewenshire, or some place up in Erkynland." The young monk did not speak Westerling as well as Septes; he had to stop and think carefully before choosing words. "He say that when Elias' siege cannot throw down Josua's castle, the High King raise up white demons from the earth, and by magic they kill everyone in the keep. He swear it is so, that he sees it himself."

Septes, who had been dabbing at the front of his robe while Rovalles spoke, now leaned forward. "Like me, Isbeorn, you know how full of superstition people can be, yes? If only this man told the story, I would call him madman and have done. But many are speaking quietly here in the Sancellan, many who say Elias has trafficked with demons and evil spirits." He touched Isgrimnur's hand with his bent fingers; the duke fought an urge to recoil. "You must have heard of the siege, even though you say you left the north before it ended. What is the truth behind these stories?"

Isgrimnur stared at the old monk for a moment, wondering if there was more to this question than met the eye. At last he sighed. This was a kindly old man with a harelip, nothing more. These were frightening times—why should Septes not try to cadge information from someone who had come from the heartland of rumor?

"I have heard little more than you," he said at last, "but I can tell you that evil things are afoot—things that godly men would rather not know about, but damn me if that makes them go away." Septes' eyebrow twitched upward again at Isgrimnur's language, but he did not interrupt. Isgrimnur, warming to the subject, spoke on. "Sides are forming, you could say, and some that look prettier are really the fouler. I can't say more than that. Don't believe everything you hear, but don't be too quick to cry 'superstition,' either . . ." He broke off, realizing that he was entering dangerous territory. There was little more he could say without attracting attention as a source of substantiation for the gossip that was doubtless flying through the Sancellan Aedonitis. He could not afford to be the subject of attention until he had learned if Princess Miriamele was indeed here.

The bits and pieces he had doled out, however, seemed to satisfy Septes. The old man leaned back, still scratching idly at the drying soup stain on his breast. "Ah," he nodded. His voice just carried above the tabletalk. "Welladay, we have heard enough fearsome stories to take what you say seriously, yes? Very seriously." He gestured for the nearest acolyte to help him up. "Thank you for sharing our meal, Isbeorn," he said. "God keep you. I hope we can speak more in the common room tonight. How long do you stay?"

"I'm not sure yet," Isgrimnur replied. "My thanks to you, too."

The old man and his two companions disappeared into the crush of retreating monks, leaving Isgrimnur to sort out his thoughts. After a moment he gave up and rose from the table.

I can't even hear myself think in here. He shook his head grimly, pushing toward the doorway. His large size helped him make rapid progress and he reached the main hallway swiftly. *Now I've gone and spouted my own piece, but I'm not a whit closer to finding poor Miriamele,* he thought sourly. *And how can I find out her whereabouts, anyway? Just ask someone if Elias' missing daughter is anywhere in the place? Oh, and she's traveling as a boy, besides. That's even better. Perhaps I'll just ask around, find out if any young monks have shown up at the Sancellan Aedonitis lately.*

He gave a bitter snort as he watched the river of habited forms swirl past.

Elysia, Mother of God, I wish Eolair was with me. That damned Hernystirman loves this kind of nonsense. He'd track her down quick enough, with his smooth ways. What am I doing here?

The Duke of Elvritshalla rubbed his fingers along his unnaturally smooth jaw. Then, startling even himself, he began to laugh at his own hopeless foolishness.

Passing priests eddied nervously around the big-bellied northern monk, who was evidently caught up in some kind of religious fit. Isgrimnur roared and bellowed with laughter until the tears coursed down his chafed pink cheeks.

Thunderstorm weather lay on the swamp like a blanket, damp and oppressively hot. Tiamak could feel the storm's yearning hunger to exist; its prickly breath made the hair stand up on his arms. What he would not give for the storm to break and a little cool rain to fall! The thought of raindrops splashing on his face and bending the leaves of the mangroves seemed like a dream of the most benevolent magic.

Tiamak sighed as he lifted his pole from the water and laid it across the thwarts of his flatboat. He stretched, trying without success to unkink the muscles of his back. He had been poling for three days and had suffered two near-sleepless nights filled with worry about what he should do. If he went to Kwanitupul and stayed there, would he be betraying his tribesmen? Could they ever understand a debt he owed to drylanders—or owed to a few drylanders, anyway?

Of course they wouldn't understand. Tiamak frowned and reached for his waterskin, sloshing a generous mouthful around before swallowing it. He had always been thought of as strange. If he did not go to Nabban to plead his people's case with Duke Benigaris, he would simply be a strange traitor. That would be the end of it as far as the elders of Village Grove were concerned.

He took his kerchief from his head and dipped it over the side of the boat into the water, then arranged it atop his hair once more. Blessedly cool water dribbled down his face and neck. The bright, long-tailed birds perched in the branches overhead stopped screeching for a moment as a dim rumble rolled across the swamp. Tiamak felt his heart beat faster.

He Who Always Steps on Sand, let the storm come soon!

His boat had begun to slow when he had stopped poling. Now the stern began to swing gradually out to the middle of the watercourse, turning him sideways so that he faced the bank—or rather, what would have been the bank if this were a dryland river. Here in the Wran it was only a tangle of clustered mangroves whose roots held in just enough sand for the colony of trees to grow and prosper. Tiamak made a resigned noise and pushed his pole back into the water once more, straightening the boat and prodding it forward through a thick clump of lilies which clutched at his passing hull like the fingers of drowning swimmers. It was several more days to Kwanitupul, and that was if the storm he was praying for did not bring heavy winds in its train, winds which might uproot trees and make this part of the Wran an unpassable snarl of roots and trunks and broken branches.

He Who Always Steps on Sand, he amended his prayer, *let a cooling but gentle storm come soon!*

His heart felt unutterably heavy. How could he choose between two such awful possibilities? He could go as far as Kwanitupul before choosing whether to stay there in accordance with Morgenes' wishes or to go on to Nabban as Older Mogahib and the rest had ordered. He tried to soothe himself with that idea, but wondered if such thinking was not in fact just like allowing a wound to fester, when instead he should grit his teeth and clean it out so the healing could start?

Tiamak thought of his mother, who had spent most of her life on her knees, tending the cookfire, grinding grain in the pestle, working every day from the darkness before dawn until it was time to crawl into the hammock at night. He had little respect for the village elders, but now he felt a sudden fear that his mother's spirit might be watching him. She would never understand her son turning his back on his people for the sake of strangers. She would want him to go to Nabban. Serve his own folk first, then take care of his personal honor, that was what his mother would say.

Thinking of her made it seem very clear. He was a Wrannaman first:

nothing would change that. He must go to Nabban. Morgenes, that kind old man, would understand his reasons. Afterward, after he had finished his duties to his people, he would go back to Kwanitupul as his drylander friends had asked.

The decision lifted part of the load of worry from Tiamak's shoulders. He decided he might as well stop soon and scare up something for a noon meal. He reached down and tested his fishing line, tied to the back of the flatboat. It seemed light; as he pulled it up he saw to his disgust that the bait had been eaten again, but whatever had dined at his expense had not waited around to pay respects. At least the hook was still there. Metal hooks were painfully expensive items—he had paid for this one with an entire day of work as an interpreter in the market at Kwanitupul. The next month at market he had found the parchment with Nisses' name on it, and had paid a full day's wages for that as well. Two expensive purchases, but the fishhook had indeed proved much sturdier than the ones he whittled of bone, which usually broke on the first snag. The Nisses parchment—he patted protectively at the oilskin bag lying at his feet—if he was correct about its origins, was a gem beyond price. Not bad work for two days' marketing.

Tiamak hauled in the line, wrapping it gently, then steered the boat over closer to the bank of mangroves. He poled along slowly, waiting until the mangrove roots gave way for a while to a short stretch of soggy dirt cluttered with waving reeds. Bringing the boat as close to the edge of the watercourse as he could, he pulled his knife from his belt and dug in the wet soil, at last turning up some spitfly roe. He wrapped the shiny things in his kerchief, saving one only to bait the hook. This done, he tossed the line back into the water to trail behind the boat. As he poled out into the middle of the stream once more, thunder grumbled in the distance. It seemed to be farther away than last time. He shook his head sadly. The storm was in no hurry.

It was late afternoon when he passed out of the overhanging thicket of mangroves and emerged into unshadowed sunlight once more. Here the waterway grew wider and deeper. A sea of reeds rolled out toward the horizon, all but motionless in the oppressive heat, crisscrossed with the shining tracks of other watercourses. The sky was gray with threatening clouds, but the sun burned brightly behind them, and Tiamak could not help but feel more lighthearted. An ibis rose, white wings flapping slowly, then settled down into the reeds a short distance away. To the south, past miles of marsh and swamp forest, he could see the dark line of the Nascadu Mountains. To the west, invisible beyond an endless prairie of cattails and mangroves, lay the sea.

Tiamak poled distractedly, momentarily caught up in a correction he had decided to make in his great work of scholarship, a revision of *The*

Sovran Remedies of the Wranna Healers. He had suddenly realized that the shape of the cattail itself might have something to do with its use among the men of the Meadow Thrithings as a marital potion, and was planning the wording of a footnote that would delicately suggest this connection without seeming too clever, when he felt a strange vibration against his back. He turned, startled, and saw that his fishing line was pulled taut, humming like the plucked string of a lute.

For a moment he was sure it must be a snag—the pull was so strong that it had imparted some of its tension to the stern of the boat—but as he leaned over he saw some silver-gray thing rise briefly toward the surface, wriggling, then dive down into the brackish water again. A fish! As long as Tiamak's arm! He gave a small cry of delight and began to pull on the line. The silver thing seemed to leap up at him. For a split instant one pale, shiny fin appeared above the water, then it vanished beneath the boat, stretching the line tight. Tiamak heaved and it gave a little, but not much. It was a strong fish. A sudden image of the line snapping and his next two days' worth of meals swimming away filled Tiamak's heart with sick horror. He lessened the tension on the fishing line. He would let the fish tire itself, then he could reel it in at his leisure. In the meantime, he would keep an eye open for a dry patch where he could build a fire. He could wrap the fish in *minog* leaves, and surely there would be wild quickweed growing somewhere nearby . . . In his thoughts he could already taste it. The heat, the recalcitrant thunderstorm, his betrayal of Morgenes (as he still saw it) and all else receded in the warm glow of the contemplated meal. He tested the line again, rejoicing at the firm, steady pull. He had not had fresh fish in weeks!

A splash impinged on his reverie. Tiamak looked up to see a rainbow of ripples spreading beside the shoreline, a couple of long stone-throws away. There was something else as well: a moment later he picked out a row of low bumps like tiny islands moving smoothly through the water toward his boat.

Crocodile! Tiamak's heart quailed. His wonderful dinner! He tugged hard at the line, but the fish was still beneath the flatboat and resisting fiercely; the line burned his palms as he struggled unsuccessfully to wrestle the fish to the surface. The crocodile was a dark blur just below the surface, the motion of its powerful tail sending eddies across the still water. Its craggy back breached for just a moment, a hundred cubits from where Tiamak sat, then it was gone—diving toward *his* fish!

There was no time to think, no time at all. His dinner, his fishing hook, his line, all would be lost if he waited a moment longer. Tiamak felt a black rage flare into life in his empty stomach and a band of pain tighten itself around his temples. His mother, had she lived to see him at this moment, would hardly have recognized her shy, clumsy son. If she had seen what he did next, she would have stumbled to the shrine of She Who

Birthed Mankind at the back wall of the family hut, then fainted dead away.

Tiamak looped the cord tied to his knife-hilt around his wrist, then flung himself over the stern of the boat. Mumbling inarticulately with anger and despair, he barely sucked in a hasty breath and closed his mouth before the green, cloudy water closed over his head.

Flailing, he opened his eyes. The sunlight filtered down through the watercourse, passing through plumes of drifting silt as through clouds. He darted a glance up at the rectangular darkness that was the bottom of his boat and saw a glittering shape hanging there. Despite his wild, heart-thumping panic, he felt a moment of satisfaction at the size of the fish lying torpid at the end of his line. Even his father Tugumak would have had to admit it was a splendid catch!

As he stroked upward, reaching toward his prize, the shimmering thing darted along the boat-bottom and slipped out of sight along the craft's far side, rising up out of Tiamak's view. The line pulled taut against the wooden hull. The Wrannaman snatched at it wildly, but it now hugged the boat so tightly that his fingers could find no purchase. He gave a little cough of dread, sending bubbles dancing outward. Hurry, he must hurry! The crocodile would be upon him in a moment!

His heartbeat boomed in the watery silence of his ears. His scrabbling fingers could not grip the line. The fish remained out of sight and out of reach, as if perversely determined that it should not suffer alone, and panic was making Tiamak clumsy. He finally gave up and pushed himself away from the bottom of the boat, kicking to bring himself upright. The fish was lost. He had to save himself.

Too late!

A dark shape slid past him and angled upward, slipping in and out of the shadow of his boat. The crocodile was not the largest he had ever seen, but it was certainly the largest he had ever been beneath. Its white belly passed over him, the tail a diminishing stripe buffeting him with its wake.

His breath was pressing on his lungs, burning to escape and fill the murky water with bubbles. He kicked and turned, his eyes feeling as though they would push from his head, and saw the blunt arrow-shape of the crocodile skimming toward him. Its jaws parted. There was a glimpse of red-shadowed darkness and an infinity of teeth. He whirled, swinging his arm, and watched the horrifyingly slow movement of the knife as he pushed it against the wall of water. The reptile thumped against his ribs, rasping him with its horny hide as he struggled out of its way. His knife bit shallowly into its flank, dragging along the armored skin for a moment before bouncing off. A thin brown-black cloud trailed the crocodile as it swam on, circling the boat once more.

Tiamak's lungs felt as though they had grown impossibly large within his chest, straining at his ribs until spots of blackness began to appear before his eyes. Why had he been such a fool? He didn't want to die like this, drowned and eaten!

Even as he tried to struggle upward toward the surface, he felt a crushing pressure enfold his leg; in the next instant, he was jerked downward. His knife spilled loose from his hand, and his arms and free leg kicked wildly as he was pulled toward the darkness of the river bottom. A belch of bubbles escaped his lips. The faces of the elders of his tribe, Mogahib and Roahog the Potter and others, seemed to press down on his dimming sight, their expressions full of weary disgust at his idiocy.

His knife-cord still looped his wrist; as he whirled down into river-darkness he struggled to find the hilt. His hands coiled against it and he summoned his strength, then leaned forward against the bottomward pull, finding the hard, rough jaws that clutched his leg. Clinging with one hand so that he could feel the crooked teeth beneath his fingers, he set the knifepoint against the leathery eyelid and pushed. The head jerked beneath his hands as the crocodile convulsed and bit down harder, which sent a bolt of scalding pain up his leg and into his heart. Another clutch of precious bubbles sprang from Tiamak's mouth. He pushed the blade in as hard as he could, his thoughts a swirling black blur of faces and nonsensical words. As he twisted at the handle in mad agony, the crocodile loosened its jaws. He pulled at its upper jaw with desperate strength, forcing it up just far enough to jerk his leg free before it snapped shut again. The water was clouding with blood. Tiamak could feel nothing beneath his knee at all, nothing above it but the fiery pain of his bursting lungs. Somewhere below him the crocodile was tying itself in dark knots on the river bottom, swimming in ever-narrowing circles. Tiamak tried to claw upward toward the remembered sun, even as he felt the spark within him dying.

He passed through many darknesses, coming at last into the light.

The daystar was in the gray sky; the cattails stood windless and silent along the edge of the water. He gasped in a lifetime's worth of hot marsh air, opening his entire body to it, then almost sank beneath the water again as it rushed into his lungs like a river shattering its dam and spilling down into a parched valley. Light of every hue gleamed before his eyes, until he felt as though he had discovered some ultimate secret. A moment later, as he saw his boat bobbing on the unsettled water a short distance away, the sense of revelation evaporated. He felt a sick, debilitating blackness again come crawling up his spine into his skull. He struggled toward the boat, his body curiously painless, as though he were nothing but a head floating upon the watercourse. He reached the side of the flatboat and clung, breathing deeply as he summoned his strength. By sheer will he pulled himself over into safety, scraping his cheek raw on the thwart, not caring in the least. The blackness overcame him at last. He stopped struggling and sank beneath its surface.

★ ★ ★

He awakened to a sky red as blood. A hot wind swept across the marshland. The blazing sky seemed inside his head as well, for he burned like a fired pot fresh from the kiln. With fingers that felt awkward as pieces of wood, he scrabbled his spare breechclout from the bottom of the boat and tied it tightly around the red ruin of his lower leg, unable to think much about the bleeding runnels that had been gouged from knee to heel. Struggling against the oblivion that was reaching out for him, he wondered absently if he would be able to walk again, then dragged himself to the edge of the boat and pulled at the fishing line which still hung over the side, trailing into green depths. With his failing strength he managed to wrestle the silver fish over the stern, letting it slide wriggling down next to him in the boat's shallow belly. The fish's eye was open; its mouth, too, as though it were trying to ask Death a question.

He rolled onto his back, staring up into the violet sky. There was a resounding crack and rumble from above. A flurry of raindrops danced on his fevered skin. Tiamak smiled as he once more fell away into darkness.

Isgrimnur got up from the bench and strode to the fireplace, turning to present his rump to the blaze. He would be off to bed in a short while, so he might as well soak up all the warmth he could before he had to return to that be-damned, arse-freezing cell.

He listened to the muted sounds of conversation that filled the common room, marveling at the diversity of accents and languages. The Sancellan Aedonitis was like a little world of its own, even more so than the Hayholt, but varied as the talk had been all evening, he was not an inch closer to solving any of his problems.

The duke had paced the near-endless halls all morning and afternoon, keeping an eye open for a suspicious pair of monks or anything else that might ease his predicament. His search had been fruitless, except to remind him of the size and power of Mother Church. He had become so frustrated by his inability to discover whether Miriamele was here or not that as the afternoon waned he had left the Sancellan Aedonitis entirely.

He took his supper in an inn partway down the Sancelline Hill, then walked quietly in the Hall of Fountains, something he had not done for many years. He and Gutrun had visited the fountains shortly before their marriage, when they had come to Nabban on a nuptial pilgrimage traditional in Isgrimnur's family. The glistening play of water and its continual music had filled him with a kind of pleasant melancholy; although his longing and worry for his wife were great, for the first time in weeks he had been able to think of her without being overwhelmed by pain. She *must* be safe—and Isorn, too. He would just believe it, for what else could he do? The rest of the family, his other son and two daughters, were in the capable hands of old Thane Tonnrud in Skoggey. Sometimes, when all was uncertain, a man just had to trust in the goodness of God.

After his walk, Isgrimnur had returned to the Sancellan, his mind calmed and ready to turn to his task once more. His companions from the morning meal had come in for a while but had left early, old Septes explaining that they kept "country hours." The duke had sat and listened long to the talk of others, but to no avail.

Much of the gossip, although couched in careful terms, seemed to be about whether Lector Ranessin would legitimize Benigaris' succession to Nabban's ducal seat. Not that anything Lector Ranessin might say would actually lift Benigaris' hind end from the throne, but the Benidrivine House and Mother Church had long ago reached a delicate balance concerning Nabban's governance. There was much worry that the lector would do something rash, like denounce Benigaris on the basis of the rumors that the new duke had betrayed his father, or had not defended him properly in the battle before Naglimund, but most of the Nabbanai priests—the Sancellan's home-grown men—were quick to assure their foreign brethren that Ranessin was an honorable and diplomatic man. The lector, they promised, would certainly do the right thing.

Duke Isgrimnur flapped the hem of his cassock, trying to force a little warm air up beneath the garment. If only the lector's honor and diplomacy could solve _everybody's_ problems . . .

Of course! That's it! Damn my ignorant eyes for not seeing it before! Isgrimnur smacked a broad hand on his thigh and chuckled fruitily. _I'll talk to the lector. Whatever he thinks, my secret will be safe with him. I'm sure Miriamele's will, too. If anyone has the authority to find her here without raising a fuss, it's His Sacredness._

The duke felt much better after this solution had presented itself. He turned and rubbed his hands before the flames a few more times, then set out across the polished wooden floor of the common room.

A small crowd at one of the arched doorways caught his attention. Several monks were standing in the open door; several others stood on the balcony outside, cold air bleeding in past them. Many of the common room's other inhabitants were protesting, or had already given up and moved nearer the fire. Isgrimnur wandered over, his hands tucked up in his voluminous sleeves as he peered over the shoulder of the hindmost monk.

"What is it?" he asked. He could see a couple of dozen men milling in the courtyard below, half of them on horseback. It seemed nothing unusual: the figures moved calmly and unhurriedly, those on foot apparently the Sancellan's guards, greeting new arrivals.

"It's the High King's counselor," the monk standing before him said. "That Pryrates fellow. He used to be here once—in the Sancellan Aedonitis, I mean. They say he's a clever one."

Isgrimnur clenched his teeth, choking down a shout of anger and surprise. He felt a hot breath of fury moving within him and stood up on his toes to see. There indeed was the priest's tiny, hairless head bobbing atop a scarlet cloak that looked orange in the gateyard torchlight. The duke found himself wondering how he could get close enough to stick a knife into the sneaking traitor. Ah, sweet God, but that would be satisfying!

But what good would it do, fool, besides the admitted good of removing Pryrates from this earth? It would not find Miriamele, and I would never escape to search for her after the deed was done. Not to mention what would happen if Pryrates did not die—p'raps he has some sorcerous shield.

No, it would not do. But if he could get in to see the lector, he would give Ranessin an earful about that devil's bastard of a red priest and his hellish counseling of the High King. But what was Pryrates doing here of all places?

Isgrimnur tramped off to bed, thoughts of mayhem denied swimming through his mind.

Twenty cubits below, Pryrates looked up to the common room balcony as though he had heard someone calling his name, his black eyes glitteringly intent, his pale head gleaming like a toadstool in the shadows of the gateyard. The spectators in the common room, separated by distance and darkness, could not see the smile that curled across the priest's gaunt face, but they could feel the sudden draught of chill air that swept down on the Sancellan Aedonitis, setting the guards' cloaks to billowing. Goosefleshed, the monks on the balcony quickly made their way inside, pushing the door shut behind them before hastening back to the fire.

12

Birdsflight

Simon and his companions left Binabik's people behind and rode southeast along the base of the Trollfells, clinging to the foothills like a nervous child unwilling to wade into deeper water. On their right, the white emptiness of the Waste stretched away into the distance.

In the middle of the gray afternoon, as they walked their horses across a thin trail of stones that made an uncertain crossing over one of Blue Mud Lake's inlet streams, a wedge of cranes flew overhead, gabbling and honking until it seemed they would rattle the sky. The birds swerved above the riders' heads, wings thrusting, then banked as one and flew into the south.

"Three months it is before they should be making that journey," Binabik said ruefully. "It is wrong, very wrong. Spring and summer have been retreated like a beaten army."

"It doesn't seem much colder than it did when we were on our way to Urmsheim," Simon offered, clutching at Homefinder's reins.

"That was in late spring," Sludig grunted, working to keep his footing on the water-slicked stones. "Now we are in midsummer."

Simon thought about that. "Oh," he said.

They stopped on the stream's far bank to share a few of the provisions that Binabik's folk had sent with them. The sun was gray and remote. Simon wondered where he would be when another summer came—*if* another summer came.

"Can the Storm King make it winter forever?" he asked.

Binabik shrugged. "That is not in my knowledge. He has been making winter very well during these Yuven- and Tiyagar-months. Let us not think of it, Simon. It will not be making our task any easier to worry over such things. Either the Master of Storms will triumph or he will not. There is nothing else for doing with what we have been given."

Simon swung himself clumsily into his saddle. He envied Sludig's practiced grace. "I'm not talking about stopping it," he said testily. "I just wondered what he was going to *do*."

"If I could know," Binabik sighed, "I would not be cursing myself for an unfit student of my good master." He whistled for Qantaqa.

They stopped again that afternoon while some daylight still remained to scavenge for firewood and give Sludig some time to instruct Simon. The Rimmersman found a long tree limb beneath the snow and broke it in half, binding a strip of rag around one end of each piece for an easier grip.

"Can't we use real swords?" Simon asked. "I'm not going to be fighting anyone with wood."

Sludig raised a skeptical eyebrow. "So? You would prefer slipping and sliding on wet ground while fighting a trained swordsman with real blades? Using this black sword, perhaps, that you cannot lift half the time?" He indicated Thorn with a jerk of his head. "I know it is cold and dreary on this journey, Simon, but are you really so anxious to die?"

Simon stared hard. "I'm not so clumsy. You told me so yourself. And Haestan taught me some things."

"In a fortnight?" Sludig's look turned to amusement. "You are brave, Simon, and lucky, too—a trait not to be overlooked—but I am trying to make you a better fighter. The next thing you fight against may not be a brutish Hunë but an armored man. Now, take your new sword and hit me."

He kicked the branch to Simon and lifted his own weapon. Simon held the tree limb before him and circled slowly. The Rimmersman was right: the snowy ground was treacherous. Before he could even take a swing at his instructor, his feet went out from under him and he toppled heavily onto his rump. He remained there, scowling furiously.

"Don't be embarrassed," Sludig said, taking a step forward and laying the end of his cudgel against Simon's chest. "When you fall down—and men do trip and stumble in battle—make sure and keep your blade up or you may not live to resume the fight."

Seeing the sense in this, Simon grunted and shoved the Rimmersman's branch away with his hand before getting onto his knees. He then rose to his feet once more and resumed his crablike circling.

"Why are you doing that?" Sludig said. "Why do you not swing at me?"

"Because you're faster than I am."

"Good. You are right." As he finished speaking, Sludig snapped his cudgel out, landing a smarting blow below Simon's ribs. "But you must stay balanced at all times. I caught you with your feet crossed one over the other." He aimed another blow, but this time Simon was able to twist his body out of the way, then return a swing of his own which Sludig deflected toward the ground.

"Now you are learning, Warrior Simon!" Binabik called. He sat beside the young fire, scratching Qantaqa's neck as he watched the cudgel-play. It was hard to tell whether it was due to the scratching or to the spectacle of Simon being thrashed, but the wolf seemed to be enjoying herself immensely: her tongue hung from her grinning mouth and her brushy tail twitched in pleasure.

Simon and the Rimmersman worked for about an hour. Simon did not land a single blow, but received quite a few in return. When he at last flopped down to rest on a flat stone by the fire-circle, he was more than willing to take a swallow of kangkang from Binabik's bag. He was willing to take a second swallow as well, and would have taken a third, but Binabik retrieved the skin bag.

"I would be doing no friendliness if I let you drink yourself drunken, Simon," the troll said firmly.

"It's just because my ribs ache."

"You have youth and will be fast healing," Binabik replied. "I am, in a way, in responsibility for your care."

Simon made a face but did not argue. It was nice that someone cared about him, he supposed, even if he did not entirely agree with the form that caring took.

Two more days of cold riding along the skirts of the Trollfells—as well as two more evenings of what the recipient began to think of as "scullion smacking"—did not do much to brighten Simon's view of the world. Many times during his instruction, as he sat on the soggy ground feeling some new part of his body throb into painful prominence, he considered telling Sludig he was no longer interested, but the memory of Haestan's pale face inside his winding cloth forced him onto his feet once more. The guardsman had wanted Simon to learn these things, to be able to defend himself and also to help defend others. Haestan had never been able to quite explain the way he felt—the Erkynlander had not been a man given to aimless talking—but he had often said that "strong folk a-bullyin' th'weak" was not right.

Simon thought back on Fengbald, Elias' ally. He had taken a troop of armored men and burned down a district of his own earldom, slaughtering with a free hand because the guild of weavers had flouted his will. It made Simon feel a little sick to remember how he had admired Fengbald and his handsome armor. Bullies, that was the proper name for the Earl of Falshire and his like—Pryrates, too, although the red priest was a bully of a subtler and more frightening sort. Simon sensed that Pryrates did not so much revel in his ability to crush those who opposed him, as Duke Fengbald and others like him did; rather, the priest used his strength with a kind of thoughtless cruelty, heeding no obstacles between himself and his unknown goals. But whichever was true, it was bullying all the same.

On more than one occasion the memory of the hairless priest was enough to bring Simon back up from the ground, swinging fiercely. Sludig would back off, eyes narrowed in concentration, until he could control Simon's fury in a way that would force the youth back into the lesson once more. The thought of Pryrates reminded Simon of why he must learn to fight—not that sword skill would be of use against the alchemist, but it might keep him alive long enough to get at Pryrates once more. The priest had many crimes to answer for, but the death of Doctor Morgenes and Simon's banishment from his own home were reasons enough to keep Pryrates' face before Simon's eyes, even as he crossed staves with Sludig in the snows of the White Waste.

Shortly after the dawning of the fourth day since they had left Blue Mud Lake, Simon awakened shivering beneath the flimsy shelter of lashed-together branches in which the foursome had spent the night. Qantaqa, who had been lying across his legs, had gone out to rejoin Binabik. The loss of her furry warmth was enough to bring Simon out into the crystal-line morning light, teeth chattering as he brushed pine needles from his hair.

Sludig was nowhere in sight, but Binabik sat on a snowy stone beside the remains of the previous night's fire, staring into the eastern sky as though contemplating the direct light of the sun. Simon turned to follow the line of Binabik's gaze, but could see nothing but the pale sun itself crawling up past the last peaks of the Trollfells.

Qantaqa, lying at the troll's feet, raised her head briefly as Simon approached crunchingly through the snow, then lay her shaggy head back down on her paws once more.

"Binabik? Are you well?" Simon asked.

The troll seemed not to hear him for a moment, then turned slowly, a slight smile creasing his face. "A good morning to you, Simon-friend," he said. "I am feeling completely well."

"Oh. I just . . . you were staring."

"Look." Binabik extended a stubby finger from the sleeve of his jacket, pointing into the east.

Simon turned to look once more, shading his eyes. "I don't see anything."

"Be looking more closely. Look to the last peak, standing on your right hand. There." He indicated an icy slope, thrown into shadow by the sun behind it.

Simon stared for some time, unwilling to admit failure. A moment before he gave up in despair, he at last saw something: dark lines running beneath the glassy face of the mountain like facets in a gemstone. He squinted, trying to make out the details.

"Do you mean those shadows?" he asked at last. Binabik nodded, a rapt expression on his face. "Well," Simon demanded, "what are they?"

"More than shadows," Binabik said quietly. "What you are there seeing are the towers of lost Tumet'ai."

"Towers inside the mountain? And what's 'Tooma-tie'?"

Binabik frowned mockingly. "Simon. You have been hearing its name several times. What kind of student did Doctor Morgenes take on? Are you remembering when I spoke with Jiriki of the *'Ua'kiza Tumet'ai nei-R'i'anis'?*"

"Sort of," Simon said uncomfortably. "What is it?"

"The song of the fall of the city of Tumet'ai, one of the great Nine Cities of the Sithi. That song is telling the tale of Tumet'ai's abandonment. Those shadows you see are its towers, imprisoned in many thousand years of ice."

"Truly?" Simon stared at the dark vertical blurs that ran like stains beneath the milky ice. He tried to see them as towers, but could not. "Why did they abandon it?" he asked.

Binabik ran his hand along the fur of Qantaqa's back. "A number of reasons there are, Simon. If you like, I will tell you part of its story later, when we are riding. It will be a help for passing the time."

"Why did they build their city on an icy mountain in the first place?" Simon asked. "That seems stupid."

Binabik looked up peevishly. "You are speaking, Simon, to one raised in the mountains, as you are no doubt able to recall. Part of manhood, I am thinking, is to ponder one's words before opening one's mouth."

"I'm sorry." Simon tried to suppress a mischievous smile. "I didn't realize that trolls actually liked living where they do."

"Simon," Binabik said sternly, "I think it would be a good thing if you went to gather up the horses."

"So, Binabik," Simon said at last, "what are the Nine Cities?"

They had been riding for an hour, tilting away at last from the base of the mountains and out onto the vast white sea of the Waste, following the line of what Binabik called the Old Tumet'ai Road, a broad causeway that had once linked the ice-bound city with its sisters to the south. There was little to see of any road now, only a few large stones still standing on either side of the trail and an occasional patch of cobbles still in place beneath the covering snow.

Simon had not asked the question out of any real eagerness to learn more history—his head was already crammed so full of strange names and places he could scarcely hold a thought—but the featureless terrain, the endless field of snow dotted with forlorn stands of trees, made him hungry for a story.

Binabik, who had ridden slightly ahead, whispered something to Qantaqa. Leaking plumes of vaporous breath, the wolf stopped in her wide tracks until Simon had caught up. Simon's mare shied and pranced away. As Qantaqa crunched inoffensively alongside, Simon patted the horse's neck, speaking low words of encouragement. After a few head-swinging paces, she was able to continue her progress with nothing more than an occasional nervous snort. For her part, the wolf paid no attention to the horse at all, her head held low as she sniffed at the snow.

"Good, Homefinder, good." Simon ran his hand down her shoulder, feeling the tremendous muscles moving beneath his fingers. He had named her and now she obeyed him! He felt himself filled with quiet joy. She was his horse now.

Binabik smiled at Simon's prideful expression. "You show her respect. That is a good thing," he said. "Too often it is that men think those who serve are doing it from inferiorness or weakness." He chuckled. "Folk who have those beliefs should ride a mount like Qantaqa, who could eat them if she chose. They would then be learning humbleness." He scratched the ridge of fur between Qantaqa's shoulders; the wolf stopped pacing for a moment to appreciate the attention, then dug forward through the snow once more.

Sludig, riding just ahead, turned to look back. "Hah! You will be a horseman as well as a fighter, is that right? Our friend Snowlock is the boldest kitchen boy in the world!"

Simon scowled, embarrassed, and felt his skin wrinkling around his cheek-scar. "That's not my name."

Sludig laughed at his discomfiture. "And what is wrong with 'Simon Snowlock' for a name? It is a true name, honorably won."

"If it is displeasing, Simon-friend," Binabik said kindly, "we will call you some other thing. But Sludig speaks rightly: your name was gained with honor, given to you by Jiriki of the highest Sithi house. The Sithi are seeing more clearly than mortals—at least in some ways. Like any of their other gifts, a name is not to be discarded with easiness. Do you remember when you held the White Arrow above the river?"

Simon did not have to think hard. The moment when he had fallen into the turbulent Aelfwent, despite all the strange adventures he had suffered since, remained a black spot in his memory. It had been his idiot pride, of course—the other side of his mooncalf nature—that had sent him down into the swirling depths. He had been trying to show Miriamele how lightly he regarded even the gifts of the Sithi. The very thought of his foolishness made him feel ill. What an ass he was! How could he ever hope Miriamele could care about him?

"I remember," was all he said, but the joy of his moment was gone. Anyone could ride a horse, even a mooncalf. Why should he grow so large in his own estimation just because he had kept an already battle-hardened mare from balking? "You were going to tell me about the Nine Cities, Binabik," he said heavily.

The troll lifted an eyebrow at Simon's despairing tone, but did not pursue the subject. Instead, he brought Qantaqa to a halt.

"Turn for a moment and be looking back," the troll said, gesturing to both Simon and Sludig. The Rimmersman made an impatient noise, but did as Binabik asked.

The sun had pulled free from the mountain's embrace. Its slanting rays now blazed along the face of the easternmost peak, laying fire along its icy cheek and throwing deep shadows in the crevices. The imprisoned towers, dark streaks at dawn, now seemed to glow with warm reddish light, like blood running through the mountain's cold arteries.

"Look well," Binabik said. "We may none of us be ever seeing that sight again. Tumet'ai was a place of highest magic, as were all the great cities of the Sithi. Their like will never again come to the light." The troll took a deep breath, then suddenly and startlingly burst out into song.

> *"T'seneí mezu y'eru,*
> *Iku'do saju-rhá,*
> *O do'ini he-huru.*
> *Tumet'ai! Zi'inu asuná!*
> *Shemisayu, nun'ai temuy'á . . ."*

Binabik's voice carried out through the windless morning, disappearing with no answering echo. "That is the beginning of the song of Tumet'ai's fall," he said solemnly. "A very old song, and one of which I am knowing only a few verses. That one I have sung means this:

> *"Towers of scarlet and silver,*
> *The daystar's herald,*
> *You have slipped into cold shadows.*
> *Tumet'ai! Hall of Dawn!*
> *First mourned and last forgotten . . ."*

The troll shook his head. "It is so much difficulty for me to make things of Sithi craft into proper words—especially in a tongue not of my birth-place. You can be forgiving, I hope." He grinned sourly. "In any case, most Sithi songs have as their root thoughts of loss and long memory, so how is a person of my short years to make their words sing?"

Simon was staring at the almost invisible towers, fading streaks in the prisoning ice.

"Where did the Sithi go who lived there?" he asked. The mournful words of Binabik's songs echoed in his thoughts: *You have slipped into cold shadows.* He could feel those shadows tightening around his heart like bands of ice. *You have slipped into cold shadows.* His face throbbed where the dragon's blood had marked him.

"Where the Sithi always go," the troll replied. "Away. To lesser places. They die, or pass into shade, or live and become less than they were." He stopped, eyes downcast as he strove to find the proper words. "They were bringing much that had beauty into the world, Simon, and much that was beautiful in the world was admired by them. It has been many times said that the world grows less fair because of their diminishing. I do not have the knowledge to tell if that is so." He thrust his hands into Qantaqa's thick pelt and urged her about once more, cantering away from the mountains. "I wanted you to remember that place, Simon . . . but do not grieve. Still there is being much of beauty in this world."

Sludig made the sign of the Tree above his cloaked breast. "I cannot say I share your love of these magical places, troll." He snapped his reins, urging his horse into a walk. "The good Lord Usires came to free us from paganism. It is no accident that the heathen demons who threaten our world are cousins to these Sithi you mourn for."

Simon felt a surge of anger. "That's stupid, Sludig. What about Jiriki? Is he a demon?"

The Rimmersman turned to him, an unhappy smile flashing in his blond beard. "No, youngling, but neither is he a magical playmate and protector, as you seem to think him. Jiriki is older and deeper than any of us can know. Like many such things, he is also more dangerous than mortals can know. God knew what He did when he aided mankind to scourge the Sithi from this land. Jiriki has been fair, but his people and ours can never live together. We are too different."

Simon choked back a furious response, turning his eyes to the snowy path before them. Sometimes he did not like Sludig very much at all.

They rode on for a while, silent but for the chuffing of breath and the scraping of their horses' hooves, before Binabik spoke again.

"You have been having luck of great rarity, Simon," he said.

"Being chased by demons, you mean?" Simon growled. "Or seeing my friends killed?"

"Please." The troll raised his small hand in a calming gesture. "I do not refer to luckiness of that sort. Clearly, it has been a terrible road we have walked. No, I meant only that you have seen three of the nine great cities. Few if any mortals can be making such a statement with truthfulness."

"Which three?"

"Tumet'ai, of which you have just seen all that is left to see, now that ice has buried her." The troll spread his fingers, counting. "Da'ai Chikiza, in Aldheorte Forest, where I received my unfortunate arrowing. And Asu'a itself, whose bones are the underpinnings of the Hayholt where you had your birth."

"The Sithi built Green Angel Tower there, and it's still standing," Simon said, remembering its pale sweep, like a white finger pointing at the sky. "I used to climb in it all the time." He thought for a moment. "Was that other place . . . the one called Enki . . . Enki. . . ?"

"Enki-e-Shao'saye?" Binabik prompted.

"Yes. Was Enki-e-Shao'saye one of the great cities?"

"It was. And we shall see its ruins, too, one day—if any remain—for it is near to where we will be finding the Stone of Farewell." He leaned low as Qantaqa leaped up and over a small rise.

"I've seen it already," Simon said. "Jiriki showed it to me in the mirror. It was beautiful—all green and gold. He called it the Summer City."

Binabik smiled. "Then you have seen four, Simon. Few of even the wisest ones can say as much after a whole length of life."

Simon considered this. Who would ever have dreamed that Morgenes' history lessons would be so important? Old cities and old stories were now part of his very life. It was strange how the future seemed tied inseparably to the past, so that both revolved through the present, like a great wheel . . .

The wheel. The shadow of the wheel . . .

An image from a dream rose before him, a great black circle pushing relentlessly downward, a huge wheel that drove everything before it. Somehow the past was forcing its way right into this very moment, casting a long shadow across the what-would-be . . .

Something was there in his mind, but just beyond reach, some occult shape that he could feel but not recognize. It was something about his dreams, something about Past and Future . . .

"I think I need to know more, Binabik," he said at last. "But there are so many things to understand, I'll never remember them all. What were the other cities?" He was momentarily distracted by a movement in the sky before him, a scatter of dark, moving shapes like breeze-blown leaves. He squinted, but saw that it was only a flock of high-soaring birds.

"About the past is a good thing to know, Simon," said the little man, "but it is deciding which things are important that separates a wise one from others. Still, although it is my guessing that the names of the Nine Cities will be little use, it is good to know of them. Once their names were known to every child in its cradle.

"*Asu'a, Da'ai Chikiza, Enki-e-Shao'saye,* and *Tumet'ai* you are knowing. *Jhiná T'seneí* lies drowned beneath the southern seas. The ruins of *Kementari* stand somewhere on Warinsten Island, birth-home of your king Prester John, but no one, I think, has seen them for years and years. Also long unseen are *Mezutu'a* and *Hikehikayo,* both lost beneath Osten Ard's northwestern mountains. The last, *Nakkiga,* now that my thought is upon it, you have already seen as well—or you have in a way . . ."

"What does that mean?"

"Nakkiga was the city the Norns built long ago in the shadow of Stormspike, before they were retreating into the great ice mountain itself. On the dream-road with Geloë and myself you visited it, but doubtless you overlooked its crumbling remains beside the mountain's immensity. So in a way, then, you have visited Nakkiga also."

Simon shuddered, remembering a vision of the endless icy halls within

Stormspike, of the ghost-white faces and burning eyes that shone in its depths. "That was as close as I ever want to be," he said. He squinted his eyes, staring at the sky. The birds still circled lazily overhead. "Are those ravens?" he asked Binabik, pointing. "They've been staying just above our heads for some time."

The troll looked upward. "Ravens, yes, and large ones they are as well." He grinned wickedly. "Perhaps they are waiting for us to fall down very dead, and so aid them in their searching for sustenance. A pity it is to disappoint them, is it not?"

Simon grunted. "Maybe they can tell I'm starving—that I won't last much longer."

Binabik nodded solemnly. "How thoughtless I am being. Of course, Simon, it is indeed true that you have had no food since breaking your fast, and—Chukku's Stones! You poor fellow! That has been an hour ago! You must be fast approaching the awful moment of finalness." Finished with this bit of sarcasm, he began to rummage in his pack, steadying himself against Qantaqa's back with his other hand. "Perhaps I can discover for you some dried fish."

"Thank you." Simon tried to sound enthusiastic—after all, any food was better than no food.

As Binabik performed his laborious search, Simon looked up at the sky once more. The swarm of black birds still hovered silently, wind-tossed beneath the somber clouds like tattered rags.

The raven strutted on the windowsill, feathers fluffed against the chill air. Others of his kind, grown fat and insolent on gibbet-leavings, crowed raucously in the leafless branches beyond the window. No other sounds drifted up from the silent, deserted courtyard.

Even as it preened its shiny black feathers, the raven kept a bright yellow eye cocked; when the goblet came flying toward it like a sling-stone, it had more than enough time to drop from the sill with a harsh cry, spreading its wings to flutter up and join its kin in the barren treetop. The dented goblet rolled in an uneven circle on the stone floor before lurching to a halt. A thin wisp of steam rose from the dark liquor that had splattered beneath the windowsill.

"I hate their eyes," King Elias said. He reached for a fresh goblet, but used this one for its proper and intended purpose. "Those damned sneaking yellow eyes." He wiped his lip. "I think they're spying on me."

"Spying, Majesty?" Guthwulf said slowly. He did not want to send Elias into one of his thunderstorm rages. "Why would birds spy?"

The high king fixed him with a green stare, then a grin split his pale face. "Oh, Guthwulf, you are so innocent, so undefiled!" He chuckled harshly. "Come, pull that chair closer. It is good to speak with an honest man once more."

The Earl of Utanyeat did as his king bade him, sliding forward until less than an ell separated his stool from the yellowing mass of the Dragonbone Chair. He kept his eyes averted from the black-scabbarded sword that hung at the High King's side.

"I do not know what you mean by 'innocent,' Elias," he said, inwardly cursing the stiffness he heard in his own voice. "God knows, we have both of us labored mightily in the Chapel of Sin in our time. However, if you mean innocent of any treachery toward my king and friend, then I accept the name gladly." He hoped he sounded more certain than he felt. The very word "treachery" made his heart gallop these days, and the rotting fruit hanging from the distant gibbet was only one reason.

Elias seemed to sense none of Guthwulf's misgivings. "No, old friend, no. I meant the word kindly." He took another swig of the dark liquid. "There are so few I can trust these days. I have a thousand, thousand enemies." The king's face took on a brooding cast which only accentuated his pallor, the lines of weariness and strain. "Pryrates is gone to Nabban, as you know," he said at last. "You may speak freely."

Guthwulf felt a sudden spark of hope. "Do you suspect *Pryrates* of treachery, sire?"

The spark was quickly extinguished.

"No, Guthwulf, you misunderstand me. I meant that I know you are not comfortable around the priest. That is not surprising: I once found his company difficult as well. But I am a different man, now. A different man." The king laughed oddly, then raised his voice to a shout. "Hangfish! Bring me more—and be swift, damn you!"

The king's new cupbearer appeared from the next room, a sloshing ewer in his pink hands. Guthwulf watched him sourly. Not only was he positive that this pop-eyed Brother Hengfisk was a spy for Pryrates, but there was something else gravely wrong with him as well. The monk's face seemed forever fixed in an idiot grin, as though he were burning up inside with some splendid joke he could not share. The Earl of Utanyeat had tried to speak to him once in the hallway, but Hengfisk had only stared at him unspeaking, his smile so wide it seemed his face might split in half. With any other servitor but the king's cupbearer, Guthwulf would have struck him for such insolence, but he was uneasy about what Elias might take offense at these days. Also, there was an unpleasant look to the half-witted monk, his skin slightly raw, as though the upper layer had burned and peeled away. Guthwulf was in no hurry to touch him.

As Hengfisk poured the dark liquid into the king's goblet, a few smoking drops spattered onto the monk's hands, but the cupbearer did not flinch. A moment later he scuttled out, still wearing his lunatic grin. Guthwulf restrained a shudder. Insanity! What had the kingdom come to?

Elias had ignored the whole episode, his eyes fixed on something beyond the window. "Pryrates does have . . . secrets," he said at last, slowly, as though carefully considering each word.

The earl forced himself to pay attention.

"But he has none from me," the king continued, "—whether he realizes it or not. One thing he thinks I do not know is that my brother Josua survived the fall of Naglimund." He raised a hand to still Guthwulf's exclamation of surprise. "Another secret-that-is-no-secret: he plans to do away with you."

"Me?" Guthwulf was caught by surprise. "Pryrates plans to kill me?" The anger that welled within him had a core of sudden fear.

The king smiled, lips pulling back from his teeth like the grin of a cornered dog. "I do not know if he plans to kill you, Wolf, but he wishes you out of the way. Pryrates thinks I place too much trust in you when he deserves all my attention." He laughed, a harsh bark.

"But . . . but Elias . . ." Guthwulf was caught offstride. "What will you do?"

"Me?" The king's gaze was unnervingly calm. "I will do nothing. And neither will you."

"What!?"

Elias leaned back into his throne, so that for a moment his face vanished in the shadow beneath the great dragon's skull. "You may protect yourself, of course," he said cheerfully. "I merely mean I cannot allow you to kill Pryrates—assuming you could, which isn't something I'm too certain of. Quite frankly, old friend, at this moment he is more important to me than you are."

The king's words hung in the air, seeming so much the stuff of madness that for a moment Guthwulf felt sure he was dreaming. As moments passed and the chill room did not waver into some other shape, he had to force himself to speak once more.

"I don't understand."

"Nor should you. Not yet." Elias leaned forward, his eyes bright as lamps burning behind thin green glass. "But someday you will, Guthwulf. I hope you live to understand everything. At this time, though, I cannot let you interfere with Pryrates, so if you feel you must leave the castle, I will understand. You are the only friend I have left. Your life is important to me."

The Earl of Utanyeat wanted to laugh at such a bizarre statement, but the sense of sick unreality would not leave him. "But not as important to you as Pryrates?"

The king's hand leaped out like a striking serpent, fastening on Guthwulf's sleeve. "Don't be a fool!" he rasped. "Pryrates is nothing! It is what Pryrates is helping me to *do* that matters. I told you that there were great things coming! But there will be a time first when things are . . . changing."

Guthwulf stared at the king's feverish face and felt something die within him. "I have sensed some of the changes, Elias," he said grimly. "I have seen others."

His old friend looked back at him, then smiled oddly. "Ah. The castle, you mean. Yes, some of the changes are happening right here. But you still do not understand."

Guthwulf was not practiced in patience. He fought to hold down his rage. "Help me to understand. Tell me what you do!"

The king shook his head. "You could not possibly make sense of it—not now, not this way." He sat back again, his face sliding into shadow once more, so that it almost seemed as though the great fanged and black-socketed head was his own. A stretching silence followed. Guthwulf listened to the bleak voices of ravens in the courtyard.

"Come here, old friend," Elias said at last, voice slow and measured. As Guthwulf looked up, the king slid his double-hilted sword part way from its scabbard. The metal gleamed darkly, black and crawling gray like the mottled belly of some ancient reptile. The ravens abruptly fell silent. "Come here," the king repeated.

The Earl of Utanyeat could not tear his eyes from the sword. The rest of the room became gray and insubstantial; the sword itself seemed to glow without light, to make the very air heavy as stone. "Will you kill me now, Elias?" Guthwulf felt his words grow weighty, each one an effort to use. "Will you save Pryrates his trouble?"

"Touch the sword, Guthwulf," Elias said. His eyes seemed to shine more brightly as the room darkened. "Come and touch the sword. Then you will understand."

"No," Guthwulf said weakly, but watched with horror as his arm moved forward as if by its own will. "I don't want to touch the damned thing . . ." Now his hand hovered just above the ugly, slow-shimmering blade.

"Damned thing?" Elias laughed, his voice seeming far away. He reached out and took his friend's hand, gentle as a lover. "You can't begin to guess. Do you know what its name is?"

Guthwulf watched his fingers slowly flatten against the bruised surface of the sword. A deadening chill crept up his arm, countless icy needles pricking his flesh. Close behind the cold came a fiery blackness. Elias' voice seemed to be falling away into the distance.

". . . *Jingizu* is its name . . ." the king called. "Its name is Sorrow . . ."

And in the midst of the dreadful fog that enwrapped his heart, through the blanket of frost that covered and then entered his eyes and ears and mouth, Guthwulf felt the sword's dreadful song of triumph. It hummed right through him, softly at first but growing ever stronger, a terrible, potent music that matched and then devoured his rhythms, that drowned out his weak and artless notes, until it had absorbed the entire song of his soul into its darkly triumphant tune.

Sorrow sang inside him, filling him. He heard it cry out with his voice, as though he had become the sword, or the sword had somehow become Guthwulf. Sorrow was alive and looking for something. Guthwulf was looking, too: he had now been subsumed in the alien melody. He and the blade were one.

Sorrow reached for its brothers.

He found them.

Two shining forms were there, just beyond his reach. Guthwulf longed to be with them, to join his proud melody to theirs, so that together they would make a music greater still. He yearned, a bloodless, warmthless desire, like a cracked bell straining to toll, like a lodestone aching for true north. They were three of a kind, he and these other two, three songs unlike any the world had heard—but each was incomplete without its fellows. He stretched toward his brothers as though to touch them, but they were too far away. Mere distance still separated them. No matter how he strained, Guthwulf could not bring them closer, could not join with them.

At last the delicate balance collapsed, sending him plunging down into an infinite nothingness, falling, falling, falling . . .

Slowly he came to himself again—Guthwulf, a man born of woman—but still he fell through blackness. He was terrified.

Time sped. He felt graveworms eating his flesh, felt himself coming apart deep within the black earth, rendered into innumerable particles that ached to scream without voices to do so; at the same moment, like a rushing wind, he flew laughing past the stars and into the endless places between life and death. For a moment the very door of Mystery swung open and a dark shadow stood beckoning in the doorway . . .

Long after Elias had sheathed the sword, Guthwulf still lay choking on the steps before the Dragonbone Chair, his eyes burning with tears, his fingers helplessly flexing.

"Now can you understand?" The king said, beaming with pleasure as though he had just given his friend a taste of a singularly splendid wine. "Do you understand why I must not fail?"

The Earl of Utanyeat got slowly to his feet. His clothes were soiled and spattered. He turned wordlessly from his liege lord and staggered across the throne room floor, pushing through the door and into the hallway without looking back.

"Do you see?" Elias shouted after him.

A trio of ravens fluttered down to the windowsill. They stood close together, their yellow eyes intent.

"Guthwulf?" Elias was no longer shouting, but still his voice carried through the silent room like a tolling bell. "Come back, old friend."

"Look, Binabik!" Simon cried. "What are those birds doing?!"

The troll followed Simon's pointing finger. The ravens were wheeling madly about the sky overhead, flying in long, looping circles.

"They are upset, perhaps," Binabik shrugged. "I do not have much knowledge of the ways of such things . . ."

"No, they're looking for something!" Simon said, excited. "They're looking for something! I know it! Just look at them!"

"But they are not leaving the air above us." Binabik raised his voice as the ravens began to call back and forth, their croaking voices sharp as blades in the still air.

Sludig had reined up his horse, too, and was staring up at the strange exhibition. He narrowed his eyes. "If this is not some deviltry," he said, "then I am not an Aedonite. The raven was Old One-Eye's bird, back in the dark days . . ." He trailed off as he saw something new. "There!" he said, pointing. "Is that not some other bird they are chasing?"

Now Simon could see it too: a smaller gray shape that flitted among the black ones, darting wildly, now this way, now that. At every turn it seemed to find one of the larger birds already there. It was tiring, Simon could see plainly, its loops becoming ever more ragged, its escapes narrower.

"It's a sparrow!" Simon cried. "Like the ones Morgenes had! They're going to kill it!"

Even as he spoke, the swooping circle of ravens seemed to sense that the quarry was nearing its limits. The whirling funnel contracted and the croaking voices rose as if in triumph. Then, just when it seemed the hunt was over, the sparrow found an open space and burst free of the black ring, darting unevenly toward a stand of fir trees half a furlong away. The ravens, shrieking, whirled in pursuit.

"I do not think it chance that such a bird should be here," Binabik said, unscrewing his walking stick to shake free his pouch of darts. "Or that the ravens would be waiting with such patientness just where we are." He grabbed Qantaqa's hackles. *"Chok, Qantaqa!"* he cried. *"Ummu chok!"*

The wolf sprang away, churning the snow beneath her broad paws. Sludig dug in his heels and his mount leaped after her. Simon, cursing beneath his breath, wrestled for a moment with Homefinder's reins. By the time he had them sorted out, she had decided to follow Sludig's horse anyway. Simon clung to her neck as they pounded over the uneven snow, hoof-churned sleet burning his eyes.

The ravens were circling the copse like a swarm of black bees. Binabik, in the lead, vanished among the close-standing trunks. Sludig went just after, his spear now in his hand. Simon had a moment to wonder how the Rimmersman would kill birds with a heavy spear, then the line of trees was looming before him as well. He pulled up on the reins, slowing his horse. He ducked his head beneath a low-hanging branch, but was not fast enough to avoid a clump of snow falling into the loose hood of his cloak and slithering down his neck.

Binabik stood beside Qantaqa at the center of the copse, the hollow tube to his mouth. The troll's cheeks puffed; a moment later a large black bundle fell down through the branches overhead, flapping in a slow circle on the white ground before it died.

"There!" Binabik said, gesturing. Sludig poked upward with his spear, rattling its point among the tree limbs as Qantaqa gave vent to a sharp, excited bark.

A black wing skimmed by Simon's face. The raven struck at the back of Sludig's head, its claws scrabbling impotently against the metal of his helm. Another one swooped down from above, squawking, whirling about the Rimmersman's arms as he plied the spear.

Why aren't I wearing a helmet? Simon thought disgustedly as he raised his hand before his suddenly vulnerable eyes.

The little copse raged with the angry voices of birds. Qantaqa had her front paws up on a tree trunk, shaking her head from side to side as if she had already caught one of them.

Something small and still as a tiny snowball dropped from the tree overhead. Binabik fell to his knees at the Rimmersman's feet and cupped it in his hands.

"I have it!" he cried. "Let us be going into the open! *Sosa, Qantaqa!*" He clambered onto the wolf's back, his hand now tucked inside his jacket. He had to duck beneath the onslaught of one of the ravens; the haft of Sludig's spear whistled through the space his head had just vacated, smacking the bird like a club, shattering it into a puff of dark feathers. A moment later the wolf had carried Binabik out from beneath the trees. Simon and Sludig quickly followed.

Despite the angry voices of the birds behind them, the open ground outside seemed remarkably still to Simon. He turned to look back. Hard yellow eyes stared from the uppermost branches, but the ravens did not follow.

"You saved the bird?" he asked.

"Let us be riding farther away," Binabik said. "Then we will look to what we have."

When they stopped, the troll took his hand from beneath his skin jacket. He opened it slowly, as though not sure what he might find there. The bird nestled inside was dead, or nearly so. It lay on its side unstirring, its ragged wounds striped with blood. There was a shred of parchment about its leg.

"I was thinking this could be," Binabik said, looking over his shoulder. The dark silhouettes of a dozen ravens sat like hunch-shouldered inquisitors in the nearest tree. "I am afraid that we are more late than we should have been."

His small finger unfurled the parchment. It had been chewed or torn until but a part of it remained. "A fragment, only," Binabik said sadly.

Simon looked at the tiny runes dotting the ragged strip. "We could go back to the trees and look for the rest," he said, disliking the idea mightily even as he said it.

The troll shook his head. "I have a sureness that the rest has found its way down a raven gullet—as would this scrap, too, and the messenger, if we had been later still." He squinted at it. "Few words am I making out, but I feel no doubt it was meant for us. See?" He pointed at a minute squiggle. "The circle and feather of the League of the Scroll. It was sent by a Scrollbearer."

"Who?" Simon asked.

"Patience, Simon-friend. Perhaps the remaining message will tell." He held the curling strip as flat as he could. "Two bits only can I read," he said. "This, saying: '. . . ry of false messengers,' and this: 'Make haste. The Storm is spr . . .' Then it is signed below with the League's mark."

"False messenger," Simon breathed, dread creeping through him. "That was the dream I had in Geloë's house. Doctor Morgenes told me to beware the false messenger." He tried to push away the memory of that dream. In it the doctor had been a charred corpse.

" 'Be wary of false messengers' is then what it is likely meaning," Binabik said, nodding his head. " 'Make haste. The Storm is spr . . .' Spreading, I am supposing."

The great fear Simon had kept suppressed for several days came crawling back. "False messenger," he repeated helplessly. "What can it mean? Who wrote it, Binabik?"

The troll shook his head. He tucked the sliver of parchment in his bag and then kneeled, scraping a hole in the snow. "It is a Scrollbearer, and there are not many now alive. It might be Jarnauga, if he still lives. There is also Dinivan in Nabban." He laid the little gray bird in the hole and tenderly covered it over.

"Dinivan?" Simon asked.

"He is the helper of the Lector Ranessin, the head of your Mother Church," Binabik said. "A very good man."

Sludig, who had stood silent, suddenly spoke. "The lector is part of your heathen circle?" he said wonderingly. "With trolls and such?"

Binabik smiled a tiny smile. "Not the lector. Father Dinivan, his helper. And it is not a 'heathen circle,' Sludig, but a band of those who wished the preserving of important knowledge—for just such times as these are." He frowned. "I am thinking of who else it might be who was writing this message to us—or to me, rather, for it is my master's arts that likely drew the bird here to me. If not one of the two I mentioned, then I cannot be saying, for Morgenes and my master Ookequk are dead. There are no other Scrollbearers I know of, unless new ones have been chosen."

"Could it be Geloë?" Simon asked.

Binabik thought for a moment, then shook his head. "She is one of the wisest of the wise, but she has never been a true Scrollbearer, and I am doubting she would use the League's rune in place of her own." He mounted up onto Qantaqa's back. "We will think of the meaning of this warning as we ride. There are many messengers who have led us to this place, and many others we will doubtlessly be meeting in days and weeks to come. Which are false? It is a puzzle of great difficulty."

"Look, the ravens are flying!" Sludig cried. Simon and Binabik turned to see the birds swarm up from the stand of trees like smoke, swirling in the gray sky before wheeling away into the northwest, their disdainful voices echoing.

"They have done what they were sent for doing," Binabik said. "Now they are headed back to Stormspike, do you suppose?"

Simon's cold fear deepened. "You mean . . . the Storm King sent them after us?"

"I have little doubt that they were meant to keep that message from our eyes," Binabik said, leaning forward to pick his walking stick from the ground.

Simon turned to follow the flight of the vanishing ravens. He almost expected to see a dark figure looming on the northern horizon, a burning red gaze in a faceless black head.

"Those storm clouds on the horizon look very dark," Simon said. "A lot darker than they did before."

"The lad's right." Sludig glowered. "That's an ugly storm gathering."

Binabik sighed. His round face was grim, too. "The last part of the message we all of us understand. The storm is spreading, in more than one way only. We have a long journeying ahead over open and unprotected country. We will need to go with all the speed that we can be making."

Qantaqa started ahead. Simon and Sludig spurred their horses forward. Prompted by something he did not understand, Simon looked back once more, although he knew what he would see.

The ravens, now little more than black specks on the wind, were fading from sight into the dark swell of the gathering storm.

13

The Stallion Clan

The prince's company came out at last onto the plains after nearly a month in the vast, ancient forest. As they broke through the last line of trees the grasslands opened before them, a floor of uneven turf shrouded by morning mist, merging seamlessly with the gray horizon.

Father Strangyeard sped his pace to catch up with Geloë. The witch woman was striding purposefully out onto the flatland, wet stems falling before her approach.

"Valada Geloë," Strangyeard said breathlessly, "ah, this is a marvelous book Morgenes has written. Marvelous! Valada Geloë, have you read this passage?" He tried to juggle the loose pages, stumbled over a tussock, and only barely retained his balance. "I think there is something here of importance. Ah, how silly of me, how foolish—there are many things of importance. What a marvelous book!"

Geloë put her hand on Leleth's shoulder, bringing the child to a halt. The little girl did not look up, but stood where she had stopped, staring out into the mists.

"Strangyeard, you will do yourself an injury," Geloë said brusquely. She looked at him expectantly. "Well?"

"Oh, dear," the archivist said. He tugged at his eyepatch self-consciously, almost losing his armful of pages in the process. "I didn't want you to stop walking. I can read and still keep up."

"I repeat: you will do yourself an injury. Read."

Before Strangyeard could do so, they were interrupted by new arrivals.

"Praise God," Isorn cried. He and Deornoth struggled out of the trees upslope. "We are out of the cursed forest and on open ground!" The pair carefully set down the litter they had been dragging, glad to rest Sangfugol's weight for a moment. Under the witch woman's ministrations, the harper was healing well and swiftly from what should have been a fatal corruption of his blood, but he still could not walk more than a few hours at a time.

Geloë turned to look back. "Praise God all you wish," she warned, "but we may regret the loss of those sheltering trees before long."

The rest of the party limped down out of the woods. Prince Josua was helping Towser, who walked dazed and unspeaking; the old man's eyes were rolled up, as though he contemplated a distant heaven hidden behind the fog-blanketed sky. Vorzheva and Duchess Gutrun walked a little way behind them.

"It has been many years since I have seen the Thrithings," Josua said, "even this tamer part. I had almost forgotten its beauty." He closed his eyes in thought for a moment, then opened them once more to gaze out toward the indistinct horizon. "It is like no other land in all of Osten Ard—some call it 'God's tabletop.' "

"If this is indeed God's tabletop," Sangfugol said with a weak smile, "my prince, He uses us for dice. Aedon save me, I am meant to sing of Jack Mundwode and his naughty bandits, not ape their forest-traipsing." He struggled out of the litter. "I need to get out of this thumping, bouncing torture device and sit down—no, the grass is fine for me. I fear my sore leg more than the wet."

"Some gratitude," Isorn said, smiling. "I think I shall show you what thumping really is, harper."

"Very well," Josua said. "We shall rest. No one stray far, and if you go more than a stone's throw, take someone with you."

"So we have escaped the forest," Deornoth sighed. "If only Einskaldir could have seen it." He thought of the Rimmersman's grave in one of the quiet glades of Shisae'ron, a simple mound marked only by his helmet and Strangyeard's wooden Tree. Even Geloë's healing skills had not been enough to save him from the terrible wounds he had received leading their escape from the Norns. Now, fierce Einskaldir would lie forever in a place of timeless calm. "He was a stern bastard, bless him." Deornoth shook his head. "He never gave up, either—but I don't think he believed we would ever get away."

"We wouldn't have, if not for him," Isorn said. "He's another mark on the list."

"List?"

"The list of what is owed to our enemies—to Skali and Elias and all the rest." Isorn's broad face was grim. "We owe them a blood feud. Someday, they will pay for what they did. And when it happens, Einskaldir will be watching in heaven. And laughing."

Deornoth could think of nothing to say. If Einskaldir could watch battles from heaven, he *would* be laughing. For all his piety, it seemed a shame that Einskaldir had missed the old pagan days of Rimmersgard, and would instead be forced to spend his eternity in the quieter environs of Aedon's paradise.

As the others milled about, Vorzheva said a quiet word to Duchess Gutrun, then walked down the short slope and onto the damp meadow.

She moved as if in a kind of dream, her eyes fixed on nothing, her track aimless and elliptical as she made her way through the damp grasses.

"Vorzheva," Josua called, his voice sharper than usual, "do not go alone. The mist is very thick and you would soon be out of sight."

"She would have to go very far before she would be out of earshot, Prince Josua," said Duchess Gutrun, leading Towser with a gentle hand on his elbow.

"That may be," Josua said, "but I would prefer we were not stumbling through the fog, shouting our presence to any listening ears. Surely you have not so soon forgotten our escort from Naglimund."

Gutrun shook her head in dismay, conceding the point. Vorzheva, seemingly oblivious to the discussion, was now only a dim upright shape slipping through the mists like a ghost.

"Damn her frowardness," Josua said grimly, staring after her.

"I will go with her." Geloë turned to Gutrun. "Keep the child close to you, please." She pointed Leleth in the general direction of the duchess, then strode off after the fast-fading Vorzheva.

Josua watched her go, then laughed unhappily. "If this is the way I command a kingdom of nine or ten," he told Deornoth, "then my brother can rest easily on the Dragonbone Chair. People used to beg to do my father John's bidding."

Even his queen? Deornoth wondered, but he did not say it. He watched the dark shape of Geloë catch up to the wraith that was Vorzheva. *If you have a proud and headstrong woman, you would be better off not to judge your success by her obedience.*

"Please, my lord," he said instead, "do not speak ill of yourself. You are hungry and tired and cold. Let me build a fire."

"No, Deornoth." Josua rubbed the stump of his wrist as though it hurt. "We will not stay so long." He turned to look back at the forest fringe and the gaping shadows that lined it. "We must move farther before we do more than pause to rest. We will stop somewhere that puts us in open ground on all sides. At least then, even though we are exposed, anything that stalks us will be exposed as well."

"A happy thought," grunted Sangfugol from his seat on the turf. "S'truth, but we are a merry band of pilgrims."

"Pilgrims on the road through hell cannot afford too much merriment," Josua said. He strode a little way out onto the greensward to stand by himself in thought.

"Then why don't you tell him?" There was exasperation in Geloë's voice, but her hawk-yellow eyes betrayed little emotion. "By bough and branch, Vorzheva, you are not a young girl, you are a woman. Why do you carry on so?"

Vorzheva's eyes were moist. "I do not know. I cannot understand him."

Geloë shook her head. "I cannot understand any of you. I have spent little of my life with human folk, and it is because of this ridiculous uncertainty—'I want this, I do not want that . . .' The animals are more sensible, it seems to me. They do what they must and do not fret over what cannot be changed." The witch woman laid a callused hand on Vorzheva's arm. "Why do you worry so about things that do not matter? Prince Josua obviously cares for you. Why do you not tell him the truth?"

Her companion sighed. "He thinks me a foolish wagon-girl. It makes him cold to me. If I tell him, it will only be worse . . . I am sorry." She angrily wiped at her face with her tattered sleeve. "It was seeing the Feluwelt again—that is what my people call this place, where the meadow runs in the forest's shadow. It brought many memories to my mind, and made me unhappy. . . ."

"Valada Geloë?" It was Father Strangyeard's voice, sourceless in the mist, but quite near. "Are you there? Valada Geloë?"

A little frustration showed itself on Geloë's stern face. "Here, Strangyeard. Is anything wrong?"

The archivist appeared, a lanky, flapping shape materializing from gray obscurity. "No, no, I just wanted to . . ." He stopped, staring at Vorzheva's tear-stained face. "Oh. Oh, I'm so terribly sorry. How rude of me. I will leave you." He turned to lurch off into the mist once more.

"Don't go!" Strangely, it was Vorzheva who spoke. "Do not leave us, Father. Walk with us."

Strangyeard looked at her, then to Geloë. "I do not wish to intrude, Lady. I fear I was thinking only of something I found in Morgenes' book." Eyepatch askew, thin fringe of reddish hair curling in the damp, he looked like a startled woodpecker. He seemed about to bolt once more, but the witch woman raised a calming hand.

"Walk with us, Strangyeard, as Vorzheva said. Perhaps your need is one for which my talents are better suited." The priest looked at her nervously. "Come. We will walk back toward the others as we talk."

Strangyeard was still carrying the loose sheaves of Morgenes' book in his hand; after a few silent paces he began to leaf through them. "I'm afraid I've lost the section," he said, shuffling the parchments. "I thought it might be significant—it was a bit about magic—The Art, that's what Morgenes called it. I'm amazed by the things he knew, quite amazed . . . I would never have dreamt . . ." A triumphant smile came to his face. "Here it is." He squinted. "Wonderful way with words . . ."

They walked several more paces in silence. "Will you read?" Geloë asked at last.

"Oh! Of course." Strangyeard cleared his throat.

"*. . . In truth, articles useful to The Art seem to fall into two broad categories,*" the priest began,

"*those whose worth is bound in themselves, and those whose worth is bound in their derivation. In contradiction to popular superstition, an herb gathered in a graveyard is not generally useful because it came from such a place, but rather because of the herb itself. Since a graveyard may be the only place that herb is found, the connection becomes established and is then almost impossible to disentangle.*

"*The other category of useful objects are usually 'made' objects, and their virtue is in their shaping or their raw beginnings. The Sithi, who have long possessed secrets of crafting hidden from mortals, made many things whose creation itself was a practice of The Art—although the Sithi would not exactly term it so. Thus, the virtue of these objects is in their making. The famous arrows of Vindaomeyo are an example: carved from common wood and fletched with the feathers of ordinary birds, yet each one is a talisman of great worth.*

"*Other objects take their power from the stuff of their making. The great swords alluded to in Nisses' lost book are examples here. All seem to derive their worth from their materials, although the crafting of each was a mighty task. Minneyar, King Fingil's sword, was made of the iron keel of his boat, iron brought to Osten Ard by the Rimmersman sea-raiders out of the lost west. Thorn, most recently the sword of Prester John's noblest knight, Sir Camaris, was forged from the glowing metals of a fallen star—like Minneyar's iron, something foreign to Osten Ard. And Sorrow, the sword that Nisses claims Ineluki of the Sithi used to slay his own father the Erl-king, was made of Sithi witchwood and iron, two elements long thought to be antithetical and unmixable. Thus, such objects derive their strength primarily, it would seem, from the unearthly origins of their substance. Stories tell, however, that powerful Spells of Making were also wound in the forging of all these three blades, so the power of the Great Swords may come from both their substance* **and** *their making.*

"*Ti-tuno, the hunting horn crafted in fabled Mezu'tua from the tooth of the dragon Hidohebhi, is another clear example of how sometimes an object of power may be made by both the crafting and the materials crafted . . .*"

Strangyeard broke off. "It goes on to talk of other things. It is all fascinating, of course—what a scholar that man was!—but I thought the section on the swords might be interesting."

Geloë nodded her head slowly. "It is. I wondered about these three swords that have become the object of our hopes. Morgenes seems to make a good argument as to the reason for their value. Perhaps they will indeed be useful against Ineluki. It is good that you found that, Strangyeard."

The priest's pink cheeks went a deeper red. "Too kind. You're too kind."

Geloë cocked her head. "I hear the others. Are you composed, Vorzheva?"

Vorzheva nodded her head. "I am not such a fool as you think me," she said quietly.

The witch woman laughed. "I do not think you a fool, particularly. I think *most* people are foolish—and I count myself as well, for here I am without a roof, wandering over the grasslands like a stray heifer. Sometimes obvious foolishness is the only answer to grave problems."

"Hmmm," said Strangyeard, baffled. "Hmmm."

The ragged band continued out onto the fog-ridden meadowlands, heading south toward the river Ymstrecca, which meandered along the breadth of the High Thrithings. They made camp on the open plain, shivering in the rain-sodden wind, huddling close to their small fire. Geloë made a soup of herbs and roots she had gathered. It was filling and warmed the stomach, but Deornoth mourned the absence of something more toothsome.

"Tomorrow let me go farther afield, my lord," he implored Josua as they sat by the fire. All the others but Geloë had wrapped themselves in their cloaks to sleep, bundled close together like a family of sleeping kittens. The witch woman had gone a-wandering. "I know I could find a hare or two, and the underbrush must be full of grouse, even in this cold summer. We have had no meat for several days!"

Josua permitted himself a chilly smile. "I wish I could say yes, faithful friend, but I need your strong arms and good wit close by. These people can scarcely walk another step—those who can still walk, that is. No, a brace of hares would be tasty indeed, but I must keep you here. Besides, Valada Geloë tells me that one can live years without tasting meat."

Deornoth grimaced. "But who would want to?" He studied his prince carefully. Josua's already slender frame had grown even thinner; the play of his bones was plain beneath the skin. With what little fat he had worn long gone, the prince's high forehead and pale eyes made him seem a statue of some ancient philosopher-monk, his gaze fixed always upon the infinite while the busy world spun on before him, ignored.

The fire hissed, working away at the damp wood. "One other question, then, my lord," Deornoth said softly. "Are we so sure of this Stone of Farewell that we should drag these sick, wounded people across the Thrithings in search of it? I speak no ill of Geloë, who is plainly a good-hearted soul, but to go so far? The edge of Erkynland is only a few leagues to the west. Surely we could find a loyal heart in one of the towns of the Hasu Vale—even if they were too frightened of your brother the king to give us shelter, we could find food and drink and warmer clothing for our wounded, surely."

Josua sighed and rubbed his eyes. "Perhaps, Deornoth, perhaps. Believe me, the thought has occurred to me." He stretched his long legs before him, nudging at the edge of the coals with his boot heel. "But we cannot risk it, nor can we spare the time. Every hour we walk in the open means more time for one of Elias' patrols to find us, or something worse to catch us unprotected. No, the only place that it seems we can go is Geloë's Stone of Farewell, so the sooner we do, the better. Erkynland is lost to us—at least for now, perhaps forever."

The prince shook his head and fell into thought once more. Deornoth sighed and poked at the fire.

They reached the banks of the Ymstrecca in the morning of their third day on the grasslands. The wide river shone faintly beneath the gray sky, a dim streak of silver passing like a dream through the dark, damp meadows. The water's voice was as muted as its sheen, a faint murmur like distant conversation.

Josua's people were content to pause and rest a while on the riverbanks, enjoying the sound and sight of the first swiftly-moving waters they had seen since deep in Aldheorte Forest. When Gutrun and Vorzheva made known their plan to follow the river downstream a short distance to where they could bathe their limbs in privacy, Josua was quick to object, worried for their safety. When Geloë offered to go with them, the prince reluctantly consented. It was difficult to think of a situation beyond the witch woman's enormous competence.

"Ah, it is somehow as if I never left," Vorzheva said, dangling her feet in the current. They had chosen a sandy bank where a stand of birch trees in midstream widened the rivercourse, shielding them from the view of their distant fellow travelers. Her voice was careless, though her face belied her. "It is like when I was a little girl." She frowned as she splashed water on the numerous scratches covering her legs. "But it is so cold!"

Duchess Gutrun had loosened the neck of her garment. She stood a little way out from the bank, the river eddying around her plump calves as she splashed water on her throat and scrubbed at her face. "It is not so bad," she laughed. "The river Gratuvask that runs by our home in Elvritshalla— now that is cold water! Every year at spring the maidens of the town go down to the river to bathe—I did when I was young." She straightened up, staring at nothing. "The men must stay inside all morning, on penalty of a beating, so the maidens can splash in the Gratuvask. And cold! The river is born from the snows of the northern mountains! You have not heard shrieking until you hear a hundred young girls plunge into a chilly river on an Avrel morning!" She laughed again. "There is a story, you know, about one young man who was determined to see the Gratuvask maidens—it is a famous tale in Rimmersland, perhaps you have heard it. . . ?" She broke off, water sluicing from her cupped hands. "Vorzheva? Are you ill?"

The Thrithings-woman was bent over, her face pale as milk. "Just a pain," she said harshly, straightening up. "It will go away soon. See, I am better now. Tell your story."

Gutrun looked at her suspiciously. Before the duchess could say anything, Geloë spoke up from her seat on the bank nearby, where she had been tidying Leleth's hair with a comb made from fishbone.

"The story must wait." The witch woman's tone was sharp. "See—we are not alone."

Vorzheva and the duchess turned to follow Geloë's pointing finger. Across the meadows, some three or four furlongs away to the south, a mounted rider stood poised on a hillock. He was much too far away for his face to be discernible, but there was little doubt he was looking in their direction. All the women stared back, even Leleth, her strange eyes wide. After several silent moments in which it seemed that no hearts beat, the solitary figure turned his horse and rode down the hillock, vanishing from sight.

"How . . . how frightening," the duchess said, clutching the neck of her dress closed with a damp hand. "Who is it? Those horrible Norns?"

"I cannot say," Geloë rasped. "But we should return to tell the others, in case Josua did not see. We must be concerned with any strangers now, be they friend or foe."

Vorzheva shuddered. Her face was still pale. "There are no friendly strangers on these grasslands," she said.

The women's news was enough to convince Josua that they could dally no longer. Unhappily, the company shouldered their few possessions and set off again, following the course of the Ymstrecca east alongside the border of the now-distant forest, a thin dark strip on the misty northern horizon.

They saw no one else all afternoon.

"These seem like fertile lands," Deornoth said as they searched for a spot to camp. "Isn't it strange that we have seen no people beside that lone rider?"

"One rider is enough." Josua was grim.

"My people have never liked it here, so near to the old forest," Vorzheva said, and shivered. "There are spirits of the dead beneath the trees."

Josua sighed. "These are things I would have laughed at a year ago. Now I have seen them, or things even worse. God save me, what a world this has become!"

Geloë looked up from where she was making a bed of grass for young Leleth. "It has always been the same world, Prince Josua," she said. "It is only that in these troubled hours things are seen more clearly. The lamps of cities blur many shadows that are plain beneath the moon."

Deornoth awoke in the deeps of night, his heart beating swiftly. He had been dreaming. King Elias had become a spindly thing of grasping claws and red eyes clinging to Prince Josua's back. Josua could not see him and did not even seem to know that his brother was there. In the dream

Deornoth tried to tell him, but Josua did not listen, only smiled as he walked through the streets of Erchester with the terrible Elias-thing riding his back like a deformed baby. Every time Josua bent to pat the head of a child or give a coin to a beggar, Elias reached out to undo the good work when Josua had passed, snatching the coin back or scratching the child's face with dirty nails. Soon an angry crowd followed behind Josua, shouting for his punishment, but the prince went blithely on, unknowing, even as Deornoth screamed and pointed at the evil thing riding the prince's shoulders.

Awake on the benighted grasslands, Deornoth shook his head, trying to pull free from the clinging sense of disquiet. Elias' dream-face, wizened and spiteful, would not leave his mind. He sat up and looked around. All the camp was sleeping but for Valada Geloë, who sat dreaming or pondering over the last coals of the dying fire.

He lay back and tried to sleep, but could not for fear the dream would return. At last disgusted by his own weak-heartedness, he got up and quietly shook out his cloak, then walked to the fire and sat down near Geloë.

The witch woman did not look up at his approach. Her face was red-splashed by firelight, eyes staring unblinkingly into the embers as though nothing else existed. Her lips were moving but no sound came forth; Deornoth felt a chill creep up the back of his neck. What was she doing? Should he wake her?

Geloë's mouth continued to work. Her voice rose to a whisper. "*. . . Amerasu, where are you? Your spirit is dim . . . and I am weak . . .*"

Deornoth's hand stopped an inch from the witch woman's rough sleeve. "*. . . If ever you share, let it be now . . .*" Geloë's voice hissed like the wind. "*Oh, please . . .*" A tear, scarlet-shot, trickled down her weathered cheek.

Her despairing whisper drove Deornoth back to his makeshift bed. He did not fall back into sleep for some time, but lay staring up at the blue-white stars.

He was awakened once more before dawn—this time by Josua. The prince shook Deornoth's arm, then lifted his handless right wrist to his lips, gesturing for silence. The knight looked up to see a clot of darkness to the west, thicker even than the general obscurity of night, approaching along the line of the river. The muffled sound of hoofbeats rolled toward them over the grass. Deornoth's heart raced. He felt on the ground for his scabbard, and was soothed only a little by the feeling of his sword hilt beneath his fingers. Josua crawled away to wake the others.

"Where is the witch woman?" Deornoth whispered urgently, but the prince was too far away to hear, so he crawled over to where Strangyeard lay. The older man, sleeping lightly, was awake in a moment.

"Be still," the knight murmured. "There are riders coming."

"Who?" Strangyeard asked. Deornoth shook his head.

The oncoming riders, still little more than shadows, split almost noise-lessly into several groups, sweeping wide around the encampment. Deornoth had to marvel at their silent horsemanship even as he cursed his party's lack of bows and arrows. A folly, to fight with swords against mounted men—if men they were. He thought he could count count two dozen attackers, although any estimate was dubious in this half-light.

Deornoth got to his feet, even as a few shadowy figures around him did the same. Josua, nearby, drew Naidel from its sheath; the sudden hiss of metal against leather seemed as loud as a shout. The surrounding figures reined up, and for a moment utter silence fell once more. Someone passing a stone's throw away would never have suspected the presence of a single soul, let alone two forces at battle-ready.

A voice broke the stillness.

"Trespassers! You walk on the land of Clan Mehrdon! Lay down your arms."

Flint rang on steel, then a torch blossomed behind the nearest figures, throwing long shadows across the campsite. Mounted men, hooded and cloaked, surrounded Josua's band with a ring of spears.

"Lay down your weapons!" the voice said again in thickly-accented Westerling. "You are prisoners of the randwarders. We will kill you if you resist." Several more torches flared alight. The night was suddenly full of armed shadows.

"Merciful Aedon!" Duchess Gutrun said from somewhere nearby. "Sweet Elysia, what now?"

A large shape pushed toward her—Isorn, going to comfort his mother.

"Do not move!" the disembodied voice barked out; a moment later one of the riders walked his horse forward, his spear point lowering, catching a glint of torchlight. "I hear women," the rider said. "Do nothing foolish and they will be spared. We are not beasts."

"And what about the rest?" Josua said, stepping forward into the light. "We have many here wounded and sick. What will you do with us?"

The rider leaned down to stare at Josua, momentarily exposing his hooded features. He had a rough face, with a shaggy, braided beard and scarred cheeks. Heavy bracelets clinked on his wrists. Deornoth felt his tension ease somewhat. At least their enemies were mortal men.

The rider spat into the dark grass. "You are prisoners. You ask no questions. The March-thane will decide." He turned to his fellows. "Ozhbern! Kunret! Round them in a circle to march!" He wheeled his horse to supervise as Josua, Deornoth, and the others were herded at spearpoint into the ring of torchlight.

"Your March-thane will be unhappy if you mistreat us," Josua said.

The leader laughed. "He will be more unhappy with me if you are not at the wagons by sun-high." He turned to one of the other riders. "All?"

"All, Hotvig. Six men, two women, one child. Only one cannot walk." He indicated Sangfugol with the butt of his spear.

"Put him on a horse," Hotvig said. "Over the saddle, no matter. We must ride fast."

Even as they were prodded into movement, Deornoth sidled closer to Josua. "It could be worse," he whispered to the prince. "It could have been the Norns who caught us instead of Thrithings-men."

The prince did not reply. Deornoth touched his arm, feeling the muscles tense as barrel staves beneath his fingers. "What's wrong, Prince Josua? Have the Thrithings-men thrown in with Elias? My lord?"

One of the riders looked down, mouth set in a humorless, gap-toothed grin. "Quiet, stone-dwellers," he snarled. "Save your breath for walking."

Josua turned a haunted face toward Deornoth. "Didn't you hear him?" the prince whispered. "Didn't you hear him?"

Deornoth was alarmed. "What?"

"Six men, two women, and a child," Josua hissed, looking from side to side. "Two women! *Where is Vorzheva?*"

The rider slapped a spear butt against his shoulder and the prince lapsed into anguished silence. They trudged on between the horsemen as dawn began to smolder in the eastern sky.

As she lay on her hard bed in the darkened servant's quarters, Rachel the Dragon imagined she could hear the gibbet creaking, even above the howling wind that skirled through the battlements. Nine more bodies, the chancellor Helfcene's among them, were swaying above the Nearulagh Gate tonight, dancing helplessly to the wind's fierce music.

Nearer at hand, somebody was crying.

"Sarrah? Is that you?" Rachel hissed. "Sarrah?"

The moaning of the gale died down. "Y—yes, mistress," came the muffled reply.

"Blessed Rhiap, what are you sobbing about? You'll wake the others!" Beside Sarrah and Rachel, there were only three other women now sleeping in the maid's quarters, but all five cots were huddled together to conserve heat in the large, chilly room.

Sarrah seemed to struggle to compose herself, but when she answered her voice was still shaken by sobs. "I'm . . . I'm afraid, M—mistress Rachel."

"Of what, fool girl, the wind?" Rachel sat up, holding the thin blanket closely around her. "It's blowing up a storm, but you've heard wind before." Torchlight bleeding beneath the doorway revealed the faint shape of Sarrah's pale face.

"It's . . . my gammer used to say . . ." The maid coughed wetly. "Gammer said that nights like this . . . are when dead spirits walk. That you . . . you can hear the voices in the w—wind."

Rachel was grateful for the darkness that hid her own discomforted shiver. If there ever would be such a night, tonight seemed a likely choice. The wind had been raging like a wounded animal since sundown, wailing among the Hayholt's chimneys and scratching at the doors and windows with insistent, twiggy fingers.

She made her voice firm. "The dead don't walk in *my* castle, idiot girl. Now go back to sleep before you give the others nightmares." Rachel lowered herself back down onto her pallet, trying to find a position that would ease her knotted back. "Go to sleep, Sarrah," she said. "The wind can't hurt you, and there'll be work in plenty tomorrow, the Good Lord knows, just a-picking up what the wind's blown down."

"I'm sorry." The pale face sank. After a few sniffling minutes, Sarrah was silent once more. Rachel stared upward into the blackness and listened to the night's restless voices.

She might have slept—it was hard to tell when all was in darkness—but Rachel knew that she had been listening to a sound beneath the windsong for some time. It was a quiet, stealthy scratching, a dry sound like bird claws on a slate roof.

Something was at the door.

She might have been sleeping, but now, suddenly, she was terribly awake. When she turned her head to the side she could see a shadow slipping along the strip of light below the door. The scratching became louder, and with it came the sound of someone crying.

"Sarrah?" Rachel whispered, thinking that the noise had awakened the maid, but there was no response. As she listened wide-eyed in the dark she knew that the strange, thin sound was coming from the hallway—from whatever stood outside her locked door.

"Please," someone whispered there, "please . . ."

Blood pounding in her head, Rachel sat up, then silently placed her bare feet on the cold stone floor. Could she be dreaming? She seemed so very wide awake, but it sounded like a boy's voice, like . . .

The scratching took on an impatient quality which quickly began to sound like fearfulness—whatever it was, she thought, it *must* be frightened, to scratch so . . . A wandering spirit, a homeless thing walking lone and lorn on this blustery night, looking for its long-vanished bed?

Rachel crept closer to the door, silent as snow. Her heart labored. The wind in the battlements stilled. She was alone in the dark with the breathing of the slumbering maids and the pitiful scraping of what stood beyond the door.

"Please," the voice said again, softly, weakly. "I'm scared . . ."

She traced the sign of the Tree on her breast, then grasped the bolt and drew it back. Though the moment of choosing was past, she drew the door open slowly: even with the choice made, she feared what she would see.

The solitary torch against the far corridor outlined the faint figure, its thatch of hair, its scarecrow-thin limbs. The face that turned to her, startled eyes showing their whites, was blackened as though burnt.

"Help me," it said, staggering through the doorway into her arms.

"Simon!" Rachel cried, and beyond all sense felt her heart overflowing. He had come back, through fire, through death. . . .

"Si . . . Simon?" the boy said, his eyes sagging closed from exhaustion and pain. "Simon's dead. He . . . he died . . . in the fire. Pryrates killed him. . . ."

He went limp in her arms. Head whirling, she pulled his sagging form through the doorway, letting him slide to the floor, then shot the bolt firmly home and went looking for a candle. The wind cried mockingly; if other voices cried within it, there were none that Rachel recognized.

"It's Jeremias, the chandler's boy," Sarrah said wonderingly as Rachel washed the dried blood from his face. In the candlelight, Jeremias' dark-socketed eyes and scratched cheeks made him seem almost a wizened old man.

"But he was a chubby thing," Rachel said. Her mind was boiling with the boy's words, but things must be done one at a time. What would these useless girls think if she let herself go all to pieces? "What's happened to him?" she growled. "He's thin as a stave."

The maids had all gathered around, blankets wrapped as cloaks around their nightdresses. Jael, no longer as stout as she had once been, owing to the greater burden of work all the remaining girls shared, stared at the senseless youth.

"I thought someone said Jeremias ran away?" she said, frowning. "Why did he come back?"

"Don't be foolish," Rachel said, trying to tug Jeremias' tattered shirt over his head without waking him. "If he had run away, how would he have gotten back into Hayholt at the middle of night? Flown?"

"Then tell us where he *has* been," one of the other girls said. It was a measure of Rachel's shock at Jeremias' entrance that this near-impertinence went completely unremarked-upon by the Mistress of Chambermaids.

"Help me turn him over," she said, working the shirt free. "We'll put him to sleep in . . . Oh! Elysia, Mother of God!" She fell into astonished silence. Sarrah burst into tears beside her.

The youth's back was crisscrossed with deep, bloody weals.

"I feel . . . I feel sick!" Jael mumbled, then lurched away.

"Don't be a fool," Rachel said, regaining her composure once more. "Splash some water on your face, then bring me the rest of the basin. This wet cloth alone won't do. And take that sheet from the bed Hepizibah used to sleep in and tear strips for bandages. Rhiap's Pain, do I have to do everything myself?"

It took the whole sheet and part of another one. His legs had been scourged, too.

★　　★　　★

Jeremias awoke just before dawn. His eyes at first roamed the room without seeing anything, but after a time he seemed to regain his wits. Sarrah, sadness and pity shining through her homely face as though it were glass, gave him some water to drink.

"Where am I?" he asked at last.

"You're in the servant's quarters, boy," Rachel said briskly. "As you should know. Now, what sort of mischief have you been up to?"

He stared at her groggily for a moment. "You're Rachel the Dragon," he said at last. Despite their weariness and fright, and the lateness of the hour, the chambermaids were hard put to suppress their smiles. Rachel, strangely, did not seem angered in the slightest.

"I'm Rachel," she agreed. "Now, where have you been, boy? We heard that you ran away."

"You thought I was Simon," Jeremias said, wonderingly, staring around the chamber. "He was my friend—but he's dead, isn't he? Am I dead?"

"You're not dead. What happened to you?" Rachel leaned forward to brush Jeremias' tangled hair out of his eyes; her hand lingered for an instant on his cheek. "You're safe now. Talk to us."

He seemed about to slide back into sleep, but after a moment he opened his eyes again. When he spoke it was more plainly than before. "I did try to run away," he said. "When the king's soldiers beat my master Jakob and drove him out the gate. I tried to run away that night, but the guards caught me. They gave me to Inch."

Rachel frowned. "That animal."

Jeremias' eyes widened. "He's worse than any animal. He's a devil. He said I would be his apprentice, down in the furnaces . . . in the forges. He thinks he's a king down there . . ." The boy's face screwed up, and he suddenly burst into tears. "He says he's . . . he's Doctor Inch, now. He beat me and . . . he used me."

Rachel leaned forward to blot his cheeks with her kerchief. The girls made the sign of the Tree.

Jeremias' sobbing diminished. "It's worse than anything . . . down there."

"You said something, boy," Rachel said briskly. "Something about the king's counselor. About Simon. Say it again."

The boy opened his brimming eyes wide. "Pryrates killed him. Simon and Morgenes. The priest went there with troops. Morgenes fought with him, but the chamber burned down and Simon and the doctor died."

"And how could you know that?" she snapped, a little harshly. "How could such as you know that?"

"Pryrates said so himself! He comes down to see Inch. Sometimes he just brags, like about killing Morgenes. Other times he helps Inch . . . h–hurt people." Jeremias was having trouble. "Sometimes . . . sometimes the priest takes people away with him . . . takes them when he goes. They don't come b–back." He fought to catch his breath. "And there's . . . other things. Other things down there. Terrible things. Oh, God, please don't send me back." He grasped Rachel's wrist with his hand. "Please hide me!"

Rachel tried to mask her shock. She deliberately closed off her thoughts about Simon and this new revelation until she could consider it all in privacy. But despite her firm self-control, Rachel felt a cold hatred running through her, a hatred unlike anything she had ever felt.

"We won't let them have you," she said. Her straightforward tone made it clear that any gainsaying of her will would bring great risk to the gainsayer. "We'll . . . we'll . . ." She broke off for a moment, non-plussed. What *would* they do? They could not hide the boy for long here in the servant's quarters, especially if he had run away from the king's forges below the Hayholt.

"What 'other things' were there?" Jael asked. Her brown, calflike eyes were puzzled.

"Hush, now," Rachel said sharply, but Jeremias was already answering.

"I d–don't know," he said. "There are . . . shadows that move. Shadows without people. And things that are there—and then they aren't. And voices . . ." he shivered, and his eyes stared past the candleflame to the darkness in the room's corner. "Voices that cry, and sing, and . . . and . . ." Tears formed in his eyes once more.

"That's enough," Rachel said sternly, displeased with herself for letting the boy talk so long. Her charges darted glances among themselves, nervous as startled sheep.

Elysia! she thought, *that's all I need—to have the last of my girls frightened out of the castle.*

"Too much talking," she said aloud. "The boy needs rest. He's so worn and beaten he has the vapors. Let him sleep."

Jeremias shook his head weakly. "I'm telling the truth," he said. "Don't let them have me!"

"We won't," Rachel said. "Go to sleep. If we can't hide you, we'll think of some way to get you out of the Hayholt. You can go to your kin, wherever they may be. We'll keep you away from that one-eyed devil Inch."

". . . And Pryrates," Jeremias said slurredly, succumbing to drowsiness. "He . . . talks . . . to the Voices . . ."

A moment later the boy was slumbering. A little of the fear seemed to lift from his hunger-thinned features. Rachel looked down at him and felt her heart grown hard as a stone in her breast. That devil-priest, Pryrates! That murderer! What kind of plague had he brought down on their house, what foulness to her beloved Hayholt?

And what had he done to her Simon?

She turned to look sternly at her wide-eyed maids. "You had all better get what sleep you can," she growled. "A little excitement doesn't mean the floors won't need scrubbing when the sun is up."

As they crawled into their beds, Rachel snuffed the candle, then lay down with her cold thoughts. Outside, the wind was still searching for a way in.

The morning sun rose above the gray blanket of clouds. It brought a diffuse light to the rolling grasslands of the High Thrithings, but could not lift the damp from the endless leagues of prairie grass and heather. Deornoth was soaked to the thighs and tired of marching.

The Thrithings-men did not stop for a meal, instead eating dried meat and fruits from their saddlebags as they rode. The prisoners were not offered any food, and were only allowed to pause for a short rest at mid-morning, during which time Deornoth and Josua quietly questioned the rest of their party about Vorzheva's whereabouts. No one had seen her leave, although Geloë said she had awakened Vorzheva at the first sound of the approaching riders.

"She was born on this land," the witch woman told the prince. "I would not worry for her too much." Geloë's own face, however, showed more than a trace of concern.

Hotvig and his men roused Josua's band after a too-short rest and the march began anew. A wind sprang up from the northwest, soft at first, then blowing stronger, until the ribbons on the Thrithings-men's saddles whipped like tournament pennants and the long grasses bent double. The prisoners labored on, shivering in their wet clothing.

Soon they began to see signs of habitation: small herds of cattle grazing on the low hills, watched over by solitary horsemen. As the sun rose closer to its noon apogee, the cattle herds they passed grew larger and closer together, until at last the prisoners found themselves following the snaking course of one of the Ymstrecca's tributaries through the very midst of an immense throng of animals. The vast herd seemed to run from horizon to horizon and contained mostly cattle of the ordinary sort, but shaggy bison and bulls with long, curving horns also grazed among them, lifting their heads to stare blearily at the passing prisoners, mouths solemnly chewing.

"It is obvious that these folk do not follow Geloë's advice on vegetable-eating," Deornoth said. "There is enough meat on the hoof here to feed all Osten Ard." He looked hopefully to his prince, but Josua's smile was a weary one.

"Many of them are sickly," Gutrun pronounced. In her husband's frequent absences, she ran the duke's household at Elvritshalla with a firm hand, and rightly considered herself a good judge of livestock. "See, and there are not many calves for such a huge herd."

One of the riders who had been listening made a noise of disgust, as if to show his disdain for the opinions of prisoners, but one of his mounted companions nodded his head and said: "It is a bad year. Many cows die birthing. Others eat but do not grow fat." The Thrithings-man's beard fluttered in the wind. "It is a bad year," he repeated.

Here and there among the great herd were circles of wagons, each circle surrounded with fences of hastily-driven posts. The wagons themselves were all wooden, with large, high wheels, but otherwise were quite different from each other. Some were tall as two or three men, wheeled cottages with wooden roofs and shuttered windows. Others were little more than a wagon-bed topped with a cloth-covered shelter, the fabric rippling and snapping in the stiff breeze. Children played in many of the enclosures or darted in and out among the milling, amiable cattle. Horses grazed in some of the paddlocks—and not just dray horses and wagon-pullers. Many were slender-limbed and wild-maned, with something light and strong as forged steel to be seen in their step even from a distance.

"Ah, God, if only we had a few beasts like those," Deornoth said wistfully. "But we have nothing to trade. I am mightily tired of walking."

Josua looked at him with a trace of sour humor. "We will be lucky if we walk away from here with our lives, Deornoth, and you are hoping for a brace of battle steeds? I would rather I had your optimism than their horses."

As the prisoners and their captors continued south, the sprawl of separate wagon-camps began to come together, clumped like mushrooms after an autumn rain. Other groups of mounted men rode in and out among the settlements; Josua's escorts exchanged shouted remarks with some of them. Soon the wagons stood so near each other that it began to seem that the prisoners traversed a city without roads.

At last they reached a large stockade, its fence posts hung with ornaments of bright metal and polished wood that clattered in the wind. Most of the riders sheared off, but Hotvig the leader and six or seven others ushered the prince's party through a swinging gate. There were several compounds within the stockade, one of them containing a score of fine horses, another a half-dozen fat and glossy heifers. In an enclosure by himself stood a huge stallion, his shaggy mane twined with red and gold ribbons. The great horse nosed the ground as they passed and did not look up—he was a monarch more used to being stared at than staring. The men escorting Josua's party touched their hands to their eyes reverently as they passed.

"It is their clan beast," Geloë said to no one in particular.

At the far end of the encampment stood a great wagon with wide, heavy-spoked wheels and a banner bearing a golden horse billowing from the roof-peak. Before it were two figures, a large man and a young girl. The girl was knotting the man's long beard into two thick braids that hung down onto his chest. Despite his age—he looked to have passed some sixty summers on the grasslands—his black hair was only faintly striped with silver and his wide frame was still knotted with muscle. He held a bowl upon his lap in his huge beringed and braceleted hands.

The riders stopped and dismounted. Hotvig strode forward to stand before him.

"We have captured several trespassers who walked the Feluwelt without your leave, March-thane: six men, two women, and a child."

The March-thane stared the prisoners up and down. His face split in a wide, crooked-toothed grin. "Prince Josua Lackhand," he said, without the least trace of surprise in his voice. "Now that your stone house is fallen, have you come to live beneath the sky like men do?" He took a long swallow from his bowl, draining it dry, then handed it to the girl and waved her away.

"Fikolmij," Josua said, bleakly amused. "So you are March-thane now."

"When the Choosing came, of all the chieftains there was only Blehmunt who would stand against me. I broke his head like an egg." Fikolmij laughed, patting at his new-braided beard, then stopped, lowering his eyebrows like a nettled bull. "Where is my daughter?"

"If that young one was yours, you just sent her away," Josua said.

Fikolmij clenched a fist in anger, then laughed again. "Stupid tricks, Josua. You know who I mean. Where is she?"

"I will tell you the truth," Josua said. "I do not know where Vorzheva is."

The March-thane looked him over speculatively. "So," he said at last. "You are not so high in the world today, stone-dweller. You are a trespasser in the Free Thrithings now, as well as a daughter-stealer. Perhaps you will seem better to me with your other hand cut off, too. I will think on it." He lifted his hairy paw and gestured carelessly to Hotvig. "Put them in one of the bull runs until I decide which ones to cut up and which to keep."

"Merciful Aedon preserve us," Father Strangyard murmured.

The March-thane chuckled, flicking a wind-blown curl of hair from his eye. "And give these city-rats a blanket or two and some food, Hotvig. Otherwise, the night air may kill them and rob my sport."

As Josua and the others were led away at spearpoint, Fikolmij turned and shouted for the girl to bring him more wine.

14

A Crown of Fire

It was a dream, Simon knew even as he dreamed it. It started in an ordinary enough fashion: he was lying in the Hayholt's great loft, hidden in tickling hay, watching the familiar figures of Shem Horsegroom and castle smith Ruben the Bear talking quietly below. Ruben, his broad arms glimmering with sweat, was hammering clankingly away at a scarlet-hot horseshoe.

Suddenly the dream took on a strange cast. Ruben's and Shem's voices changed, until they sounded nothing like their real selves. Simon could now hear the conversation perfectly well, but the smith's hammer was silent as it struck the gleaming iron.

". . . But I have done all you asked for," Shem abruptly said in a queer, rasping tone. *"I brought King Elias to you."*

"You presume too much," Ruben replied. His voice was like nothing Simon had ever heard, cold and remote as the wind in a high mountain pass. *"You know nothing of what we want . . . of what He wants."* There was more wrong with the blacksmith than just his voice: a feeling of wrongness emanated from him, a black and bottomless lake hidden beneath a crust of thin ice. How could Ruben seem so evil, even in a dream—kind, slow-talking Ruben?

Shem's lined face smiled cheerfully, but his words sounded strained. *"I do not care. I will do anything He wishes. I ask little in return."*

"You ask a great deal more than any other mortal would," Reuben replied. *"Not only do you dare to call on the Red Hand, you have the temerity to demand favors."* He was chill and uncaring as graveyard dirt. *"You do not even know what you ask. You are a child, priest, and you grasp at gleaming things because they seem pretty. You may cut yourself on something jagged and find that you bleed to death."*

"I don't care." Shem spoke with a lunatic firmness. *"I don't care. Teach me the Words of Changing. The Dark One owes me . . . he is obligated . . ."*

Ruben threw back his head in wild laughter. A crown of flames seemed to blaze about his head. *"Obligated?"* he gasped. The sound of his amusement was terrifying. *"Our master? To you?"* He laughed again, and suddenly the blacksmith's skin began blistering. Little gouts of smoke jetted into the air as Ruben's flesh burned away, peeling back to reveal a shifting kernel of flame beneath, pulsating with reddish light like a coal fanned by wind. *"You will live to see His final triumph. That is more reward than most mortals can expect!"*

"Please!" Even as Ruben flared, Shem had begun to shrink, becoming small and gray as a charred parchment. His tiny arm waved, crumbling. *"Please, undying one, please."* His voice was oddly light, fraught with a kind of slyness. *"I will ask nothing further—I will not speak of the Dark One again. Forgive a mortal fool. Teach me the Word!"*

Where Ruben had stood, a living flame glowed. *"Very well, priest. There is, perhaps, little risk in giving you this dangerous but final toy. The Lord of All will be taking this world back soon enough—there is nothing you can do that He cannot make undone. Very well. I will teach you the Word, but the pain will be great. No Change is without some cost."* Laughter bubbled again in the unearthly voice. *"You will scream . . ."*

"I don't care!" Shem said, his ashy form swirling away now into darkness, as did the shadowed smithy and then the hayloft itself. *"I don't care! I must know. . . !"* Finally, even the glowing thing that had been Ruben became only a bright point in the blackness . . . a star. . . .

Simon awakened, breathless as a drowning man, his heart thudding in his chest. There *was* a single star overhead, peeping through the hole in the top of their sleeping shelter like a blue-white eye. He gasped.

Binabik lifted his head from Qantaqa's shaggy neck. The troll was half-asleep, but struggling toward full wakefulness. "What is wrong, Simon?" he asked. "Were you having a dream that frightened?"

Simon shook his head. The tide of fear was ebbing a little, but he was sure it had been more than just a night fantasy. It had seemed that an actual conversation was taking place nearby, a conversation that his sleeping mind had woven neatly into the stuff of his dream—a mundane happening that he had experienced many times. What was strange and frightening was that there were no other speakers anywhere about: Sludig was snoring, Binabik obviously new-wakened.

"It's nothing," Simon said, struggling to speak evenly. He crawled to the front of their lean-to, mindful of the bruises from the evening's stave-practice, and pushed his head out to look around. The first star he had seen had a great deal of company—a spatter of tiny white lights across the night sky. The clouds had been driven away by the brisk wind, the night was clear and cold, and the unrelieved monotony of the White Waste stretched away on every side. There was not another living thing to be seen anywhere beneath the ivory moon.

So it *had* only been a dream, a dream of how old Shem Horsegroom might speak with Pryrates' croaking tongue, and how Ruben the Bear might speak with the sepulchral tones of nothing on God's living earth. . . .

"Simon?" Binabik asked sleepily. "Are you. . . ?"

He was frightened, but if he was to be a man he could not run to cry on someone's shoulder every time he had a bad dream. "It's nothing." He crawled shivering back to his cloak. "I'm well."

But it seemed so real. The branches of their flimsy shelter creaked, wind-handled. *So real. Like they were talking in my head . . .*

Taking the silver sparrow's fragmentary message to heart, they rode from first light to last every day, trying to outpace the coming storm. Simon's mock-combats with Sludig now took place by firelight, so that he had scarcely a moment to spend alone from the moment he rose until he tumbled into exhausted sleep at the end of each day. The days of riding passed in a procession of sameness: the endless, humped fields of white, the dark tangles of stunted trees, the numbing insistence of the wind. Simon was grateful for his thickening beard: without it, he often thought, the relentless wind might rub away his face, down to the very bones.

It seemed that the wind had already worn away the face of the land, leaving behind little that was remarkable or distinct. Had it not been for the widening line of forest on the horizon, he could have supposed that every morning found them back at the same cold, bleak starting place. Thinking morosely about his own warm bed in the Hayholt, he decided that even if the Storm King himself were to move into the castle, his minions numerous as snowflakes, Simon could still live happily in the servant's quarters. He wanted a home desperately. He was close to the point where he would take a mattress in Hell if the Devil would lend him a pillow.

As days wore by, the storm continued to grow behind them, a black pillar rising ominously in the northwestern sky. Great cloudy arms clutched at the firmament like the branches of a heaven-spanning tree. Lightning flickered between them.

"It's not moving very fast," Simon said one day as they ate a sparse noontime meal. There was more nervousness in his voice than he would have liked.

Binabik nodded. "It grows, but its spreading is slow. That is something for being thankful about." He wore an unusually dispirited expression. "The slower it is moving, the longer we are not beneath it—for I am thinking that when it comes, it will bring a darkness with it that will not be passing away, as with storms of the ordinary type."

"What do you mean?" Now the tremor was plain to hear.

"It is not a storm with just snow and rain," Binabik said carefully. "My thought is that it is exactly meant to bring fear where it goes. It rises from

Stormspike. It has the look of something full of unnaturalness." He raised his palms apologetically. "It is spreading, but as you said, not with great swiftness."

I do not know about such things," Sludig said, "but I must admit I'm happy we will be off the Waste soon. I wouldn't want to get caught in the open in any storm, and that one looks truly nasty." He turned toward the south and squinted. "Two days until we reach Aldheorte," he said. "That will be some protection."

Binabik sighed. "I hope you are right, but I am fearing that there will be no protection against this storm—or that the protection must be something other than forest trees or roofs."

"Do you mean the swords?" Simon asked quietly.

The little man shrugged. "Perhaps. If we are finding all three, perhaps winter can be kept at spear-length—or even pushed back. But first we must go to where Geloë tells us. Otherwise, it is only worrying about things we cannot be changing; that is foolishness." He mustered a smile. " 'When your teeth are gone,' we Qanuc say, 'learn to like mush.' "

The next morning, their seventh on the Waste, came laden with foul weather. Although the storm in the north was still only an inky blotch defacing the far horizon, steely gray clouds had gathered overhead, their edges stripped into sooty tatters by the rising wind. By noon, when the sun had vanished from view entirely behind the dismal pall, the snow began to fly.

"This is terrible," Simon shouted, eyes narrowed against the stinging sleet. Despite his heavy leather gloves, his fingers were swiftly growing numb. "We're blinded! Shouldn't we stop and make shelter?"

Binabik, a small, snow-covered shadow atop Qantaqa's back, turned and called back to him: "If we go a little farther, we will reach the crossroads!"

"Crossroads!" Sludig bellowed. "In this wilderness?!"

"Ride nearer," Binabik cried. "I will be explaining."

Simon and the Rimmersman brought their mounts closer to the striding wolf. Binabik lifted his hand to his mouth, but still the wind's roar threatened to carry off his words. "Not far beyond here, I am thinking, this Old Tumet'ai Road meets the White Way, that is running along the northern edge of the forest. At the crossroad may be shelter, or at least the trees should be of more thickness there, closer to the woods. Let us go riding on a while longer. If there is nothing in that spot, we will make our camp there despite it."

"As long as we stop well before dark, troll," Sludig bellowed. "You are clever, but your cleverness may not be enough to make a decent camp in darkness in this blizzard. Having lived through all the madness I have seen, I do not want to die in the snow like a lost cow!"

Simon said nothing, saving his strength so he could more fully appreciate his misery. Aedon, it was cold! Would there never be an end to snow?

They rode on through the bleak, icy afternoon. Simon's mare plodded slowly, ankling through the new drifts. Simon leaned his head close to her mane, trying to stay out of the wind. The world seemed as formless and white as the inside of a flour cask, and only slightly more habitable.

The sun was quite invisible, but a dimming of the already scarce light suggested that the afternoon was fading fast. Binabik, however, did not seem inclined to stop. As they passed yet one more unprepossessing stand of evergreens, Simon could stand it no longer.

"I'm freezing, Binabik!" he shouted angrily above the wind. "And it's getting dark! There's another bunch of trees gone and we're still riding. Well, it's almost night! By God's bloody Tree, I'm not going to go any farther!"

"Simon . . ." Binabik began, striving to assume a placating tone while yelling at the top of his lungs.

"There's something in the road!" Sludig cried hoarsely. "*Vaer!* Something ahead! A troll!"

Binabik squinted. "It is being no such thing," he shouted indignantly. "No Qanuc would be foolish enough to go wandering alone in such weather!"

Simon stared into the swirling gray dimness before them. "I don't see anything."

"As neither do I." Binabik brushed snow from his hood lining.

"I saw something," Sludig growled. "I may be snow-blinded, but I am not mad."

"An animal, that is most likely," the troll said. "Or, if we are unlucky, one of the diggers as a scout. Perhaps it *is* time to make shelter and fire, as you said, Simon. There is a stand of trees that looks to make better sheltering just ahead. There, over the rise."

The companions chose the most protected spot they could find. Simon and Sludig wove branches among the tree trunks for a windbreak while Binabik, with the help of his yellow fire-powder, set flame to damp wood and began to boil water for broth. The weather was so unremittingly foul and cold that after sharing the thin soup, they all curled up in their cloaks and lay shivering. The wind was too loud for any but shouted conversation. Despite the proximity of his friends, Simon was alone with his cheerless thoughts until sleep came.

Simon woke with Qantaqa's steaming breath on his face. The wolf whined and nudged him with her great head, rolling him halfway over. He sat up, blinking in the weak rays of morning sun filtering into the copse. Snow drifts had piled against the woven branches, making a wall that kept the wind at bay, so the smoke from Binabik's campfire rose almost undisturbed.

"Good morning, Simon-friend," Binabik said. "We have survived through the storm."

Simon gently pushed Qantaqa's head out of his side. She made a noise of frustration, then backed away. Her muzzle was red-daubed.

"She has been unsettled all the morning," Binabik laughed. "I am thinking that the many frozen squirrels and birds and such who have tumbled from the trees have fed her well, however."

"Where's Sludig?"

"He is seeing to the horses." Binabik poked at the fire. "I convinced him to take them downslope in the open, so the horses would not be stepping on my morning meal or your face." He lifted a bowl. "This is the last of the broth. Since our dried meat is now almost finished, I suggest you enjoy it. Meals may be scarce if our own hunting must be relied on."

Simon shivered as he wiped a handful of snow on his face. "But won't we reach the forest soon?"

Binabik patiently offered the bowl again. "Just so, but we will be traveling along it rather than through. It is a route more circuitous but less time-consuming, since we will not be cutting through underbrush. Also, in this frozen summer there may be few animals who are not sleeping in their dens and nests. Thus, if you are not soon taking this soup from my hands, I will drink it myself. I am no more interested in starving than you, as well as a great deal more sensible."

"Sorry. Thank you." Simon hunched over the bowl, enjoying a deep breath of the rising scent before he drank.

"You may be washing the bowl when you have finished," the troll sniffed. "A nice bowl is a luxurious thing to have on a journey of such dangerousness."

Simon smiled. "You sound like Rachel the Dragon."

"I have not met this Dragon-Rachel," Binabik said as he stood up, brushing snow from his breeches, "but if she was given charge of you, she must have been a person of great patientness and kindness."

Simon chortled.

They reached the crossroads in late morning. The meeting of the two roads was marked only by a gaunt finger of stone set upright in the frozen ground. Gray-green lichen, seemingly impervious to frost, clung to it grimly.

"The Old Tumet'ai Road runs through the forest." Binabik gestured to the barely distinguishable path of the south road, which coiled away through a stand of firs. "Since I am thinking it is nevermore used and likely quite overgrown, we should instead follow the White Way. Perhaps we will find some deserted habitations where we may be finding supplies."

The White Way proved a slightly newer road than the one leading from the ancient site of Tumet'ai. There were a few marks of recent human visitation—a rusted and broken iron wheel-rim dangling from a roadside branch, where it had doubtless been thrown by an irate wagon owner; a sharpened spoke perhaps used as a tent-spike, discarded by the shoulder; a circle of charred stones half-covered in snow.

"Who lives out here?" Simon asked. "Why is there a road at all?"

"There were once several small settlements east of St. Skendi's monastery," Sludig said. "You remember Skendi's—the snow-buried place we passed on our way to the dragon-mountain. There were even a few towns here—Sovebek, Grinsaby, some others, as I remember. I think also that a century or so ago, people traveled this way around the great forest when they came north from the Thrithings, so there may have been a few inns."

"In days more than a century gone," Binabik intoned, "this part of the world was being much traveled. We Qanuc—some of us, that is to say—traveled farther south in summer, sometimes to the edges of the lowlander countries. Also, the Sithi themselves were everywhere in their wandering. It is only in these late and sad days that all this land has become empty of voices."

"It does seem empty now," Simon said. "It seems like no one could live here anymore."

They followed the winding course of the road through the short afternoon. The trees were gradually becoming thicker here at the forest's edge, in spots growing so closely about the road that it seemed as if the companions had already entered Aldheorte, whether they wished to or not. At last they came to another standing stone, this one leaning forlornly by the roadside, with no crossing or other possible landmark in sight. Sludig dismounted to take a closer look.

"There are runes on it, but faint and weathered." He peeled back some of the frozen moss. "I think they say that Grinsaby is nearby." He looked up, smiling in his frosty beard. "Someplace with a roof or two, perhaps, even if nothing else. That would be a nice change." His step a little springier, the Rimmersman vaulted back into his saddle. Simon, too, was heartened. Even a deserted town would be a vast improvement over the comfortless waste.

The words of Binabik's song came back to him. *You have slipped into cold shadows . . .* He felt a moment's pang of loneliness. Perhaps the town would not be deserted, after all. Maybe there would be an inn with a fire, and food . . .

As Simon yearned for the comforts of civilization, the sun vanished for good behind the forest. The wind rose and the early northern twilight came down upon them.

There was still light in the sky, but the snowy landscape had turned blue and gray, soaking up shadow like a rag dipped in ink. Simon and his companions were nearly ready to stop and make camp, and were discussing the subject in loud voices over the monotonous wind when they came upon the first outbuildings of Grinsaby.

As if to disappoint even Sludig's modest hopes, the roofs of these abandoned cottages had collapsed under the weight of snow. The paddocks and gardens were also long untended, knee-deep in swirling white. Simon had seen so many emptied towns in his northern sojourn that it was hard to believe that the Frostmarch and the Waste had once been inhabited, that people had led their lives here just as they did in the green fields of Erkynland. He ached for his own home, for familiar places and familiar weather. Or had winter already crawled over the entire land?

They rode on. Soon Grinsaby's deserted houses began to appear in greater profusion on either side of the road Binabik had named the White Way. Some still bore traces of their once-residents—a rusted axe with a rotted handle standing in a chopping block before a snow-buried front door; an upright broom sticking out of the roadside drifts like a flag or the tail of a frozen animal—but most of the dwellings were as empty and desolate as skulls.

"Where do we stop?" Sludig called. "I think we may not find a roof after all."

"We may not, so let us be looking for good walls," Binabik replied. He was about to say more when Simon tugged at his arm.

"Look! It *is* a troll! Sludig was right!" Simon pointed off to the side of the road, where a short figure stood motionless but for its wind-flung cloak. The last rays of sunlight had found a thin spot in the forest fringe behind Grinsaby, throwing the stranger into relief.

"Be looking yourself," Binabik said grumpily, but his eyes were fixed warily on the stranger. "It is no troll." The figure beside the road was very small, wearing a thin hooded cloak. Bare, bluish skin showed where the breeches-legs failed to meet the top of his boots.

"It's a little boy." After amending his earlier identification, Simon steered Homefinder toward the edge of the road. His two companions followed. "He must be freezing to death!"

As they rode toward him, the child looked up, snow flecking his dark brows and lashes. He stared at the approaching trio, then turned and began to run.

"Stop," Simon called, "we won't hurt you!"

"Halad, künde!" Sludig shouted. The retreating form stopped and turned, staring. Sludig rode a few ells closer, then climbed down from his horse and walked forward slowly. *"Vjer sommen marroven, künde,"* he said, extending a hand. The boy stared at him suspiciously, but made no further move toward flight. The child seemed to be no more than seven or eight years old and thin as the handle of a butter churn, judging by the bits of him showing. His hands were full of acorns.

"I'm cold," the boy said in fair Westerling.

Sludig looked surprised, but smiled and nodded. "Come on, then, lad." He gently took the acorns and poured them into his cloak pocket, then gathered up the unresisting child in his strong arms. "It's all right, then. We'll help you." The Rimmersman placed the dark-haired stranger on the front of his saddle, wrapping his cloak around him so that the boy's head seemed to grow from Sludig's now-broad belly. "Can we find a place to make camp now, troll?" he growled.

Binabik nodded. "Of course."

He urged Qantaqa ahead. The boy watched the wolf with wide but unworried eyes as Simon and Sludig spurred after. Snow was rapidly filling in the hollow where the boy had stood.

As they rode on through the empty town, Sludig brought out his skin of kangkang and let the newcomer have a short drink. The boy coughed, but otherwise seemed unsurprised by the bitter Qanuc liquor. Simon decided he might be older than first appearance made him seem: there was a precision to his movements that made him seem less like a child. Some of his apparent youth, Simon guessed, might be due to his large eyes and slender frame.

"What's your name, lad?" Sludig asked at last.

The boy looked him over calmly. "Vren," he said at last, the word fluidly and oddly accented. He tugged at the drinking skin, but Sludig shook his head and put it back in his saddle bag.

" 'Friend'?" Simon asked, puzzled.

" 'Vren,' I am thinking he said," Binabik replied. "It is a Hyrkaman name, and I am thinking he might be a Hyrka."

"Look at that black hair," Sludig said. "The color of his skin, too. He is a Hyrka, or I am no Rimmersman. But what is he doing alone in the snow?"

The Hyrkas, Simon knew, were a footloose people accounted good with horses and skilled in games at which other people lost money. He had seen many at the great market in Erchester. "Do the Hyrkas live out here, in the White Waste?"

Sludig frowned. "I've never heard of such—but I have seen many things of late I would have have believed in Elvritshalla. I thought they lived mainly in the cities and on the grasslands with the Thrithings-folk."

Binabik reached up and patted the boy with a small hand. "So have I been taught, although there are some who also are living beyond the Waste, in the empty steppe-lands to the east."

After they had ridden farther, Sludig dismounted again to search for signs of habitation. He returned, shaking his head, and went to Vren. The child's brown eyes gazed unflinchingly back at him. "Where do you live?" the Rimmersman asked.

"With Skodi," was the reply.

"Is that near?" Binabik asked. The boy shrugged. "Where are your parents?" The gesture was repeated.

The troll turned to his companions. "Perhaps Skodi is the name of his mother. Or it might be a name of some other town name near to Grinsaby-village. It is also being possible he has strayed from a caravan of wagons—although these roads, I have sureness, are not much used at the best of times. How could he survive long in fearful winter days like these. . . ?" He shrugged, a movement oddly similar to the child's.

"Will he stay with us?" Simon asked. Sludig made an exasperated noise but said nothing. Simon turned on the Rimmersman angrily. "We can't leave him here to die!"

Binabik waved a placating finger. "No, do not fear that we would. In any case, I suspect that there must be more people than Vren who are living here."

Sludig stood up. "The troll is right: there must be folk here. Anyway, the idea of taking a child with us is foolish."

"That is what some were saying of Simon," Binabik responded quietly. "But I am having agreement with your first statement. Let us find his home."

"He can ride with me for a while," Simon said. The Rimmersman made a wry face, but handed over the unresisting child. Simon wrapped the boy in his cloak as Sludig had done.

"Sleep now, Vren," he whispered. The wind moaned through the ruined houses. "You're with friends, now. We'll take you home."

The boy stared back at him, solemn as a petty cleric at a public ceremony. A small hand snaked out from beneath the jacket to pat Homefinder's back. With Vren's slender form resting against his chest, Simon took his reins in one hand so he could drape an arm around the boy's midsection. He felt very old and very responsible.

Will I ever be a father? he wondered as they tramped on through the gathering dark. *Have sons?* He thought about it for a moment. *Daughters?*

All the people he knew, it seemed, had lost their fathers—Binabik's in a snowslide, Prince Josua's to old age. Jeremias the chandler's boy, Simon remembered, had lost his to the chest-fever; Princess Miriamele's sire might as well be dead. He thought about his own father, drowned before he was born. Were fathers just that way, like cats and dogs, making children and then going away?

"Sludig!" he called, "do you have a father?"

The Rimmersman turned, an irritated expression on his face. "What do you mean by that, boy?"

"I mean is he alive?"

"For all I know," the Rimmersman snorted. "And little I care, either. The old devil could be in Hell and it would not bother me." He turned back to the snow-shrouded road.

I will not be a father like that, Simon decided, clutching the child a little closer. Vren moved uneasily beneath Simon's cloak. *I'll stay with my son. We'll have a home, and I won't go away.*

But who would be the mother? A series of confusing images, random as snowflakes, flurried before his mind's eye: Miriamele distant on her tower balcony at the Hayholt, the maid Hepzibah, cross old Rachel, and angry-eyed Lady Vorzheva. And where would his home be? He looked around at the vast whiteness of the Waste and the approaching shadow of Aldheorte. How could anyone hope to stay in one place in this mad world? To promise that to a child would be a lie. Home? He would be lucky to find a place to get out of the wind for a night.

His unhappy laugh set Vren to squirming; Simon pulled the cloak tighter around them both.

As they approached the eastern outskirts of Grinsaby they still had not seen a living soul. Neither had there been any evidence of recent habitation. They had questioned Vren closely, but had been unable to elicit any information other than the name "Skodi."

"Is Skodi your father?" Simon asked.

"It is a woman's name," Sludig offered. "A Rimmerswoman's name."

Simon tried again. "Is Skodi your mother?"

The boy shook his head. "I live with Skodi," he said, his words so clear despite the accent that Simon wondered again if the boy was not older than they had guessed.

There were still a few desolate settlements perched among the low hills along the White Way, but they were appearing more and more infrequently. Night had come on, filling the spaces between trees with inky shadows. The company had ridden too long—and too far past eating-time by Simon's reckoning. Darkness now made their search impractical. Binabik was just setting a pitchy pine limb alight to use as a torch when Simon saw a gleam of light through the forest, some distance from the road.

"Look there!" he cried. "I think it's a fire!" The distant white-blanketed trees seemed to glow redly.

"Skodi's house! Skodi's house!" the boy said, bouncing so that Simon had to restrain him. "She'll be happy!"

The company sat for a moment, eyeing the flickering light.

"We go carefully," Sludig said, flexing the fingers that clutched his Qanuc spear. "It is a damned odd place to live. We have no assurance these folks will be friendly."

Simon felt a sudden inner chill at Sludig's words. If only Thorn were reliable enough for him to carry at his side! He felt his bone knife in its scabbard and was reassured.

"I will ride ahead," Binabik said. "I am smaller and Qantaqa is more quiet. We will go to have a look." He murmured a word; the wolf slid off the road through the long shadows, her tail waving like a puff of smoke.

A few minutes passed. Simon and Sludig rode slowly along the snowy downs, not talking. Staring at the warm light that shimmered in the treetops, Simon had fallen into a sort of shallow dream when he was startled by the troll's abrupt reappearance. Qantaqa grinned hugely, her red tongue hanging from her mouth.

"It is an old abbey, I am thinking," Binabik said, his face almost hidden in the darkness of his hood. "There is a bonfire in the dooryard and several people who are around it, but they look to be children. I was seeing no horses, no sign of anyone waiting to ambush."

They rode quietly forward to the crest of a low hill. The fire burned before them at the bottom of a tree-lined clearing, surrounded by small, dancing silhouettes. Behind them loomed the red-tinted stone walls and cracked mortar of the abbey. It was an old building that had suffered beneath the weather's rough handling: the long roof had collapsed in several places, the holes gaping at the stars like mouths. Many of the surrounding trees also seemed to have pushed their limbs right through the small windows, as though trying to escape the cold.

As they sat looking, Vren slithered free beneath Simon's arm and hopped down from the saddle, tumbling into the show. He stood, shaking like a dog, then pelted down the hill toward the bonfire. Some of the small shapes turned at his approach with glad cries. Vren stood among them for a moment, waving his arms excitedly, then pushed through the abbey's front door and disappeared into the warm glow.

When long moments had passed and no one came back out again, Simon looked inquiringly at Binabik and Sludig.

"It is certainly seeming to be his home," Binabik said.

"Should we go on our way?" Simon asked, hoping they would say no. Sludig looked him over, then grunted in exasperation.

"It would be foolish to pass the chance of a warm night," the Rimmersman said grudgingly. "And we are ready to make camp. But no word of who we are or what we do. We are soldiers run away from the garrison at Skoggey, should any ask."

Binabik smiled. "I approve of your logic, although I am doubting I can be mistaken for a Rimmserman warrior. Let us go and see Vren's home."

They cantered down into the dell. The small figures, perhaps half a dozen in all, had resumed their dancing game, but as Simon and the others approached they paused and fell silent. They were only raggedly-dressed children, as Binabik had suggested.

All eyes now turned to the new arrivals. Simon felt himself subjected to a thorough scrutiny. The children seemed to range in age from three or four up to Vren's age or a little older, and seemed to be of no one type. There was a little girl who shared Vren's black hair and dark eyes, but also two or three others so fair they could be nothing but Rimmersgarders. All wore expressions of wide-eyed caution. As Simon and his friends dismounted, heads turned almost in unison to watch. No one spoke.

"Hello," Simon said. The boy nearest him stared sullenly, his face lapped in firelight. "Is your mother here?" The boy continued to stare.

"The child we brought went inside," Sludig said. "That is undoubtedly where the grown folk are." He hefted his spear thoughtfully and a half-dozen pairs of eyes warily followed his movement. The Rimmersman took the spear with him toward the abbey door which Vren had swung shut behind him, then propped it against the pitted mortar of the wall.

He gave his silent audience a meaningful look. "No one may touch this," he said. "Understood? *Gjal es, künden!*" He patted his scabbarded sword, then lifted a fist and thumped on the door. Simon looked back at Thorn, a hide-wrapped bundle on one of the packhorses. He wondered whether he should bring it with him, but decided that would draw more attention than was best. Still, it rankled. So many sacrifices to get the black sword, just to leave it strapped to the saddle like an old broomstick.

"Binabik," he said quietly, pointing at the concealed sword. "Do you think. . . ?"

The troll shook his head. "Little need for concern, I am certain," the troll whispered. "In any case, even if these children were to steal it, I am guessing they would have a difficult time carrying it away."

The heavy door swung slowly open. Little Vren stood in the doorway. "Come in, you men. Skodi says come in."

Binabik dismounted. Qantaqa sniffed the air for a moment, then bounded away in the direction they had come. The children by the fire watched her departure raptly.

"Let her hunt," Binabik said. "She is not happy walking inside a people-house. Come, Simon, we have been offered some hospitality." He stepped past Sludig and followed Vren inside.

A fire nearly as large as the bonfire in the dooryard was roaring and crackling in the grate, throwing wild, flickering shadows on the cob-webbed plaster. Simon's first impression of the room was of some kind of animal nest. Great piles of clothes and straw and other more unusual articles were piled haphazardly on every dirty surface.

"Welcome, strangers," someone said. "I'm Skodi. Do you have any food? The children are very hungry."

She was sitting in a chair close to the fire, with several children younger than those in the yard clambering over her lap or sitting at her feet. Simon's first thought was that she was another child herself—albeit a very large one—but after a moment's inspection he could see that she was his own age or even a little older. Her white-blonde hair, colorless as spider silk, framed a round face that might have been quite pretty, despite a few blemishes, if she had not been so fat. Her pale blue eyes stared avidly at the new arrivals.

Sludig looked at her suspiciously, uncomfortable in such close sur-roundings. "Food? We have little, mistress . . ." he considered for a moment, ". . . but you are welcome to share."

She waved her hand airily. Her chubby pink arm nearly dislodged a sleeping toddler. "It's not important. We always get by." As Sludig had predicted, she spoke Westerling with a heavy Rimmersgard accent. "Sit down and tell me the news of the world." She frowned, pursing her red lips. "There may be some beer somewhere. You men like beer, don't you? Vren, go find some beer. And where are those oak-nuts I sent you for?"

Sludig looked up suddenly. "Oh." Sheepishly, he produced Vren's acorns from his cloak pocket.

"Good," Skodi said. "Now beer."

"Yes, Skodi." Vren scuttled off down an aisle of stacked stools, vanishing into the shadows.

"How is it, if we may be asking, that you can live out here?" Binabik said. "It seems a place of great isolation."

Skodi had been staring at him avidly. Now her eyebrows lifted in surprise. "I thought you were a child!" She sounded disappointed. "But you are a little man."

"Qanuc, my lady." Binabik sketched a bow. "What your people call 'trolls.' "

"A troll!" She clapped her hands in excitement. This time, one of the children did slither off her rounded lap into the blankets coiled at her feet. The little one did not wake, and another quickly crawled up to take the spot the first had vacated. "So wonderful! We have never had a troll here!" She turned and called into the darkness. "Vren! Where is the beer for these men?"

"Where did all these children come from?" Simon asked wonderingly. "Are they all yours?"

A defensive look came to the girl's face. "Yes. They are now. Their parents did not want them, so Skodi keeps them instead."

"Well . . ." Simon was nonplussed. "Well, that's very kind of you. But how do you feed them? You said they were hungry."

"Yes, it is kind," Skodi said, smiling now. "It is kind of me, but that is how I was taught. Lord Usires said to shelter the children."

"Aye," Sludig grumbled. 'That's so."

Vren came back into the firelight balancing a jar of beer and several cracked bowls. The pile swayed dangerously, but with help he was able to set them down and pour beer for all three travelers. The wind had risen, making the flames billow in the grate.

"This is a very good fire," Sludig said as he wiped froth from his mustache. "You must have had a difficult time finding dry wood in yesterday's storm."

'Oh, Vren chopped for me early in the spring." She reached out and patted the boy's head with her plump hand. "He butchers and cooks, too. He is my good boy, Vren is."

"Is there no one here who is older?" Binabik asked. "I am meaning nothing discourteous, but you seem young to raise these children in solitude."

Skodi looked at him carefully before answering. "I told you. Their mothers and fathers have gone away. There is no one here but us. But we do very well, don't we, Vren?"

"Yes, Skodi." The little boy's eyes were growing heavy. He snuggled himself against her leg, basking in the warmth of the fire.

"So," she said at last, "you said that you had some food. Why do you not get it, then we can share. We can find the makings of a meal somewhere here. Wake up, Vren, you lazy thing!" She cuffed him lightly on the side of the head. "Wake up! It's time to make supper!"

"Don't wake him," Simon said, feeling sorry for the little black-haired boy. "We'll take care of the meal."

"Nonsense," Skodi said. She gave the protesting Vren a gentle shake. "He loves to make supper. You go and get what you have. You will stay the night, yes? Then you should stable your horses. I think the stable is around the side of the courtyard. Vren, get up, you lazy lump! Where is the stable?"

The forest had grown close around the back of the abbey where the stables were located. The old trees, dusted with snow, swayed mournfully as Simon and his companions threw dry straw onto the floor of one of the stalls and dumped snow into the trough to melt. The stable seemed to have been used occasionally—there were blackened torches in the cressets, and the crumbling walls had been haphazardly patched—but it was hard to guess when the most recent occasion might have been.

"Shall we bring all our things inside?" Simon asked.

"I am thinking so," Binabik replied, loosening the belly-strap on one of the packhorses. "I doubt the children would steal anything that was not food, but who can say what might become mislaid?"

The smell of wet horses was strong. Simon rubbed Homefinder's hard flank. "Don't you think it's strange that no one lives here but children?"

Sludig laughed shortly. "The young woman is older than you, Snowlock—and quite a lot of woman at that. Girls her age often have children of their own."

Simon blushed, but his irritated reply was forestalled by Binabik. "I am thinking," the troll said, "that Simon speaks with good sense. There are things unclear about this place. It will do no harm to ask more questions of our hostess."

Simon wrapped Thorn in his cloak before carrying it back through the snow to the abbey. The changeable sword was at this moment quite light. It also seemed to throb slightly, although Simon knew that might be no more than his chilled, trembling hands. When little Vren let them back inside, Simon placed Thorn near the hearth where they would sleep and piled several of their saddlebags atop it, as though to immobilize a sleeping beast that might wake and flail about.

Supper was an odd mixture of unusual food and strange conversation. Beside the remains of dried fruit and meat provided by the three travelers, Skodi and her young charges put out bowls of bitter acorns and sour berries. Scavenging, Vren found a molding but edible cheese somewhere in the abbey's ruined larder, along with several more jars of musky Rimmersgard beer. With this they managed to make a meal that served the whole company, albeit meagerly: the children all assembled numbered a dozen or more.

Binabik found little time to ask questions during the meal. Those of Skodi's charges who were old enough to go outside stood up to relate fanciful stories of various adventures they had encountered that day, stories so exaggerated as to be obviously untrue. One little girl told of flying to the top of a mighty pine tree to steal a feather from a magical jaybird. Another, one of the older boys, swore that he had found a chest of ogre's gold in a cave in the forest. Vren, when his turn came, calmly informed his listeners that while gathering acorns he had been pursued by an icy demon with glinting blue eyes, and that Simon and his two companions had saved him from the frosty menace's clutches, smiting it with their swords until it shattered into icicles.

Skodi held the smaller children on her lap as she ate, each in its turn, and listened to each story with an expression of envious fascination. She rewarded those she enjoyed most by giving the teller an extra morsel of food, which was eagerly accepted—indeed, Simon decided, the reward was probably the main reason for the fabulous nature of the stories.

There was something about Skodi's face that Simon found captivating. Despite her great size, there was a delicacy to her girlish features and a brightness to her eyes and smile that transfixed him. At certain moments, as she laughed breathlessly at one of the children's inventions, or turned so that the firelight played glinting in her flaxen hair, she seemed quite beautiful; at others, when she greedily snatched a handful of berries from one of the smaller the children and stuffed her wide mouth, or when her spellbound appreciation of the story-telling for a moment resembled mere idiocy, he found her repellent.

A few times she caught Simon staring. The glances she returned to him frightened him a little, even as they made him blush. Skodi, for all her bulk, wore a hungering look that would not have been out of place on a starveling beggar.

"So," she said when Vren had finished his wild tale, "you are even braver men than I guessed." She smiled hugely at Simon. "We will sleep well tonight, knowing you are under our roof. You do not think Vren's ice-demon has brothers, do you?"

'I am thinking it is not likely," Binabik said with a gentle smile. "You need not be fearing any such demon while we are staying here in your home. In return, we have much gratitude for a roof and a hearth for warming."

"Oh, no," Skodi said, her eyes wide, "it is me who is grateful. We do not get many visitors. Vren, help clear a place for the men to sleep. Vren, do you hear me?"

Vren was staring intently at Simon, an unfathomable expression in his dark eyes.

"Your mentioning of guests, my lady," Binabik began, "—it brings to my mind a question I had meant to be asking you. How is it that you and these children have come to be in such a place of isolation. . . ?"

"The storms came. Others ran away. We had nowhere else to go." Her brisk words poorly concealed her wounded tone. "None of us were wanted—none of the children, nor Skodi either." The subject discussed, her voice warmed again. "Now it is time for the little ones to sleep. Come, all of you, help me up." Several of her wards scurried to assist Skodi in levering her large body up out of the chair. As she moved slowly toward the door at the back of the room, a pair of sleeping children clinging to her like baby bats, she called: "Vren will help you find your way. Bring the candle when you come, Vren." She disappeared into the shadows.

Simon awakened from an uneasy sleep in the depths of night, filled with confused panic by the red-touched and starless darkness, and also by a faint thread of sound that wove itself in and out of the muted tapestry of windsong. It took some moments to remember that they slept near the hearth of the old abbey, warmed by dreaming coals and sheltered from the elements by the roof and decaying walls. The noise was Qantaqa's lonely howl, floating distantly. Simon's fear faded a little, but did not disappear.

Was that a dream I had last night? Shem and Ruben and the voices? Was it truly just a mad fancy, or was it as real as it seemed . . . as it sounded?

Ever since the night of his escape from the Hayholt, he had not felt a master of his own destiny. That same Stoning Night, when he had somehow felt Pryrates' repellent thoughts and had unwillingly shared in the ritual as Elias received the terrible gift of the sword Sorrow, Simon had wondered if he was even a master of his own mind. His dreams had become vivid far beyond the realms of mere night-wandering. The dream at Geloë's house, in which a cadaverous Morgenes had warned him of a false messenger, and the repeated visitations of the great, all-crushing wheel and of the tree-that-was-a-tower, white among the stars— these seemed too insistent, too powerful to be just unsettled sleep. And now, in his dreams the night before, he heard heard Pryrates talking to some unearthly thing as clearly as if Simon listened at a keyhole. These were not anything like the dreams of his life before this last terrible year.

When Binabik and Geloë had taken him on the Road of Dreams, the vision he experienced there had felt much like these others—like dreaming, but with a wild and indescribable potency of vision. Perhaps somehow, because of Pryrates on the hilltop or something else, a door had opened in him that sometimes led to the dream-road. That seemed like madness, but what did not in this topsy-turvy age? The dreams must be important—when he awoke, it was with the sense of something infinitely crucial slipping away—but terrifyingly, he had no idea what they might mean.

Qantaqa's mournful cry sounded again through the storm that blew beyond the abbey's walls. Simon wondered that the troll did to get up to soothe his mount, but the sound of Binabik's and Sludig's snoring continued unabated. Simon tried to rise, determined to at least offer her the chance to come in—she sounded so lone and lorn, and it was so very cold outside—but found that a heavy languor clutched his limbs, so that he could not force himself up. He struggled, but to no avail. His limbs were no more responsive than if they had been carved of ash-wood.

Simon suddenly felt terribly sleepy. He fought his drowsiness, but it pulled him relentlessly downward; Qantaqa's distant howl faded and he went sliding as though down a long slope, back toward unknowingness. . . .

When he woke again, the last coals had burned black and the abbey was in utter darkness. A cold hand was touching his face. He gasped with horror, but air barely filled his lungs. His body still felt heavy as stone, without the power of movement.

"Pretty," Skodi whispered, a deeper shadow, sensed rather than seen, looming tall and wide above him. She stroked his cheek. "Just got your beard, too. You are a pretty one. I will keep you."

Simon strove helplessly to wriggle from beneath her touch.

"They don't want you, either, do they?" Skodi said, crooning as though to a baby. "I can feel it. Skodi knows. Cast out, you were. I can hear it in your head. But that is not why I had Vren bring you."

She settled down beside him in the dark, folding into a crouch like a tent pulling loose from its stakes. "Skodi knows what you have. I heard it singing in my ears, saw it in my dreams. Lady Silver Mask wants it. Her Lord Red Eyes does, too. They want the sword, the black sword, and when I give it to them they will be nice to me. They will love Skodi and give her presents." She caught a lock of his hair between her plump fingers and gave it a sharp pull. The twinge of pain seemed far away. A moment later, as if in recompense, she ran her hand carefully over Simon's head and face.

"Pretty," she said at last. "A friend for me—a friend my age. That is what I have waited for. I will take away those dreams that are bothering you. I will take away all your dreams. I can do that, you know." She lowered her whispering voice even further, and Simon realized for the first time that the heavy breathing of his two friends had ceased. He wondered if they were lying silent in the darkness, waiting to save him. If that was so, he prayed they would act soon. His heart seemed as nerveless as his leaden limbs, but fear beat through him, aching like a secret pulse. "They drove me out of Haethstad," Skodi muttered. "My own family and neighbors. Said I was a witch. Said I put curses on people. Drove me out." Horribly, she began to snuffle. When she spoke again, her words were garbled by tears. "I sh–sh–showed them. When Father was drunk and sleeping, I stabbed Mother with his knife and then put it back in his hand. He killed himself." Her laugh was bitter but remorseless. "I could always see things others could not, think of things they would not. Then, when the deep winter came and would not go away, I began to be able to *do* things. Now I can do things no one else can do." Her voice rose triumphantly. "I am growing stronger all the time. Stronger and stronger. When I give Lady Silver Mask and Lord Red Eyes the sword they're looking for, the singing black sword I heard in my dreams, then I'll be like they are. Then the children and I will make everyone sorry."

As she spoke, she absently slid her cold hand from Simon's forehead down into his shirt, letting it play over his naked chest as if she petted a dog. The wind had stilled, and in the dreadful silence of its abatement he suddenly knew that his friends had been taken away. There was no one in the lightless room but Skodi and Simon.

"But I will keep *you*," she said. "I will keep you for myself."

15

Within God's Walls

Father Dinivan toyed with his food, staring into his bowl as though some helpful message might be written there in olive pits and breadcrumbs. Candles burned fiercely the length of the table. Pryrates' voice was loud and harsh as a brazen gong.

"... So you see, Your Sacredness, all that King Elias wishes is your acceptance of one fact: Mother Church's provenance may be men's souls, but she has no right to interfere in the disposition of men's corporeal forms by their legitimate monarch." The hairless priest grinned in self-satisfaction. Dinivan's heart sank to see the lector smile dully in return. Surely Ranessin must know that Elias was as much as declaring that God's shepherd on earth had less right to power than an earthly king? Why did he sit and say nothing?

The lector slowly nodded his head. He looked across the table to Pryrates, then briefly to Duke Benigaris, new master of Nabban, who appeared a trifle nervous beneath the lector's scrutiny, hurriedly wiping grease from his chin with the back of a brocaded sleeve. This Feast of Hlafmansa Eve was usually only a religious and ceremonial occasion. Although Dinivan knew him to be utterly the creature of Pryrates' master Elias, at this moment the duke seemed to be wishing for more ceremony and less confrontation.

"The High King and his emissary Pryrates wish only the best for Mother Church, Sacredness," Benigaris said gruffly, unable to hold Ranessin's gaze, as though he saw his rumored murder of his father mirrored there. "We should listen to what Pryrates says." He addressed his trencher once more, wherein he found more convivial company.

"We are considering all that Pryrates has to say," the lector responded mildly. Silence fell upon the table once more. Fat Velligis and the other escritors present returned to their own meals, obviously pleased that the long-feared confrontation seemed to have been averted.

Dinivan lowered his eyes to the remains of his supper. A young priest who hovered at his elbow refilled Dinivan's goblet with water—it had seemed a good night to avoid wine—and reached forward to take his bowl, but Dinivan waved him back. It was better to have something to concentrate on, if only to avoid looking at viperous Pryrates, who was not bothering to hide his immense pleasure at discomfiting the church hierarchy.

Absently pushing breadcrumbs with his knife, Dinivan marveled at how inseparably the great and the mundane were linked. This ultimatum from King Elias and the lector's response might one day seem an event of unforgettable magnitude, like that day long ago when the third Larexes had declared Lord Sulis heretic and apostate, sending that magnificent and troubled man into exile. But even during *that* momentous event, Dinivan reflected, there had probably been priests who scratched their noses, or stared at the ceiling, or silently bemoaned their aching joints as they sat within the very crucible of history—even as Dinivan now poked at his own supper-leavings and Duke Benigaris belched and loosened his belt. So men always would be, ape and angel mixed, their animal nature chafing at the restraints of civilization even as they reached for Heaven or for Hell. It was amusing, really . . . or should have been.

As Escritor Velligis tried to initiate a more soothing supper-table conversation, Dinivan suddenly felt an odd trembling in his fingers: the table was shuddering gently beneath his hands. *Earthquake* was his first thought, but then the olive pits in his bowl began to slide together slowly, forming themselves into runes before his astonished eyes. He looked up, startled, but no one else at the banquet table appeared to notice anything amiss. Velligis droned on, his chubby face gleaming with sweat; the other guests watched him, politely feigning interest.

Creeping like insects, the leavings in Dinivan's bowl had merged to form two sneering words: "SCROLL PIG." Sickened, he looked up to meet Pryrates' shark-black eyes. The alchemist wore a look of vast amusement. One of his white fingers was waving above the tablecloth, as if sketching upon the insubstantial air. Then, as Dinivan watched, Pryrates waggled all his digits at once. The crumbs and olive stones in Dinivan's bowl abruptly tumbled apart, whatever forces that had bound them now dispersed.

Dinivan's hand rose defensively to grasp the chain that lay beneath his cassock, feeling for the hidden scroll; Pryrates' grin widened in almost childish glee. Dinivan found his usual optimism melting before the red priest's unmistakable confidence. He suddenly realized what a thin and breakable reed his own life actually was.

". . . They are not, I suppose, truly dangerous . . ." Velligis was blathering, "but it is a dreadful blow to the dignity of Mother Church, these barbarians settling themselves afire in public squares, a dreadful blow—as much as daring the church to stop them! It is a kind of contagious madness, I am told, carried by bad airs. I no longer go out without a kerchief to wear over my nose and mouth . . . ."

"But perhaps the Fire Dancers are not mad," Pryrates said lightly. "Perhaps their dreams are more . . . *real* . . . than you would like to believe."

"That is . . . that is . . ." Velligis spluttered, but Pryrates ignored him, his obscenely empty eyes still fixed on Dinivan.

He fears no excess now, Dinivan thought. The realization seemed an unbearable burden. *Nothing binds him any longer. His terrible curiosity has become a heedless and insatiable hunger.*

Had that been when the world had begun to go wrong? When Dinivan and his fellow Scrollbearers had brought Pryrates into their secret councils? They had opened their hearts and treasured archives to the young priest, respecting the honed sharpness of Pryrates' mind for a long time before the rot at the center of him could no longer be mistaken. They had driven him from their midst, then—but too late, it seemed. Far, far too late. Like Dinivan, the priest sat at the tables of the mighty, but Pryrates' red star was now ascending, while Dinivan's track seemed murky and obscured.

Was there anything more he could do? He had sent messages to the two Scrollbearers still living, Jarnauga and Ookequk's apprentice, though he had heard from neither in some time. He had also sent suggestions or instructions to others of good faith, like the forest-woman Geloë and little Tiamak in the marshy Wran. He had brought Princess Miriamele safely to the Sancellan Aedonitis and made her tell her story to the lector. He had tended all the trees as Morgenes would have wished: all he could do now was wait and see what fruit might come. . . .

Slipping Pryrates' troubling gaze, Dinivan looked around the lector's dining hall, trying to take note of details. If this was to be a momentous night, for good or ill, he might as well try to remember all he could. Perhaps in some future—a brighter one than he could now envision—he would be an old man standing at the shoulder of some young artisan, offering corrections: "No, it wasn't like that at all! I was *there* . . ." He smiled, forgetting his worries for a moment. What a happy thought—to survive the cares of these dark days, to live with no greater responsibility than being an annoyance to some poor artist laboring to complete a commission!

His moment of reverie ended abruptly, arrested by the sight of a familiar face in the arched doorway that led to the kitchens. What was Cadrach doing here? He had been in the Sancellan Aedonitis scarcely a week and would have no business that could bring him near the lector's private quarters, so he could only be spying on the lector's supper guests. Was it only curiosity, or was Cadrach . . . Padreic . . . feeling the tug of old loyalties? Of *conflicting* loyalties?

Even as these thoughts flashed through Dinivan's head, the monk's face fell back into the shadows of the door and was gone from sight. A moment later a server marched through with a wide salver, making it obvious that Cadrach had vanished from the archway entirely.

Now, as if in counterpoint to Dinivan's confusion, the lector rose suddenly from his tall chair at the head of the table. Ranessin's kind face was somber; the shadows thrown by the bright candlelight made him seem ancient and bowed with troubles.

He silenced prattling Velligis with a single wave of his hand. "We have thought," the lector said slowly. His white-haired head seemed remote as a snow-capped mountain. "The world as you speak of it, Pryrates, makes a certain kind of sense. There is weight to its logic. We have heard similar things from Duke Benigaris and his frequent envoy, Count Aspitis."

"Earl Aspitis," Benigaris said abruptly, his heavy face flushed. He had drunk a great deal of the lector's wine. "Earl," he continued heedlessly. "King Elias made him an earl at *my* request. As a gesture of his friendship to Nabban."

Ranessin's slender features curled in a poorly-concealed look of disgust. "We know you and the High King are close, Benigaris. And we know that you yourself rule Nabban. But you are at our table now, in God's house—*my* table—and we bid you to remain silent until Mother Church's highest priest finishes speaking."

Dinivan was shocked by the lector's angry tone—Ranessin was ordinarily the mildest of men—but found himself heartened by such unexpected strength. Benigaris' mustache quivered angrily, but he reached for his wine-cup with the clumsiness of an embarrassed child.

Ranessin's blue eyes were now fixed on Pryrates. He continued in the stately manner he so seldom used, but which seemed so natural when he did. "As we said, the world which you and Elias and Benigaris preach makes a certain kind of sense. It is a world where alchemists and monarchs decide the fate not only of men's corporeal forms, but of their souls as well, and where the king's minions encourage deluded souls to burn themselves for the glory of false idols if it suits their purposes. A world where the uncertainty of an invisible God is replaced by the certainty of a black, burning spirit who dwells on this earth, in the heart of a mountain of ice."

Pryrates' hairless brows shot up at this; Dinivan felt a moment of cold joy. Good. So the creature could still be surprised.

"Hear me!" Ranessin's voice gained force, so that for a moment it seemed that not only the room had fallen silent, but the whole world with it, as though in that instant the candlelit table rode the very cusp of Creation. "This world—*your* world, the world you preach to us with your sly words—is not the world of Mother Church. We have long known of a dark angel who strides the earth, whose bleak hand reaches out to trouble all the hearts of Osten Ard—but *our* scourge is the Arch-fiend himself, the implacable foe of God's light. Whether your ally is truly our Enemy of

countless millennia or just another vicious minion of darkness, Mother Church has always stood against his like . . . and always shall."

Everyone in the room seemed to hold their breath for an endless moment.

"You do not know what you say, old man." Pryrates' voice was a sulfurous hiss. "You grow feeble and your mind wanders . . ."

Shockingly, not one of the escritors raised their voices in protest or dissent. They stared, wide-eyed, as Ranessin leaned across the table and calmly engaged the priest's angry stare. Light seemed to quail and almost die throughout the banquet hall, leaving only the two illuminated, one scarlet, one white, their shadows stretching, stretching . . .

"Lies, hatred, and greed," the lector said softly. "They are familiar, age-old enemies. It matters not beneath whose banner they march." He stood up, a slim, pale shape, and lifted a hand. Dinivan felt again the fierce, uncontrollable love that had driven him to bend his back in supplication before the mystery of Man's divine purpose, to bind his life over into the service of this humble and wonderful man, and to the church that lived in his person.

With cold deliberation, Ranessin drew the sign of the Tree in the air before him. The table seemed to shudder again beneath Dinivan's hand; this time he could not believe it the alchemist's doing. "You have opened doors that should have remained closed for all time, Pryrates," the lector proclaimed. "In your pride and folly, you and the High King have brought a ponderous evil into a world which already groaned beneath a mighty burden of suffering. Our church—*my* church—will fight you for every soul, until the very Day of Weighing-Out dawns. I declare you *excommunicate*, and King Elias with you, and also banish from the arms of Mother Church any who follow you into darkness and error." His arm swept down, once, twice. *"Duos Onenpodensis, Feata Vorum Lexeran. Duos Onenpodensis, Feata Vorum Lexeran!"*

No clap of thunder of horn of judgment followed the Lector's booming words, only the distant peal of the Clavean bell tolling the hour. Pryrates stood slowly, his face pale as wax, his mouth twisted in a trembling grimace.

"You have made a horrible mistake," he rasped. "You are a foolish old man and your great Mother Church is a child's toy made of parchment and glue." He was quivering with surprised fury. "We shall put a torch to it ere long. The howling will be great when it burns. *You have made a mistake.*"

He turned and stalked from the dining hall, his bootheels clocking on the tiled floor, his robes billowing like flame. Dinivan thought he heard a terrible intimation of holocaust in the priest's departing footsteps, of a great and final conflagration, a black scorching of the pages of history.

❧

Miriamele was sewing a wooden button onto her cloak when someone rapped on the door. Startled, she slid off the cot and padded to answer, her bare feet chill against the cold floor.

"Who is it?"

"Open the door, Prin . . . Malachias. Please open the door."

She drew the bolt. Cadrach stood in the poorly lit hallway, his sweaty face gleaming in the candlelight. He pushed past her into the small cell and elbowed the door shut so abruptly that Miriamele felt a breeze as it swept by her nose.

"Are you mad?" she demanded. "You cannot just push in like this!"

"Please, Princess . . ."

"Get out! Now!"

"Lady . . ." Astonishingly, Cadrach fell to his knees. His normally ruddy face was quite pale. "We must flee the Sancellan Aedonitis. Tonight."

She stared down. "You *have* gone mad." Her tone was imperious. "What are you talking about? Have you stolen something? I don't know if I should protect you any longer, and I certainly will not go charging out of . . ."

He cut her off in mid-speech. "No. It is nothing I have done—at least, nothing I have done tonight—and the danger is not to me so much as to you. But that danger is very great. We must flee!"

For several moments Miriamele could not think of a thing to say. Cadrach indeed looked very frightened, a change from his usual veiled expression.

He broke the silence at last. "Please, my lady, I know I have been a faithless companion, but I have done some good, as well. Please trust me this once. You are in terrible danger!"

"Danger from what?"

"Pryrates is here."

She felt a wave of relief wash over her. Cadrach's wild words had frightened her after all. "Idiot. I know that. I spoke to the lector yesterday. I know all about Pryrates."

The stocky monk rose to his feet. His jaw was set in a very determined way. "That is one of the most foolish things you have ever said, Princess. You know very little about him, and you should be grateful for that. Grateful!" He reached out and seized her arm.

"Stop that! How dare you!" She tried to slap at his face, but Cadrach leaned away from the blow, maintaining his grip. He was surprisingly strong.

"Saint Muirfath's Bones!" he hissed. "Don't be such a fool, Miriamele!" He leaned toward her, holding her gaze with his own wide eyes. There was, she fleetingly noticed, no smell of wine about him. "If I must treat you like a child, I will," the monk growled. He pushed her backward until she toppled onto the cot, then stood over her, angry yet fearful. "The lector has declared Pryrates and your father excommunicate. Do you know what that means?"

"Yes!" she said, her voice almost a shout. "I'm glad!"

"But Pryrates is *not* glad, and something bad will happen. It will happen very soon. You should not be here when it does."

"Bad? What do you mean? Pryrates is alone in the Sancellan. He came with half a dozen of my father's guardsmen. What can he do?"

"And you claim to know all about him." Cadrach shook his head in disgust, then turned and began scooping Miriamele's loose clothing and few possessions into her traveling bag. "I, for one," he said, "do not want to see whatever he will be getting up to."

She watched him for a moment, dumbfounded. Who was this person who looked like Cadrach, but shouted and ordered and grabbed her arm like a river-barge bravo? "I will not go anywhere until I talk to Father Dinivan," she said at last. Some of the edge had disappeared from her voice.

"Splendid," Cadrach said. "Whatever you wish. Just prepare yourself to go. I'm sure that Dinivan will agree with me—if we can find him at all."

Reluctantly, she bent to help him. "Just tell me this," she said. "Do you swear that we're in danger? And that it's not something you did?"

He stopped. For the first time since he had entered the room, Cadrach's odd half-smile appeared, but this one twisted his face into a mask of terrible sorrow. "We have all done things that we regret, Miriamele. I have made mistakes that set God the Highest to weeping on His great throne." He shook his head, angry at wasting time with talk. "But this danger is real and immediate, and there is nothing we can either of us do to make it less. Thus, we shall flee. Cowards always survive."

Seeing his face, Miriamele suddenly did not ever want to know what Cadrach had done to make him hate himself so much. She shuddered and turned away, looking for her boots.

The Sancellan Aedonitis seemed strangely deserted, even for the late evening hour. A few priests had gathered in the various common rooms where they sat gossiping in hushed tones; a handful more strode the corridors with lighted candles, on errands of one sort or another. Except for these few, the halls were empty. The torches burned fitfully in their sockets, as though troubled by restless breezes.

Miriamele and Cadrach were in a deserted upstairs gallery, passing from the chambers where visiting churchmen stayed and into the administrative and ceremonial heart of God's House, when the monk pulled Miriamele over to a shadowed window alcove.

"Put the candle down and come look," he said quietly. She wedged the taper in a crevice between two tiles and leaned forward. The cold air struck her face like a slap.

"What should I look at?"

"There, below. Do you see all those men with torches?" He tried to point within the confines of the narrow window. Miriamele could see at least a score of men in the courtyard below, amored and cloaked, bearing spears on their shoulders.

"Yes," she said slowly. The soldiers did not appear to be doing much more than warming their hands at the courtyard fire-cairns. "So?"

"Those are from Duke Benigaris' household guard," Cadrach said grimly. "Someone is expecting trouble tonight, and expecting it to be here."

"But I thought soldiers were never allowed to bear arms in the Sancellan Aedonitis." The spearpoints caught the torchlight like tongues of flame.

"Ah, but Duke Benigaris himself is a guest here tonight, since he attended the lector's banquet."

"Why didn't he go back to the Sancellan Mahistrevis?" She stepped away from the drafty window. "It's not very far."

"An excellent question," Cadrach replied, a sour smile playing over his shadow-striped face. "Why indeed?"

Duke Isgrimnur tested Kvalnir's keen edge with his thumb and nodded with satisfaction. He slipped his whetstone and jar of oil back into his bag. There was something very calming about sharpening his sword. A pity he had to leave it behind. He sighed and wrapped it in rags once more, then pushed it underneath his pallet.

It wouldn't do to go see the lector carrying a sword, he thought, *no matter how much better it'd make me feel. I doubt his guards would take kindly to it.*

Not that Isgrimnur was going to see the lector directly. It was very unlikely that a strange monk would be allowed into the Shepherd of Mother Church's bedchamber, but Dinivan's chambers were close by. The lector's secretary had no guards. Also, Dinivan knew Isgrimnur and thought highly of him. When the priest realized who his late-night visitor really was, he would listen carefully to what the duke had to say.

Still, Isgrimnur felt his stomach fluttering, as it had before countless battles. That had been the reason he'd brought out his sword: Kvalnir hadn't been unsheathed more than twice since he'd left Naglimund, and certainly hadn't seen any duty that would have dulled her Dverning-forged blade, but honing his sword gave a man something to do when the waiting became difficult. There was something in the air tonight, a queasy expectancy that reminded Isgrimnur of the shores of Clodu during the Battle of the Lakelands.

Even King John, blooded war-hawk that he was, had been nervous *that* night, knowing that ten thousand Thrithings-men waited somewhere in the darkness beyond the sentry fires, and knowing also that the plains-dwellers were no adherents of orderly dawn starting-times for battles or any other such conventions of civilized warfare.

Prester John had come to the fire that night, joining his young Rimmersman friend—Isgrimnur had not yet inherited his father's dukedom—for a jug of wine and a bit of conversation. As they talked, the king had taken stone and polishing rag to fabled Bright-Nail. They spent the night yarning away, a little self-consciously at first, with many a pause to listen for unusual noises, then with increasing ease as dawn approached and it became obvious the Thrithings-men planned no nighttime raids.

John told Isgrimnur tales of his youth on Warinsten—which he described as an island of backward and superstition-plagued bumpkins—and of his early travels on the mainland of Osten Ard. Isgrimnur was fascinated by these unexpected glimpses of the king's early life: Prester John was already nearly fifty years old as they sat by the fire at Lake Clodu, and to the young Rimmersman might as well have been king since the beginning of time. But when asked about his legendary destruction of the red worm Shurakai, John had waved the question away like an irritating fly. He proved no more willing to discuss how he had received Bright-Nail, saying that those stories were overtold and tiresome.

Now, forty years later, in a monk's cell at the Sancellan Aedonitis, Isgrimnur remembered and smiled. John's nervous whetting of Bright-Nail was the closest the duke had ever seen his lord come to anything approaching fear—fear about combat, at least.

The duke snorted. Now, with that good old man two years in his grave, here sat his friend Isgrimnur, moping about when there were tasks to be done for the good of John's kingdom.

Lord willing, Dinivan will be my herald. He's a clever man. He'll put Lector Ranessin on my side and we'll track Miriamele down.

He pulled his hood low on his head, then opened the doorway, letting the torchlight spill in from the corridor. He recrossed the room to put out the candle. It wouldn't do to have it fall over on his pallet and catch the place on fire.

Cadrach was becoming increasingly agitated. They had been waiting inside Dinivan's study for some time; high above, the Clavean bell had just sounded the eleventh hour.

"He is not returning, Princess, and I do not know where his private chambers are. We must go."

Miriamele was peering into the lector's great audience hall through the curtain at the back of the secretary's work room. Lit by only a single torch, the painted figures on the high ceiling seemed to swim in muddy water. "Knowing Dinivan, his private chambers are probably close to where he works," she said. The monk's worried tone made her feel a little superior once more. "He'll come back here. He left all his candles burning, didn't he? Why are you so worried?"

Cadrach looked up from Dinivan's papers, which he had been surreptitiously examining. "*I* was at the banquet tonight. I saw Pyrates' face. He is a man not accustomed to being balked."

"How do you know that? And what were you doing at the banquet?"

"Doing what was necessary. Keeping an eye open."

Miriamele let the drapery slide back into place. "You are full of hidden talents, aren't you? Where did you learn to open a door without a key, like you did to this room?"

Cadrach looked stung. "You said you wanted to see him, my lady. You insisted on coming here. I thought it was better we came inside than stand around in the halls waiting for the lector's guards to go by, or one of the other priests who might want to know what we were doing in this part of the Sancellan."

"Lock-pick, spy, kidnapper—unusual talents for a monk."

"You may make fun if you wish, Princess." He seemed almost ashamed. "I have not had the life of my choice, or rather, I suppose, my choices have not been good ones. But spare me your nasty jibes until we are out of here and safe."

She slid into Dinivan's chair and rubbed her cold hands together, fixing the monk with her best level gaze. "Where do you come from, Cadrach?"

He shook his head. "I do not wish to talk of such things. I grow increasingly doubtful that Dinivan will return. We must go."

"No. And if you don't stop saying that, I will scream. Then we'll see how *that* will go down with the lector's guards, won't we?"

Cadrach peeked out into the hallway, then quickly closed the door again. For all the chill, his tonsured hair hung on the side of his head in sweaty strands. "My lady, I beg you, I am beseeching you, for your own life and safety, please let us leave now. It is approaching midnight and the danger is increasing every moment. Just . . . *believe* me!" Now he sounded truly desperate. "We cannot wait any longer . . ."

"You're wrong." Miriamele was enjoying the way that things had shifted back in her direction. She put her booted feet up on Dinivan's cluttered table. "I can wait all night if need be." She tried to fix Cadrach with a stern eye once more, but he was pacing behind her, out of sight. "And we are not going to go fleeing into the night like idiots without talking to Dinivan first. I trust him a great deal more than I trust you."

"As you should, I suppose," Cadrach sighed. He sketched the sign of the Tree in the air, then lifted one of Dinivan's heavy books and smashed it down on top of her head, tumbling her senseless to the carpeted floor. Cursing himself, he bent to lift her, then stopped as he heard voices in the corridor.

"You really must go," the lector said sleepily. He was propped up in his wide bed, a copy of *En Semblis Aedonitis* open on his lap. "I shall read for a short while. You really must get some rest yourself, Dinivan. It has been a very trying day for all."

His secretary turned from his inspection of the painted panels on the wall. "Very well, but don't read long, Sacredness."

"I won't. My eyes tire very quickly by candlelight."

Dinivan stared at the old man for a moment, then impulsively knelt and took the lector's right hand, kissing the ilenite ring he wore. "Bless you, Your Sacredness."

Ranessin looked at him with worried fondness. "You must indeed be overtired, dear friend. Your behavior is quite unusual."

Dinivan stood. "You have just excommunicated the High King, Sacredness. That makes for a somewhat unusual day, does it not?"

The lector waved his hand dismissively. "Not that it will do anything. The king and Pryrates will do as they please. The people will wait to see what happens. Elias is not the first ruler to suffer Mother Church's censure."

"Then why do it? Why pit ourselves against him?"

Ranessin stared at him shrewdly. "You speak as though this excommunication was not your own fondest hope. You of all people know why, Dinivan: we must speak out when evil shows itself, whether there is any hope of changing it or not." He closed the book before him. "I really am too tired even to read. Tell the truth, Dinivan. Is there much hope?"

The priest looked at him, surprised. "Why do you ask me, Sacredness?"

"Again you are ingenuous, my son. I know that there are many things with which you do not trouble a weary old man. I also know that there are good reasons for your secrecy. But tell me, from your own knowledge—is there hope?"

"There is always hope, Sacredness. You taught me that."

"Ah." Ranessin's smile was oddly satisfied. He settled down into his cushions.

Dinivan turned to the young acolyte who slept at the foot of the lector's bed. "Make sure you bolt the door behind me when I go." The youth, who had been dozing, nodded his head. "And do not let anyone into your master's chamber this night."

"No, Father, I won't."

"Good." Dinivan stepped to the heavy door. "Good night, Sacredness. God be with you."

"And you," Ranessin said, muffled in his pillows. As Dinivan stepped out into the hallway the acolyte shuffled over to push the door closed.

The hall was even more poorly lit than the lector's bedchamber. Dinivan squinted anxiously until he spotted the lector's four guards standing at attention against the shadowed wall, swords scabbarded at their sides, pikes in their mailed fists. He let out his breath in relief, then walked toward them down the long, high-arched corridor. Perhaps he should ask for another two pairs to join these. He wouldn't be sure of the lector's safety until Pryrates had gone back to the Hayholt and treacherous Benigaris had returned to the ducal palace.

He rubbed his eyes as he approached the guards. He did indeed feel very tired, wrung out and hung up to dry. He would just stop and get some things from his workroom, then go to bed. Morning services were only a few hours away . . .

"Ho, Captain," he said to the one whose helmet bore the white plume, "I think it might be best if you called . . . called . . ." He broke off, staring. The guard's eyes gleamed like pinpoints in the depth of his helm, but they were fixed on some point beyond Dinivan, as were the eyes of his companions. They were all as motionless as statues. "Captain?" He touched the man's arm, which was rigid as stone. "In the name of Usires Aedon," he muttered, "what has happened here?"

"They do not see or hear you."

It was a familiar rasping voice. Dinivan whirled to see a glint of red at the far end of the hallway.

"Devil! What have you done!?"

"They are sleeping," Pryrates laughed. "In the morning, they will remember nothing. How the villains got past them to kill the lector will be a mystery. Perhaps it will be viewed by some—the Fire Dancers, for instance—as a kind of . . . *black miracle.*"

Poisonous fear crawled up from Dinivan's stomach, mixing with his anger. *"You will not harm the lector."*

"And who will stop me? You?" Pryrates' laugh turned scornful. "You can try anything you wish, little man. Scream if you like—no one will hear anything that happens in this hallway until I leave."

"Then I will prevent you myself." Dinivan reached into his robe and pulled forth the Tree that hung around his neck.

"Oh, Dinivan, you have missed your calling." The alchemist stepped forward, the torch light burnishing the arc of his hairless head. "Instead of lector's secretary, you should have sought a position as God's own fool. You cannot stop me. You have no idea of the wisdom I have discovered, the powers I command."

Dinivan stood his ground as Pryrates advanced, bootheels echoing through the corridor. "If selling your immortal soul on the cheap is wisdom, I am happy to have none of it." His fear mounting, he fought to keep his voice steady.

Pryrates' reptilian smile widened. "That is your mistake—you and all those timid fools who call themselves Scrollbearers. The League of the

Scroll! A gossip society for whimpering, quibbling, would-be scholars. And you, Dinivan, are the worst of all. You have sold your own soul for superstitions and reassurances. Instead of opening your eyes to the mysteries of the infinite, you have hidden yourself among the callus-kneed ring-kissers of the church."

Rage flooded through Dinivan's frame, momentarily reversing the tide of terror. *"Stand back!"* he shouted, lifting his Tree before him. It seemed to glow, as though the wood itself smoldered. "You will go no farther, servant of evil masters, unless you kill me first."

Pryrates eyes widened in mock-astonishment. "Ah. So the little priest has teeth! Well, then, we shall play the game your way . . . and I will show you some teeth of my own." He lifted his hands over his head. The alchemist's scarlet robes billowed as though a wild wind gusted through the hallway. The torches rippled in their sockets, then blew out.

"And remember this . . ." Pryrates hissed in darkness. "I command the Words of Changing now! *I am no one's servant!*"

The Tree in Dinivan's hand flared more brightly, but Pryrates remained sunken in shadow. The alchemist's voice rose, chanting in a language whose very sound made Dinivan's ears ache and wrapped a band of agony about his throat.

"In the name of God the Highest . . ." Dinivan shouted, but as Pryrates' chant mounted toward a triumphant climax it seemed to tear the words of prayer from his mouth almost before they were spoken. Dinivan choked. "In the name of . . ." His voice fell silent. In the shadows before him, Pryrates' spell had become a grunting, gasping parody of speech as the alchemist suffered through some agonizing transformation.

Where Pryrates had stood a roiling, unrecognizable shadow now flailed, writhing in knotted loops that grew larger and larger until even the starlight was blotted out and the hallway sank into unbreachable blackness. Ponderous lungs wheezed like a blacksmith's bellows. A deadening, ancient cold filled the corridor with unseen frost.

Dinivan flung himself forward with a shout of terrified rage, trying to strike the invisible thing with his Holy Tree, but instead found himself caught up like a doll by some massive yet horribly insubstantial appendage. They struggled, lost in the freezing darkness. Dinivan gasped as he felt something pushing its way into his terrified thoughts, scraping inside his head with burning fingers, trying to pry open his very mind like a jam jar. He fought back with all his strength, struggling to hold the image of Holy Aedon in his flickering thoughts; he thought he heard the thing that held him gasp in pain.

But the shadow only seemed to grow more substantial. Its grip tightened around him, a horrible bone-cracking fist of jelly and lead. Sour, cold breath fluttered against his cheek like the kiss of nightmare.

"In the name of God . . . and the League . . ." Dinivan groaned. The

animal noises and terrible labored breathing began to fade away. Angels
of painful, burning light filled his head, dancing to welcome the darkness,
deafening him with their silent song.

Cadrach dragged Miriamele's limp form out into the hallway, swearing
panicky oaths to various saints, gods, and demons. The only light was the
thin blue of starlight bleeding in through the windows high overhead, but
it was difficult not to see the huddled figure of the priest laying like a
discarded puppet in the center of the corridor a few steps away. It was
equally impossible to ignore the ghastly cries and shrieks coming from the
lector's chamber at the end of the hall, where the thick wooden door lay
splintered across the floor.

The noises ceased abruptly, ending on a drawn-out wail of despair that
dwindled at last to a gurgling hiss. Cadrach's face filled with horror. He
bent and swept up the princess, heaving her over his shoulder, then
crouched awkwardly to pick up their bag of possessions. He straightened
and staggered away from the destruction at the far end of the hall, fighting
to stay on his feet.

Around the corner the passageway widened, but there also the torches
had been extinguished. He thought he could see the shadowy forms of
armored men standing sentry, but they were motionless as relics. The
unhurried echo of booted feet sounded in the arched hall behind him.
Cadrach hurried forward, cursing the slippery tiles.

The passage turned once more, opening into the great entrance chamber, but as he scurried through the arch he struck something solid as a wall
of adamant, although he had seen nothing in the doorway but air. Stunned,
he tripped and tumbled backward. Miriamele slid from his shoulder to
the hard floor.

The sound of approaching bootheels grew louder. Cadrach reached
forward in a fit of panic, encountering an unnatural wall, an invisible but
unyielding *something*. More transparent than crystal, it showed clearly
every detail of the torchlit chamber beyond.

"Ah, please, don't let him have her," the monk murmured, clawing
with desperate fingers, searching for some flaw in the invisible barrier.
"Please!"

His questing was in vain. The wall was seamless.

Cadrach kneeled before the doorway, head slowly sinking to his chest as
the approaching footfalls grew louder. The unmoving monk might have
been a prisoner waiting at the executioner's block. Suddenly, he looked
up.

"Wait!" he hissed. "Think, idiot man, think!" He shook his head and
took a deep breath, then released it and took one more. He held his palm

before the archway and spoke a single quiet word. A wash of cold air blew past him, ruffling the tapestries in the entrance chamber. The barrier was gone.

He dragged Miriamele through, pulling her across the floor and into one of the archways opening off the grand chamber. They disappeared from sight just as Pryrates' red-robed figure appeared in the doorway where the unseen impediment had been. Dim sounds of alarm were beginning to filter through the halls.

The red priest paused as though surprised to find his barrier gone. Nevertheless, he turned and sketched a gesture in the direction from which he had come, as though to sweep away whatever traces of his handiwork might remain.

His voice boomed, reverberating down the corridors in all directions. "Murder!" he cried. "Murderers are in God's house!" As the echoes died away he smiled briefly and set off toward the chambers where he stayed as the lector's guest.

Struck by a thought, Pryrates stopped suddenly in the archway and turned to survey the chamber. He lifted his hand once more, fingers flexing. One of the torches gouted sparks, then spat out a tongue of flame which leaped across to a row of tapestries lining the wall. The ancient weavings blazed, fire licking upward at the great ceiling beams and spreading rapidly from wall to wall. In the hallway beyond, other fires were also blooming.

The alchemist grinned. "One must give omens their due," he said to no one present, then departed, chuckling. All around, the babble of confused and frightened voices began to fill the byways of the Sancellan Aedonitis.

Duke Isgrimnur congratulated himself for bringing a candle. The hallway was black as tar. Where were the sentries? Why weren't the torches lit?

Whatever the problem was, the Sancellan was awakening all around him. He heard someone shout boldly of murder, which set his heart swiftly beating; this was followed by other, more distant cries. For a few moments he considered returning to his tiny room, but decided that perhaps the confusion was for the best. Whatever the cause of the alarm really was—and he doubted it was murder—it might mean he would be able to find the lector's secretary without having to answer wearisome questions from the lector's guards.

The candle in its wooden holder threw Isgrimnur's shadow high against the walls of the great entrance hall. As the sounds of approaching discovery grew, he wracked his brain for the proper exit from the chamber. He chose the archway that seemed likeliest.

A short distance past the second turning of the hallway, he found himself in a wide gallery. A robed figure lay sprawled on the floor amid a tangle of draperies, beneath the unperturbed stare of several armed guards.

Are they statues, then? he wondered. *But, damn me, statuary never looked like that. See, that one there is leaning as though he were whispering to the other.* He stared up at the unseeing eyes that gleamed within the helms and felt his skin crawling. *Aedon save us. Black sorcery, that's what it is.*

To his despair, he recognized the body on the floor the moment he turned it over. Dinivan's face seemed bluish, even by the dim candlelight. Thin stripes of blood had run forward from his ears, drying on his cheek like red tears. His body felt like a sack of broken twigs.

"Elysia, Mother of God, what's happened here?" the duke groaned aloud.

Dinivan's eyes fluttered open, startling Isgimnur so that he almost let the priest's head fall back against the tiles. Dinivan's gaze wandered for a moment before fixing on him. It might have been the candle Isgrimnur awkwardly held, but the priest's eyes seemed to burn with a strange spark. Whatever the case, Isgrimnur knew it was a spark that would not last long.

"Lector . . ." Dinivan breathed. Isgrimnur leaned closer. "Look . . . to . . . lector."

"Dinivan, it's me," he said. "Duke Isgrimnur. I've come looking for Miriamele."

"Lector," the priest said stubbornly, his bloodied lips struggling to form the word. Isgrimnur sat up.

"Very well." He looked helplessly for something to cushion the priest's wounded head, but could find nothing. He let Dinivan down, then rose and walked to the end of the hallway. There was little doubt which room was the lector's—the door lay in great shards, and even the marble around the door-frame was scorched and crumbled. There was even less doubt about Lector Ranessin's fate. Isgrimnur took one look around the ruined chamber, then turned and retreated hurriedly into the corridor. Blood had been smeared across the walls as if by a huge brush. The mangled forms of Mother Church's leader and his young servant were barely recognizable as human: their corpses had been spared no indignities. Even Isgrimnur's old soldier's heart quailed at the sight of so much blood.

Flames were flickering in the far archway when the duke returned, but he steeled himself to ignore them for a moment. Time for thought of escape later. He took Dinivan's cold hand.

"The lector is dead. Can you help me find Princess Miriamele?"

The priest breathed raggedly for a moment. The light in his eyes was fading. "She's . . . here," he said slowly. "Called . . . Malachias. Ask room-warden." He gasped for air. "Take her . . . to . . . Kwanitupul . . . to *Pelippa's Bowl.* Tiamak is . . . there."

Isgrimnur's eyes filled with tears. This man should be dead. There could be nothing keeping him alive but sheer will. "I'll find her," he said. "I'll keep her safe."

Dinivan suddenly seemed to recognize him. "Tell Josua," he panted. "I fear . . . *false messengers.*"

"What does that mean?" Isgrimnur asked, but Dinivan was silent, his free hand crawling across his chest like a dying spider, fumbling hopelessly at the neck of his robe. Isgrimnur gently pulled out Dinivan's Holy Tree and laid it on his chest, but the priest shook his head feebly, trying once more to reach inside his robe. Isgrimnur lifted out a golden scroll and quill pendant on a chain. The catch broke as he held it; the chain spilled out into the damp hair at Dinivan's neck like a tiny, gleaming snake.

"Give . . . Tiamak," Dinivan rasped. Isgrimnur could barely hear him over the clamor of approaching voices and the crackle of flames in the corridor beyond. The duke slipped it into the pocket of his monk's robe, then looked up, startled by a sudden movement nearby. One of the immobile guards, illuminated by pulsing fireglow, was swaying in place. A moment later he fell forward with a crash, his helmet skittering across the tiles. The toppled soldier groaned.

When Isgrimnur looked down again, the light had fled Dinivan's eyes.

16

The Unhomed

The darkness in the abbey was complete, the silence marred only by Simon's ragged breath. Then Skodi spoke again, her voice no longer whisperingly sweet.

"Stand up."

Some force seemed to tug at him, a pressure delicate as a cobweb but strong as iron. His muscles flexed against his will, but he resisted. A short time before he had struggled to rise—now, he strained to lie still.

"Why do you fight me?" Skodi asked petulantly. Her chilly hand brushed across his chest and down onto the quivering skin of his stomach. He flinched, and control of his limbs slipped away as the girl's will closed on him like a fist. A forceful but intangible pull brought him to his feet. He swayed in the darkness, unable to find his balance. "We will give them the sword," Skodi crooned, "the black sword—oh, we will get such lovely presents . . ."

"Where . . . are . . . my friends?" Simon croaked.

"Hush, silly. Go out to the yard."

He stumbled helplessly through the darkened room, barking his shins on hidden obstacles, lurching like a clumsily manipulated puppet.

"Here," Skodi said. The abbey's front door swung open on grating hinges, filling the room with baleful reddish light. She stood in the doorway, pale hair fluttering in the swirling wind. "Come, now, Simon. What a night this is! A *wild* night."

The bonfire in the dooryard blazed even higher than it had when the travelers arrived, a beacon of flame that reached the height of the sloping roof and threw the abbey's cracked walls into red relief. Skodi's children, the young and old alike, were feeding all manner of strange objects into the fire: broken chairs and other bits of ruined furniture, and deadwood from the surrounding forest that burned with a ceaseless hiss of steam. In fact, the bonfire's eager wardens seemed to be throwing everything they could find into the blaze, without regard for suitability—rocks and animal bones, cracked pottery, and shards of colored glass from the abbey's decaying windows. As the flames roared and leaped in the surging wind, the children's eyes caught the light, glowing like the yellow orbs of foxes.

Simon tottered out onto the snowy courtyard with Skodi following close behind. A keening howl lanced through the night, a wretched, lonely sound. Slow as a sunning tortoise, Simon swiveled his head toward the green-eyed shape crouched atop the hill that overlooked the clearing. Simon felt an instant of hope as it lifted its muzzle and moaned again.

"Qantaqa!" he cried; the name fell strangely from his stiff jaws and slack lips. The wolf came no closer than the hill-crest. She howled once more, a cry of fear and frustration as clear as if it had been spoken with a human tongue.

"Nasty animal," Skodi said with distaste. "Child-eater. Moon-shouter. It won't come near Skodi's house. It won't break my charm." She stared hard at the green eyes and Qantaqa's baying became a whimper of pain. A moment later the wolf turned and vanished from the rise. Simon cursed inwardly and struggled again to break free, but he was still as helpless as a kitten dangled by the scruff. Only his head seemed his own, and every movement was painfully difficult. He turned slowly, looking for Binabik and Sludig, then stopped, eyes widening.

Two crumpled shapes, one small, one large, lay on the frosty ground against the abbey's rotted plaster front. Simon's tears froze into stinging ice on his cheek as something tugged his head back around and drew him another unwilling step toward the fire.

"Wait," Skodi said. Her voluminous white nightdress flapped in the wind. Her feet were bare. "I do not want you too close. You might be burned and that would spoil you. Stand there." She pointed a plump arm at a spot a couple of paces away. As if he were an extension of her hand, Simon found himself trudging unsteadily across the thawing mud to the spot she had indicated.

"Vren!" Skodi cried. She seemed gripped by maniacal good cheer. "Where is that rope? Where are you?"

The dark-haired boy appeared in the abbey's front doorway. "Here, Skodi."

"Tie his pretty wrists."

Vren shot forward, skittering over the icy ground. He grasped Simon's limp hands and pulled them behind his back, then deftly bound him with a length of rope.

"Why are you doing this, Vren?" Simon gasped. "We were kind to you."

The Hyrka boy ignored him, pulling the knots tight. When he had finished, he put his small hands on Simon's hips and pushed him toward where Binabik and Sludig lay huddled.

Like Simon, both had their hands trussed behind their backs. Binabik's eyes rolled to meet Simon's, the whites gleaming in the fire-shadowed yard. Sludig was breathing but insensible, a strand of spittle frozen on his blond beard.

"Simon-friend," the troll rasped, each word a labor. The little man drew breath as if to say more, but instead fell back into silence.

Across the yard, Skodi had bent to draw a circle in the melting snow, trickling a handful of reddish powder from her fist. When that was finished, she began to scrape runes into the muddy ground, her tongue clenched between her teeth like a studious child. Vren stood a short distance away, swiveling his head from Skodi to Simon and back again, face empty of all emotion but a sort of animal watchfulness.

Finished stoking the fire, the children were huddled near the wall of the abbey. One of the youngest girls sat on the ground in her thin shift, sobbing quietly; an older boy patted her head in a perfunctory way that seemed meant to comfort her. They all watched Skodi's movements with fascinated attention. The wind had blown the fire into a rippling pillar, which painted their sober little faces with vermillion light.

"Now, where is Honsa?" Skodi called, clutching her nightdress closer to her body as she straightened up. "Honsa!?"

"I'll get her, Skodi," Vren said. He slipped into the shadows at the corner of the abbey, vanishing from sight, then reappeared a few moments later with a black-haired Hyrka girl a year or two older than himself. A heavy basket swung between them, bumping and jostling across the uneven ground until they set it down by Skodi's swollen feet and scampered back to the crowd of watching children. Once there, Vren squatted in front of the little group and pulled a knife from his belt, then began to nervously shred the end of his remaining hank of rope. Simon could feel the boy's tension from across the yard. He wondered dully what the cause might be.

Skodi reached into the basket and lifted out a skull whose mandible clung by only a few knots of dried flesh, so that the eyeless face seemed to gape in surprise. The bulging basket, Simon now saw, was full of skulls. He suddenly felt sure he knew what had happened to the parents of all these children. His numbed body shivered reflexively, but he perceived the movement only dimly, as though it happened to someone else who was some distance away. Nearby, dark-eyed Vren picked at the end of rope with his gleaming blade, his features set in a brooding scowl. Simon remembered with a sinking heart how Skodi had said that beside his other chores, Vren butchered and cooked for her.

Skodi held the skull before her, her oddly pretty face utterly absorbed—a scholar studying a table of high mathematical formulae. She swayed from side to side like a boat in high wind, nightdress flapping, and began to sing in her high-pitched, childish voice.

"In a hole, in a hole."

Skodi piped,

". . . in the ground, in a hole, where the wet-nosed mole
sings a song of cold stone, and of mud and gray bone,
a quiet, small song all the chill, dark night long
as he digs in the deep, where the white worms creep,
and the dead all sleep, with their eyes full of earth
where the beetles give birth, laying little white eggs,
and their brittle black legs go scrape, scrape, scrape,
and the dark, like a cape, covers all just the same,
darkness hiding their shame as it covered their names,
the names of the dead, all gone, all fled,
empty winds, empty heads,
Above grass grows on stone, fields lie fallow, unsown
all is gone that they've known
so they wail in the deep, crying out in their sleep,
without eyes, still they weep, calling out for what's lost,
in the darkness they toss, under pitweed and moss
in the deeps of the grave, neither master or slave,
has now feature or fame, needs knowledge or name,
but they long to come back, and they stare through the cracks
at the dim sun above, and they curse cruel love,
and the peace lost in life, think of worry and strife,
ruined child or wife,
all the troubles that burned, dreadful lessons unlearned,
still they long to return, to return, to return,
they long to return.
Return!

In a hole, in the ground, under old barrow-mound,
where skin, bone, and blood turn to jelly-soft mud,
and the rotting world sings . . .

Skodi's song went on and on, circling downward like a black whirlpool in a weed-strewn and unfrequented pond. Simon felt himself sinking with it, tugged by its insistent rhythms until the flames and the naked stars and the gleaming eyes of children blurred together into streaks of light, and his heart spiraled down into darkness. His mind could feel no connection with his shackled body, or with the actions of those around him. A bleak hiss of idiot noise filled his thoughts. Bleak shapes moved across the snowy courtyard, unimportant as ants.

Now one of the shapes took the round, pale object in its hand and tossed it into the fire, throwing a fistful of powder in after it. A plume of scarlet smoke belched forth, trailing off into the sky and obscuring Simon's view. When it cleared, the fire was burning as brightly as before, but a heavier darkness seemed to have settled over the courtyard. The red light that splashed the buildings had become subdued, old as sunset on a dying world. The wind had failed, but a deeper cold crept through the abbey's grounds. Though his body was no longer fully his own, still Simon could feel the intense chill crawling right into his bones.

"Come to me, Lady Silver Mask!" the largest of the figures cried. "Speak with me, Lord Red Eyes! I want to trade with you! I have a pretty thing you will like!"

The wind had not returned, but the bonfire began to waver from side to side, bulging and shuddering like some great animal struggling inside a sack. The cold intensified. The stars dimmed. A shadowy mouth and two empty black eye-smudges formed in the flames.

"I have a present for you!" the large one shouted gleefully. Simon, drifting, remembered that her name was Skodi. Several of the children were crying, voices muffled despite the curious stillness.

The face in the fire contorted. A low, grumbling roar spilled from the yawning black mouth, slow and deep as the creaking of a mountain's roots. If words were part of that drone, they were indistinguishable. A moment later, the features began to shimmer and fade.

"Stay!" Skodi cried. "Why do you go away?" She looked around wildly, flapping her large arms; her exhilarated expression was gone. "The sword!" she shrieked at the covey of children. "Stop crying, you stupid oxes! Where is the sword? Vren!"

"Inside, Skodi," the little boy said. He was holding one of the smaller children on his lap. Despite the curious sense of dislocation—or perhaps because of it—Simon could not help noticing that Vren's arms were bare and thin beneath his ragged coat.

"Then get it, you fool!" she cried, hopping up and down in a leviathan jig of rage. The face in the flames was now barely distinguishable. "Get it!"

Vren stood up quickly, letting the child in his lap slide to the ground, where it joined its wails to the general cacophony. Vren sped into the house and Skodi turned to the billowing flames once more. "Come back, come back," she coaxed the diminishing face, "I have a present for my Lord and Lady."

Skodi's grip on him seemed to diminish somewhat. Simon felt himself slipping back into his body once more—a curious feeling, like donning a cloak of softly tickling feathers.

Vren appeared in the doorway, pale face solemn. "Too heavy," he called. "Honsa, Endë, you others, come here! Come and help!" Several of the children came creeping across the snow toward the abbey at his call, looking over their shoulders at the groaning bonfire and their gesticulating caretaker. They followed Vren into the shadowed interior like a string of nervous goslings.

Skodi turned again, her round cheeks flushed, her rosy lips trembling. "Vren! Bring me the sword, you lazy thing! Hurry!"

He stuck his head out of the doorway. "Heavy, Skodi, it's heavy like a stone!"

Skodi abruptly turned her mad eyes on Simon. "It's *your* sword, isn't it?" The face had vanished from the flames, but the stars, pale as balls of ice, still barely smoldered in the night sky; the bonfire still rippled and danced, untouched by any wind. "You know how to move it, don't you?" Her gaze was almost intolerable.

Simon said nothing, fighting inwardly with all his might to prevent himself from babbling like a drunkard, from spilling to those compelling eyes every thought he'd ever had.

"I *must* give it to them," she hissed. "They are searching for it, I know! My dreams told me that they are. The Lord and Lady will make me . . . a *power.*" She began to laugh, a girlish trill that frightened him as much as anything that had happened since the sun had set. "Oh, pretty Simon," she giggled, "what a wild night! Go and bring me your black sword." She turned and shouted at the empty doorway. "Vren! Come untie his hands!"

Vren popped out into the open, glaring furiously. "No!" he screamed. "He's bad! He'll get away! *He'll hurt you!*"

Skodi's face froze into an unpleasant mask. "Do what I say, Vren. Untie him."

The boy loped forward, stiff with rage, tears standing in his eyes. He roughly pulled Simon's hands out behind and thrust the knife blade between the cords. Vren's breath came in constricted gasps as he sawed the ropes away; when Simon's hands fell free, the Hyrka boy turned and sped back to the abbey.

Simon stood, rubbing his wrists slowly, and thought about simply running away. Skodi had turned her back on him and was crooning imploringly to the bonfire. He looked out of the corner of his eye to Binabik and Sludig. The Rimmersman still lay without movement, but the troll was struggling against his bonds.

"Take . . . take the sword and run, friend Simon!" Binabik whispered. "We will be escaping . . . somehow . . ."

Skodi's voice cut through the darkness. "The sword!" Simon felt himself turning helplessly from his friend, compelled beyond any possibility of resistance. He marched toward the abbey as though prodded by an invisible hand.

Inside, the children were crouched in the darkened hearth-corner, still tugging without success at Thorn. Vren glared as Simon entered, but stepped out of his way. Simon kneeled before the sword, a hard, angular bundle shrouded in rags and hides. He unwrapped it with hands that felt curiously blunted.

As he grasped the corded hilt, the firelight spilling through the doorway painted a stripe of glowing red along Thorn's black length. The sword shuddered beneath his fingers in a way he had not felt before, a tremble almost of hunger or anticipation. For the first time Simon felt Thorn to be something unutterably and loathsomely alien, but he could no more drop it from his hands than he could run away. He lifted it. The blade did not feel painfully heavy, as it sometimes did, but it still had a strange weightiness, as though he dragged it up from the muck at the bottom of a pond.

He found himself compelled toward the doorway. Somehow, even though she could not see him, Skodi could still move him like a straw doll. He let himself be tugged back out to the red-lit courtyard.

"Come here, Simon," she said as he emerged, spreading her arms like a loving mother. "Come stand in the circle with me."

"He has a sword!" Vren shrieked from the doorway. "He'll hurt you!"

Skodi laughed dismissively. "He will not. Skodi is too strong. Besides, he is my new pet. He likes me, don't you?" She reached out her hand toward Simon. Thorn seemed to be swollen full with some awful, sluggish life. "Don't break the circle," she said lightly, as though they played a game. Skodi clasped his arm and pulled him to her, helping him to lift his clumsy foot over the circle of reddish dust. "Now they will be able to see the sword!" She glowed with her triumph. One of her warm pink hands clasped his atop Thorn's hilt, the other coiled around his neck, pulling him against her pulpy breasts and stomach. The heat of the fire softened him like wax; the push of Skodi's body against his was like a smothering fever-dream. He stood half-a-head taller, but had no more power to resist her than if he had been an infant. What sort of witch was this girl?

Skodi began to shout in piercing Rimmerspakk as she swayed against him. The lines of a face began to reform in the bonfire. Through tears that the heat forced from his eyes, Simon saw the unstable black mouth opening and closing like a shark's. A cold and dreadful presence came down upon them—questing, questing, sniffing for them with predatory patience.

The voice roared at them. This time Simon could hear speech in the jumble of sound, unrecognizable words that made his very teeth ache.

Skodi gasped in excitement. "It is one of Lord Red Eye's highest servants, just as I hoped! Look, sir, look! The present you want!" She forced Simon to lift Thorn, then stared eagerly at the shadowy thing moving in the blaze as it spoke again. Her exhilarated grin soured. "It does not understand me," she whispered against Simon's neck with the easy familiarity of a lover. "It cannot find the right road. I feared this. My charm alone is not strong enough. Skodi has to do something she did not want to do." She turned her head outward. "Vren! We must have blood! Get the bowl and bring me some of the tall one's blood."

Simon tried to cry out, but could not. The heat within the circle was lifting Skodi's fine hair like wisps of pale smoke. Her eyes seemed flat and inhuman as potshards. "Blood, Vren!"

The boy stood over Sludig, an earthenware bowl in one hand, the blade of the knife—huge in Vren's small fingers—lying against the Rimmersman's neck. Vren turned to look back at Skodi, ignoring Binabik as the troll struggled on the ground nearby.

"That is right, the big one!" Skodi cried. "I want to keep the little one! Hurry, Vren, you stupid squirrel, I need blood for the fire now! The messenger will go away!"

Vren lifted his knife.

"And bring it carefully!" Skodi cried. "Don't spill any inside the circle. You know how the little ones swarm when charms are spoken, how hungry they are."

The Hyrka boy suddenly whirled and came stalking toward Skodi and Simon, his face suffused with anger and fear. "No!" he screamed. For a moment Simon felt a rush of hope, thinking that the boy meant to strike Skodi down. "No!" Vren shrieked again, waving the knife in the air as tears coursed down his cheeks. "Why are you keeping them? Why are you keeping *him!?*" He jabbed his blade in Simon's direction. "He's too old, Skodi! He's bad! Not like me!"

"What are you doing, Vren?" Skodi narrowed her eyes in alarm as the boy leaped forward toward the circle. The blade swept up, red-gleaming. Simon's muscles burned as he strove to throw himself out of the boy's path, but he was clenched in a hand of stone. Sweat sluiced into his eyes.

"You can't like *him!*" Vren screeched. With a croaking shriek, Simon managed to squirm just enough for the blade aimed at his ribs to miss and tear along his back instead, leaving a track of cold silvery pain. Something in the fire bellowed like a bull, then the darkness fell in on top of Simon, blotting out the faded stars.

Eolair had left her alone for a moment while he went back through the great doorway to fetch another lamp.

As she waited for the Count of Nad Mullach's return, Maegwin gazed happily down at the vast stone city in the cavern below. A great burden had been lifted from her. Here was the city of the Sithi, of Hernystir's allies of old. She had found it! For a while, Maegwin had begun to believe herself as mad as Eolair and the others thought, but here it stood.

It had come to her at first as a certain disorder in her dreams—troubled dreams that were already dark and chaotic, full of the suffering faces of her beloved dead. Then other images began to seep through. These new dreams showed her a beautiful city rippling with banners, a city of flowers and captivating music, hidden from war and bloodshed. But these visions that appeared in the last, fleeting moments of sleep, although preferable to her nightmares, had not helped to calm her. Rather, in their richness and exotic wonder, they had inflamed Maegwin with fear for her own troubled mind. Soon, in her wanderings through Grianspog's tunnels, she had also begun to hear whispering in the earth's depths, chanting voices unlike anything she had ever experienced.

The idea of the ancient city had grown and flowered until it became far more important than anything happening within reach of sunlight. Sunlight brought evil: the daystar was a beacon for disaster, a lamp that the enemies of Hernystir could use to seek out and destroy her people. Only in the deeps did safety lie, down among the roots of the earth where the heroes and gods of elder days still lived, where the cruel winter could not go.

Now, as she stood above this fantastic stone city—*her* city—a vast sense of satisfaction spread over her. For the first time since her father King Lluth had gone away to battle Skali Sharp-nose, she felt peace. True, the stone towers and domes spread across the rock canyon below did not much resemble the airy summer-city of her dreams, but there seemed small doubt that this was a place crafted by inhuman hands, and it stood in a place where no Hernystiri had walked since time out of mind. If it was not the dwelling place of the deathless Sithi, then what was it? Of course it was their city; that seemed laughably obvious.

"Maegwin?" Eolair called, slipping through the half-open door. "Where are you?" The worry in his voice brought a tiny smile to her face, but she hid it from him.

"I am here, of course, Count. Where you bade me stay."

He came and stood at her shoulder, gazing down. "Gods of stock and stone," he said, shaking his head, "it *is* miraculous."

Maegwin's smile came back. "What else would you expect of such a place? Let's go down and find those who live here. Our people are in great need, you know."

Eolair looked at her carefully. "Princess, I doubt very much that anyone is living there. Do you see anything moving? And no lights are burning but our own."

"What makes you think that the Peaceful Ones cannot see in darkness?" she said, laughing at the foolishness of men in general and clever ones like the count in particular. Her heart was racing so that the laugh threatened to get away from her. Safety! It was a breathtaking thought. How could anything harm them in the lap of Hernystir's ancient protectors?

"Very well, my lady," Eolair said slowly. "We will go down a short way, if these stairs are to be trusted. But your people are worrying about you," he grimaced, "—and me, too, before long. We must return quickly. We can always come back again later, with more folk."

"Certainly." She fluttered her hand to show how little such concerns affected her. They would return with *all* her people, of course. This was the place they would live forever, out of reach of Skali and Elias and the rest of the blood-soaked madmen above ground.

Eolair grasped her elbow, guiding her with almost laughable caution. She herself felt the urge to skip down the rough-hewn stairs. What could hurt them here?

They descended like two small stars falling into a great abyss, the flames of their lamps reflecting from the pale stone roofs below. Their footsteps echoed out through the great cavern and rebounded from the invisible ceiling to be repeated in countless reverberations, returning to them as a rush of pattering sound like the velvet wings of a million bats.

For all its completeness, the city nevertheless seemed skeletal. Its interconnected buildings were tiled in a thousand colors of pale stone, ranging from the white of a first snow through endless wan shades of sand and pearl and sooty gray. The round windows stared like unseeing eyes. The polished stone streets gleamed like the tracks of wandering snails.

They were halfway down the stairs when Eolair pulled up short, clasping Maegwin's arm close against his side. In the lamplight his worried face seemed almost translucent; she fancied suddenly that she could see everything that was in his mind.

"We have gone far enough, Lady," he said. "Your people will be hunting for us."

"My people?" she asked, pulling away. "Are they not your people, too? Or are you now far above a mere tribe of cringing cave-dwellers, Count?"

"That is not what I mean, Maegwin, and you know it," he said harshly.

That looks like pain in your eyes, Eolair, she thought. *Does it hurt you so to be yoked to a madwoman? How could I have been fool enough to love you when I could never hope for more than polite forbearance in return?*

Aloud, she said: "You are free to go whenever you wish, Count. You doubted me. Now perhaps you are frightened that you might have to face those whose existence you denied. I, however, am not going anywhere but down to the city."

Eolair's fine features wrinkled in frustration. As he unknowingly wiped a smear of lampblack onto his chin, Maegwin wondered suddenly what *she* looked like. The long, obsessive hours of searching and digging and chipping away at the bolt that secured the great door floated in her mind like a poorly-remembered dream. How long had she been down here in the depths? She stared at her dirt-caked hands with a growing sense of horror—she must indeed look the part of madwoman—then pushed the thought away in disgust. What did such things matter at an hour like this?

"I cannot let you lose yourself in this place, Lady," Eolair said at last.

"Then come with me or bully me all the way back to your wretched camp, noble count." She suddenly did not like the way she sounded, but it was said and she would not take it back.

Eolair did not show the anger she expected; instead, a weary resignation crept over his features. The pain she had seen before did not go away, but rather seemed to sink deeper, spreading into the very lines of his face. "You made a promise to me, Maegwin. Before I opened the door, you said you would heed my decision. I did not believe you an oath-breaker. I know your father never was."

Maegwin pulled back, stung. "Do not throw my father up to me!"

Eolair shook his head. "Still, my lady, you promised me."

Maegwin stared at him. Something in his careful, clever face took hold of her so that she did not hurry away down the stairs as she had intended. An inner voice mocked her stupidity, but she faced him squarely.

"You are only partly correct, Count Eolair," she said slowly. "You could not open it yourself, if you remember. I had to help you."

He looked at her closely. "So, then?"

"So, then, a compromise. I know you think me headstrong or worse, but I do still want your friendship, Eolair. You have been good to my father's house."

"A bargain, Maegwin?" he asked expressionlessly.

"If you will let us walk down to the bottom of the stairs—just until we can set foot on the tiles of the city—I will turn around and go back with you . . . if that is what you wish. I promise."

A weary smile touched Eolair's lips. "You promise, do you?"

"I swear by Bagba's Herd." She touched her soiled hand to her breast.

"Better you should swear by Black Cuamh, down here." He grimaced in frustration. His long tail of hair had shed its ribbon and lay black across his shoulders. "Very well. I don't like the idea of trying to carry you back up these stairs against your will."

"You couldn't," Maegwin said, pleased. "I am too strong. Come, let's go faster. As you said, people are waiting for us."

They passed down the steps in silence, Maegwin reveling in the safety of shadows and stone mountains, Eolair lost in his own unvoiced thoughts. They watched their feet, fearful of a misstep despite the stairway's great width. The stairs were pitted, crazed with cracks as though the earth had shifted in uneasy sleep, but the stonecraft was beautiful and subtle. The lamplight revealed traces of intricate designs that coiled across the steps and onto the wall above the staircase, scribings delicate as the fronds of young ferns or the shingled feathers of hummingbirds. Maegwin could not help turning to Eolair with a smile of satisfaction.

"Do you see!?" She held her lamp up to the wall. "How could this be work of any mere mortals?"

"I see it, Lady," Eolair responded somberly. "But there is no such wall on the other side of the stairs." He indicated the drop-off to the canyon below. Despite the distance they had already traveled downward, it was still far enough to kill someone handily. "Please don't look at the carvings so closely that you stumble over the edge."

Maegwin curtseyed. "I will be careful, Count."

Eolair frowned, perhaps at her frivolity, but only nodded.

The great stairway opened out at the bottom a like fan, spreading onto the canyon floor. Away from the overhanging cavern wall, the glow of their lamps seemed to diminish, the light not strong enough to dispel the deep and overwhelming dark. Buildings which had seemed cunning as carved toys from the height of the canyon rim now loomed above them, a fantastic array of shadowed domes and spiraling towers that tapered up into the blackness like impossible stalagmites. Bridges of living stone stretched from the cavern walls to the towers, winding in and about the spires like ribbons. Its various parts tied together with narrow integuments of stone, the city seemed more like a single, breathingly vital thing than an artifact of lifeless rock—but it was surely empty.

"The Sithi are long gone, Lady, if they ever lived here." Eolair was solemn, but Maegwin thought she heard a certain satisfaction in his tone. "It is time to return."

Maegwin gave him a look of disgust. Had the man no curiosity at all? "Then what is that?" she asked, pointing to a faint glow near the center of of the shadowed city. "If that is not lamplight, then I am a Rimmersman."

The count stared. "It does look like it," he said cautiously. "But it might be something else. Light leaking down from above."

"I have been in the tunnels a long while," Maegwin said. "Surely it is well past sunset aboveground." She turned and touched his arm. "Come, Eolair, please! Don't be such an old man! How could you leave this place without knowing?"

The Count of Nad Mullach frowned, but she could see other emotions struggling beneath the surface. He did wish to know, that was plain. It was just this transparency that had captured her heart. How could he be an envoy to all the courts of Osten Ard and yet sometimes be as uncloudedly obvious as a child?

"Please?" she said.

He checked the oil in the lamps before answering. "Very well. But only to set your mind at ease. I do not doubt that you have found a place that once belonged to the Sithi, or to men of old who had skills we have lost, but they are long vanished. They cannot save us from our fate."

"Whatever you say, Count. Hurry now!"

She tugged him forward, into the city.

Despite her confident words, the stone byways did indeed seem long-deserted. Dust sifted beneath their feet, eddying listlessly. After they had walked awhile, Maegwin found her enthusiasm begin to diminish, her thoughts turning melancholy as the lamplight threw the jutting towers and swooping spans into grotesque relief. She was again reminded of bones, as though they wandered through the time-scoured rib cage of some impossible beast. Following the twisting streets through the abandoned city, she began to feel herself swallowed up. For the first time the utterness of these depths, the sheer furlongs of stone between herself and the sun, seemed oppressive.

They passed innumerable empty holes in the carved stone facades, holes whose smooth edges had once been tight-filled by doors. Maegwin imagined eyes staring out at her from the darkened entrances—not malicious eyes, but sad ones, eyes that gazed at the trespassers with more regret than anger.

Surrounded by proud ruins, Lluth's daughter felt herself weighted down by all that her people had not become, all that they could never be. Given the entirety of the world's sunlit fields in which to run, the Hernystiri tribes had let themselves be driven into caves in the mountain. Even their gods had deserted them. At least these Sithi had left their memorial in magnificently crafted stone. Maegwin's people built of wood, and even the bones of Hernystir's warriors now bleaching on the Inniscrich would disappear with the passing of years. Soon there would be nothing left of her people at all.

Unless someone saved them. But surely none but the Sithi could do that—and where had they gone? Was Eolair right? Were they indeed dead? She had been sure they had gone deep into the earth, but perhaps they had passed on to some other place.

She stole a glance at Eolair. The count was walking silently beside her, staring up at the city's splendid towers like a farmer from the Circoille fringes on his first visit to Hernysadharc. Watching his thin-nosed face, his bedraggled tail of black hair, she suddenly felt her love for him come surging up from the place where she had thought it prisoned, a helpless love as painful and undeniable as grief. Maegwin's memory went flying back almost a score of years to the first day she had seen him.

She had been only a girl, but already tall as a grown woman, she recalled with disgust. She had been standing behind her father's chair in the Taig's great hall when the new Count of Nad Mullach arrived for his ritual pledge of loyalty. Eolair had seemed so young that day, slender and bright-eyed as a fox, nervous, but almost giddy with pride. *Seemed* young? He had *been* young: scarcely more than twenty-two years old, full of the suppressed laughter of anxious youth. He had caught Maegwin's eye as she peered curiously around the high back of Lluth's chair. She had blushed scarlet as a berry. Eolair had smiled then, showing her those bright, small, sharp teeth, and it had felt as though he took a gentle bite of her heart.

It had meant nothing to him, of course. Maegwin knew that. She was only a girl then, but already fated to become the king's gawky spinster daughter, a woman who lavished her attention on pigs and horses and birds with broken wings, and knocked things off tabletops because she could never remember to walk and sit and carry herself delicately, as a lady should. No, he had meant nothing more than a fretful smile at a wide-eyed young girl, but with that unwitting smile Eolair had caught her forever in an unbreakable net. . . .

Her thoughts were interrupted as the walled road they had chosen ended before a broad, squat tower whose surface crawled with ornate stone vines and translucent stone flowers. A wide doorway gaped darkly like a toothless mouth. Eolair looked at the shadowed entrance suspiciously before stepping forward to peer inside.

The interior of the tower seemed oddly spacious, despite the close-hovering shadows. A stairway choked with rubble curled away up one inner wall, and a descending stairway passed around the circumference of the tower in the opposite direction. When they drew their lamps back outside the door, a glimmer of light—only the faintest of sheens—seemed to brighten the air where this downward passage disappeared from view.

Maegwin took a deep breath. Astonishingly, she felt no fear at being in such a mad place. "We will turn back whenever you say."

"That staircase is far too treacherous," Eolair replied. "We should go back now." He hesitated, torn between curiosity and responsibility. There was indeed an unarguable gleam of light from the downtrack. Maegwin stared at it, but said nothing. The count sighed. "We will just go a little way on the other path, instead."

They followed the downward path, spiraling for what seemed a furlong into the depths until they leveled out at last in a broad, low-ceilinged passageway. The walls and roof were carved with tangled vines and grasses and flowers, a panorama of vegetation that could only grow far above, beneath sun and sky. The interwoven strands of stem and vine ran endlessly along the wall beside them in a tapestry of stone. Despite the immensity of the panels, no part of the wall seemed carved with exactly the same design as any other. The great carvings themselves were composed of many kinds of rock, of an almost infinite variety of hues and textures, but the panels were no mosaic of individual tiles as was the patterned floor. Rather, the very stone itself seemed to have grown in exact and pleasing shapes, as a hedge coaxed and pruned by gardeners might mimic the form of an animal or bird.

"By the gods of Earth and Sky," she breathed.

"We must turn back, Maegwin." There was little conviction in Eolair's voice. Here in the deeps, time seemed to have slowed almost to a stop.

They walked on, examining the fantastic carvings in silence. At last, the lamplight was supplemented by a more diffuse glow from the tunnel's far end. Maegwin and the count stepped out of the passageway and into the open, where the shadowed ceiling of the huge cavern once more arched distantly overhead.

They stood on a broad fan of tiles above a great and shallow bowl of stone.

The arena, three stone-throws across, was lined all about with benches of pale, crumbling chert, as though the deserted bowl had been the site of worship or vast spectacle. A misty white light glowed in the open space of the bowl's center, like an invalid sun.

"Cuamh and Brynioch!" Eolair swore quietly. There was a distant and anxious edge to his voice. "What is it?"

A great, angular crystal stood on an altar of dull granite in the middle of the arena, shimmering like a corpse-candle. The stone was milky white, smooth-faced but rough-edged as a jagged chunk of quartz. Its strange and subtle light slowly brightened, then died, then brightened again, so that the ancient benches standing nearest seemed almost to flicker in and out of existence with every scintillation.

Pale light washed over them as they approached the strange object; the chill air began to seem distinctly warmer. Maegwin felt a moment of breathlessness at the queer splendor of the thing. For long moments she and Eolair stood looking into the snowy glare, watching subtle colors chase each other through the stone's depths, marigold and coral and shy lavender, shifting like quicksilver.

"It's beautiful," she said at last.

"Aye."

They lingered, transfixed. At last, with obvious reluctance, the Count of Nad Mullach turned away. "But there is nothing else here, Lady. Nothing."

Before Maegwin could speak, the white stone suddenly blazed, radiance swelling and blossoming like the birth of a heaven-star, until the blinding glare seemed to fill the cavern. Maegwin battled to orient herself in the sea of terrifying brilliance. She reached out for the Count of Nad Mullach. Blasted by light, Eolair's face had blurred until his features were almost indistinguishable. His far side had vanished into absolute shadow so that he seemed but half a man.

"What is happening?!" she cried. "Is the stone burning up?!"

"Lady!" Eolair snatched at her, trying to pull her back from the glare. "Are you hurt?"

"Ruyan's Children!"

Maegwin reeled back in shock, stumbling unaware into Eolair's protective grasp. The stone had spoken with the voice of a woman, a voice that surrounded them as though mouths spoke from every side.

"Why do you not answer me!? Three times now have I called to you. I no longer have the strength! I will not be able to try again!"

The words were spoken in a tongue Maegwin had never heard, but still their meaning was somehow as clear as if spoken in her own Hernystiri, as powerful as if the woman's voice were inside her head. Was this the madness she had feared? But Eolair, too, had clapped his hands over his ears, beset by the same unnatural voice.

"Ruyan's Folk! I beg you, forget our old strife, the wrongs that were done! A greater enemy now threatens us both!"

The voice spoke as though with a great effort. Weariness and sorrow was in it, but something also of immense power, a strength that set Maegwin's skin to tingling. She held her hands splay-fingered before her eyes and squinted into the heart of the glare, but could see nothing. The light that beat out at her seemed almost to push like a strong wind. Could some person be standing in the midst of that staggering incandescence? Or could it somehow be the stone itself that spoke? She found herself sorrowing for whoever or whatever should call out so desperately, even as she fought against the lunatic idea of a shouting stone.

"Who are you?!" Maegwin cried. "Why are you in the stone!? Get out of my ears!"

"What? Someone is there at last? Praise to the Garden!" Unexpected hope flared in the voice, supplanting weariness for a moment. *"Oh, ancient kindred, black evil threatens our adopted land! I crave answers to my questions . . . questions that might save us all!"*

"Lady!"

Maegwin at last noticed that Eolair was holding tightly to her waist. "It will not hurt me!" she told him. She moved a little closer to the stone, pulling against his strong arms. "What questions?" she shouted. "We are Hernystiri. I am the daughter of King Lluth-ubh-Llythinn! Who are you? are you in the stone? Are you here in the city?"

The light from the stone dimmed and began to flicker. There was a pause before the voice came back, more muted than before. *"Are you Tinukeda'ya? I hear you only faintly,"* the woman said. *"It is too late! You are fading away. If you can still hear me, and would give aid against a shared enemy, come to us in Jao é-Tinukai'i. Some among you must know where it is."* Her voice grew softer still, until it was barely a whisper, tickling the insides of Maegwin's ears. The stone had lapsed back into fitful gleaming. *"Many are searching for the three Great Swords. Listen! This might be the salvation of us all, or the destruction."* The stone pulsed. *"This is all the Year-Dancing Grove could tell me, all the leaves would sing . . ."* Despair welled up in her dying voice. *"I have failed. I have grown too weak. First Grandmother has failed . . . I can see only darkness coming. . . ."*

The soft words at last were gone. The speaking stone dimmed to a smear of pale light before Maegwin's eyes. "I could not help her, Eolair." She felt quite empty. "We did nothing. And she was so sad!"

Eolair gently released her from his grasp. "We do not understand enough to help anyone, Lady," he said softly. "We are in need of help ourselves."

Maegwin stepped away from him, fighting back angry tears. Hadn't he felt the woman's goodness, her sorrow? Maegwin felt as though she had watched a wonderful bird thrashing in a trap just beyond her reach.

Turning to Eolair, she was startled to see moving sparks in the darkness beyond. She blinked, but it was no phantasm of her dazzled eyes. A procession of dim lights was moving toward them, wending its way down the aisles of the shadowed arena.

Eolair followed her stare. "Murhagh's Shield!" he swore, "I knew I was right to mistrust this place!" He fumbled for his sword hilt. "Behind me, Maegwin!"

"Hide from those who will save us?" She darted around his restraining hand as the bobbing lights approached. "It is the Sithi at last!" The lights, pink and white, wavered like fireflies as she took a step forward. "Peaceful Ones!" she cried. "Your old allies need you!"

The words that whispered out of the shadows came from no mortal throat. Maegwin was filled with wild excitement, certain now that her dreams had spoken truly. The new voice spoke an antique Hernystiri that had not been heard beneath the sunlight for centuries. Oddly, there seemed also a touch of fear in its words.

"Our allies are gone to bones and dust, now, as with most of our folk. What kind of creatures be you, that fear not the Shard?"

The speaker and his fellows slowly came forward into the light. Maegwin, who had thought herself ready for anything, felt as though the bedrock swayed beneath her. She clutched at Eolair's sword arm as the Count of Nad Mullach hissed in surprise.

It was their eyes that seemed so strange at first, great round eyes with no whites. Blinking in the lampglare, the four newcomers seemed frightened creatures of the forest night. Man-tall but achingly slender, they clutched shining rods of some translucent gemstone in their long, spidery fingers. Fine, pale hair hung down around their bony faces; their features were delicate, but they wore rough clothes of fur and dusty leather, knobbed at knees and elbows.

Eolair's sword rasped out of the scabbard, gleaming pinkly in the light of the crystal rods. "Stand back! What are you?"

The being nearest took a step backward, then drew up, its thin face evidencing nervous surprise. "But it is you who be trespassers here. Ah, you *do* be Children of Hern, as we did suspect. Mortals." He turned and said something to his fellows in a language like a murmur of song. They nodded gravely, then all four pairs of saucer eyes turned to Maegwin and Eolair once more. "No, we have spoken on this, and only meet it is that you make shift to name yourselves."

Marveling at how the dream had turned, Maegwin steadied herself on Eolair's arm and spoke. "We . . . we are . . . I am Maegwin, daughter of King Lluth. This is Eolair, Count of Nad Mullach."

The strange creatures' heads bobbled on their slender necks; they spoke melodically among themselves once more. Maegwin and the count shared a look of stunned disbelief, then turned as the one who had spoken before made a discreet noise in his throat.

"You speak with good grace. So, be you gentlefolk among your kind, in truth? And promise you mean no harm? Sadly, it has been long since we have had dealings with Hern's Folk, and we are sore ignorant of their doings. We were affrighted when you spoke to the Shard."

Eolair swallowed. "Who are you? And what is this place?"

The leader stared at him for a long moment, the reflection of the lamp-flame bright in his great eyes. "Yis-fidri am I. My companions hight Sho-vennae, Imai-an, and Yis-hadra, who is my good wife." They bowed their heads in turn as he named them. "This city is called Mezutu'a."

Maegwin was fascinated by Yis-fidri and his friends, but a nagging doubt was making itself felt at the back of her mind. They were certainly strange, but they were not what she had expected. . . .

"You cannot be the Sithi," she said. "Where are they? Are you their servants?"

The strangers looked at her with alarm on their wide-eyed faces, then took a few pattering steps backward and joined briefly in chiming colloquy. After a moment, Yis-fidri turned and spoke a little more harshly than he had before.

"We served others once, but that was long ages agone. Have they sent you for us? We will not go back." For all his defiant tone, there was something tremendously pathetic in Yis-fidri's wagging head and huge, mournful eyes. "What did the Shard tell you?"

Eolair shook his head, confused. "Forgive us if we are rude, but we have never seen any like you. We were not sent to look for you. We did not even know you existed."

"The Shard? Do you mean the stone?" Maegwin asked. "It said many things. I will try to remember them. But who are you then, if you are not the Sithi?"

Yis-fidri did not answer, but slowly lifted his crystal, extending his spindly hand until the rod's rosy light burned heatlessly beside Maegwin's face. "By your aspect, Hern's people stand not so much changed since we Tinukeda'ya of the mountains last knew them," he said wistfully. "How is it we are forgotten already—have so many generations of mortals come and gone? Surely it was only a few turnings of the earth since your northern tribesmen, the bearded ones, did know us?" His thin face grew distant. "The northerners called us Dvernings, and brought us gifts so we would craft for them."

Eolair stepped forward. "You are the ones our ancestors called *Domhaini*? But we thought they were legend only, or at least were long dead. You are . . . the dwarrows?"

Yis-fidri showed a mild frown. "Legend? You do be of Hern's folk, be you not? Who was it, think you, that *taught* your ancestors to mine these mountains in days agone? We did. As to names, what matter? Dwarrow to some mortals, Dverning or Domhaini to others." He waved his long fingers, slowly, sadly. "Only words. We are Tinukeda'ya. We came from the Garden and we can never return."

Eolair sheathed his sword with a clang that echoed through the cavern. "You sought for the Peaceful Ones, Princess! This is as strange or stranger! A city in the mountain's heart! The dwarrows out of our oldest legends! Has the world below gone as mad as the world above?"

Maegwin was scarcely less astonished than Eolair, but found herself with little to say. As she stared at the dwarrows, she mourned; the black cloud that had lifted for a while seemed to roll back over her mind.

"But you are not the Sithi," she said at last, voice flat. "They are not here. They will not help us."

Yis-fidri's companions moved up, so that they formed a semicircle around the huddled pair. Watching Maegwin and Eolair worriedly, the wide-eyed dwarrows seemed poised to bolt.

"If you came searching for the Zida'ya—those who you name Sithi," Yis-fidri said carefully, "then that is of deep interest to us indeed, since we brought us here to hide from them." He nodded slowly. "Long ago did we refuse to bend any longer to their will, to their overweening injustice, and so we escaped. We thought they had forgotten us, but they have not. Now that we are weary and few, they seek to capture us once more." A dim fire was kindled in Yis-fidri's eyes. "They even call to us through the Shard, the Witness which has been silent for many long years. They mock us with their tricks, trying to lure us back."

"You are hiding from the Sithi?" Eolair asked, confused. "But why?"

"We did serve them once, Hern's Child. We fled. Now they would cozen us into coming back. They speak of swords to lure us—for they know that such crafting was always our delight, and the Great Swords some of our highest works. They ask us of mortals we have never met nor heard of—and what would we have to do with mortals now? You are the first we have seen in a long age."

The Count of Nad Mullach waited for Yis-Fidri to continue. When it appeared he would not, Eolair asked: "Mortals? Like us? What mortals do they name to you?"

"The Zida'ya woman—First Grandmother, as she is called—spoke several times of . . ." the dwarrow conferred briefly with his fellows, ". . . of Handless Josua.' "

"Handless. . . ! Gods of earth and stream, do you mean *Josua Lackhand?!*" Eolair stared, astounded. "Oh, heaven, this *is* madness!" He sat down heavily on one of the decaying benches.

Maegwin slumped beside him. Her mind was already reeling beneath such weariness and disappointment that she had no strength left to be surprised, but when she at last turned away from the mild, wide eyes of the puzzled dwarrows to look to Eolair, the count's face was that of a man struck by lightning in his own house.

Simon awakened from a flight through black spaces and screaming winds. The howling continued, but a red light bloomed before his eyes as the darkness receded.

"Vren, you little fool!" someone was shrieking close by. "There is blood in the circle!"

When he tried to take a breath, Simon felt something pushing down on him, so that his lungs had to strain for air. He wondered briefly if a roof had fallen on him. Fire? The red light danced and billowed. Was the Hayholt on fire?

He could see a vast shape now, dressed in flapping white. The figure seemed to have grown tall as the trees, looming far into the sky. It took long moments before he realized he was lying on the icy ground, that Skodi was standing over him, screaming at someone. How long. . . ?

The little boy Vren flailed on the ground a few cubits away, his hands holding his throat, eyes bulging in his dark face. Untouched and unapproached, he was kicking his feet wildly, heels drumming on the frozen mud. Somewhere nearby, Qantaqa was mournfully howling.

"You are bad!" Skodi screamed, her face gone pinkish-purple with rage. "Bad Vren! Spilled blood! They will swarm! Bad!" She gasped in a great breath and bellowed. *"Punishment!"* The little boy writhed like a smashed snake.

Beyond Skodi, a shadowy face watched from the center of the rippling fire, its unstable mouth moving in laughter. A moment later the bottomless black eyes settled on Simon, their sudden touch like an icy tongue pressed against his face. He tried to scream, but some great weight was pushing on his back.

Little fly, a voice whispered in his head, heavy and dark as mud. It was a voice that had haunted many dreams, a voice of red eyes and burning darkness. *We meet you in the strangest places . . . and you have that sword, as well. We must tell the master about you. He will be very interested.* There was a pause; the thing in the fire seemed to grow larger, the eyes cold black pits in the heart of an inferno. *Why, look at you, manchild,* it purred, *you are bleeding. . . .*

Simon drew his shaking hand out from beneath his body, wondering why it seemed strange that it should respond to his will. When he disentangled it from Thorn's hilt, he saw that the trembling fingers were indeed covered with slick red blood.

"Punished!" Skodi was shrieking, her childlike voice cracking. "Everyone will be punished! We were to give presents to the Lord and Lady!" The wolf howled again, closer.

Vren had gone limp, facedown in the mud at Skodi's feet. As Simon stared distractedly, the ground seemed to bulge, obscuring his view of the boy's pale, crumpled form. A moment later another bulge appeared close by, quivering; the half-thawed earth parted with a crunching, sucking sound. A thin dark arm and long-nailed hand lifted from the agitated soil, reaching toward the dim stars with fingers spread like the petals of a black flower. Another hand snaked up beside it, followed by a pale-eyed head scarcely bigger than an apple. A needle-toothed grin split the wizened face, twitching the scraggly black whiskers.

Simon squirmed, unable to cry out. A dozen bulges blistered the earth of the courtyard, then a dozen more. In a moment the diggers were seething up from below like maggots from a burst carcass.

"*Bukken!*" Skodi shrilled in alarm. "Bukken! Vren, you little fool, I told you not to spill blood in the charm-circle!" She waved her fat arms at the diggers, who swarmed over the shrieking children like a plague of chittering rats. "I punished him!" she screamed, pointing at the unmoving child. "Go away!" She turned to the bonfire. "Make them go away, Sir! Make them go away!"

The fire fluttered in the chill wind, but the face only watched.

"Help! Simon!" Binabik's voice was hoarse with fear. "Help us! We are still tied!"

Simon rolled over painfully, trying to pull his knees beneath him. His back was clenched in an immovable knot, as though he had been kicked by a horse. The air before his eyes seemed full of shining snowflakes.

"Binabik!" he groaned. A wave of squealing black shapes split off from the main cluster, flowing away from the children and toward the abbey wall where Sludig and the troll lay.

"Stop! I will make you!" Skodi had clamped her hands over her ears, as though to shield herself from the children's pitiful screams. A small foot, pallid as a mushroom, emerged briefly from the knot of diggers, then was swallowed up again. "*Stop!*"

The ground suddenly erupted all about her, gouts of gelatinous mud spattering her nightdress. A flurry of spidery arms wrapped around her broad calves, then a swarm of diggers were climbing her legs as though they were tree trunks. Her nightdress bulged as they swarmed up beneath it in ever-increasing numbers, until at last the thin fabric split like an overstuffed bag, revealing a squirming mass of eyes and scrawny legs and taloned hands that almost completely obscured her doughy flesh. Skodi's mouth pulled wide to scream and a serpentine arm pushed into it, disappearing to the shoulder. The girl's pale eyes bulged.

Simon had finally dragged himself into a half-crouch when a gray shape flashed past him, bowling into the slithering, squeaking mass that had been Skodi and tumbling it to the ground. The diggers' mewing cries rose in pitch, quickly becoming trills of fear as Qantaqa snapped necks and crushed skulls, throwing small bodies in the air with gleeful abandon. A moment later she was through and racing toward the throng of creatures that had descended on Binabik and Sludig.

The fire had flared up to a great height. The unformed thing within it laughed. Simon's could feel its terrible amusement sapping him, sucking the life from him.

This is amusing, little fly, is it not? Why don't you come closer and we will watch together.

Simon tried to ignore the pull of the voice, the insistent power of its words. He clambered agonizingly to his feet and staggered away from the fire and the thing that lurked within it. He used Thorn as a crutch, propping himself, though the hilt slid treacherously beneath his blood-damped hand. The slash Vren had made across his back was a cold ache, a numbness that was still somehow painful.

The thing Skodi had summoned continued to taunt him, its voice echoing inside his head, playing with him like a cruel child with a captured insect.

Little fly, where are you going? Come here. The master will want to meet you. . . .

It was a terrible struggle to keep walking in the other direction; life seemed to be running out of him like sand. The diggers' squeals and Qantaqa's wet, joyful growl had become no more than a faint roaring in his ears.

For a long moment he did not even notice the talons grasping at his legs; when at last he looked down into the spider-egg eyes of the Bukken, it was as though he stared through a window into some other world, a horrible place that was fortuitously separated from his own. It was not until the scrabbling claws began to shred the legs of his breeches and score the flesh beneath that the dreamlike state fell away. With a shout of horror, he smashed the wrinkled face with a balled fist. More were climbing his legs. He kicked them away with moans of disgust, but they seemed as numberless as termites.

Thorn shivered again in his hands. Without thinking, Simon lifted it and sent the black blade whistling into a clump of prancing creatures. He felt it hum, as though it sang silently. Grown marvelously light, Thorn sheared heads and arms like grass stems until dark ichor ran down the bladed in streams. Every swing sent fiery pain lancing through Simon's back, but at the same time he felt mad exhilaration course though him. Long moments after all the diggers around him had died or fled, he was still hacking at the tangled corpses.

My, you are a fierce fly, aren't you? Come to us. The voice seemed to reach into his head as into an open wound, and he squirmed in disgust. *Tonight is a great night, a wild night.*

"Simon!" Binabik's muffled cry at last cut through his frenzy of hatred. "Simon! Unbind us!"

You know we will win, little fly. Even at this instant, far away in the south, one of your greatest allies falls . . . despairs . . . dies . . .

Simon turned and staggered toward the troll. Qantaqa, her muzzle blood-washed to the ears, was keeping a hopping, shrilling throng of diggers at bay. Simon lifted Thorn once more and began to cut his way through the Bukken, smashing them down in bunches until at last they scattered from his path. The voice in his head seemed to be crooning almost wordlessly. The fire-washed courtyard shimmered before his eyes.

He bent to cut the troll's bonds and a great wave of dizziness almost toppled him to the ground. Binabik rubbed the rope against Thorn's cutting edge for a moment until the pieces fell aside. The little man tried briefly to rub life back into his wrists, then turned to Sludig. After picking at the knot for a moment, he turned to Simon.

"Here, lend your sword to this cutting," he began, then stared. "*Chukku's Stones!* Simon, you are all of blood on your back!"

Blood will open the doorway, manchild. Come to us!

Simon tried to speak to Binabik but could not. Instead, he thrust Thorn forward, clumsily pinking Sludig's back with the point. The Rimmersman, coming slowly back to wakefulness, groaned.

"While he slept they struck his head with a stone," Binabik said mournfully. "Because of his bigness, I am thinking. Me they only tied." He sawed Sludig's bonds against Thorn until they, too, fell slithering to the snowy ground. "We must be reaching the horses," the troll said to Simon. "Have you sufficent strength?"

He nodded. His head felt far too heavy for his neck and the roaring in his thoughts was giving way to a frightening emptiness. For the second time that night he felt his inner self beginning to float free from its confining shell, but this time he feared there would be no returning. He forced himself to remain standing as Binabik coaxed the bleary Rimmersman to his feet.

The master is waiting in the Chamber of the Well. . . .

"All we may do is run for the stables," Binabik shouted over the wolf's menacing snarl. She had forced the diggers back, so that several yards of open ground stood between the ring of Bukken and Simon's friends. "With Qantaqa leading, we can perhaps be getting there, but we must not slow or hesitate."

Simon swayed. "Get the saddlebags," he said. "In the abbey."

The little man stared at him incredulously. "Foolishness!"

"No." Simon shook his head drunkenly. "I won't go . . . without . . . White Arrow. She . . . they . . . won't take that." He stared out across the dooryard at the heaving mass of diggers gathered where Skodi had stood.

You will stand before the Singing Harp, you will hear His sweet voice. . . .

"Simon," Binabik began, then briefly swung his hand in the Qanuc ward against madmen. "You are barely able for standing," he grunted. "I will go."

Before Simon could respond, the troll had vanished through the door into the abbey's lightless interior. Long moments later he returned, dragging the saddlebags behind him.

"We will hang most on Sludig," Binabik said, eyeing the waiting diggers apprehensively. "He is too full of sleepiness to fight, so he will be our pack-ram."

Come to us!

As the troll draped the bags over the bemused Rimmersman, Simon looked out at the circle of pale, naked eyes. The waiting diggers clicked and chittered quietly as though talking among themselves. Many wore tatters of crude clothing; some had rough, jagged-bladed knives clutched in their spindly fists. They stared back at him, swaying like rows of black poppies.

"Are you now ready, Simon?" Binabik whispered. Simon nodded, lifting Thorn before him. The blade had been light as a switch, but now it suddenly seemed heavy as stone. It was all he could do to hold it before him.

"*Nihut*, Qantaqa!" the troll shouted. The wolf sprang forward, jaws wide. Diggers piped in fear as Qantaqa plowed a furrow through flailing arms and gnashing teeth. Simon followed, swinging Thorn heavily from side to side to side to side.

Come. There are endless cold halls below Nakkiga. The Lightless Ones are singing, waiting to welcome you. Come to us!

Time seemed to fold in on itself. The world closed down into a tunnel of red light and white eyes. The throb of pain in his back seemed to grow as rhythmic as his heartbeat, and the aperture of his vision alternately spread and shut as he stumbled forward. A roar of voices as continuous as the sea washed over him, voices both within and without. He swung the sword, felt it bite, then shook it free and swung again. Things reached for him as he passed. Some caught and tore at his skin.

The tunnel narrowed to black for a while, then opened up for a few moments sometime later. Sludig, who was saying words too quiet for Simon to hear, was helping him up onto Homefinder's back, pushing Thorn through the saddle-loops. They were surrounded by stone walls, but as Simon drove his heels into his horse's ribs, the walls were suddenly gone and he was beneath the tree-slashed night sky, the stars glimmering overhead.

Now is the time, manchild. The door is opened by blood! Come, join us in our celebrations!

"No!" Simon heard his own voice shouting. "Leave me alone!"

He spurred ahead, leaping out into the forest. Binabik and Sludig, not yet mounted, shouted after him, but their words were lost in the din inside his head.

The door is open! Come to us!

The stars were speaking to him, telling him to sleep, that when he awoke he would be far away from . . . eyes in the fire . . . from . . . Skodi . . . from . . . clawing fingers . . . from . . . he would be far away from . . .

The door is open! Come to us!

He rode heedlessly through the snowy woods trying to outrun the terrible voice. Branches tore at his face. Stars peered coldly down through the trees. Time passed, perhaps hours, but still he rode wildly onward. Homefinder seemed to feel his frenzy. Her hooves flung clouds of snow as they pounded through the darkness. Simon was alone, his friends far behind, but still the fire-thing spoke gleefully inside his thoughts.

Come, manchild! Come, dragon-burned! It is a wild night! We await you beneath the ice-mountain. . . .

The words in Simon's head were a swarm of fiery bees. He writhed in the saddle, striking at himself, slapping at his ears and face as he tried to drive the voice away. Even as he flailed, something loomed abruptly before him—a patch of blackness deeper than the night. In a split instant he felt his heart falter, but it was only a tree. A tree!

His headlong flight was too madly swift to avoid the obstacle. He was struck as though by a giant hand and thrown from Homefinder's saddle, tumbling through nothingness. He was falling. The stars were fading.

Black night came down and covered all.

17

A Wager of Little Value

The afternoon had worn away. The wind-scoured sky stretched above the grasslands like a purple awning. The first stars were coming out. Deornoth, wrapped in a coarse blanket against the chill, stared up at the faint points of light and wondered if God had finally turned away His face.

Josua's people were huddled together in a bull run, a long, narrow pen of wooden palings driven deep into the earth and lashed together with rope. For all their seeming flimsiness—in many places there were gaps so wide that Deornoth could slip through his entire arm and most of his shoulder—the walls were strong as mortared stone.

As he looked around at his fellow prisoners, Deornoth's gaze stopped on Geloë. The witch woman held Leleth in her lap, singing quietly into the child's ear as they both stared up at the darkening sky.

"It seems madness that we should escape from Norns and diggers to end here." Deornoth could not keep an aggrieved tone from his voice. "Geloë, you know charms and spells. Could you not have magicked our captors somehow—put them to sleep, or turned yourself into a ravening beast and attacked them?"

"Deornoth," Josua said warningly, but the forest woman needed no defending.

"You understand little, Sir Deornoth, of how The Art works," Geloë replied sharply. "First of all, what you call 'magic' has its cost. If it could be easily used to defeat a dozen armed men, the armies of princes would be full of hired wizards. Secondly, we have not been harmed yet. I am no Pryrates: I do not waste my strength in puppet plays for the bored and curious. I have a greater enemy to occupy my thoughts, more dangerous by far than anyone in this encampment."

As if giving such a long answer exasperated her—and indeed, Geloë seldom said so much at once—she fell silent, turning away to stare at the firmament once more.

Frustrated with himself, Deornoth shrugged off his blanket and stood. Had it come to this? What sort of knight was he, that berated an old woman for not saving him from danger? A shiver of anger and disgust traveled through him; he clenched and unclenched his fists helplessly. What could he do? What strength did any of this ragged band have left to do anything?

Isorn was comforting his mother. Duchess Gutrun's remarkable courage had held though any number of horrors, but she seemed to have reached her limit. Sangfugol was crippled. Towser had virtually given in to madness. The old man lay curled on the ground, his eyes fixed witlessly on nothing, seamed lips trembling as Father Strangyeard tried to help him drink from a bowl of water. Deornoth felt another wave of despair rise and break within him as he walked slowly to the muddy log on which Prince Josua sat, chin on hand.

The manacle that had once prisoned him in Elias' dungeon still dangled on the prince's slender wrist. Josua's thin face was painted with deep shadows, but the whites of his eyes gleamed as he watched Deornoth slump down beside him. For a long while the two did not speak. The sounds of lowing cattle and the shout and clatter of horsemen could be heard all around as the Thrithings-men brought in their herds for the night.

"Welladay, friend," the prince said at last. "I said it was a poor game at best, did I not?"

"We have done what we could, Highness. No one could have done more than you."

"Someone has." For a moment, Josua seemed to regain his dry humor. "He is sitting his skeletal throne in the Hayholt, drinking and eating before a roaring fire, while we sit waiting in the slaughter pen."

"He has made a foul bargain, Prince. The king will regret his choice."

"But we, I fear, will not be around when the reckoning comes." Josua sighed. "I am almost sorriest for you, Deornoth. You have been the most faithful of knights. If you had only found a better lord to be faithful to . . ."

"Please, Highness." In his present mood, such words brought Deornoth real pain. "There is no one I would rather serve outside the Kingdom of Heaven."

Josua looked at him from the sides of his eyes, but did not reply. A party of horsemen rode past the stockade, the palings rippling as the horses thundered by.

"We are far from that kingdom, Deornoth," the prince said at last, "but at the same time only a few breaths away." His face was now hidden in darkness. "But death frightens me little. It is the hopes I have crushed that weigh down my soul."

"Josua," Deornoth began, but the prince's hand on his arm stilled him.

"Say nothing. It is no more than the truth. I have been a lodestar for disaster since the moment I drew breath. My mother died birthing me, and my father's greatest friend Camaris died soon after. My brother's wife died in my care. Her only child has escaped my guardianship to suffer Aedon only knows what fate. Naglimund, a keep built to hold siege for years, fell beneath me in weeks; countless innocents died horribly."

"I cannot listen to this, my prince. Would you take all the world's betrayals on your own back? You did everything that you could!"

"Did I?" Josua asked seriously, as though he debated a point of theology with the Usirean brothers. "I wonder. If things are fated, then perhaps I am merely a sorry strand in God the Highest's tapestry. But some say that one chooses everything, even the bad."

"Foolishness."

"Perhaps. But there is no doubting that an evil star has hung over all I have undertaken. Hah! How the angels and devils both must have laughed when I swore I would take back the Dragonbone Chair! Me, with my ragtag army of priests and jugglers and women!" The prince laughed bitterly.

Deornoth felt anger boiling inside him once more, but this time it was his liege lord who was the cause. It was almost breathtaking. He had never thought he could feel like this.

"My prince," he said between clenched teeth, "you have become a fool, a damnable fool. Priests, jugglers, and women! An army of mounted knights could scarcely have done more than your women and jugglers—and certainly could not have been braver!" Shaking with fury, he rose and stalked away across the muddy compound. The stars seemed almost to tilt in the sky.

A hand closed on his shoulder, pulling him around with surprising strength. Josua stood stiffly as he held Deornoth at arm's length. The prince jutted his head forward on his long neck, a bird of prey preparing to stoop.

"And what have I done to you, Deornoth, that you speak so to me?" His voice was tight.

At any other moment Deornoth would have fallen to his knees, ashamed at his own disrespectfulness. Now, he stilled his trembling muscles and took a breath before he spoke. "I can love you, Joshua, yet hate what you say."

The prince stared at him, his expression indecipherable in the evening dark. "I spoke badly of our companions. That was wrong. But I said nothing ill of you, Sir Deornoth . . ."

"Elysia, Mother of God, Josua!" Deornoth almost sobbed, "I care nothing for myself! And as for the others, that was only a careless remark that you made out of weariness. I know you meant nothing by it. No, it is *you* who are the victim of your own cruelest treatment! *That* is why you are a fool!"

Josua stiffened. "What?"

Deornoth threw his arms up in the air, filled with the sort of giddy madness felt on Midsummer's Eve, when all wore masks and told the truth. But here in the bull run there were no masks. "You are a better enemy to yourself than Elias can ever be," he shouted, not caring anymore who heard. "Your blame, your guilt, your failed duty! If Usires Aedon were to return to Nabban today, and again be hung on the Tree in the temple garden, you would find a way to blame it on yourself! No matter who is speaking the evil, I will listen to a fine man slandered *no longer!*"

Josua stared as if stunned. The terrible silence was broken by the creak of the wooden gate. Half a dozen men with spears pushed into the stockade, led by the one named Hotvig who had captured them on the Ymstrecca's banks. He strode forward, peering around the shadowed pen.

"Josua? Come here."

"What do you want?" the prince asked quietly.

"The March-thane has called for you. Now." Two of Hotvig's men moved up, lowering their spear points. Deornoth tried to catch Josua's eye, but the prince turned away and walked out slowly between the two Thrithings-men. Hotvig pulled the high gate shut behind them. The wooden bolt creaked back into place.

"You don't think that . . . that they will harm him, do you, Deornoth?" Strangyeard asked. "They wouldn't hurt the prince, would they?"

Deornoth sank down onto the muddy ground, tears rolling down his cheeks.

The interior of Fikolmij's wagon smelled of grease and smoke and oiled leather. The March-thane looked up from his joint of beef to nod Hotvig back out the door, then returned his attention to his meal, leaving Josua to stand and wait. They were not alone. The man standing beside Fikolmij was half a head taller than Josua and only slightly less muscled than the broad March-thane himself. His face, clean-shaven but for long mustaches, was covered with scars too regular to be accidental. He returned the prince's stare with undisguised contempt. One hand, clatteringly laden with bracelets, dropped to caress the hilt of his long curved sword.

Josua held this one's narrowed eyes for a moment, then casually allowed his glance to slide away, taking in the vast array of harnesses and saddles hanging from the wagon's walls and ceiling, their myriad silver buckles glittering in the firelight.

"You have discovered some of the virtues of comfort, Fikolmij," Josua said, eyeing the rugs and stitched cushions scattered over the floor boards.

The March-thane looked up, then spat into the fire-trough. "Pfah. I sleep beneath stars, as I always have. But I need someplace safe from listening ears." He bit at the joint and chewed vigorously. "I am no stone-dweller, who wears a shell like a soft-skinned snail." A piece of clanking bone rattled into the trough.

"It has been some time since I have slept behind walls or in a bed myself, Fikolmij. You can see that. Did you bring me here to call me soft? If so, have done and let me go back to my people. Or did you bring me here to kill me? The fellow beside you has somewhat the look of a head-chopper."

Fikolmij dropped the denuded bone into the fire and grinned hugely, his eyes red as a boar's. "You don't know him? He knows you. Don't you, Utvart?"

"I know him." He had a deep voice.

The March-thane now leaned forward, peering at the prince intently. "By the Four-Footed," he laughed, "Prince Josua has more gray hairs than old Fikolmij! Living in your stone houses makes a man old fast."

Josua smiled thinly. "I have had a difficult spring."

"You have! You have!" Fikolmij was enjoying himself immensely. He picked up a bowl and tilted it to his mouth.

"What do you want of me, Fikolmij?"

"It is not me that wants, Josua, despite your sin against me. It is Utvart here." He nodded at his glowering companion. "We spoke of age. Utvart has only a few years less than you, but he does not wear a man's beard. Do you know why?"

Utvart stirred, rubbing his fingers on his pommel. "I have no wife," he rumbled.

Josua looked from man to man, but said nothing.

"You are a clever man, Prince Josua," Fikolmij said slowly, then took another long draught. "You see the problem. Utvart's bride was stolen. He has sworn never to marry until the one who stole her is dead."

"Dead," Utvart echoed.

Josua's lip curled. "I stole no one's bride. Vorzheva came to me after I had left your camp. She begged to go away with me."

Fikolmij slammed the bowl down, splashing dark beer into the fire trough, which hissed as if startled. "Curse you, did your father have no male children!? What true man hides behind a woman, or allows one to have her way? Her bride-price was set! All was agreed!"

"Vorzheva had not agreed."

The March-thane rose from his stool, staring at Josua as though the prince were a poisonous serpent. Fikolmij's corded arms trembled. "You stone-dwellers are a pestilence. One day the men of the Free Thrithings will drive you into the sea and burn away your rotting cities with clean fire."

Josua eyed him evenly. "The men of the Thrithings have tried that before. It is how we met, you and I. Or have you forgotten the uncomfortable fact of our alliance—an alliance against your own people?"

Fikolmij spat again, and this time did not bother to aim for the trough. "It was a chance to increase my strength. It worked. I stand today unquestioned lord of the High Thrithings." He stared at Josua as if daring him to argue. "Besides, that treaty was with your father. For a stone-dweller, he was a mighty man. You are a thin shadow of him."

Josua's face was empty. "I am tired of talking. Kill me if you wish, but do not bore me."

Fikolmij leaped forward. His broad fist crashed against the side of Josua's head and the prince crumpled to his knees. "Proud talk, worm! I should kill you with my own hands!" The March-thane stood over Josua, his barrel chest heaving. *"Where is my daughter!?"*

"I don't know."

Fikolmij grabbed Joshua's tattered shirt and pulled the prince onto his feet. Watching, Utvart swayed gently from side to side, his eyes dreamy. "And you don't care, either, do you? By the Grass Thunderer, I have dreamed of smashing you—dreamed of it! Tell me of my Vorzheva, child-stealer. Did you at least marry her?"

A bleeding welt showed at Josua's temple. He stared back. "We did not wish to marry . . ."

Another blow rocked the prince's head. Blood started from his upper lip and nose. "How you laughed at old Fikolmij when you sat in your stone house, eh?" the March-thane hissed. "Stole his daughter and made her your whore, then did not have to pay a single horse for her! You laughed, didn't you?" He slapped hard at the prince's face; pearls of blood flew through the air. "You thought you could cut off my stones and run away." The March-thane struck again, but though fresh blood seeped from Josua's nose, this blow was softer, dealt with a kind of savage affection. "You are clever, Lackhand. Clever. But Fikolmij is no gelding."

"Vorzheva . . . is . . . no . . . whore."

Fikolmij propelled him back against the wagon's door. The prince left his arms dangling, making no attempt to defend himself as he was struck twice more. "You stole what was mine," Fikolmij snarled, his face so close to Josua's that his braided beard rubbed on the prince's bloody shirtfront. "What would you call her, then? What did you use her for?"

Josua's red-smeared face, despite his injuries, had been full of a terrible calmness. Now, it seemed to break apart, dissolving into grief.

"I . . . used her badly . . ." He hung his head.

Utvart strode forward, drawing his sword from its tooled and beaded scabbard. The tip clicked against a ceiling beam. "Let me kill him," he breathed. "Slow."

Fikolmij looked up, eyes squinting fiercely. Sweat dripped from his face as he looked from Utvart to Josua, then lifted his thick-knuckled fist over the prince's head.

"Let *me*," Utvart pleaded.

The March-thane hammered three times against the wall. The harnesses swayed, tinkling. "Hotvig!" he roared.

The wagon door opened. Hotvig entered, pushing a slender figure before him. The pair stopped just within the doorway.

"You heard all!" Fikolmij bellowed. "You betrayed your clan and me . . . for *this!*" He gave Josua's shoulder a push. The prince fell back against the wall and slid to the floor.

Vorzheva burst into tears. Hotvig's restraining hand held her back as she leaned forward to touch the prince. Josua slowly lifted his head, staring at her distractedly from eyes that were beginning to swell shut. "You are alive," was all he said.

She tried to pull away from her captor, but Hotvig grasped her close, ignoring the nails that raked at his arm, leaning his head away when she tried to reach his eyes.

"Randwarders caught her in the outer grazing march," Fikolmij growled. He slapped at her lightly, angered by her struggling. "Be still, you faithless bitch! I should have drowned you in the Umstrejha at birth. You are worse than your mother, and she was the evilest cow I have ever known. Why do you waste your tears on this piece of dung?" He prodded Josua with his foot.

The prince's absorbed look had returned. He regarded the March-thane with dispassionate interest for a moment before turning to Vorzheva. "I am glad you are safe."

"Safe!" Vorzheva laughed shrilly. "I love a man who does not want me. The man who *does* want me would use me like a brood mare and beat me if I ever left my knees!" She struggled in Hotvig's grasp, turning to face Utvart, who had lowered his sword to the floor. "Oh, I remember you, Utvart! Why did I run away, except to get away from you, you raper of children—and of young sheep when you cannot get a child! You, who love your scars more than you ever could a woman. I would rather be dead than your bride!"

Grim-faced Utvart said nothing, but Fikolmij snorted in dour amusement. "By the Four-Footed, I had almost forgotten that jagged knife you have for a tongue, daughter. Maybe Josua here is happy to feel the blows of fists for a change, eh? As for what you prefer, kill yourself the moment the marriage ride is over if you wish. I only want my bride-price and the honor of the Stallion Clan made good."

"There are better ways to do that than slaughtering helpless prisoners," a new voice said.

All heads turned—even Josua's, though he moved carefully. Geloë stood in the doorway, arms spread to the lintel, cloak rippling in the wind.

"They have escaped from the bull run!" Fikolmij shouted wrathfully. "Don't move, woman! Hotvig, saddle and bring the rest back. Someone will howl for this!"

Geloë stepped into the wagon, which was rapidly becoming crowded. With a muffled curse, Hotvig pushed past her and out into the darkness. The witch woman calmly pulled the door closed behind him. "He will find them still penned," she said. "Only I can come and go as I please."

Utvart lifted his broad blade and held it near her neck. Geloë's hooded yellow eyes touched his and the tall Thrithings-man stepped back a pace, brandishing the sword as though he were menaced.

Fikolmij looked her up and down with puzzlement and guarded anger. "What is your business, old woman?"

Released from Hotvig's grip, Vorzheva had dropped to her knees and crawled past her father to dab at Josua's face with her tattered cloak. The prince gently caught her hand, holding it away as Geloë spoke.

"I said, I come and go as I please. For now, I choose to be here."

"You are in my wagon, old woman." The March-thane wiped sweat from his forehead with a hairy arm.

"You thought to hold Geloë your prisoner, Fikolmij. That was foolish. Still, I have come to give you advice, in hopes that you have more sense than you have shown so far this day."

He seemed to fight an urge to strike out once more. Seeing his struggle, his strained look, Geloë nodded her head and smiled grimly.

"You have heard of me."

"I have heard of a devil-woman with your name, one who lurks in the forest and steals the souls of men," Fikolmij grunted. Utvart stood close behind him, mouth set in a tight line, but the tall man's eyes were wide, and shifted as though he made certain of where the doors and windows were.

"You have heard many false rumors, I am sure," Geloë said, "but there is some truth behind them, however twisted it may have become. That truth is in the tales that say I make a bad enemy, Fikolmij." She blinked slowly, as an owl blinks when it catches sight of something small and helpless. "A bad enemy."

The March-thane pulled his beard. "I do not fear you, woman, but I do not trifle with demons needlessly. You are no use to me. Go away, then, and I will not trouble you, but do not meddle in what does not concern you."

"Fool of a horse-lord!" Geloë flung up her arm, cloak trailing like a black wing. The door burst open behind her. The wind that swept in extinguished the lamps and plunged the wagon into near-darkness, leaving only the fire glowing scarlet in its trough like a door into Hell. Somebody cursed fearfully, barely audible above the moaning inrush. "I told you," Geloë cried, "I go where I please!" The door swung shut again, although the witch woman had not moved. The wind was gone. She leaned forward so that her yellow eyes reflected restless flames. "What happens to these people *does* concern me—and concerns you as well, although you are too ignorant to know it. Our enemy is your enemy, and he is greater than you can understand, Fikolmij. When he comes, he will sweep across your fields like a grassfire."

"Hah!" The March-thane smirked, but the nervous edge was not gone from his voice. "Do not preach to me. I know all about your enemy, King Elias. He is no more a man than Josua here. The Thrithings-men do not fear him."

Before Geloë could respond there was a rap at the door, which swung open to reveal Hotvig, bearing his spear and a puzzled expression. He was only a young man, despite his heavy beard, and he regarded the witch woman with undisguised dismay as he spoke to his chieftain.

"The prisoners are still in the bull run. None of the men outside saw this one leave. The gate is locked, and there are no holes in the fence."

Fikolmij grunted and waved his hand. "I know." The March-thane's gaze shifted to Geloë for a brooding moment, then he smiled slowly. "Come here," he ordered Hotvig, then whispered into the rider's ear.

"It will be done," Hotvig said, darting a nervous glance at Geloë before going out again.

"So," Fikolmij said, and smiled broadly, showing most of his crooked teeth. "You think I should set this dog free to run away." He shoved Josua with his foot, earning a swift glare of hatred from his daughter. "What if I do not?" he asked cheerfully.

Geloë narrowed her eyes. "As I told you, March-thane: I make a bad enemy."

Fikomij chortled. "And what shall you do to me, when I have told my men to kill the remaining prisoners unless I come to them myself before the next watch of the night to say otherwise?" He patted his hands on his belly in contentment. "I do not doubt you have charms and spells that can harm me, but now our blades are at each other's throats, are they not?" In the corner of the wagon Utvart growled, as if excited by the image invoked.

"Oh, horse-lord, may the world be preserved from such as you," Geloë said disgustedly. "I hoped to convince you to help us, which would be for your good as much as ours." She shook her head. "Now, as you say, our knives are out. Who knows if they may be put away without causing many deaths?"

"I do not fear your threats," Fikolmij growled.

Geloë stared at him for a moment, then looked at Josua, who was still seated on the floor watching all that transpired with odd placidity. Lastly, she turned her gaze on Utvart. The tall man scowled fiercely, not at all comfortable under her scrutiny. "I think there is still one favor I can do for you, March-thane Fikolmij."

"I need no . . ."

"Quiet!" Geloë shouted. The March-thane fell silent, balling his fists, his reddened eyes bulging. "You are about to break your own laws," she said. "The laws of the High Thrithings. I will help you avoid that."

"What madness are you speaking, devil-woman?!" he raged. "I am the lord of the clans!"

"The clan councils honor no man as March-thane who breaks their old laws," she replied. "I know this. I know many things."

With a sweep of his arm, Fikolmij sent a bowl flying from atop his stool to clatter against the wagon's far wall. "What law? Tell me what law or I will throttle you even though you burn me to ashes!"

"The laws of bride-price and betrothal." Geloë pointed at Josua. "You would kill this man, but he is her betrothed. If another—" she indicated brooding Utvart, "—wishes to have her, he must fight for her. Is that not true, Thane?"

Fikolmij smiled, a great rancid grin that spread across his face like a stain. "You have outsmarted yourself, meddler. They are not betrothed. Josua admitted that from his own lips. I would break no law to kill him. Utvart stands ready to pay the bride-price."

Geloë looked at him intently. "They are not married and Josua has not asked her. This is true. But have you forgotten your own customs, Fikolmij of the Stallion-Clan? There are other forms of betrothal."

He spat. "None but fathering . . ." he broke off, forehead wrinkling in a sudden thought. "A child?"

Geloë said nothing.

Vorzheva did not look up. Her face was hidden by her dark hair, but her hand, which had stroked the prince's bloodied cheek, froze like a snake-startled rabbit.

"It is true," she said finally.

Josua's face was a complicated puzzle of emotions, made even harder to read by the elaborate tracing of bruises and weals. "You. . . ? How long have you known. . . ? You said nothing . . ."

"I have known since just before Naglimund fell," Vorzheva said. "I feared to tell you."

Josua watched the tears cutting new tracks along her dusty cheeks. He lifted his hand to touch her arm briefly before allowing it to drop back into his lap, then looked from Vorzheva up to Geloë. The witch woman held his eye for a long moment; some communicated thought seemed to pass between them.

"By the Four-Footed," Fikolmij growled at last, bemused. "A child-betrothal, is it? If it's even his, that is."

"It *is* his, you pig!" Vorzheva said fiercely. "It could be no one else's."

Utvart stepped forward, boot buckles chinking. His swordpoint thumped down into the floor boards, sinking half an inch into the wood. "A challenge, then," he said. "To the death we fight." He looked to Geloë and his expression became cautious. "Vorzheva, the March-thane's daughter, she is spoils." Turning back to the prince, he tugged his sword free. The great curved glade came loose as lightly as a feather. "A challenge." Josua's eyes were hard as he spoke through torn lips. "God hears."

Deornoth stared down at his prince's battered features. "In the morning!?" he cried, loud enough to draw a scowl from one of the guards. The Thrithings-men, bundled in heavy woolen cloaks against the chill, did not look pleased with their assignment in the windy bull run. "Why do they not just kill you cleanly?"

"It is a chance," Joshua said, then surrendered to a fit of coughing.

"What chance?" Deornoth said bitterly. "That a one-handed man who has been beaten bloody can get up in the morning and outfight a giant? Merciful Aedon, if I could only get my hands on that snake Fikolmij . . ."

Josua's only reply was to spit bloodily into the mud.

"The prince is correct," Geloë said. "It is a chance. Anything is better than nothing."

The witch woman had returned to the bull run to tend the prince. The guards had stepped back quickly to let her pass: something of her nature had traveled through the camp in swift whispers. Fikolmij's daughter had not come with her. Vorzheva had been locked in her father's wagon, tears of sorrow and anger still damp on her face.

"But you had him at a disadvantage," Deornoth said to the witchwoman. "Why did you not strike then? Why did you let him send guards?"

Geloë's yellow eyes glittered in the torchlight. "I had no advantage at all. I told you once, Sir Deornoth, I cannot make warlike magic. I escaped this stockade, yes, but other than that it was all bluff. Now, if you will be silent about what you do not know, I will put my true skills to their proper use." She returned her attention to the prince.

*How **did** she escape the stockade?* Deornoth could not help wondering. One moment Geloë had been wandering in the shadows at the far end of the bull run, the next she had been gone.

He shook his head. It was useless to argue, and he had been little else but useless of late. He touched Josua's thin arm. "If I may be of any help, my prince, only ask." He dropped to his knees, then looked briefly to the witch woman. "I apologize for my unthinking words, Valada Geloë."

She grunted an acknowledgment. Deornoth rose and walked away.

The rest of the starveling band was seated by the other fire. The Thrithings-men, being not entirely without mercy, had given them brush and twigs with which to build it. They were not merciless, Deornoth thought, but not stupid, either: such poor fuel would provide heat—barely—but could not be used as a weapon, as could a flaming brand. The thought of weapons set him to musing as he seated himself between Sangfugol and Father Strangyeard.

"This is a foul way to end things," he said. "You have heard what has happened to Josua?"

Strangyeard swung his slender hands. "They are untutored barbarians, these grasslanders. Mother Elysia, I know all men are equal in God's eyes, but this is atrocious! I mean to say, even ignorance is not an excuse for such . . ." He trailed off fretfully.

Sangfugol sat up, wincing at the pain in his leg. Anyone who knew him would have been astonished: the harper, previously meticulous in grooming and dress almost to the point of comedy, was as ragged, soiled, and burr-covered as a haystack vagabond. "And if Josua dies?" he said quietly. "He is my master and I love him, I suppose, but if he dies—*what happens to us?*"

"If we are lucky, we will be little better than slaves," Deornoth said, hearing his own words as if from another's lips. He felt quite hollow. How had things come to such a point? A year earlier the world had been as regular as supper bread. "If we are *unlucky* . . ." he continued, but did not finish his thought—nor did he need to.

"It will be worse on the women," Sangfugol whispered, looking over to Duchess Gutrun, who held sleeping Leleth on her lap. "These men are ungodly brutes. Have you seen the scars they give themselves?"

"Isorn," Deornoth called suddenly. "Come here, if you please."

Duke Isgrimnur's son crawled around the meager fire to sit near them.

"I think," Deornoth said, "that we must prepare ourselves to do something tomorrow when Josua is made to fight."

Strangyeard looked up, worried. "But we are so few . . . half a dozen in the midst of thousands."

Isorn nodded, a grim little smile showing on his wide face. "At least we can choose the way we die. I will not let them have my mother." The smile vanished. "By Usires, I swear I would kill her first."

Sangfugol looked around as if hoping they would reveal their joke. "But we have no weapons!" he whispered urgently. "Are you mad? Perhaps we might live if we do nothing, but if we make trouble we will certainly die."

Deornoth shook his head. "No, harper. If we do not fight, we will certainly be less than men, whether they kill us or not. We will be less than dogs, who at least rip the bear's guts as he kills them." His gaze traveled from face to face. "Sangfugol," he said at last, "we must plan. Why don't you sing a song against the chance of any of these cow-herders wondering why we are gathered or what we speak of."

"A song? What do you mean?"

"A song. A long, boring song about the virtues of quiet surrender. If it comes to an end and we are still talking, begin again."

The harper was plainly agitated. "I know no tune like that!"

"Then make one up, Song-bird," Isorn laughed. "We have been too long without music, anyway. If we die tomorrow, we should live tonight."

"Make it a part of your plans, if you will," Sangfugol said, "that I would prefer not to die at all." He sat up straighter and began to hum tunelessly, searching for words. "I am frightened," he said at last.

"So are we," Deornoth replied. "Sing."

Fikolmij swaggered into the bull run soon after dawn touched the gray sky. The March-thane of the High Thrithings wore a heavy embroidered wool cloak and a rugged gold stallion on a chain around his neck. He seemed to be in an expansive mood.

"So the reckoning comes," he laughed, then spat upon the ground. His wrists were weighty with metal bracelets. "Do you feel fit, Josua Lackhand?"

"I have felt fitter," Josua said, tugging on his boot. "Do you have my sword?"

Fikolmij waved; Hotvig stepped forward bearing Naidel in its sheath. The young Thrithings-man watched the prince curiously as Josua drew the sword belt around his hips, managing adroitly despite his missing hand. When it was buckled, Josua drew Naidel out, holding the slender blade up to catch the morning light. Hotvig stepped back respectfully. "May I have a whetstone?" Josua asked. "The edge is dull."

The March-thane chuckled and produced his own kit from a pouch on his wide belt. "Sharpen it, stone-dweller, sharpen it. We want the only the best sport, as you have at your city tournaments. But this will not be quite the same as your castle-games, will it?"

Josua shrugged, smearing a thin film of oil along Naidel's cutting surface. "I have never cared much for those, either."

Fikolmij's eyes narrowed. "You seem very fit indeed, after the lesson I gave you last night. Has this witch cast some spell on you? That would be dishonorable."

Joshua shrugged again to show how little he cared about Fikolmij's ideas of honor, but Geloë stepped forward. "There have been no charms, no spells."

Fikolmij eyed her distrustfully for a moment, then turned back to Josua. "Very well. My men will bring you when you are ready. I am glad to see you up. It will make for a better fight." The March-thane strutted out of the paddock, followed closely by three of his guard.

Deornoth, who had watched the whole exchange, cursed quietly. He knew what effort it had taken his prince to act so unconcerned. He and Isorn had helped Josua climb to his feet in the hour just before first light. Even after the healing draught Geloë had given him—an unmagical concoction to bolster Josua's strength; Geloë had bitterly regretted the lack of a sprig of mockfoil to make it truly efficacious—the prince had still found it difficult to dress himself. The beating Fikolmij had given him had taken a terrible toll on his undernourished frame. Deornoth secretly doubted that Josua would even be able to stand after swinging a blade for a short while.

Father Strangyeard approached the prince. "Your Highness, is there truly no other way? I know the Thrithings-men are barbaric, but God despises none of His creations. He has put the spark of mercy in every breast. Perhaps . . ."

"It is not the Thrithings-men who wish this," Josua told the one-eyed priest kindly, "it is Fikolmij. He bears an old hatred for me and my house, one that even he will not fully admit."

"But I thought the Stallion Clan fought for your father in the Thrithings War," Isorn said. "Why should he hate you?"

"Because it was with my father's help that he became war-thane of the High Thrithings. He cannot forgive the fact that it was the stone-dwellers, as he calls us, who gave him the power his own people would not. Then his daughter ran from him and I took her with me, losing him a bride-price of horses. To our friend the March-thane, that is a terrible dishonor. No, there are no words, priestly or otherwise, that will make Fikolmij forget."

Josua took a last look at Naidel's keen blade, then slid it back into its sheath. He gazed around at his assembled people. "Heads high," he said. The prince seemed strangely clear-eyed and cheerful. "Death is no enemy. God has prepared a place for us all, I am sure." He walked to the gate in the fence. Fikolmij's guards opened it, then formed a spear-bristling escort as Josua walked across the wagon-city.

A swift, cool breeze was blowing across the grasslands, an invisible hand that ruffled the meadows and thrummed in the tentlines. The low hills were dotted with grazing cattle. Scores of grimy children who had been dodging in and out among the wagons left their games to follow Josua and his makeshift court as they trudged toward the March-thane's paddock.

Deornoth looked at the faces of children and their parents as they came to join the swelling procession. Where he expected to see hatred or bloodlust, he found only eager expectancy—the same eagerness he had seen as a child on his brothers' and sisters' faces when the High King's Guard or a painted peddler's wagon had passed their Hewenshire freeholding. These people hoped only for some excitement. It was unfortunate that it would take somebody's death, most likely that of his beloved prince, to provide it.

Golden ribbons flapped on the fenceposts of Fikolmij's enclosure, as if this were a festival day. The March-thane sat on a stool before his wagon door. Several more bejeweled Thrithings-men—other clan leaders, Deornoth guessed—were seated on the ground beside him. Several women of various ages stood nearby, and one of them was Vorzheva. The March-thane's daughter no longer wore the rags of her court dress. She had been dressed in a more traditional clan costume, a hooded wool dress with a heavy belt studded with colorful stones and a band across her forehead that tied at the back of her hood. Unlike the other women, whose bands were of dark hues, Vorzheva wore a white ribbon—no doubt indicating, Deornoth reflected sourly, a bride for sale.

As Josua and his followers stepped through the gate, the prince and Vorzheva caught each others' eyes. Josua deliberately made the sign of the Tree on his chest, then kissed his hand and touched it to that spot. Vorzheva turned away as if to hide tears.

Fikolmij stood and began to speak to the assembled crowd, slipping back and forth between Westerling and the harsh Thrithings dialect as he held forth to the seated dignitaries and the other clanfolk gathered around the paddock fences. As the March-thane roared on, Deornoth slipped forward between the half-dozen spearmen who had followed Josua into the enclosure and moved to his prince's side.

"Highness," he said quietly, laying a hand on his shoulder. The prince started, as if woken from a dream.

"Ah. It's you."

"I wanted to beg your forgiveness, my prince, before . . . before whatever happens. You are the kindest lord a man could want. I had no right to speak to you as I did yesterday."

Josua smiled sadly. "You had every right. I only wish I had more time to think about the things you said. I have indeed been far too self-absorbed of late. It was the act of a friend to point that out."

Deornoth fell to a knee, pulling Josua's hand to his lips. "The Lord bless you, Josua," he said quickly. "Bless you. And do not close too swiftly with that brute."

The prince thoughtfully watched Deornoth rise. "I may have to. I fear I have not the strength to wait long. If I see any chance at all, I must take it."

Deornoth tried to speak again, but his throat was too tight. He clasped Josua's hand, then retreated.

A ragged volley of shouts and cheers rose from the crowd as Utvart climbed over the paddock fence and took his place before Fikolmij. Josua's adversary stripped off his cowhide vest and displayed his muscular torso, which had been rubbed with fat until it glistened. Seeing this, Deornoth frowned: Utvart would be able to move quickly, and the fat would help him keep warm.

The Thrithing-man's curved sword had been thrust scabbardless through his broad belt, his long hair pulled into a knot at the back of his head.

Utvart wore a bracelet on each arm, and several earrings dangled against his jaw. He had daubed his scars with red and black paint, making himself seem a kind of demon.

Now he pulled his sword from his belt and lifted it over his head, engendering another chorus of shouts. "Come, Lackhand," he boomed. "Utvart is waiting."

Father Strangyeard was praying aloud as Josua walked forward across the enclosure. Deornoth found that rather than soothing or reassuring him, the priest's words rubbed on his nerves until he had to step away; after a moment's consideration, he moved to a spot along the fence just to the side of one of the guards. He looked up and saw Isorn staring. Deornoth shifted his chin in a virtually undetectible nod; Isorn eased over toward the wall also, until he stood a few yards from Deornoth.

Josua had left his cloak with Duchess Gutrun, who cradled it like a child. Beside her stood Leleth, dirty fist clutching the duchess' tattered skirt. Geloë was a short distance away, her yellow stare hooded.

As Deornoth surveyed the group, other eyes met his and slid away, as if fearing to maintain too lengthy a contact. Sangfugol quietly began to sing.

"So, son of Prester John, you come before the Free Folk of the Thrithings a little less great than you once were," Fikolmij grinned. His clansmen laughed and whispered.

"Only in my possessions," Josua said calmly. "As a matter of fact, I would like to propose a wager, Fikolmij—between the two of us, you and me."

The March-thane laughed, surprised. "Brave words, Josua, proud words coming from a man who knows he will soon die." Fikolmij looked him over calculatingly. "What kind of wager?"

The prince slapped his scabbard. "I propose to bet on this and my good left hand."

"Good, since it is your only hand," Fikolmij smirked. His clansmen roared.

"That is as may be. If Utvart defeats me, he gets Vorzheva and you get her bride-price, is that not true?"

"Thirteen horses." The March-thane was smug. "What of it?"

"Simply this. Vorzheva is already mine. We are betrothed. If I survive, I gain nothing new." His eyes met Vorzheva's across the crowd of watchers, then moved back to her father with cold regard.

"You gain your life!" Fikolmij spluttered. "In any case, it is foolish to talk. You will not survive."

Utvart, waiting impatiently, allowed himself a thin smile at his thane's words.

"That is why I wish to make a wager with you," Josua said. "With you, Fikolmij. Between men." Some of the clansmen chuckled at this; Fikolmij looked around angrily until they fell silent.

"Speak on."

"It will be a wager of little value, Fikolmij, the kind that bold-willed men make without hesitation in the cities of my people. If *I* win, you will give me the same price you are asking from Utvart." Josua smiled. "I will choose thirteen horses from you."

There was an undertone of anger in Fikolmij's hoarse voice. "Why should I wager with you at all? A wager is only a wager if both sides risk something. What could you possibly have that I want?" His expression turned cunning. "And what do you have that I cannot simply take from your people when you are dead?"

"Honor."

Fikolmij drew back in surprise. The whispers around him intensified. "By the Four-Footed, what does that mean?! I care little for your soft-hearted, stone-dweller's honor."

"Ah," Josua said with a ghost of a smile, *"but your own?"*

The prince turned suddenly to face the crowd of Thrithings-folk who hung over the fences of Fikolmij's great paddock. A ripple of quiet talk ran through the throng. "Free men and women of the High Thrithings!" he cried. "You have come to see me killed." A bray of laughter greeted this statement. A clod of dirt hurtled toward Josua, missing him by only a few cubits and rolling past Fikolmij's clansmen, who glared out at the assembly. "I have offered your March-thane a wager. I swear that the Aedon, god of the stone-dwellers, will save me—and that I will beat Utvart."

"That would be something to see!" one of the crowd bellowed in heavily-accented Westerling. There was more laughter. Fikolmij stood and moved toward Josua as if to silence him, but after looking around at the shouting spectators seemed to think better of it. Instead, he crossed his arms over his broad chest and watched sullenly. "What do you wager, little man?" one of the clansmen near the front shouted.

"All that remains to me: my honor and the honor of my people." Josua drew Naidel from its sheath and lifted it high. His shirt sleeve fell back; Elias' rusted manacle, which he still wore around his left wrist, caught the faint morning light like a band of blood. "I am the son of Prester John, the High King who you remember well. Fikolmij knew him best of all of you." The crowd murmured. The March-thane growled his discontent at this show.

"Here is my wager," Josua shouted. "If I fall to Utvart, I swear it will prove that our god Usires Aedon is weak, and that Fikolmij speaks true when he says that he is stronger than the stone-dwellers. You will know that your March-thane's Stallion is mightier than the Dragon and Tree of John's house, which is the greatest house in all the city-lands of Osten Ard."

A chorus of shouting voices rose. Josua calmly surveyed the crowd. "What does Fikolmij wager?" someone cried at last. Utvart, standing only a few ells away, was glowering at Josua, obviously furious at how his thunder had been stolen, but just as obviously unsure as to whether Josua's wager could somehow increase his own glory when he slaughtered this crippled city-dweller.

"As many horses as Vorzheva's bride-price. And my people and I to go free and unhindered," Josua said. "Not much when matched against the honor of a prince of Erkynland."

"A prince with no house!" someone catcalled, but a host of other voices drowned out the heckler, exhorting Fikolmij to take the wager, crying that he would be a fool to let this stone-dweller show him up. The March-thane, features twisted in poorly-hidden rage, let the crowd's urgings wash over him like rain. He looked quite ready to grasp Josua's neck in his hands and throttle the prince himself.

"So. It is done," he snarled at last, lifting his arm in a gesture of acceptance. The watchers cheered. "By the Grass Thunderer, you have heard him. The wager is set. My horses against his empty words. Now, let this foolishness come to a swift end." Much of the March-thane's enjoyment seemed to have evaporated. He leaned forward, speaking low so that only Josua could hear. "When you are dead, I will kill your women and children with my own hands. Slowly. No man makes me butt of a joke before my clans and steals my rightful horses." Fikolmij turned and stalked back to his stool, frowning at the jests from his randwarders.

As Josua unbuckled and cast away his sword belt, Utvart stepped forward, corded arms gleaming as he lifted his heavy blade.

"You talk and talk and talk, little man," the grasslander snarled. "You talk too much."

A moment later he bounded across the intervening space in three long strides, his sword swinging in a great arc. Naidel flashed up, deflecting the blow with a dull chime, but before Josua could bring his slim blade up for a cut of his own, Utvart had whirled and begun another powerful, two-handed sweep. Josua again managed to sidestep Utvart's attack, but this time the curved sword rang hard against the prince's guard and Naidel almost flew from his hand. He staggered back a few steps across the muddy turf before he could regain his balance. Utvart grinned fiercely and began circling, forcing Josua to turn quickly so the prince could keep his left shoulder facing the Thrithings-man. Utvart feinted, then lunged. Josua's boot heel slid on the hoof-trampled ground, forcing him to drop to one knee. He managed to turn Utvart's thrust, but as the big man pulled his blade free it sawed back across Josua's sword arm, freeing a ribbon of blood.

The prince rose carefully. Utvart showed his teeth and continued circling. A trickle of red dripped from the back of Josua's hand. The prince
wiped it on the leg of his breeches, then raised it again quickly as Utvart
feigned another thrust. Moments later the blood was again dribbling
down Josua's wrist and onto his hilt.

Deornoth thought he understood the strange business of the wager—
Josua was hoping to make Fikolmij and Utvart angry in the hope it would
lead to some sort of mistake—but the prince's idea had all too obviously
not succeeded. The March-thane was indeed furious, but Josua was not
battling Fikolmij, and Utvart did not seem as hot-headed as the prince had
probably hoped. Instead, the Thrithings-man was proving himself a canny
fighter. Rather than relying blindly on his superior strength and reach, he
was wearing Josua down with heavy blows, then springing away before
the prince could counter.

As he watched the one-sided combat, Deornoth felt his heart falling like
a stone. It had been foolish to think anything else could happen. Josua was
a fine swordsman, but he would have had trouble with one like Utvart at
the best of times. Today, the prince was injured and poorly-rested, weak
as a stripling. It was only a matter of time. . . .

Deornoth turned to Isorn. The young Rimmersman shook his head
grimly: he, too, understood that Josua was fighting a defensive action,
putting off the inevitable as long as possible. Isorn lifted his eyebrow
inquiringly. *Now?*

Father Strangyeard's murmured prayers were a counterpoint to the
shouting throng. The guards around them were staring raptly, eyes wide,
spears held only loosely. Deornoth lifted his hand. *Wait* . . .

Blood was rilling from two more wounds, a slash on Josua's left wrist
and a broad gouge in his leg. The prince wiped sweat from his forehead
and left a broad scarlet smear across his face, as though he sought to match
Utvart's painted scars.

Josua stumbled back, ducking awkwardly beneath another of Utvart's
swinging attacks, then tensed and lunged forward. His thrust ended harm-
lessly, well short of Utvart's oiled stomach. The Thrithings-man, silent to
this point, laughed harshly and cut again. Josua blocked, then attacked.
Utvart's eyes widened, and for a moment the paddock echoed with the
percussive sound of steel on steel. Most of the throng were up and
shouting. Slender Naidel and Utvart's long sword spun in and out through
an intricate dance of silver light, ringing their own accompaniment.

The Thrithings-man's mouth stretched in a grimace of wild glee, but
Josua's face was ashen, his bloodless lips pursed and his gray eyes burning
with some last reserve of strength. Two of the Thrithings-man's powerful
swings were clangingly rebuffed, then Josua's swift lunge drew a bright

red line along Utvart's ribs. Some in the watching crowd shouted and clapped at this evidence that the fight was not yet over, but Utvart narrowed his eyes in anger and surged forward, raining blows like a blacksmith hammering at an anvil. Staggered, Josua could only retreat, trying to keep Naidel up before him, the thin strip of steel his only shield. The prince's weak attempt at a counter-thrust was carelessly knocked aside, then one of Utvart's bludgeoning swipes banged off the prince's guard and struck his head. Josua lurched backward for several loose-jointed steps before slumping to his knees, blood coursing from a spot just above his ear. He lifted Naidel before him as though to ward off more blows, but his eyes were bleary and the sword wavered like a willow limb.

The noise of the throng rose to a howl. Fikolmij was on his feet, beard blowing in the sharp wind, clenched fist in the air like an angry god calling down the thunder of the heavens. Utvart approached Josua slowly, still surprisingly cautious, as though he expected some stone-dweller trick, but the prince was clearly beaten, struggling to rise from his knees, the stump of his right wrist slipping in the mud.

A different kind of noise suddenly arose from the far side of the paddock. The crowd's attention grudgingly turned toward the source. There was an eddying of bodies near where the prisoners stood, and spears flailing like grass-stems. A woman's shriek of amazement was followed immediately by a man's cry of pain. A moment later a pair of bodies broke free from the press. Deornoth held one of the Thrithings guards, his elbow around the man's throat. The knight's other hand clasped the guard's spear just below the head, its sharp point pushed snug against the man's belly.

"Tell your other riders to stand back, horse-lord, or these men will die." Deornoth prodded at his captive's belly. The man grunted but did not cry out. A spot of blood appeared on his dun-colored shirt.

Fikolmij stepped forward, flushed with wrath, his braided beard quivering on his jaws. "Are you mad? Are you madmen? By The Four-Footed, I will crush you all!"

"Then your clansmen will die as well. We do not like to kill in cold blood, but we will not stand by and see our prince murdered after you beat him until he could not fight."

The crowd murmured unhappily, but Fikolmij, seething with rage, paid no attention. He raised his braceleted arm to call for his warriors, but a voice lanced out.

"No!" It was Josua, climbing totteringly to his feet. "Let them go, Deornoth."

The knight stared in amazement. "But, Highness . . ."

"Let them go." He paused to find breath. "I will fight my own battle. If you love me, release them." Josua rubbed blood from his eyes, blinking.

Deornoth turned to Isorn and Sangfugol, who held spears on three more guards. They returned his astonished stare. "Release them," he said at last. "The prince bids us release them."

Isorn and Sangfugol lowered their spears, allowing the Thrithings-men to step away. They promptly did, scrambling out of reach of the spear points before they remembered their original roles as captors and stopped, muttering angrily. Isorn ignored them. Beside him, the harper was trembling like a wounded bird. Geloë, who had not moved through all the furor, shifted her yellow eyes back to Josua.

"Come, Utvart," the prince said haltingly, his smile a bitter slash of white across a bloody mask. "Forget them. We are not finished."

Fikolmij, who stood close by, champing with his open mouth as though at a bit, started to say something. He never had the chance.

Utvart leaped forward, battering at Josua's guard. The moment's respite had not returned Josua's strength: he fell backward unsteadily before the Thrithings-man's attack, fending off the curved blade only by the slimmest of margins. At last a swinging blow slid past, nicking Josua's chest, then the following attack landed the flat of Utvart's blade on Josua's elbow, springing Naidel from his grasp. The prince scuttled after it, but as his fingers closed on the bloody hilt his feet slipped from beneath him and he sprawled on the trampled turf.

Seeing his advantage, Utvart lunged forward. Josua was able to lift his sword and turn the stroke downward, but his awkward position as he rose from the ground allowed Utvart to grapple him in a hugely-muscled arm and begin to pull the prince in toward the cutting edge of the curved sword. Josua brought up his knee and right arm to try to hold his attacker at bay, then managed to raise his other arm, keeping his blade locked against Utvart's guard, but the stronger Thrithings-man pushed his sword up slowly against the prince's stiffened wrist, forcing Naidel back as the crescent blade rose toward Josua's throat. The prince's lips skinned back in a grimace of ultimate exertion and sinews knotted along his slender arm. For a moment, his supreme effort halted the rising blade. The two men stood grappling chest to chest. Sensing the prince's flagging strength, Utvart tightened his grip around his smaller foe and smiled, drawing Josua toward him in a movement almost ritually slow. Despite the agonized play of the prince's muscles, the long edge of the curved blade continued inexorably upward, coming lovingly to rest against the side of Josua's throat.

The crowd stopped shouting. Somewhere overhead a crane threw out its clattering call, then silence swept back over the field.

"Now," the Thrithings-man exulted, breaking his long silence, "Utvart kills you."

Josua suddenly ceased resisting and flung himself forward into his enemy's grasp, snapping his head to one side. The curved blade slid along the outside of his neck, slicing the flesh deeply, but in that fractional instant of freedom the prince drove a knee into Utvart's groin.

As Utvart grunted in painful surprise, Josua hooked a foot around the Thrithings-man's calf and pushed against him. Utvart could not find his balance and tumbled backward. Josua fell with him, the Thrithings-man's blade flailing past his shoulder. When Utvart struck the ground with a hiss of released breath, Naidel snaked free. A moment later its point slid beneath the Thrithings-man's chin and was hammered upward a hand's-width or more, through the jaw and into the braincase.

Josua rolled himself free of Utvart's spastic clutch and struggled to his feet, dripping scarlet. He stood for a moment, legs shaking, arms dangling limp and helpless, and stared at the body on the ground before him.

"Tall man," he gasped, "it is . . . *you* . . . who talks too much."

A moment later his eyes rolled up beneath his lids and he fell heavily across the Thrithings-man's chest. They lay together, their blood commingling, and across the entire grasslands it seemed that nothing spoke or moved for a long time. Then the shouting began.

PART THREE

Storm's Heart

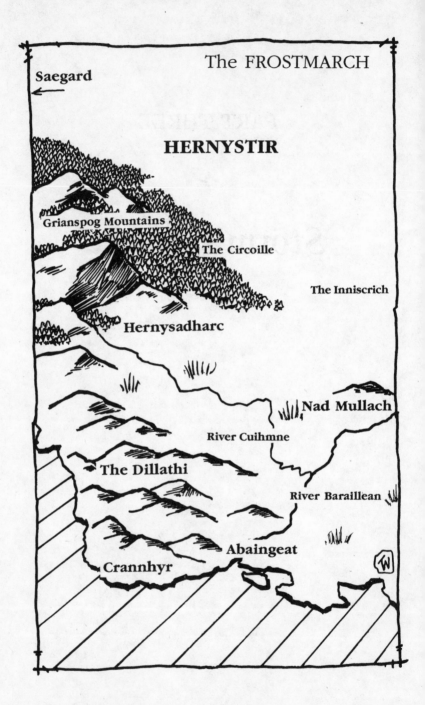

The FROSTMARCH

Saegard

HERNYSTIR

Grianspog Mountains

The Circoille

The Inniscrich

Hernysadharc

Nad Mullach

River Cuihmne

The Dillathi

River Baraillean

Abaingeat

Crannhyr

18

The Lost Garden

After a long sojourn in soundless velvet emptiness, Simon returned at last to the dim borderlands between sleep and waking. He came to awareness in darkness, on the edge of dream, and realized that once again a voice was speaking within his thoughts, as on the nightmarish flight out of Skodi's abbey. Some door had been opened inside him: now it seemed that anything might enter.

But *this* uninvited guest was not the taunting flame-thing, the Storm King's minion. The new voice was as different from that ghastly other as the quick from the dead. The new voice did not mock or threaten—in fact, it did not even seem to be speaking to Simon at all.

It was a womanly voice, musical yet strong, shining in Simon's lightless dream like a beacon. Though its words were sorrowful, it brought him a strange sense of comfort. Even though Simon knew that he slept, and was sure that it would only be the work of an instant to wake into the real world, the voice captivated him so that he did not wish to awaken just yet. Remembering the wise, beautiful face he had seen in Jiriki's mirror, he was content to hover on the edge of wakefulness and listen, for this was the same voice, the same person. Somehow, when that door into Simon had been opened, it was the mirror-woman who had come through. Simon was infinitely thankful for that. He remembered a little of what the Red Hand had promised him, and even in the shelter of sleep he felt frost upon his heart.

"Beloved Hakatri, my beautiful son," the woman's voice said, *"how I miss you. I know you are beyond hearing or beyond replying, but I cannot help speaking as though you were before me. Too many times have the People danced the year's end since you went into the West. Hearts grow cold, and the world grows colder still."*

Simon realized that even though the voice sang through his dream, these words were not meant for his ears. He felt like a beggar child spying on a rich and powerful family through a crack in a wall. But just as the wealthy family might have sorrows a beggar could not understand—miseries unrelated to hunger or cold or physical pain—so the voice in Simon's dream, for all its majesty, seemed weighted with quiet anguish.

"In some ways, it seems only the turning of a handful of moon-faces since the Two Families left Venyha Do'sae, the land of our birth across the Great Sea. Ah, Hakatri, if only you could have seen our boats as they swept across the fierce waves! Of silverwood they were crafted, with sails of bright cloth, brave and beautiful as flying fish. As a child I rode in the bow as the waves parted, and I was surrounded by a cloud of scintillant, sparkling seafoam! Then, when our boats touched the soil of this land, we cried. We had escaped the shadow of Unbeing and won our way to freedom.

"But instead, Hakatri, we found that we had not truly escaped shadow at all, but only replaced one sort with another—and this shadow was growing inside us.

"Of course, it was long before we realized it. The new shadow grew slowly, first in our hearts, then in our eyes and hands, but now the evil it caused has become greater than anyone could have suspected. It is stretching across all this land that we loved, the land to which we hastened long ago as to the arms of a lover—or as a son to the arms of his mother . . .

"Our new land has become as shadowed as the old one, Hakatri, and that is our fault. But now your brother, who was ruined by that shadow, has himself become an even more terrible darkness. He casts a pall over all he once loved.

"Oh, by the Garden that is Vanished, it is hard to lose your sons!"

Something else was now competing for his attention, but Simon could only lie helplessly, unwilling or unable to awaken. It seemed that somewhere outside of this dream-that-was-not-a-dream, his name was being called. Did he have friends or family who searched for him? It did not matter. He could not break away from the woman. Her terrible sadness twisted within him like a sharpened stick or a bit of broken pot: it would be cruel to leave her alone with her sorrow. At last the voices that faintly called for him vanished.

The woman's presence remained. It seemed that she wept. Simon did not know her, and could not guess to whom she spoke, but he wept with her.

Guthwulf was feeling confused and irritated. As he sat polishing his shield he tried to listen to the report of his castellain, who had just ridden down from Guthwulf's hold in Utanyeat. He was not having much luck with either chore.

The earl spat citril juice into the floor rushes. "Say it again, man, you are making no sense at all."

The castellain, a round-bellied, ferret-eyed fellow, firmly repressed a sigh of weariness—Guthwulf was not the kind of master before whom one displayed imperfect patience—and started in again on his explanation.

"It is simply this, Lord: your holdings in Utanyeat are nearly empty. Wulfholt is deserted but for a few servants. Almost all the peasants have left. There will be no one to bring in the oats or barley, and harvest can wait little more than a fortnight."

"My serfs have left?" Guthwulf stared distractedly at the boar and silver spears that sparkled on his black shield, the spearheads picked out in mother-of-pearl. He had loved that coat of arms, once, loved it as he would a child. "How do they dare leave? Who but me has fed the ugly louts all these years? Well, hire others for harvest, but do not let those who fled come back again. Not ever."

Now the castellain did make the smallest noise of despair. "My lord, Earl Guthwulf, I fear you have not been listening to me. There are not enough free folk left in Utanyeat to hire. The barons, your liege men, have their own problems and few workers to spare. Fields everywhere in eastern and northern Erkynland are going to seed unharvested. Skali of Kaldskryke's army across the river in Hernystir has cut a swath through all the border towns near Utanyeat, and will probably cross the river soon, having exhausted Lluth's country."

"Lluth is dead, I am told," Guthwulf said slowly. He himself had been in King Lluth's house, the Taig. His blood had flowed hot in his veins as he insulted the sheep-herder king in the midst of Lluth's own court. That had been a few scant months ago. Why did he feel so terrible now, so unmanned? "Why are all these villains running away from their rightful homes?"

The castellain looked at him queerly, as though Guthwulf had suddenly asked which direction was up. "Why? Because of the wars and looting on their border, the chaos of the Frostmarch. And the White Foxes, of course."

"The White Foxes?"

"Surely you know of the White Foxes, Lord." The castellain was almost openly skeptical. "Surely, since they came to the aid of the army you commanded at Naglimund."

Guthwulf looked up, pawing reflectively at his upper lip. "The Norns, you mean?"

"Yes, Lord. White Foxes is the name the common people give them, because of their corpse-pale skin and foxy eyes." He suppressed a shudder. "White Foxes."

"But what of them, man?" the earl demanded. When there was no immediate answer, his voice began to rise. "What do they have to do with my harvest, Aedon shake your soul?"

"Why, they are coming south, Earl Guthwulf," the castellain said, surprised. "They are leaving their nest in Naglimund's ruins. People who must sleep in the open have seen them walking the hills by darkness, like ghosts. They travel at night, a few at a time, and always moving southward—heading for the Hayholt." He looked around nervously, as if only now realizing what he had said. "Coming *here.*"

After the castellain left, Guthwulf sat a long time drinking from a stoup of wine. He picked up his helm to polish it, staring at the ivory tusks that lifted from the crest, then put it back down, untouched. His heart was not in the task, even though the king expected him to lead the Erkynguard into the field a few days hence and his armor had not been thoroughly looked-to since the siege of Naglimund. Things had not gone right at all since the siege. The castle seemed ghost-ridden, and that damnable gray sword and its two blade-brothers haunted his dreams until he almost feared to go to bed, to fall asleep. . . .

He set the wine down and stared at the flickering candle, then felt his melancholy spirits lift a little. At least he had not been imagining things. The countless odd night-sounds, the untethered shadows in the halls and commons, Elias' vanishing midnight visitors, all these and more had begun to make the Earl of Utanyeat doubt his own good mind. When the king had forced him to touch that cursed sword, Guthwulf had become sure that, whether by sorcery or no, some crack in his thoughts had let madness in to destroy him. But it was no whim, no fancy—the castellain had confirmed it. The Norns were coming to the Hayholt. The White Foxes were coming.

Guthwulf pulled his knife from his sheath and sent it whickering end over end into the door. It stuck, quivering in the heavy oak. He shuffled across the chamber and pulled it loose, then threw again, fetching it out with a swift jerk of his hand. The wind shrilled in the trees outside. Guthwulf bared his teeth. The knife thumped into the wood once more.

Simon lay suspended in a sleep that was not sleep, and the voice in his head spoke on.

"*. . . You see, Hakatri, my quietest son, perhaps that was where our troubles began. I spoke a moment ago of the Two Families, as though we twain were the only survivors of Venyha Do'sae, but it was the boats of the Tinukeda'ya that brought us across the Great Sea. Neither we Zida'ya nor our brethren the Hikeda'ya would have lived to reach this land had it not been for Ruyan the Navigator and his people—but to our shame, we treated the Ocean Children as badly here as we had in the garden-lands beyond the sea. When most of Ruyan's folk at last departed, going forth into this new land on their own, that, I think, was when the shadow first began to grow. Oh, Hakatri, we were mad to bring those old injustices to this new place, wrongs that should have died with our home in the Uttermost East. . . .*"

The clown mask bobbed before Tiamak's eyes, gleaming with firelight, covered with strange plumes and horns. For a moment he felt confused. How had the Wind Festival come so soon? Surely the annual celebration of He Who Bends the Trees was months away? But here was one of the wind-clowns bowing and dancing before him—and what other explanation could there be for the way Tiamak's head ached but an excessive intake of fern beer, a sure sign that Festival Days were here?

The wind-clown made a soft clicking noise as it tugged at something in Tiamak's hand. What could the clown be doing? Then he remembered. It wanted his coin, of course: everyone was expected to carry beads or pieces of money for He Who Bends the Trees. The clowns gathered these glittering tributes in clay jars to shake at the sky, making a rattling, roaring noise that was the chief music of the Festival—a noise that brought the good will of the Tree-Bender, so that he would keep harmful winds and floods at bay.

Tiamak knew he should let the clown have his coin—wasn't that what he had brought it for?—but still, there was something about the insinuating way the wind-clown pawed at him that made Tiamak uncomfortable. The clown's mask winked and leered; Tiamak, fighting a growing sense of unease, clutched the metal more tightly. What was wrong. . . ?

As his vision suddenly cleared, his eyes widened in horror. The bobbing clown mask became the chitinous face of a ghant, hanging only a scant cubit above his boat, suspended by a vine from a branch that overhung the river. The ghant was prodding gently with its insectile claw, patiently trying to poke Tiamak's knife loose from his sleep-sweaty grasp.

The little man shouted with disgust and threw himself back toward the stern of his flatboat. The ghant rasped and clicked its mouth-feelers, waving a plated foreleg as though trying to reassure him that it had all been a mistake. A moment later Tiamak swept up his steering pole, swinging it broadside so that he caught the ghant before it could scurry back up the vine. There was a loud clack and the ghant flew out across the river, legs curled like a singed spider. It made only a small splash as it disappeared into the green water.

Tiamak shuddered in repugnance as he waited for it to bob back to the surface. A chorus of dry clacking came from above his head and he looked up quickly to see half a dozen more ghants, each the size of a large monkey, staring down at him from the safety of the upper branches. Their expressionless black eyes glittered. Tiamak had little doubt that if they guessed he could not stand, they would be upon him in a moment; still, it seemed strange for ghants to attack any full-grown human, even an injured one. Strange or not, he could only hope they didn't realize how weak he really was, or what sort of injuries the bloody bandage on his leg signified.

"That's right, you ugly bugs!" he shouted, brandishing his steering pole and knife. His own cry made his head hurt. Wincing, he prayed silently that he didn't faint from the exertion; if he did, he felt sure he would never wake up. "Come on down and I'll give you the same lesson I did your friend!"

The ghants chittered at him with offhanded malice, as much as to say that there was no hurry; if they didn't get him today, some other ghants would soon enough. Crusty, lichen-dotted carapaces scraped against the willow branches as the ghants dragged themselves higher up into the tree. Resisting a fit of shivers, Tiamak calmly but deliberately poled his flatboat toward the center of the watercourse, out from beneath the low-hanging limbs.

The sun, which had been only midway up the morning sky when he noticed it last, had moved shockingly far past the meridian. He must have fallen asleep sitting up, despite the early hour. His fever had taken a great deal out of him. It seemed to have abated, at least for the present, but he was still dreadfully weak, and his injured leg throbbed as if it were aflame.

Tiamak's sudden laugh was raw and unpleasant. To think that two days ago he had been making grand decisions about where he would go, about which of the mighty folk clamoring for his services would be lucky enough to get him and which would have to wait! He remembered that he had decided to go to Nabban as his tribal elders had requested, and to let Kwanitupul go for now, a decision that had caused him many hours of worrying deliberation. Now his careful choice had been reversed in a freakish instant. He would be lucky if he even made it to Kwanitupul alive: the long journey to Nabban was simply inconceivable. He had lost blood and was sick with wound-spite. None of the proper herbs to treat such an injury grew in this part of the Wran. Also, just to insure his continuing misery, a nest of ghants had now spotted him and made him out as soon-to-be easy pickings!

His heart raced. A gray cloud of weakness was descending on him. He reached a slender hand down into the rivercourse, then splashed cold water onto his face. That filthy thing had actually been touching him, sly as a pickpocket, trying to dislodge his knife so its brethren might drop on him unresisted. How could anyone think that ghants were only animals? Some of his tribesmen claimed that they were nothing but the overgrown bugs or crabs they much resembled, but Tiamak had seen the terrible intelligence lurking behind those remorseless jet eyes. The ghants might be products of They Who Breathe Darkness rather than She Who Birthed Mankind—as Older Mogahib so often proclaimed—but that did not make them stupid.

He swiftly surveyed the contents of his boat to make sure nothing had been taken by the ghants before he had awakened. All his meager lot—a few rags of formal clothing, the Summoning Stick from the tribal elders, a few cooking things, his throwing-sling, and his Nisses scroll in its oilskin bag—lay scattered in the bottom of the flatboat. Everything seemed as it should be.

Lying in the hull nearby were the skeletal remains of the fish whose capture had begun these latest troubles. Some time during the last two days of chills and madness he must have eaten most of it, unless birds had picked the bones naked while he slept. Tiamak tried to remember how the fever-time had passed, but all he could summon were visions of poling endlessly down the watercourse while the sky and water bled color like glaze running from a poorly-fired pot. Had he remembered to make a fire and boil the marsh-water before washing out his wound? He seemed to have a vague recollection of trying to lay a spark to some tinder piled in his clay cooking-bowl, but had no idea whether a fire had ever caught there.

Trying to remember made Tiamak's head swim. It was useless to fret over what had or had not happened, he told himself. He was obviously still sick; his only chance was to make his way to Kwanitupul before the fever returned. With a regretful head shake he dropped the fish carcass overboard—the size of the skeleton confirmed that it had indeed been a splendid fish—then donned his shirt as another bout of shivers ran through him. He slumped back against the stern of the boat, then reached for the hat he had woven from sand-palm fronds during his journey's first day. He pulled it down low in an effort to keep the harsh midday sun out of his smarting eyes. After dabbing a little more water on his eyelids, he began to push with the pole, laboriously forcing the flatboat along the wide channel while his aching muscles protested with every stroke.

The fever did return sometime during the night. When Tiamak escaped its clutches once more, it was to find himself floating in lazy circles, his flatboat becalmed in a marshy backwater. His leg, although swollen and tremendously painful, did not seem markedly worse. With luck, if he could get to Kwanitupul soon he would not lose it.

Shaking loose the cobwebs of sleep, he offered yet another prayer to He Who Always Steps on Sand—whose existence, despite Tiamak's generally skeptical nature, had come to seem a great deal more conceivable since the misadventure with the crocodile. Whether this weakening of his disbelief was due to the mind-dizzying fever, or to a resurgence of true faith brought on by the nearness of death, Tiamak did not much care. Neither did he scrutinize his feelings about the matter very deeply. The fact was, he did not want to be a one-legged scholar—or worse, a dead scholar. If the gods did not help him, then there was no resource available to him in this treacherous marsh other than his own fast-failing resolve. Faced with those simple alternatives, Tiamak prayed.

He poled himself out of this latest backwater, at last reaching a place where several waterways came together. It was hard to tell exactly how he had wandered to this point, but using the newly-kindled stars as a reference—especially the Loon and the shining-pawed Otter—he was able to orient himself toward Kwanitupul and the sea. He kept his barge-pole moving until dawn, when he could no longer ignore his weary mind and wounded body crying out for rest. Fighting to keep his eyes open, he floated down the watercourse a little farther, poking in the muddy bank until at last he located a large stone which he levered free. This he secured to his fishing line and dumped it over the side to act as an anchor so he could remain moored in an uncovered section of the waterway as he took his desperately-needed sleep, safely away from tree-clinging ghants and other unwanted company.

Now able to preserve the gains made by his poling, Tiamak made better time. He lost half of the next afternoon (his eighth or ninth since leaving home, he guessed) to another resurgence of fever, but was able to push on a bit during the evening, and even continue after dark in order to make up some of his lost time. He discovered that there were far fewer biting and stinging insects once the sun had vanished into the western swamp; this and the oddly pleasant blue glow of twilight made such a nice change from his sun-battered afternoons that he celebrated by finally eating the rather forlorn-looking river-apple he had found on a branch overhanging the watercourse. River-apples were usually gone by this late in the year, those which had escaped the birds falling free at last to drift on the eddying water, bobbing like fisherman's floats until their seeds wound up at last in some mud-dam or root-tangled clump of soil. Tiamak had considered the find a good omen. He had put it aside after many expressions of thanks to beneficent deities, knowing he would enjoy it more if he savored the thought of it for a while.

The first bite through the rind of the river-apple was sour, but the pale flesh nearer the middle was wonderfully sweet. Tiamak, who had been surviving for days on waterbugs and edible grasses and leaves, was so overcome by the taste of the fruit that he nearly fell into a swoon. He had to put most of it aside for later.

Kwanitupul could have been said to occupy the northern shore of the upper prong of the Bay of Firannos, except that there was no real shore in that location: Kwanitupul lay on the Wran's northernmost fringe, but it was still very much a part of the greater marsh.

What had once been a minor trading village made up of a few score tree-houses and stilted huts had grown vast when the merchants of Nabban and Perdruin and the Southern Islands discovered the array of valuable things that came from the Wran's unreachable interior—unreachable by any except the Wrannamen, of course. Exotic feathers for ladies' gowns, dried mud for dyes, apothecarical powders and minerals of unequaled rarity and potency, all these things and many more kept the bazaars of Kwanitupul thriving with merchants and traders from up and down the coast. Since there was no land worthy of the name, pilings were driven deep into the mud instead, and shallow-drafted boats were laden with powdered stone and mortar and allowed to sink along the banks of the swampy waterways. Across these foundations countless huts and walk-ways had sprung up.

As Kwanitupul grew, Nabbanai and Perdruinese drifted in to share its dilapidated precincts with the native Wrannamen, until the trading city had spread its way over many miles of canals and swaying bridges, growing across and clogging the outer byways of the swamp like water-hyacinth. Its ramshackle eminence now dominated the Bay of Firannos as its older and larger sister Ansis Pelippé did the Bay of Emettin and Osten Ard's north-central coast.

Still dizzy with fever, Tiamak found himself at last drifting up out of the swamp's wild interior into the increasingly crowded arterial water-ways of Kwanitupul. At first, only a few other flatboats shared the green water with him, and these were almost entirely poled by other Wrannamen, many wearing feathery tribal finery in honor of their first visit to the grandest marsh-village of all. Farther into Kwanitupul the canals were choked with a host of other crafts—not only small boats like Tiamak's, but ships of all size and design, from the beautifully carved and canopied barks of rich merchants to huge grain ships and barges carrying cut stone that slid along the waterways like imperious whales, forcing smaller boats to scatter or risk being swamped in their rolling wake.

Tiamak normally enjoyed the sights of Kwanitupul enormously—although, unlike his tribesmen, *he* had seen Ansis Pelippé and the other port cities of Perdruin, beside which Kwanitupul was only a slightly shabby copy. Now, however, his fever was upon him once more. The lapping of water and the shouts of Kwanitupulis seemed curiously distant; the waterways he had traveled many times before were forbiddingly unfamiliar.

He wracked his wandering mind for the name of the inn to which he had been directed to go. In his letter, the one whose delivery had martyred Tiamak's gallant pigeon Ink-daub, Father Dinivan had told him . . . told him . . .

You are sorely needed. Yes, he remembered that part. The fever made it so hard to think . . . *Go to Kwanitupul*, Dinivan had written, *stay at the inn we have spoken of, and wait there until I can tell you more.* And what else had the priest said? *More than lives may depend on you.*

But what inn had they spoken of? Tiamak, startled by a smear of color before his unfocused gaze, looked up in time to prevent his boat sliding in front of a larger vessel with two flaring eyes painted on its hull. This boat's owner jumped up and down in the bow, waving a fist at Tiamak as he drifted past. The man's mouth was moving, but Tiamak heard only a dull roaring in his ears as he poled out of the wake. What inn?

"Pelippa's Bowl!" The name struck him like lightning out of the sky. He did not realize he had shouted it aloud, but such was the din of the waterway that his indiscretion mattered little.

Pelippa's Bowl: an inn Dinivan had mentioned in a letter, because it was run by a woman who had once been a nun of Saint Pelippa's order—Tiamak could not summon the woman's name—and who still liked to talk theology and philosophy. Morgenes had stayed there whenever he traveled in the Wran, because the old man liked the proprietress and her irreverent but thoughtful mind.

As these memories came back to him, Tiamak felt his weary spirits lifted. Perhaps Dinivan would join him at the inn! Or, even better, perhaps Morgenes himself was staying there, which would explain why Tiamak's latest messages to the old man's home at the Hayholt in Erkynland had gone unanswered. Whatever the case, with the names of his Scrollbearer friends to offer as currency, he was certain that he would find a bed and a sympathetic ear at *Pelippa's Bowl!*

Still fever-addled, but with a more hopeful heart, Tiamak bent his aching back to the pole once more. His frail boat skimmed along Kwanitupul's greasy green waterways.

The strange presence in Simon's head spoke on. The spell of the woman's voice held him gently prisoned, enwrapped in a charm that seemed to have no seam or flaw. He was in perfect darkness, as in the moment just before the final tumble into sleep, but his thoughts were as janglingly active as those of a man who only pretends to slumber while his enemies scheme across the room. He did not awaken, but neither did he pass into forgetfulness. Instead, the voice spoke on, and the words summoned images of beauty and horror:

". . . And although you have gone away, Hakatri—to death or the Ultimate West, I know not which—I shall say these things to you; for in truth, no one knows the way time flows on the Road of Dreams, or where it is that thoughts may wander that have been cast out on the scales of the Greater Worm or on the other Witnesses. It could be that somewhere . . . or somewhen . . . you will hear these words and know of your family and your people.

"Also, I have need just to speak with you, my beloved son, though you have been long absent.

"You know that your brother blamed himself for your terrible wounding. When

you went away at last into the West in search of heart's-ease, he became cold and discontented.

"I will not tell you all the story of the maraudings of the ship-men, those fierce mortals from across the sea. Some hint of their coming you had before you went away, and some would say that it was these Rimmersmen who struck the greatest blow against us; for they threw down Asu'a, our great house, and those of us who survived were driven into exile. Some would say that the Rimmersmen were our greatest foes, yet others might say that our most terrible wound came when your brother Ineluki raised his hand against your father, Iyu'unigato—your father; my husband—and slew him there in the great hall of Asu'a.

"Still others would say our shadow first grew in the deeps of time, in Venyha Do'sae, the Lost Garden, and that we brought it with us in our hearts. They would say that even those born here in our new land—like you, my son—came into the world with that shadow already staining your innermost selves, so that there has been no innocence anywhere since the world was young.

"And that is the problem with shadows, Hakatri. At first consideration they seem to be quite simple—a matter only of something that stands before the light. But that which is shadowed from one side may from another angle show as a brilliant reflection. What is covered by shadow one day may die in harsh sunlight another day, and the world will be lessened by its passing. Not everything that thrives in shadow is bad, my son . . ."

Pelippa's Bowl . . . Pelippa's Bowl . . .

Tiamak was finding it difficult to think. He repeated the name distractedly a few more times, having momentarily forgotten what it meant, then realized he was looking at a swinging signboard that bore the painted image of a golden bowl. He squinted at it woozily for a few moments, unable to remember exactly how he had wound up in this spot, then began looking around for a place to tie his boat.

The sign of the Bowl hung over the door of a large but rather undistinguished-looking inn in a backwater section of the warehouse district. The rickety structure seemed to sag between two larger buildings, like a drunk with a crony at each elbow. An armada of small and medium-sized flatboats bobbed in the waterway below, tied at the building's crude wharf or lashed directly to the pilings that held the building and its slovenly fellows above water. The inn was surprisingly quiet, as if both the guests and ostlers were sleeping.

Tiamak's fever had returned strongly and his exertions had left him very little strength. He balefully regarded the rope ladder that depended from the landing. It was badly tangled: even reaching up with the steering pole he came short of the lowest rung by a good cubit. He considered jumping to make up the last bit of distance, but even in his diminished state Tiamak realized that when one was too weak to swim, there would be few things more foolish than jumping up and down in a small boat. At last, stymied, he called hoarsely for assistance.

If this was one of Morgenes' favorite hostelries, he thought muzzily some time later, then the doctor had a high tolerance for slackness. He renewed his braying cry, marveling at the pained quality of his own voice as it echoed through this unfrequented area of Kwanitupul. At last, a white-haired head appeared in the doorway above and remained there for long moments, regarding Tiamak as though he were some interesting but unsolvable puzzle. At last the head's owner left the safety of the doorway and came forward. It was an old Perdruinese or Nabbanai man, tall and well-built, whose handsome pink face wore the simple expression of a young child. He stopped and squatted at the edge of the landing, looking down at Tiamak with a pleasant smile.

"The ladder." Tiamak waved his steering pole. "I can't reach the ladder."

The old man looked kindly from Tiamak to the ladder, then seemed for some time to reflect gravely on the whole question. At last he nodded, his smile widening. Tiamak, despite extreme weariness and the pain of his throbbing leg, found himself smiling back at this strange old bird. After this exchange of unspoken good cheer had gone on for some little while, the man abruptly turned and disappeared back into the doorway.

Tiamak howled despairingly, but the old man reappeared a few moments later with a boat-hook clutched in his long-fingered hand which he used to jiggle the ladder free; it uncoiled the rest of the way and the bottom splashed into the green water. Tiamak, after a moment of muddled deliberation, took a few things from the boat and began to climb. The Wrannaman found he had to stop twice during the short three-fathom trip to rest. His crocodile-bitten leg was burning with a pain like fire.

By the time he reached the top his head was reeling worse than it had all day. The old man had gone, but when Tiamak dragged the heavy door open and hobbled through he found him again, now sitting in the corner of an enclosed courtyard on a pile of blankets that looked as though they served as his bed, surrounded by skeins of rope and various other tools. Most of the space in the damp courtyard was taken by a pair of upturned boat-hulls. One had been badly slashed, as though by a sharp rock. The other was half-painted.

As Tiamak made his way around the jars of white paint that cluttered the path across the courtyard, the old man smiled foolishly at him once more, then settled back into his blankets as though to fall asleep.

The door at the far side of the courtyard led into the inn itself. This bottom floor seemed to contain only a dowdy common room with a handful of stools and a few long tables. A sour-faced Perdruinese woman, heavy-armed and with gray-shot hair, stood pouring beer from one jug to another.

"What do you want?" she said.

Tiamak paused in the doorway. "Are you . . ." he at last remembered the former nun's name, ". . . Xorastra?"

The woman made a face. "Dead three years. She was my aunt. Mad as a mudlark. Who are you? You're a swamp man, aren't you? We don't take beads or feathers here for payment."

"I need a place to stay. My leg is injured. I am a friend of Father Dinivan and of Doctor Morgenes Ercestres."

"Never heard of them. Blessed Elysia, but you do speak decent Perdruinese for a savage, don't you? We have no rooms available. You can sleep with old Ceallio out there. He's simple-minded but he does no harm. Six cintis a night, nine if you want food." She turned away, gesturing absently at the courtyard beyond.

As she finished speaking a trio of children thundered down the stairs, smacking at each other with switches, laughing and shrieking. They almost knocked Tiamak down as they pushed past him and went through into the courtyard.

"I must have help with my leg." Tiamak swayed as dizziness washed over him. "Here." He reached into his belt-pouch and pulled out the two gold Imperators he had been saving for years. He had brought them with him for just such an emergency, and what good would money be to him if he died? "Please, I have gold."

Xorastra's niece turned. Her eyes bulged. "Rhiappa and her large Pirates!" she swore. "Look at that, now!"

"Please, good lady. I can bring you back many more of these." He couldn't, but there was a much better chance this woman would help keep him alive if she thought he could. "Just get a barber or a healer to see to my leg, and give me food and a place to sleep."

Her mouth, still gaping in surprise at the appearance of the glittering golden coins, widened even further as Tiamak pitched over at her feet, senseless as a stone.

" . . . But although not everything that thrives in shadow is bad, Hakatri, still much that hides in darkness does so to keep its evil hidden from all eyes."

Simon was beginning to lose himself in this strange dream, to feel as though it were to him that the patient, pained voice spoke: he felt bad for having been so long absent, for bringing further suffering to such a high yet afflicted soul.

"Your brother has long hidden his plans beneath a cloak of shadow. The year-end was danced countless times after Asu'a's fall before we had even a hint that he still lived—if his spectral existence can be called life. Long he plotted in darkness, hundreds of years of black-minded deliberation before the first steps were taken. *Now, with his plan marching forward, there is so much still hidden in shadow. I think and I watch, I wonder and I guess, but the subtlety of his design eludes my old eyes. I have seen many things since first I saw leaves fall in Osten Ard, but I cannot make sense of this. What does he plan? What does your brother Ineluki mean to do. . . ?"*

The stars seemed very naked over Stormspike, gleaming white as polished bone, cold as knobs of ice. Ingen Jegger thought them very beautiful.

He stood beside his horse on the road before the mountain. The bitter wind whistled through the ivory muzzle of his snarling, dog-faced helm. Even his Norn-stallion, bred in the world's blackest, coldest stables, was doing its best to duck the brutal sleet that the wind flung like arrows—but Ingen Jegger was exalted. The shrill of the wind was a lullabye, the sting of freezing sleet a caress. Ingen's mistress had set him a great task.

"No other Queen's Hunter has ever been granted such a responsibility," she had told him as the indigo light of the Well filled the Chamber of the Harp. As she spoke, the groans of the Singing Harp—a great, translucent and ever-changing *thing* cloaked by the mists of the Well—had made the very stones of Stormspike shudder. "We have brought you back from the outlands of Death's Country." Utuk'ku's glittering mask threw back the Well's blue radiance so fiercely that her face was obscured, as though a flame burned between shoulders and crown. "We have also given you weapons and wisdom no other Queen's Hunter has ever had. Now we offer you a task of terrible difficulty, a task like no one, mortal or immortal, has ever faced."

"I will do it, Lady," he had said, and his heart had throbbed within him as though it would burst from joy.

Standing now on the royal roadway, Ingen Jegger looked at the ruins of the old city that lay all about him, skeletal litter on the lower slopes of the great ice-mountain. When the huntsman's progenitors were scarcely more than savages, he thought, ancient Nakkiga had stood beneath the night sky in her full beauty, a needle-forest of alabaster and white witchwood, a chalcedony necklace around the mountain's throat. Before the huntsman's people had known fire, the Hikeda'ya had built pillared chambers within the very mountain itself, each chamber blazing with a million crystalline facets of glittering lamplight, a galaxy of stars burning in the darkness of the earth.

And now he, Ingen Jegger, was their chosen instrument! He wore the mantle no mortal had ever borne! Even to one of his training, of his horrifying discipline, it was a maddening thought.

The wind gentled. His steed made a noise of impatience, a large pale shape beside him in the flurrying snow. He stroked the horse with his gloved hand, letting his touch rest on its powerful neck, feeling the quick pulse of life. He put a boot into the stirrup and lifted himself into the saddle, then whistled for Niku'a. A few moments later the great white hound appeared on a rise nearby. Nearly as large as the huntsman's horse, Niku'a filled the night with his steaming breath; the dog's short fur was pearled with mist so that it glowed like moonlit marble.

"Come," Ingen Jegger hissed. "Great deeds lie before us!" The road stretched before him, leading down from the heights and into the unsuspecting lands of sleeping men. "Death is behind us."

He spurred his horse forward. The hooves fell on the icy road like hammers.

"*. . . And so in a way I am blinded to your brother's machinations.*" The voice in Simon's head was growing more and more faint now, withering like a rose lingered past its season. "*I have been forced to my own stratagems— and poor, weak games they seem when placed against the swarms of Nakkiga and the enduring, deathless hatred of the Red Hand. Worst of all, I do not know what I am fighting, although I believe I am now discerning the first faint shapes. If I have even a glimmer of the truth, it is horrible. Horrible.*

"*Ineluki's game has begun. He was the child of my loins; I cannot shirk my responsibility. Two sons I had, Hakatri. Two sons I have lost.*"

The woman's voice was only a whisper, the merest breath, but still Simon could feel its bitterness. "*The eldest are always the loneliest, my quiet one, but no one should be left behind for so long by those whom they had loved . . .*"

And then she was gone.

Simon awakened slowly out of the extended darkness that had held him. His ears seemed to echo strangely, as though the absence of the voice to which he had listened so long left a greater emptiness. When he opened his eyes, light flowed in, dazzling him; when he closed them, rings of bright color spun before his shuttered lids. He assayed a more careful view of the world and found that he was in a tiny forest dell blanketed in new-fallen snow. Pale morning light streamed down through the overhanging trees, silvering the naked branches and speckling the forest floor.

He was very cold. He was also completely alone.

"Binabik!" he cried. "Qantaqa!" A moment later he added "Sludig!" as an afterthought. There was no reply.

Simon untangled himself from his cloak and clambered unsteadily to his feet. He shook off a coating of powdery snow, then stood for a moment rubbing his head to clear the shadows. The dingle mounted up steeply on either side of him; judging by the array of torn branches piercing his shirt and breeches, he had tumbled down from above. He felt himself gingerly, but other than the long, healing wound on his back and some ugly toothmarks on his leg, he seemed only bruised and scraped and very, very stiff. He grabbed a protruding root in his hand and clambered painfully up the side of the dell. His legs were trembling as he scrambled over the edge and stood up. A monotonous profusion of snow-robed trees stretched away in all directions. There was no sign of his friends or his horse; in fact, there was no sign of anything but endless white forest.

Simon tried to remember how he had come to this place, but drew only a shuddering memory of the last mad hours in Skodi's abbey, of a hateful, icy voice that had plagued him, and of riding into blackness. Afterward there had been a gentler, sadder voice that had spoken long in his dreams.

He looked around, hoping at least to find a saddlebag, but with no luck. His empty scabbard was tied to his leg; after some searching, he finally spotted the bone knife from Yiqanuc lying at the bottom of the dingle. With many a self-pitying curse, Simon climbed back down to retrieve it. He felt a little better to have something sharp close to hand, but it was a very tiny consolation. When he reached the top once more and looked around at the inhospitable expanse of wintery woods, a sense of desertion and fear crept over him that had been absent for a long while. He had lost everything—everything! The sword Thorn, the White Arrow, the things that he had won, all were gone! And his friends were gone, too.

"Binabik!" he screamed. Echoes fled and vanished. "Binabik! Sludig! Help me!" Why had they deserted him? Why?

He shouted for his friends again, over and over as he stumbled back and forth across the forest clearing.

His voice hoarse, his many cries unanswered, Simon slumped down on a rock at last and fought back tears. Men shouldn't cry just because they were lost. Men didn't do that sort of thing. The world seemed to shimmer a little, but it was only the fierce cold that made his eyes sting so. Men shouldn't cry, no matter how terrible things had gotten. . . .

He put his hands in his cloak pocket to ease the chill and felt the rough carvings of Jiriki's mirror beneath his fingers. He lifted it out. Gray sky was reflected there, as though the looking glass were full of clouds.

He held the scale of the Greater Worm before him. "Jiriki," he murmured, breathing on the shiny surface as though his own warmth might lend the thing a kind of life. "I need help! *Help me!*" The only face that looked back was his own, wearing a pale scar and a sparse red beard. "Help me."

Snow began to fall once more.

19

Children of the Navigator

Miriamele awakened slowly and unpleasantly. The pounding in her head was not helped at all by the side-to-side swaying of the floor, and she was unhappily reminded of a particular Aedonmansa supper at the palace in Meremund when she was nine years of age. An indulgent servant had allowed her to drink three goblets of wine; the wine had been watered, but Miriamele had still become very ill, throwing up all over her new Aedontide frock and spoiling it beyond reclamation.

That long-ago bout of stomach-sickness had been preceded by just such a sway as she was now feeling, as though she were aboard a boat rocking up and down in the midst of the ocean. The morning following her drunken adventure she had remained in bed with a horrific headache—a pain almost as bad as the one she was experiencing now. What grotesque indulgence had led her to this dreadful pass?

She opened her eyes. The room was fairly dark, the roofbeams overhead heavy and crudely cut. The mattress on which she was lying was impossibly uncomfortable, and the room would not stop its terrible tilting. Had she been so drunk that she had fallen and struck her head badly? Perhaps she had split her crown and was even now dying. . . ?

Cadrach.

The thought came to her suddenly. In fact, she remembered, she hadn't been drinking or doing anything of the sort. She had been waiting in Father Dinivan's workroom, and . . . and . . .

And Cadrach had struck her. He had said they could not wait any longer. She had said they would. Then he had said something else and hit her on the head with something heavy. Her poor head! And to think that for a foolish moment she had regretted trying to drown him!

Miriamele struggled to her feet, holding her head between her hands as though to keep the pieces together. It was just as well she was bent double: the ceiling was so low that she could not have stood up. But the swaying! Elysia, Mother of God, it was worse than being drunk! It seemed mad that being cuffed on the head could make things veer and wobble so. It was indeed just like being on a ship. . . .

She *was* on a ship, and a ship under sail at that. The realization came suddenly from a subtle amalgam of clues: the movement of the floor, the faint but definite creaking of timbers, the thin, saltier-than-usual scent of the air. How had this happened?

It was hard to make out anything in the near-blackness, but as far as Miriamele could tell she was surrounded by casks and barrels. She was in the hold of a ship, that was certain. As she squinted into the darkness, another sound began to make itself heard, something that had been there all along, but was only now becoming clear.

Someone was snoring.

Miriamele was immediately filled with a mixture of rage and fear. If it was Cadrach, she would find him and strangle him. If it was *not* Cadrach— Merciful Aedon, who could say how she had wound up on this boat, or what the mad monk might have done that had made them both fugitives? If she revealed herself, it might be to a stowaway's death sentence. But if it was Cadrach—oh, she so wanted to catch hold of his flabby neck. . . !

She hunkered down between a pair of casks; the sudden movement sent a stabbing pain down the back of her neck. Slowly and quietly, she began to crawl toward the source of the rasping noise. Whoever was burring and mumbling so did not seem apt to be sleeping lightly, but there was no sense taking unnecessary risks.

A sudden thumping from overhead set her cowering both from possible discovery and the painful noise itself. When nothing followed but softer repetitions, Miriamele decided it was only the normal business of the ship going on above. She continued to stalk her snoring prey through the rows of close-stacked barrels.

By the time she was a few cubits away from the snorer, she no longer felt even the slightest doubt—she had heard that sodden, drunken rumble too many nights to mistake it.

At last she crouched over him. Feeling with her hand, she located the empty jug curled in the crook of his arm with which he'd besotted himself. Above that, she felt Cadrach's unmistakable round face, the wine-sour breath piping wetly in and out of his open mouth as he snored and muttered. The feel of him filled her with fury. It would be so easy just to crack his sodden skull with the plundered jar, or topple one of the leaning barrel towers to crush him like a bug. Hadn't he plagued her since she had met him? He had stolen from her and sold her to her enemies like a slave, and now he had struck her and dragged her by force out of God's house. Whatever else she was, whatever her father had become, she was still a princess of the blood of King Prester John and Queen Ebekah. No drunkard of a monk had a right to lay hands on her! No man! No one. . . !

Her anger, which had been curling and spiraling higher within her like the flames of a wind-tortured fire, blazed up and then abruptly vanished. Tears choked her; sobs thudded painfully in her chest.

Cadrach stopped snoring. His slurred, querulous voice rose from the darkness before her. "My lady?"

For a moment she did not move; then, sucking in a fierce gasp of breath, she struck out at the invisible monk. She made only the most incidental contact, but it was enough to locate him in the darkness. Her next blow landed stingingly on something. "You whoreson rogue!" she hissed, then struck again.

Cadrach let out a muffled cry of pain, scrambling away from her so that her fingers struck nothing but the hold's damp floorboards. "Why . . . why do you. . . ?" he muttered. "Lady, I saved your life!"

"Liar!" she spat, and burst into tears once more.

"No, Princess, it is surely the truth. I'm sorry I hit you, but I had no choice."

"Damnable liar!"

"No!" His voice was surprisingly firm. "And keep quiet. We dare not be discovered. We must stay down here until we can sneak off at nightfall."

She sniffled angrily and wiped her nose on the back of her sleeve. "Dullard!" she said. "Fool! Sneak where? We're at sea!"

There was a moment of silence. "We can't be . . ." the monk said weakly. "We can't be. . . ."

"Can't you feel that up-and-down dipping? You never did know anything about boats, you treacherous little man. That's no rocking at anchor in the harbor. That's sea-swell." Her anger was ebbing, leaving her empty and stupefied. She fought its going. "Now, if you don't tell me how we wound up on this boat and how we're going to get off, I'm going to make you wish you had never left Crannhyr—or wherever you truly came from."

"Oh, gods of my people," Cadrach groaned, "I have been a fool. They must have cast off while we were asleep. . . ."

"While *you* were asleep, drunkenly asleep. *I* had been beaten senseless!"

"Ah, you speak the truth, my lady. I wish you didn't. I did drink myself into forgetfulness, princess, but there was much to forget."

"If you mean hitting me, I won't *let* you forget."

There was another silence in the darkness of the hold. The monk's voice, when it came at last, was strangely wistful. "Please, Miriamele. Princess. I have done wrong many times, but in this I did only what I thought best."

She was indignant. "What you thought best! Of all the arrogance. . . !"

"Father Dinivan is dead, Lady." His words spilled out swiftly. "So is Ranessin, Lector of Mother Church. Pryrates killed them both in the very heart of the Sancellan Aedonitis."

She tried to speak, but something seemed stuck in her throat. "They're. . . ?"

"Dead, Princess. By tomorrow morning the news will be traveling like wildfire all across the face of Osten Ard."

It was hard to think about, hard to understand. Sweet, homely Father Dinivan, who had blushed like a boy! And the lector, who was going to make everything right, somehow. Now, nothing would be right. Nothing ever again.

"Are you telling the truth?" she asked at last.

"I wish I were not, Lady. I wish this were only another of my long index of falsehoods, but it is not. Pryrates rules Mother Church, or as good as. Your only true friends in Nabban are dead, and that is why we are hiding in the hold of a ship that was floating at anchor in the docks below the Sancellan . . ."

The monk found it hard to finish, but the odd catch in his voice finally convinced her beyond any doubting. The darkness in the ship's belly seemed to grow. In the immeasurable time that followed, when it seemed that all the tears she had held back since leaving home came welling up at once, Miriamele felt as though that black shroud of despair had grown to enfold all the world.

"So where are we?" she asked at last. Clasping her knees, she rocked slowly back and forth in countermotion to the swaying of the ship.

Cadrach's mournful voice whispered out of the darkness. "I do not know, my lady. As I told you, I brought us to a boat that was anchored beneath the Sancellan. It was dark."

Miriamele strove to compose herself, grateful that no one could see her tear-reddened face. "Yes, but whose ship? What did it look like? Whose mark was on the sail?"

"I know little of boats, Princess, you know that. It is a boat, a large one. The sails were furled. I think there was a bird of prey painted on the bow, but the lamps burned very low."

"What bird?" she asked urgently.

"A fish hawk, I think, or some such. Black and gold."

"An osprey." Miriamele sat up straight, drumming her fingers agitatedly against her leg. "That is the Prevan House. I wish I knew how they stood, but it has been so long since I lived here! Perhaps they are supporters of my late uncle and would take us to safety." She smiled wryly—for her own benefit only, since the darkness hid her from the monk. "But where would that be?"

"Believe me, Lady," Cadrach said fervently. "At this moment, the coldest, darkest, inner chambers of Stormspike would be safer for us than the Sancellan Aedonitis. I told you, Lector Ranessin has been thrown down and murdered! Can you imagine how Pryrates' power must have grown that he would slay the lector right in God's own house?"

Miriamele's fingers suddenly stopped drumming. "That was an odd thing to say. What do you know of Stormspike and its inner chambers, Cadrach?"

The uneasy truce that shock and horror had built seemed suddenly very foolish. Miriamele's quick-flaring anger masked a sudden fear. Who was this monk, who knew so much and acted so oddly? And here she was once more, trusting him, trapped in a dark place into which he himself had led her. "I asked you a question."

"My lady," Cadrach said, hesitant as he searched for words. "There are many things . . ."

He broke off suddenly. A wrenching noise echoed through the hold; bright torchlight stabbed down as the hatch door rose. Blinking, the princess and Cadrach threw themselves among the piled casks, squirming for shelter like earthworms in a shovel-turn of soil. Miriamele caught a brief glimpse of a cloaked figure climbing backward down the ladder. She curled herself back against the inner wall of the hold and drew her legs up before her, hiding her face beneath her down-dropping hood.

The one who had entered the hold made very little noise, picking carefully between the stacks of provisions. Miriamele's speeding heart seemed to jump in her breast as the footsteps came to a sudden halt just a few cubits away. She held her breath in her straining lungs until it seemed she would burst. The sound of the surf was as loud in her ears as the bellowing of a bull, but a strange musical humming floated beneath it like the drowsy murmur of bees. Then the drone abruptly stopped.

"Why do you hide here?" a voice asked; a dry finger touched her face. Miriamele's pent-up breath flew out explosively and her eyes snapped open. The voice exclaimed: "Ah, but you are only a child!"

The one who bent over her had pale golden skin and large, wide-set dark eyes that peered from beneath a fringe of white hair. She seemed aged and frail: her hooded robe could not hide the slightness of her frame.

"A Niskie!" Miriamele gasped, then lifted her hand to her mouth.

"Why should that surprise you?" the other said, thin brows arching. Her skin was netted with fine wrinkles, but her movements were precise. "Where better to find a Niskie than on a deep-water ship? No, the question, stranger-girl, is why are *you* here?" She turned toward the shadows where the monk still hid. "And that question also goes for you, man. Why are you skulking in the hold?"

When there was no immediate answer from either stowaway, she shook her head. "Then I suppose I must call for the ship's master . . ."

"No, please," Miriamele said. "Cadrach, come out. Niskies have sharp ears." She smiled in what she hoped was a conciliatory manner. "If we had known it was you, we would not have bothered. It is foolish to try to hide from a Niskie."

"Yes." Their discoverer nodded, pleased. "Now tell me: who are you?"

"Malachias . . ." Miriamele stopped, realizing that her gender had already been identified. "*Marya,* that is. That's me. Cadrach is my companion." The monk, crawling out from a bulky fold of sailcloth, grunted.

"Good." The Niskie smiled in tight-lipped satisfaction. "My name is Gan Itai. *Eadne Cloud* is my ship. I sing the kilpa down."

Cadrach was staring. "Sing the kilpa down? What does that mean?"

"You said you were well-traveled," Miriamele broke in. "Everyone knows that you can't take a boat out to deep sea without a Niskie to sing the songs that keep the kilpa away. You know what kilpa are, don't you?"

"I have heard of them, yes," Cadrach said shortly. He turned his curious gaze back to Gan Itai, who rocked back and forth, listening. "You are of the Tinukeda'ya, are you not?"

The Niskie's mouth widened in a toothless grin. "We are Navigator's Children, yes. Long ago we came back to the sea, and by the sea we stayed. Now, tell Gan Itai what you do on this ship."

Miriamele looked at Cadrach, but the monk seemed absorbed in thought. The torchlight showed his pale face beaded with sweat. Whether from the shock of discovery or something else, the fog of his drunkenness seemed to have burned away. His small eyes were troubled but clear. "We cannot tell all," the princess answered. "We have done no wrong, but our lives are in danger, so we are hiding."

Gan Itai narrowed her long eyes and pursed her lips meditatively. "I must tell the ship's master you are here," she said at last. "If that is wrong, I am sorry, but I owe first allegiance to *Eadne Cloud*. Stowaways are always reported. No harm must come to my ship."

"We wouldn't hurt the ship," Miriamele said desperately, but the Niskie was moving swiftly toward the ladder, her nimbleness belying her apparent frailty.

"I regret, but I do what I must. Ruyan's Folk have laws that cannot be overthrown." She shook her head and disappeared through the hatchway. A splash of dawn-lit sky showed briefly before the hatch door thumped down once more.

Miriamele slumped back against a barrel. "Elysia save us. What will we do? What if this boat belongs to enemies?"

"As far as I am concerned, it is boats themselves which are the enemies." Cadrach shrugged fatalistically. "My hiding us on one was foolishness beyond understanding. As to discovery . . ." he waved his plump hand dismissively. "It was inevitable once the boat actually put to sea, but anything is better than staying in the Sancellan Aedonitis." He wiped sweat from his face. "Ah, me, my stomach feels dreadful. As a wise man stated, 'There are three kinds of people—the living, the dead, and those at sea.'" His expression of disgust changed to one of contemplation. "But Niskies! I have met the living Tinukeda'ya! Bones of Anaxos, but the world is full of odd tales!"

Before Miriamele could ask him what that meant, they heard the sound of heavy boots on the deck overhead. Deep voices spoke, then the hatch door creaked up and the opening was abruptly filled with torchlight and long shadows.

Maegwin sat in a crumbling ancient arena, in the midst of a mysterious stone city hidden deep in the heart of a mountain, face to face with four creatures out of the legends of ancient days. Before her stood a great, shining stone that had spoken to her as though it were a person. Still, she was unutterably disappointed.

"The Sithi," she murmured quietly. "I thought the Sithi would be here."

Eolair looked at her with seeming dispassion, then turned back to the saucer-eyed dwarrows once more. "This is very strange. How do you know the name of Josua Lackhand?"

Yis-fidri seemed uncomfortable. The earth-dweller's bony face bobbed at the end of his slender neck like a sunflower on its stem. "Why do you seek the Sithi? What do you want with our old masters?"

Maegwin let out a sigh.

"It was only a thin hope," Eolair said quickly. "The Lady Maegwin thought they might help us, as they aided our people in days past. Hernystir has been invaded."

"And this Handless Josua of whom the Sithi spoke—is he the invader, or is he one of Hern's children, like you?" Yis-fidri and his fellows leaned forward solemnly.

"Josua Lackhand is no Hernystirman, but neither is he an invader. He is one of the chiefs in the great war that rages on the surface." Eolair spoke carefully. "Our people have been invaded by Josua's enemies. Thus, it could be said Josua fights for us—if he still lives."

"Josua is dead," Maegwin said dully. The weight of earth and stone around her pressed down, squeezing out her breath. What was the point in all this blather? These spindly creatures were not the Sithi. This was not the city of banners and sweet music she had seen in her dreams. Her plans had come to nothing.

"That may not be so, my lady," Eolair said quietly. "When I was last afield, I heard rumors that he still lived, rumors that had more than a slight sound of truth to them." He turned back to the patient dwarrows. "Please tell us where you heard Josua's name. We are not your enemies."

Yis-fidri was not so easily swayed. "And does this Handless Josua fight for our old masters the Sithi, or against them?"

Eolair pondered before speaking. "We mortals know nothing of the Sithi and their battles. Josua is probably as ignorant as we."

Yis-fidri pointed to the gleaming, shimmering chunk of stone at the center of the arena. "But it was the First Grandmother of the Zida'ya—the Sithi—who spoke to you through the Shard!" He sounded perversely pleased, as though he had caught Eolair in a pointless fib.

"We did not know *whose* voice it was. We are strangers here, and we are strangers to your . . . your Shard."

"Ah." Yis-fidri and the others huddled and spoke in their own tongue, the words flying back and forth like rippling chimes. At last they straightened.

"We will trust you. We believe that you be honorable folk," Yis-fidri said. "Even if we did not, you have seen now where the last dwarrows live. Unless we make an end to you, we can only hope you will not reveal us to our former masters." He laughed sadly, his dark gaze nervously roaming the shadows. "And we are not folk who can compel others by force. We are weak, old . . ." The dwarrow struggled to compose himself. "No more is saved by holding knowledge back. So, all our people can now return to this place, the Site of Witness."

Yis-hadra, the one Yis-fidri had named as his wife, lifted her hand. She beckoned into the darkness at the top of the great bowl, then called out in the musical dwarrow-tongue.

Lights appeared and came drifting silently down the aisles of the arena, perhaps three dozen in all, each a gleaming rose crystal clutched in the hands of a dwarrow. Their large heads and wide, solemn eyes made them seem distorted children, grotesque but not frightening.

Unlike Yis-fidri's foursome, these new dwarrows seemed afraid to approach Maegwin and Eolair too closely. Instead, they passed slowly down the stone pathways and seated themselves here and there among the hundreds upon hundreds of benches, faces turned toward the gleaming Shard, thin fingers clutching their crystals. Like a dying galaxy, the vast, gloomy bowl was pricked with dim stars.

"They were cold," Yis-fidri whispered. "They are happy to come back to the warmth."

Maegwin jumped, startled after the long quiet. The realization came to her abruptly that here beneath the world's crust there were no birds singing, no rustling of wind-tossed trees; the city seemed almost constructed of silence.

Eolair looked around at the ring of solemn eyes before turning back to Yis-fidri. "But you and your people seemed afraid of this place."

The dwarrow looked embarrassed. "The voices of our old masters frighten us, yes. But the Shard is warm and great Mezutu'a's halls and streets are cold."

The Count of Nad Mullach took a deep breath. "Please, then. If you believe we mean you no harm, explain to us how you know Josua's name."

"Our Witness—the Shard. As we told you. The Sithi have called to us here at the Site of Witness, asking of this Josua, and of the Great Swords. The Shard was long silent, but lately it has begun speaking to us again, for the first time in recent memory."

"Speaking?" Eolair asked. "As it spoke to us? What *is* the Shard?"

"Old, it is. One of the oldest of all the Witnesses." Yis-fidri's worried tone returned. His cohorts wagged their heads, narrow faces uneasy. "Long has it been silent. None did speak to us."

"What do you mean?" The count looked at Maegwin to see if she shared his puzzlement. She avoided his eyes. The Shard pulsed with gentle, milky light as Eolair tried again. "I am afraid I cannot understand you. What is a Witness?"

The dwarrow considered carefully, looking for words to explain something that had never before needed explaining.

"In days long past," he finally said, "we and others of the Gardenborn did speak through the particular objects that could act as Witnesses: Stones and Scales, Pools and Pyres. Through these things—and through some others, like Nakkiga's great Harp—the world of the Gardenborn was tied together with strands of thought and speech. But we Tinukeda'ya had forgotten much even before mighty Asu'a fell, and had grown far apart from those who lived there . . . those who we had once served."

"Asu'a?" Eolair said. "I have heard that name before. . . ."

Maegwin, only half-listening, watched the coruscating colors of the Shard dart like bright fish below the crystal's surface. On the benches all around, the dwarrows watched, too, their faces grim, as though their hunger for its radiance shamed them.

"When Asu'a fell," Yis-fidri continued, "the seldom-speaking became silence. The Speakfire in Hikehikayo and the Shard here in Mezutu'a were voiceless. Do you see, we dwarrows had lost the Art of their using. Thus, when the Zida'ya spoke to us no more, we Tinukeda'ya could no longer master the Witnesses, even to speak among ourselves."

Eolair pondered. "How did you forget the art of using these things?" he asked at last. "How could it be lost among even such few as there are of you?" He gestured to the silent ones sitting around the stone bowl. "You are immortal, are you not?"

Yis-fidri's wife Yis-hadra threw back her head and moaned, startling both Maegwin and the count. Sho-vennae and Imai-an, Yis-fidri's other two companions, joined her. Their lament turned into a kind of eerie, sorrowful song that rose to the cavern ceiling and echoed in the darkness above. The other dwarrows turned to watch, heads slowly swaying like a field of gray and white dandelions.

Yis-fidri lowered his heavy lids and cupped his chin in trembling fingers. When the moaning had died away, he looked up.

"No, Hern's Child," he said slowly, "we are not immortal. It is true we are far longer-lived than you mortals be, unless your race has much changed. But unlike Zida'ya and Hikeda'ya—our old overlords, Sithi and Norn—we do not live on and on, eternal as the mountains. Nay, Death comes for us as for your folk, like a thief and a reaver." Anger touched his face. "Mayhap our once-masters were of somewhat different blood since back in the Garden of our old stories, whence came all the Firstborn; mayhap then we are just of shorter-lived stock. Either that, or there was in truth some secret kept from us, who were after all deemed only their servers and vassals." He turned to his wife and gently touched her cheek. Yis-hadra hid her face against his shoulder, her long neck graceful as a swan's. "Some of us died, some left, and The Art of the Witnesses has escaped us."

Eolair shook his head, confused. "I am listening carefully, Yis-fidri, but I fear I still do not understand all the riddles in what you say. The voice that spoke to us from the stone—the one you called the grandmother of the Sithi—said that Great Swords are being sought. What does Prince Josua have to do with any of this?"

Yis-fidri raised his hand. "Come with us to a better place for speaking. I fear that your presence has bewildered some of our folk. It has been beyond the lives of most of us since Sudhoda'ya were among us." He stood up with a creak of leather, unfolding his spindly limbs like a locust climbing a stalk of wheat. "We will continue in the Pattern Hall." His expression became apologetic. "Also, Hern's Folk, I am tired and hungry." He shook his head. "I have not talked so much in a long age."

Imai-an and Sho-vennae stayed behind, perhaps to explain to their shy fellows what sort of creatures the mortals were. Maegwin saw them gather the other dwarrows together in a solemn group at the center of the giant bowl, huddling near the inconstant light of the Shard. Only an hour before she had been brimming with anticipation and excitement, but now Maegwin was glad to see the arena disappearing behind them. Wonder had turned to unease. A structure like the Site of Witness should stretch beneath an open sky filled with stars, as did the circuses of Nabban or the great theater of Erchester, not crouch beneath a firmament of dead black basalt. Anyway, there was no help for the Hernystiri here.

Yis-fidri and Yis-hadra led them through Mezutu'a's deserted byways, crystal rods glowing in the murk like swamp-ghosts as they wound through the narrow streets, across broad, echoing squares and over icicle-slender bridges with only shadowed emptiness below.

The lamps that Maegwin and Eolair had brought down to the subterranean city had guttered and gone out. The soft, roseate glow of the dwarrow's batons cast the only light. Mezutu'a's lines seemed softer now than they had by lamplight, the city's edges gentler, rounded as though by wind and rain. But Maegwin knew that here in the deeps of the earth no such weather had troubled the ancient walls.

She found her thoughts straying even from such wonderfully strange sights as these, returning instead to the trick that had been played upon her. The Sithi were not here. In fact, if the remaining Peaceful Ones were calling for the help of a diminished tribe like the dwarrows, they were probably in worse straits than Maegwin's own folk.

So here was the end of her hope of assistance—at least of earthly aid. There would be no rescue for her people, unless she herself could think of some way. Why had the gods sent Maegwin such dreams, only to dash them to pieces? Had Brynioch, Mircha, Rhynn and the rest truly turned their back on the Hernystiri? Many of her people, crouched in the cave above, already thought it dangerous even to fight back against Skali's invading army—as though the gods' will was so clearly against Lluth's tribe that to resist would be to insult the minions of heaven. Was *that* the lesson, both of her dreams about the lost Sithi and the actuality of Yis-fidri's frightened folk? Had the gods brought her here only to show her that the Hernystiri, too, would soon diminish and fade, as the proud Sithi and crafty dwarrows had themselves been brought low?

Maegwin straightened her shoulders. She could not let such qualms frighten her. She was Lluth's daughter . . . the king's daughter. She would think of something. The error was in relying on the fallible creatures of earth, men *or* Sithi. The gods would send to her. They would—they *must*—give her some further sign, some plan, even in the midst of her despair.

Her sigh drew a curious glance from Eolair. "Lady? Are you sick?"

She waved away his concerns.

"Once all this city was full-lit," Yis-fidri announced suddenly, waving an elongated hand. "The mountain-heart all besparkled, yes."

"Who lived here, Yis-fidri?" the count asked.

"Our people. *Tinukeda'ya*. But most of our kind are long gone. A few are here, and some few lived in Hikehikayo in the northern mountains, a smaller city than this." His face twisted. "Until they were made to leave."

"Made to leave? By what?"

Yis-fidri shook his head, palpating his long chin with his fingers. "That would be a great wrong to say. Unkind it would be to bring our evil on Hern's innocent children. Fear not. Our few remaining folk there fled, leaving the evil behind them."

His wife Yis-hadra said something in the fluttering dwarrow tongue.

"True, that is true," Yis-fidri said regretfully. He blinked his vast eyes. "Our people have left those mountains behind. We *hope* that they have left the evil behind as well."

Eolair looked at Maegwin in a way she supposed was somehow significant. The talk had mostly slipped past her, immersed as she was in the greater problems of her unhomed people. She smiled sadly, letting the Count of Nad Mullach know that his laboring after such fruitless details

did not go unnoticed or unappreciated, then lapsed back into silent contemplation once more.

Count Eolair shifted his disconcerted glance from Lluth's daughter back
to the dwarrows. "Can you tell me of this evil?"

Yis-fidri looked at him speculatively. "No," he said at last. "I have not
the right to share so much, for all you be noble persons among your kind.
Mayhap when I have had a greater while to think, you will hear more.
Content yourself." He would say nothing further concerning the subject.

Silent now but for the quiet noise of footsteps, the odd procession crept
on through the ancient city, lights bobbing like fireflies.

The Pattern Hall was a dome only slightly smaller in circumference than
the Site of Witness, set low in the midst of a forest of towers, surrounded
by a moat of rock sculpted to resemble the waves of a crashing sea. The
dome itself was fluted like a sea shell, constructed of some fair stone that
did not shine like the rose-crystal rods, but nevertheless seemed faintly
radiant.

"The Ocean Indefinite and Eternal," said Yis-fidri with a gesture at the
spiky stone waves. "Our birth-home was an island in the sea that sur-
rounds all. We Tinukeda'ya built those craft that took all the Gardenborn
across that water. Ruyan Vé, the greatest of our folk, steered the ships and
brought us here to this land, safe out of destruction." A light came to the
dwarrow's saucerlike eyes, a note of triumph to his voice. He wagged his
head firmly, as though to emphasize the importance of what he said.
"Without us, no ships would have been. All, both masters *and* servants,
would have passed into Unbeing." After a moment he blinked and looked
around, the fire abruptly gone. "Come, Hern-folk," he said. "Hie we
down to the *Banipha-sha-zé*—the Pattern Hall."

His wife Yis-hadra beckoned, then led Maegwin and the count around
the frozen gray ocean to the back of the dome, which sat off-center in the
moat like the yoke of an egg. A ramp curled down into the shadowed
depths.

"This is where my husband and I dwell," Yis-hadra said. She spoke
Hernystiri more haltingly than her husband. "We are keepers of this
place."

The inside of the Pattern Hall was dark, but as Yis-hadra entered before
them, she drew her hands along the walls. Where her long fingers touched,
stones began to glow with a pale light, yellower than that given off by the
rods.

Maegwin saw Eolair's sharp profile hovering beside her, spectral and
dreamlike. She was beginning to feel the burden of her long, strenuous
day; her knees were growing weak, her thoughts furry. How had Eolair
ever let her do such a foolish thing, she wondered? He should have . . .
have . . . have what? Knocked her senseless? Carried her kicking and

screeching back to the surface? She would have hated him if he had. Maegwin ran her hands through her matted hair. If only none of these terrible things had ever happened, if only life at the Taig had gone on its small, foolish way, with her father and Gwythinn alive, with winter in its proper place. . . .

"Maegwin!" The count took her elbow. "You almost hit your head against the doorway."

She shook off his hand and bent to pass through. "I saw it."

The room beyond slowly revealed itself as Yis-hadra touched more stones into radiant life. It was circular, the walls pocked every few paces by a low doorway. The doors themselves were carved of dressed stone and hinged with tarnished bronze. Their surfaces were covered with runic letters unlike anything Maegwin had seen, different even than the great gates that had led her to Mezutu'a in the first place.

"Seat yourself, if you please," Yis-fidri said, gesturing to a row of granite stools, solid upcroppings that rose like mushrooms beside a low stone table. "We will prepare food. Will you dine with us?"

Eolair looked at her, but Maegwin pretended to be looking in the other direction. She was desperately tired and confused, full of regret. The Sithi were not here. These bent, flawed creatures could be no help against the likes of Skali and King Elias. There was no earthly help coming.

"You are very kind, Yis-fidri," the count said. "We will be pleased to share your table."

A great show was made of lighting a tiny bed of coals in a trough set into the stone floor. Yis-fidri's anxious care with them suggested that such fuel was hard to find, and used only for very special occasions.

Maegwin could not help noticing the strangely graceful way that the dwarrows moved as they fetched the ingredients of their meal. Despite their awkward, stiff-limbed gaits, they stepped in and out of the two doors at the room's opposite end and slid around obstacles with an odd, dancing fluidity, and seemed almost to caress each other in passing with their tuneful, pattering speech. She knew she watched a pair of ancient lovers, both enfeebled, but so accustomed to each other that they had become two limbs of the same body. Now that the strangeness of the dwarrows' owl-eyed appearance had worn away, Maegwin observed their quiet interactions and felt certain that they were just what they seemed—a couple who might have seen terror and sorrow, but whose happiness with each other spanned centuries.

"Come now," Yis-fidri said at last, pouring something from a stone ewer into bowls for Maegwin and the count. "Drink."

"What is it?" Maegwin asked quietly. She sniffed the liquid, but could discern nothing unusual in its smell.

"Water, Hern-child," Yis-fidri said, puzzlement plain his voice. "Do your folk no longer drink water?"

"We do," Maegwin smiled, lifting the bowl to her lips. She had forgotten how long it had been since she had last sipped from her water skin, but it must have been hours. The water ran down her throat in gulps, cold and sweet as iced honey. It had a taste she could not identify, something stony but clean. If it were a color, she decided, it would have been the blue of new evening.

"Wonderful!" She let Yis-fidri pour her another bowl.

The dwarrows next produced a dish piled high with pieces of white, faintly luminous fungus, and other bowls with things in them that Maegwin was sinkingly sure were some kind of many-legged bugs. These had been wrapped in leaves and roasted over the coals. The spell cast by the draught of delicious water abruptly vanished and Maegwin found herself tottering once more on the edge of a terrible homesickness.

Eolair manfully took a few bites of fungus—it was not by chance that he was deemed the best court envoy in Osten Ard—and ostentatiously chewed and swallowed one of the leggy morsels, then settled down to rearranging his supper in a way that resembled eating. If Maegwin had needed any additional proof, the expression on his chewing face was enough to keep the contents of her own bowl far from her mouth.

"So, Yis-fidri, why is your house called the Pattern Hall?" the Count of Nad Mullach asked. He quietly let a few blackened grubs fall from his fingertips and down into the hem of his cloak.

"We shall show that to you when eating is finished," Yis-hadra said proudly.

"Then, if it is not impolite, may I ask you of some other things? Our time here is growing short." Eolair shrugged. "I must return this lady to our people in the caverns above."

Maegwin bit back a sneering remark. Return this lady, indeed!

"Ask, Hern's child."

"You spoke of a mortal, one we know as Josua Lackhand. And the voice from the stone said something about Great Swords. What are these swords, and what do they have to do with Josua?"

Yis-fidri scraped with his spoon-shaped fingers at a fragment of fungus on his chin. "I must begin before the beginning, as we say." He looked from Eolair to Maegwin and back. "In days agone, our folk made for a king of the northern men a sword. That king betrayed his bargain. When the time came to pay, the mortal king instead argued, then slew the leader of our folk. That king hight Elvrit, first master of Rimmersgard. The sword dwarrow-forged for him, he named Minneyar."

"I have heard this legend," Eolair said.

Yis-fidri held up a spidery hand. "You have not heard all, Count Eolair, if I have recalled your name aright. Bitter was our curse on that blade, and closely did we watch it, though it was far from us. Such is dwarrow-work, that nothing we have forged is ever far from our hearts or our

sight. Minneyar brought much sadness to Fingil and his tribe, for all it
was a mighty weapon."

He took a swallow of water to clear his throat. Yis-hadra tenderly
watched his face, her hand atop his. "We told you that our Witnesses
have stood unused for centuries of silence. Then, little more than one year
ago, the Shard spoke to us—or rather, something spoke to us *through* the
Shard, as in the elder days.

"That which spoke was someone or something who we knew not,
something that used the Speakfire in the old dwarrow-home of Hikehikayo,
something that talked to us in gentle and persuasive words. Strange
enough was it to hear Shard and Speakfire talking as of old, but we also
remembered the evil that had driven our fellows from their home—an evil
of which you mortals need not hear, for it would throw you into great
fear—so we trusted this stranger not. Also, as long as it had been since we
had last used the Witnesses, still some for us remembered the elder days
and what it felt like when the Ziday'a did speak to us then.

"*This was not the same.* Whatever stood before the Speakfire in the north
seemed more like a cold breath of Unbeing than a living creature, for all
its kindly words."

Yis-hadra moaned softly beside him. Maegwin, caught up in the
dwarrow's story despite herself, felt a chill travel through her.

"That which spoke," Yis-fidri continued, "wished to know of the
sword Minneyar. It knew we had been the blade's makers and it knew
that we dwarrows are bound to our work even after it has gone from us,
as one who has lost a hand often feels it still at the end of his arm. The
thing that spoke to us from Witness to Witness asked if the northern king
Fingil had indeed taken the sword Minneyar into Asu'a when he conquered that great place, and was it there still."

"*Asu'a,*" Eolair breathed. "Of course—the Hayholt."

"That is its mortal name," Yis-fidri nodded. "We were frightened by
this strange and fearful voice. You must understand, we have been as
castaways for more years than your people can dream. It was obvious that
some new power had arisen in the world, but one that nevertheless did
command the old Arts. But we do not wish any of our old masters to find
us and take us back, so at first we made no answer."

The dwarrow leaned forward on his padded elbows. "Then, a short
time ago—a few of the Moon-woman's changes, as you would reckon it
beneath the sky—the Shard spoke again. This time it did speak with the
voice of the eldest of the Sithi, the voice you heard. She also asked us of
Minneyar. With her, also, we were silent."

"Because you fear they will make you their servants again."

"Yes, Hern's man. Unless you have ever fled from bondage, you will
not understand that terror. Our masters are ageless. We are not. They
retain the old lore. We diminish." Yis-fidri rocked back and forth on his

stool, the ancient leather of his garments rubbing and squeaking like crickets.

"But we knew something neither of our questioners did," he said finally; there was a gleam in his round eye unlike anything the surface dwellers had yet seen. "Do you see, our masters think the sword Minneyar never left Asu'a, and that is true. But the one who found the sword there beneath the castle, the one you call King John Prester, had it reforged and made new. Under the name of Bright-Nail, he carried it all across the world and back."

The Count of Nad Mullach whistled, a low, surprised trill. "So Bright-Nail was the old Scourge of the North, Fingil's Minneyar. Strange! What other secrets did Prester John take to his grave above the Kynslagh, I wonder?" He paused. "But, Yis-fidri, still we do not understand . . ."

"Patience." The dwarrow showed a wintry smile. "You could never tend and harvest balky stone as we do, you quick-blooded Children. Patience." He took a breath. "The mistress of the Zida'ya told us that this sword, one of the Great Swords, was somehow much concerned with events now transpiring, and with the fate of the mortal prince named Handless Josua . . ."

"Josua Lackhand."

"Yes. But we think that is trickery, for she also said that this sword might be somehow vital against that same evil that had driven our tribesfolk out of Hikehikayo, and that the same evil soon might threaten all that walked above or below ground. How could the fate of any mortal man affect the squabblings of immortals?" The dwarrow's voice quavered. "It is another trap, to play on our fear. She wishes us to seek her help, so we will fall into their clutch once more. Did you not hear her? 'Come to us at Jao é-Tinukai'i.' Was ever a trap more cold-bloodedly baited before the victim's eyes?"

"So," the count said at last, "somehow Josua's survival is tied to this blade?"

Yis-fidri shot him a worried glance. "So she claimed. But how could she say his fate is tied to that of Minneyar when she did not even know it had been reforged? She said that none but us did know this thing, and that possibly many fates—perhaps the threads of *all* fate—were tied to three great swords, of which Minneyar was one."

Yis-fidri stood, a haunted look upon his face. "And I will tell you a terrible, terrible thing," he said miserably. "Even though we cannot trust our once-masters, we fear that they may be telling the truth. Mayhap a great doom *has* come into the world. If so, we dwarrows may have brought it on."

Eolair looked around, struggling to make sense of what he had heard. "But why, Yis-fidri? Bright-Nail's history might be a deep and dark secret, but you dwarrows did not tell it to anyone. When the Shard spoke to us, *we* said nothing of it, because we did not know the tale. No secrets have been told. What doom have you brought on?"

The dwarrow was deeply pained. "I . . . did not tell you all. One last time before your arrival, the Shard called to us. It was the fearsome stranger from Hikehikayo asking again of the sword Minneyar—that cursed sword." He slumped bonelessly back onto the stool. "This time there was only one of us at the Site of Witness—young Sho-vennae, who you have met. He was alone and the voice laid a great fear upon him. It threatened, then it promised, then threatened again." Yis-fidri slapped his wide palm on the table. "You must understand, he was afraid! We are all afraid! We are not what we were." He lowered his eyes as if shamed, then looked up to find his wife's gaze. He seemed to gain courage. "At last, Sho-vennae's terror did overwhelm him. He told the stranger the tale of Minneyar, of how it was reforged and became Bright-Nail." Yis-fidri's shook his great head. "Poor Sho-vennae. We should never have let him stand watch at the Shard alone. May the Garden forgive us. Do you see, you Hern's folk, our former masters may have lied to us, but still we fear that no good can come out of the darkness in Hikehikayo. If the First Grandmother of the Sithi has told the truth, who knows what power we have given to evil?"

Maegwin hardly heard him. She was losing the thread of Yis-fidri's speech, dully registering bits and pieces while her weary mind swirled with thoughts of her own failure. She had misunderstood the gods' will. She needed to be free, to have time to herself, time to think.

Count Eolair sat thinking for a long while; the room was full of brooding silence. At last, Yis-fidri stood.

"You have shared our table," he said. "Let us show you our prizes, then you may go back to the bright, airy surface."

Eolair and Maegwin, still silent, let themselves be led across the round room and through one of the doors. They followed the dwarrows down a long, sloping hallway before coming at last to a deeper chamber whose outer walls were as complicated as a maze, angling in and out so that everywhere Maegwin looked there were surfaces covered with carved stone.

"In this chamber and others below it are the Patterns," Yis-fidri said. "Long the dwarrows have delved, and widely. Every tunnel, every deep place we dug is there. This is the history of our folk, and we two are the keepers of it." He waved his hand proudly. "Maps of bright Kementari, the labyrinth of Jhiná-T'seneí, the tunnels beneath the mountains Rimmersmen call Vestivegg, and those that honeycomb the mountains above our heads—all here. The catacombs of Zae-y'miritha are long-buried and silent . . . but here they live!"

Eolair turned slowly, looking from surface to surface. The interior of the great chamber was as intricate as a many-faceted stone; each facet, every angle and niche, was covered with delicate maps carved into the living stone. "And you said that you have maps of the tunnels that run here, throughout the Grianspog?" he asked slowly.

"With certainty, Count Eolair," Yis-fidri said. Being among the Patterns seemed to have restored life to his sagging frame. "Those and more."

"If we could have those, it would be a great help to us in our own struggle."

Maegwin turned on the count, irritation finally bubbling to the surface. "What, shall we carry a thousandweight of stone up to our caves? Or climb down here to this lost place every time we must choose a fork in the path?"

"No," said Eolair, "but like the Aedonite monks, we could copy them onto parchment, and so have them where we need them." His eyes shone. "There must be tunnels we never dreamed of! Our raids on Skali's camps will truly seem like magic! See, Maegwin, you *have* brought great assistance to your people after all—a help greater than swords and spears!" He turned to Yis-fidri. "Would you allow us to do such a thing?"

Worried, the dwarrow turned to his wife. As the sound of their conversation chimed back and forth, Maegwin watched the count. Eolair was walking from wall to wall, squinting up at the angled walls and their beetle-busy carvings. She fought a rising tide of anger. Did he think he was doing her a kindness when he complimented her on this "discovery?" She had been looking for help from the shining, legendary Sithi, not a gaggle of scarecrows with their dusty tunnel-maps. Tunnels! Maegwin had been the one who had rediscovered the tunnels in the first place! How dare he try and placate her?

As she felt herself caught between fury and loneliness and loss, a sudden realization cut through her confused thoughts like a knife.

Eolair must go away.

She could have no peace, she could never understand what the gods meant her to do, as long as he was around. His presence turned her into a child, a whining, moody thing unfit to lead her people out of these dangerous straits.

Yis-fidri turned at last. "My wife and I must speak with our people before anything can be decided. This would be a new thing, and could not be done lightly."

"Of course," said Eolair. His voice was calm, but Maegwin could hear the suppressed excitement. "Of course, whatever may be best for your people. We will go away now and come back to you in a day or two, or whenever you say. But tell them that it will perhaps save Hern's folk, whom the dwarrows often helped before. The Hernystiri have never thought anything but good of you."

Maegwin had another thought. "Are there tunnels near the Hayholt?"

Yis-hadra nodded. "Yes. Asu'a, as we call it, was delved deep as well as built high. Now its bones lie beneath the castle of mortal kings, but the earth underneath that castle is still alive with our diggings."

"And are those maps here, too?"

"Of course," the dwarrow replied proudly.

With a satisfied nod, Maegwin turned on the Count of Nad Mullach. "There," she said. "That is the final answer I sought. A course lies open before us: we would be traitors to our own folk not to take it." She lapsed into grave silence.

Eolair rose to the bait. "What do you mean, Princess?"

"You *must* find Josua, Count Eolair," she said abruptly. She was pleased at the calm authority in her voice. "You heard what Yis-fidri said at the table. This matter of the sword is of utmost importance. I was already thinking that Prince Josua must be informed, in case there is a chance this knowledge can be used to defeat Elias. You and I know that as long as the High King prospers, Skali Sharp-nose will remain at our necks like a knife. Go find Josua and tell him the secret of the sword. That will be the deed that saves our people."

In truth, Maegwin did not quite remember all the details of the dwarrow's tale—she had been occupied with her own dire thoughts—but she remembered that it had something to do with Josua and his father's sword.

Eolair was astonished. "Go to Josua?! What do you say, Lady? We have no idea where he is, or if he even lives. Do you ask me to leave our people in their need to go rabbiting off on such a fool's mission?"

"You claimed you heard that he was alive," she responded coldly. "Only a short while ago you were lecturing me on the chance of his survival. Can we afford to assume he is dead?"

It was hard to tell from his practiced expression what he was thinking. Maegwin took a breath before beginning again. "In any case, Count Eolair, you fail to see the full importance of what these folk have told us. Maps of our tunnels are important, yes—but we can now send to Josua maps of Elias' stronghold, and of the secret entrances that could be the High King's undoing." Listening to herself, it *did* suddenly seem like a good plan. "You know that Skali will never loosen his grip on our land as long as Elias rules at his back in the Hayholt."

Eolair shook his head. "To many questions, my lady, too many questions. There is merit in what you say, certainly. Let us think about it. It will take us days to make semblances of all these maps. Surely it will be better if we consider it carefully, if we talk with Criobhan and the other knights."

Maegwin wanted to set the hook now, while Eolair was hesitating. She feared that more time would mean time for the count to think of another solution, and for her to sink back into her inclarity of purpose. Being near him made her heart heavy as stone. She needed him to go away—she felt it now as a deep longing. She wanted him gone, so the pain and confusion would stop. How was it he could cloud her wits this way?

She made her face cold. "I do not like your resistance, Count. In fact, you seem to be doing precious little here, if you have time to follow me down holes in the ground. You might be better employed on a task that has some chance of saving us from our current situation." Maegwin smiled, purposefully mocking. She was proud of how well she hid her true feelings, but this cruelty, however necessary, filled her with horror.

What kind of creature am I becoming? she wondered even as she carefully watched Eolair's reaction. *Is this statecraft?* She felt a moment of panic. *Am I being a fool? No, it is better he goes away—but if this is how kings and queens must see their wills accomplished, Bagba's Herd, what a terrible thing!*

Aloud, she added, "Besides, Count, you are pledged to my father's house—just in case you had forgotten. If you wish to flaunt the first request Lluth's daughter has made of you, I cannot prevent you, but the gods will know and judge." Eolair started to speak. Maegwin lifted a hand to stop him—a very dirty hand, she could not help noticing. "I will not argue with you, Count Eolair. Do as you are told, or do not. That is all."

Eolair's eyes narrowed, as though he saw her truly for the first time and did not like what he now saw. His contemptuous expression leaned against her heart like an impossibly heavy stone, but there was no turning back.

The count waited a long time before answering. "Very well, Lady," he said quietly, "I will do as you command. I do not know where this sudden fancy—fancy! It seems a kind of madness!—has come from. If you had asked my counsel in this thing and treated me as your family's friend instead of a vassal, I would have heeded your wish happily. Instead you will have my obedience, but there will be little love with it. You thought to act the queen, but instead you have proved yourself only a callow child after all."

"Be silent," she said hoarsely.

The dwarrows stared at Eolair and Maegwin curiously, as if they performed a quaint but inscrutable pantomime. The lights of the Pattern Hall dimmed for a moment, and shadows grew monstrously tall among the labyrinthine walls of stone. A moment later the pale light flared once more, illuminating the darker corners, but a certain shadow had taken up residence in Maegwin's heart and would not be dismissed.

The *Eadne Cloud*'s crew did not handle Miriamele and Cadrach gently as they routed the pair from the hold, but neither were they especially brutal. The sailors seemed more than a little amused by such an unexpected couple of stowaways. As the captives appeared beneath the lightening sky, the crewmen jeered mockingly, speculating on the vices of monks who took young women as companions, and on the virtue of young women who allowed themselves to be so taken.

Miriamele stared back defiantly, undaunted by their rough manners. Despite the well-known sailor's custom of going bearded, many of the *Cloud*'s crew were smooth-cheeked, not yet old enough to grow whiskers: she herself had seen more in a year, she felt sure, than these youths had seen in their whole lives.

Still, it was clear the *Eadne Cloud* was no plodding merchantman, no carrack bobbing like a washing tub as it carefully hugged the coastline, but a lithe ocean-rider. A child of river-fronted and sea-wrapped Meremund, Miriamele could tell the ship's quality just by the spritely way the deck rolled beneath her feet and by the sound of the white sails crackling overhead as they drank deeply of the daybreak wind.

An hour earlier, Miriamele had despaired. Now she found herself taking great breaths, her heart rising once more. Even a whipping from the captain would be bearable. She was alive and upon the open sea. The sun was rising into the morning sky, a beacon of continuing hope.

A glance at the standard snapping on the mainmast confirmed that Cadrach had been correct. The Prevan osprey flew there, ocher and black. If only she had found more time to talk to Dinivan, to find out more news of the Nabbanai court and where the Prevan house and others stood. . . .

She turned to whisper a warning to Cadrach about the need for secrecy, but was brought up sharply before a wooden stairway by the sailor at her side, who even in the stiff breeze smelled excessively of salt-pork.

The man on the quarterdeck turned to look down upon them. Miriamele, startled, sucked in a sharply audible breath of air. His was not a face she knew, nor did he seem to recognize her. He was, however, very, *very* handsome. Dressed in black breeches, jacket, and boots, each minutely wrought with gilt piping, with a brilliant cloth-of-gold cape swirling around him and the wind blowing his golden-blond hair, this strange nobleman seemed a sun god out of ancient legends.

"Kneel down, you louts," one of the sailors hissed. Cadrach dropped immediately. Miriamele, nonplussed, complied more slowly. She was unable to take her eyes off the golden man's face.

"These are they, Lord," the sailor said. "The ones the Niskie found. As you see, one's a girl."

"As I see," the man replied dryly. "You two remain kneeling," he directed Miriamele and Cadrach. "You men, go. We need more sail if we are to make Grenamman tonight."

"Yes, Lord."

As the sailors moved off hurriedly, the one they called lord turned to finish his conversation with a burly, bearded man that Miriamele guessed was the captain. The nobleman glanced at the prisoners once more before making his leonine way off the quarterdeck. Miriamele thought his eyes might have lingered on her longer than curiosity alone would dictate, and felt an unfamiliar tingle run through her—half fear, half excitement—as she turned to watch him go. A pair of manservants scurried after him, trying to keep his wind-whipped cloak from snagging on anything. Then, for a brief instant, the golden-haired man looked back. Catching her eye, he smiled.

The burly captain stared down at Cadrach and Miriamele with poorly hidden disgust. "Earl says he'll decide what to do with you after his morning meal," he growled, then spat expertly with the wind. "Women and monks—what could be worse luck, and especially in these times? I'd throw you over if the master didn't happen to be aboard."

"Who . . . who *is* the master of this ship?" Miriamele asked quietly.

"You don't recognize the crest, doxy? You didn't recognize milord when he was standing in front of you? Aspitis Preves, Earl of Drina and Eadne is master of this ship—and you'd better hope he takes a liking to you or you'll find yourself sleeping in kilpa beds." He spat more gray citril juice.

Cadrach, already pale, looked ill at the captain's words, but Miriamele barely heard. She was thinking of Aspitis' golden hair and bold eyes, and wondering how in the midst of such danger she could suddenly feel so unexpectedly fascinated.

20

A Thousand Steps

"There. Now you have witnessed for yourself." Binabik gestured at Qantaqa with helpless disgust. The wolf sat on her haunches, ears flattened and hackles raised, her gray pelt starred with snowflakes. "Qinkipa's Eyes!" the troll swore, "if I could be making her do it, have assurance that I would. She will walk back toward the abbey, but only to stay at my side and no more." He turned to his mount again. "Qantaqa! Simon *mosoq! Ummu!*" He shook his head. "She will not."

"What's wrong with her?" Sludig kicked at the ground, lifting a cloud of snow into the biting wind. "Every hour we do not find him the trail grows fainter. And if the boy is hurt, every hour leaves him nearer to death."

"Daughter of the Mountains, Rimmersman," Binabik shouted, "every hour of every day is leaving *all* of us nearer to death." He blinked his reddened eyes. "Of course we have need for haste. Do you think *I* do not care for Simon? Why have we been at trudging here and there since sunup? If I could exchange Qantaqa's nose for mine, I would with certainty! But she was badly frightened by the horror at Skodi's abbey, I am thinking— see! It is only with reluctance she is even following!"

Qantaqa had again balked. As Binabik looked back, she dipped her massive head and whined, barely audible against the rising wind.

Sludig slapped his leather-clad hands on his legs with a wet smack. "Damn me, troll, I know! But we need her nose! We don't even know where the boy went, or why he won't answer us. We have been shouting for hours!"

Binabik shook his head morosely. "That is what gives me the most worry. We did not go far before finding his horse—half of a league at the most. We have been twice that distantness now, and most of the way returning, but still no sign of Simon is there to see."

The Rimmersman squinted into the flurrying snow. "Come. If he's fallen off, he'd probably make his way back down his own tracks . . .

while they lasted. Let's drag the wolf a little farther, head back toward the abbey. All the way back this time. Maybe if she actually smells the boy close by, she will do better." He urged his mount and the trailing pack-horses forward. Binabik grimaced and whistled for Qantaqa. The wolf came reluctantly.

"I am not liking this storm that comes," the troll called; only a short distance ahead, the Rimmersman had already become a bulky blur. "Not any bit. This is the outrider for the darkness we saw gathering in the north near Stormspike. It is coming down with great swiftness."

"I know it," Sludig shouted over his shoulder. "Soon we will have to look to our own safety, whether we find the boy or not."

Binabik nodded, then thumped his hand sharply against his jacketed chest, once, twice, then a third time. Unless the gods of his people were watching, no one saw his anguished gesture.

The abbey, lately the scene of such wild horror, had become a quiet, snow-draped sepulcher. The mounds of drifting snow obscured most signs of what had become of Skodi and her young charges, but could not hide all. Qantaqa would not approach within an arrow's flight of the silent walls; Binabik and Sludig themselves only crossed into the abbey's door-yard long enough to make certain that Simon was not one of the still, white-shrouded forms, then left hurriedly.

When they had put a thousand paces between themselves and the abbey, they stopped and stood silently for a while, sharing long swallows from a bottle of kangkang as they listened to the mournful wind. Qantaqa, obviously happy to be heading away from that dire place once more, sniffed briefly at the air before curling up at Binabik's feet.

"Holy Aedon, troll," Sludig said at last, "what manner of witch was that girl Skodi, anyway? I have never seen anything to match it. Was she one of the Storm King's followers?"

"Only in the way that those like her do what the Storm King wishes, whether they are knowing it or not. She had power, but she was hoping to *become* a Power—which, I am thinking, is very different. A little Norn Queen with her own little band of followers was what she was wishing to be. Times of war and strife are the arising times of new forces. The old order begins its changing, and those like Skodi appear, seeking to make a mark."

"I only thank blessed God for wiping out the whole nest of them to the smallest pup." Sludig shivered and scowled. "No good could have come from any of those witchlets surviving."

Binabik looked at him curiously. "The innocent can be molded, as those children were, but sometimes luck is granting that they can be molded back. I have little belief in evil beyond redeeming, Sludig."

"Oh?" The Rimmersman laughed harshly. "What about your Storm King? What good thing could you possibly say about such a black-hearted hellspawn as that?"

"Once he loved his people more than his own life," Binabik said quietly.

The sun made a surprisingly swift crossing through the murky sky. By the time they halted again, early twilight was approaching. They had twice more covered the distance between the abbey and the spot in the deep woods that they had decided on as the outermost point. All their shouting and beating of bushes had been to no avail: Simon remained unfound, and now darkness and fresh storms were fast approaching.

"Aedon's Blood," Sludig said in disgust, then patted Simon's gray mare, which was roped to the train of pack horses. "At least we did not lose the damnable sword as well." He waved a hand at Thorn, but did not touch it. Where the black sword was visible through the loose swaddling, snowflakes lit upon its surface and slid away, leaving it free of the white that spattered everything else. "It makes our decision more difficult, though. If the lad and the sword were lost together, we would have no choice but to search."

Binabik looked up with angry eyes. "What 'decision' do you speak about?"

"We can't very well abandon everything for the stripling, troll. I'm fond of him, the good Lord knows, but we have our duty to Prince Josua. You and the other book-readers keep saying that Josua needs this blade or we are all doomed. Should we ignore that to hunt for a lost boy? Then we would be more foolish than the boy was for getting lost in the first place."

"Simon is not foolish." Binabik buried his face in the ruff of Qantaqa's neck for a long moment. "And I am tired of being an oath-breaker. I swore for his protection." The troll's voice was muffled by the wolf's pelt, but the straining edge was unmistakable.

"We are forced to difficult choices, troll."

Binabik looked up. His usually mild brown gaze had turned flinty. "Do not be speaking to me of *choices*. Do not go teaching me about *difficulty*. Take the sword. On my master's grave I swore to protect Simon. To me, nothing else has more importance."

"Then you are the most foolish of all," Sludig growled. "We are down to two left while the world freezes around us. Would you send me alone with the sword that could save your people and mine? All so you need not be an oath-breaker to a dead master?"

Binabik straightened. His eyes brimmed with angry tears. "Do not dare speak to me of my oath," he hissed. "I am taking no advice from a witless *Croohok!*"

Sludig raised a gloved fist as though to strike at the little man. The Rimmersman stared at his own trembling hand, then turned and stalked out of the clearing. Binabik did not look up to see him ago, but instead returned to stroking Qantaqa's shaggy back. A tear ran down his cheek and vanished into the fur of his hood.

Minutes passed without even a bird's cry.

"Troll?" Sludig stood at the edge of the glade, just beyond the horses. Binabik still would not look up. "Listen, man," Sludig continued, "you must listen to me." The Rimmersman still hung back, like an unexpected guest waiting to be invited indoors. "Once, soon after we first met, I told you that you knew nothing of honor. I wished to go and kill Storfot, Thane of Vestvennby, for his insults to Duke Isgrimnur. You said I should not go. You said that my lord Isgrimnur had given me a task to perform, and that putting that task's fulfillment in jeopardy was neither brave or honorable, but foolish."

The troll continued to rub distractedly along Qantaqa's back.

"Binabik, I know you are honorable. You know I am the same. We have a bad choice to make, but it is not right that allies should fight and throw insults like stones at each other."

The troll still did not reply, but his hands fell from the wolf and into his lap. He crouched unspeaking for long moments, chin on chest.

"I have been disgracing myself, Sludig," he said at last. "You are right to be hurling my own words back into my face. I beg for your pardon, although I have done nothing for its deserving." He turned an unhappy face up to the Rimmersman, who took a few steps back into the clearing.

"We cannot afford to search for Simon forever," Sludig said quietly. "That is a truth separate from love and friendship."

"You are not wrong," Binabik said. He shook his head slowly. "Not wrong." He stood and moved toward the bearded soldier, extending a small hand. "If you can show forgiving of my stupidity . . ."

"There is nothing to forgive." His broad palm clasped Binabik's, engulfing it.

A weary smile flitted across the troll's face. "Then one favor there is I will ask. Let us be making a fire here during tonight and tomorrow night, and we will call for Simon. If we are finding no trace of him, then the morning after tomorrow we will walk on toward the Stone of Farewell. Otherwise, I will feel as though I have deserted him without proper searching."

Sludig nodded gravely. "Fairly spoken. Now, we should gather wood. Night is coming on quickly."

"The cold wind is not lessening, either," Binabik said, frowning. "An unhappy thought for all who are out of doors without shelter."

Brother Hengfisk, the king's unpleasant cupbearer, gestured to the doorway. The monk's grin was as derangedly fixed as ever, as though he struggled with some monstrous humor only barely held in check. The Earl of Utanyeat stepped through the door and silent Hengfisk scuttled away down the stairs, leaving the earl standing just inside the bell chamber.

Guthwulf took a moment to catch his breath. It was a very long climb up the tower steps and the earl had not been sleeping well lately.

"You called for me, Highness?" he said at last.

The king stood hunched over the sill of one of the high-arched windows, his heavy cloak glinting in the torchlight like a fly's glass-green back. Although the afternoon was only half gone, the sky outside was evening-dark, purple and sullen gray. The curve of Elias' shoulders made Guthwulf think of a vulture. The king wore the heavy gray sword scabbarded at his side; seeing it, the earl shivered uncontrollably.

"The storm is almost upon us," Elias said without turning. "Have you been this high in Green Angel Tower before?"

Guthwulf forced himself to speak casually. "I have been in the entry hall. Perhaps once to the chaplain's rooms on the second floor. Never this high, sire."

"It is a strange place," the king said, his gaze still fixed on something beyond the northwestern window. "This place, Green Angel Tower, was once the center of the greatest kingdom Osten Ard has ever seen. Did you know that, Guthwulf?" Elias swung away from the window. His eyes were bright, but his face was drawn and lined as though his iron crown were cinched too tightly about his brow.

"Do you mean your father's kingdom, Highness?" the earl asked, puzzled and more than a little fearful. He had felt only a kind of dread when he had received this latest summons. This man was no longer his old friend. At times the king seemed almost unchanged, but Guthwulf could not ignore the underlying reality: the Elias he had known might as well be dead. However, the gallows in Battle Square and the spikes atop the Nearulagh Gate were now crowded with the mortal remains of those who had upset this new Elias in some way or other. Guthwulf knew to keep his mouth well shut and do what he was told—at least for a while longer.

"Not my father's, idiot. For the love of God, my hand stretches over a far realer kingdom than his ever did. My father had King Lluth on his very doorstep; now there are no other kings but me." Elias' moment of bad temper faded as he waved his arm expansively. "No, Guthwulf, there are more things in this world than such as you can even dream of. This was once the capital of a mighty empire—vaster than Fingil's Greater Rimmersgard, older than the Nabban of the Imperators, stronger in lore than lost Khandia." His voice sank so that it was almost lost in the call of the wind. "But with his help, I will make this castle the seat of an even greater kingdom."

"Whose help, Highness?" Guthwulf could not refrain from asking. He felt a surge of cold jealousy. "Pryrates?"

Elias looked at him oddly for a moment, then burst into laughter. "Pryrates! Guthwulf, you are artless as a child!"

The Earl of the Utanyeat bit the inside of his cheek to hold back the angry—and potentially fatal—words. He clenched and unclenched his scarred fists. "Yes, my king," he said at last.

The king was once more staring out the window. Above his head, the great bells slept in dark clusters. Thunder muttered somewhere far away. "But the priest does keep secrets from me," Elias said. "He knows my power is growing as my understanding increases, and so he tries to hide things from me. Do you see that, Guthwulf?" He pointed out the window. "Well, Fires of Hell, man, how can you see from there?" the king snarled. "Come closer! Do you fear the wind will freeze you?" He laughed strangely.

Guthwulf reluctantly stepped forward, thinking of what Elias had been like before this insanity had begun to creep in: quick-tempered, yes, but not inconstant as a spring breeze; fond of jokes, but with the bluff humor of a soldier, not this mocking and incomprehensible wit. It was growing harder and harder for Guthwulf to recall that other man, his friend. Ironically, it seemed that the madder Elias became, the more he grew to resemble his brother Josua.

"There." The king gestured across the damp rooftops of the Hayholt toward the gray bulk of Hjeldin's Tower, squatting along the Inner Bailey's northern wall. "I gave that to Pryrates to use for his various endeavours—his *investigations,* if you will—and now he keeps it always locked; he will not even give a key to his king. For my safety, he says." Elias glared across at the priest's brooding tower, gray as the sky, upper windows of thick red glass. "He is growing very proud, the alchemist."

"Banish him, Elias—or destroy him!" Guthwulf spoke without thinking, then decided to press on. "You know I have always spoken to you as a friend, blunt when it was needed. And you know I am no craven who whimpers when a little blood is spilled or a few bones are cracked. But that man is poisonous as a serpent and far more dangerous. He will stab you in the back. Only say the word and I will kill him." When he finished he found that his heart was racing, as in the hour before battle.

The king stared for a moment, then laughed again. "Ah, there is the Wolf I knew. No, no, old friend, I told you once before: *I need Pryrates,* and I will use whatever I need to perform the grand task before me. Neither will he stab me in the back, for you see, he needs me, too. The alchemist uses me—or thinks he does."

Thunder pealed again in the distance as Elias stepped away from the window and laid his hand on Guthwulf's arm. The earl could feel the radiating cold right through his heavy sleeve. "But I do not want Pryrates to kill you," the king said, "—and kill you he would, make no mistake. His courier arrived today from Nabban. The letter tells me that negotiations with the lector are going very well, and that Pryrates will be back in a few days. That is why it was a happy thought to send you out to the High Thrithings at the head of my knights. Young Fengbald was pressing for the command, but you have always been of great service to me, and—more importantly—you will then be out of the red priest's path until he has done what I need."

"I am grateful for the chance to serve, my king," Guthwulf said slowly, several kinds of anger and fear swelling venomously within him. To think that the Earl of Utanyeat had come to such sneaking and bowing!

What if he were to grab Elias, he thought suddenly, wildly—just grab the king and then fling himself over the window's low railing, both of them plunging down over a hundred cubits to smash like eggs. Usires the Ransomer, what a relief it would be to end this festering brain-sickness that had crept all through the Hayholt and through Guthwulf himself! His mind reeled. Aloud, he only said: "Are you sure that these rumors of your brother are not just that? Rumors only, the imaginings of complaining peasants? I find it hard to believe that anything could have survived . . . could have survived Naglimund." One step, he thought, just one, then the two of them would be gliding down through the heavy air. It would all be over in moments and the long dark sleep would begin. . . .

Elias moved away from the window, breaking the spell. Guthwulf felt chill sweat beading on his forehead. "I do not heed 'rumors,' my dear Utanyeat. I am Elias the High King, and I *know*." He stalked to a window on the tower's far side, one that faced southeast, into the teeth of the wind. His hair swirled, black as a crow's wing. "There." He pointed out across the choppy, leaden-hued Kynslagh into the murky distance. A flash of lightning briefly illuminated the deep wells of his eyes. "Josua lives, indeed, and he is *somewhere . . . out . . . there*. I have received word from a trusted source." Thunder came, chasing the lightning. "Pryrates tells me my energies could be better spent. He tells me not to worry about my brother. If I had not seen a thousand kinds of proof of Pryrates' black and empty heart, I would think he felt sorry for Josua, so strongly does he argue against this mission. But I will do as I please. I am the king and I want Josua dead." Another lightning flare etched his face, which was twisted like a ritual mask. The king's voice strained; for a moment it seemed that only his white-knuckled grasp upon the stone sill kept him from toppling. "And I want my daughter back. *Back.* I want Miriamele back. She has disobeyed her father, joining with his enemies . . . with *my* enemies. She must be *punished*."

Guthwulf could think of nothing to say. He nodded his head, trying to dispel the terrible thoughts that now surged within him like a well filling with black water. The king and his cursed sword! Even now, Guthwulf felt the blade's presence sickening him. He would go to the Thrithings and hunt for Josua, if that was what Elias wished. At least he would be out of this horrible castle with its night sounds, its fearful servants and mad, mourning king. He would be able to think again. The earl would breathe unsullied air and keep the company of soldiers once more, men with whose thoughts and conversation he was comfortable.

Thunder rang through the chamber, setting the bells to humming. "I will do as you say, my king," he said.

"Of course," Elias nodded, calm again. "Of course."

Scowling Guthwulf had gone away, but the king stayed for some time, staring out into the cloudy sky, listening to the wind as carefully as if he understood its mournful tongue. Rachel, Mistress of Chambermaids, was beginning to feel very uncomfortable in her cramped hiding place. Still, she had learned what she needed to know. Her mind was full of ideas quite beyond her usual concerns: lately, Rachel the Dragon had found herself thinking thoughts she had never dreamed possible.

Wrinkling her nose against the harsh but familiar scent of polishing grease, she peeked out of the crack between the stone doorframe and the warped wooden door. The king was still as a statue, gazing off into nothingness. Rachel was again filled with horror at her own transgression. Spying like the most slatternly, brought-in-just-for-the-holy-days servant girl! And on the High King! Elias *was* the son of her beloved King John—even if he couldn't hope to match up to his father—and Rachel, the Hayholt's last bastion of rectitude, was spying on him.

The thought make her feel faint and weak; the odoriferous grease did not help. She leaned against the wall of the bell-ringer's closet and was grateful for its narrow confines. Between the stacks of rope, the bell hooks and grease pots and brick walls standing close at either shoulder, she could not topple over even if she tried.

She had not meant to spy, of course—not really. She had heard the voices as she was examining the woefully dirty stairs at Green Angel Tower's third floor. She had stepped quietly out of the spiraling passageway into a curtained alcove so as not to seem to be listening to the king's business, for she had recognized Elias' voice almost immediately. The king had climbed past, speaking as though to the grinning monk Hengfisk who accompanied him everywhere, but his words had seemed like babbling nonsense to Rachel. "Whispers from Nakkiga," he had said, and "songs of the upper air." He had spoken of "listening for the cry of the witnesses," and "the day of the hilltop bargain coming soon," and of things even less understandable.

The pop-eyed monk followed at the king's bootheels, as he always did these days. The mad words of Elias washed over him, but the monk only nodded ceaselessly as he scrambled along behind—the king's grinning shadow.

Fascinated and excited in a way she had not felt for some time, Rachel had found herself following through the shadows a few ells behind the pair as they climbed what seemed a thousand steps up the tower's long stairway. The king's litany of incomprehensibles had continued until at last he and the monk disappeared into the bell chamber. Feeling her age and the throbbing of her infirm back, she had remained on the floor below. Leaning against the oddly-tiled stone walls, fighting for breath, she had wondered again at her own boldness. An open workroom lay before her. A great pulley had been spread in pieces on top of a sawdust-mantled block; a sledge lay on the floor nearby, as though its owner had disappeared in midswing. There was only the main room and a curtained alcove beside the stairwell: thus, when the monk suddenly came pattering back down the steps, there had truly been no choice but to bolt for the alcove.

At the far end of the niche she had discovered a wooden ladder leading up into darkness. Knowing she was caught between the king above and whoever his cupbearer might bring from below, she had seen no other choice but to climb upward in search of a more secure hiding place: anyone walking too close to the alcove might brush the curtain aside and reveal her, delivering Rachel up to humiliation or worse.

Worse. The thought of the heads rotting like black fruit atop Nearulagh gate spurred her old bones up the ladder, which turned out to lead straight to the bell-ringer's closet.

So it had not really been her fault, had it? She had not truly meant to spy—she had been virtually forced to listen to Elias' confusing conversation with the Earl of Utanyeat. Surely good Saint Rhiap would understand, she told herself, and would intercede on Rachel's behalf when it came time to read from the Great Scroll in Heaven's anteroom.

She peered out through the door-crack again. The king had moved to another window—this one facing north, into the churning black heart of the approaching storm—but otherwise seemed no nearer to leaving. Rachel was beginning to feel panicky. People used to say that Elias spent many sleepless nights at work with Pryrates in Hjeldin's Tower. Was it the king's particular madness to walk around in towers until the break of dawn? It was only afternoon now. Rachel felt another bout of dizziness. Was she to be trapped in here forever?

Her eyes, wildly darting, lit upon something carved on the inside of the bolted door and widened in surprise.

Somebody had scratched the name *Miriamele* into the wood. The letters were cut deeply, as though whoever had done it had been trapped like Rachel, fidgeting away the time. But who would be here in the first place that might do such a thing?

For a moment she thought of Simon, remembering how the boy would climb like an ape and get into trouble that others could not even find. He had loved Green Angel Tower—wasn't it just a bit before King John died that Simon had knocked over Barnabas the sexton downstairs? Rachel smiled faintly. The boy had been a very devil.

Thinking of Simon, she abruptly remembered what the chandler's boy Jeremias had said. The smile dissolved from her face. *Pryrates.* Pryrates had killed her boy. When she thought of the alchemist, Rachel felt a hatred that burned and bubbled like quicklime, a hatred quite unlike anything she had ever felt in her life.

Rachel shook her head, dizzied. It was horrifying to think about Pryrates. What Jeremias told her about the hairless priest gave her ideas, black thoughts she had not known she was capable of thinking.

Frightened by the power of her feelings, she forced her attention back to the wall carving.

Squinting at the careful letters, Rachel decided that, whatever other mischief Simon had gotten into, this carving was not his doing. It was far too neat. Even with Morgenes' instruction, Simon's writing had wandered across a page like a drunken beetle. These letters were made by someone educated. But who would carve the princess' name in such an out of the way place? Barnabas the sexton used this closet, no doubt, but the idea of that sour, juiceless, leathery old lizard carving Miriamele's name laboriously into the door beggared even Rachel's imagination, and Rachel could imagine men committing virtually *any* evil or stupidity if freed from the proper influence of women. Even so, sexton Barnabas as a pining lover was too much to conceive.

Her thoughts were wandering, Rachel chided herself angrily. Was she indeed so old and fearful that she must distract herself at a time when she had many important things to think about? A plan had been forming in her mind since the night she and the other chambermaids had rescued Jeremias, but a part of her wanted to forget about it, wanted things to just be the way they once were.

Nothing will ever be the same, you old fool. Face up to it.

It was harder and harder to hide from such decisions these days. Confronted with the runaway chandler's lad, Rachel and her charges had eventually realized that there was no solution but to help him escape, so they had smuggled him out of the Hayholt one day's end, Jeremias disguised as a chambermaid returning home to Erchester. As she watched the ill-used boy go limping to safety, Rachel had been seized by a revelation: the evil haunting her home could be ignored no longer. And, she now thought grimly, where the Mistress of Chambermaids saw that which was foul, she must make it clean.

Rachel heard the scuffling of heavy boots across the white stone floor of the bell-chamber and risked a peek through the narrow opening. The king's green-cloaked form was just disappearing through the doorway. She listened as his steps descended and grew fainter, then waited a long while after they had passed from her hearing altogether before she clambered back down the ladder. She stepped out from behind the curtain into the airiness of the stairwell, then patted at her forehead and cheeks, which were damp with perspiration despite the cold stone. Stepping carefully and quietly, she began to descend.

The king's conversation had told her much that she needed to know. Now, she must only wait and think. Surely planning such a thing could not be half as complicated as commanding a spring cleaning? And, in a way, that was what she planned, was it not?

Her old bones aching, but her face stretched in an odd smile that would have set her chambermaids to shuddering, Rachel walked slowly down Green Angel Tower's endless stairway.

Binabik's eyes would not meet Sludig's across the cookfire. Instead, the troll swept his sad pile of knuckle-bones back into their bag. He had cast them several times that morning. The results seemed to give him little pleasure.

Sighing, the troll pocketed the sack, then turned and poked in the ashes of the fire with a stick, digging out their breakfast, a cache of nuts that he had located and dug from the frozen ground. It was a bitterly cold day, and their saddlebags were empty of food: Binabik was not above stealing from squirrels.

"Do not speak," the troll said abruptly. After an hour of silence, Sludig had just opened his mouth. "Please, Sludig, for a moment be saying nothing. Just the flask of kangkang from your pocket I am asking for."

The Rimmersman sadly handed over the flask. Binabik took a long swallow, then wiped the sleeve of his jacket across his mouth. The sleeve made another pass across the troll's eyes.

"A promise I made," he said quietly. "I was asking for two night's fires and you gave them. Now I must be fulfilling the oath that of all I would be most happily breaking. We must take the sword to the Stone of Farewell."

Sludig began to speak, but instead accepted the flask back from Binabik and took a deep draught.

Qantaqa returned from a hunting foray to discover the troll and the Rimmersman wordlessly bundling their few belongings onto the pack-horses. The wolf watched them for a moment, then uttered a low moan of distress and danced away. She curled up at the edge of the clearing and peered solemnly at Binabik and Sludig over the fence of her brushy tail.

Binabik lifted the White Arrow out of the saddle bag and held it up, then pressed its wooden shaft against his cheek; the arrow shone more brightly than the powdery snow lying all around. He tucked the arrow back into the bag. "I will be back for you," the little man said to no one present. "I will find you."

He called for Qantaqa. Sludig swung up into his own saddle and they vanished into the forest, the string of pack horses following. The downsifting snow began to fill in their footprints. By the time the muffled sounds of their passage faded, all trace of their presence in the clearing was gone.

Sitting in one place lamenting his fate wasn't going to do him much good, Simon decided. In any case, the sky was becoming unpleasantly dark for mid-morning and snow was beginning to fall more heavily. He stared ruefully at the looking glass. Whatever Jiriki's mirror might be, the Sithi prince had spoken truth when he said that it would not bring him magically to Simon's side. He put it back in his cloak and stood up, rubbing his hands.

It was possible that Binabik and Sludig were still somewhere close by: perhaps, like Simon, they had also been tumbled from their mounts and were in need of help. He had no idea how long he had lain helplessly in the grip of sleep, listening to the Sitha-woman speaking through his dreams—it might have been hours or days. His companions could still be close by, or they might have given up on him. They could be leagues away.

Pondering the bleak possibilities, he began walking in what he hoped was an expanding spiral, something he dimly remembered Binabik suggesting as a good thing to do when people were lost. It was difficult to know if this spiral-walking was *exactly* the right thing to do, however, since he was not sure precisely who was lost. Also, he had not paid particularly close attention when the little man had explained how one calculated this spiral—the troll's woodcraft lecture had concerned the movement of sun, the coloration of bark and leaves, the direction certain tree roots sprouted as they lay in running water, but at the time Binabik had been explaining these things, Simon had been watching a three-legged lizard slowly limping along the Aldheorte Forest floor. It was a shame Binabik had not tried to make his explanation a little more interesting, Simon thought, but it was too late to do anything about it now.

He tramped on through the thickening snowfall as the sun rose invisibly behind the smother of clouds. The brief afternoon arrived, then almost immediately began preparing to leave. The wind blew and the storm seized Aldheorte in its frosty fingers and squeezed. The cold jabbed at Simon through his cloak, which began to feel as thin as a lady's summer veil; it had seemed adequate while he was still in the company of friends, but when he thought about it, he could not remember the last time he had felt truly warm.

As the day of unrewarded snow-trudging dragged on, his stomach began to ache as well. He had last eaten in Skodi's house—the memory of the meal and its aftermath dislodged one of the few remaining shivers that the cold wind had not yet discovered. Who could say how much time had passed since then?

Holy Aedon, he prayed, *give me food.* The thought became a sort of verse that echoed over and over in his head in time with the crunching of snow beneath his boots.

Unfortunately, this was a problem that would not go away by thinking of something else. Neither had it gotten as bad as it could get: Simon knew he could not get any more lost than he was at that moment, but he could become a great deal more hungry.

In his time with Binabik and the soldiers he had gotten used to others doing the hunting and gathering; when he had helped, it was usually at someone else's direction. Suddenly he was as alone as he had been during those first awful days in Aldheorte after he had fled the Hayholt. He had been dreadfully hungry then, and had survived until the troll found him, but that had not been winter weather. He had also been able to pilfer from isolated freeholdings. Now he wandered in a frozen and unpeopled wilderness that made his earlier sojourn in the forest seem an afternoon outing.

The storm winds rose in pitch. The very air seemed to grow suddenly colder, sending Simon into a fresh spasm of trembling. As the forest began to darken ever so slightly, sending the first warning that even this weak daylight could not last forever, Simon found himself fighting back a rising surge of horror. All day long he had tried to ignore the faint scrabbling of its claws: at times he had felt as though he walked along the edge of an abyss, a pit which had no bottom, no limit.

In a situation like this, Simon realized, it would be very easy to go mad—not to spring suddenly into arm-waving lunacy, like a beggerman ranting on Tavern Row, but rather to slip over into quiet madness. He would make some unrecognized misstep and topple slowly, helplessly into the abyss whose nearness seemed at that moment so unarguably clear. He would fall and fall until he did not even remember that he was falling anymore. His real life, his memories, the friends and the home he had once had, all would dwindle until they were nothing but ancient, dusty objects inside a head like a boarded-up cottage.

Was that what dying was like, he suddenly wondered? Did a part of you stay in your body, as in Skodi's ghastly song? Did you lie in the earth and feel your thoughts dwindling away bit by bit, like a sandbar broken down and carried off by a flowing stream? And now that he thought of it, would that be so terrible after all—to lie in the damp and dark and just slowly cease to be? Might it not be better than the frantic concerns of the living, the useless struggle against impossible odds, the panicky and pointless flight from death's ultimate victory?

To give in. To just stop fighting . . .

It had a pacific sound to it, like a sad but pretty song. It seemed a gentle promise, a kiss before sleeping . . .

Simon was falling forward. Shocked into alertness, he threw out a hand and steadied himself against the trunk of a skeletal birch. His heart was beating very swiftly.

He saw with astonishment that snow had gathered thickly on his shoulders and boots, as though he had stood in this place for a long time—but it had seemed like the merest instant! He shook his head and slapped at his cheeks with gloved fingers until the stinging brought life surging back through his body. He growled at himself. To almost fall asleep standing up! To freeze on your feet! What kind of a mooncalf was he?!

No. He growled again and shook his head. Binabik and Sludig had said he was almost a man: he would not prove them wrong so easily. It was cold and he was hungry, that was all. He would not cry and give up like a lowly apprentice scullion locked out of the kitchen. Simon had seen and done many things. He had survived worse than this.

But what should he do?

He couldn't solve the lack of food immediately, he knew, but that wasn't so bad. One thing Binabik had said that Simon remembered very well was that a person could go a long time without food, but could not survive a single night in the cold without shelter. For this reason, the troll always said, fire was very, very important.

But Simon had no fire, nor could he make one.

As he considered this grim fact, he kept walking. Despite the fast-increasing darkness he hoped to find a better camping place before he stopped. The snow was falling faster now, and at the moment he was slogging along the bottom of a long, shallow canyon. He wanted to find higher ground, someplace where he would not have to dig his way out if he survived the night. Thinking about this, Simon felt a painful smile form on his cracked lips. With the dreadful luck he had been having, the high place he chose would probably be struck by lightning.

He laughed hoarsely and was momentarily heartened by the sound of his own mirth, but the wind snatched it away before he could savor it.

The spot he chose was a stand of hemlocks clustered atop a low hill like white-caped sentries. He would have preferred the shelter of several large stones—or better still, a cave—but his luck was not so generous. He ignored the gurglings of his empty stomach as he briefly surveyed the little copse, then set to work pressing snow into hard lumps. These he piled between the trees on the windward side, pressing and smoothing them together until he had a serviceable wall that reached to a little above his knees.

As the last light started to bleed from the sky, Simon began pulling branches from the surrounding hemlocks. He pilled them near the base of his snow-bulwark until he had made a bed of springy needles nearly as high as the wall. Not yet content, he continued his way around the clearing, using his Qanuc knife to cut branches by the handful until a pile of equal size lay beside the first. He stopped for a moment, breathing heavily, and felt the chill air suck the warmth away from his exposed face as abruptly as if he had been fitted with a mask of sleet.

Suddenly aware of the enormity of trying to stay warm during the wintery night to come—and of the fact that if he decided wrong, he might not wake up the following morning—he was spurred to a feverish renewal of his efforts. He shored up the snow wall, making it a little taller and much thicker, then built a lower wall supported by tree trunks on the other side of the first pile of branches. He raced around the copse cutting more branches—his gloves were now so resinous that he could not separate the fingers, and could only remove his hand from his knife by stepping on the blade first—until the height of both piles equaled that of his windward wall. By now it was almost too dark to see: even the great trees were rapidly blurring into murky smudges against the near-luminous snow.

He lay down on his bed of branches, bending his knees and pulling his long legs up against his body so that they would benefit as much as possible from being wrapped in his cloak, then began to pull the remaining branches over himself. He tried his best, with clumsy, sticky fingers, to weave them together so that there were no large exposed areas, and ended by reaching awkwardly up through the hemlock blanket to drag the last few branches over his head. He then turned his face sideways so that it was mostly hidden in his hood. The position was miserably uncomfortable and unnatural in the extreme, but he could feel his own warm breath whispering in the pocket of the hood; for this little while at least, he stopped shivering.

He had been so exhausted when he lay down that Simon expected to be asleep in a matter of moments, despite the tickling branches and his cramped legs. Instead, he found himself growing gradually more wakeful as the first hour of night wore on. The cold, while not as sharply biting as when he had earlier walked through the forest into the teeth of the wind, nevertheless sneaked through his meager shelter and seeped down into his bones and flesh. It was a dull and relentless sort of cold, patient as stone.

The chill was bad enough, but though the thunder of his breathing and the drumbeat of his heart were loud in his ears, he could hear other, stranger noises as well. He had forgotten how differently the night forest sounded when no friend slept nearby. The wind moaned achingly through the trees; other sounds seemed ominously stealthy, yet were loud enough to be heard even above the lamenting wind. After all the horrors he had seen, he harbored no idle hopes that the night was innocent of dangers—surely he was hearing damned souls crying in the storm, and lumbering Hunën prowling the forest in search of warm blood!

As the night marched on, Simon felt black dread rising once more. He was all alone! He was a lost, doomed fool of a mooncalf who should never have dabbled in the affairs of his betters! Even if he survived the night, even if he was spared the clutches of some gibbering, faceless nightwalker, it would only be to starve in the daylight! Certainly he could last a few days, perhaps weeks if he was lucky, but from what Binabik had told him it was many leagues to the Stone of Farewell—and that was assuming that he knew how to get there at all, and could find his way through Aldheorte's unsympathetic depths to do so. Simon knew he did not possess the woodcraft to survive a long exile in the wild: he was no Jack Mundwode, not even close. Similarly, there was almost no chance that anyone who could help would pass through this remote part of the northeastern forest, especially in such hellish weather.

Worst of all, his friends were long gone. In the middle of the afternoon he had suddenly found himself in a fit of panicky shouting, repeating their names over and over again until his throat felt rough as a butcher's block. At the last, just before his voice gave out, he thought he had been screaming the names of the dead. That was the most frightening thought of all, a path that ran very close to the abyss: shout for the dead today, speak to them tomorrow, join them soon after—in a living death of irredeemeable madness if nothing else, and that might be worse than actually dying.

He lay beneath the branches and shivered, but no longer from only the chill. Darkness rose within him and Simon struggled against it. He didn't want to die yet, that he knew—but did it matter? There seemed to be nothing he could do about it one way or the other.

But I will not die here, he decided at last, pretending for a moment he had been offered some choice. He felt for his own desperation and began to smooth it down and push it back, quieting it like a frightened horse. *I've touched dragon blood. I won a Sithi White Arrow. It all means something, doesn't it?*

He didn't know if it *did* all mean something, but he suddenly wanted very much to live.

I won't die yet. I want to see Binabik again, and Josua . . . and Miriamele. And I want to see Pryrates and Elias suffer for what they did. I want a home again, a warm bed—oh, merciful Usires, if you really are real, let me have a home again! Don't let me die in the cold! Let me find a home . . . a home . . . let me find a home. . . !

Sleep was conquering him at last. He seemed to hear his own voice echoing down an old stone well. At last he slid away from cold and painful thoughts into a warmer place.

He survived that night and six more nights after it, each followed by a morning of terrible, frigid stiffness, of solitude and increasing hunger.

The unseasonal cold had killed many of Spring's children in the womb, but some plants had managed to bud and flower in the brief, false season of warmth before the deadly winter returned to stay. Binabik and the Sithi had both given him flowers to eat, but Simon had no idea if there were right or wrong kinds of flowers. He ate what few he could find. They did not fill him up, but neither did they kill him. Patches of bitter yellow grass—*very* bitter—had survived beneath some of the snow hummocks as well, and he made full use of all he could find. Once, in a moment of starved unreason, he even tried to eat a handful of fir needles. They tasted astoundingly dreadful, and the sap and his own froth made a sticky, half-frozen mess of his downy beard.

One day, when his longing for something solid to eat had become a maddening obsession, a chill-baffled beetle wandered across his path. Rachel the Dragon had held a very firm line on the almost incalculable filthiness of such vermin, but Simon's stomach had become a far more powerful force than even Rachel's training. He could not let this opportunity pass.

Despite his hollow gut, the first one proved very difficult. When he felt the tiny legs moving within his mouth, he gagged and spit the beetle into the snow. Its aimless kicking made him want to be sick, but a moment later he snatched it up again, then chewed and swallowed it as quickly as he could. The beetle's texture was that of a delicate, slightly flexible nutshell, the taste little more than a musty tang. When an hour had passed with none of Rachel's dire predictions coming to pass, Simon began to watch the ground carefully in hope of a few more such slow-moving morsels.

Different than his great hunger, and in some ways worse, was the continuing cold: when he could find and devour a fistful of lutegrass, his hunger was for a moment made less, and when he had hiked the first morning hour, his muscles stopped aching for a short time . . . but after that initial moment when he first crawled into his forest-bed, he was never warm again. When he ceased moving even for a few short moments he began to shiver uncontrollably. The chill was so relentless that it began to seem that it pursued him like an enemy. He cursed at it weakly, swinging his arms through the air as though the malevolent cold was something he could strike, as he had struck at the dragon Igjarjuk, but cold was everywhere and nowhere; it had no black blood to spill.

There was nothing that Simon could do but walk. So, during all the painful hours of daylight, from the time his cramped limbs forced him from his makeshift bed each morning to the hour when the sun finally withdrew from the sodden gray sky, he walked almost ceaselessly southward. The rhythm of his shuffling feet became as much a part of the cycle of life as the rise and fall of the wind, the passage of the sun, the settling of snowflakes. He walked because it kept him warm; he walked south because he dimly remembered Binabik saying that the Stone of Farewell stood in the grasslands south of Aldheorte. He knew he could never survive a journey through the entire forest, a passage across a vast nation of trees and snow, but he had to have some destination: the endless tramping was easier if all he had to do was let the occluded sun pass from his left to his right.

He also walked because when he stood still the cold began to bring strange, frightening visions. Sometimes he saw faces in the contorted trunks of trees and heard voices speaking his name and the names of strangers. Other times the snowy forest seemed a thicket of towers; the sparse greenery was transformed into leaping flames and his heart tolled in his ears like a doomful bell.

But most importantly, Simon walked because there was nothing else he could do. If he did not keep moving, he would die—and Simon was not ready to die.

> *"Bug now, don't run, don't flitter*
> *Taste bitter, don't care, don't care*
> *Bug stay, happy day, tasty bite*
> *Don't fight . . ."*

It was late morning, the seventh day since his awakening. Simon was stalking. A spotted brown and gray beetle—larger and possibly more succulent than the small black variety which he had made a staple of his diet—was picking its way across the trunk of a white cedar. Simon had snatched at it once, some twenty ells back, but this beetle had wings—and surely that proved its tastiness, since it had to work so hard to remain uneaten!—and had gone humming away most ungracefully. It had not flown far. A second attempt had also failed, which had led to this most recent landing place.

He was singing to himself; whether he sang out loud or not, he didn't know. The beetle didn't seem to mind, so Simon kept it up.

> *"Beetle sleep, don't creep, trust me*
> *Stand still, stand still, tasty crumb*
> *Here I come, through the snow, don't go . . ."*

Simon, his eyes screwed down in a hunter's squint, was moving as slowly as his trembling, ill-nourished body would permit. He wanted this bettle. He *needed* this beetle. Feeling a shiver beginning to well up inside of him, a shiver that would spoil his careful approach, he lunged. His palms slapped eagerly against the bark, but when he brought his cupped hands up to his face to peer within he saw that he held nothing.

"What do you want it for?" someone asked. Simon, who had carried on more than a few conversations with strange voices during these last days, had already opened his mouth to reply when his heart suddenly began hammering in his chest. He whirled, but no one was there.

Now it's begun, the going-mad has begun . . . was all he had time to think before someone tapped him on his shoulder. He spun again and almost fell down.

"Here. I caught it." The beetle, curiously lifeless, hovered in the air before him. A moment later he saw that it hung from the fingers of a white-gloved hand. The hand's owner stepped out from behind the cedar tree. "I don't know what you will do with it. Do your people eat these things? I had never heard that."

For a brief instant he thought Jiriki had come—the golden-eyed face was framed by a cloud of pale lavender hair, Jiriki's own odd shade, and feathered braids hung beside each up-slanting cheekbone—but after a long, staring instant he realized it was not his friend.

The stranger's face was very slender, but still slightly rounder than Jiriki's. As with the prince, the alien architecture made some of this Sitha's expressions seem cold or cruel or even faintly animalistic, yet still strangely beautiful. The newcomer seemed younger and more unguarded than Jiriki: her face—he had just realized that the stranger was female—changed swiftly from expression to expression even as he watched, like an exchange of subtle masks. Despite what seemed the fluidity and energy of youth, Simon saw that deep in the cat-calm, golden eyes, this stranger shared with Jiriki the ancient Sithi light.

"Seoman," she said, then laughed whisperingly. Her white-clad finger touched his brow, light and strong as a bird's wing. "Seoman Snowlock."

Simon was quivering. "Wh . . . wh . . . who. . . ?"

"Aditu." Her eyes were faintly mocking. "My mother named me Aditu no-Sa'onserei. I have been sent for you."

"S–sent? B–b–by. . . ?"

Aditu tilted her head to one side, stretching her neck sinuously, and regarded Simon as someone might an untidy but interesting animal that crouched on the doorstep. "By my brother, manchild. By Jiriki, of course." She stared as Simon began to sway gently from side to side. "Why do you look so strange?"

"Were you . . . in my dreams?" he asked plaintively.

She continued to watch curiously as he abruptly sat down in the snow beside her bare feet.

★   ★   ★

"Certainly I have boots," Aditu said later. Somehow she had built a fire, scraping away the snow and stacking the wood right beside the spot where Simon had crumpled, then igniting it with some swift movement of her slender fingers. Simon stared intently into the flames, trying to make his mind work properly once more. "I just wanted to take them off so I could approach more quietly." She eyed him blandly. "I did not know what it was that could make such a blundering noise, but it was you, of course. Still, there *is* something fine about the feel of snow on the skin."

Simon shuddered, thinking of ice against bare toes. "How did you find me?"

"The mirror. Its song is very powerful."

"So . . . so if I had lost the mirror, you w—wouldn't have found me?"

Aditu looked at him solemnly. "Oh, I would have found you eventually, but mortals are frail creatures. There might not have been much of interest left to find." She flashed her teeth in what he guessed was a smile. She seemed both more and less human than Jiriki—almost childishly flippant at times, but in other ways far more exotic and alien than her brother. Many of the traits Simon had observed in Jiriki, the feline grace and dispassion, seemed even more pronounced in his sister.

As Simon rocked back and forth, still not absolutely sure he was awake and sane, Aditu reached inside her white coat—which, with her white breeches, had made her all but indistinguishable against the snow—and removed a package wrapped in shiny cloth. She handed it to him. He poked clumsily at the wrappings for some time before he was able to expose what was inside: a loaf of golden-brown bread that seemed oven-fresh, and a handful of fat pink berries.

Simon had to eat his meal in very small bites to avoid making himself ill; even so, each less-than-a-mouthful seemed like time spent in paradise.

"Where did you find these?" he asked through a faceful of berries.

Aidtu looked at him for a long time, as if debating some important decision. When she spoke, it was with what seemed an air of carelessness. "You will soon see. I will take you there—but such a thing has never happened before."

Simon did not pursue this cryptic last remark. Instead, he asked: "But where are you taking me?"

"To my brother, as he asked me to," Aditu said. She looked solemn, but a wild light gleamed in her eyes. "To the home of our people—*Jao é-Tinukai'i.*"

Simon finished chewing and swallowed. "I will go anywhere there is a fire."

21

Prince of Grass

"Say nothing," Hotvig murmured, "but look to the redcoat there by the fence."

Deornoth followed the Thrithings-man's subtle gesture until his gaze lit on a roan stallion. The horse regarded Deornoth warily, stepping from side to side as though he might bolt at any moment.

"Ah, yes." Deornoth nodded his head. "He is a proud one." He turned. "Did you see this one, my prince?"

Josua, who was leaning against the gate at the far side of the paddock, waved his hand. The prince's head was wrapped in linen bandages, and he moved as slowly as if all of his bones were broken, but he had insisted on coming out to assist in claiming the fruits of his wager. Fikolmij, apoplectic with rage at the idea of watching Josua picking thirteen Thrithings horses from the March-thane's own pens, had sent his randwarder Hotvig in his place. Instead of mirroring his thane's attitude, Hotvig seemed rather taken with the visitors and with Prince Josua in particular. On the grasslands a one-handed man did not often kill an opponent half again his size.

"What's the red's name?" Josua asked Fikolmij's horsekeeper, a wiry, ancient man with a tiny wisp of hair on the top of his head.

"Vinyafod," this one said shortly, then turned his back.

"It means "Wind-foot" . . . Prince Josua." Hotvig pronounced the title awkwardly. The randwarder went and slipped a rope about the stallion's neck, then led the balking animal to the prince.

Josua smiled as he looked the horse up and down, then boldly reached up and pulled at its lower lip, exposing the teeth. The stallion shook his head and pulled away, but Josua grabbed the lip again. After a few nervous head-shakes, the horse at last allowed himself to be examined, the only sign of anxiety his blinking eyes. "Well, he is certainly one we shall take east with us," Josua said, "—although I doubt that will please Fikolmij."

"It will not," Hotvig said solemnly. "If his honor was not held up before all the clans, he would kill you just for coming near these horses. This Vinyafod was one that Fikolmij demanded specially as part of Blehmunt's booty when Fikolmij became leader of the clans."

Josua nodded solemnly. "I don't want the March-thane so angry that he follows and murders us, pledge or no pledge. Deornoth, I give you leave to pick the rest; I trust your eye better than mine. We will take Vinyafod, that is certain—as a matter of fact, I think I will claim him for my own. I am tired of limping from here to there. But as I said, let us not cull the herd so thoroughly that we force Fikolmij to dishonor himself."

"I will choose carefully, sire." Deornoth strode across the paddock. The horsekeeper saw him coming and tried to sidle away, but Deornoth hooked the old man's elbow and began asking questions. The keeper was hard-pressed to pretend he could not understand.

Josua watched with a faint smile on his face, shifting his balance from one foot to another to spare his aching body. Hotvig watched the prince from the corner of his eye for a long time before he spoke.

"You said you go east, Josua. Why?"

The prince looked at him curiously. "There are many reasons, some of which I cannot discuss. But mostly it is because I must find a place to make a stand against my brother and the evil that he has done."

Hotvig nodded his head with exaggerated seriousness. "It seems that you have kinsmen who feel as you do."

Josua's expression turned to puzzlement. "What do you mean?"

"There are others of your kind—other stone-dwellers—who have begun to settle east of here. That is why Fikolmij brought us so far north of our usual grazing areas for this season, to make sure that the newcomers were not crossing onto our lands." A grin crossed Hotvig's scarred face. "There were other reasons for our clan coming here, too. The March-thane of the Meadow Thrithings tried to steal away some of our randwarders at the last Gathering of Clans, so Fikolmij wanted his people far away from the Meadow Thrithings. Fikolmij is feared, but not well-loved. Many wagons have already left the Stallion Clan. . . ."

Josua waved impatiently. The bickering between the Thrithings clans was legendary. "What about the stone-dwellers you spoke of? Who are they?"

Hotvig shrugged and fingered his braided beard. "Who can say? They came from the west—whole families, some traveling in carts as our people do, some on foot—but they were not our people, not Thrithings-men. We heard of them from our outriders when we were at the second-to-last Gathering, but they passed through the north of the High Thrithings and were gone."

"How many?"

Again the Thrithings-man shrugged. "Stories say as many as in two or three of our small clans."

"So, perhaps a hundred or two." The prince seemed to momentarily escape his pain, for his face brightened as he pondered this news.

"But that is not all, Prince Josua," Hotvig said earnestly. "That was one group. Other companies have trickled past since then. I have myself seen two hand's worth or so all counted. They are poor, though, and they have no horses, so we let them pass out of our lands."

"You did not let my folk pass and we had not a pony between us." Josua's smile was sardonic.

"That is because Fikolmij knew it was you. The randwarders had watched your people for several days."

Deornoth approached, the grumbling horsekeeper in tow. "I have chosen, Highness. Let me show you." He pointed to a long-legged bay. "Since you have picked red Vinyafod for your own, Prince Josua, I have selected this one for myself. *Vildalix* is his name—Wild-shine."

"He is splendid," Josua said, laughing. "You see, Deornoth, I remembered what you said about Thrithings horses. Now you have some, just as you asked."

Deornoth looked at Josua's bandages. "The price was too high, sire." His eyes were sorrowful.

"Show me the rest of our new herd," said Josua.

Vorzheva came out to meet the prince as he and the others returned from the paddock. Hotvig took one look at her face and slipped away.

"You are foolish to be up walking!" The thane's daughter turned to Deornoth. "How could you keep him out so long? He is very unwell!"

Deornoth said nothing, but only bowed. Josua smiled. "Peace, Lady," the prince said. "The fault is not Sir Deornoth's. I wanted to see the horses, since I am most assuredly going to ride and not walk from here." He chuckled ruefully. "Not that I could walk more than a furlong these days in any case, even if my life were in the balance. But I will get stronger."

"Not if you stand in the cold." Vorzheva leveled her sharp-eyed glance at Deornoth as if daring him to argue. She took Josua's arm, adjusting her pace to his halting strides, and together all three went back toward the camp.

The prince's company was still housed in the bull run. Fikolmij had snarled that just because he had lost a wager was no reason that he must treat miserable stone-dwellers like clansmen, but several of the more high-minded Thrithings-folk had brought blankets and ropes and tent stakes. Fikolmij was not a king: while the people lending assistance to the former prisoners gave the March-thane's camp a wide berth, neither were they ashamed or afraid to go against his wishes.

Led by practical Duchess Gutrun, Josua's people had quickly made of these contributions a secure shelter, closed on three sides and double-roofed with blankets of heavy wool. This served to keep out the worst of the cold rains, which seemed to increase in strength daily.

Above the Thrithings the gray-black sky hung threateningly close, as though the very grasslands had been lifted up by giant hands. This spell of bad weather, which had lasted nearly a week straight and off and on for over a month, would have been unusual even in early spring. It was now high summer, however, and the people of the Stallion Clan were openly worried.

"Come, my lady," Josua said as they reached the enclosure. "Let you and I walk a little while longer."

"You should not walk more!" Vorzheva said indignantly. "Not with your wounds! You must sit and have some hot wine."

"Nevertheless," Josua said firmly, "let us walk. I will look forward to the wine. Deornoth, if you would pardon us. . . ?"

Deornoth nodded and bowed, turning at the gate in the bull run fence. He watched the prince's laborious progress for a moment before he went inside.

Josua's victory over Utvart had brought certain amenities. Like his lady, the prince had exchanged his rags for newer garb, and now wore the soft leather breeches, boots, and baggy-sleeved wool shirt of a randwarder, a bright scarf knotted across his brow in place of his princely diadem. Vorzheva wore a voluminous gray dress, rolled and belted at the hips in the Thrithings manner to lift the hem above the wet grass, leaving visible her thick woolen leggings and low boots. She had discarded her white bride-band.

"Why do you take me away from the others to talk?" Vorzheva demanded. Her defiant tone was belied by apprehensive eyes. "What do you say that must be hidden?"

"Not hidden," Josua said, twining his arm around hers. "I only wished to speak where we would not be interrupted."

"My people do not hide things," she said. "We cannot, since we live so close."

Josua nodded his head. "I only wished to say that I am sorry, Lady, very sorry."

"Sorry?"

"Yes. I have treated you badly, as I admitted in your father's wagon. I have not given you the respect you deserve."

Vorzheva's face twisted, somewhere between joy and anguish. "Ah, still you do not understand me, Prince Josua of Erkynland. I do not care for respect, not if that is all you give me. I want your attention. I want your heart! If you give me that, then you can give to me all the . . . the not-respect . . ."

Quietly: "Disrespect."

". . . All the disrespect you want. Do not treat me like you do the farmers who come to you for justice. I do not want your careful thinking, your measuring, your talking, talking, talking . . ." An angry tear was quickly wiped away. "Just give your heart, you damned stone-dweller!"

They stopped, standing in wind-rippled grass to their knees. "I try," he said.

"No, you do not," she hissed bitterly. "You have that other woman's face in your heart, your brother's wife. Men! You are all little boys, you keep old loves in your heart like polished stones you have found. How can I fight a dead woman!? I cannot grab her, I cannot slap her, I cannot drive her away or follow you when you go to her!" She stood breathing heavily, her legs wide-set as though braced for battle. Her hands dropped to her stomach and her look changed. "But you did not give her a child. You gave one to me."

Josua looked helplessly at her pale face, at the rosy flush of her cheeks and her cloud of black hair. A movement caught his eye: a rabbit, emerging from a thatch of tall grass, stopped for a moment and rose on its hindquarters to look around. Its dark, round eye touched his. A moment later it sprang forward and was gone, a thin gray shadow skimming the meadow.

"You have done nothing wrong, Lady," he said. "Nothing but attach yourself to a brooding ghost of a man." He smiled sadly, then laughed. "But in a way, I suppose, I have been reborn. I have been allowed to live when surely I ought to have died, so I must take that as an omen and see my life differently. You will bear our child, and we will be married when we reach the Stone of Farewell."

A touch of indignation returned to Vorzheva's dark eyes. "We will be married here, before my people," she said firmly. "We are betrothed: now they will see and stop speaking behind their hands."

"But Lady," he began, "we have need of haste . . ."

"Have you no honor?" she demanded. "What if you are killed before we reach this place? The child in me will be a bastard . . . and I will not even be a widow."

Josua began to speak, but instead broke into laughter once more. He reached his arm around her and pulled her close, unmindful of his injuries. She resisted for a moment, then allowed herself to be embraced, but retained her frown. "Lady, you are right," the prince said, smiling. "It shall not be put off. Father Strangyeard will marry us and I will be a good husband to you and keep you safe. And if I die before we reach our destination, you will be the finest widow on the grasslands." He kissed her. For a while they stood in the rain, faces pressed close together.

"You are trembling," Vorzheva said at last, but her own voice seemed the unsteady thing. She pulled free of Josua's embrace. "You have stood and walked too long. If you die before we marry, it will spoil everything." Her look was softer, but still some trace of apprehension remained, an edge of fear that would not go away. Josua took her hand and lifted it to his lips. They turned and walked slowly back toward the encampment, as carefully as if they were both very, very old.

"I must leave," Geloë announced that evening. Josua's people huddled around the fire as fierce winds strummed at the walls of their makeshift shelter.

"I hope you do not mean that," Josua said. "We have need of your wisdom."

Deornoth felt himself both glad and sorry at the thought of the witch woman leaving.

"We will all meet again, and soon," she said. "But I must go ahead to the Stone of Farewell. Now that you are safe, there are things I must do there before you come."

"What things?" Deornoth heard the edge of suspicion in his own voice and was embarrassed by his lack of charity, but no one else seemed to notice.

"There will be . . ." Geloë searched for words, ". . . shadows there. And sounds. And faint traces like the ripples left behind when a pebble drops into a stream. It is vital that I try to read these before people come tramping around."

"And what will these things tell you?" Josua asked.

Geloë shook her graying head. "I do not know. Perhaps nothing. But the Stone stands in a special and powerful place; it may be that there are things I can learn. We face an immortal enemy; perhaps we can find some clue toward his defeat among the vestiges of his immortal people." She turned to Duchess Gutrun, who cradled sleeping Leleth in her lap. "Will you keep the child until you see me again?"

Gutrun nodded. "Of course."

"Why do you not take her with you?" Deornoth asked. "You said she helped to . . . to center your skills in some way."

Firelight glinted in Geloë's great eyes. "True. But she cannot travel in the way I must travel." The witch woman stood, tucking her breeches into her heavy boots. "And I will do best traveling by night."

"But you will miss our marriage!" Vorzheva exclaimed. "Father Strangyeard is to marry Josua and me at morning-time."

Those who had not yet heard offered congratulations; Josua received all as calmly and graciously as if he stood again in his throne room at Naglimund. Vorzheva's smiles at last dissolved into what were surely happy tears, which she cried on Gutrun's accommodating shoulder. Leleth, who had awakened and rolled out of the duchess' lap to stare silently at the ruckus, was quickly scooped up into the thin arms of Father Strangyeard.

"This is good news Vorzheva, Prince Josua, but I cannot stay," Geloë said. "I do not think you will miss me. I am not much for entertainments or merrymaking and I am feeling particularly pressed. I had wished to leave yesterday, but stayed to see that you actually claimed your horses." She gestured out toward the darkness beyond the shelter, where the prince's new steeds shifted and snorted in their own enclosure. "Now I can wait no longer."

After brief private conversations with Josua and Strangyeard and a few words whispered into Leleth's ear—words which the little girl received as impassively as if listening to the ocean's voice echoing in a sea shell—Geloë said her brisk farewells and strode out into the night, threadbare cloak snapping in the brisk wind.

Deornoth, who sat closest to the edge of the shelter, leaned his head out a short time later. He had heard a mournful echo sweeping down from the wind-raked sky, but when he looked up he caught only a momentary glimpse of some shadowy, winged thing passing before the gelid moon.

Deornoth was standing his watch—they had not become so trusting of the Thrithings-men that they had lost their sense—when Josua limped out to join him.

"The stars have barely swung around," Deornoth whispered. "Look, there is the Lamp, scarcely moved." He pointed to a dim flare in the cloudy night sky. "It is not your turn for hours, Highness. Go back to bed."

"I cannot sleep."

Deornoth was sure his smile was invisible in the darkness. "It is not uncommon to have worries and doubts on the night before a wedding, sire."

"It's not that, Deornoth. My worries and my self-doubts, as once you so correctly pointed out, are trivial. There are larger matters to think of."

Deornoth wrapped the collar of his cloak tighter around his neck during the moment of silence. The night had grown very chill.

"I am happy to be alive," Josua said at last, "but I do feel a bit like a mouse that the cat has allowed to run into the corner. Alive, yes, but for how long? Far worse than even my brother's evil, now the Hand of the North is reaching out." He sighed. "Once I nurtured a hope that Jarnauga's tale was untrue, despite all the evidence, but the moment I saw those white faces staring up at me from before the walls of Naglimund, something within me died. No, do not worry, good Deornoth," the prince said hastily, "I am not about to run maundering, as I know you secretly dread. I have taken your admonitions to heart." He laughed sourly. "But at the same time, I tell only the truth. There are hatreds that run through this world like blood, hot and lively. All my studies of evil with the Usirean brothers, all their learned considerations of the Devil and his work, never made that so clear as one instant staring into those black eyes. The world has a dark underbelly, Deornoth. I wonder if maybe it is better not to seek after knowledge."

"But surely God put such things on the earth to test our faith, Prince Josua," Deornoth ventured at last. "If no one ever saw evil, who would fear Hell?"

"Who indeed?" The prince's tone changed. "But this is not why I came out to speak to you. Leave it to Josua to turn any conversation into a dour and doomful one." He laughed again; this time it seemed more cheerful. "Actually, I came to ask you to stand for me when Vorzheva and I are married in the morning."

"Prince Josua, I am honored. Gladly—I will do it gladly."

"You have been the most loyal of friends, Deornoth."

"You are the best lord a man could have."

"I did not say 'liege man' or 'knight,' Deornoth." Josua spoke firmly, but with a hint of good humor in his voice. "I said 'friend'—but do not think that standing for me is an honor bereft of responsibility. It is not." He became serious. "I have not had a splendid history of caring for those dear to me, Deornoth my friend. You may protest, but it is a simple fact. Thus, if something happens to me, I want your word that you will look after Vorzheva and our child."

"Of course, my prince."

"Say it." Then, more gently: "Swear it to me."

"I swear by the honor of Blessed Elysia that I will protect the welfare of Lady Vorzheva and the child she carries as if they were my own family. I will lay down my life without hesitation, if need be."

Josua clasped the knight's wrist and held it for a moment. "Good. Many thanks. The Lord bless you, Deornoth."

"May He bless you, too, Prince Josua."

The prince sighed. "And all the rest as well. Did you know, Deornoth, that tomorrow is the first day of Anitul? That means tomorrow is Hlafmansa. There are many absent friends to whom our blessings should go this night—many who no doubt are far closer to the fearful face of darkness than we are."

Deornoth saw the shadow beside him move abruptly as the prince made the sign of the Tree. They shared a long moment of silence before Josua spoke again. "May God bless us all and deliver us from evil."

The men were up with the darkling dawn, saddling the horses and packing the supplies gained when Josua had traded two of his new steeds for a quantity of food and clothing. Since Leleth would ride with Duchess Gutrun, and Towser and Sangfugol would share a horse, four horses remained to carry goods.

When the mounts had been readied, the men returned to the bull run. They found it surrounded by more than a few curious Thrithings-folk.

"What, have you made some announcement?" Josua demanded crossly. Vorzheva eyed him unblinkingly. She had donned the white bride-band once more.

"Do you think my people would not notice you loading the horses?" she snapped. "Besides, what is the use of being married if it is done like thieves stealing by night?" She strutted away, the wide skirt of her wedding dress swirling. A moment later she returned, leading the wide-eyed young girl who had been waiting on Fikolmij when Josua's folk had first come as prisoners to the wagon camp. "This is Hyara, my youngest sister," Vorzheva explained. "She will be married someday, so I want her to see that it is not always frightful."

"I will do my best to look like a nice person to marry," Josua said, arching an eyebrow. Hyara stared back at him, anxious as a startled fawn.

Vorzheva insisted that they be married beneath the open sky and before the eyes of her clanfolk. The wedding party made its way out from beneath the roof of blankets, Father Strangyeard mumbling fretfully as he tried to remember the important sections of the marriage ceremony—he had not, of course, been able to bring a Book of the Aedon from Naglimund, and had never performed a marriage before. Of the principals, he was clearly the most nervous. Young Hyara, sensing a kindred spirit, walked so close to him that she was almost between his feet, adding to the priest's discomfiture.

It was not surprising to see a cheerful and curious crowd of Thrithings-folk assembled along the edges of the bull run—a crowd not greatly different in mood, Deornoth reflected, than that which had come to watch Josua be cut into slivers. It was a little disconcerting to see among them the mother and sisters of he who had failed to slice Josua up, the late Utvart. This group of women, dressed identically in dresses and scarves of dark mourning blue, stared balefully at the emerging stone-dwellers, their mouths pulled tight in uniform expressions of ill-regard.

If the attendance of Utvart's family was surprising, the appearance of Fikolmij on the scene was even more so. The March-thane, who had taken his foul temper and virtually gone into hiding after Josua's victory, now came swaggering through the camp to the bull run, trailed by a handful of scarred randwarders. Although the gray dawn was not an hour passed, Fikolmij's red-eyed stare had the look of drunkenness.

"By the Grass-Thunderer!" he bellowed, "surely you did not think I would let my daughter and her horse-rich husband be wedded without coming to share their happiness!?" He slapped his broad belly and guffawed. "Go on! Go on! We are waiting to see how marriages are done in the mazes of the stone-dwellers!"

At the sound of her father's roar, little Hyara took a step backward and looked wildly around, preparing to flee. Deornoth reached out and gently took her elbow, holding it loosely until she gathered courage to move forward and stand at Vorzheva's side once more. Hopelessly rattled, Father Strangyeard started the *Mansa Connoyis*—the Prayer of Joining— several times without success, each time losing his way after a few lines and stuttering to a halt like a millwheel whose ox was balking in the traces. Each failed attempt drew more laughter from Fikolmij and his randwarders. The archive-master's already pink face grew redder and redder. At last, Josua leaned forward and whispered in his ear.

"You are a Scrollbearer now, Father, as was your friend Jarnauga." He spoke so quietly that none but Strangyeard could hear. "Surely a simple *mansa* is child's play for you, whatever the distractions."

"One-eye speaks the marriage for One-hand!" Fikolmij shouted.

Strangyeard tugged self-consciously at his patch, then grimly nodded his head. "You . . . you are right, Prince Josua. Forgive me. Let us continue."

Speaking each word carefully, Strangyeard worked his way through the long ritual as though wading in high and treacherous waters. The March-thane and his jibing cronies shouted louder and louder, but the priest would no longer be deterred. At last, the crowd of watching Thrithings-folk became restive, tiring of Fikolmij's rudeness. Every time another graceless jest echoed across the bull run, the murmur grew louder.

As Strangyeard neared the end of the prayer, Hotvig appeared on horseback out of the west. He was windblown and disheveled, as though he had ridden fast in his return to the wagon-city.

The rider sat dazedly surveying the scene for a moment, then swung down from the saddle and trotted to his thane's side. He spoke rapidly, then pointed back in the direction from which he had come. Fikolmij nodded, grinning hugely, then turned and said something to the other randwarders which set them rocking with laughter. A look of confusion came over Hotvig's face—confusion which soon turned to anger. As Fikolmij and the others continued to chortle over the news he had brought, the young Thrithings-man strode to the fence around the bull run and waved for Isorn's attention. Hotvig spoke into Isorn's ear; the Rimmerman's eyes widened. When Father Strangyeard paused in his recital a few moments and bent to look for the bowl of water he had filled earlier and put by for this moment in the prayer, Isgrimnur's son pushed away from the fence and marched directly to Prince Josua's side.

"Forgive me, Josua," Isorn hissed, "but Hotvig says there are three score armored riders coming down on the wagon camp. They are less than a league away and riding hard. The leader's coat is a falcon in scarlet and silver."

Startled, Josua looked up. "Fengbald! What is that whoreson doing here?!"

"Fengbald?" Deornoth echoed, astounded. It seemed a name from another age. "Fengbald?"

A rustle of wonder went through the crowd at this odd turn to the ceremony.

"Josua," Vorzheva said tightly, "how can you talk of these things now?"

"I am truly sorry, my lady, but we have little choice." He turned to Strangyeard, who stood staring, his increasingly confident rhythms again disrupted. "Go on to the final part," Josua directed him.

"Wha . . . what?"

"The final part, man. Come, then, hurry to it! I won't have it said I left my lady unmarried against my promise, but if we stand much longer she will be a widow before the *mansa* is over." He gave the priest a gentle shove. "The end, Strangyeard!"

The archivist's one eye bulged. *"May the love of the Ransomer, His mother Elysia, and His Father the All-Highest bless this joining. May . . . may your lives be long and your love be longer still. You are married."* He waved his hands anxiously. "That's . . . that's it. You are married, just as it says."

Josua leaned and kissed the astonished Vorzheva, then grabbed her wrist and pulled her toward the paddock gate while Isorn hurried the rest of their party after them.

"Are you so anxious for your wedding night, Josua?" Fikolmij smirked. He and his randwarders pushed toward the gate as the crowd shouted questions at their thane. "You seem to be in a hurry to leave."

"And you know why," Deornoth shouted at him, his palm itching on the hilt of his sword. "You knew they were coming, didn't you? You treacherous dog!"

"Watch your tongue, little man," Fikolmij growled. "I only said I would not hinder your going. I sent word to the king's men long ago—in the hour when you first crossed over into my Thrithings." He laughed heartily. "So I broke no promises. But if you wish to fight my men and me before the Erkynlanders get here, come ahead. Otherwise, you had better get on your new ponies and ride away."

Vorzheva pulled away from Josua as they passed through the gate and into the crush of Thrithings-folk. She reached her father in a few steps and slapped him stingingly across the face.

"You killed my mother," she shouted, "but someday I will kill you!" Before he could grab her, she sprang back to Josua's side. Naidel whisked out of the prince's sheath and swayed menacingly, a flickering tongue of light beneath the dim sky. Fikolmij stared at Josua, eyes bulging, face crimson with rage. With a visible effort, the March-thane subdued his anger and contemptuously turned his back.

"Go, ride for your lives," he growled. "I do not break my word over a woman's feeble blows."

Hotvig followed as they hustled toward the paddock where the horses were waiting. "The thane was right about one thing, Josua, Vorzheva," he called. "You must indeed ride for your lives. You have an hour's start and your horses are rested, so all is not lost. Some of the others will help me slow them down."

Deornoth stared. "You'll. . . ? But Fikolmij wants us caught."

Hotvig shook his head roughly. "Not all favor the March-thane. Where do you go?"

Josua thought for a moment. "Please do not let our enemies hear of this, Hotvig." He lowered his voice a little. "We go north of where the rivers meet, to a place called the Stone of Farewell."

The Thrithings-man looked at him strangely. "I have heard something of it," he said. "Go swiftly, then. It is possible we will see each other again." Hotvig turned and gave Vorzheva a long look, then bowed his head briefly. "Make these people know that not all Thrithings-folk are like your father." Hotvig turned and walked away.

"No more time to talk!" Josua cried. "To horse!"

The outermost grazing lands of the wagon-camp were disappearing behind them. Despite the injured and inexperienced riders, the long strides of Vinyafod and his fellows ate up the ground. The grass flew away beneath their hooves.

"This is becoming sickeningly familiar," Josua shouted across to Deornoth and Isorn.

"What?"

"Running! Pursued by superior forces!" Josua waved his arm. "I am tired of showing my backside, whether to my brother or the Storm King's minions!"

Deornoth looked up at the clotted sky, then over his shoulder. Only a few lone cows dotted the rearward horizon: there was no sign of pursuing riders. "We must find a place to make our stronghold, Prince Josua!" he called.

"That's right!" Isorn shouted. "People will come flocking to your banner then, you'll see!"

"And how will they find us?" Josua called back with a mocking smile. "These people, how will they find us?"

"They will, somehow," Isorn shouted, "—everybody else does!" He whooped with laughter. The prince and Deornoth joined in. Vorzheva and the others stared at them as if they were mad.

"Ride on!" Josua cried. "I am married and an outlaw!"

The sun made no clear appearance all day. When the dim light at last began to wane and the pall of approaching evening spread across the stormy sky, the prince's party chose a spot and made camp.

They had ridden due north from the wagon-city until they reached the Ymstrecca in early afternoon, crossing the river at a muddy ford whose banks were pockmarked with hoofprints. Josua had decided that traveling eastward would be safer on the far side of the Ymstrecca, where they would be within an hour's swift ride to the forest. If Fengbald continued to pursue them, they would at least have a chance to spur toward the dark trees and perhaps evade the superior force in Aldheorte's tangled depths.

Despite this caution, there had been no sign of the High King's horsemen all afternoon. The night's watches also passed uneventfully. After breaking their fast at sunrise on dried meat and bread, they were mounted and on their way. They kept their pace swift, but fear of pursuit was lessening by the hour: if Hotvig and others had done something to slow Fengbald, they seemed to have made a good job of it. The only real misfortune was the suffering of those who were unaccustomed to riding on horseback. The cold, gray morning was full of regretful noises as they rode on into the east.

On the second day's journey across the green but comfortless land, the travelers began to see large roofed wagons and blowsy cottages of mud and sticks dotted along the Ymstrecca's banks. In two or three places a few huts had even grown together in a tiny settlement, like slow-moving beasts seeking each other's company upon the dark plain. The chill grasslands were thick with mist and the travelers could not see far or clearly, but the inhabitants of these huddling-spots did not seem to be Thrithings-folk.

"Hotvig spoke aright," Josua mused as they passed by one such settlement. A handful of dim figures bobbed in the gray ribbon of the Ymstrecca that wound beside the huts—settlers casting their fish nets. "I think they are Erkynlanders. See, that cottage has a holy Tree painted on its side! But why are they here? Our folk have never lived in this land."

"Upheaval, crops ruined," Strangyeard said. "Goodness, how people must be suffering in Erchester! Terrible!"

"They are more likely God-fearing folk who know Elias deals with devils," Gutrun said. She clasped Leleth tighter against her considerable bosom, as though to protect the child from the High King's communicants.

"Should we not tell them who you are, sire?" Deornoth asked. "There is safety in numbers, and we have been few for very long. Besides, if they are Erkynlanders, you are their rightful prince."

Josua gazed at the distant camp, then shook his head. "They may have come out here to escape *all* princes, rightful or otherwise. Also, if we are followed, why put innocents in danger by giving them knowledge of our names and destination? No, as you said, when we have a stronghold we will make ourselves known. They can then come to us if they wish, and not because we have swept down on them with swords and horses."

Deornoth kept his expression carefully neutral, but inside he was disappointed. They were in dire need of allies. Why did Josua insist on being so damnably careful and correct? Some things about his prince, it was obvious, would never change.

As the riders continued across the brooding steppe, the weather grew steadily worse, as though they were abroad at the turning of winter instead of the earliest days of Anitul-month in what should be high summer. Flurries of snow came riding on the back of the north wind, and the impossibly broad sky had gone a perpetual gray, dreary as fireplace ash.

Even as the landscape on either side grew more dismal and uninviting, the travelers began to encounter larger settlements along the Ymstrecca's banks, settlements that seemed not to have grown so much as accumulated. As the river carried brambles and sticks and silt before sloughing them off at convenient sandbars, so the very substance of these settlements, both people and materials, seemed to have arrived in this strange and only slightly hospitable place by chance, lodging as in some narrow spot while the force that had carried them so far swept on without them.

Josua's people rode silently past these tiny, ramshackle hamlets, embryonic towns almost as forbidding as the land itself, each made up of perhaps a dozen crude shelters. Few living things could be seen outside the flimsy walls, but wisps of smoke from their cooking fires twined on the wind.

A second, third, and fourth night beneath the cloud-hidden stars took the prince's exiles to the edge of the Stefflod river-valley. The evening of the fifth day brought more snow and bitter cold, but the darkness also gleamed with lights: torches and campfires, hundreds of fires that filled the neck of the valley like a bowl of gems. The travelers had found the largest settlement yet, a near-city of flimsy shelters nestled in the trough of the shallow valley where the Ymstrecca and the Stefflod came together. After a long journey across the empty plain, it was a heartening sight.

"Still we go like thieves, Prince Josua," Deornoth whispered crossly. "You are the son of Prester John, my lord. Why must we skulk into this crofter's clutter acting—and looking—like footpads?"

Josua smiled. He had not changed his travel-stained Thrithings clothes, although one of the things he had bartered for had been extra garments. "You are no longer begging my pardon for your forwardness as once as you once did, Deornoth. No, do not apologize. We have been through too much together for me to disapprove. You are right, we are not coming down into this place as a prince and his court—we make a sorry court, in any case. We shall instead find out what we can and not put our women and young Leleth and the rest in any unnecessary danger." He turned to Isorn, who was the third and to this point quietest member of the trio. "If anything, we will want to allay suspicion that we are anything but ordinary travelers. You, Isorn, look especially well-fed: your size alone might make some of these poor folk afraid." He chuckled and poked the brawny young Rimmersman in the side. Isorn, taken unawares by the prince's sudden lightheartedness, stumbled and almost fell.

"I cannot make myself small, Josua," he grunted. "Be thankful I am not as big as my father, or your poor folk might run screaming into the night at the sight of me."

"Ah, how I miss Isgrimnur," Josua said. "May the Aedon indeed look after your father, that good man, and bring him back to us safely."

"My mother misses him very much and fears for him," Isorn said quietly, "but she does not say so." His good-natured face was solemn.

Josua looked at him keenly. "Yes, your family is not one for breast-beating."

"All the same," Deornoth suddenly said, "the duke can certainly make a ruckus when he is displeased! I remember when he first found out that Skali was coming to King John's funeral. He threw a chair through Bishop Domitis' screen and broke it to bits! *Ouch!* Damn me!" Laughing, Deornoth tripped on a hummock in the darkness. Tonight's misted moon was stinting with her light. "Hold the torch closer, Isorn. Why are we walking and leading our horses, in any case?"

"Because if *you* break a leg, you can ride," the prince said dryly. "If your new mount Vildalix breaks his, will you carry him?"

Deornoth granted the point grudgingly.

Talking quietly of Isorn's father and his legendary temper—the expression of which was almost always followed, as soon as the duke calmed down, by horrified apologies—they made their way down the grassy slope and toward the lights of the nearest fires. The rest of their party had built camp at the valley's edge; the fire Duchess Gutrun tended was a shrinking beacon on the high ground behind them.

A gang of shivering, starveling dogs barked and scattered as the three-some approached the settlement. A few shadowy figures looked up from their fires or stood cross-armed in the door-flaps of shabby huts, watching the strangers pass, but if there was any sense that Josua and his comrades did not belong, no one challenged them. From the snippets of speech they picked up as they passed, it was clear that these settlers were indeed mostly Erkynlanders, speaking both the old country speech and Westerling. Here and there a Hernystiri burr could be heard as well.

A woman stood in the open space between two houses, talking to her neighbor about the rabbit her son had brought home and how they had steamed it with sourgrass for Hlafmansa. It was odd, Deornoth thought, to hear people speaking of such mundane things here in the mist of the empty grassland, as if there might be a church hidden behind a rock where they would go for the morning prayer, or an ostler's shop under a leaf where they could buy beer to drink with their rabbit stew.

The woman, of middle years, red-faced and raw-boned, turned at their approach and surveyed them with a look of mixed apprehension and interest. Deornoth and Isorn stepped to one side to pass around her, but Josua halted.

"We wish you a pleasant evening, goodwife," the prince said, inclining his head in a sort of bow. "Do you know where we could get a bit of food? We are travelers and have good money to pay. Has someone got something to sell?"

The woman looked him over carefully, then turned an eye on his companions. "There are no taverns and no inns here," she said grimly. "Everyone keeps what they have."

Josua nodded slowly, as if sifting particles of purest golden wisdom from her discourse. "And what is the name of this place?" he asked. "It is not on any map."

"Shouldn't think so," she snorted. "Wasn't here two summers ago. It doesn't have a name, not truly, but some call it Gadrinsett."

"Gadrinsett," Josua repeated. *"Gathering-place."*

"Not that anyone's gathering *for* anything." She made a face. "Just can't go any farther."

"And why is that?" Josua asked.

The woman ignored this last question, looking the prince up and down once more in a calculating manner. "Here," she said at last, "if you want food and you'll pay for it, I might be able to do something for you. Show me your money first."

Josua showed her a handful of cintis and quinis-pieces that he had brought in his purse out of Naglimund. The woman shook her head.

"Can't take the bronze. Some folk farther along the river might trade for the silver, so I'll take a chance on one o' them. D'you have aught else to trade? Leather straps from broken saddle? Buckles? Extra clothes?" She looked at Josua's outfit and smirked. "No, I doubt you've got extra clothes. Come on then, I'll give you some soup and you can tell me any news." She waved to her friend—who had remained at a safe distance, watching the whole exchange open-mouthed—then led them back through the cluster of huts.

The woman's name was Ielda, and although she mentioned several times that her man might return at any moment, Deornoth guessed that this was mostly to forestall any thoughts of robbery that three strangers might have; he saw no sign of any living husband around her camp, which centered around an outdoor fire and small, rickety cottage. She did have several children, their genders somewhat blurred by dirt and evening darkness. These came out to watch the prince and his friends with the same wide-eyed attention they might have given to a snake swallowing a frog.

After receiving a quinis-piece, which immediately vanished into her dress, Ielda poured them each a bowl of thin soup, then procured from somewhere a jar of beer that she said her man had brought with him from Falshire where they had previously lived. Seeing that jar hardened in Deornoth's mind the notion that her husband was dead: what man could live in this Godforsaken hole, yet leave beer so long undrunk?

Josua thanked her gravely. The three of them passed the jar around several times before thinking to ask Ielda if she would like some herself. She accepted with a gracious nod and took several healthy swallows. Her children discussed this among themselves in a strange pidgin language consisting mostly of grunts, a few recognizable words, and repeated cuffings to the head and shoulders.

The pleasures of company and conversation soon began to work on Ielda. Reserved at first, before long she was holding forth quite knowledgeably on everything there was to know about Gadrinsett and her fellow squatters. Untutored, she nevertheless had a sly wit, and although the travelers were chiefly interested in finding the way to their destination—Geloë's instructions had not been very precise—they found themselves enjoying Ielda's imitations of her various neighbors.

Like many of Gadrinsett's other inhabitants, Ielda and her family had fled Falshire when Fengbald and the Erkynguard had burned down the city's wool district—a punishment for the resistance of the wool merchants' guild to one of Elias' less popular proclamations. Ielda also explained that Gadrinsett was even larger than Josua's folk had first guessed: it continued for a way down the valley, she said, but the hills loomed high enough that the camp fires at the far end were blocked from view.

The reason it was the stopping place for so many, Ielda said, was that the land beyond the spot where the Stefflod and Ymstrecca joined was ill-omened and dangerous.

"Full of fairy-rings it is," she said earnestly, "and there are mounds where spirits dance at night. That's why those folk that live in the Thrithings leave us in peace—they wouldn't live here anyway." Her voice dropped and her eyes grew large. "One great hill there is where witches meet, full of terrible warlock-stones—worse even than Thisterborg by Erchester, if you've heard tell of *that* evil place. Not far from it is a city where devils once lived, an unholy, unnatural city. Terrible magicks is what that land across the river's full of—some women here have had children stolen away. One had a changeling left in return, pointed ears and all!"

"That warlock-hill sounds a fearsome place indeed," Josua said, an expression of great seriousness on his long face. When the woman looked down at her lap, where she was mixing flour and water in a bowl, he caught Deornoth's gaze and winked. "Where is it?"

Ielda pointed into the darkness. "Straight that way, up the Stefflod. You're wise to avoid it." She stopped, frowning. "And where *are* you going, sirs?"

Deornoth chimed in before Josua could speak. "Actually, we are traveling knights who hope to lend our swords to a grand task. We have heard that Prince Josua, the younger son of High King John the Presbyter, has come here into the eastern lands, where he plots the overthrow of his wicked brother, King Elias." Trying not to smile, Deornoth ignored Josua's irritated gestures. "We have come to join that noble cause."

Ielda, who had stopped kneading the dough for a moment to stare, made a snorting noise and resumed her labor. "Prince Josua? Here on the grasslands? That's a clever joke. Not that I wouldn't like to see something done. Things just haven't been right since old Prester John died, bless him." She made a stern face, but her eyes suddenly gleamed wetly. "It's been hard for us all, so hard . . ."

She stood abruptly and laid out the flattened balls of dough on a clean heated stone at the edge of the fire; they began to quietly sizzle. "I'm just going to see my friend," Ielda said, "and find out if she has a bit more beer we can borrow. I won't tell her what you said about the prince, because she'd just laugh. Watch those cakes close now while I go—they're for the children to eat in the morning." She got up and walked out of the circle of firelight, dabbing at her eyes with a dirty shawl.

"What kind of foolishness is this, Deornoth?" Josua asked crossly.

"But did you hear? People like this are waiting for you to do something. You are their prince." It seemed so obvious. Surely Josua could see?

"Prince of what? Prince of ruins, prince of empty lands and grass? I have nothing to offer these folk . . . yet." He got up and walked to the edge of the camp. Ielda's children peered out at him, a cluster of white-rimmed eyes gleaming in the darkened doorway.

"But how will you gain anything without folk to follow you?" Isorn asked. "Deornoth is right. If Fengbald now knows where we are, it is only a matter of time until Elias brings his full anger to bear on us."

"Suspicion may keep these people away from the Stone of Farewell, but it will not keep Earl Guthwulf and the High King's army at bay," said Deornoth.

"If the king on the Dragonbone Chair is going to bring his armies down on us," Josua replied hotly, throwing his hand up in a gesture of frustration, "a few hundred Gadrinsett-folk will be no more than feathers in a gale against them. That is all the more reason not to drag them in. We few at least can vanish into Aldheorte once more if we must, but these folk cannot."

"Again we plan to retreat, Prince Josua," Deornoth replied angrily. "You are tired of it yourself—you said as much!"

The three were still arguing when Ielda returned. They broke off into guilty silence, wondering how much she might have heard. Their conversation, however, was the last thing on her mind.

"My cakes!" she shrieked, then pulled them off the hot rock one after the other, making little cries of pain as she burned her fingers. Each cake was charred black as Pryrates' soul. "You monsters! How could you? Talking all your high-flown nonsense about the prince, then letting my cakes burn!" She turned and smacked ineffectually at Isorn's broad shoulders.

"My apologies, goodwife Ielda," Josua said, producing another quinis-piece. "Please take this and forgive us . . ."

"Money!" she cried, even as she took the coin, "What about my cakes? Will I give my children money to eat tomorrow morning when they are crying!?" She snatched up a broom of bound twigs and swung lustily at Deornoth's head, almost knocking him off the rock on which he sat. He bounded quickly to his feet and joined Josua and Isorn in full retreat.

"Don't come 'round here any more!" she shouted after them. "Swords-for-hire indeed! Cake-burners! The prince is dead, my friend said—and your talk can't bring him back!"

Her angry cries slowly faded into the distance as Josua and his companions stumbled back to their horses and made their way out past the fringes of Gadrinsett.

"At least," Josua said after they had walked a while, "we have a good idea of where the Stone of Farewell lies."

"We learned more than that, Highness," Deornoth said, half-smiling. "We saw how your name still inspires passion among your subjects."

"You may be the Prince of Grass, Josua," Isorn added, "but you are definitely *not* the King of Cakes."

Josua looked at them both disgustedly. "I would appreciate," he said slowly, "going back to camp in silence."

22

Through the Summer Gate

"It is not a road that takes us there," Aditu said sternly. "It is a sort of song."

Simon frowned in irritation. He had asked a simple question, but in her maddening Sithi way, Jiriki's sister had once more given an answer that was no answer. It was too cold to stand around talking nonsense. He tried again.

"If there's no road, it must still be in some direction. What direction is it, then?"

"In. Into the forest's heart."

Simon peered up at the sun to try and orient himself. "So, it's . . . that way?" He pointed south, the direction in which he had been traveling.

"Not quite. Sometimes. But that would more often be when you wished to enter through the Gate of Rains. That is not right at this time of year. No, it is the Summer Gate that we seek, and that is a different song altogether."

"You keep saying a song. How can you get to a thing by a song?"

"How. . . ?" She appeared to consider this carefully. She inspected Simon. "You have a strange way of thinking. Do you know how to play *shent*?"

"No. What does that have to do with anything?"

"You might be an interesting player—I wonder if anyone ever has played with a mortal? None of my folk would ask such a question as you did. I must teach you the rules."

Simon grumbled his confusion, but Aditu lifted a slim-fingered hand to halt his questions. She stood very quietly, her web of lavender hair trembling in the breeze, everything else still; in her white clothing she was nearly invisible against the snow drifts. She seemed to have fallen asleep standing, like a stork swaying on one leg among the reeds, but her lustrous eyes remained open. At last she began to breathe deeply, letting the air out again with a chuffing hiss. The exhalations gradually became a crooning, humming sound that hardly seemed to come from Aditu at all. The wind, which had been a cold-fingered push on Simon's cheek, abruptly changed direction.

No, he realized a moment later, it was more than just an altering of the wind. Rather, it seemed that the whole of creation had moved ever so slightly—a frightening sensation that brought on a moment of dizziness. As a child he had sometimes whirled himself around and around in a circle; when he stopped, the world would continue to reel about him. This dizziness felt much like that, yet calmer, as though the world that spun beneath his feet moved as deliberately as the unfolding petals of a flower.

Aditu's wordless, airy drone solidified into a litany of unfamiliar Sithi speech, then trailed off into silent breathing once more. The drab light slipping down through the snowbound trees seemed to have gained some warmer color, an infinitesimal shift of hue that leavened the gray with blue and gold. The silence stretched.

"Is this magic?" Simon heard his voice shatter the stillness like the braying of a donkey. He immediately felt foolish. Aditu swung her head to look at him, but her expression showed no anger.

"I am not sure what you mean," she said. "It is how we find a hidden place, and Jao é-Tinukai'i is indeed hidden. But there is no power in the words themselves, if that is what you ask. They could be spoken in any language. They help the searcher to remember certain signs, certain paths. If that is not what you mean by 'magic,' I am sorry to disappoint you."

She did not look very sorry. Her mischievous smile had come back.

"I shouldn't have interrupted," Simon muttered. "I always asked my friend Doctor Morgenes to show me magic. He never did." The thought of the old man brought back a memory of a sunny morning in the doctor's dusty chamber, the sound of Morgenes mumbling and musing to himself while Simon swept. With that memory came a fierce pang of regret. All those things were gone.

"Morgenes . . ." Aditu said musingly. "I saw him once, when he visited my uncle in our lodge. He was a pretty young man."

"Young man?" Simon stared again at her thin, waiflike face. "Doctor Morgenes?"

The Sitha suddenly became serious once more. "We should delay no longer. Would you like me to sing the song in your tongue? It could cause no harm that is worse than the trouble we are already brewing, you and I."

"Trouble?" Confusion was piling on confusion, but Aditu had taken her odd stance once more. He had a sudden feeling that he must speak quickly, as though a door were being closed. "Yes, please, in my tongue!"

She settled on the balls of her feet, poised like a cricket on a branch. After breathing measuredly for a moment, she again began to chant. The song slowly became recognizable, the clumsy, blocky sounds of Simon's Westerling speech softening and turning liquid, the words running and flowing together like melting wax.

"The Serpent's dreaming eye is green,"

she sang, her eyes fixed on the icicles that hung like jeweled pennants from the branches of a dying hemlock. The fire absent from the muted sun now burned in their scintillant depths.

"His track is moon-silver.
Only the Woman-with-a-net can see
The secret places that he goes . . ."

Aditu's hand drifted out from her side and hung in the air for a long moment before Simon realized that he was expected to take it. He grasped her fingers in his gloved hand, but she pulled free. For a moment he thought he had guessed wrong, that he had forced some unwanted, oafish intimacy on this golden-eyed creature, but as her fingers flexed impatiently he realized in a rush of confusing feelings that she wanted his bare hand. He pulled his leather mitten off with his teeth, then clasped her slender wrist with fingers warm and moist from their residence in the glove. She gently but firmly pulled her wrist away, this time sliding her hand against his own; her cool fingers curled around his. With a head-shake like a cat awakened from a nap, she repeated the words she had sung:

"The Serpent's dreaming eye is green,
His track is moon-silver.
Only the Woman-with-a-net can see
The secret places that he goes . . ."

Aditu led him forward, ducking beneath the hemlock bough and its burden of icicles. The stiff, snow-salted breeze that clawed at his face brought tears into his eyes. The forest before him was suddenly distorted, as though he were trapped inside one of the icicles, staring out. He heard his boots crunching in the snow, but it seemed to be happening at a great distance, as though his head floated treetop-high.

"Wind-child wears an indigo crown,

Aditu crooned. They walked, but if felt more like floating, or swimming.

"His boots are of rabbit skin.

Invisible is he to Moon-mother's stare,
But she can hear his cautious breathing . . ."

They turned and clambered down into what should have been a gulley
lined with evergreens; instead, to Simon's misted eyes the tree limbs
resembled shadowy arms reaching out to enfold the two travelers. Branches
swatted at his thighs as he passed, their scent spicy and strong. Sap-
covered needles clung to his breeches. The wind—which breathed
whisperingly among the swaying branches—was a little more moist, but
still shiveringly cold.

". . . Yellow is the dust on old Tortoise's shell."

Aditu paused before a bank of umber stone, which thrust from the
snow at the bottom of the gulley like the wall of a ruined house. As she
stood singing before it, the sunlight that fell through the trees abruptly
shifted its angle; the shadows in the crevices of stone deepened, then
overtopped their clefts like flooding rivers, sliding across the face of the
rock as though the hidden sun were plummeting swiftly toward its evening berth.

"He goes in deep places,"

she chanted,

"Bedded beneath the dry rock,
He counts his own heartbeats in chalky shadow . . ."

They curved around the massive stone and suddenly found themselves
on a down-slanting bank. Smaller outcroppings of dusky rock, pale pink
and sandy brown, pushed up through the snowy ground. The trees that
loomed against the sky were a darker green here, and full of quiet birdsong.
Winter's bite was noticeably less.

They had traveled, but it seemed they had also passed from one kind of
day to another, as though they somehow walked at right angles to the
normal world, moving unrestrainedly as the angels that Simon had been
told flew here and there at God's bidding. How could that be?

Staring up past the trees into the featureless gray sky, Aditu's hand
clutched in his, Simon wondered if he might indeed have died. Might this
solemn creature beside him—whose eyes seemed fixed on things he could
not see—be escorting his soul to some final destination, while his lifeless
body lay somewhere in the forest, slowly vanishing beneath a blanket of
drifting snow?

Is it warm in Heaven? he wondered absently.

He rubbed at his face with his free hand and felt the reassuring pain of his chapped skin. In any case, it mattered little: he was going where this one led him. His contented helplessness was such that he felt he could no more remove his hand from hers than remove his head from his body.

> *". . . Cloud-song waves a scarlet torch:*
> *A ruby beneath a gray sea.*
> *She smells of cedar bark,*
> *And wears ivory at her breast . . ."*

Aditu's voice rose and fell, her song's slow, thoughtful cadence blending with the birdsong as the waters of one river would meld indistinguishably into the flow of another. Each verse in the endless stream, each cycle of names and colors, was a jeweled puzzle whose solution always seemed to be at Simon's fingertips but never revealed itself. By the time he thought he might be making sense of something, it was gone, and something new was dancing on the forest air.

The two travelers passed from the bank of stones into deep shade, entering a thicket of dark green hedges pearled with tiny white flowers. The foliage was damp, the snow underfoot soggy and unstable. Simon clasped Aditu's hand more firmly. He tried to wipe his eyes, which had blurred again. The little white flowers smelled of wax and cinnamon.

> *". . . The Otter's eye is pebble-brown.*
> *He slides beneath ten wet leaves;*
> *When he dances in diamond streams,*
> *The Lantern-bearer laughs . . ."*

And now, joining with the rising and falling melody of Aditu's song and the delicate trill of birds, came the sound of water splashing in shallow pools, tuneful as a musical instrument made of fragile glass. Shimmering light sparkled on melting snowdrops; as he listened in wonderment, Simon looked all around at the starry gleam of sun through water. The tree branches seemed to be dripping light.

They walked beside a small but active stream whose joyful voice reverberated through the tree-pillared forest halls. Melting snow lay atop the stones and rich black earth lay beneath the damp leaves. Simon's head was whirling. Aditu's melody ran through all his thoughts, just as the stream slid around and over the polished stones that made its bed. How long had they been walking? It had seemed only a few steps at first, but now it suddenly seemed they had marched for hours—days! And why was the snow vanishing away? Just moments ago it had covered everything!

Spring! he thought, and felt a nervous but exultant laughter bubbling inside him *I think we're walking into Spring!*

They strode on beside the stream. Aditu's music chimed on and on like the water. The sun had vanished. Sunset was blooming in the sky like a rose, singeing all of Aldheorte's leaves and branches and trunks with fiery light, touching the stones with crimson. As Simon watched, the blaze flared and died in the sky, then was swiftly supplanted by spreading purple, which itself was devoured in turn by sable darkness. The world seemed to be spinning faster beneath him, but he still felt firmly grounded: one foot followed the other, and Aditu's hand was firm in his.

> ". . . *Stone-listener's mantle is black as jet,*
> *His rings shine like stars,*

As she sang these words, a scattering of white stars indeed appeared against the vault of the heavens. They blossomed and faded in a succession of shifting patterns. Half-realized faces and forms coalesced, pricked in starlight against the blackness, then dissolved again just as rapidly.

> *Nine he wears; but his naked finger*
> *Lifts and tastes the southerly breeze . . ."*

As he walked beneath the velvet-black sky and wheeling stars, Simon felt as if an entire lifetime might be passing with incredible swiftness; simultaneously, the night journey seemed but a single moment of near-infinite duration. Time itself seemed to sweep through him, leaving behind a wild mixture of scents and sounds. Aldheorte had become a single living thing that changed all around him as the deathly chill melted away and the warmth came pushing through. Even in darkness he could sense the immense, almost convulsive alterations.

As they walked in bright starlight beside the chattering, laughing river, Simon thought he could sense green leaves springing from bare boughs and vibrant flowers forcing their way out of the frozen ground, fragile petals unfurling like the wings of butterflies. The forest seemed to be shaking off winter like a snake shrugging its old, useless skin.

Aditu's song wound through everything like a single golden thread in a tapestry woven of muted colors.

> ". . . *Violet are the shadows in Lynx's ears.*
> *He hears the sun rising;*
> *His tread sends the cricket to sleep,*
> *And wakes the white rose . . ."*

Morning light began to permeate Aldheorte, spreading evenly, as though it had no single source. The forest seemed alive, every leaf and branch poised, waiting. The air was filled with a thousand sounds and numberless scents, with birdsong and bee-drone, the musk of living earth, the sweet rot of toadstools, the dry charm of pollen. Unmuffled by clouds, the sun climbed into a sky that showed purest pale blue between the towering treetops.

> *". . . Sky-singer's cape is buckled in gold,"*

Aditu sang triumphantly, and the forest seemed to throb around them as though it had one vast and indivisible pulse.

> *"His hair is full of nightingale feathers.*
> *Every three paces he casts pearls behind,*
> *And saffron flowers before him . . ."*

She stopped in her tracks and released Simon's hand; his arm fell to his side, limp as a boned fish. Aditu stood on her toes and stretched, lifting her upraised palms to the sun. Her waist was very slender.

It took a long time before Simon could speak. "Are we . . ." he tried at last, "are we. . . ?"

"No, but we have traveled the most difficult part," she said, then turned on him with a droll look. "I thought you would break my hand, you clutched so hard."

Simon remembered her calm, strong grip and thought how unlikely that was. He smiled dazedly, shaking his head. "I have never . . ." He couldn't make the words come. "How far have we come?"

She seemed to find this a surprising question and thought hard for a moment. "Quite far into the forest," she said at last. "Quite far in."

"Did you make the winter go away by magic?" he asked, turning in a stumbling circle. On all sides the snow was gone. The morning light knifed down through the trees and splashed on the crush of damp leaves underfoot. A spider web quivered, afire in a column of sunlight.

"The winter has not gone away," she said. "We have gone away from the winter."

"What?"

"The winter you speak of is false—as you know. Here, in the forest's true heart is a place the storm and cold have not penetrated."

Simon thought he understood what she was saying. "So you are keeping the winter away by magic."

Aditu frowned. "That word again. Here the world dances its true dance. That which would *change* such a truth is 'magic'—dangerous magic—or so it seems to me." She turned away, obviously tiring of the subject. There was little of imposture in Aditu's character, at least when it was a matter of her time being wasted in niceties. "We are almost there now, so there is no need to rest. Are you hungry or thirsty?"

Simon realized that he was ravenous, as if he had not eaten for days. "Yes! Both."

Without another word, Aditu slipped between the trees and vanished, leaving Simon standing alone by the stream. "Stay," she called, her voice echoing so that it seemed to come from every side at once. A few moments later she reappeared with a reddish sphere held delicately in each hand. *"Kraile,"* she said. "Sunfruits. Eat them."

The first sunfruit proved sweet and full of yellowy juice, with a spicy aftertaste that made him quickly bite into the second. By the time he had finished both, his hunger was pleasantly blunted.

"Now, come," she said. "I would like to reach *Shao Irigú* by noon today."

"What's 'Shao Irigú'—and what day is it today, anyway?"

Aditu looked annoyed, if such a mundane expression could be said to exist on so exotic a face. "Shao Irigú is the Summer Gate, of course. As for the other, I cannot do all the measurements. That is for those like First Grandmother. I think you have a moon-span you call 'Ahn-ee-tool'?"

"Anitul is a month, yes."

"That is as much as I can say. It is that 'month,' by your reckoning."

Now it was Simon's turn to be annoyed: he could have told her that much himself—although months did tend to sneak past when one was on the road. What he had been hoping to discover, in a roundabout way, was how long it had taken them to get here. It would have been easy to ask straight out, of course, but somehow he knew that the answer Aditu gave him would not be very satisfying.

The Sitha-woman moved forward. Simon scrambled after her. Despite his irritation, he more than half-hoped she would ask for his hand again, but that part of the journey seemed to be over. Aditu picked her way down the slope beside the stream without looking back to see if he was following.

Nearly deafened by the cheerful cacophony of birds in the trees overhead, bewildered by all that had happened, Simon opened his mouth to complain about her evasions, then stopped suddenly in his tracks, shamed by his own short-sightedness. His weariness and crossness abruptly fell away, as though he had sloughed off a heavy blanket of snow dragged with him out of winter. This *was* a wild sort of magic, whatever Aditu said! To have been in a deadly storm—a storm that covered all the northern world, as far as he could tell—and then to follow a song into sunlight and clear skies! This was as good as anything Simon had ever heard in one of Shem Horsegroom's stories. This was an adventure even Jack Mundwode never had. Simon the scullion was going to the Kingdom of the Fair Folk!

He hastened after her, chortling. Aditu looked back at him curiously.

*   *   *

As the weather had changed during their strange journey, so, too, had the vegetation: the evergreens and low shrubs in which Simon had been snowbound and lost had given way to oak and birch and white ash, their interlaced branches bound with flowering creepers, making an overhead canopy colorful as a stained glass ceiling but far more delicate. Ferns and wood sorrel blanketed the stones and fallen trees, covering Aldheorte's floor with a bumpy counterpane of green. Mushrooms crouched hiding in pools of shadow like deserting soldiers, while other pale but oddly beautiful fungi clung to the trunks of trees like the steps of spiraling staircases. The morning sun sprinkled all with a light like fine silver and gold dust.

The stream had cut a gentle gorge in its passage, winding down into a valley whose bottom was obscured by close-leaning trees. As Simon and Aditu picked their way carefully over the slippery rocks that lined the gorge, the stream filled the air around them with fine spray. The watercourse splashed into a series of narrow ponds that grew successively larger down the hillside, each one spilling over into the one below. The ponds were overhung by aspen and drooping willows, the surrounding stones slickly furred in rich green moss.

Simon sat down on one to rest his ankles and catch his breath.

"We will be there before too much longer," Aditu said, almost kindly.

"I'm fine." He stretched out his legs before him, staring critically at his cracked boots. Too much snow had ruined the leather—but why should he worry about that now? "I'm fine," he repeated.

Aditu sat down on the stone beside him and looked up to the skies. There was something quite marvelous about her face, something that he had never seen in her brother, despite the distinct familial resemblance: Jiriki had been very interesting to look at, but Simon thought that Aditu was lovely.

"Beautiful," he murmured.

"What?" Aditu turned to look at him questioningly, as though she did not know the word.

"Beautiful," Simon repeated. "Everything is very beautiful here." He cursed himself for a coward and took a deep breath. "You are beautiful, too, Lady," he finally added.

Aditu stared at him for a moment, her golden eyes puzzled, her mouth creased in what seemed a tiny frown. Then she abruptly burst into a peal of hissing laughter. Simon felt himself redden.

"Don't look so angry." She laughed again. "You are a very beautiful Snowlock, Seoman. I am glad you are happy." Her swift touch on his hand was like ice on a hot forehead. "Come," Aditu said, "we will go on now."

The water, uninterested in their doings, continued on its own way, belling and splashing beside them as they made their way down toward the valley. Scrambling over the rocks as he struggled to keep up with light-stepping Aditu, Simon wondered if just this once he might actually have said the right thing. She certainly didn't seem angry at his forwardness. Still, he resolved to continue thinking carefully before he spoke. These Sithi were damnably unpredictable!

When they had nearly reached level ground, they stopped before a pair of towering hemlocks whose trunks seemed vast enough to be the columns upholding Heaven. Where these mighty trees thrust up between their smaller neighbors into unshadowed sunshine, tangled nets of flowering creepers grew like an arbor between the two trunks, trailing blossom-laden vines that hung almost to the ground and quivered in the wind. The grumble of bees was loudest from the flowers, but they swarmed everywhere among the creepers, stolid laborers in gold and black, wings glistening.

"Stop," Aditu said. "Do not so lightly pass through the Summer Gate."

Despite the power and beauty of the great hemlocks, Simon was surprised. "*This* is the gate? Two trees?"

Aditu looked very serious. "We left all monuments of stone behind when we fled Asu'a the Eastward-Looking, Seoman. Now, Jiriki bade me tell you something before you entered Shao Irigú. My brother said that no matter what may occur later, you have been given the rarest of all honors. You have been brought to a place in which no mortal has ever set foot. Do you understand that? *No mortal has ever walked in beneath this gate.*"

"Oh?" Simon was startled by her words. He looked around quickly, fearing he might see some disapproving audience. "But . . . but I just wanted someone to help me. I was starving . . ."

"Come," she said, "Jiriki will be waiting." Aditu took a step forward, then turned. "And do not look so worried," she smiled. "It *is* a great honor, it is true, but you are *Hikka Staja*—an Arrow-Bearer. Jiriki does not break the oldest rules for just anyone."

Simon was passing beneath the great trees before he understood what Aditu had said. "Break the rules?"

Aditu was moving quickly now, almost skipping, swift and sure-footed as a deer as she made her way along the path that stretched downhill from the Summer Gate. The forest here seemed just as wild but more accommodating. Trees as old and grand as these could never have known the touch of an axe, yet they stopped just short of the path; their hanging branches would not brush the head of any but the tallest traveler.

They followed this winding path for no little way, traveling on a rise just a short distance above the floor of the valley. The forest was so thick-shrouded with trees on either side of the path that Simon could never see more than a stone's throw before him, and began to feel as though he stood in one place while an endless succession of mossy trunks marched past him. The air had become positively warm. The wild river—which, judging from its noisy voice, snaked a parallel course along the valley floor not a hundred cubits away—filled the forest air with delicate mist. The sleepy hum of bees and other insects washed over Simon like a healthy swallow of Binabik's hunt-liquor.

He had almost forgotten himself entirely, and was dreamily following Aditu by sheer repetition of left foot, right foot, left foot, when the Sitha-woman drew him to a halt. To their left the curtain of trees fell away, revealing the valley floor.

"Turn," she said, suddenly whispering. "Remember, Seoman, you are the first of your kind to see Jao é-Tinukai'i—the Boat on the Ocean of Trees."

It was nothing like a boat, of course, but Simon understood the name in an instant. Stretched between treetop and ground, and from trunk to trunk and bough to bough, the billowing sheets of cloth in a thousand diverse colors resembled at first sight nothing so much as exquisite sails—indeed, for that first moment the entire valley floor seemed in truth a vast and incredible ship.

Some of these expanses of brilliantly gleaming cloth had been stretched and tented to make roofs. Others twined about the trunks of trees, or spanned from bough to ground to form translucent walls. Some simply heaved and snapped in the wind, bound to the highest branches with shiny cords and allowed to wave. The whole city undulated with every shift of the wind, like a seaweed forest on the ocean floor bowing gracefully with the tide.

The cloth and binding cords mirrored with subtle differences the hues of the forest all around, so that in places the additions were barely discernible from that which had grown naturally. In fact, as Simon peered closer, overwhelmed with Jao é-Tinukai'i's subtle and fragile beauty, he saw that in many places the forest and city appeared to have truly been shaped as one, so that they blended together with unearthly harmony. The river which meandered along the center of the valley floor was more subdued here, but still full of relentless, ringing music; the rippling light it reflected onto the city's shifting facades added to the illusion of watery depth. Simon thought he could also see the silvery tracks of other streams weaving in and out through the trees.

The forest floor between the houses—if such they were—was covered with thick greenery, mostly springy clover. This grew like a carpet everywhere but on the paths of dark earth that had been lined with shimmering white stone. A few of the gracefully haphazard bridges that spanned the waterway were also constructed of this same stone. Beside these paths, strange birds with fanlike, iridescent tails of green and blue and yellow strutted or flapped unsteadily back and forth between earth and the lowest branches of the surrounding trees, all the while uttering harsh and somewhat foolish-sounding cries. There were other flashes of incandescent color among the upper branches, birds as brilliantly-feathered as the fantails but considerably more mellifluous of voice.

Warm, gentle winds lifted an essence of spices and tree sap and summer grass to Simon's nose; the avian choir fluted a thousand different songs that somehow fit together like a terrifyingly beautiful puzzle. The marvelous city stretched away before him into the sunlit forest, a Heaven more welcoming than any he had ever envisioned.

"It's . . . wonderful," Simon breathed.

"Come," Aditu said. "Jiriki awaits you in his house."

She beckoned. When he didn't move, she gently took his hand and led him. Simon stared around in delight and awe as they followed a cross-trail down off the rise and onto the outermost path of the valley floor. The rustling of silken folds and the murmuring river blended their melodies together beneath the birdsong, creating a new sound that was altogether different, but still infinitely satisfying.

There was a long time of looking, smelling, and listening before Simon ever began thinking once more. "Where is everyone?" he asked at last. In all of the city within his sight, a space easily twice the size of Battle Square back in Erchester, he could not see a single living soul.

"We are a solitary folk, Seoman," Aditu said. "We stay largely to ourselves, except at certain times. Also, it is midday now, when many of our people like to leave the city and go out walking. I am surprised we saw no one near the Pools."

Despite her reasonable words, Simon thought he sensed something troubling the Sitha, as though she herself was not quite sure she spoke the truth. But he had no way of knowing: expressions or behaviors that meant something definite among those with whom Simon had grown up were almost useless as standards by which to judge any of the Sitha he had met. Nevertheless, he felt fairly sure that something was troubling his guide, and that it might very well be the emptiness Simon had noticed.

A large wildcat strode imperiously onto the pathway before them. For a startled moment, Simon felt his heart speed to a frenzied pace. Despite the creature's size, Aditu did not break stride, walking toward it as calmly as if it were not there. With a flip of its stubby tail, the wildcat abruptly bounded away and vanished into the undergrowth, leaving only the bouncing fronds of a fern to show it had existed at all.

Clearly, Simon realized, birds were not the only creatures who roamed unhindered through Jao é-Tinukai'i. Beside the path, the coats of foxes—seldom seen at night, let alone bright noon—glimmered like flames in the tangled brush. Hares and squirrels stared incuriously at the pair as they passed. Simon felt quite sure that if he leaned down toward any of them they would move unhurriedly out of his fumbling reach, discommoded for a moment but utterly unafraid.

They crossed a bridge over one of the river-forks, then turned and followed the watercourse down a long corridor of willows. A ribbon of white cloth wound in and out among the trees on their left, wrapped about trunks and looped over branches. As they passed farther down the row of willow sentries, the initial ribbon was joined by another. These two snaked in and out, crossing behind and before each other as though engaged in a kind of static dance.

Soon more white ribbons of different widths began to appear, woven into the growing pattern in knots of fantastic intricacy. These weavings at first made up only simple forms, but soon Simon and Aditu began to pass increasingly complex pictures that hung in the spaces framed by the willow trunks: blazing suns, cloudy skies overhanging oceans covered with jagged waves, leaping animals, figures in flowing robes or filigreed armor, all formed by interlaced knots. As the first plain pictures became entire tapestries of tangled light and shadow, Simon understood that he watched an unfolding story. The ever-growing tapestry of knotted fabric portrayed people who loved and fought in a gardenlike land of incredible strangeness, a place where plants and creatures thrived whose forms seemed obscure even though precisely rendered by the unknown weaver's masterful, magical hands.

Then, as the tapestry eloquently showed, something began to go wrong. Only ribbons of white were used, but still Simon could almost see the dark stain that began to spread through the people's lives and hearts, the way it sickened them. Brother fought brother, and what had been a place of unmatched beauty was blighted beyond hope. Some of the people began building ships . . .

"Here," Aditu said, startling him. The tapestry had led them to a whirlpool swirl of pale fabric, an inward-leading spiral that appeared to lead up a gentle hill. On the right, beside this odd door, the tapestry leaped away across the river, trembling in the bright air like a bridge of silk. Where the taut ribbons of the tapestry vaulted the splashing stream, the knots portrayed eight magnificent ships at sea, cresting woven waves. The tapestry touched the willows on the far side and turned, winding back up the watercourse in the direction from which Simon and Aditu had come, stretching away from tree to tree until it could no longer be seen.

Aditu's hand touched his arm and Simon shivered. Walking in someone else's dream, he had forgotten himself. He followed her through the doorway and up a set of stairs carefully cut into the hillside, then paved with colorful smooth stones. Like everything else, the corridor through which they walked was made of rippling, translucent cloth: the walls were white near the door, gradually darkening to pale blue and turquoise. In her white clothes Aditu reflected this shifting light, so that as she walked before him, she, too, seemed to change color.

Simon trailed his fingers along the wall and found that it was as exquisitely soft as it looked, but curiously strong; it slid beneath his hand as smoothly as gold wire, yet was warm to the touch as the down of a baby bird and quivered with the wind's every breath.

The featureless corridor soon opened up into a large, high-ceilinged room that, but for the instability of its walls, looked much like a room in any fine house. The turquoise hue of the cloth near the entrance shaded imperceptibly into ultramarine. A low table of dark wood stood near one wall, with cushions scattered all around it. On the table sat a board painted in many colors; Simon thought it a map until he recognized it as a place to play the game called shent, which he had seen Jiriki do in his hunting lodge. He remembered Aditu's challenge. The pieces, he guessed, were in the intricate wooden box sitting beside it on the table top. The only other item on the table was a stone vase containing a single branch from a flowering apple tree.

"Sit down, Snowlock, please." Aditu waved her hand. "I believe Jiriki has a visitor."

Before Simon could follow her suggestion, the room's far wall began to billow. A section flew up as if it had torn free. Someone dressed in bright green, whose braided hair was a jarringly contrasting shade of red, stepped through.

Simon was surprised at how quickly he recognized Jiriki's uncle, Khendraja'aro. The Sitha was muttering gruffly in what seemed to be fury—seemed, because Simon could see no discernible emotion on his face at all. Then Khendraja'aro looked up and spotted Simon. His angular face blanched, as though the blood had run out of him like water from an upended pail.

"Sudhoda'ya! Isi-isi'ye-a Sudhoda'ya!" he gasped, his voice full of an anger so astonished as to seem like something else altogether.

Khendraja'aro dragged his slender, beringed hand slowly across his eyes and face as if trying to wipe away the sight of gangly Simon. Unable to do so, Jiriki's uncle hissed in almost feline alarm, then turned on Aditu and began to speak to her in rapid, quietly liquid Sithi that nonetheless strengthened the suggestion of spitting rage. Aditu absorbed his tirade expressionlessly, her deep, gold-shot eyes wide but unfrightened. When Khendraja'aro had finished, she answered him calmly. Her uncle turned and regarded Simon once more, making a series of strangely sinuous gestures with his splayed fingers as he listened to her measured response.

Khendraja'ro took a deep breath, letting a preternatural calm overtake him until he stood motionless as a pillar of stone. Only his bright eyes seemed alive, burning in his face like lamps. After several moments of this overwhelming stillness he walked from the room without a word or sideways glance, padding silently down the corridor to the door of Jiriki's house.

Simon was shaken by the unmistakable force of Khendraja'aro's anger. "You said something about breaking rules. . . ?" he asked.

Aditu smiled strangely. "Courage, Snowlock. You are *Hikka Staja*." She brushed her fingers through her hair, a curiously human gesture, then pointed to the flap where her uncle had entered. "Let us go in to my brother."

They stepped through into sunlight. This room, too, was made of fluttering cloth, but the fabric of one long wall had been rolled and drawn up to the ceiling; beyond this opening the hill dropped away for some dozen paces. Below lay a shallow, peaceful backwater of the same river that passed before Jiriki's front door, a wide pond with a narrow inlet neck, surrounded by reeds and quivering aspens. Little red-and-brown birds hopped about on the rocks at the center of the pond, like conquerors strutting the battlements of a captured stronghold. At pond's edge a bale of turtles basked in the sun streaming down through the trees.

"In the evening the crickets are quite splendid here."

Simon turned to see Jiriki, who had apparently been standing in the shadows at the opposite end of the room.

"Welcome to Jao é-Tinukai'i, Seoman," he said. "We are well-met."

"Jiriki!" Simon sprang forward. Without thinking, he grasped the slender Sitha in a tight embrace. The prince tensed for a moment, then relaxed. His firm hand patted Simon's back. "You never said farewell," Simon said, then pulled away, embarrassed.

"I did not," Jiriki agreed. He wore a long, loose robe of some thin blue cloth, belted at the waist with a wide red band; his feet were bare. His lavender hair descended in braids before either ear, and was gathered atop his head with a comb of pale, polished wood.

"I would have died in the woods if you had not helped me," Simon said abruptly, then gave an awkward laugh. "If Aditu had not come, that is." He turned to look at her; Jiriki's sister was watching intently. She nodded her head in acknowledgment. "I would have died." He realized as he spoke that it was absolutely true. He had begun the process of dying when Aditu had found him, growing more distant each day from the business of life.

"So." Jiriki folded his arms before him. "I am honored I could help. It still does not discharge my obligation, however. I owed you *two* lives. You are my *Hikka Staja*, Seoman, and so you will remain." He looked over to his sister. "The butterflies have gathered."

Aditu replied in their lyric tongue, but Jiriki held up his hand.

"Speak in a way that Seoman can understand. He is my guest."

She stared at him for a moment. "We met Khendraja'aro. He is not happy."

"Uncle has not been happy since Asu'a fell. No plans of mine are likely to change that."

"It is more than that, Willow-switch, and you know it." Aditu stared hard at him, but her face remained dispassionate. She turned to look briefly at Simon; for a moment, embarrassment seemed to darken her cheeks. "It is strange to speak this tongue."

"These are strange days, Rabbit—and *you* know *that*." Jiriki lifted his hands toward the sunlight. "Ah, what an afternoon. We must go, now, all of us. The butterflies have gathered, as I said. I speak lightly of Khendraja'aro, but my heart is uneasy."

Simon stared at him, completely baffled.

"First allow me to take off this ridiculous clothing," Aditu said. She slipped away through another hidden door so quickly that she seemed to melt into shadow.

Jiriki led Simon toward the front of his house. "We will wait for her below. You and I have much to speak about, Seoman, but first we must go to the Yásira."

"Why did she call you . . . Willow-switch?" Of all his countless questions, this was the only one he could put into words.

"Why do I call you Snowlock?" Jiriki looked closely at Simon's face, then smiled his charming, feral smile. "It is good to see you well, manchild."

"Let us be off," Aditu said. She had come up behind Simon so soundlessly that he gasped in surprise. When he turned a moment later, he gasped again. Aditu had shed her heavy snow-clothing for a dress that was little more than a wisp of glimmering, nearly transparent white cloth belted with a ribbon of sunset orange. Her slim hips and small breasts were clearly silhouetted beneath the loose garment. Simon felt his face grow hot. He had grown up with the chambermaids, but they had moved him out many years before sending him to sleep with the other scullions. Such near-nakedness was more than disconcerting. He realized he was staring and turned hurriedly away, his face coloring. One hand made an involuntary Tree before his chest.

Aditu's laugh was like rain. "I am happy to be shed of all that! It was *cold* where the manchild was, Jiriki! Cold!"

"You are right, Aditu," Jiriki said grimly. "We find the winter outside easy to forget when it is still summer in our home. Now, it is off to the Yásira, where some do not want to believe that winter exists at all."

He led the way out his strange entry hall to the sunsplashed corridor of willows beside the river. Aditu followed him. Simon brought up the rear, still blushing furiously, with no choice but to watch her springy, swaying walk.

With the added distraction of Aditu in her summer finery, Simon did not think about much of anything for a while, but even Jiriki's lissome sister and Jao é-Tinukai'i's myriad other glories could not distract him forever. Several things had been said lately that were beginning to worry him: Khendraja'aro was angry with him, apparently, and Simon had distinctly heard Aditu say something about breaking rules. What exactly was happening?

"Where are we going, Jiriki?" he asked at last.

"The Yásira." The Sitha gestured ahead. "There, do you see?"

Simon stared, shielding his eyes from the strong sunlight. There were so many distractions here, and the sunlight itself was one of the strongest. Only a few days before he had been wondering if he would ever be warm again. Why was he yet again allowing himself to be dragged somewhere else, when all he wanted to do was flop down on his back in the clover and sleep. . . ?

At first the Yásira seemed like nothing so much as a grand and oddly-shaped tent, a tent whose center pole mounted fifty ells into the air, made of a fabric more shifting and colorful than any of Jao é-Tinukai'i's other beautiful structures. It took another two dozen paces before Simon realized that the center pole was a gigantic ash tree with wide-spreading branches, whose crown rose into the forest sky high above the Yásira itself. He drew another hundred paces closer before he saw why the fabric of the vast tent shimmered so.

Butterflies.

Trailing to the ground from the ash tree's widest branches were a thousand threads, so slender that they seemed little more than parallel glints of light as they fell a hand-span apart all around the tree. Clinging to these strands from top to bottom, lazily fanning their iridescent wings, huddling so closely that they overlapped each other like the shingles on some impossible roof were . . . a million, million butterflies. They were of every color imaginable, orange and wine-red, oxblood and tangerine, cerulean blue, daffodil yellow, velvet black as the night sky. The quiet whisper of their wings was everywhere, as if the warm summer air itself had been given voice. They moved sluggishly, as though near sleep, but were otherwise bound in no way that Simon could see. Countless chips of vibrant moving color, the butterflies shattered the sunlight like an incomparable treasury of living gems.

In that moment, as Simon first saw it, the Yásira seemed the breathing, glowing center of Creation. He stopped and abruptly burst into helpless tears.

Jiriki did not see Simon's overwhelmed response. "The little wings are restless," he said. "S'hue Khendraja'aro has brought the word."

Simon sniffled and wiped at his eyes. Faced with the Yásira, he suddenly thought he could understand the bitterness of Ineluki, the Storm King's hatred for childish, destructive mankind. Shamed, Simon listened to Jiriki's words as though from a great distance. The Sitha prince was saying something about his uncle—was Khendraja'aro talking to the butterflies? Simon didn't care any longer. This was all just too much for him. He didn't want to think; he wanted to lie down. He wanted to sleep.

Jiriki had at last noticed his distress. He took Simon carefully by the elbow and guided him toward the Yásira. At the front of the mad, glorious structure, butterfly-laden strands trailed on either side of a wooden doorway, which was no more than a simple carved frame wound round with trailing roses. Aditu had already stepped through, and now Jiriki led Simon in.

If the effect of the butterflies from outside was one of gleaming magnificence, the view from within was entirely different. The multicolored shafts of light leaked down through the living roof, as if through stained glass that had somehow become unstable. The great ash tree that was the Yásira's spine stood bathed in a thousand shifting hues; Simon was again reminded of some strange forest thriving beneath the inconstant ocean. This time, however, he was beginning to find the thought a little much to bear. He felt almost as though he were drowning, floundering helplessly in an opulence he could not entirely understand.

The great chamber had few furnishings. Beautiful rugs lay scattered everywhere, but in many places the grass grew uncovered. Shallow pools gleamed here and there, flowering bushes and stones around them, all things just as they were outside. The only differences were the butterflies and the Sithi.

The chamber was full of Sithi-folk, male and female, in costumes as variegated as the wings of the butterflies that quivered overhead. One by one at first, then in clusters, they turned to look at the new arrivals, hundreds of calm, catlike eyes agleam in the shifting light. What seemed to Simon a quiet but malicious hiss rose from the multitude. He wanted to run away, and actually made a brief, stumbling attempt, but Jiriki's grip on his arm was gently unbreakable. He found himself led forward to a rise of earth before the base of the tree. A tall, moss-netted stone stood there like an admonishing finger sunken in the grassy ground. On low couches before it sat two Sithi dressed in splendid pale robes, a woman and a man.

The man, who was seated closest, looked up at Simon and Jiriki's approach. His hair, tied high atop his head, was jet black, and he wore a crown of carved white birchwood. He had the same angular golden features as Jiriki, but there was something drawn at the corners of his narrow eyes and thin mouth that suggested a life of great length filled with vast but subtle disappointment. The woman who sat beside him on his left hand had hair of a deep, coppery red; she, too, wore a circlet of birchwood on her brow. Long white feathers hung from her many braids, and she wore several bracelets and rings as black and shiny as the hair of the man beside her. Of all the Sithi Simon had seen, her face was the most immobile, the most rigidly serene. Both man and woman had an air of age and subtlety and stillness, but it was the quiet of a dark old pond in a shadowed wood, the calm of a sky filled with motionless thunderheads: it seemed entirely possible that such placidity might hide something dangerous—dangerous to callow mortals, at least.

"You must bow, Seoman," Jiriki said quietly. Simon, as much because of his shaking legs as anything else, lowered himself to his knees. The smell of the warm turf was strong in his nostrils.

"Seoman Snowlock, manchild," Jiriki said loudly, "know you are come before Shima'onari, King of the Zida'ya, Lord of Jao é-Tinukai'i, and Likimeya, Queen of the Dawn-Children, Lady of the House of Year-Dancing."

Still kneeling, Simon looked up dizzily. All eyes were focused on him, as though he were a singularly inappropriate gift. Shima'onari at last said something to Jiriki, words as harsh-sounding as anything Simon had yet heard the Sithi tongue produce.

"No, Father," Jiriki said. "Whatever else, we must not so lightly turn our backs on our traditions. A guest is a guest. I beg you, speak words that Seoman can understand."

Shima'onari's thin face pinched in a frown. When he spoke at last, he proved far less facile with the Westerling tongue than his son and daughter.

"So. You are the manchild that saved Jiriki's life." He nodded his head slowly, but did not seem very pleased. "I do not know if you can understand this, but my son has done a very bad thing. He has brought you here against all laws of our people—you, a mortal." He straightened up, looking from face to face among the Sithi-folk that surrounded them. "What is done is done, my people, my family," he called. "No harm can come to this manchild: we have not sunk so far. We owe him honor as *Hikka Staja*—as bearer of a White Arrow." He turned back to Simon, and a look of infinite sadness crept over his face. "But neither can you leave, manchild. We cannot let you leave. So you will stay forever. You will grow old and die with us, here in Jao é-Tinukai'i."

The wings of a million butterflies murmured and whispered.

"Stay. . . ?" Simon turned, uncomprehending, to Jiriki. The prince's usually imperturbable face was an ashen mask of shock and sorrow.

* * *

Simon was silent as they walked back to Jiriki's house. Afternoon was slowly fading into twilight; the cooling valley was alive with the smells and sounds of untainted summer.

The Sitha did nothing to break the silence, guiding Simon along the tangled paths with nods and gentle touches. As they approached the river that ran past Jiriki's door, Sithi voices lifted in song somewhere in the overhanging hills. The melody that spilled echoing over the valley was an intricately constructed series of descending figures: sweet, but with a touch of dissonance winding through it, like a fox dodging in and out among rainy hedgerows. There was something unquestionably liquid about the song; after a moment, Simon realized that the invisible musicians were in some way singing along with the noise of the river itself.

A flute joined in, ruffling the surface of the music like wind on the watercourse. Simon was abruptly and painfully struck by the strangeness of this place; loneliness welled within him, an aching emptiness that could not be filled by Jiriki or any of his alien kind. For all its beauty, Jao é-Tinukai'i was no better than a cage. Caged animals, Simon knew, languished and soon died.

"What will I do?" he said hopelessly.

Jiriki stared at the glinting river, smiling sadly. "Walk. Think. Learn how to play shent. In Jao é-Tinukai'i, there are many ways to pass time."

As they walked toward Jiriki's door the water-song cascaded down from the tree-mantled hillside, surrounding them with mournful music that seemed ever-changing but unhurried, patient as the river itself.

23

Deep Waters

"By Elysia the Mother," Aspitis Preves said, "what a terrible time you have had of it, Lady Marya!" The earl lifted his cup to drink but found it empty. He tapped his fingers on the cloth as his pale squire hurried forward to pour more wine. "To think that the daughter of a nobleman should be so ill-treated in our city."

The trio sat around the earl's circular table as the remains of a more than adequate supper were cleared away by a page. Flickering lamplight threw distorted shadows on the walls; outside, the wind sawed in the rigging. Two of the earl's hounds brawled over a bone beneath the table.

"Your Lordship is too kind." Miriamele shook her head. "My father's barony is very small, just a freeholding, really. One of the smallest baronies in Cellodshire."

"Ah, then your father must know Godwig?" Aspitis' Westerling was a little difficult to understand, and not only because it was his second tongue: the goblet in his hand had been drained and filled several times.

"Of course. He is the most powerful of all the barons there—the king's strong hand in Cellodshire." Thinking of the despicable, braying Godwig, Miriamele found it hard to keep her expression pleasant, even while looking on the goldenly handsome Aspitis. She darted a glance at Cadrach, who was sunk in some dark mood, his brow furrowed like a thunderhead.

He thinks I'm saying too much, Miriamele decided. She felt a flash of anger. *But who is **he** to make faces? He got us into this trap; now, thanks to me, instead of us going over the side as kilpa food, we're at the master's table drinking wine and eating good Lakeland cheese.*

"But I am still astonished by your ill fortune, Lady," Aspitis said. "I had heard that these Fire Dancers were a problem in the provinces, and I have seen a few heretical madmen preaching the Fire Dancer creed in Nabban's public places—but the idea that they would actually dare to lay hands on a noblewoman!"

"An Erkynlandish noblewoman, a very unimportant one," Miriamele said hastily, worried she might have gone too far in her improvisation. "And I was dressed to travel to my new convent home. They had no idea of my position."

"That is immaterial." Aspitis waved his hand airily, almost knocking over the candle on the tabletop with his trailing sleeve. He had shed the finery he wore on the quarterdeck, choosing instead a long, simple robe like those worn by knights during their vigil. But for a delicate gold Tree on a chain about his neck, his only adornment was the insignia of the Prevan House woven on each sleeve; the osprey wings wrapped his forearms like climbing flames. Miriamele was favorable impressed that a wealthy young man like Aspitis would greet guests in such modest attire. "Immaterial," he repeated. "These people are heretics and worse. Besides, a noblewoman from Erkynland is no different than one of Nabban's own Fifty Families. Noble blood is the same throughout Osten Ard, and like a spring of sweet water in an arid wilderness, must be protected at all costs." He leaned forward and gently touched her arm through her sleeve. "Had I been there, Lady Marya, I would have given my life before letting one of them mishandle you." He leaned back and patted the hilt of his scabbarded sword, studiedly casual. "But if I had been forced to make that ultimate sacrifice, I would have insisted that a few of them accompany me."

"Oh," said Miriamele. "Oh." She took a deep breath, a little overwhelmed. "But really, Earl Aspitis, there is no need to worry. We escaped quite safely—it's just that we had to flee to your boat and hide. It was dark, you see, and Father Cadrach . . ."

"Brother," the monk said sourly from across the table. He took a draught of wine.

". . . *Brother* Cadrach said that this would be the safest place. So we hid ourselves in the cargo hold. We are sorry for the imposition, Earl, and we thank you for your kindness. If you will only put us ashore at the next port . . ."

"Leave you out among the islands somewhere? Nonsense." Aspitis leaned forward, fixing her with his brown eyes. He had a dangerous smile, Miriamele realized, but it did not frighten her as much as she knew it should. "You will ride out the voyage with us, then we may put you safe back in Nabban where you belong. It will be little more than a fortnight, Lady. We will treat you well—both you and your guardian." He briefly turned his smile on Cadrach, who did not seem to share Aspitis' good humor. "I think I even have some clothes on board that will fit you, Lady. They should suit your beauty better than your . . . traveling clothes."

"How nice!" Miriamele said, then remembered her imposture. "If it meets with Brother Cadrach's approval."

"You have women's clothes on board?" Cadrach asked, eyebrow raised.

"Left by my sister." Aspitis' smile was untroubled.

"Your sister." He grunted. "Yes. Well, I shall have to think on it."

Miriamele started to raise her voice to the monk, then remembered her situation. She strove to look obedient, but silently cursed him. Why shouldn't she be allowed to wear nice clothes for a change?

As the earl began to talk animatedly of his family's great keep beside Lake Eadne—ironically, a freehold that Miriamele had visited when a very young child, although she did not now remember it—there was a rap at the door. One of Aspitis' pages went to answer it.

"I come to speak with the ship's lord," a breathy voice said.

"Come in, my friend," Aspitis said. "You have all met, of course. Gan Itai, you were the one who found Lady Marya and her guardian, yes?"

"That is true, Earl Aspitis," the Niskie nodded. Her black eyes twinkled as they reflected the lamplight.

"If you would be so good as to come back in a while," Aspitis said to the sea watcher, "then we will talk."

"No, please, Earl Aspitis." Miriamele stood. "You've been very kind, but we should not keep you any longer. Come, Brother Cadrach."

"Keep me?" Aspitis put a hand to his breast. "Should I complain at being the victim of such lovely company? Lady Marya, you must think me a dullard indeed." He bowed and took her hand, holding it for a lingering moment against his lips. "I hope you do not think me too forward, sweet lady." He snapped his fingers for a page. "Young Thures will show you to your beds. I have put the captain out of his cabin. You will sleep there."

"Oh, but we couldn't take the captain's . . ."

"He spoke out of turn and did not show you proper respect, Lady Marya. He is lucky I do not hang him—but I am willing to forgive. He is a simple man, not used to women on his ships. A few nights sleeping at general quarters with his crew will do him no harm." He dragged fingers through his curly hair, then waved his hand. "Go on, Thures, lead them."

He bowed to Miriamele again, then smiled politely at Cadrach. This time Cadrach returned the smile, but it seemed little more than a baring of teeth. The little page, lantern held carefully before him, led his charges out the door.

Aspitis stood silent a while in thought, then found the wine ewer and poured himself another gobletful, which he drank off in a long swallow. At last he spoke.

"So, Gan Itai, it is unusual for you to come here—and it is even more unusual for you to leave the bow at night. Are the waters so untroubled that your song is not needed?"

The Niskie shook her head slowly. "No, Ship's Master. The waters are very troubled, but for this moment they are safe, and I wished to come and tell you that I am disturbed."

"Disturbed? By the girl? Surely Niskies are not superstitious like sailors."

"Not like sailors, no." She pulled her hood forward, hiding all but her bright eyes. "The girl and the monk, even if they are not what they say, are the least of my worries. There is a great storm coming down from the north."

Aspitis looked up at Gan Itai. "You left the bow to tell me that?" he asked mockingly. "I have known that since before we set sail. The captain says we will be out of deep waters before the storm reaches us."

"That may be, but there are great shoals of kilpa moving in from the northern seas, as if they are swimming before the storm. Their song is fierce and cold, Earl Aspitis; they seem to come up from the blackest water, from the deepest trenches. I have never heard the like."

Aspitis stared for a moment, his whole aspect slightly out of kilter, as though the wine had finally begun to effect him. "*Eadne Cloud* has many important tasks to perform for Duke Benigaris," he said. "You must do what it is your life's work to do." He lowered his head into the palms of his hands. "I am tired, Gan Itai. Go back to the bow. I need to sleep."

The Niskie watched him for a moment, full of imponderable gravity, then bowed gracefully and backed out of the door, letting it fall shut behind her with a quiet thump. Earl Aspitis leaned forward across the table, pillowing his head on his forearms in the circle of lamplight.

It is good to be around a nobleman once more," Miriamele said. "They are full of themselves, yes, but they do understand how to show a woman respect."

Cadrach snorted from his pallet on the floor. "I find it hard to believe you could see any value in that ringleted fop, Princess."

"Hush!" Miriamele hissed. "Idiot! Don't speak so loudly! And don't call me that. I am Lady Marya, remember."

The monk made another noise of disgust. "A noblewoman chased by Fire Dancers. That was a pretty tale to spin."

"It worked, didn't it?"

"Yes, and now we must spend our time with Earl Aspitis, who will ask question after question. If you had only said you were a poor tailor's daughter who had hidden in fear for her virtue, or some such, the earl would leave us alone and put us off at the first island where they take on water and provisions."

"And make us work like dogs until then—if he didn't just throw us into the sea. I, for one, am growing tired of this disguise. It is bad enough I have been an acolyte monk all this time, now should I be a tailor's daughter as well?"

Although she could not see him in the darkened cabin, Miriamele knew by the sound of his voice that Cadrach was shaking his heavy head in disagreement. "No, no, no. Do you understand nothing, Lady? We are not choosing parts like a children's game, we are struggling to stay alive. Dinivan, the man who brought us here, has been *killed*. Do you understand? Your father and your uncle are at war. The war is spreading. They have killed the lector, the Ransomer's chief priest on the face of Osten Ard, and they will stop at nothing, Lady! It is no game!"

Miriamele choked back an angry reply, thinking instead about what Cadrach had said. "Then why didn't Earl Aspitis say anything about the lector? Surely it's the kind of thing people would talk about. Or did you make that up as well?"

"Lady, Ranessin was only killed late last night. We left early in the morning." The monk struggled to keep his patience. "The Sancellan Aedonitis and the Escritorial Council may not announce what has happened for a day or two. Please, believe what I say is true, or we will both come to a terrible end."

"Hmmph." Miriamele lay back, pulling the blanket up to her chin. The feeling of the boat rocking was quite soothing. "It seems that if it weren't for my inventiveness and the earl's good manners, we might have come to a terrible end already."

"Think what you like, Lady," Cadrach said heavily, "but do not, I beg you, extend your trust to others any farther than you have with me."

He fell silent. Miriamele waited for sleep. An odd, hauntingly alien melody floated on the air, timeless and arrhythmic as the roar of the sea, persistent as the rising and falling wind. Somewhere in the darkness outside, Gan Itai was singing the kilpa down.

Eolair rode down out of the heights of the Grianspog Mountains in the midst of the summer's worst snowstorm. The secret trails that he and his men had so laboriously cut through the forest only weeks before were now buried beneath three cubits of drifting white. The dismal skies hung oppressively close, like the ceiling of a tomb. His saddlebags were crammed with carefully-drawn maps, his head with brooding thoughts.

Eolair knew there was no use pretending that the land was suffering only a long bout of freakish weather. A grievous sickness was spreading over Osten Ard. Perhaps Josua and his father's sword truly were tied up in something vaster than the wars of men.

The Count of Nad Mullach was suddenly reminded of his own words, uttered over the King's Great Table a year before—Gods of earth and sky, he thought, but didn't it seem a lifetime since those relatively peaceful days! *"Evil is abroad . . ."* he had told the assembled knights that day. *"It is not only bandits who prey on travelers and cause the disappearance of isolated farmers. The people of the North are afraid . . ."*

Not only bandits . . . Eolair shook his head, disgusted with himself. He had been so caught up in the day-to-day matters of his people's struggle to survive that he had failed to heed his own warning. There were indeed greater menaces to fear than Skali of Kaldskryke and his cutthroat army.

Eolair had heard stories told by survivors of the fall of Naglimund, the bewildered accounts of a ghostly army raised by Elias the High King. From the days of his childhood Eolair had heard tales of the White Foxes, demons who lived in the blackest, coldest lands of the uttermost north, who appeared like a plague, then vanished again. All during this last year the Frostmarch dwellers had whispered over their night-fires of just such pale demons. How foolish that Eolair of all people should not have realized the truth behind these tales—had he not spoken of just that at the Great Table!?

But what could it all mean? If they were truly involved, why should creatures like these White Foxes side with Elias? Could it have something to do with that monstrous priest Pryrates?

The Count of Nad Mullach sighed, then leaned far to the side to help his horse balance as they made their way down a treacherous hill path. Perhaps for all her foolishness, Maegwin had been right to set this task for him. But still, that was no justification for the way in which she had done it. Why should she treat him as she did in the underground city, after all he had done for her family and the faithful service he had given her father King Lluth? The terror and strangeness of their situation might be the reason for such unkindness, but it was no excuse.

Such thoughtlessness was yet another odd change in Maegwin's demeanor, the latest of many. He feared for her deeply, but could think of no way to help. She despised his solicitousness, and seemed to think he was little more than a sly courtier—Eolair, who hated falsity, yet had been driven to master it in the loyal service of her father! When he tried to help, she insulted him and turned her back: he could only watch her sickening as the land around him had sickened, her mind filling with strange fancies. He could do nothing.

Eolair was two days making his way down through the silent valleys of the Grianspog, with only his own cold thoughts for company.

It was astonishing to see how quickly Skali was making his occupation of Hernystir permanent. Not content with taking over those houses and buildings still standing in Hernysadharc and the surrounding villages, the Thane of Kaldskryke had begun to construct new ones, great longhouses of rough-hewn timbers. The Circoille Forest fringe was shrinking rapidly, replaced by a growing expanse of mutilated tree stumps.

Eolair made his way along the ridgetops, watching the antlike figures swarming over the flatlands below. The clatter of hammer on wedge rang through the snowy hills.

He could not at first understand why Skali should need to build more dwelling places: the conqueror's army, while of good size, was hardly so vast that it could not harbor itself in the Hernystiri's abandoned dwellings. It was only when Eolair looked away to the lowering northern skies that he realized what was happening.

All Skali's Rimmersfolk must be coming here from the North—old and young, women and children. He stared down at the tiny, industrious shapes. *If it's snowing in Hernysadharc in late Tiyagar-month, it must be a frozen hell up by Naarved and Skoggey. Bagba bite me, what a thought! Skali has chased us into the caves. Now he will move his Rimmersgarders onto our captured lands.*

Despite all that his folk had already suffered at the hands of Skali Sharp-nose's warriors, despite King Lluth struck down, Prince Gwythinn tortured and dismembered, and hundreds of Eolair's own brave Mullachi dead beneath the gray skies of the western meadows, the count found suddenly and to his surprise that he contained depths of anger and raw hatred yet unplumbed. Skali's men strutting in the roads of Hernysadharc was bad enough, but the thought of them bringing their women and families to live on Hernystiri land filled Eolair with an unchanneled rage stronger than he had felt since the first Hernystirmen had fallen at the Inniscrich. Helpless on the ridgetop, he cursed the invaders and promised himself that he would see Skali's jackals whipped howling back to Kaldskryke—those who did not die on the precious Hernystiri soil that they had usurped.

Suddenly, the Count of Nad Mullach longed for the purity of battle. The Hernystiri forces had been so savaged at Inniscrich that they had been unable to fight anything but rearguard actions since. Now they had been driven into hiding in the Grianspog and there was little they could do but harrass the victors. Gods, he thought, but it would be fine to swing steel in the open once more, to line up breast to breast with shields flashing sunlight and sound the charge! The count knew it was a foolish craving, knew himself for a careful man who always preferred talking sensibly to fighting, but just now he craved simplicity. Open warfare, for all its witless violence and horror, could seem a sort of beautiful idiocy into which one could throw oneself as into the arms of a lover.

Now the call of that compelling but dangerous lover was growing stronger. Whole nations seemingly on the march, topsy-turvy weather, mad men ruling and dire legends come to life—how he suddenly longed for simple things!

But even as he yearned for unthinking release, Eolair knew that he would hate its coming to be: the fruits of violence did not necessarily go to the just or the wise.

Eolair skirted Hernysadharc's westernmost outposts and circled far around the largest encampments of Skali's Rimmersmen, who had spread across the meadowlands beneath Hernystir's capital. He rode instead through the hilly country called the Dillathi, which stood like a bulwark along Hernystir's coast as if to prevent invasion by sea. Indeed, the Dillathi would have presented a nearly impossible problem for any would-be conqueror, but the invasion which had undone Hernystir had come from the opposite direction.

The highland folk were a suspicious lot, but they had grown used to war-fugitives in the past year, so Eolair was able to find welcome in a few houses. Those who took him in were far more interested in his news than the fact that their guest was the Count of Nad Mullach. These were days when gossip was the most valued coin in the country.

So far from the cities, no one had known much of Prince Josua in the first place, let alone how his struggle with the High King might be somehow connected to Hernystir's plight. No one in the Dillathi country had the slightest idea of whether King Elias' brother Josua was alive or dead, let alone where he might be. But the highlanders had heard of their own King Lluth's mortal wounding from the tales of wanderering soldiers, survivors of the fighting at the Inniscrich. Thus, Eolair's hosts were usually heartened to discover from him that Lluth's daughter still lived, and that a Hernystiri court-in-exile of sorts still existed. Before the war they had thought little of what the king in the Taig said or did, but he had been part of their lives nonetheless. Eolair guessed they found it reassuring that at least a shadow of the old kingdom remained, as though the continued existence of Lluth's family somehow assured that the Rimmersmen would eventually be forced out.

Coming down out of the Dillathi, Eolair steered wide of high-walled Crannhyr, Hernystir's strangest and most insular city, guiding his horse instead toward Abaingeat at the mouth of the River Baraillean. He was unsurprised to find that the Hernystirmen of Abaingeat had found a way to live under the heavy hands of both Elias and Skali; Abaingeaters had a reputation for flexibility. It was a common joke in other parts of the country to refer to the port city as "Extremely North Perdruin" because of the shared affection for profits and dislike of politics—the kind of politics that interfered with business, anyway.

It was also in Abaingeat that Eolair received his first real clue to Josua's whereabouts, and it happened in a very typical Abaingeat way.

Eolair shared a supper table with a Nabbanai priest in an inn along the waterfront. The wind was howling and rain was beating on the roof, making the common room rumble like a drum. Under the very eyes of bearded Rimmersmen and haughty Erkynlanders—Hernystir's new conquerors—the good father, who had perhaps had one tankard of ale too many, told Eolair a disjointed but fascinating story. He had just arrived from the Sancellan Aedonitis in Nabban, and he swore that he had been told by someone there, someone he characterized as "the most important priest in the Sancellan," that Josua Lackhand had survived Naglimund.

with seven other survivors, had made his way eastward through the grasslands to safety. These facts had been told to him, the priest said, only under the condition of his complete discretion.

Immediately after telling this tale, Eolair's companion, full of drunken remorse, begged him swear to secrecy—as, the count felt sure, the priest had begged many other recipients of this same secret. Eolair agreed with a commendably straight face.

There were several things that interested Eolair about this tale. The exact number of survivors in Josua's party seemed a possible indication of its authenticity, although he had to admit it sounded almost like a legend in the making: The One-Handed Prince and his Gallant Seven. Also, the priest's contrition about blurting out the secret seemed genuine. He had not told the tale to make himself appear more grand; rather, he was simply the kind of man who could not keep a confidence to save his soul.

This, of course, raised a question. Why would a man of some importance to Mother Church, as the priest's informant supposedly was, entrust such a vital piece of intelligence to a numbwit on whose flushed, foolish face untrustworthiness was clearly written? Surely no one could expect this cheerful drunkard to keep anything to himself, let alone keep hidden a subject of such interest in the war-torn North?

Eolair was puzzled but intrigued. As thunder growled over the Frostmarch, the Count of Nad Mullach began to consider a journey to the grassy country beyond Erkynland.

Later that night, coming back from the stables—Eolair never trusted others to take proper care of his horse, a habit that had benefited him more often than not—he stopped outside the inn's front door. A fierce wind laden with snow blew down the street, banging the shuttered windows. Beyond the docks the sea murmured uneasily. All of Abaingeat's inhabitants seemed to have vanished. The midnight city was a ghost ship, floating captainless beneath the moon.

Strange lights played across the northern sky: yellow and indigo and a violet like the after-image of lightning. The horizon pulsed with rippling, radiant bands unlike anything Eolair had ever seen, at once chilling and yet incredibly vital. Compared to silent Abaingeat, the North seemed wildly alive, and for a mad moment the count wondered if it was worth fighting any more. The world he had known was gone, and nothing could bring it back. Perhaps it would be better just to accept . . .

He smacked his gloved hands together. The clap echoed dully and faded. He shook his head, trying to shake the leadenness from his thoughts. The lights were compelling indeed.

And where would he go now? It was a ride of several weeks to the meadowlands beyond Hasu Vale of which the priest had spoken. Eolair knew he could cling to the coastline, passing Meremund and Wentmouth, but that would mean riding as a lone traveler through an Erkynland that owed its complete allegiance to the High King. Or, he could let the shimmering aurora draw him north instead, to his home in Nad Mullach. His keep was occupied by Skali's reavers, but those of his people who survived in the countryside would give him shelter and news, and also a chance to rest and reprovision himself for the remainder of his long journey. From there he could turn east and pass Erchester to the north, moving in the protective shadow of the great forest.

Pondering, he stared at the spectral glow in the northern sky. It made for a very chilly light.

The waves were choppy, the dark sky wild with tattered, ominous clouds. A zigzag of lightning flared on the blackened horizon.

Cadrach gripped the railing and groaned as the *Eadne Cloud* lifted high, then settled once more into the trough of a wave. Overhead the sails popped in the strong wind, percussive bursts of sound like whipcracks. "Oh, Brynioch of the Skies," the monk implored, "take this tempest away!"

"This is barely a storm at all," Miriamele said derisively. "You've never been in a real sea-storm."

Cadrach made a gulping sound. "Nor do I want to be."

"Besides, what are you doing, praying to pagan gods? I thought you were an Aedonite monk."

"I have been praying for Usires' intercession all afternoon," Cadrach said, his face pale as fish-flesh. "I thought it time to try something different." He rose on tiptoes and leaned farther out over the railing. Miriamele turned her head away. A moment later the monk settled back, wiping his mouth with his sleeve. A spatter of rain drifted across the deck.

"And you, Lady," he said, "does nothing bother you?"

She bit back a mocking reply. He looked truly pathetic, his few strands of hair pasted flat, his eyes dark-rimmed. "Many things, but not being on a boat at sea."

"Count yourself blessed," he mumbled, then turned back to sag against the rail once more. Instead, his eyes widened. He screeched in shock and tumbled backward, falling rump-first to the deck.

"Bones of Anaxos!" he shouted. "Save us! What is it?!"

Miriamele stepped to the rail to see a gray head bobbing in the saddle of the waves. It was vaguely manlike, hairless yet unscaled, sleek as a dolphin, with a red-rimmed, toothless mouth and eyes like rotting black-berries. The flexible mouth rounded into a circle as though it would sing. It gave out a strange, gurgling hoot, then slipped beneath the waves, showing a glimpse of long-toed, webbed feet as it dove. A moment later the nub of head appeared again a little closer to the ship. It watched them.

Miriamele's stomach fluttered. "Kilpa," she whispered.

"It is horrible," Cadrach said, still crouching below the wale. "It has the face of a damned soul."

The empty black eyes followed Miriamele as she moved a few steps up the railing. She understood the monk clearly. The kilpa was far more horrifying than any mere animal could be, no matter how savage—so dreadfully near-human, yet so devoid of anything that looked like human feeling or understanding.

"I have not seen one in years," she said slowly, unable to tear her eyes away. "I don't think I have ever seen one so close." Her thoughts tumbled back to her childhood, to a trip she had taken with her mother Hylissa from Nabban to the island of Vinitta. Kilpa had glided in and out of their wake, and to the younger Miriamele they had seemed almost sportive, like porpoises or flying fish. Seeing this one so closely, she now understood why her mother had hastily dragged her from the rail. She shuddered.

"You say that you have seen them before, my lady?" a voice asked. She whirled to find Aspitis standing behind her, his hand resting on crouching Cadrach's shoulder. The monk looked quite sick.

"On a long-ago visit to . . . to Wentmouth," she said hastily. "They are terrible, aren't they?"

Aspitis nodded slowly, staring at Miriamele rather than the slick gray thing bobbing off the stern rail. "I hadn't realized that kilpa traveled into cold northern waters," he said.

"Doesn't Gan Itai keep them away?" she said, trying to change the subject. "Why has this one come so close?"

"Because the Niskie is exhausted and is sleeping for a while, and also because the kilpa have become very bold." Aspitis bent and picked a square-headed iron nail off the deck, then pitched it at the silent watcher. It splashed a foot from the kilpa's noseless, earless head. The black eyes did not blink. "They are more active than I have ever heard of, these days," the earl said. "They have swarmed several small craft since the winter, and even a few large ones." He hurriedly raised a hand on which gold rings sparkled. "But fear not, Lady Marya. There is no better singer than my Gan Itai."

"That thing is a horror and I am ill." Cadrach groaned. "I must go and lie myself down." He ignored Aspitis' proffered hand and clambered to his feet, then went stumbling away.

The earl turned and shouted instructions to the crewmen swarming in the wind-buffeted rigging. "We must reef the sails," he said by way of explanation. "There is a very fierce storm coming, and we can only ride it out." As if to underscore his point, lightning flashed once more on the northern horizon. "Perhaps you would be good enough to join me for my evening meal." Thunder came rolling across the swells; a flurry of rain swept over them. "That way, your guardian can be given some privacy to recuperate, and you need not be without company if the storm grows frightening." He smiled, showing even teeth.

Miriamele felt tempted but cautious. There was an impression of coiled strength to Aspitis, as though some potential were being hidden so as not to frighten. In a way, it reminded her of old Duke Isgrimnur, who treated women with gentle, almost excessive deference, as though his blundering bluffness might at any time escape his control and burst forth to shock and offend. Aspitis, too, seemed to hold something in check. It was a quality she found intriguing.

"Thank you, your Lordship," she said at last. "I would be honored—you will have to excuse me, though, if I must leave from time to time to see that Brother Cadrach is not suffering too badly for want of aid or company."

"Did you not," Aspitis said, smoothly taking her arm, "you would not be the good and gentle lady that you are. I can see that you two are as close as family, that you respect Cadrach as you would a beloved uncle."

Miriamele could not help looking over her shoulder as Aspitis led her across the deck, beneath the crewmen shouting at each other in the rigging so they could be heard above the wail of the wind. The kilpa still floated in the rough green seas, watching solemnly as a priest, its open mouth a round black hole.

The earl's squire, a thin, whey-faced young man with a resentful frown, directed the two pages as they loaded the table with fruit and bread and white cheese. Thures, the smaller of the pages, tottered out beneath the weight of a salver bearing a cold joint of beef. The boy stayed to assist, handing the squire a new carving untensil each time that artist impatiently waved his hand. The little page seemed clever—his dark eyes watched the pasty-faced squire intently for the slightest sign—but the bad-tempered older boy nevertheless found several opportunities to cuff him for his slowness.

"You seem very comfortable on a ship, Lady Marya," Aspitis said, smiling as he filled a wine goblet from a beautiful brass ewer. He had his other page carry it around the table to her. "Have you been at sea before? It is a long way from Cellodshire to what we in Nabban call the *Veir Maynis*—the Great Green."

Miriamele silently cursed herself. Perhaps Cadrach was right. She should have thought of a simpler story to tell. "Yes. I mean, no, I haven't. Not really." She took a long, studied sip of wine, forcing herself to smile back at the earl despite its sourness. "We traveled on shipboard down the Gleniwent several times. I have been on the Kynslagh as well." She took another long sip and realized she had emptied the goblet. She set it down, embarrassed. What would this man think of her?

"Who is 'we'?"

"I beg your pardon?" She guiltily pushed the goblet away, but Aspitis took this as a sign and refilled it, pushing it back to her side of the rimmed table with an understanding smile. As the cabin pitched with the boat's motion, the wine threatened to overtop the edge of the goblet. Miriamele picked it up, holding it very gingerly.

"I said, who is 'we', Lady Marya, if I may ask? You and your guardian? You and your family? You mentioned your father, Baron . . . Baron . . ." He frowned. "A thousand apologies, I've forgotten his name."

Miriamele had forgotten also. She covered her moment of panic with another sip of wine; it became rather a long sip as she struggled with her memory. The name she had chosen came back at last. She swallowed.

"Baron Seoman."

"Of course—Baron Seoman. Was that who took you down the Gleniwent?"

She nodded her head, hoping not to get into any further trouble.

"And your mother?"

"Dead."

"Ah." Aspitis' golden face became somber as a cloud-curtained sun. "Forgive me. I am being rude, asking so many questions. I am terribly sorry to hear that."

Miriamele had a moment of inspiration. "She died in the plague last year."

The earl nodded. "So many did. Tell me, Lady Marya—if you will allow me one last and quite forward question—is there a special man to whom you are promised?"

"No," she answered quickly, then wondered if she could have given a better and less potentially troublesome answer. She took a deep breath, holding the earl's gaze. The pomander that scented the cabin air was rich in her nostrils. "No," she repeated. He was very handsome.

"Ah." Aspitis nodded gravely. With his youthful face and head of brilliant curls, he seemed almost a child play-acting as an adult. "But see, you have not eaten anything, Lady. Does the fare displease you?"

"Oh, no, Earl Aspitis!" she said breathlessly, looking for a spot to put her wine goblet down so she could pick up her knife. She noticed that the cup was empty. Aspitis saw her look and leaned forward with the ewer.

As she picked at her food, Apitis talked. As if in apology for his earlier interrogation, he kept his conversation airy as swansdown, speaking mostly of odd or silly things that happened at the Nabbanai court. To hear him talk, it was quite a glittering place. He told stories well and soon had her laughing—in fact, with the rocking of the ship and the walls of the small, lamplit cabin pressing in upon her, she began to wonder if she was laughing too much. The whole thing felt rather dreamlike. She was having difficulty keeping her eyes squarely on Aspitis' smiling face.

As she suddenly realized that she could no longer see the earl at all, a hand came to rest lightly upon her shoulder: Aspitis was behind her, still talking about the ladies of the court. Through the wine fumes that filled her head, she could feel his touch, weighty and hot.

". . . But of course their beauty is that rather . . . *arranged* beauty, if you know what I mean, Marya. I do not mean to be cruel, but sometimes when Duchess Nessalanta is caught in a breeze, the powder flies off her like snow from a mountaintop!" Aspitis' hand squeezed gently, then moved to her other shoulder as he altered his stance. On the way, his fingers trailed gently across the nape of her neck. She shuddered. "Do not misunderstand me," he said, "I would defend to the death the honor and beauty of our courtly Nabbanai women—but in my heart there is nothing so fine as the unimproved loveliness of a country girl." His hand moved to her neck again, the touch delicate as a thrush's wing. "*You* are such a beauty, Lady Marya. I am so pleased to have met you. I had forgotten what it was to see a face that needed no embellishment . . ."

The room spun. Miriamele abruptly straightened and her elbow toppled the wine cup. A few drops like blood pooled on her hand towel. "I must go outside," she said. "I must have some air."

"My lady," Aspitis said, concern plain in his voice, "are you ill? I hope it is not my poor table that has offended your gentle constitution."

She waved a hand, trying to placate him, wanting only to be out of the glaring lamplight and the stiflingly warm, perfumed air. "No, no. I just want to go outside."

"But there is a storm, my lady. You would be soaked. I can't allow it."

She stumbled a few steps toward the door. "Please. I'm ill."

The earl shrugged helplessly. "Let me at least get you a warm cloak that will keep out most of the damp." He clapped for his pages, who were trapped with the unpleasant squire in the tiny room that served as both larder and kitchen. One of the pages began to go through a large chest in search of an appropriate garment while Miriamele stood by miserably. She was at last outfitted in a musty-smelling wool cloak with a hood; Aspitis, similarly dressed, took her elbow and guided her up onto the deck.

The wind was blowing in earnest. Torrents of rain sliced down, turning to cascades of sparkling gold as they passed through the guttering lamplight, then vanishing back into blackness. Thunder drummed.

"Let us at least sit beneath the canopy, Lady Marya," Aspitis cried, "or we will both of us catch some terrible ague!" He led her aft, where a red-striped sailcloth awning stretched between the wales, humming as it vibrated in the strong wind. A steersman in a flapping cloak bowed his head as they ducked beneath the cloth, but kept his hands firmly clasped on the tiller. The pair sat down on a pile of dampened rugs.

"Thank you," Miriamele said. "You are kind. I feel very foolish to trouble you."

"I only worry that this is a cure worse than the illness," Aspitis said, smiling. "If my physician were to hear of this, he would be leeching me for brain fever before I could blink."

Miriamele laughed and shivered in quick succession. Despite the chill, the tangy sea air had vastly improved her outlook. She no longer felt as though she might faint—in fact, she felt so much better that she did not object when the Earl of Eadne and Drina slipped a solicitous arm around her shoulders.

"You are a strange but fascinating young woman, Lady Marya," Aspitis whispered, barely audible above the moan of the wind. His breath was warm against the chilled flesh of her ear. "I feel there is some mystery about you. Are all country girls so full of moods?"

Miriamele was very definitely of two minds about the tingling that was running right through her. Fear and excitement seemed dangerously intermixed. "Don't," she said at last.

"Don't what, Marya?" Even as the storm roared and flailed outside, Aspitis' touch was solemn, silken.

A flurry of confusing images seemed to sweep in on the wind—her father's cold, distant face, young Simon crookedly smiling, the riverbanks of the Aelfwent flashing past, flickering with light and shadow. Her blood was warm and loud in her ears.

"No," she said, pulling free of the earl's clinging arm. She scrambled forward until she was out from under the canopy and could straighten up. The rain smacked wetly against her face.

"But Marya . . ."

"Thank you for the lovely supper, Earl Aspitis. I have been a great deal of trouble and I beg your forgiveness."

"No forgiveness need be sought, my lady."

"Then I will bid you goodnight." She stood, buffeted by the strong wind, and made her way unsteadily down to the deck, then followed the cabin wall to the ladder down into the narrow corridor. She stepped through the door into the cabin she shared with Cadrach. She stood in darkness and listened to the monks's even, sonorous breathing, thankful that he did not wake. A few moments later came the sound of Aspitis' boots on the ladder rungs; his cabin door opened, then closed behind him.

For a long while Miriamele leaned against the door. Her heart beat as swiftly as if she been hiding for her life's preservation.

Was this love? Fear? What kind of spell did the golden-haired earl cast that she should feel so wild, so pursued? She was breathless and confused as a flushed hare.

The thought of lying on her bed, trying to sleep while her thoughts raced and Cadrach snored on the floor, was intolerable. She opened the cabin door a crack and listened, then slipped out into the corridor and onto the deck once more. Despite the rain pelting down, the storm seemed to have lessened. The deck still pitched so that she could not make her way forward without keeping a hand on the shrouds, but the sea had calmed considerably.

A trill of disquieting but curiously seductive melody drew her along. The song curved and recurved, stitching the stormy night like a thread of silver-green. By turns it was soft or hearty or piercingly loud, but the changes unfolded so joinlessly that it was impossible to remember what had been happening a moment before, or to understand how anything different than what was happening at this particular moment could even exist.

Gan Itai sat cross-legged in the forecastle, head thrown back so that her hood fell loosely on her shoulders and her white hair streamed in the breeze. Her eyes were closed. She swayed from side to side, as though her song were a fast-moving river which took every bit of her concentration to ride.

Miriamele drew her own hooded cloak close and settled into the dubious shelter of the ship's wale to listen.

The Niskie's song went on for what seemed an hour, sliding smoothly from pitch to pitch and pace to pace. Sometimes her liquid words seemed arrows that flew outward to spark and sting, other times an array of gems that dazzled with smoldering colors. Through it all ran a deeper melody that never entirely disappeared, a melody which seemed to speak of peaceful green depths, of sleep, and of the coming of a heavy, comforting silence.

Miriamele awakened with a little start. When she lifted her head, it was to see Gan Itai regarding her curiously from the forecastle. Now that the Niskie had stopped singing, the roar of the ocean seemed curiously flat and tuneless.

"What are you doing, child?"

Miriamele was oddly embarrassed. She had never been so near a singing Niskie before. It almost seemed that she had been spying on some very private thing.

"I came out on deck to get some air. I was having supper with Earl Aspitis and felt sick." She took a breath to still her shaking voice. "You sing wonderfully."

Gan Itai smiled slyly. "That is true, or the *Eadne Cloud* would not have made so many safe voyages. Come, sit by me and talk. I need not sing for a while, and the late watches are lonely."

Miriamele climbed up, seating herself beside the Niskie. "Do you get tired, singing?" she asked.

Gan Itai laughed quietly. "Does a mother grow tired raising her children? Of course, but it is what I do."

Miriamele stole a glance at Gan Itai's wrinkled face. The Niskie's eyes peered out from beneath her white brows, fixed on the spray and swells.

"Why did Cadrach call you Tinook . . ." She tried to remember the word.

"*Tinukeda'ya*. Because that is what we are: Ocean Children. Your guardian is learned."

"But what does it mean?"

"It means we always lived on the ocean. Even in the far-away Garden, we dwelt always at land's end. It has only been since we came to this place that some of the Navigator's Children have been changed. Some have left the sea entirely, which is as hard for me to understand as if someone were to stop breathing and claim that was a good way to live." She shook her head, pursing her thin lips.

"Where are your people from?"

"Far away. Osten Ard is only our most recent home."

Miriamele sat for a while, thinking. "I always thought that Niskies were just like Wrannamen. You *look* very much like Wrannamen."

Gan Itai laughed sibilantly. "I have heard," she said, "that though they are different, some animals grow to look like each other because they do the same things. Perhaps the Wrannamen, like the Tinukeda'ya, have bowed their heads for too long." She laughed again, but Miriamele did not think it was a happy laugh. "And you, child," the Niskie said at last, "it is your turn to answer questions. Why are you here?"

Miriamele stared, caught off balance. "What?"

"Why are you here? I have thought about what you said, and I am not sure I believe you."

"Earl Aspitis does," Miriamele said, a little defiantly.

"That may be true, but I am altogether different." Gan Itai turned her gaze on Miriamele. Even in the dim lamplight, the Niskie's eyes glittered like anthracite. "Speak to me."

Miriamele shooked her head and tried to pull away, but a thin, strong hand closed on her arm. "I am sorry," Gan Itai said. "I have frightened you. Let me put your mind at ease. I have decided that there is no harm in you—no harm to the *Eadne Cloud*, at least, which is what I care about. I am considered peculiar among my folk because I judge quickly. When I like something or someone, I like it." She chuckled dryly. "I have decided that I like you, Marya—if that is your name. It shall be your name for now, if you wish. You need never fear me, not old Gan Itai."

Bewildered by the night, by wine, and by this latest of many unusual feelings, Miriamele began to weep.

"Now, child, now . . ." Gan Itai's gentle, spidery hand patted her back.

"*I have no home.*" Miriamele fought her tears. She felt herself on the verge of saying things she should not say, no matter how much she wished to be unburdened. "I am . . . a fugitive."

"Who pursues you?"

Miriamele shook her head. Spray arched high over the bow as the ship 'nosed down into another trough. "I cannot say, but I am in terrible danger. That's why I had to hide on the boat."

"And the monk? Your learned guardian? Is he not in danger, too?"

Miriamele was brought up short by Gan Itai's question. There was much she had not had time to think about. "Yes, I suppose he is."

The Niskie nodded, as if satisfied. "Fear not. Your secret is safe with me."

"You won't tell Aspitis . . . the earl?"

Gan Itai shook her head. "My own allegiances are more complex than you can know. But I cannot promise you he will remain ignorant. He is a clever one, *Eadne Cloud*'s master."

"I know." Miriamele's reply was heartfelt.

The mounting storm flung down another wash of rain. Gan Itai leaned forward, staring out into the wind-tossed sea. "House of Vé, they do not stay down long! Curse them, but they are strong!" She turned to Miriamele. "I think it is time for me to sing once more. It would probably be good for you to get below deck."

Miriamele awkwardly thanked the Niskie for her companionship, then stood and made her way down the slippery ladder and off the forecastle. Thunder growled like a beast hunting them through the darkness. She wondered suddenly, desperately, if she had been a fool to open her heart to this strange creature.

At the hatchway she stopped, cocking her head. In the black night behind her, Gan Itai's song had been lifted against the storm once more, a slender ribbon offered to hold back the angry sea.

24

Dogs of Erchester

Josua's company rode north along the banks of the river Stefflod, heading upstream from the juncture with the Ymstrecca through grassland rumpled with low hills. Soon the downs began to rise higher on either side, so that the prince's folk found themselves traveling through a meadowed river-valley, a wide trough of land with the watercourse at its center.

The Stefflod wound along beneath the somber sky, shining dully as a vein of tarnished silver. Like the Ymstrecca, its song at first seemed muffled, but Deornoth thought this river had a queer undertone to its murmuring, as though it hid the voices of a great whispering throng. Sometimes the noise of the water seemed to rise in what was almost a thread of melody, clear as a succession of pealing bells. A moment later, as Deornoth strained to hear what it was that had captured his attention, nothing sounded but the mutter and rush of moving water.

The light playing upon the Stefflod's surface was just as dreamily inconstant. Despite the overcast, the water glimmered at times as though cold-burning stars were rolling and bumping along the river's bottom. At other moments the gleam heightened to a sparkle like a froth of jewels. Then—just as suddenly, whether the sun was showing or cloud-hidden— the waterway would again become dark and unreflective as lead.

"Strange, isn't it?" Father Strangyeard said. "For all the things we've seen . . . my goodness, the world still has more to show us, doesn't it?"

"There's something very . . . alive about it." Deornoth squinted. A curl of light seemed to wriggle on the river's agitated skin, like a radiant fish struggling against the current.

"Well, it is all . . . hmmm . . . all part of God," Strangyeard said, making the sign of the Tree on his breast, "so of course it *is* alive." He squinted too, frowning slightly. "But I do know what you mean, Sir Deornoth."

The valley that had gradually risen around them seemed to take much of its character from the river. Willow trees stood sleepily beside the water-course, shivering as they bent to the cold water like women washing their hair. As the riders traveled farther, the river widened and slowed. Thickets of reeds appeared along the banks, resplendent with birds who shrieked from their bowers to warn all their tribe that strangers walked the land.

Strangers, Deornoth thought. *That is what we suddenly seem here. As if we have passed out of the lands meant for our folk and crossed over into someone else's domain.* He remembered Geloë's words on that night, weeks back, when they had first met her in the forest:

"*Sometimes you men are like lizards, sunning on the stones of a crumbled house, thinking: 'what a nice basking spot someone built for me.'*" The witch woman had frowned as she spoke.

She told us we were in Sithi lands, he recalled. *Now we are again entering their fields, that is all. That is why things seem so strange.*

Somehow this did not dispel his unsettled feeling.

They made camp in a meadow. The low grass was dotted here and there with fairy-rings, as the woman Ielda had called them, perfect circles of small white toadstools that shone faintly against the dark turf as twilight came on. Duchess Gutrun did not like the idea of sleeping so near to these rings, but Father Strangyeard sensibly pointed out that the people of Gadrinsett said the whole of this land belonged to the "fairies," so the proximity of a mushroom ring meant little. Gutrun, more concerned for the safety of the child Leleth than herself, gave in with reservations.

A small fire, made with willow branches they had gathered during the journey, helped to dispel some of the strangeness. The prince's party ate and talked quietly long into the evening. Old Towser, who had been sleeping so long and so deeply during the journey that he hardly seemed one of their company anymore, but more like a piece of baggage, awakened and lay staring at the night sky.

"The stars aren't right," he said at last, so quietly that none heard him. He repeated himself more loudly. Josua came to kneel beside him, taking the jester's trembling hand in his.

"What is it, Towser?"

"The stars, they aren't right." The old man pulled his fingers free from the prince's grip and gestured upward. "There's the Lamp, but it's got one star more than it should. And where's the Crook? It shouldn't be gone 'til harvest time. And there's others there I don't know at all." His lip quivered. "We're all dead. We've gone through into the Shadow Land like my grandmother used to tell of. We're dead."

"Come, now," Josua said gently. "We are not dead. We are simply in a different place, and you have been in and out of dreams."

Towser fixed him with a surprisingly sharp eye. "It is Anitul-month, is it not? Don't think I am crazy-old yet, no matter what I have been through. I have stared at summer skies for nearly twice your lifetime, young prince. We may be in a different place, but all Osten Ard shares the same stars—does it not?"

Josua was silent for a while. A thin babble of voices rose from the campfire behind him. "I did not mean to say you had lost your wits, old friend. We are in a strange place, and who knows what stars may shine upon us? In any case, there is nothing to be done about it." He took the old man's hand again. "Why do you not come and sit closer to the fire? I think it would be comforting to have us all together, at least for a little while."

Towser nodded and let Josua help him rise. "A little warmth would not go amiss, my prince. I feel a growing cold in my bones . . . and I don't like it."

"All the better, then, to sit near the fire on a damp night." He led the old jester back.

The fire had dimmed to embers and Towser's unfamiliar stars were wheeling in the sky overhead. Josua looked up when a hand touched his shoulder. Vorzheva had a blanket draped over her arm.

"Come, Josua," she said. "Let us go and make our bed by the riverside."

He looked around at the others, all sleeping but Deornoth and Strangyeard, who talked quietly on the far side of the fire. "I do not think I should leave my people alone."

"Leave your people?" she said. There was an edge of anger in her voice, but a moment later it gave way to a quiet laugh. She shook her head and her black hair fell across her face. "You will never change. I am your wife now, do you remember that? We have gone four nights as if our marriage had never happened because you feared pursuit by the king's soldiers and wished to be close to the others. Do you still fear?"

He looked up at her. His lip curled in a smile. "Not tonight." He rose and put his arm about her slender waist, feeling the strong muscles of her back. "Let us go down by the river."

Josua left his boots by the fire circle and together they went barefoot through the damp grass until the glow of the coals had disappeared behind them. The murmur of the river grew louder as they made their way down to the sandy verge. Vorzheva unfurled the blanket and sank down upon it. Josua joined her, pulling his heavy cloak over them both. For a while they lay in silence beside the dark Stefflod, watching the moon holding court among her stars. Vorzheva's head rested on Josua's chest, her river-washed hair against his cheek.

"Do not think that because our wedding was foreshortened, it meant any less to me," he said finally. "I promise you that one day we will have our lives back as they were meant to be. You shall be the lady of a great house, not an exile in the wilderness."

"Gods of my clan! You are a fool, Josua," she said. "Do you think that I care what kind of house I live in?" She turned and kissed him, wriggling closer against his body. "Fool, fool, fool." Her breath was hot against his face.

They spoke no more. The stars gleamed in the sky and the river sang to them.

Deornoth awakened just after dawn to the sound of Leleth crying. It took him a moment to realize why that seemed so strange. It was the first sound he had heard the child make.

Even as the last shreds of dream fell away—he had stood before a great white tree whose leaves were flames—he was clawing for the hilt of his sword. He sat up to see Duchess Gutrun holding the little girl on her lap. Beside her, Father Strangyeard had poked his head tortoiselike from beneath his cloak; the priest's wispy red hair was dew-dampened.

"What is it?" Deornoth asked.

Gutrun shook her head. "I don't know. She woke me up with her crying, the poor thing." The duchess tried to cradle Leleth against her breast, but the child pulled back. She continued to cry, her eyes wide open, staring at the sky. "What's the matter, little one, what's the matter?" Gutrun crooned.

Leleth tugged her hand free from the woman's embrace and tremblingly pointed toward the northern horizon. Deornoth could see nothing but a black fist of clouds in the most distant part of the sky. "Is something out there?" he asked.

The child's cries died away to hiccoughing sobs. She pointed again at the horizon, then turned away to huddle in Gutrun's lap, face hidden.

"It's just a bad dream, that's all," the duchess soothed. "There now, little one, just a bad dream. . . ."

Josua was suddenly standing before them, Naidel unsheathed in his hand. The prince wore nothing but his breeches; his slender frame gleamed pallidly in the dawnlight. "What is it?" he demanded.

Deornoth pointed to the darkened horizon. "The child saw something there that made her cry."

Josua stared grimly. "We who saw Naglimund's last days would do well to pay attention. That is an ugly knot of stormclouds." He looked around at the wet grasslands. "We are all tired," he said, "but we must make a faster pace. I do not like the look of that storm any more than did the child. I doubt we will find any shelter on these open plains until we reach Geloë's Stone of Farewell." He turned and shouted to Isorn and the others, who were just waking up. "Saddle up. We will break our fast as we travel. Come, there is no longer such a thing as a simple storm. If I can help it, we will not be caught by this one."

*   *   *

The river valley continued to deepen. The vegetation began to grow thicker and more lush, the sparse meadowland now broken by freestanding groves of birches and alders, as well as thickets of strange trees with silvery leaves and slim trunks deep-furred in moss.

The prince's party had little time to admire this new greenery. They rode at a fierce pace all day, stopping only for a brief rest in afternoon, then continuing on until long after the sun had dropped behind the horizon and twilight had sapped the brightest colors from the land. The threatening stormclouds now obscured much of the northern sky.

As the rest made a circle of stones and built a healthy blaze—firewood was now in broad supply—Deornoth and Isorn took the horses down to the river.

"At least we are no longer on foot," Isorn said, uncinching the buckle on a set of saddlebags, which slid to the grass with a soft thump. "That is something worth thanking Aedon's goodness for."

"True." Deornoth patted Vildalix. The drops of perspiration on the horse's neck had already chilled in the evening breeze. Deornoth rubbed him dry with a saddle blanket before moving on to Josua's horse Vinyafod. "We have precious little else to be thankful for."

"We are alive," Isorn said reprovingly, his wide face serious. "My wife and children are alive and safe with Tonnrud in Skoggey, and I am here to protect my mother." He pointedly avoided mentioning his father Isgrimnur, from whom there had been no word since the duke had left Naglimund.

Deornoth said nothing, understanding the worry Isorn must feel. He knew well the love his Rimmersman friend felt for the duke. In a way, he envied Isorn, and wished his feelings for his own father could be so admirable. Deornoth was unable to fulfill God's command for sons to honor their sires. Despite his knightly ideals, he had never been able to feel anything but the most grudging respect and no love whatsoever for the pinch-souled old tyrant who had made Deornoth's boyhood a misery.

"Isorn," he said at last, considering, "someday, when things are as they were before—before all this happened—and we are telling our grandchildren about it, what will we say?" The breeze blew harder, making the willow branches slap together.

His friend did not respond. After a moment, Deornoth stood up and looked across Vinyafod's back to where Isorn stood a few ells away, holding the horses' reins as they drank from the river. The Rimmersman was only a faint silhouette against the purple-gray evening sky. "Isorn?"

"Look to the south, Deornoth," he said, his voice strained. "There are torches."

Away across the grasslands, back down the Stefflod in the direction from which they had come, a swarm of tiny lights moved across the land.

"Merciful Aedon," Deornoth groaned, "it is Fengbald and his men. They have caught us up after all." He turned and gave Vinyafod a light slap on the flanks, causing the charger to take a few prancing steps forward. "No rest for you yet, fellow." He and Isorn sprinted up the bank toward the wind-whipped flames that marked their camp.

". . . And they are less than a league away," Isorn finished breathlessly. "Down by the river we could see the lights clearly."

Josua's face was composed, but noticeably pale in the firelight. "God has given us a hard test, to let us get so far and then pull the trap shut." He sighed. The eyes of all watched him in fearful fascination. "Well, at least we must kick out the fire and ride on. Perhaps if we can find a thick enough copse of trees to hide in, and if they have no hounds, they may pass us by. Then we can think of what other plan might suffice."

As they clambered into their saddles once more, Josua turned to Deornoth. "We brought two bows as part of our booty from Fikolmij's camp, did we not?"

Deornoth nodded.

"Good. You and Isorn take them." The prince laughed grimly, brandishing the stump of his right wrist. "I am not much of a bowman, but I think we will have need of a little arrow-play."

Deornoth nodded again, wearily.

They rode swiftly, though all the party sensed that they could not do so for long. The Thrithings horses ran gamely, but it had already been a long day's trek before the company had stopped. Vinyafod and Vildalix seemed as though they had several hours left in them, but some of the other mounts were clearly winded; their riders were scarcely stronger. As his horse moved beneath him and the moonlit grasslands rolled past, Deornoth could almost feel his will to resist ebbing away, draining like sand through the neck of an hourglass.

We have come ten times as far as anyone would have dreamed possible, he thought, clinging tightly to the reins as Vildalix topped one of the meadow downs and plunged down the opposite slope like a boat breasting a wave. *There is no dishonor in failing now. What more can God expect than that we give our all?* He looked back. The rest of the party was beginning to fall behind. Deornoth pulled up on the reins, slowing his charger until he was in the midst of the company once more. God might be ready to reward them with a hero's place in Heaven, but he could not give up the struggle while innocents like the duchess and the child were at risk.

Isorn was beside him now, clutching Leleth on the saddle before him. The young Rimmersman's face was a gray blur in the moonlight, but Deornoth did not need to see his friend to know the anger and determination written on his broad features.

He looked back once more. For all their haste, the rippling torches had gained ground on them, closing the distance in the last two hours until they trailed the prince's folk by less than a dozen furlongs.

"Slow up!" Josua cried behind him in the darkness. "If we run farther, we will have no strength left to fight. There is a grove of trees atop the rise there. That is where we will make a stand."

They followed the prince up the slope. The cold wind had risen and the trees bent and thrashed, branches scraping together. In the darkness the pale, swaying trunks seemed white-robed spirits lamenting some terrible circumstance.

"Here." The prince ushered them past the outermost circle of trees. "Where are those bows, Sir Deornoth?" His voice was flat.

"At my saddle, Prince Josua." Deornoth heard the awful formality echoed in his own tones, as though they all participated in some ritual. He loosed the two bows and flung one to Isorn, who had handed Leleth over to his mother to free his hands. As Deornoth and the young Rimmersman strung the supple ashwood, Father Strangyeard accepted an extra dagger from Sangfugol. He held it unhappily, as though he pinched a serpent's tail. "What will Usires think?" he said mournfully. "What will my God think of me?"

"He will know you fought to save the lives of women and children," Isorn said shortly, nocking one of their few arrows.

"Now we wait," Joshua hissed. "We stay close together, in case I see a chance for us to run once more, and we wait."

The minutes stretched as taut as the bowstring beneath Deornoth's fingers. The nightbirds had gone silent in the trees overhead, but for one whose eerie, whispering call echoed over and over until Deornoth wished he could put an arrow through its feathered throat. A sound as of distant and continuous drumming began to separate itself from the droning murmur of the Stefflod, growing ever louder. Deornoth thought he could feel the ground beginning to shudder beneath his feet. He suddenly wondered if blood had ever been shed in this seemingly uninhabited land before. Had the roots of these pale trees ever drunk of things other than water? The great oaks around the battlefield at the Knock were said to have gorged on blood until their pith was rosy pink.

The thunder of hoofbeats rose until it was louder than Deornoth's own heart drumming in his ears. He lifted his bow but did not bend it, saving his strength for the moment it would be needed. A swirl of flickering lights appeared on the meadow below them. The headlong flight of the horsemen slowed, as though they somehow sensed the prince's folk hiding in the grove above them. As they reined up, the flames of their streaming torches bobbed upright once more, blooming like orange flowers.

"They are nearly two dozen," Isorn said unhappily.

"I will take the first," Deornoth whispered. "You take the second."

"Hold," said Josua quietly. "Not until I say."

The leader got down from his horse, bending to the ground so that he disappeared out of the glow of torchlight. When he stood his pale, hooded face turned to look up the slope, so that it almost seemed to Deornoth he had sighted them in the fastness of the shadows. Deornoth lowered his arrowhead until it pointed at the cloaked chest beneath the faint moon of face.

"Steady now," Josua murmured, "a moment more . . ."

There was a rush and clatter in the branches overhead. A dark shape battered at Deornoth's head, startling him so that the arrow flew free, high above its intended mark. Deornoth shouted in alarm and staggered back, raising his hands to protect his eyes, but whatever had struck him was gone.

"Stop!" a voice cried from the trees above, a creaking, whistlingly inhuman voice. "Stop!"

Isorn, who had stared in stupefaction as Deornoth swatted at nothing, turned grimly and lowered his own arrow to the target. "Demons!" he growled, pulling his bowstring back to his ear.

"Josua?" somebody called from the meadow below. "Prince Josua? Are you there?"

There was a moment of silence. "Aedon be praised," Josua breathed. He pushed his way through the crackling undergrowth and strode out into the full light of the moon, his cloak billowing like a sail in the fierce wind. "I am here!" he shouted.

"What is he doing?" Isorn hissed frantically. Vorzheva let out a small cry of anguish, but Deornoth, too, had recognized the voice.

"Josua?" the leader of the horsemen cried. "It is Hotvig of the Stallion Clan." He pushed back his hood to show his beard and wind-tossed yellow hair. "We have followed you for days!"

"Hotvig!" Vorzheva shouted anxiously. "Is my father with you?"

The Thrithings-man laughed harshly. "Not him, Lady Vorzheva. The March-thane is no happier with me than he is with you or your husband!"

As the randwarder and Josua clasped hands, the rest of the prince's party emerged from the copse of trees, tight-strung muscles trembling, babbling among themselves with relief.

"There is much to tell, Josua," Hotvig said as his fellow riders came up the slope to join them. "First, though, we must make a fire. We have been riding fast as the Grass Thunderer himself. We are cold and very tired."

"Indeed," Josua smiled. "A fire."

Deornoth stepped forward and took Hotvig's hand in his. "Praise Usires' mercy," he said. "We thought you were Fengbald, the High King's man. I was a moment from loosing an arrow into your heart, but something struck my hand in the darkness."

"You may praise Usires," a dry voice said, "but I had something to do with it, too."

Geloë came out of the trees behind them, marching down the slope and into the circle of torchlight. The witch woman, Deornoth realized with a start, wore a cloak and breeches that came from his own saddlebag. Her feet were unshod.

"Valada Geloë!" Josua said in wonderment. "You come unlooked-for."

"You may not have looked for me, Prince Josua, but I looked for you. And a good thing that I did, else this night might have ended in bloodshed."

"It was you that struck me before I could let my arrow fly?" Deornoth said slowly. "But how. . . ?"

"Time enough for stories later," Geloë said, then kneeled as Leleth pulled free of Gutrun's clutch to run into the wise woman's arms with a wordless cry of pleasure. As she embraced the child, Geloë's huge yellow eyes held Deornoth's gaze; he felt a shiver travel down his backbone. "Time enough for stories later," she repeated. "Now it is time to make a fire. The moon is far along in her journey. If you are on your horses by dawn tomorrow, you will reach the Stone of Farewell before dark." She looked up at the northern sky. "And perhaps before the storm, as well."

The sky was tar-black with angry clouds. The rain was turning into sleet. Rachel the Dragon, chilled and storm-battered, stepped into the lee of a building on Ironmonger's Street for a moment's rest. The byways of Erchester were empty but for flurrying hailstones and a solitary figure carrying a large bundle on its back as it trudged away through the mud toward Main Row.

Probably leaving for the countryside, carrying all his wordly goods, she thought bitterly. *Another one gone, and who could blame him? It's like the plague has run through this city.*

Shivering, she set out once more.

Despite the vicious weather, many of the doors along Ironmonger's Street swung back and forth unlatched, opening to giving a glimpse of empty blackness beyond, banging closed with a sound like breaking bones. It was indeed much as if some pestilence had devastated Erchester, but it was a scourge of fear rather than disease that was driving out the city's denizens. This, in turn, had forced the Mistress of Chambermaids to walk the entire length of the ironmongery district before she could find someone to sell her what she needed. She carried her new purchase under her cloak and against her bosom, hidden from the sight of passersby—of which there were obviously few—and perhaps, she hoped, somehow also hidden from the eyes of a disapproving God.

The irony was that there had been no necessity to walk through the savage winds and deserted streets: any of several hundred implements in the Hayholt's kitchen would have admirably suited her bill of particulars.

But this was her own plan and her own decision. To take what she needed from Judith's cupboards might put the fat Mistress of Kitchens in jeopardy, and Judith was one of the few castle folk for whom Rachel felt respect. More importantly, it truly *was* Rachel's own plan, and in a way it had been necessary for her to walk one more time through Erchester's haunted alleyways: it was helping her work up the courage to do what must be done.

Spring cleaning, she reminded herself grimly. A shrill, un-Rachel-like laugh escaped her lips. *Spring cleaning in midsummer, with snow on the way.* She shook her head, feeling a momentary urge to sit down in the muddy street and cry. *That's enough, old woman*, she told herself, as she often did. *There's work to be done, and no rest this side of Heaven.*

If there had been any doubts that the Day of Weighing-Out was almost at hand, just as foretold in the holy Book of the Aedon, Rachel had only to think back to the comet that had appeared in the sky during the spring of Elias' regnal year. At the time, with the optimism of those days not long past, many had thought it a sign of a new age and a new beginning for Osten Ard. Now it was clear as well water that it had instead prophesied the last days of Trial and Doom. And what else, she upbraided herself, could such a hellish red slash in the sky mean? It was only blind foolishness that could have made anyone think otherwise.

Welladay, she thought, peering from beneath her hood at the desolate shops of Main Row, *we have all made our bed of pain: now God will make us lie in it. In His anger and wisdom He's given us plague and drought, and now unnatural storms. And who could ask for a plainer sign than the poor old lector dying so horribly?*

The shocking news had swept through the castle and city below like flame. Folk had spoken of little else for the last week: Lector Ranessin was dead, murdered in his bed by some terrible pagans called Fire Dancers. These godless monsters had also set part of the Sancellan Aedonitis ablaze. Rachel had seen the lector when he came for John's funeral, a fine and holy man. Now, in this dreadful year of years, he, too, had been stuck down.

Lord save our souls. The holy lector murdered, and demons and spirits walking the night, even in the Hayholt itself. She shuddered, thinking of the sight she had seen from the window of the servant's quarters one night not long ago. Lured to the window, not by any sound or sight, but rather by some undefinable feeling, she had silently left her sleeping charges and clambered up onto a stool, leaning on the window casement to look out on the Hedge Garden below. There, amid the shadowy shapes of the hedge-animals, had stood a circle of silent, black-robed figures. Almost breathless with terror, Rachel had rubbed at her old and treacherous eyes, but the figures were no dream or illusion. Even as she stared, one of the hooded shapes had turned to look up at her, its eyes black holes in a corpse-white face. She had run back and leaped into her hard bed, pulling the blanket up over her face to lie in sweaty, sleepless fear until dawn.

Before this year of derangement, Rachel had trusted her own judgment with the same iron faith she extended to her God, her king, and the sanctity of tidiness. After the comet came, and particularly since Simon's cruel death, that faith had been badly shaken. The two days following her midnight vision she wandered through the castle in a daze, mind only half on her chores, wondering if she had turned into the kind of daft old woman she had vowed to die before becoming.

But as she quickly discovered, if the Mistress of Chambermaids was mad, it was a contagious madness. Many others had also seen such pallid-faced specters. The diminished marketplace along Erchester's Main Row was full of whispered talk about the things that walked by night in both countryside and city. Some said that they were ghosts of Elias' victims, unable to sleep while their heads were spiked above the Nearulagh Gate. Others said that Pryrates and the king had struck a deal with the Devil himself, that these undead hell-wights had thrown down Naglimund on Elias' behalf and now waited upon his bidding for further unholy tasks.

Rachel the Dragon had once believed in nothing that Father Dreosan did not include in his catalog of churchly acceptabilities, and had doubted that even the Prince of Demons himself could bar her way in a pinch, since she had both blessed Usires the Ransomer and common sense on her side. Rachel was now as much of a believer as her most superstitious chambermaid, because *she had seen.* With her own two eyes, she had seen the hosts of Hell in her castle's Hedge Garden. There could be little doubt that the Day of Weighing-Out was at hand.

Rachel was dragged from her brooding thoughts by a noise in the street ahead. She looked up, shielding her eyes from the stinging sleet. A pack of dogs was fighting over something in the muddy road, snarling and baying as they dragged it back and forth. She moved to the side of the road, hugging the walls of the buildings. There were always dogs running loose in Erchester's streets, but with so few people left they had become wild in a way they had never been before. The ironmonger had told her that several dogs had leaped through a window in Cooper's Alley and attacked a woman in her bed, biting her so badly that she bled to death. Thinking of this, Rachel felt a tremor of fear run right through her. She stopped, wondering if she should walk past the creatures or not. She looked up and down the road, but there was no one else about. A pair of dim figures moved in the distance a couple of furlongs off, much too far away to be of any help. She swallowed and moved forward, dragging the fingers of one hand along the wall, the other clutching her purchase close against her body. As she edged past the struggling hounds she looked around for an open doorway, just to be safe.

It was hard to tell just what they were fighting for, since both dogs and prize were splattered with dark mud. One of the curs looked up from the roil of lean bellies and bony haunches, mouth stretched in a tongue-lolling, idiot grin as it watched Rachel pass. The soiled snout and gaping jaw suddenly put her in mind of some sinner condemned to the ultimate pit, a lost soul that had forgotten whatever it had once known of beauty or happiness. The beast stared silently as hailstones pitted the muddy street.

Its attention caught once more by the struggles of its fellows, the dog turned away at last. With a snarl, it dove back into the thrashing pile.

Tears starting in her eyes, Rachel lowered her head and struggled against the wind, hurrying back toward the Hayholt.

Guthwulf stood beside the king on a balcony that overlooked the courtyard of the Inner Bailey. Elias seemed in an unusually cheerful mood, considering the unimpressive size of the crowd that had been brought into the Hayholt to watch the mustering-out of the Erkynguard.

Guthwulf had heard the rumors that passed among his fighting men, stories of the night-terrors that were emptying the halls of the Hayholt and the houses of Erchester. Not only had comparatively few folk appeared to see the king, but the mood of those gathered was restive; Guthwulf did not think he would like to walk unarmed through such a crowd while wearing the sash that proclaimed him King's Hand.

"Damnable weather, isn't it?" Elias said, his green eyes intent on the milling riders who labored to hold their horses in place beneath the pelting hail. "Oddly cold for Anitul, don't you think, Wolf?"

Guthwulf turned in surprise, wondering if the king made a strange joke. The upside-down weather had been the chief topic of conversation throughout the castle for months. It was far, far more than 'oddly cold.' Such weather was terrifyingly wrong, and had added in no little part to the earl's feeling of impending disaster.

"Yes, sire," was all he said. There was no longer any question in his mind. He would lead the Erkynguard out, as Elias requested, but once he and the troops were beyond the king's immediate reach, Guthwulf himself would never return. Let heedless, criminal idiots like Fengbald do the king's bidding. Guthwulf would take those Erkynguards who were willing, along with his own loyal Utanyeaters, and offer his services to Elias' brother Josua. Or, if the prince's survival were nothing more than rumor, the earl and those who followed him would go someplace where they could make their own rules, out of reach of this fever-brained creature who had once been his friend.

Elias patted him stiffly on the shoulder, then leaned forward and waved an imperious hand. Two of the Erkynguard lifted their long horns and played the muster-call, and the hundred or so guardsmen redoubled their efforts to form their balking mounts into a line. The king's emerald dragon-banner whipped in the wind, threatening to pull free from its bearer's grasp. Only a few of the watching crowd cheered, their voices all but buried by the noise of wind and pattering sleet.

"Perhaps you should let me go down to them, Majesty," Guthwulf said quietly. "The horses are anxious in this storm. If they bolt, they will be among the crowd in a moment."

Elias frowned. "What, do you worry about a little blood beneath their hooves? They are battle-bred: it will not harm them." He turned his gaze onto the Earl of Utanyeat. His eyes were so alien that Guthwulf flinched helplessly. "That is the way it is, you know," Elias continued, lips spreading in a smile. "You can either grind down that which stands before you, or else be ground down yourself. There is no middle ground, friend Guthwulf."

The earl bore the king's glance for a long moment, then looked away, staring miserably at the crowd below. What did that mean? Did Elias suspect? Was this whole show only an elaborate setting for the king to denounce his old comrade and send Guthwulf's head to join the others that now clustered thick as blackberries atop the Nearulagh Gate?

"Ah, my king," rasped a familiar voice, "are you taking a little air? I could wish you a better day for it."

Pryates stood in the curtained archway behind the balcony, teeth bared in a vulpine grin. The priest wore a great hooded cloak over his usual scarlet robe.

"I am glad to see you here," Elias said. "I hope you are rested after your long journey yesterday."

"Yes, Highness. It was an unsettling trip, but a night in my own bed in Hjeldin's Tower has done wonders. I am ready to do your bidding." The priest made a little mock bow, the top of his pale bald head revealed for a moment like a new moon before he straightened and looked to Guthwulf. "And the Earl of Utanyeat. Good morningtide to you, Guthwulf. I hear you are riding forth in the king's behalf."

Guthwulf looked at Pryates with cold distaste. "Against your advice, I am told."

The alchemist shrugged, as if to show that his personal reservations were of little account. "I do think there are perhaps more important matters with which His Majesty should concern himself than a search for his brother. Josua's power was broken at Naglimund: I see little need in pursuing him. Like a seed on stony ground, I think he will find no purchase, no place to grow strong. No one would dare flaunt the High King's Ward by giving such a renegade shelter." He shrugged again. "But I am only a counselor. The king knows his own mind."

Elias, staring down at the quiet assembly in the courtyard below, seemed to have ignored the entire conversation. He rubbed absently at the iron crown on his brow, as though it caused him some discomfort. Guthwulf thought the king's skin had a sickly, transparent look.

"Strange days," Elias said, half to himself. "Strange days . . ."

"Strange days indeed," Guthwulf agreed, drawn to reckless conversation. "Priest, I hear you were in the Sancellan on the very night of the lector's assassination."

Pryrates nodded soberly. "A ghastly thing. Some mad cult of heretics, I hear. I hope Velligis, the new lector, will soon root them out."

"Ranessin will be missed," Guthwulf said slowly. "He was a popular and well-respected man, even among those who do not accept the True Faith."

"Yes, he was a powerful man," Pryrates said. His black eyes glinted as he gazed sidelong at the king. Elias still did not look up, but an expression of pain seemed to flit across his pallid features. "A very powerful man," the red priest repeated.

"My people do not seem happy," the king murmured, leaning out against the stone railing. The scabbard of his massive double-hilted sword scraped the stone and Guthwulf suppressed a shudder. The dreams that still haunted him, the dreams of that foul sword and its two brother blades!

Pryrates moved forward to the king's side. The Earl of Utanyeat edged away, unwilling to touch even the alchemist's cloak. As he turned, he saw a blur of movement from the archway—billowing curtains, a pale face, a dull glint of exposed metal. An instant later a howling shriek echoed through the courtyard.

"Murderer!"

Pryrates staggered back from the railing, a knife handle standing between his shoulder blades.

The next moments passed with dreadful slowness: the lassitude of Guthwulf's movements and the dull, doomed progression of his thoughts made him feel as though he and all the others on the balcony were suddenly immersed in choking, clinging mud. The alchemist turned to face his attacker, a wild-eyed old woman who had been thrown down to the stone floor behind him by the priest's spasmodic reaction. Pryrates' lips skinned back from his teeth in a horrible doglike grin of agony and fury. His naked fist lifted in the air and a weird gray-yellow glow began to play about it. Smoke seeped from his fingers and around the knife wagging in his back, and for a moment the very light in the sky seemed to dim. Elias had turned as well, his mouth a black hole of surprise in his face, his eyes bulging with a panicky horror such as Guthwulf had never dreamed he would see on the king's face. The woman on the floor was scrabbling at the stone tiles as if swimming in some thick fluid, trying to drag herself away from the priest.

Pryrates' black eyes seemed almost to have fallen back into his head. For a moment, a leering, scarlet-robed skeleton stood over the old woman, bony hand smoldering into incandescence.

Guthwulf never knew what spurred his next action. A commoner had attacked the king's counselor, and the Earl of Utanyeat was King's Hand; nevertheless, he found himself suddenly lurching forward. The noise of the crowd, the storm, his own heartbeat, all swelled together into a single hammering pulse as Guthwulf grappled with Pryrates. The priest's spindly form was solid as iron beneath his hands. Pryrates' head turned, agonizingly slowly. His eyes burned into Guthwulf's. The earl felt himself abruptly pulled out of his own body and sent spinning down into a dark pit. There was a flash of fire and a blast of incredible heat, as though he had fallen into one of the forge-furnaces beneath the great castle, then a howling blackness took him away.

When Guthwulf awakened, he was still in darkness. His body seemed one dull ache of pain. Droplets of moisture pattered lightly on his face and the smell of wet stone was in his nostrils.

". . . I did not even see her," a voice was saying. After a moment, Guthwulf was able to identify it as the king's, although there was a subtle, chiming tone to it that he had not marked before. "By God's head, to think that I have become so slow and preoccupied." The king's laugh had a fearful tinge. "I was sure she had come for me."

Guthwulf tried to respond to Elias, but found that he could not form the proper sounds. It was dark, so dark that he could not make out the king's form. He wondered if he had been brought to his own room, and how long he had been senseless.

"*I* saw her," Pryrates rasped. His voice, too, had taken on a ringing sound. "She may have escaped me for a moment, but by the Black Eon, the scrubbing-bitch will pay."

Guthwulf, still struggling for speech, found himself amazed that Pryrates should be able to speak at all, let alone be standing while the Earl of Utanyeat lay on the ground.

"I suppose now I shall have to wait for Fengbald to return before I can send out the Erkynguard—or perhaps one of the younger lords could lead them?" The king sighed wearily. "Poor Wolf." There seemed in his strangely tuneful voice little sympathy.

"He should not have touched me," Pryrates said contemptuously. "He interfered and the slattern escaped. Perhaps he was in league with her."

"No, no, I do not think so. He was always loyal. Always."

Poor Wolf? What, did they think he was dead? Guthwulf strained to make his muscles work. Had they brought him to some curtained room to lie in waiting for burial? He fought for mastery of his body, but all his limbs seemed coldly unresponsive.

A horrible thought came to him suddenly. Perhaps he *was* dead—for who, after all, had ever returned to say what it was like? Only Usires Himself, and he was the son of God. Oh, merciful Aedon, would he have to stay trapped in his body like a prisoner in a forgotten cell, even as they laid him in the wormy ground? He felt a scream building within him. Would it be like the dream when he touched the sword? God save him. Merciful Aedon . . .

"I am going, Elias. I will find her, even if I must crush the stones of the servant's quarters into dust and flay the skin off of every chambermaid." Pryrates spoke with a sort of sweetness, as though the savor of this thought was as splendid as wine. "I will see that people are punished."

"But surely you should rest," Elias said mildly, as though speaking to a froward child. "Your injury . . ."

"The pain I inflict on the chamber-mistress will take my own pain away," the alchemist said shortly. "I am well. I have grown strong, Elias. It will take more than a single knife thrust to dispatch me."

"Ah." The king's voice was emotionless. "Good. That is good."

Guthwulf heard Pryrates' bootheels clocking against the tiled stone floor, striding away. There was no sound of a door opening and closing, but another shower of moisture spattered the Earl of Utanyeat's face. This time he felt the chill of the water.

"L . . . L . . . 'Lias," he managed to say at last.

"Guthwulf!" the king said, gently surprised. "You live?"

"Wh . . . where. . . ?"

"Where is what?"

". . . Me."

"You are on the balcony, where you had your . . . accident."

How could that be? Had it not been morning time when they had watched the Erkynguard muster? Had he lain here lifelessly until evening? Why hadn't they moved him to a more comfortable place?

". . . He's right, you know," Elias was saying. "You really shouldn't have interfered. What did you think you were doing?" The odd ringing sound was beginning to fade from his voice. "It was very foolish. I told you to stay away from the priest, didn't I?"

". . . Can't see . . . ." Guthwulf managed at last.

"I'm not surprised," Elias said calmly. "Your face is badly burned, especially around your eyes. They look very bad. I was certain you were dead—but you're not." The king's voice was distant. "It's a pity, old comrade, but I told you to watch out for Pryrates."

"Blind?" Guthwulf said, his voice hoarse, throat seizing in a painful spasm. "Blind?!"

His rasping howl broke across the commons, bouncing from wall to stone wall until it seemed a hundred Guthwulfs were screaming. As he vented his agony, the king patted him on the head as though soothing an old dog.

The river valley waited for the oncoming storm. The chilly air warmed and grew heavy. The Stefflod murmured uneasily and the sky was gravid with angry-looking clouds. The travelers found themselves speaking softly, as if they rode past the sleeping form of some huge beast who might be awakened by disrespectful loudness or levity.

Hotvig and his men had decided to ride back to the rest of their party, who were nearly four score all told, men, women, and children. Hotvig's clanfolk and their wagons were following as swiftly as they could, but they were no match for the speed of unencumbered riders.

"I am still amazed that your people would uproot themselves to follow us into an unknown and ill-omened wilderness," Josua said at their parting.

Hotvig grinned, showing a gap in his teeth earned in some past brawl. "Uproot? There is no such word to the folk of the Stallion Clan. Our roots are in our wagons and our saddles."

"But surely your clansmen are worried about riding into such strange territory?"

A brief look of concern flickered across the Thrithings-man's face, quickly supplanted by an expression of disdainful pride. "You forget, Prince Josua, that they are my kinfolk. I told them, 'If stone-dwellers can ride there without fear, can the people of the Free Thrithings shy away?' They follow me." He pulled at his beard and grinned once more. "Besides, it is worth many risks to get out from under Fikolmij's hand."

"And you are sure he will not pursue you?" the prince asked.

Hotvig shook his head. "As I told you last night, the March-thane has lost face because of you. Anyway, our clans often split into smaller clan-families. It is our right as people of the Free Thrithings. The last thing Fikolmij can do now is to try to keep us few from leaving the greater clan. That would prove beyond doubt that he is losing his hold on the reins."

When they had all gathered around the fire after their encounter in the dark, Hotvig had explained how Fikolmij's treatment of his daughter and Prince Josua had caused much disgruntled talk around the wagons of the Stallion Clan. Fikolmij had never been a popular leader, but he had been respected as a powerful fighter and clever strategist. To see him so bedeviled by the mere presence of stone-dwellers, to the point where he would lend aid to Fengbald and others of the High King's men without consulting his clan chiefs, had made many wonder out loud whether Fikolmij was still capable of lording it as March-thane of all of the High Thrithings.

When Earl Fengbald had arrived with his fifty or so armored men, swaggering into the wagon camp like conquerors, Hotvig and some of the other randwarders had brought the men of their own clan-families to Fikolmij's wagon. The March-thane had wished to set the Erkynlanders quickly on the trail of Josua's party, but Hotvig and the others had stood against their leader.

"No stone-dwellers go armed across the Stallion Clan's fields without a gathering of chiefs to say they can," Hotvig had cried, and his fellows had echoed him. Fikolmij had fumed and threatened, but the laws of the Free Thrithings were the only immutable things in the clan-folk's nomadic existence. The argument had ended with Hotvig and the other randwarders telling Earl Fengbald—"a foolish, dangerous man who likes himself well," as Hotvig described him—that the only way the High King's men could pursue Josua was to go around the Stallion Clan's territory. Fengbald, outnumbered by ten to one or more, had no choice but to ride away, taking the shortest route back off the High Thrithings. The Earl of Falshire had made many angry threats before departing, promising that the grasslanders' long days of freedom were over, that High King Elias would come soon and knock the wheels off their wagons once and for all.

Unsurprisingly, this public thwarting of Fikolmij's authority brought on a terrible argument that several times almost erupted into deadly bloodshed. The disputing ceased only when Hotvig and several other randwarders took their families and followed Josua, leaving Fikolmij behind to curse and lick his wounds, his strength as March-thane weakened but by no means ended.

"No, he will not follow us," Hotvig repeated. "That would say to all the clans that mighty Fikolmij cannot survive the loss of our few wagons, and that the stone-dwellers and their feuds are more important to the March-thane of all the High Thrithings than his own people. Now, we clan exiles will live near you for a while at your Farewell Stone and talk among ourselves about what we will do."

"I cannot tell you how grateful I am for your help," Josua said solemnly. "You have saved our lives. If Fengbald and his soldiers had caught us, we would be going back to the Hayholt in chains. Then there would be no one to stop my brother."

Hotvig looked at him keenly. "You may think so, but you do not know the strength of the Free Thrithings if you think we would be so easily overcome." He hefted his long spear. "Already the men of the Meadow Thrithings are making things very difficult for the stone-dwellers of Nabban."

Father Strangyeard, who had been listening carefully, made a worried face. "The king is not the only one we fear, Hotvig."

The Thrithings-man nodded. "So you told me. And I would hear more, but now I must go back for the rest of my people. If your destination is as close as the woman says," he indicated Geloë with careful respect, "then look for us before sunset tomorrow. The wagons can go no faster."

"But do not delay," the wise woman said. "I did not speak lightly when I said we must make haste ahead of this storm."

"No one can ride like grasslander horsemen," Hotvig said sternly. "And our wagon-teams are not much slower. We will be with you before tomorrow's night." He laughed, again showing his missing tooth. "Leave it to city folk to find stone in the middle of the meadowlands, then want to make their home there. Still," he said to the prince, "I knew when you killed Utvart that things would never be the same for anyone. My father taught me to trust my hand and my heart." He grinned. "My luck, too. I bet one of my foals on you, Josua, in your fighting with Utvart. My friends were ashamed to best me so easily, but they took my wager," He laughed loudly. "You won four good horses for me!" He turned his mount toward the south, waving. "Soon we will meet again!"

"And no arrows this time," cried Deornoth.

"Go safely," Josua called as Hotvig and his men spurred away across the green lands.

Heartened by the encounter with the Thrithings-folk, the travelers rode cheerfully through the morning despite the threatening skies. When they stopped briefly to take their midday meal and water the horses, Sangfugol even convinced Father Strangyeard to sing with him. The priest's surprisingly sweet voice blended well with the harper's, and if Father Strangyeard did not quite understand what "The Ballad of Round-Heeled Moirah" was about, his enjoyment was the greater for it, and for the laughing praise given to him after.

When they were in the saddle once more, Deornoth found himself riding beside Geloë, who cradled Leleth before her on the saddle. She rode flawlessly, as one of long experience; Deornoth found himself wondering once more what the wise woman's strange history might be. She was also still wearing the spare clothing he had brought out of the wagon-camp, as if she had come to that fateful copse of trees naked. After thinking for a while about why that might be, and remembering the clawed thing that had struck at him in darkness, Deornoth decided that there were some things about which a God-fearing knight should not inquire.

"Forgive me, Valada Geloë," he said, "but you look very grim. Is there something important you have not told us yet?" He indicated Sangfugol and Strangyeard, laughing with Duchess Gutrun as they rode. "Are we singing in the lich-yard, as the old saying goes?"

Geloë continued to watch the sky. From her lap, Leleth looked at him as though he were an interesting rock. "I fear many things, Sir Deornoth," Geloë said at last. "The problem with being a 'wise woman' is that sometimes you know just enough to be truly afraid, while still not having any better answers than might the youngest child. I fear this coming storm. The one who is our true enemy—I will not say his name here in this land, not in the open—is reaching the summit of his power. We have already seen in this cold summer how his pride and anger speak in the winds and clouds. Now, black weather is swirling out of the north. I am sure it is *his* storm: if I am right, it will bring woe to those who resist him."

Deornoth found himself following her gaze. Suddenly, the ominous clouds seemed an inky hand stretching across the sky from the north, blindly but patiently searching. The idea of waiting for that hand to find them sent a poisonous dread twisting through him, so that he had to look down at his saddle for a moment before he could lift his eyes to Geloë's yellow stare.

"I understand," he said.

Sunlight bled fitfully through chinks in the clouds. The wind turned, blowing into their faces, heavy and moist. As they followed the line of the valley, a broad bend in the Stefflod revealed for the first time the old forest, the Aldheorte. The great wood was much nearer than Deornoth would have guessed—the party's return on horseback had been far swifter than their straggling march out across the Thrithings. Because of their descent into the river valley, the forest now stood on the heights above them, a solid line of vegetation like dark cliffs along the valley's northern rim.

"It is not far now," Geloë said.

They rode on through the afternoon as the curtained sun slid down the sky, glowing behind the gray murk. Another turn in the river's course brought them around a cluster of shallow hills. They stopped short.

"Merciful Aedon," Deornoth breathed to himself.

"*Sesuad'ra,*" Geloë said. "There stands the Stone of Farewell."

"That's no stone," Sangfugol said disbelievingly. "That's a mountain!"

A great hill rose from the valley floor before them. Unlike its low, rounded neighbors, Sesuad'ra thrust up from the meadows like the head of a buried giant, bearded with trees, crowned with angular stones that stood along the ridgeline. Beyond the spiky stones some shimmering whiteness lay along the hill's very peak. An immense, upward-straining slab of weathered rock and clinging brush, Sesuad'ra loomed some five hundred cubits above the river. The uneven sunlight washed across the hill in wavering bands, so that the entire mass almost seemed to turn and watch them as they rode slowly down the watercourse.

"It is much like Thisterborg, near the Hayholt," Josua said wonderingly.

"That's no stone," Sangfugol repeated stubbornly, shaking his head.

Geloë laughed harshly. "It is all stone. Sesuad'ra is a part of the very bones of the earth, thrust free of her body in the pain of the Days of Fire, but still reaching down into the very center of the world."

Father Strangyeard was eyeing the massive hill nervously. "And we are going to . . . are going to . . . stay there? Live there?"

The witch woman smiled. "We have permission."

As they neared, it became apparent that the Stone was not so sheer as distance made it seem. A path, a lighter streak through the choking trees and brush, snaked its way around the base of the hill, then appeared again farther up, spiraling summitward around the circumference of the rock until it disappeared near the crest.

"How can trees live on such a stone, let alone thrive?" Deornoth asked. "Can they grow in the very rock?"

"Sesuad'ra has been broken and worn over the eons of its existence," Geloë answered. "Plants will ever find a way, and they themselves help to further break the stone until it is crumbled to a dirt scarcely less rich than found on a Hewenshire freeholding."

Deornoth frowned slightly at this reference to his birthplace, then wondered how the wise woman knew of his father's farm. He had certainly never mentioned it to her.

Soon they were walking in the sudden twilight of the hill's long shadow, whipped by a chilly wind. The path that began at Sesuad'ra's base lay before them, hugging the hillside, a trampled cut of grass and moss overhung by trees and twining creepers.

"And we are going up?" Duchess Gutrun asked in some consternation. "Up into this place?"

"Of course," Geloë said, a touch of impatience in her rough voice. "It is the highest ground for leagues. We have need of high ground just now. Besides, there are other reasons—must I explain them all again?"

"No, Valada Geloë, please lead us," Josua said. The prince seemed fired by some inner flame, his pale face alight with excitement. "This is what we have been searching for. This is where we will begin the long road back." His face slackened somewhat. "I do wonder, though, how Hotvig and his folk will feel about leaving their wagons below. It is a pity there is no way to get them up the hill."

The wise woman waved her callused hand. "You worry too soon. Step ahead and you will have a surprise."

They rode forward. Beneath the straggling grass the path that wound up the hillside was as smooth as one of old Naglimund's hallways and wide enough for any wagon.

"But how can this be?" Josua asked.

"You forget," Geloë responded, "this is a Sithi place. Beneath this bramble is the road they built. It takes many, many centuries to destroy the handiwork of the Zida'ya."

Josua was not cheered. "I am amazed, but now I am even more worried. What will keep our enemies from climbing as easily as we do?"

Geloë snorted in disgust. "First, it is easier to defend a high place than to take it from below. Secondly, the nature of the place itself is against it. Third, and perhaps most importantly, our enemy's own rage may outsmart him and ensure our survival—at least for a while."

"How so?" the prince demanded.

"You will see." Geloë spurred her horse up the path, Leleth bobbing on the saddle before her. The child's wide brown eyes took in everything without any show of feeling. Josua shrugged and followed.

Deornoth turned to see Vorzheva sitting upright on her horse, face set in lines of grim fear. "What is it, my lady?" he asked. "Is something amiss?"

She offered a nervous smile. "My people have hated and feared this valley forever. Hotvig is a clan-man and would not show it, but he fears this place, too." She sighed shakily. "Now I must follow my husband up on this unnatural rock. I am afraid."

For the first time since his prince had brought this odd woman to live in the castle at Naglimund, Deornoth felt his heart opening to her, filling with admiration. "We are all deathly afraid, my lady," he said. "The rest of us are just not as honest as you."

He tapped gently with his heels at Vildalix's ribs and followed Vorzheva up the path.

The road was overhung with trailing vines and the tangled branches of trees, forcing the travelers to spend as much time ducking their heads as they did riding upright. As they slowly circled out of the shadow, like ants walking the perimeter of a sundial, the mist that clung to the hill lent an unusual sparkle to the afternoon glow.

Deornoth thought that the smell of the place was what seemed strangest of all. Sesuad'ra gave off a scent of timeless growth, of water and roots and damp earth in a place long undisturbed. There was an air of peace here, of slow, careful thought, but also a disturbing sensation of watchfulness. From time to time the stillness was broken by the trill of unseen birds whose songs were as somber and hesitant as children whispering in a high-ceilinged hall.

As the grassy meadow began to drop away below them, the travelers passed posts of standing stone, time-smoothed white shapes almost twice a man's height that had in their unrecognizable outlines some hint of movement, of life. They passed the first as the path brought them around into direct sunlight for the first time.

"Marking pillars," Geloë called over her shoulder. "One for each of the moons in the year. We'll pass a dozen every time we circle around the hill until we reach the summit. They were carved to look like animals and birds once, I think."

Deornoth stared at the rounded nob that might have been a head and wondered what beast it had once represented. Weathered by wind and rain, it was now as shapeless as melted wax, faceless as the forgotten dead. He shivered and make the sign of the Tree on his breast.

A little while later Geloë stopped and pointed downward toward the northwest part of the valley, where the rim of the old forest reached out almost to the very banks of the Stefflod. The river was a tiny streak of quicksilver along the valley's emerald floor.

"Just beyond the river," she said, "do you see?" She gestured again at the forest's dark breakfront, which might have been a frozen sea-wave awaiting only spring's thaw before it swept across the low ground. "There, in the forest's fringe. Those are the ruins of Enki-e-Shao'saye, which some say was the most beautiful city ever built in Osten Ard since the world began."

As his companions whispered and shaded their eyes, Deornoth moved to the edge of the path, squinting at the distant forest. He saw nothing but what might have been a crumbled wall of lavender, a flash of gold.

"There's not much to see," he said quietly.

"Not in this age," Geloë replied.

Up they climbed as the day waned. Each time they circled around to the hill's northern slope, coming out of shade into ever-decreasing afternoon light, they could see the spreading knot of blackness on the horizon. The storm was moving in swiftly. It had now swallowed the far borders of great Aldheorte, so that all the north seemed a gray uncertainty.

As they finished their twelfth circuit around the hill, passing the one hundred and forty-fourth of the marking pillars—a small enough diversion, but still Deornoth had kept score—the travelers emerged at last from the shadowing greenery, clambering up a final slope until they stood on the hill's windy summit. The sun had fallen away into the west; only a reddish sliver remained.

The top of the hill was nearly flat and scarcely less wide than Sesuad'ra's base. All around its perimeter jutted fingers of upright stone, not smoothed like the marking pillars, but great, raw standing stones, each as tall as four men, made of the same gray rock veined with white and pink that formed the hill.

In the center of the plateau, in the midst of a field of waving grass, stood a vast, low building of opalescent stone, tinged with the sunset's red glow.

At first it seemed a temple of some sort, like the great old buildings of Nabban from the days of the Imperium, but its lines were plainer. Its unassuming but affecting style made it seem almost to spring from the hill itself. It was plain that this structure *belonged* on this windy hilltop, beneath this incredibly wide sky. The grandeur and self-interest that spoke from every angle of houses of human worship, however finely wrought, was a language alien to whoever had built this. The passage of unguessable years had in places brought its walls to collapse. Unhindered for centuries, trees had thrust up through the building's very roof, or pushed their way in at the arched doorways like unwanted guests. Still, the simplicity and beauty of the place were so plain—and at the same time so inhuman—that for a long time no one ventured to speak.

"We are here," Josua said at last, his tones solemn but exalted. "After all our danger and all our suffering, we have found a place where we can stop and say: *we go no farther.*"

"It is not forever, Prince Josua." Geloë spoke gently, as if unwilling to break his mood, but the prince was already striding confidently across the hilltop toward the white walls.

"It need not be forever," he called. "But for now, we will be safe!" He turned and waved his hand for the others to follow, then continued turning, gazing around him on all sides. "I take back what I said!" he shouted to Geloë. "With a few good folk behind me, I could make a stand here and Sir Camaris himself could not defeat me, not with all the knights of my father's Great Table at his side!"

He bounded away toward the pale walls that now showed a touch of blue. Evening was coming on. The others went after him, talking quietly among themselves as they passed through the swaying grass.

25

Petals in a Wind Storm

"It's a stupid game," Simon said. "It doesn't make any sense."

Aditu lifted an eyebrow.

"It doesn't!" he insisted. "I mean, look! You could win if you just moved here . . ." he pointed, "and there . . ." he pointed again. Looking up, he found Aditu's golden eyes upon him, laughing, mocking. "Couldn't you. . . ?" he finished.

"Of course, Seoman." She moved the polished stones across the gaming board as he had suggested, from one golden island to another over a sea of sapphire-blue waves. The mock-ocean was surrounded by scarlet flames and murky gray clouds. "But then the game is over, and only the shallowest waters have been explored."

Simon shook his head. He had struggled for days to learn the complex rules of shent, only to discover that what he had been taught were only the rudiments. How could he learn a game that people did not play to win? But Aditu did not try to lose either, as far as Simon could tell. Instead, it seemed as though the issue was to make the game interesting by introducing themes and puzzles, most of which were as far beyond Simon's comprehension as the mechanisms of the rainbow.

"If you will not take offense," Aditu said, smiling, "may I instead show you another way?" She put the markers back in their previous locations. "If I use these Songs of mine to build a Bridge here . . ."—a quick flurry of movements—"then you can cross to the Isles of the Cloud of Exile."

"But why do you want to help me?" Somewhere, as if in the very fabric of the mutable walls, a stringed instrument began to sound; if Simon had not known that they were quite alone within the airy nectarine halls of Aditu's house, he would have thought a musician played in the next wind-shifting room. He had stopped wondering about such things, but could not still a reflexive shudder; the music felt eerie and delicate as a small and excessively-legged something walking across his skin. "How can you win a game when you keep helping the other person?"

Aditu leaned back from the gaming board. In her own home she wore just as little as she did on the walkways of Jao é-Tinukai'i, if not less. Simon, who still could not look comfortably on the abundance of her golden limbs, stared hard at the playing pieces.

"Manchild," she said, "I think you can learn. I think you are learning. But remember, we Zida'ya have been playing this game since time before time. First Grandmother says it came with us from the Garden that is Lost." She laid a placatory hand on Simon's arm, raising goosebumps there. "Shent can be played to amuse, only. I have played games that were nothing but gossip and friendly mockery, and all strategies were turned to that end. Other games one can only win by almost losing. I have also experienced games where both players truly *strove* to lose—although it took years for one to succeed." Some memory brought a flick of smile. "Do you not see, Snowlock, winning and losing are only the walls within which the game takes place. Inside the House of Shent . . ." she paused, a frown touching her mercurial face like a shadow. "It is hard to say in your tongue." The frown disappeared. "Perhaps that is why it seems so difficult for you. The thing is, within the House of Shent it is the coming and going, the visitors—friends and enemies both—the births and deaths, all of these things that matter." She gestured around her at her own habitation, the floors deep in sweet grass, the rooms tangled with the branches of tiny flowering trees. Some of the trees, Simon had discovered, had fierce little thorns. "As with all dwellings," she said, "of mortals and immortals both, it is the living that makes a house—not the doors, not the walls."

She rose and stretched. Simon watched covertly, struggling to keep his frowning mask even as her graceful movements caused his heart to leap painfully. "We will continue our play tomorrow," she said. "I think you are learning, although you do not know it yet. Shent has lessons even for Sudhoda'ya, Seoman."

Simon knew that she was bored and that it was time for him to leave. He was terribly conscious of never overstaying his welcome. He hated it when the Sithi were kind and understanding with him, as though he were a stupid animal that did not know better.

"I should go, Aditu."

She did not ask him to stay. Anger and regret and a sort of deep physical frustration all struggled within him as he bowed his head briefly, then turned and made his way out between the swaying blossoms. The afternoon light glowed through the orange and rose walls, as if he moved inside the very heart of a sunset.

He stood outside Aditu's house for some time, looking out past the shimmering mist thrown up from the cataract that played beside her doorway. The valley was umber and gold, slashed with the darker green of the tree-covered hills and the bright emerald of tended meadows. To look at, Jao é-Tinukai'i seemed straightforward as sun and rain. Like any other place, it had rocks and plants and trees and houses—but it also had the Sithi, the folk who lived in these houses, and Simon had grown quite sure that he would never understand them. Like the minute and secret life that teemed in the black earth beneath the valley's placid grass, Simon now realized that Jao é-Tinukai'i was crowded with things beyond his comprehension. He had already found out how little he understood when he had embarked upon an attempt at escape, soon after being sentenced to a lifetime's imprisonment among these gentle captors.

He had waited three full days after his sentence had been delivered by Shima'onari. Such patience, Simon had felt sure, demonstrated a cold-blooded subtlety of maneuver worthy of the great Camaris. Looking back a fortnight later, such ignorance was already laughable. What had he thought he was doing. . . ?

On the fourth day of his sentence, in late afternoon while the prince was away, Simon walked out of Jiriki's house. He crossed the river quickly but—he hoped—unobtrusively, clambering over a narrow bridge, then headed back toward the spot where Aditu had first brought him to the valley. The cloth-knotted mural that led to Jiriki's house continued on the river's far side as well, spanning from tree to tree. The sections Simon passed seemed to show the survivors of some great disaster bringing their boats to a new land—the Sithi coming to Osten Ard?—and building great cities, empires in the forests and mountains. There were other details, too, signs woven into the tapestry that suggested strife and sorrow had not been left behind in the blighted homeland, but Simon was in too much of a hurry to stop and look closely.

After making his way down the river path for some distance he turned off at last and headed for the heavy undergrowth at the base of the hills, where he hoped to make up in stealth what he lost in time. There were not many Sithi about, but he was certain that any one of them would sound the alarm at the sight of their prisoner traveling toward the boundaries of Jao é-Tinukai'i, so he slid through the trees as carefully as he could, keeping away from the common paths. Despite the exhilaration of escape, he felt more than a pang of guilt: Jiriki would doubtless suffer some punishment for letting the mortal captive slip away. Still, Simon owed a responsibility to his other friends that outweighed even the multimillennial laws of the Sithi.

No one saw him, or at lease no one made an attempt to stop him. By the time several hours had passed, he had moved into what seemed a wilder, less tamed section of the old forest, and was certain he had made his escape. His entire trip with Aditu, from the Pools to Jiriki's door, had taken less than two hours. He had now gone easily twice that, straight back along the river.

But when Simon crept down from the cover of the thickest vegetation, it was to find himself still in Jao é-Tinukai'i, albeit in a part he had not yet seen.

He stood in the middle of a shadowed, dusky clearing. The trees all around were draped with fine, silky streamers like spiderwebs; the afternoon sun set them gleaming, so that the forest seemed wound in a fiery net. In the middle of the clearing an oval door of moss-matted white wood had been built into the trunk of a huge oak, around which the silk hung so thickly that the tree itself was barely visible. He paused for a moment, wondering what undersized hermit would live here, in a tree on the outskirts of the city. Next to the beautiful, rippling folds of Jiriki's house or the other graceful constructions of Jao é-Tinukai'i, let alone the living magnificence of the Yásira, this place seemed backward, as though whoever dwelled here hid himself from even the slow pace of the Sithi. But despite its aura of age and isolation, the spidersilk house seemed in no way menacing. The clearing was empty and peaceful, comfortable in its unimportance. The air was dusty but pleasant, like the pockets of a beloved aunt. Here the rest of Jao é-Tinukai'i seemed only a memory of vibrant life. A person could linger here beneath the silk-draped trees while the very world crumbled away outside. . . .

As Simon stood watching the undulating strands, a mourning dove hooted softly. He abruptly remembered his mission. How long had he stood here, staring like a fool? What if the owner of this strange house had come out, or returned from some errand? Then the hue and cry would go up and he would be caught like a rat.

Frustrated by this first error in reckoning, Simon hurried back into the forest. He had misjudged his time, that was all. Another hour's hiking would carry him beyond the city's fringe and back through the Summer Gate. Then, with the hoarded provisions he had quietly stolen from the prince's generous table, he would head due south until he reached the edge of the forest. He might die in the attempt, but that was what heroes did. This he knew.

Simon's willingness to become a dead hero seemed to have little effect on the subtleties of Jao é-Tinukai'i. When he emerged at last from the dense brush, the sun now far across the sky toward evening, it was to find himself up to his knees in the golden grass of open woodland before the mighty Yásira, where he stood dumbstruck before the shimmering, shifting wings of the butterflies.

How could this be? He had followed the river carefully. It had never been out of his sight for more than a few steps, and always it had flowed in the same direction. The sun had seemed to move correctly across the sky. His journey into this place with Aditu would be printed on his heart forever—he could not forget a single detail!—but nevertheless, he had walked more than half the afternoon to travel a distance of a few hundred paces.

With this realization, the strength flowed from his body. He fell to the warm, damp ground and lay with his face against the turf, as though he had been struck a blow.

Jiriki's house had many rooms, one of which he had given to Simon to be his own, but the prince seemed to spend most of his own time in the open-sided chamber where Simon had first met him on arriving in Jao é-Tinukai'i. As the earliest weeks of his confinement passed it became Simon's habit to spend each evening there with Jiriki, sitting on the gentle slope above the water while the light gradually dimmed from the sky, watching the shadows lengthen and the glassy pond grow darker. As the last gleam of the sunset vanished from between the branches the pond became a somber mirror, stars blooming in its violet depths.

Simon had never really listened to the sounds of oncoming night, but Jiriki's often silent company encouraged him to give ear to the songs of cricket and frog, to begin to hear the sighing of wind in the trees as something other than a warning to pull his hat down tightly over his ears. At times, as he sank into the swelling evening, he felt he was on the verge of some great understanding. A sense of being more than himself stole over him, of what it felt like to live in a world that cared little for cities or castles or the worries of the folk who built them. Sometimes he was frightened by the size of this world, by the limitless depths of the evening sky salted with cold stars.

But for all these unfamiliar insights, he still remained Simon: most of the time he was merely frustrated.

"Surely he didn't mean it." He licked the juice of a just-devoured pear from his fingers, then peevishly flung the core across the grassy verge. Beside him, Jiriki was toying with the stem that remained from his own. This was Simon's fifteenth evening in Jao é-Tinukai'i—or was it the sixteenth? "Stay here until I die? That's madness!" He had not, of course, told Jiriki of his failed attempt at escape, but neither could he pretend to be satisfied with his captivity.

Jiriki made what Simon had come to recognize as an unhappy face, a subtle thinning of the lips, a hooding of his upturned, feline eyes. "They are my parents," the Sitha said. "They are Shima'onari and Likimeya, Lords of the Zida'ya, and what they decide is as unchangeable as the wheel of seasons."

"But then why did you bring me here? You broke *that* rule!"

"There was no rule to break. Not truly." Jiriki twitched the stem once more between his long fingers, then flicked it into the pond. A tiny circle spread to show where it had fallen. "It was always an unspoken law, but that is different than a Word of Command. It is traditional among the Dawn Children that we may do what we please unless it goes against a Word of Command, but this business of bringing a mortal here cuts to the heart of the things that have divided our people since time out of mind. I can only ask you to forgive me, Seoman. It was a risk, and I had no right to gamble with your life. However, I have come to believe that for once— and hear me, *only* this once—you mortals may be right and my folk may be wrong. This spreading winter threatens many things beside the king- doms of the Sudhoda'ya."

Simon lay back, staring up at the brightening stars. He tried to smother the feeling of desperation that rose inside him. "Might your parents change their minds?"

"They might," Jiriki said slowly. "They are wise, and would be kind if they could. But do not let your hopes rise too high. We Zida'ya never hasten to decisions, especially difficult ones. What might seem to them a reasonable time to ponder could be years, and such waiting is hard for mortals to bear."

"Years!" Simon was horrified. He suddenly understood the beast that would gnaw off its own leg to escape a trap. "Years!"

"I am sorry, Seoman." Jiriki's voice was hoarse as though with great pain, but his golden features still showed little emotion. "There is one hopeful sign, but do not read too much into it. The butterflies remain."

"What?"

"At the Yásira. They gather when great decisions are to be made. They have not flown, so there are things still unresolved."

"What things?" Despite Jiriki's warning, Simon felt a surge of hope.

"I do not know." He shook his head. "Now is the time for me to stay away. At this moment, I am not my father's and mother's favored voice, so I must wait before I go to them again to make my arguments. Fortu- nately, First Grandmother Amerasu seems to have concerns about my parents' actions—my father's, especially." He smiled wryly. "Her words carry great weight."

Amerasu. Simon knew that name. He inhaled deeply of the night. Suddenly it came back to him: a face more beautiful and yet undeniably more ancient than even those of Jiriki's ageless parents. Simon sat up.

"Do you know, Jiriki, I saw her face once in the mirror—Amerasu, the one you call First Grandmother."

"In the mirror? In the dragon-scale mirror?"

Simon nodded. "I know I wasn't supposed to use it unless I was calling for your help, but what happened . . . it was an accident." He proceeded to describe his strange encounter with Amerasu and the terrifying appear- ance of silver-masked Utuk'ku.

Jiriki seemed to have entirely forgotten the crickets, despite the splendor of their song. "I did not forbid you to use the mirror, Seoman," he said.

"What is surprising is that you were able to see anything but natural reflection. That is odd." He made an unfamiliar gesture with his hand. "I must talk to First Grandmother about this. Very odd."

"May I come?" Simon asked.

"No, Seoman Snowlock," Jiriki smiled. "No one goes to see Amerasu the Ship-Born without her invitation. Even Root and Bough—what you would call her nearest kin—must ask very respectfully for such a favor. You do not know how astonishing it is that you saw her in my mirror. You are a menace, manchild."

"A menace? Me?"

The Sitha laughed. "Your presence is what I refer to." He touched Simon lightly on the shoulder. "You are without precedent, Snowlock. Completely unknown and unforeseen." He rose. "I will move on this. I am anxious myself for something to do."

Simon, who had never been good at waiting, was left alone with the pond, the crickets, and the unreachable stars.

It all seemed so strange. One moment he had been fighting for his life, perhaps even for the survival of all Osten Ard, struggling against bone-weariness and dark magic and terrible odds; a moment later he had been snatched out of winter and dropped headlong into summer, out of hideous danger and into . . . boredom.

But, Simon realized, it was not even so simple as that. Just because he had been removed from the world did not mean that the problems he had left behind were solved. On the contrary: somewhere out there, living or dead in the snowy woods beyond Jao é-Tinukai'i, was his horse Homefinder and its terrible burden—the sword Thorn, for which Simon and his friends had crossed hundreds of leagues and shed precious blood. Men and Sithi alike had died to find that blade for Josua. Now, with the sword perhaps lost in the forest, Simon had been imprisoned as offhandedly as Rachel had once locked him in one of the Hayholt's dark pantries for some trifling misdeed.

Simon had told Jiriki about the lost sword, but the Sitha had only shrugged, infuriatingly placid. There was nothing to be done.

Simon looked up. He had wandered far up the riverbank in the stillness of early afternoon; Jiriki's house, with its tapestry of knots, had fallen out of sight behind him. He sat down on a stone and watched a white egret stilt out into one of the river's shallow backwaters, bright eye staring obliquely, pretending disinterest to allay the fears of any wary fish.

He was sure that at least three weeks had passed since he had come to the valley. For the last few days his imprisonment had seemed almost a sort of terribly dull joke, one that had gone on too long and now threatened to spoil everyone's enjoyment.

What can I do?! In frustration, he scrabbled up a twig from the dirt and sent it spinning out onto the water. *There's no way to leave!*

Thinking back on the grand failure of his first escape and the other confirming experiments that had followed, Simon made a noise of disgust and threw another twig out onto the river. Every attempt to find his way out had left him back in the center of Jao é-Tinukai'i.

How could I have been such a mooncalf? he thought sourly. *Why should I think it would be so easy to walk away from here, when Aditu and I had to walk clear out of winter to arrive?* The stick whirled for a moment, spinning like a weathervane, then was sucked under by the gentle current.

That's me, he thought. *That's what I'll be like as far as these Sithi-folk are concerned. I'll be around for a little while, then before they even realize I'm getting old, I'll be dead.* The thought brought a lump of terror into his throat. Suddenly, he wanted nothing more than to be around his own short-lived kind—even Rachel the Dragon—rather than these soft-spoken, cat-eyed immortals.

Filled with restlessness, he sprang up from the riverbank, kicking his way through the reeds as he pushed back toward the path. He almost bumped into someone: a Sitha-man, dressed only in a pair of thin, loose-fitting blue breeches, who stood in the undergrowth and gazed out toward the river. For a moment, Simon thought this stranger had been spying on him, but the fine-boned face showed no expression at Simon's approach. The Sitha continued to stare out past him as the youth walked by. The stranger was singing quietly to himself, a breathy melody of sibilances and pauses. His attention was fixed on a tree growing out of the riverbank, half-submerged in the current.

Simon could not restrain a grunt of irritation. What was wrong with these people? They wandered around like sleepwalkers, said things that made no sense—even Jiriki sometimes talked mysterious, circular non-sense, and the prince was by far the most direct of this tribe—and they all looked at Simon as though he were an insect. When they bothered to notice him at all.

Several times Simon had encountered Sithi who he was certain were Ki'ushapo and Sijandi, the pair who had accompanied Jiriki and Simon's company north from the Aldheorte to the base of Urmsheim, but the Sithi showed no recognition, made no sign of greeting. Simon could not swear beyond any doubt that the faces were theirs, but something in the way they steadfastly avoided his eye assured him that he was correct.

After the journey across the northern waste, both Jiriki's kinsman An'nai and the Erkynlandish soldier Grimmric had died on the dragon-mountain Urmsheim, beneath the icy waterfall known as the Uduntree. They had been buried together, mortal and immortal, something which Jiriki had said was unprecedented, a binding between their two races unknown for centuries. Now Simon, a mortal, had come to forbidden Jao é-Tinukai'i.

Ki'ushapo and Sijandi might not approve of his being here, but they *knew* he had saved their prince Jiriki, and they knew Simon was *Hikka Staja*, an Arrow-Bearer—so why should they avoid him so completely? If Simon was wrong in his identification, it should still be simple enough for the real pair to seek him out, since he was the only one of his kind among their folk. Were they so angry at his being here that they could not even greet him? Were they in some way embarrassed for Jiriki, that the prince should have brought such a creature to their secret valley? Then why did they not say so, or say *something*? At least Jiriki's uncle Khendraja'aro made his dislike of mortals plain and public.

Thinking of these slights put Simon in a foul humor. He muddled his way up the stream bank, fuming. It took all his restraint not to turn back to the river-watching Sitha and shove his handsome, alien face into the mud.

Simon struck out across the valley, not with any idea of escape this time, but rather to walk off some of his restless irritation. His stiff-legged strides carried him past several more Sithi. Most walked by themselves, although a few strolled in unspeaking pairs. Some looked at him with unblinking interest, others did not seem to notice him at all. One group of four sat quietly listening to the singing of a fifth, their eyes intent on the delicate gliding movements of the singer's hands.

Merciful Aedon, he grumbled to himself, *what are they thinking about all the time? They're worse than Doctor Morgenes!* Although the doctor, too, had been prone to long silences, unbroken but for his distracted, tuneless humming, at least at the end of a day he would unstop a jug of beer and teach Simon some history, or make suggestions about his apprentice's rather blobby handwriting.

Simon kicked a fir cone and watched it roll. He did have to admit that the Sithi were beautiful. Their grace, the flowing line of their garments, their serene faces, all made him feel like some mud-covered mongrel bumping against the table linens of a great lord's house. Though his captivity infuriated him, sometimes a cruel inner voice whispered that it was only justice. He had no right to be in this place, and having come, an urchin like Simon should never be allowed to return and sully the immortals with his tales. Like Jack Mundwode's man Osgal in the story, he had gone down into a fairy-mound. The world could never be the same.

Simon's pace slowed from an angry march to a slouch. Before long, he began to hear the steady ringing of water on stone. He looked up from his grass-stained boots to discover that he had wandered right across the valley into the shade of the hills. A stirring of hope made itself felt inside him. He was near the Pools, as Aditu had called them; the Summer Gate stood nearby. It seemed that by not thinking about finding his way out, he had been able to do what he had failed so miserably to accomplish in days past.

Trying to imitate the degree of not-caring that had brought him this far, Simon wandered off the path, angling toward the sound of splashing water, staring up into the overarching trees with what he hoped was suitable nonchalance. Within a few steps he had left the sunlight and entered the cool shadow of the hills, where he made his way up grass-tangled slopes carpeted in shy blue gilly-flowers and white starblooms. As the song of falling water grew louder he had to restrain himself from breaking into a run; instead, he stopped to rest against a tree, precisely as if he were in the middle of a contemplative walk. He stared at the stripes of sunshine lancing down through the leaves and listened to his own grad-ually slowing breath. Then, just when he had nearly forgotten where he was going—did he only fancy that he could hear the rush of water suddenly increase?—he started up the hill once more.

As he reached the summit of this first slope, certain that he would see the bottommost of the Pools before him, he found himself standing instead on the rim of a circular valley. The valley's upper slopes were covered by a host of white birch trees whose leaves were just now turning summer-yellow. They rattled softly in the breeze, like bits of golden parchment. Beyond the birches, the next level of the valley was thickly grown with silvery-leaved trees that trembled as the wind continued its sweep down toward the valley floor.

At the base of the circular valley, in the depths within the ring of silver leaves, lay a vegetative darkness that Simon's eyes could not pierce. Whatever things grew there also took the wind in their turn: a sort of clattering whisper arose from the valley's shadowed deeps, a sound that might have been the scraping of breeze-blown leaves and branches, or just as easily the hiss of a thousand slim knives being drawn from a thousand delicate sheaths.

Simon let out his pent-up breath. The scent of the valley rose up to him, musty and bittersweet. He caught the smell of growing things, a pungent odor like mown grass, but also a deep and intoxicating spiciness reminis-cent of the bowls of hippocras Morgenes had mulled on cold evenings. He took another whiff and felt strangely drunken. There were other scents, too, a dozen, a hundred—he could smell roses growing against an old stone wall, stable muck, rain puffing on dusty ground, the salty tang of blood, and the similar but by no means identical odor of sea-brine. He shivered like a wet dog and felt himself drawn a few steps down the slope.

"I am sorry. You may not go there."

Simon whirled to see a Sitha-woman standing on the hilltop behind him. For a moment he thought it was Aditu. This one wore a wisp of cloth around her loins and nothing else. Her skin was red-golden in the slanting sunlight.

"What. . . ?"

"You may not go there." She spoke his mortal tongue carefully. There was no ill humor on her face. "I am sorry, but you may not." She took a step forward and looked at him curiously. "You are the Sudhoda'ya who saved Jiriki."

"So? Who are you?" he asked sullenly. He didn't want to look at her breasts, her slim but well-muscled legs, but it was nearly impossible not to. He felt himself growing angry.

"My mother named me Maye'sa," she said, making each word too precisely, as if Simon's language were a trick she had learned but never before performed. Her white hair was streaked with gold and black. Staring at her long, coiled tresses—a safe place to let his eyes rest—Simon suddenly realized that *all* the Sitha had white hair, that the myriad of different rainbow colors that made them seem like outlandish birds were just dyes. Even Jiriki, with his odd, heather-flower shade—dyes! Artifice! Just like the harlot-women that Father Dreosan had ranted about during his sermons in the Hayholt chapel! Simon felt his anger deepening. He turned his back on the Sitha-woman and started downward into the valley.

"Come back, Seoman Snowlock," she called. "That is the Year-Dancing Grove. You may not go there."

"Stop me," he growled. Maybe she would put an arrow in his back. He had seen Aditu's terrifying facility with a bow just a few mornings before, when Jiriki's sister had put four arrows side by side into a tree limb at fifty paces. He had little doubt that others of her sex were just as competent, but at this moment he cared little. "Kill me if you want to," he added, then wondered if such a remark might strain his luck.

Half-hunching his shoulders, he strode down the slope into the whispering birches. No arrow came, so he risked a backward look. The one called Maye'sa still stood where he had left her. Her thin face seemed puzzled.

He began to run down the hillside, past row after row of white, papery-barked trunks. After a moment, he noticed that the slope was leveling off. When he found himself beginning to run uphill he stopped, then walked until he found a spot from which he could look about and discover where he was. The entirety of the great bowl still lay beneath him, but he had somehow moved around the valley's rim from the spot where the Sitha-woman stood, watching.

Swearing in fury, he started down the slope once more, but experienced the same feeling of leveling, swiftly followed by the resumption of an upward slant. He had gotten no closer to the bottom—he was still, as far as he could tell, only a third of the way through the ring of birch trees.

Attempts to turn away from the uphill slope also met with failure. The wind sighed in the branches, the birch leaves rustled, and Simon felt himself struggling as though in a dream, making no headway despite all his exertions. At last, in a paroxysm of frustration, he closed his eyes and ran. His terror turned into a moment of heady exhilaration as he felt the ground sloping away beneath his feet. Tree branches slapped at his face, but some peculiar luck kept him from striking any of the hundreds of trunks that lay in the path of his headlong flight.

When he stopped and opened his eyes, he was back at the top of the hillside once more. Maye'sa stood before him, her gauzy bit of skirt fluttering in the restless breeze.

"I told you, you may not go into the Year-Dancing Grove," she said, explaining a painful truth to a child. "Did you think you could?" Stretching her sinuous neck, she shook her head. Her eyes were wide, inquisitive. "Strange creature."

She vanished back down the hillside toward Jao é-Tinukai'i. A few moments later, Simon followed. Head down, watching his boot toes scuffing through the grass, he soon found himself standing on the path before Jiriki's house. Evening was coming on and the crickets were singing by the river-pond.

"Very good, Seoman," Aditu said the next day. She examined the shent board, nodding. "Misdirection! To go away from that which you wish to gain. You are learning."

"It doesn't always work," he said glumly.

Her eyes glittered. "No. Sometimes you need a deeper strategy. But it is a beginning."

Binabik and Sludig had not come far into the forest, only deep enough to shelter their camp from the bitter wind sweeping down the plains, a wind whose voice had become a ceaseless howling. The horses shifted uneasily on their tethers, and even Qantaqa seemed restless. She had just returned from her third excursion into the forest, and now sat with ears erect, as though listening for some expected but nonetheless dire warning. Her eyes gleamed with reflected firelight.

"Do you think we are any safer here, little man?" Sludig asked, sharpening his swore. "I think I would rather face the empty plains than his forest."

Binabik frowned. "Perhaps, but would you rather also be facing hairy giants like those we saw?"

The White Way, the great road that spanned the northern borders of Aldheorte, had turned at last by the forest's easternmost edge, leading them south for the first time since they had come down off the Old Tumet'ai Road with Simon many days earlier. Not long after the southward turn, they had spotted a group of white shapes moving in the distance behind them—shapes that they both realized could be nothing but Hunën. The giants, once unwilling to leave their hunting lands at the foot of Stormspike, now seemed to range the length and breadth of the northland. Remembering the destruction that a band of these creatures had wreaked on their large traveling party, neither troll nor Rimmersgarder had any false hopes that the two of them could survive an encounter with the shaggy monstrosities.

"What makes you sure we are any safer because we have come a few furlongs into the woods?" demanded Sludig.

"Nothing that is certain," Binabik admitted, "but I know that the small, creeping diggers are reluctant to tunnel into Aldheorte. Perhaps the giants may be having similar reluctance."

Sludig snorted and made the blade rasp loudly on the whetstone. "And the Hunë that Josua killed near Naglimund, when the boy Simon was found? That one was in the forest, was it not?"

"That giant was driven to there," Binabik said irritably. He pushed the second of the leaf-wrapped birds into the coals. "There are no promises in life, Sludig, but it seems to me smarter to take fewer chances."

After a short silence, the Rimmersman spoke up. "You speak rightly, troll. I am only tired. I wish we would get where we are going, to this Farewell Stone! I would like to give Josua his damnable sword, then sleep for a week. In a bed."

Binabik smiled. "With certainty. But it is not Josua's sword, or at least I am not sure it is meant for him." He stood and took the long bundle from where it leaned against a tree. "I am not sure what it is for at all." Binabik's fingers unwrapped the blade, allowing its dark surface to show. The firelight revealed no more than its dark outlines. "Do you see?" Binabik said, hefting the bundle in his arms. "Thorn now seems to think it is acceptable for a small troll to carry it."

"Don't talk about it as if it were alive," Sludig said, sketching a hasty Tree in the air. "That is against nature."

Binabik eyed him. "It may not be alive, as a bear or a bird or a man is alive, but there is something in it that is more than sword-metal. You know that, Sludig."

"That may be." The Rimmersman frowned. "No, curse it, I do know. That is why I do not like speaking of it. I have dreams about the cave where we found the thing."

"That is not surprising to me," the troll said softly. "That was a fearsome place."

"But it is not just the place—not even the worm, or Grimmric's death. I dream of the damnable sword, little man. It was laying there among those bones as though it *waited* for us. Cold, cold, like a snake in its den . . ."

Sludig trailed off. Binabik watched him, but said nothing.

The Rimmersman sighed. "And I still do not understand what good having it will do Josua."

"No more do I, but it is a powerful thing. It is good to remember that."

Binabik stroked the glinting surface as he might the back of a cat. "Look at it, Sludig. We have been so caught up in our trials and losses that we have almost been forgetting Thorn. This is an object that is making legends! Perhaps it is the greatest weapon ever to have come to light in Osten Ard—greater than Hern's spear Oinduth, greater than Chukku's sling."

"Powerful it may be," Sludig grumbled, "but I have doubts as to how lucky it is. It didn't save Sir Camaris, did it?"

Binabik showed a small, secretive smile. "But he did not have it when he was swept over the side in Firannos Bay: Towser the jester told that to us. That is why we were able to discover it on the dragon-mountain. Otherwise it would be at ocean's bottom—like Camaris."

The wind shrieked, rattling the branches overhead. Sludig waited an appropriate interval, then moved closer to the comforting fire. "How could such a great knight fall off a boat? God grant that I die more honorably, in battle. It only proves to me, if I had any doubts, that boats are things best left alone."

Binabik's yellow grin widened. "To be hearing such words from one whose ancestors were the greatest sailors mankind has known!" His expression grew serious. "Although it must be told that some doubt Camaris was swept into the sea. Some there are who say that he was drowning himself."

"What? Why in Usires' name would he do such a thing?" Sludig poked at the fire indignantly.

The troll shrugged. "It is only being rumor, but I do not ignore such things. Morgenes' writings are filled with many strange stories. Qinkipa! How I wish I had found more time for reading the doctor's book! One thing Morgenes was telling in his life-story of Prester John was that Sir Camaris was much like our Prince Josua: a man of strange, melancholy moods. Also, he was much in admiration of John's queen, Ebekah. King Prester John had made Camaris her special protector. When the Rose of Hernysadharc—as many were naming her—died in the birthing of Josua, Camaris was said to be much upset. He grew fell and strange, and railed against his God and Heaven. He gave up sword and armor and other things, as one who takes up a life of religion—or, as one who knows he will die. He was making his way back to his home in Vinitta after a pilgrimage to the Sancellan Aedonitis. In a storm he was lost in the ocean off Harcha-island."

Binabik leaned forward and began pulling the wrapped birds out of the fire, exerting caution so as not to burn his stubby fingers. The fire crackled and the wind moaned.

"Welladay," Sludig said at last. "What you say only makes me more sure that I will avoid the high and the mighty whenever possible. But for Duke Isgrimnur, who has a good level head on his shoulders, the rest of them are drifty and foolish as geese. Your Prince Josua, if you will pardon my saying it, first among them."

Binabik's grin returned. "He is not *my* Prince Josua, and he *is*—what was your wording?—drifty. But not foolish. Not foolish at all. And he may be our last hope for staving off the coming storm." As though he had stumbled into an uncomfortable subject, the troll busied himself with their supper. He pushed a smoking bird over to the Rimmersman. "Here. Have something to eat. Perhaps if the Hunën are enjoying the cold weather, they will be leaving us alone. We can then gain ourselves a good night sleeping."

"We will need it. We have a long road before we can give away this damnable sword."

"But we owe it to those who have fallen," Binabik said, staring out into the dark reaches of the surrounding forest. "We do not have the freedom of making a failure."

As they ate, Qantaqa rose and paced about the campsite, listening intently to the wailing wind.

Snow was blowing savagely across the Waste, flung hard enough by the howling wind to strip the very bark from the trees along the Aldheorte's ragged north fringe. The great hound, not hindered in the least by such unfriendly weather, bounded lightly back through the blinding flurries, stone-hard muscles coiling and uncoiling beneath its short fur. When the dog reached Ingen's side, the Queen's Huntsman reached into his vest and produced a length of gnarled, dried meat that had at one end something suspiciously like a fingernail. The white hound crunched it in a second, then stood peering out into the darkness, cloudy little eyes full of eagerness to be moving once more. Ingen scratched carefully behind the dog's ears, his gloved fingers trailing across a bulgingly muscled jaw that could crush rock.

"Yes, Niku'a" the huntsman whispered, voice echoing within his helm. His own eyes were as madly intent as those of the hound. "You have the scent now, do you not? Ah, the Queen will be so proud. My name will be sung until the sun turns black and rotten and drops from the sky."

He lifted his helmet and let the stinging wind batter his face. As certainly as he knew that frosty stars shone somewhere above the darkness, so, too, he knew that his quarry was still before him, and that he drew nearer to it with every day that passed. At this moment he did not feel himself to be the stolid, tireless hound that was his sigil, and whose snarling face made the mask of his helm; he was instead some subtler, more feline predator, a creature of fierce but quiet joy. He felt the freezing night on his face and knew that nothing that lived beneath the black sky could escape him for long.

Ingen Jegger slid the crystalline dagger from his sleeve and held it before him, staring at it as though it were a mirror in which he could see himself, the Ingen who had feared to die in obscurity. Catching some hardy beam of moonlight or starshine, the translucent blade burned with a chilly blue fire; its carvings seemed to writhe like serpents beneath his fingers. This was all he had dreamed, and more. The Queen in the Silver Mask had set him a great task, a task befitting the making of a legend. Soon—he felt it with a certainty that made him tremble—soon that task would be accomplished. Ingen let the dagger slide back into his sleeve.

"Go, Niku'a," he whispered, as though the hidden stars might betray him if they heard. "It is time to hunt our prey to ground. We will run." Ingen vaulted into the saddle. His patient mount stirred as if awakening.

The snow swirled, blowing through the empty night where a moment before a man, a horse, and a dog had stood.

The afternoon light was failing, the translucent walls of Jiriki's house gradually growing darker. Aditu had brought a meal of fruit and warm bread to Simon's room, an act of kindness for which he would have been even more appreciative had she not stayed to annoy him. It was not that Simon did not enjoy Aditu's company or admire her exotic beauty: it was, in fact, her very beauty and shamelessness that disturbed him, making it especially difficult to concentrate on such mundane tasks as eating.

Aditu trailed a finger up his backbone once more. Simon nearly choked on a mouthful of bread.

"Don't do that!"

The Sitha-woman made an interested face. "Why not? Does it cause you pain?"

"No! Of course not. It tickles." He turned away sulkily, inwardly regretting his lack of manners—but not much. He was feeling, as he usually did around Aditu, quite flummoxed. Jiriki, for all his alien ways, had never made Simon think of himself as a cloddish mortal: beside Aditu, Simon felt himself to be made of mud.

She was attired today in little but feathers and jeweled beads and a few strips of fabric. Her body gleamed with scented oils.

"Tickles? But is that bad?" she asked. "I do not wish to hurt you or make you uncomfortable, Seoman. It is just that you are so—" she searched for the proper word, "—so unusual, and I have seldom been near your kind." She seemed to be enjoying his discomfiture. "You are very wide here . . ." She ran a finger from one of his shoulders to the other, sighing as this occasioned another muffled yelp. "It is clear you are not made like our folk."

Simon, who had slid out of reach once more, grunted. He was uncomfortable around her, that was a simple fact. Her presence had begun to make him feel as though he had some kind of damnable *itch*, and in his solitude he had come to both yearn for and yet fear her arrivals. Every time he stole a glance at her slim body, displayed with an immodesty that still shocked him to the depths of his being, he found himself remembering the thundering sermons of Father Dreosan. Simon was astonished to discover that the priest, whom he had always thought an idiot, had been right after all—the devil *did* make snares for the flesh. Just watching Aditu's lissome, catlike movements filled Simon with a squirming consciousness of sin. It was the more terrible, he knew, because Jiriki's sister was not even of his own kind.

As the priest had taught, Simon tried to keep the pure face of Elysia the Mother of God before him when he was confronted by the temptation of flesh. Back in the Hayholt, Simon had seen that face in hundreds of paintings and sculptures, in countless candlelit shrines, but now he was alarmed to find his memory turning traitor. In recollection, the eyes of Usires' sainted mother seemed more playful and more . . . *feline* . . . than could possibly be proper or holy.

Despite this discomfort, in his loneliness he was still grateful to Aditu for all her attentions, however perfunctory he sometimes thought them to be, and however careless of Simon's feelings her teasing sometimes became. He was most grateful for the meals. Jiriki was seldom at home of late, and Simon was more than a little uncertain about which of the fruits, vegetables, and less familiar plants growing in the prince's extensive forest gardens could be safely eaten. There was no one but the prince's sister on whom he could rely. Even among the first family—the "Root and Bough" as Jiriki had phrased it—there seemed to be nothing like servants. Everyone fended for themselves, as befitted the Sithi's solitary habits. Simon knew that the Sithi kept animals, or rather, that the valley was full of animals that came when they were called. The goats and sheep must allow themselves to be milked, for the meals Aditu brought him often included fragrant cheeses, but the Sithi seemed to eat no meat. Simon often thought longingly about all those trusting animals wandering the paths of Jao é-Tinukai'i. He knew he would never dare do anything about it, but— Aedon!—wouldn't a leg of mutton be a fine thing to have!

Aditu poked him again. Simon stolidly ignored her. She got up and walked past the nest of soft blankets that was Simon's bed, stopping before the billowing blue wall. The wall had been scarlet when Jiriki first brought him, but Simon's Sitha host had somehow changed its color to this more soothing cerulean. When Aditu brushed it with her long-fingered hand, the fabric slid away like a drawn curtain, revealing another, larger room beyond.

"Let us return to our game," she said. "You are too serious, manchild."

"I will never be able to learn it," Simon muttered.

"You do not apply yourself. Jiriki claims you have a good mind—although my brother has been wrong before." Aditu reached into a fold in the wall and produced a crystal sphere which began to glow at her touch. She placed it on a simple tripod of wood, letting its light spread through the darkened room, then took a carved wooden case from beneath the colorful shent board and removed the polished stones that served as playing pieces. "I think I had just made myself an acre of Woodlarks. Come, Seoman, play and don't pout. You had a good idea the other day, a very clever idea—fleeing that which you truly sought." She stroked his arm, making the hairs stand up, and gave him one of her strange Sithi smiles, full of impenetrable significance.

"Seoman has other games to play tonight."

Jiriki stood in the doorway, dressed in what appeared to be ceremonial attire, an intricately embroidered robe in varied shades of yellow and blue. He wore soft gray boots. His sword Indreju dangled at his hip in a scabbard of the same gray stuff, and three long white heron feathers were braided into his hair. "He has received a summons."

Aditu carefully set the pieces on the board. "I shall have to play by myself, then—unless you are staying, Willow-switch." She gazed from beneath lowered lids.

Jiriki shook his head. "No, sister. I must be Seoman's guide."

"Where am I going?" Simon asked. "Summoned by who?"

"By First Grandmother." Jiriki lifted his hand and made a brief but solemn gesture. "Amerasu the Ship-Born has asked to see you."

Walking in silence beneath the stars, Simon thought about the things he had seen since leaving the Hayholt. To think that once he had feared he would live and die a castle-drudge! Was there to be no end to the strange places he must go, to the strange people he must meet? Amerasu might be able to help him, but still he was growing weary of strangeness. Then again, he realized with a flutter of panic, if Amerasu or some other did *not* come to his aid, the lovely but limited vistas of Jao é-Tinukai'i might be all he would ever see again.

But the strangest thing, he thought suddenly, was that no matter where he went or what he saw, he always seemed to remain the same old Simon—a little less mooncalfish, perhaps, but not very different from the clumsy kitchen boy who had lived at the Hayholt. Those distant, peaceful days seemed utterly gone, vanished without hope of reclamation, but the Simon who had lived them was still very much present. Morgenes had told him once to make his home in his own head. That way, home could never be taken from him. Was this what the doctor meant? To be the same person no matter where you went, no matter what madness occurred? Somehow, that didn't seem quite right.

"I will not burden you with instructions," Jiriki said suddenly, startling him. "There are special rites to be performed before meeting the First Grandmother, but you do not know them, nor could you perform all of them even if they were told to you. I do not think that cause to worry, however. I believe Amerasu wishes to see you because of who you are and what you have seen, not because she wishes you to watch you perform the Six Songs of Respectful Request."

"The six *what?*"

"It is not important. But remember this: although First Grandmother is of the same family as Aditu and myself, we are both children of the Last Days. Amerasu Ship-Born was one of the first speaking creatures to set foot on Osten Ard. I say this not to frighten," he added hurriedly, seeing Simon's distressed, moonlit expression, "but only to have you know she is different even than my father and mother."

The silence returned as Simon pondered this. Could the handsome, sad-faced woman he had seen really be one of the oldest living things in the world? He did not doubt Jiriki, but his own wildest thoughts stretched to their limits still could not encompass the prince's words.

The winding path led them across a stone bridge. Once over the river, they made their way into the more heavily wooded part of the valley. Simon did his best to take note of what paths they took, but found that the memories quickly melted away, insubstantial as starlight. He remembered only that they crossed several more streams, each seeming slightly more melodious than the last, until they finally entered into a part of the forest that seemed quieter. Among these thickly knotted trees even the cricket songs were hushed. The tree branches swayed, but the wind was silent.

When they finally stopped, Simon found to his surprise that they stood before the tall, cobwebbed tree he had found in his first attempt at escape. Faint lights shone through the tangle of silken threads, as though the great tree wore a glowing cloak.

"I was here before," Simon said slowly. The warm, still air made him feel at once drowsy and yet keenly alert.

The prince looked at him and said nothing, but led him toward the oak. Jiriki set his hand to the moss-covered door, set so deeply into the bark that the tree might have grown around it.

"We have permission," he said quietly. The door swung silently inward.

Beyond the doorway was an impossible thing: a narrow hallway that stretched away before him, as silk-tangled as the front of the oak-house. Tiny lights no larger than fireflies burned within the matted threads, filling the passageway with their flickering light. Simon, who could have sworn guiltlessly on a holy Tree that nothing lay behind the spreading oak but more trees, took a step back through the doorframe to see where such a hallway could possibly be hidden—could it pass down into the ground, somehow?—but Jiriki took his elbow and gently steered him across the threshold once more. The door fell shut behind them.

They were completely surrounded by lights and silken webs, as though they moved through the clouds and among the stars. The curious sleepiness was still upon Simon: every detail was sharp and clear, but he had no idea how long they spent walking in the scintillant passage. They came at last to a more open place, a chamber that smelled of cedar and plum blossoms and other scents more difficult to identify. The minute and inconstant lights were fewer here, and the wide room was full of long, shuddery shadows. From time to time the walls creaked, as though he and Jiriki stood in the hold of a ship, or inside the trunk of a tree far larger than any Simon had ever seen. He heard a sound as of water slowly dripping, like the last drops of a rainstorm trickling from willow branches into a pool. Half-visible shapes lined the dark walls, things shaped like people; they might have been statues, for they were certainly very still.

As Simon stared, his eyes not yet adjusted to the diminished light, something brushed against his leg. He jumped and cried out, but a moment later the flickering lights showed him a waving tail that could only belong to a cat; the creature swiftly vanished into the darkness along the walls. Simon caught his breath.

Strange as the place was, he decided, there was nothing truly frightening about it. The shadowy chamber had an air of warmth and serenity unlike anything he had experienced thus far in Jao é-Tinukai'i. Judith, the Hayholt's plump kitchen mistress, would almost have called it cozy.

"Welcome to my house," a voice said from the darkness. The pinpricks of light grew brighter around one of the shadowy figures, revealing a white-haired head and the back of a tall chair. "Come closer, manchild. I can see you there, but I doubt you can see me."

"First Grandmother has very sharp sight," Jiriki said; Simon thought he could detect a trace of amusement in the Sitha's voice. He stepped forward. The golden light revealed the ancient yet youthful face he had seen in Jiriki's mirror.

"You are in the presence of Amerasu y'Senditu no'e-Sa'onserei, the Ship-Born," intoned Jiriki from behind him. "Show respect, Seoman Snowlock."

Simon felt no compunction about doing so. He kneeled on wobbling legs and lowered his head before her.

"Stand up, mortal boy," she said quietly. Her voice was deep and smooth. It tugged at Simon's memory. Had their short contact through the mirror burned itself so deeply on his mind?" "Hmmm," she murmured. "You are taller even than my young Willow-switch. Will you find the manchild a stool, Jiriki, so I do not have to stare up at him? Get yourself one, too."

When Simon was seated beside Jiriki, Amerasu inspected him carefully. Simon felt suddenly tongue-tied, but curiosity vied with shyness. He stole return glances while doing his best to avoid her almost frighteningly deep eyes.

She was much as he remembered her: shining white hair, skin tight-stretched over her fine bones. Other than the measureless depths of her stare, the only hint of the immense age to which Jiriki had alluded was in the careful deliberation with which she assayed every movement, as though her skeleton were fragile as dried parchment. Still, she was very beautiful. Caught in the web of her regard, Simon imagined that in the dawn of the world Amerasu might have been as terrifyingly, blindingly splendid to look upon as the face of the sun.

"So," she said finally. "You are out of your depths, little fish."

Simon nodded.

"Are you enjoying your visit to Jao é-Tinukai'i? You are one of the first of your kind to come here."

Jiriki sat up straighter. "*One* of the first, wise Amerasu? Not *the* first?"

She ignored him, keeping her gaze fixed on Simon. He felt himself drawn gently but helplessly into her spell of command, a wriggling fish pulled inexorably toward the water's blinding surface. "Speak, manchild. What do you think?"

"I . . . I am honored to visit," he said at last, then swallowed. His throat was very dry. "Honored. But . . . but I don't want to stay in this valley. Not forever."

Amerasu leaned back in her chair. He felt himself held more loosely, though the power of her presence was still strongly upon him. "I am not surprised." She took a long breath, smiling sadly. "But you would have to be prisoned here a long while before you would be as weary of this life as I am."

Jiriki stirred. "Should I leave, First Grandmother?"

His question gave Simon a faint tremor of fright. He could feel the Sitha-woman's great kindness and great pain—but she was so fearfully strong! He knew that if she wished, she could keep him here forever, just with the power of her voice and those compelling, labyrinthine eyes.

"Should I leave?" Jiriki asked again.

"I know it pains you to hear me speak so, Willow-switch," Amerasu said. "But you are dearest of all my young ones and you are strong. You can hear truth." She shifted slowly in her chair, long-fingered hand settling on the breast of her white robe. "You, too, manchild, have known loss. That is in your face. But though every loss is grave, the lives as well as losses of mortals appear and fade as swiftly as the seasons turn the leaves. I do not mean to be cruel. Neither do I seek pity—but not you or any other mortal has seen the dry centuries roll past, the hungry millennia, seen the very light and color sucked out of your world until nothing remains but juiceless memories." Strangely, as she spoke her face seemed to grow more youthful, as though her grief were the most vital thing left in her. Now Simon could see much more than a hint of her former splendor. He lowered his head, unable to speak.

"Of course you have not," she said, a slight tremor in her voice. "I have. That is why I am here, in the dark. It is not that I fear the light, or that I am not strong enough to stand day's brightness." She laughed, a sound like a whipoorwill's mournful call. "No, it is only that in darkness I can see the lost days and faces of the past more clearly."

Simon looked up. "You had two sons," he said quietly. He had realized why her voice seemed so familiar. "One of them went away."

Amerasu's face hardened. "Both of them are gone. What have you told him, Jiriki? These are not tales for the small hearts of mortals."

"I told him nothing, First Grandmother."

She leaned forward intently. "Tell me of my sons. What old legends do you know?"

Simon swallowed. "One son was hurt by a dragon. He had to go away. He was burned—like me." He touched his own scarred cheek. "The other . . . the other is the Storm King." As he whispered this last, Simon looked around, as though something might step toward him out of the deep shadows. The walls creaked and water dripped, but that was all.

"How do you know this?"

"I heard your voice in a dream." Simon searched for words. "You spoke in my head for a long time when I was sleeping."

The Sitha-woman's beautiful face was grave. She stared at him as though something hidden within him threatened her. "Do not be afraid, manchild," she said at last, reaching out with her slender hands. "Do not fear. And forgive me."

Amerasu's cool, dry fingers touched Simon's face. The lights streamed like shreds of lightning, then flickered and faded, dropping the chamber into utter darkness. Her grip seemed to tighten. The blackness sang.

There was no pain, but somehow Amerasu was inside his head, a forceful presence so intimately connected to him at that moment that he felt shockingly, terrifyingly raw, an exposure far more profound than any merely physical nakedness. Sensing his terror, she calmed him, cradling his secret self like a panicking bird until he was no longer afraid. First Grandmother then began to pick delicately through his memories, probing him with gentle but purposeful thoroughness.

Dizzy snatches of thought and dream fluttered past, swirling like flower petals in a windstorm—Morgenes and his countless books, Miriamele singing, seemingly meaningless fragments of conversation from Simon's days in the Hayholt. The night of Thisterborg and the dreadful gray sword spread though his mind like a dark stain, followed by the silver face of Utuk'ku and the three swords from his vision in the house of Geloë. Plump Skodi and the thing that had laughed in the courtyard flames whirled and melted into the lunacy of the Uduntree and the emotionless eyes of the great white worm Igjarjuk. Thorn was there, too, a black slash across the light of recollection. As the memories flew by, he again felt the burning pain of the dragon's blood and the fearful sense of connection to the spinning world, the sickening vastness of the hope and pain of all living things. At last, like the tatters of a dream, the pictures faded.

The lights came back slowly. Simon's head was cradled in Jiriki's lap. The wound on his cheek was throbbing.

"Forgive me, First Grandmother," Jiriki said as though from a great distance, "but was that necessary? He would have told you all he knew."

Amerasu was silent for a long time. When she spoke, it was with great effort. Her voice seemed older than before. "He could not have told me all, Willow-switch. Those things that to me seem most important, he is not even aware that he knows." She turned her eyes down to Simon, her face full of weary kindness. "I am truly sorry, manchild. I had no right to plunder you that way, but I am old and frightened and I have little patience left. Now, I am more frightened than ever."

She tried to pull herself up. Jiriki reached out to help, and she rose unsteadily from her chair and vanished into the shadows. She returned a moment later with a cup of water, which she held to Simon's lips with her own hands. He drank thirstily. The water was cold and sweet, with just a savor of wood and earth, as though it had been scooped from the trunk of a hollow tree. In her white robe, Simon thought, Amerasu looked like some pale and radiant saint from a church picture.

"What . . . did you do?" he asked as he sat up. There was a buzzing sound in his ears and small shining flecks dancing before his eyes.

"Learned what I needed to learn," Amerasu said. "I knew that I had seen you in Jiriki's mirror, but I thought that a fluke, a mischance. The Road of Dreams has changed much of late, and has become as obscure and unpredictable to even the experienced as it once was for those who only traveled it in sleep. I see now that our earlier meeting was no accident of fate."

"Do you mean that your meeting with Simon was intended by someone, First Grandmother?" Jiriki said.

"No. I mean only that the boundaries between those worlds and ours are beginning to weaken. Someone like this manchild, who has been pulled one way and another, who through true chance or some unimaginable design has been dragged into many powerful and dangerous connections between the dream world and the waking . . ." She trailed off, seating herself carefully once more before continuing. "It is as though he lived on the edge of a great wood. When the trees begin to spread outward, it is his house that first has roots across the threshold. When the wolves of the forest begin to grow hungry, it is beneath his window that they first come howling."

Simon struggled to speak. "What did you learn . . . from my memories? About . . . about Ineluki?"

Her face became impassive. "Too much. I believe I now understand my son's terrible, subtle design, but I must think a while longer. Even in this hour, I must not be frightened into foolish haste." She lifted a hand to her brow. "If I am correct, our danger is graver than we ever guessed. I must speak to Shima'onari and Likimeya. I only hope they listen—and that time has not passed us by. We may be starting to dig the well as our houses burn down."

Jiriki helped Simon sit up. "My father and mother must listen. Everyone knows your wisdom, First Grandmother."

Amerasu smiled sadly. "Once, the women of the House Sa'onserei were the keepers of lore. The final word belonged to the eldest of the house. When Jenjiyana of the Nightingales saw the right of things, she spoke and it was so. Since the Flight, things have changed." Her hand fluttered in the air like a bird alighting. "I am certain your mother will listen to reason. Your father is good, Jiriki, but in some ways he dwells even more deeply in the past than I do." She shook her head. "Forgive me. I am weary and I have much to think about. Otherwise, I would not talk so uncarefully, and especially in front of this boy." She extended her hand toward Simon, brushing his cheek with her fingertip. The pain of his old burn became less. As he looked at her solemn face and the weight she seemed to carry, he reached up and touched her retreating hand.

"Jiriki spoke to you truthfully, manchild," she said. "For better or for worse, you *have* been marked. I only wish I could give you some word to help you on your journey."

The light faded again. Simon let Jirki lead him out in darkness.

26

Painted Eyes

Miriamele leaned against the railing, watching the bustle and activity of the docks. Vinitta was not a large island, but its ruling Benidrivine house had provided Nabban's final two Imperators, as well as its three dukes under Prester John's kingship. It had also been the birthplace of the legendary Camaris, but even so great a knight was accorded only a middling-high place in Vinitta's luminous, hero-studded history. The port was a busy one: with Benigaris on the ducal throne, the fortunes of Vinitta still ran high.

Aspitis Preves and his captain had gone down into the town to accomplish their business. What that might be, Miriamele could not say. The earl had intimated that he had some important mission direct from Duke Benigaris, but that was as far as he would discuss the subject. Aspitis had bade both Miriamele and Cadrach stay on board until he returned, suggesting that the port was not the place for a noble lady to wander, and that he had not enough men-at-arms available to handle his own affairs safely and still detach a pair of soldiers for their protection.

Miriamele knew what this meant. Whatever Aspitis thought of her, however he valued her beauty and company, he did not intend to give her the chance to slip away. Perhaps he harbored some doubts about her story, or simply worried that she might be persuaded to leave by Cadrach, who had made little attempt to disguise his growing hatred of the Earl of Eadne and Drina.

She sighed, gazing sadly at the rows of tented booths that ran along the dockfront, each one festooned with flags and crammed with goods for sale. Hawkers cried their wares as they shuffled along the road, carrying their stock on their backs in huge, overstuffed bags. Dancers and musicians performed for coins, and the sailors of various boats mingled with Vinitta's residents in a shouting, laughing, swearing throng. Despite the dark skies and intermittent flurries of rain, the crowds that swarmed the waterfront seemed bent on making a cheerful ruckus. Miriamele's heart ached to join them.

Cadrach stood beside her, pink face paler than usual. The monk had not spoken much since Aspitis' pronouncement; he had watched the earl's party leave the *Eadne Cloud* with much the same sour expression as he now leveled on the activity below.

"God," he said, "but it makes a man sick to see such heedlessness." It was not exactly clear what his remark addressed, but Miriamele felt it rankle nonetheless.

"And you," she snapped. "You are better? A drunkard and coward?"

Cadrach's large head came around, moving as ponderously as a millwheel. "It is my very heedfulness that makes me so, Lady. I have watched *too* carefully."

"Watched what? Oh, never mind. I am not in the mood for one of your roundabout lectures." She shivered with anger, but could not summon the sense of righteousness she sought. Cadrach had grown more remote over the last few days, observing her from what seemed a disapproving distance. This irritated her, but the continuing flirtation between herself and the earl made even Miriamele somewhat uncomfortable. It was hard to feel truly justified in her irritation, but it was harder still to have Cadrach's gray eyes staring at her as though she were a child or a misbehaving animal. "Why don't you go and complain to some of the sailors?" she said at last. "See how well *they'll* listen to you."

The monk folded his arms. He spoke patiently, but did not meet her eyes. "Will you not listen to me, Lady? This last time? My advice is not half so bad as you make out and you know it. How long will you listen to the honeyed words of this . . . this court beauty? You are like his little bird that he takes from the cage to play with, then puts back. He does not care for you."

"You are a strange person to talk of that, Brother Cadrach. The earl has given us the captain's cabin, fed us at his own table, and treated me with complete respect." Her heart sped a little as she remembered Aspitis' mouth at her ear, his firm, gentle touch. "You, on the other hand, have lied to me, taken money for my freedom, and struck me senseless. Only a madman could put himself forward as the better friend after all that."

Now Cadrach did lift his eyes, holding her gaze for a long moment. He seemed to be looking for something, and his probing inspection brought warmth to her cheeks. She made a mocking face and turned away.

"Very well, Lady," he said. From the corner of his eye she saw him shrug and walk off down the deck. "It seems they teach little of kindness or forgiving in Usires' church these days," he said over his shoulder.

Miriamele blinked back angry tears. "You are the religious man, Cadrach, not me. If that is true, you are the best example!" She did not receive much pleasure from her own harsh rejoinder.

*   *   *

When she had tired of watching the dockyard crowds, Miriamele went down to her cabin. The monk was sitting there, staring resolutely at nothing. Miriamele did not want to speak to him, so she turned and made her way above deck once more, then paced restlessly back and forth along the length of the *Eadne Cloud.* Those of the ship's crew who had remained on board were refitting her for the outgoing voyage, some clambering in the rigging checking the state of the sails, others effecting various small repairs here and there about the deck. This was to be their only night on Vinitta, so the crewmen fairly flew through their tasks in a hurry to get ashore.

Soon Miriamele found herself at the rail by the top of the gangplank, staring down once more at the eddying citizenry of the island. As the cool, moist wind ruffled her hair, she found herself thinking about what Cadrach had said. Could he be right? She knew that Aspitis had a flattering tongue, but could it be possible he did not care for her at all? Miriamele remembered their first night on deck, and the other sweet and secret kisses he had stolen from her since, and knew that the monk was wrong. She did not pretend that Aspitis loved her with all his soul—she doubted that her face tormented him at sleeping time, as his did to her—but she also knew beyond question that he was fond of her, and that was more than could be said of the other men she knew. Her father had wanted her to marry that horrible, drunken braggart Fengbald, and her uncle Josua had just wanted her to sit quietly and not cause him any trouble.

But there was Simon . . . she thought, and felt a flicker of warmth cut through the gray morning. He had been sweet in his foolish way, yet brave as any of the noblemen she had seen. But he was a scullion and she a king's daughter . . . and what did it matter anyway? They were on opposite sides of the world. They would never meet again.

Something touched her arm, startling her. She whirled to find the wrinkled face of Gan Itai gazing up into hers. The Niskie's usual look of wily good humor was absent.

"Girl, I need to speak to you," the old one said.

"Wh–what?" Something in the Niskie's expression was alarming.

"I had a dream. A dream about you—and about bad times." Gan Itai ducked her head, then turned and looked out to sea before turning back. "The dream said you were in danger, Miri . . ."

The Niskie broke off, looking past Miriamele's shoulder. The princess leaned forward. Had she misheard, or had Gan Itai been about to call her by her true name? But that could not be: no one beside Cadrach knew who she was, and she doubted that the monk would have told anyone on the ship—what such news might bring was too unpredictable, and Cadrach was trapped out on the ocean just as she was. No, it must have been only the Niskie's odd way of speaking.

"Ho! Lovely lady!" A cheerful voice rang up from dockside. "It is a wet morning, but perhaps you would like to see Vinitta?"

Miriamele whirled. Aspitis stood at the base of the gangplank with his men-at-arms. The earl wore a beautiful blue cloak and shiny boots. His hair danced in the wind.

"Oh, yes!" she said, pleased and excited. How wonderful it would be to get off this ship! "I'll be right down!"

When she turned, Gan Itai had vanished. Miriamele frowned slightly, puzzled. She suddenly thought of the monk sitting stone-faced in the cabin they shared and felt a twinge of pity for him.

"Shall I bring Brother Cadrach?" she called down.

Aspitis laughed. "Certainly! We may find use in having a holy man with us who can talk us out of temptations! That way we may come back with a few cintis-pieces left in our purses!"

Miriamele ran downstairs to tell Cadrach. He looked at her oddly, but drew on his boots, then carefully chose just the right heavy cloak before following her back up the ladder.

The wind rose and the rainshowers became heavier. Although at first it was enough merely to walk along the busy waterfront with the handsome, sociable earl beside her, soon Miriamele's excitement at being off the ship began to wear away. Despite the pushing crowd, Vinitta's narrow streets seemed sad and gray. When Aspitis bought her a chain of bluebells from a flower seller and tenderly hung them around her neck, she found it all she could do to smile for him.

It is the weather, she guessed. *This unnatural weather has turned high summer into a dismal gray murk and put the cold right into my bones.*

She thought of her father sitting alone in his room, of the chilly, distant face he sometimes wore like a mask—a mask that he had come to wear more and more frequently in her last months in the Hayholt. *Cold bones and cold hearts,* she sang quietly to herself as the Earl of Eadne led his party down Vinitta's rain-slicked byways.

> *Cold bones and cold hearts*
> *Lie in the rain in battle's wake,*
> *On chilly beach by Clodu-lake,*
> *'Til Aedon's trumpet calls . . .*

Just before noon Aspitis took them into an eating hall, where Miriamele immediately felt her flagging spirits begin to revive. The hall had a high ceiling, but the three large fire pits kept it warm and cheery while at the same time filling the air with smoke and the smell of roasting meat. Many others had decided the hall might be a nice place to be on this bitter morning: the rafters echoed with the tumult of diners and drinkers. The master of the hall and his several assistants were being worked to the utmost, thumping jugs of beer and bowls of wine onto the wooden tables, then snatching the proffered coins in a single continuous movement.

A crude stage had been set up at the hall's far end. At the moment a boy was juggling between acts of a puppet play, doing his best to keep several sticks in the air while suffering the drunken jests of spectators, using his feet—his only available extremities—to stop the occasional coin that came bouncing up onto the stage.

"Will you have something to eat, fair lady?" Aspitis asked. When Miriamele nodded shyly, he dispatched two of his men-at-arms. His other guardsmen unceremoniously removed a large family from one of the pitted tables. Soon the original pair of soldiers returned with a crackling haunch of lamb, bread, onions, and a generous supply of wine.

A bowlful soon drove away much of Miriamele's chill, and she found that the morning's walk had given her a considerable appetite. The noon bell had scarcely rung before her food was gone. She readjusted her position on the seat, trying to avoid an unladylike belch.

"Look," she said, "they're starting the puppet play. Can we watch?"

"Certainly," Aspitis said, waving his hand generously. "Certainly. You will forgive me if I do not come with you. I have not finished my meal. Besides, it looks like a Usires play. You will not think me disrespectful if I say that, living in the lap of Mother Church, I see them frequently enough—in all varieties, from the grandest to the meanest." He turned and signaled one of his men to accompany her. "It is not a good idea for a well-dressed gentle lady like yourself to go unprotected among the milling crowd."

"I am done eating," Cadrach said, standing. "I will come too, Lady Marya." The monk fell in beside the earl's guardsman.

The play was in full swing. The spectators, especially the children, shrieked with delight as the puppets capered and smacked each other with their slapping-sticks. Miriamele, too, laughed as Usires tricked Crexis into bending over, then delivered a kick in the seat to the evil Imperator, but her smile soon faded. Instead of his usual horns, Crexis wore what looked like a crown of antlers. For some reason this filled her with unease. There was also something panicky and desperate in Usires' high-pitched voice, and the puppet's painted, upturned eyes seemed unutterably sad. She turned to find Cadrach looking at her somberly.

"So we labor to build our little dams," the monk said, barely audible above the shouting throng, "while the waters rise all around us." He made the sign of the Tree above his gray vestments.

Before she could ask him what he meant, a rising howl from the crowd drew her attention back to the puppet stage. Usires had been caught and hung wrongside-up on the Execution Tree, wooden head dangling. As Crexis the Goat prodded the helpless savior, another puppet appeared, rising from the darkness. This one was clothed all in orange and red tatters of cloth; as it swayed from side to side in an eerie dance, the rags swirled, as though the puppet were covered with licking flames. Its head was a black, faceless knob, and it carried a small wooden sword the color of mud.

"Here comes the Fire Dancer to throw you down into the dark earth!" Crexis squealed. The Imperator did a little dance of joy.

"I do not live by the sword," the puppet Usires said. *"A sword cannot harm that which is God within me, that which is silence and peace."* Miriamele almost believed she could see its motionless lips mouthing the words.

"You can be silent forever, then—and worship your God in pieces!" the Imperator shouted triumphantly as the faceless Fire Dancer began to hack with its sword. The laughing, screaming crowd grew louder, a sound like hounds at the kill. Miriamele felt dizzy, taken as though with a sudden fever. Fear growing within her, she turned away from the stage.

Cadrach no longer stood beside her.

Miriamele turned to the guardsman on the other side. The soldier, seeing her questioning look, whirled in search of the monk. Cadrach was nowhere to be seen.

A search of the eating hall by Aspitis and his men turned up no trace of the Hernystirman. The earl marched his party back to the *Eadne Cloud* through the windswept streets, his furious mood mirroring the angry skies. He was silent all the long walk back to the ship.

Sinetris the fisherman looked the new arrival up and down. The stranger was a full head taller than him, broad as a gate, and soaking wet from the rain that hammered on the ceiling of the boat stall. Sinetris weighed the advantages and disadvantages of circling slowly around this newcomer until he could address the man from outside the tiny shelter. The disadvantages of such a plan were clear: it was the kind of day today that made even the hardiest shiver by the fire and praise God for roofs. Also, it was Sinetris' own stall, and it seemed terribly unfair that he should have to go outside so that this stranger could growl and champ and suck up all the air while the fisherman stood miserably in the storm.

The advantages, however, were equally clear. If he were outside, Sinetris could run for his life when this panting madman finally became murderous.

"I don't know what you're saying, Father. There are no boats out today. You see how it is." Sinetris gestured out at the sheeting rain, flung almost sideways by the force of the wind.

The religious man stared at him furiously. The gigantic monk, if that was indeed what he was, had gone quite red and mottled in the face, and his eyebrows twitched. Strangely enough, Sinetris thought the monk seemed to be growing a beard: his whiskers were longer than even a week's razorless travel would cause. To the best of the fisherman's knowledge, Aedonite monks did not wear beards. Then, again, this one was some kind of barbarous northerner by his accent, a Rimmersman or some such: Sinetris supposed that those born beyond the River Gleniwent would be capable of just about any eccentricity. As he looked at the ragged whiskers and the chafed pink skin gleaming beneath, his unwholesome opinion of the monk grew more pronounced. This was definitely a man with whom to have as little to do as possible.

"I don't think you understand me, fisherman," the monk hissed, leaning forward and squinting in a truly frightening way. "I have come nearly through Hell itself to get this far. I'm told that you are the only one who would take his boat out in such bad weather—and that the reason is because you overcharge." A beefy hand closed on Sinetris' arm, occasioning a squeal of shock. "Splendid. Cheat me, rob me, I don't care. But I'm going downcoast to Kwanitipul and I'm tired of asking people to take me. Do you understand?"

"B–but you could go overland!" Senitris squeaked. "This is no weather to be on the water . . ."

"And how long would it take to go overland from here?"

"A day! Two, perhaps! Not long!"

The monk's grip on his arm tightened cruelly. "You lie, little man. In this weather, through that marshy ground, it would take me a solid fortnight. But you're rather hoping I'll try, though, aren't you? Hoping I'll go away and sink into the mud somewhere?" An unpleasant smile flitted across the monk's broad face.

"No, Father! No! I would never think so of a holy man!"

"That's strange, because your fellow fishermen tell me you've cheated everyone, monks and priests by the score among 'em! Well, you shall have your chance to help a man of God—and you shall have your just and more than ample payment."

Sinetris burst into tears, impressing even himself. "But Eminence! We truly dare not go out in such weather!" As he said it, he realized that for once he was telling the truth and not merely trying to raise his price. This was weather that only a fool would brave. His pleading took on a note of greater desperation. "We will drown—you, God's holiest priest, and poor Sinetris, hard-working husband and father to seven lovely children!"

"You have no children, and pity the woman who will ever be your wife. I talked to your fishing-fellows, don't you remember? You are the scum that even Perdruin the Mercenary has driven from her shores. Now, name your price, damn you. I must get to Kwanitipul as soon as possible."

Sinetris sniffled a bit to give himself time to think. The standard ferrying charge was one quinis, but with rough weather—and they certainly had that today, with no exaggeration—three or even four quinis would not be out of line.

"Three gold Imperators." He waited for the bellow of anger. When none came, he thought for a delirious moment he might have made his summer's income in two days. Then he saw the pink face drawing close, until the monk's breath was hot on his cheeks.

"You worm," the monk said softly. "There is a difference between simple robbery and rape. I think I should just fold you up like a napkin and take the damnable boat—leaving a gold Imperator for your imaginary widow and seven nonexistent brats, which is more than the whole leaky thing is worth."

"Two gold Imperators, Eminence? One for my imag . . . widow, one to purchase a mansa for my poor soul at the church?"

"One, and you know that is a gross overpayment. It is only because I am in a hurry. And we will leave now."

"Now? But the boat is not fitted out. . . ! "

"I'll watch." The monk let go of Sinetris' throbbing wrist and folded his arms across his broad chest. "Go ahead, now. Hop to it!"

"But kind Father, what about my gold piece. . . ? "

"When we get to Kwanitupul. Do not fear you will be cheated, as you have cheated others. Am I not a man of God?" The strange monk laughed.

Sinetris, snuffling quietly, went looking for his oars.

"You said you had more gold!" Charystra, the proprietress of the inn known as *Pelippa's Bowl* put on a practiced look of disgust. "I treated you like a prince—you, a little marsh-man—and you lied to me! I should have known better than to trust a dirty Wrannaman."

Tiamak struggled to keep his temper. "I think, good lady, that you have done very well from me. I paid you on arrival with two gold Imperators."

She snorted. "Well, it's all spent."

"In a fortnight? You accuse me of lying, Charystra, but that might as well be theft."

"How dare you speak that way to me! You had the best accommodations and the services of the best healer in Kwanitupul."

The ache of Tiamak's wounds only added to his anger. "If you are referring to that drunken person who came to twist my leg and hurt me, I am sure his fee was scarcely more than a bottle or two of fern beer. As a matter of fact, he appeared to have enjoyed the payments of a few other victims before he came here."

The irony! To think that Tiamak, author of the soon-to-be definitive revision of *Sovran Remedys of the Wranna Healers*, should be forced into the care of a dryland butcher!

"Anyway, I am lucky I kept my leg," he growled. "Besides, you moved me out of the best accommodations quickly enough." Tiamak waved his thin arm at the nest of blankets he now shared with Ceallio, the simpleminded door keeper.

The innkeeper's frown turned into a smirk. "Aren't you very high and cocksure for a marsh-man? Well, get on with you, then. Go to some other inn and see if they'll treat a Wrannaman as kindly as Charystra has."

Tiamak choked back a furious reply. He knew he must not let his anger get the better of him. He was being dreadfully cheated by this woman, but that was how things always went when Wrannamen put their fortunes in the hands of drylanders. He had already failed his tribe, on whose behalf he had sworn to go to Nabban and argue their case against higher tribute. If he were thrown out of *Pelippa's Bowl*, he would fail Morgenes as well, who had explicitly asked for him to stay at this inn until he was needed.

Tiamak offered a short prayer for patience to He Who Always Steps on Sand. If his staying in such a place was so important to Dinivan and Morgenes, couldn't they at least have sent him money with which to pay for it? He took a deep breath, hating to grovel before this red-faced woman.

"It is foolish to fight, good lady," he said finally. "I am still expecting that my friend will show up, bringing more gold." Tiamak forced himself to smile. "Until then, I think I still have some little bit of my two Imperators remaining. Surely it is not all spent quite yet? If I have to leave, someone else will be earning gold for giving *their* best accommodations to me and my friend."

She stared at him for a moment, weighing the advantages of throwing him out against the possibility of future money-gouging. "Well . . ." she said grudgingly, "perhaps out of the goodness of my heart I could let you stay another three days. But no meals, mind you. You'll have to come up with more coins, or else find your own food. I set a lavish table for my guests and can't afford to give it away."

Tiamak knew that the lavish table consisted mostly of thin soup and dried bread, but also knew that even such meager fare was better than nothing. He would have to feed himself somehow. He was used to going long on little provender, but he was still quite weak from his leg wounds and resulting illness. How he would love to bounce a sling-stone off this woman's mocking face!

"Very fair, my lady." He gritted his teeth. "Very fair."

"My friends always say I'm too good."

Charystra swaggered back into the common room, leaving Tiamak to cover his head with his odoriferous blanket and contemplate the grim state of his affairs.

*   *   *

Tiamak lay sleeplessly in the dark. His mind was spinning, but he could think of no solution to his problems. He could barely walk. He was stranded without resources in a strange place, among bandit drylanders. It seemed that They Who Watch and Shape had conspired to torment him.

The old man Ceallio grunted in his sleep and rolled over, his long arm flopping heavily against Tiamak's face. Painfully thumped, the Wrannaman moaned and sat up. It was no use being upset with the ancient simpleton: Ceallio was no more to blame for their uncomfortable proximity than was Tiamak himself. The Wrannaman wondered if Ceallio was upset at having to share his bed, but somehow he doubted it. The cheerful old man was as guileless as a child; he seemed to accept everything that came his way— blows, kicks, and curses included—as acts of fate, unfathomable and un- avoidable as thunderstorms.

Thinking of evil weather, Tiamak shivered. The hovering storm that had turned the air of the Wran and all the southern coast hot and sticky as broth had fallen at last, drenching Kwanitupul in unseasonable rains. The normally placid canals had turned choppy and unpredictable. Most ships rode at anchor, slowing the business of the thriving port city to a crawl. The heavy storm had also nearly choked off the flow of new visitors, which was another reason for Charystra's unpleasantness.

Tonight the rain had stopped for the first time in several days. Not long after Tiamak had crawled into his insufficient bed, the constant rattle on the roof had suddenly gone silent, a silence so deep it seemed almost like another noise. Perhaps, he thought, it was this unaccustomed silence that made it so hard to sleep.

Shivering again, Tiamak tried to pull his blanket closer about him, but the old man beside him had caught up the whole tangle in a death-grip. Despite his advanced age, the fool seemed to be a great deal stronger than Tiamak, who even before his unfortunate brush with the crocodile had never been robust, even by the standards of his small-boned people. The Wrannaman ceased struggling for the covers; Ceallio gurgled and mur- mured in the throes of some dream of past happiness. Tiamak frowned. Why had he ever left his house in the banyan tree, in his beloved, familiar swamp? It was not much, but it was his. And unlike this drafty, damp boat-house, it had always been warm. . . .

This was more than just night-cold, he realized suddenly, wracked by more shivers. There was a chill in the air that pierced the chest like daggers. He initiated another doomed struggle for blankets, then sat up again in despair. Perhaps the door had been left open?

Giving vent to a full-throated groan of anguish, he crawled away from his bed, forcing himself to stand. His leg throbbed and burned. The tosspot healer had said that his poultices would take the pain away soon enough, but Tiamak had little faith in such an obvious drunkard, and so far his doubts had been borne out. He limped slowly across the rough wood floor, doing his best to avoid the two upended boats that dominated the room. He managed to stay near the wall and thus evade these large obstacles, but a hard stool leaped up before him and cruelly battered his good shin, so that for a moment Tiamak had to stop and bite his lip as he rubbed the leg, holding in a screech of pain and anger that he feared would have no ending. Why had he and he alone been singled out for such ill treatment?

When he could walk once more, he continued with even more care, so that his journey to the door seemed to take hours. When he reached it at last he discovered to his immense disappointment that the door was shut; there seemed little more he could do to prevent himself from spending a sleepless and freezing night. As he thumped his hand against the frame in frustration, the door swung open to reveal the empty pier outside, a dim gray rectangle in the moonlight. A blast of chill air rolled over him, but before he could grasp the elusive handle and pull the door closed again, something caught his eye. Baffled, he took a couple of limping steps out through the doorway. There was something odd about the fine mist that floated down through the moonlight.

A long moment passed before Tiamak realized that it was not rain that dotted his outstretched palm, but rather tiny flakes of white. He had never seen this thing before—no Wrannaman ever had—but he was unusually well-read, and had also heard it described many times in his student days. It took only a moment for him to understand the significance of the downy flakes and the vapor that rose from his own lips to drift and dissipate on the night air.

Snow was falling on Kwanitupul, in the heart of summer.

Miriamele lay in her bed in darkness and wept until she was too tired to weep any longer. As *Eadne Cloud* rocked at anchor in Vinitta's harbor, she felt loneliness pressing down on her like a great weight.

It was not so much Cadrach's betrayal: despite her moments of weakness toward him, the monk had shown his true colors long ago. It was rather that he was her last link with her true self, with her past life. As if an anchor-rope had been cut, she felt herself suddenly adrift in a sea of strangers.

Cadrach's desertion had not been a complete surprise. So little good feeling remained between the two of them that it seemed only circumstance had kept him from deserting her earlier. She looked back on the cool deliberateness he had shown in selecting his traveling cloak before they left the boat and saw that he had clearly anticipated this escape, at least from the moment they had been summoned down to Vinitta. In a way, he had tried to warn her, hadn't he? On the deck he had asked her to listen, saying "this last time."

The monk's betrayal was unsurprising, but the pain was no less heavy for that. A long-anticipated blow had fallen at last.

Desertion and indifference. That seemed to be the thread that ran through her life. Her mother had died, her father had changed into something cold and uncaring, her uncle Josua had only wished her out of his way—he would deny it, no doubt, but it had been plain in his every word and expression. For a while she had thought Dinivan and his master the lector could shelter her, but they had died and left her friendless. Although she knew it was not even remotely their fault, she still could not forgive.

No one would help her. The kinder ones, like Simon and the troll or dear old Duke Isgrimnur, were absent or powerless. Now Cadrach, too, had left her.

There must be something inside of her that pushed others away, Miriamele brooded—some stain like the dark discoloration in the white stone canals of Meremund, hidden until the tide went out. Or maybe it was not in her at all, but in the souls of those around her, those who could not stay rooted to obligation, who could not remember their duty to a young woman.

And what of Aspitis, the golden earl? She had little hope that he would prove more responsible than the others, but at least he cared for her. At least he wanted her for something.

Perhaps when all was over, when her father had reshaped the world in whatever way pleased his corrupt fancy, she would be able to find a home somewhere. She would be happy with a small house by the sea, would gladly shed her unwanted royalty like an old snakeskin. But until then, what should she do?

Miriamele rolled over and pushed her face into the rough blanket, feeling the bed and the entire ship moving in the sea's gentle but insistent grip. It was all too much, too many thoughts, too many questions. She felt quite strengthless. She wanted only to be held, to be protected, to let time slip away until she could wake into a better world.

She cried quietly, fretfully, anchorless on the edge of sleep.

The afternoon slipped past. Miriamele lay in the darkness of her cabin, wandering in and out of dreams.

Somewhere above, the lookout cried sunset; no other sound intruded but the lap of waves and the muffled cry of sea birds. The ship was all but deserted, the sailing men ashore in Vinitta.

Miriamele was not surprised when the cabin door quietly opened at last and a weight pressed down on the bed beside her.

Aspitis' finger traced her features. Miriamele turned away, wishing she could pull the shadows over her like a blanket, wishing she were a child again, living beside an ocean that was still innocent of kilpa, an ocean upon whose waves storms touched only lightly and disappeared at the sun's golden rising.

"My lady . . ." he whispered. "Ah, I am so sorry. You have been badly treated."

Miriamele said nothing, but his voice seemed a soothing balm to her painful thoughts. He spoke again, telling her of her beauty and kindness. In her feverish sadness the words were little more than nonsense, but his voice was sweet and reassuring. She felt calmed by it, gentled like a nervous horse. When he slid beneath the sheet she felt his skin against hers, warm and smooth and firm. She murmured in protest, but softly, with no real strength: in a way, this, too, seemed a kindness.

His mouth was at her neck. His hands moved over her with calm possessiveness, as though he handled some lovely thing that belonged only to him. Tears came to her again. Full of loneliness, she let herself be drawn into his embrace, but she could not suffer his touch unfeelingly. While a part of her yearned only to be held, to be drawn into a reassuring warmth, a safe harbor like the one in which *Eadne Cloud* rocked gently at anchor, untroubled by the storms that swept the great ocean, a different self wished to break free and run madly into danger. Still another shadow huddled deeper within her, a shape of dark regret, tied to her heart with chains of iron.

The thin light leaking in at the doorframe caught glimmering in his hair as Aspitis pressed himself against her. What if someone should come in? There was no latch, no latch on the door. She struggled. Mistaking her fear, he whispered soothing things about her beauty.

Each curl of his hair was intricate, textured and individual as a tree. His head seemed a forest, his dark form looming like a distant mountainside. She cried out softly, unable to resist such implacability.

Time slid by in the shadows and Miriamele felt herself drifting away. Aspitis once more began to speak.

He loved her, her goodness and wit and loveliness.

His words, like caresses, were blind but enflaming. She did not care for flattering talk, but felt her resistance melting before his strength and sureness. He cared for her, at least a little. He could hide her away in darkness, pull it around her like a cloak. She would disappear into the deeps of a sheltering forest until the world was right again.

The boat swayed gently on the cradling waters.

He would protect her from those who would harm her, he said. He would never desert her.

She gave herself up to him at last. There was pain, but there were also promises. Miriamele had hoped for nothing more. In a way, it was a lesson the world had already taught her.

★ ★ ★

Awash with strange new feelings, not completely comfortable with any of them, Miriamele sat quietly across the dining table from Aspitis, pushing food from one side of her plate to the other. She could not understand why the earl had forced her to come sit with him in the brightly candlelit room. She could not understand why she was not even slightly in love.

A soldier rapped at the doorway, then entered.

"We've caught him, Lord," the guardsman said. His satisfaction at having redressed the earlier error of the monk's escape was plain in his voice. Miriamele, seated across the table from Earl Aspitis, felt herself stiffen.

The guardsman stepped aside and two of his fellows brought Cadrach in, slumped between them. The monk seemed to be having trouble keeping his head up. Had they beaten him? Miriamele felt a sickening pang of regret. She had half-hoped that Cadrach would just vanish, so that she would never have to see him again. It was easier to hate him when he was not around.

"He's drunk, Lord Aspitis," the guardsman said. "Stinking. We found him in the *Feathered Eel*, down on the east dock. He'd already bought a place out on a Perdruinese merchantman, but the fool got pissed and diced it away."

Cadrach looked up blearily, his face slack with despair. Even from across the table, Miriamele could smell the stink of wine. "Was 'bout t'win it back, too. Would've." He shook his head. "Maybe not. Luck's gone bad. Water's rising . . ."

Aspitis rose and strode around the table. He reached out a hand and grasped the monk's chin, pressing with his strong fingers until the flesh bulged between them. He forced Cadrach's pink face upward until their eyes met.

The earl turned to Miriamele. "Has he tried to do this before, Lady Marya?"

Miriamele nodded helplessly. She wished she were somewhere else. "More or less."

Aspitis returned his attention to the monk. "What a strange man. Why does he not just leave your father's service instead of sneaking away like a thief?" The earl turned to his squire. "And you are sure nothing is missing?"

The squire shook his head. "Nothing, Lord."

Cadrach tried to pull his head free from Aspitis' restraining fingers. "Had m'own gold. Stole nothing. Need t'get away . . ." His eyes fixed uncertainly on Miriamele, his voice took on a note of added desperation. "Dangerous . . . storm will get us. Danger."

The Earl of Eadne let go of the monk's chin and wiped his fingers on the tablecloth. "Afraid of a storm? I knew he was not a good sailor, but still . . . that is very strange. If he were *my* liege man, his back would be flayed for this trick. Still, the fellow shall certainly not be rewarded for deserting his innocent ward. Neither shall he share a cabin with you any more, Lady Marya." The earl's smile was stiffy reassuring. "He may have gone mad, or have conceived some drunken fancy. He says danger, but *he* is the dangerous one as I see it. He will be confined on the *Eadne Cloud* until I return you to Nabban, and we shall then hand him over to Mother Church for discipline."

"Confine him?" Miriamele asked. "That is not . . ."

"I may not leave him loose to plague you or worry you, my lady." The earl turned to his guardsmen. "The hold will do nicely for him. Give him water and bread, but put the leg irons on him."

"Oh, no!" Miriamele was genuinely horrified. However much she despised the monk and his cowardly treachery, the thought of any living thing forced to wear a chain, trapped in a dark hold. . . .

"Please, my lady." Aspitis' voice was soft but firm. "I must have order on my ship. I gave you sanctuary, and this man with you. He was your guardian. He betrayed your trust. I still am not sure he has not stolen something from me, or perhaps thinks to sell some intelligence of my mission here in Vinitta. No, I am afraid you must leave such men's business to me, pretty Marya." He waved his hand; Cadrach was led out, staggering between his escorts.

Miriamele felt her eyes blurring with tears. They spilled over and she lurched suddenly from her chair. "Excuse me, Earl Aspitis," she mumbled, feeling her way along the table toward the door. "I wish to lie down."

He caught her before she reached the handle, grasping her arm and pulling her smoothly around. The heat of him was very close. She averted her face, conscious of how foolish she must look, eyes red-rimmed and cheeks wet. "Please, my lord. Let the monk go."

"I know you must feel quite lost, pretty Marya," Aspitis said softly. "Do not fear. I promised that I would keep you safe."

She felt herself yielding, becoming pliant. Her strength seemed to be draining away. She was so tired of running and hiding. She had only wanted someone to hold her, to make everything go away. . . .

Miriamele shivered and pulled away. "No. It is wrong. Wrong! If you do not let him go, I will not stay on this ship!" She pushed out through the door, stumbling blindly.

Aspitis caught her long before she reached the ladder to the deck. The sea watcher Gan Itai was crooning quietly in the darkness above.

"You are upset, Lady," he said. "You must lie down, as you said yourself."

She struggled, but his grip was firm. "I demand that you release me! I do not wish to stay here any longer. I will go ashore and find my own passage from Vinitta."

"No, my lady, you will not."

She gasped. "Let go of my arm. You're hurting me."

Somewhere above, Gan Itai's song seemed to falter.

Aspitis leaned forward. His face was very close to hers. "I think there are things that must be made clear between us." He laughed shortly. "As a matter of fact, there is *much* for us to talk about—later. You will go to your cabin now. I will finish my supper and then come to you."

"I won't go."

"You will."

He said it with such quiet certainty that her angry reply caught in her throat as fear clutched her. Aspitis pulled her close against him, then turned and forced her along the passageway.

The sea watcher's song had stopped. Now it began again, rising and fading as Gan Itai murmured to the night and the quiet sea.

27

The Black Sled

"**They** are getting close," Sludig gasped. "If your Farewell Stone is more than half a league from here, little man, we will have to turn and fight."

Shaking the water from his hood, Binabik leaned forward across Qantaqa's neck. The wolf's tongue lolled and her sides heaved like a blacksmith's bellows. They had been traveling without a stop since daybreak, fleeing through the storm-battered forest.

"I wish I could be telling you that it is near, Sludig. I do not know how much distance remains, but I fear it is most of a day's riding." The troll stroked Qantaqa's sodden fur. "A brave run, old friend." She ignored him, absorbed in drinking rainwater from the hollow stump of a tree.

"The giants are hunting us," Sludig said grimly. "They have developed a taste for man-meat." He shook his head. "When we make our stand at last, some of them will regret that."

Binabik frowned. "I have too little size to be a satisfying morsel, so I will not waste their time by being caught. That way, no one will be having regrets."

The Rimmersman steered his mount over to the stump. Trembling with the cold, parched despite the pelting rain, the horse was heedless of the wolf a handsbreadth away.

As their steeds drank, a long rumbling howl lifted above the wind, blood-freezingly close.

"Damn me!" Sludig spat, slapping his palm against his sword-hilt. "They are no farther behind us than they were an hour ago! Do they run fast as horses?"

"Near to it, it is seeming," Binabik said. "I am thinking we should move deeper into the forest. The thicker trees may slow them."

"You thought getting off the flatlands would slow them, too," Sludig said, reining his reluctant horse away from the hollow stump.

"If we live, then you can be telling me all my incorrectness," Binabik growled. He took a tight grip on the thick fur that mantled Qantaqa's neck. "Now, unless you have been thinking of ways to fly, we should ride."

Another deep, coughing cry came down the wind.

Sludig's sword swished from side to side, clearing the brush as they pushed their way down the long, wooded slope. "My blade will be dull when I have greatest need," he complained.

Binabik, who was leading the string of balking horses, tripped and fell to the muddy earth, then slid a short way down the hillside. The horses milled nervously, confined to the path Sludig had hacked in the swarming undergrowth. Struggling to keep his balance in the mud, the troll got up and tracked down the bridle of the lead horse.

"Qinkipa of the Snows! This storm is never-ending!"

They took most of the noon hour to make their way down the slope. It appeared that Binabik's reliance on the forest cover had been at least partially correct: the occasional howls of the Hunën became a little fainter, although they never faded completely. The forest appeared to be growing thinner. The trees were still huge, but not as monumental as their kin that grew closer to Aldheorte's center.

The trees, alder and oak and tall hemlock, were garlanded in looping vines. The grass and undergrowth grew thick, and even in this queerly cold season a few yellow and blue wildflowers lifted their heads up from the mud, bobbing beneath the heavy rain. Had it not been for the torrent and the biting wind, this arm of the southern forest would have been a place of rare beauty.

They reached the base of the slope at last and clambered onto a low shelf of stone to scrape the worst of the mud from their boots and clothing before riding once more. Sludig looked back up the hillside, then lifted a pointing finger.

"Elysia's mercy, little man, look."

Far up the slope but still horribly near, a half-dozen white shapes were pushing their way through the foliage, long arms swinging like Nascadu apes. One lifted its head, the face a black hole against the pale, shaggy fur. A cry of thundering menace rang down the rainy hillside and Sludig's horse pranced in terror beneath him.

"It is a race," Binabik said. His round, brown face had gone quite pale. "For this moment, they are having the best of it."

Qantaqa leaped from the shelf of stone, bearing the troll with her. Sludig and his mount were just behind, leading the other horses. Hooves drummed on the sodden ground.

In their haste and ill-suppressed fear, it was some while before they noticed that the ground, while still overgrown, had become unusually flat.

They rode beside long-empty riverbeds that were now filled anew with rushing, foaming rainwater. Here and there bits of root-gnawed stone stood along the banks, covered with centuries of moss and clinging vines.

"These look like bridges, or the bones of broken buildings," Sludig called as they rode.

"They are," Binabik replied. "It means we are nearing our goal, I hope. This is a place where once the Sithi had a great city." He leaned forward, hugging Qantaqa's neck as she leaped over a fallen trunk.

"Do you think it will keep the giants at bay?" Sludig asked. "You said that the diggers did not like the places that the Sithi lived."

"They do not like the forest and the forest does not like them," the troll said, gentling Qantaqa to a halt. "The giant Hunën seem to be having no such trouble—perhaps because they are less clever, or less easily frightened. Or because they are not digging. I do not know." He tilted his head, listening. It was hard to hear anything over the relentless hissing patter of rain on leaves, but for the moment the surroundings seemed innocent of danger. "We will follow the flowing water." He pointed to the new-grown river hurrying past them, laden with broken branches knocked loose by the storm. "Sesuad'ra, the Stone of Farewell, is in the valley beside the forest's ending, very close to the city Enki-e-Shao'saye—on whose outskirts we are sitting." He gestured around him with his stubby, mittened hand. "The river must be flowing down to the valley, so it is sense for us to accompany it."

"Less talking, then—more accompanying," Sludig said.

"I have been speaking, in my day," Binabik said with a certain stiffness, "to more appreciative ears." With a shrug, he urged Qantaqa forward.

They rode past countless remnants of the vast and long untenanted city. Fragments of old walls shimmered in the undergrowth, masses of pale, crumbled brick forlorn as lost sheep; in other spots the foundations of eroded towers lay exposed, curved and empty as ancient jawbones, choked with parasitic moss. Unlike Da'ai Chikiza, the forest had done more than grow into Enki-e-Shao'saye: there was virtually nothing left of this city but faint traces. The forest, it seemed, had always been a part of the place, but over the millennia it had become a destroyer, smothering the elaborate stonework in a mass of snaking foliage, enfolding it with roots and branches that patiently unmade even the matchless products of the Sithi builders, returning all to mud and damp sand.

There was little inspiration in the crumbling ruins of Enki-e-Shao'saye. They seemed only to demonstrate that even the Sithi were bound within the sweep of time; that any work of hands, however exalted, must come at last to ignoble result.

Binabik and Sludig found a clearer path running beside the river bank and began to make better time, winding their way through the rain-soaked forest. They heard nothing but the sounds of their own passage and were glad of it. Just as the troll had predicted, the land began to slope more acutely, falling away toward the southwest. Despite its swerving course, the river was moving in that direction as well, the water gaining speed and becoming possessed of what almost seemed like enthusiasm. It positively threw itself at its banks, as if desiring to be everywhere at once; the gouts of water that flew up at obstructions in the river bed seemed to leap higher than they normally should, as though this watercourse, granted a temporary life, labored to prove to some stern riverine deities its fitness for continued survival.

"Almost out of the forest," Binabik panted from Qantaqa's bobbing back. "See how the trees are now thinning? See, there is light between them ahead!"

Indeed, the stand of trees just before them seemed poised at the outermost rim of the earth. Instead of more mottled green foliage, beyond them lay only a wall of fathomless, featureless gray, as though the world's builders had run short of inspiration.

"You are right, little man," Sludig said excitedly. "Forest's end! Now, if we are within a short ride of this sanctuary of yours, we may shake those whoreson giants after all!"

"Unless my scrolls are none of them correct," Binabik replied as they cantered down the last length of slope. "It is not much distance from forest's edge to the Stone of Farewell."

He broke off as they reached the final line of trees. Qantaqa stopped abruptly, head held low, sniffing the air. Sludig reined up alongside. "Blessed Usires," the Rimmersman breathed.

The slope abruptly fell away before them, dropping at a much steeper angle to the wide valley below. Sesuad'ra loomed there, dark and secretive in its shroud of trees, a bony thrust of stone standing far above the valley bottom. Its height was particularly apparent because it was entirely surrounded by a flat plain of water.

The valley was flooded. The Stone of Farewell, a great fist that seemed to defy the rain-lashed skies, had become an island in a gray and restless sea. Binabik and Sludig were perched at the forest's edge only a half-league away from their goal, but every cubit of valley floor that lay between was covered by fathoms of floodwater.

Even as they stared, a roar echoed through the forest behind them, distant but still frighteningly close. Whatever magic remained to Enki-e-Shao'saye was too weak to discourage the hungry giants.

"Aedon, troll, we are caught like flies in a honey jar," Sludig said, a tremor of fear creeping into his voice for the first time. "We are backed against the edge of the world. Even if we fight and stave off their first attack, there is no escape!"

Binabik stroked Qantaqa's head. The wolf's hackles were up; she whimpered beneath his touch as though she ached to return the challenge floating down the wind. "Peace, Sludig, we must be thinking." He turned to squint down the precipitous slope. "I fear you are right about one thing. We are never to be leading horses down this grade."

"And what would we do at the bottom, in any case?" Sludig growled. Rain dribbled from his beard-braids. "That is no mud puddle! This is an ocean! Did your scrolls mention that?!"

Binabik waggled his head angrily. His hair hung in his eyes, pasted to his forehead by the rain. "Look up, Sludig, look up! The sky is full of water, and it is all being dropped down on us, courtesy of our enemy." He spat in disgust. "This is perhaps become an ocean now, but a week ago it was a valley only, just as the scrolls say." A worried look crossed his face. "I am wondering if Josua and the rest were caught in low ground! Daughter of the Snows, what a thought! If so, we might as well make our stand in this place—at the world's end, as you call it. Thorn's journey will stop here."

Sludig flung himself down out of the saddle, skidding briefly in the mud. He strode to the lead packhorse and detached the bundled length of the black sword. He hefted it easily, carrying it back to Binabik in one hand. "Your 'living sword' seems eager for battle," he said sourly. "I am half-tempted to see what it can do, though it may turn anvil-heavy on me in midstroke."

"No," Binabik said shortly. "My people are not fond of running from a fight, but neither is it time for us to be singing Croohok death-songs and be going happily to glorious defeat. Our quest is not yet given over."

Sludig glowered. "Then what do you say, troll? Shall we fly to that far rock?"

The little man hissed in frustration. "No, but first we can look for some other way for getting down." He gestured at the river thundering past them, which disappeared down the steep wooded slope. "This is not the only waterway. It could be that others will lead us down in a more gradual path to the valley."

"And then what?" Sludig demanded. "Swim?"

"If necessary." As Binabik spoke, the hunting cry of their pursuers rose again, setting the horses to milling and bumping in panic. "Take the horse, Sludig," Binabik said. "There is still chance we may win free."

"If so, you are a magical troll indeed. I will name you a Sithi and you can live forever."

"Do not joke here," Binabik said. "Do not mock." He slid from Qantaqa's back, then whispered something in the wolf's ear. With a bound, she was away through the dripping vegetation, tracking eastward along the face of the slope. Sludig and the troll followed as best they could, cutting a trail that the horses could follow.

Qantaqa, swift as a racing shadow now that the weight of her rider had been lifted from her back, soon found an angled traverse down the cliffside.

Despite the sticky, treacherous footing, they were able to make their way slowly down from the high promontory, gradually approaching the lowest edge of the forest, now the shore of a wind-tormented sea.

The forest did not come to a sudden ending, but rather disappeared into the rain-rippled water. In some places the tops of submerged trees still protruded above the surface, little islands of rippling leaves. Naked branches thrust up from the gray flood beside them like the hands of drowning men.

Sludig's horse pulled up just at the water's edge and the Rimmersman vaulted down to stand ankle-deep in muddy water. "I am not sure I see the improvement, troll," he said, surveying the scene. "At least before we were on high ground."

"Cut branches," Binabik said, clambering through the mud toward him. "Long ones, as many as you can be finding. We will build a raft."

"You are mad!" Sludig snapped.

"Perhaps. But you are the strong one, so you must be the cutter. I have rope in the packs for binding the limbs together, and I can do that. Hurry!"

Sludig snorted, but set himself to work. Within moments his sword was smacking dully against wood.

"If my axes had not been lost on this foolish quest," he panted, "I could build you a whole longhouse in the time it will take me to chop a tree with this poor blade."

Binabik said nothing, intent on lashing together the rough spars Sludig had already knocked loose. When he had finished with what was available, he went searching for loose wood. He discovered another tributary nearby that dropped down into a narrow gulley before emptying at last into the greater flood. A treasure trove of loose limbs had accumulated in the narrowest spot. Binabik grabbed them up by the armful, hurrying back and forth between the river and the place where Sludig labored.

"Qantaqa cannot swim so far," Binabik grunted as he carried the last useful batch. His eyes had drifted to the distant bulk of Sesuad'ra. "But I cannot be leaving her to find her own way. There is no way for knowing how long this storm will last. She might never find me again." He dumped the wood, frowning, then bent to his knots once more, his fingers threading loops of slender cord around the damp wood. "I cannot make this raft big enough for all three, not and take that of our belongings which we must be saving. There is no time."

"Then we will take turns being in the water," Sludig said. He shuddered, staring at the rain-pocked flood. "Elysia, Mother of God, but I hate the thought of it."

"Clever Sludig! You are right. We need only make it big enough for one of us to rest while the other two are swimming, and we will go into the water one after the other." Binabik allowed himself a thin smile. "You

Rimmersmen have not lost all your seagoing blood, I see." As he redoubled his efforts, a furious groan rolled through the woods. They looked
up, startled, to see a massive white shape on the promontory only a few
short furlongs away.

"God curse them!" Sludig moaned, hacking frenziedly at a slender
trunk. "Why do they pursue us! Do they seek the sword?"

Binabik shook his head. "Almost done," he said. "Two more long ones
I am needing."

The white figure on the hillside above quickly became several figures, a
pack of furious ghosts that raised their long arms against the storming sky.
The giants' voices rolled and boomed across the water, as though they
threatened not just the puny creatures below, but the Stone of Farewell
itself, squatting in serene insolence just beyond their reach.

"Done," Binabik said, tying the last knot. "Let us move it to the water.
If it is not floating, you will have that fight you so desire, Sludig."

It did float, once they had pushed it out past the tangle of drowned
undergrowth. Above the storm came the dull crackling of vegetation
being smashed aside as the giants came pushing their way down the
muddy hillside. Sludig carefully tossed Thorn onto the damp logs. Binabik
hastened back to loot the saddlebags. He dragged one leather sack over
unopened, and flung it out to Sludig, who stood waist-deep in the murky
water. "Those things are belonging to Simon," the troll called. "They
should not be lost." Sludig shrugged, but pushed the bag on beside the
wrapped sword.

"What about the horses?" Sludig shouted. The howl of their pursuers
was growing louder.

"What can we do?" Binabik said helplessly. "We must set them free!"
He drew his knife and slashed the bridle-traces from Sludig's mount, then
rapidly cut the belly-straps of the packhorses as well, so that their burdens
slid down onto the muddy turf.

"Hurry, troll!" Sludig cried. "They are very close!"

Binabik looked around, his face screwed up in desperate thought. He
bent and rifled one last saddlebag, pulling a few articles out before pelting
down the slope once more and out into the water.

"Get on," growled Sludig.

"Qantaqa!" Binabik shouted. "Come!"

The wolf snarled as she turned to face the ruckus of the oncoming
giants. The horses were rushing in all directions, whinnying with fright.
Suddenly, Sludig's mount broke away through the trees toward the east
and the others swiftly followed. The giants were now quite plain, a few
hundred paces up the hill and descending rapidly, their leathery black faces
gaping as they howled their hunting song. The Hunën carried great clubs
which they whickered back and forth like hollow reeds, smashing a pathway through the knotted trees and shrubbery.

"Qantaqa!" Binabik shouted, panic in his voice. *"Ummu ninit! Ummu sosa!"* The wolf turned and bounded toward them, breasting the water then paddling furiously. Sludig pushed off, taking a few more steps down the submerged slope until his feet no longer touched the bottom. Before they were thirty cubits from the water's edge, Qantaqa had caught them. She scrambled over Sludig's back onto the raft, setting it rocking treacherously and almost sinking the Rimmersman.

"No, Qantaqa!" Binabik cried.

"Let her be!" Sludig gurgled. "Reach down and paddle!"

The first giant burst from the forest behind them, howling with rage. His shaggy head twisted from side to side as if he sought some other angle to head off his prey's escape. When none was apparent, he strode forward into the water. He went several steps before he suddenly fell forward with a splash, disappearing from view for a moment beneath the water. When he surfaced an instant later he was thrashing madly, dirty white fur festooned with branches. He raised his chin and barked thunderously at the storm, as though demanding help. His fellows swarmed on the shore behind him, hooting and groaning with frustrated bloodlust.

The first giant swam awkwardly and unhappily back to the shallows. He stood up, streaming with water, and reached down an apelike arm to pull loose a massive tree limb thick as a man's leg. Grunting, he flung it through the air. The limb hit the water beside the raft with a tremendous splash, tearing Sludig's cheek with a jutting branch and nearly upsetting the crude boat. Stunned, Sludig foundered. Binabik disentangled himself from Qantaqa and leaned forward, hooking the toes of his boots into gaps between the beams of the pitching raft. The little man clutched the Rimmersman's wrist with both hands until Sludig recovered. The giants hurled more missiles, but none came as close as the first. Their thwarted bellows seemed to rumble across all the flooded valley.

Cursing giants and rafts equally, Sludig pushed off with his long Qanuc spear until they at last floated free of clinging branches. He began to kick, pushing the raft and its unlikely cargo out across the chill gray water toward the shadowy stone.

Eolair rode east from his ancestral home of Nad Mullach beneath night skies a-flicker with strange lights. The countryside around his captured stronghold had proved less hospitable than he had hoped. Many of his people had already been driven away by the misfortunes of war and the terrible weather, and those who remained were reluctant to open their doors to a stranger—even if that stranger claimed to be the ruling count. Occupied Hernystir was a land held prisoner more by fear than by enemy soldiers.

Few others were abroad by night, which was when Eolair did most of his traveling. Even Skali of Kaldskryke's men, despite their conquerors' crowns, seemed reluctant to stir forth, as if taking on the character of those they had conquered. In this grim summer of snow and restless spirits, even the war's victors bowed before a greater power.

Eolair was more than ever certain that he must find Josua, if the prince still lived. Maegwin might have sent him on this quest because of some odd or spiteful notion, but now it seemed laughably apparent that the north of Osten Ard had fallen beneath a shadow of more than human origin, and that the riddle of the sword Bright-Nail might very well have something to do with it. Why else would the gods have arranged that Eolair should be in that monstrously strange city beneath the ground, or that he should meet its even stranger denizens? The Count of Nad Mullach was a pragmatist by nature. His long years of service to the king had hardened his heart to fantasy, but at the same time his experience of diplomacy had also made him mistrustful of excessive coincidence. To suggest that there was no overriding supernatural element to the summer-that-was-winter, the reappearance of creatures out of legend, and the sudden importance of forgotten but near-mythical swords was to close one's eyes to a reality as plain as the mountains and the seas.

Also, despite all his endless days in the court of Erkynland, Nabban, and Perdruin, and for all his cautious words to Maegwin, Eolair was a Herynstirman. More than any other mortal men, the Hernystiri *remembered*.

As Eolair rode into Erkynland, across bleak Utanyeat toward the battle site of Ach Samrath, the storm grew stronger. The snow, however unseasonable, had until now fallen only moderately, as it might in the early days of Novander. Now the winds were rising, changing the flat countryside into a flurrying landscape of white nothingness. The cold was so fierce that he was forced to abandon night riding altogether for a few days, but he worried little about being recognized: the roads and countryside were all but deserted even at gray, blustery noon. He noted with sour satisfaction that Utanyeat—the earldom of Guthwulf, one of High King Elias' favorites—was as storm-wounded as any of Hernystir. There was some justice, after all.

Trekking endlessly through white emptiness, he found himself thinking often of his people left behind, but especially of Maegwin. Although in some ways she had become almost as wild and intractable as a beast since the death of her father and brother, he had always felt great affection toward her. That was not yet gone, but it was hard not to feel betrayed by her treatment of him, no matter how well he thought he understood its cause. Still, he could not bring himself to hate her. He had been a special friend to her since she had been a little girl, making a point of speaking with her whenever he was at court, letting her show him the Taig's gardens, as well as the pigs and chickens to which she gave names, and which she treated with the same annoyed fondness a mother might show her reckless children.

As she grew, becoming as tall as a man—but none the less comely for it—Eolair had watched her also become steadily more reserved, only occasionally showing the flashes of girlishness which had so delighted him before. She seemed to turn inward, like a rosebush balked by an over-hanging roof that coiled in on itself until its own thorns rubbed its stems raw. She still reserved special attention for Eolair, but that attention was more and more confusing, more and more made up of awkward silences and her angry self-recriminations.

For a while he had thought she cared for him as more than just a friend of her family and distant kinsman. He had wondered whether two such solitary folk could ever find their way together—Eolair, for all his easy speech and cleverness, had always felt that the best part of himself was hidden far beneath the surface, just as his quiet hill-keep at Nad Mullach stood remote from the bustle of the Taig. But even as he had finally begun to think in earnest about Maegwin—even as his admiration for her honesty and for her impatience with nonsense had begun to ripen into something deeper—she had turned cold to him. She seemed to have decided that Eolair was only another of the legion of idlers and flatterers that surrounded King Lluth.

One long afternoon in eastern Utanyeat, as the snow stung his face and he wandered far away in thought, he suddenly wondered: *Was I wrong? Did she care for me all that time?* It was a horrifying thought, because it suddenly turned the world he knew on its head and gave vastly different meaning to everything that had transpired between them since Maegwin had become a woman.

Have I been blind? But if that were so, why should she act so backwardly to me? Have I not always treated her with respect and kindness?

After turning the idea over in his head for a long hour, he put it away again. It was too uncomfortable to consider any longer here in the middle of nowhere, with months or more between now and when he could see her again.

And she had sent him away in anger, had she not?

The wind picked restlessly at the unsettled snow.

He rode past Ach Samrath on a morning when the storm had abated somewhat, stopping his horse on a rise above the ancient battlefield where Prince Sinnach and ten thousand of his Hernystirmen had been destroyed by Fingil of Rimmersgard and the treachery of the Thrithings-lord Niyunort. As on the few other occasions he had visited this site, Eolair felt a shiver climb through him as he looked down at the great, flat field, but this time it was not prompted by the grisly past. With the freezing wind on his face and the cold, blank face of the north staring down at him, he suddenly realized that by the time this new and greater war had ended—whether on a battlefield or beneath a remorseless tide of black winter—it might be in a frenzy of death that would make Ach Samrath seem a petty dispute.

He rode on, his anger turning to ice inside him. Who had set this great thing in motion? Who had set this evil wheel to turning? Had it been Elias, or his pet serpent Pryrates? If so, there should be a special Hell prepared for them. Eolair only hoped he would be around to see them sent there— maybe on the end of Prester John's Bright-Nail, if the subterranean dwarrows spoke rightly.

As Eolair came to the edge of Aldheorte, he reverted once more to night riding. The storm's teeth seemed a little duller here in Elias' realm, only a dozen leagues from the outskirts of Erchester, and he also thought it safer not to count on the infrequency of meeting other travelers any longer— here, that infrequent other traveler was likely to be one of the High King's Erkynguard.

Beneath the shadow of the great wood, the silent, snow-blanketed farmlands seemed to wait apprehensively for whatever might come next, as though this storm were only the precursor of some darker deed. Eolair knew that these were his own feelings, but also felt strongly that they were not his alone: a sense of dread hung over Erkynland, filling the air like a terrible, will-sapping fog. The few lone farmers and woodsmen whose wagons he saw on the road did not respond to his greetings except to make the sign of the Tree as they passed him on the moonless roads, as though Eolair might be some demon or walking dead man. But their torches revealed that it was their own faces that had gone slack and pale as the masks of corpses, as though the fearful winds and constant snow had leached the very life from them.

He approached Thisterborg. The great hill stood only a few leagues from Erchester's gates, and was the closest he would come to the Hayholt— from which, on certain of the blackest nights, he could almost feel Elias' sleepless malice burning like a torch in a high tower. It was only the High King, he reminded himself, a mortal man whom he had once respected, although never liked. Whatever mad plans Elias had made, whatever dreadful bargains, he was still only a man.

Thisterborg's peak seemed to flicker as the count drew nearer, as though high on the hillcrest great watchfires burned. Eolair wondered if Elias had made it a guard post, but could think of no reason why. Did the High King fear some invasion from the ancient forest, the Aldheorte? It mattered little, in any case. Eolair was firmly resolved to circle Thisterborg on the far side from Erchester, and felt no urge whatsoever to investigate the mysterious lights. The black hill had an evil reputation that extended back far beyond the days of even Elias' father, King John. Stories about Thisterborg were many, none of them pleasant to hear. In such days as these, Eolair wished he could avoid coming any closer than a league or so, but the forest—another dubious place to be at night—and the walls of Erchester prevented such a judiciously wide swing.

He had just started around the north of the hill, his mount picking its way through the ever-thickening trees of Aldheorte's fringe, when he felt a wave of fear sweep over him that was unlike anything he had ever experienced. His heart hammered and a chill sweat broke out on his face, then turned almost immediately to fragile ice; Eolair felt like a fieldmouse that, too late for escape, suddenly perceived the stooping hawk. He had to restrain himself from digging in his spurs and riding madly in whatever direction he was already facing. He whirled, looking wildly for whatever might be the cause of such dreadful terror, but could see nothing.

At last he slapped his horse's flank and rode a short distance farther into the shielding trees. Whatever had caused him to feel this way, it seemed a product of the unprotected snows rather than the shadowy forest.

The storm was much less fierce here, as it had been since he had entered Aldheorte's lee: but for a sprinkling of snow, the sky was clear. A vast yellow moon hung in the eastern sky, turning all the landscape to a sickly shade of bone. The Count of Nad Mullach looked up at the looming bulk of Thisterborg, wondering if that could be the source of his sudden fright, but could see or hear nothing extraordinary. A part of him wondered if he had not been riding too long alone with his morbid thoughts, but that part was easily ignored. Eolair was a Hernystirman. Herynstiri remembered.

A thin sound, an unidentifiable but persistent scraping, began to make itself heard. He looked down from secretive Thisterborg and turned his gaze westward across the snows, toward the direction from which he had come. Something was moving slowly across the white plain.

The chill of fear grew deeper, spreading through him like a prickling frost. As his horse moved uncomfortably, Eolair put a trembling hand on its neck; the beast, as if it perceived his own terror, suddenly became very still. Their twin plumes of breath were the only moving things in the shadow of the trees.

The scraping grew louder. Eolair could now see the shapes moving closer over the snows, a mass of luminous white followed by a lump of blackness. Then, with the stark unreality of a nightmare, the gleaming shapes came clear.

It was a team of white goats, shaggy pelts glowing as though with captured moonlight. Their eyes were red as embers, and their heads seemed somehow gravely *wrong*: when he thought of it afterward he could never say why, except that the shapes of their hairless muzzles seemed to suggest some kind of unpleasant intelligence. The goats, nine in all, drew behind them a great black sled; it was the sound of the runners crunching through the snow that he had heard. Seated on the sled was a hooded figure that even across a distance of some hundred cubits seemed too large. Several other, smaller black-robed figures marched solemnly alongside, hoods tilted downward like monks in meditation.

An almost uncontrollable horror ran up Eolair's spine. His horse had turned to stone beneath him, as if fright had stopped its heart and left it dead upon its feet. The ghastly procession scraped past, agonizingly slow, silent but for the noise of the sled. Just as the robed figures were about to vanish into the darkness of Thisterborg's lowest slopes, one of the hooded shapes turned, showing Eolair what he fancied was a flash of skeletal white face, black holes that might have been eyes. The part of his shrieking thoughts that was still coherent thanked the gods of his and all other peoples for the shadows of the forest's fringe. The hooded eyes turned away at last. The sled and its escort vanished into the snowy woods of Thisterborg.

Eolair stood a long time, allowing himself to tremble, but did not move from the spot until he was sure it was safe. His teeth had been so tightly clenched that his jaws ached. He felt as though he had been stripped raw and tumbled down a long black hole. When he dared to move at last, he threw himself onto his horse's neck and galloped away into the east as swiftly as he could. His mount, eager as he, needed no spurs, no crop. They whirled away in a cloud of snow.

As Eolair fled Thisterborg and its mysteries, running eastward beneath the mocking moon, he knew that everything he had feared was true, and that there were things in the world that were worse even than his fears.

Ingen Jegger stood beneath the spreading arms of a black hemlock, unmindful of the bitter wind or the frost growing in his close-cropped beard. But for the impatient life in his pale blue eyes, he might have been a luckless traveler, frozen to death waiting for a morning's warmth that came too late.

The huge white hound crouching in the snow at his feet stirred, then made an inquiring sound like the scrape of rusty hinges.

"Hungry, Niku'a?" A look almost of fondness ran across Ingen's taut features. "Quiet. Soon, you will have your fill."

Motionless, Ingen watched and listened, sifting the night like a whiskered beast of prey. The moon crept from one gap in the overhanging trees to another. The forest, but for the wind, was silent.

"Ah." Satisfied, he took a few steps and shook the snow from his cloak. "Now, Niku'a. Call your brothers and sisters. Howl up the Stormspike pack! It is time for the last chase."

Niku'a leaped up, quivering with excitement. As if it had understood Ingen's every word, the great hound trotted out into the middle of the clearing before settling back on its haunches and lifting its snout to the sky. Powerful throat muscles convulsed, and a coughing howl shattered the night. Even as the first echoes died, Niku'a's strident voice burst out again, hacking and baying. The very branches of the trees trembled.

They waited, Ingen's gloved hand resting on the dog's wide head. Time passed. Niku'a's cloudy white eyes gleamed as the moon slid along between the trees. At last, as night's coldest hour crept in, the faint cries of hounds came sweeping down the wind.

The belling rose until it filled the forest. A host of white shapes appeared from the darkness, filtering into the clearing like four-legged ghosts. The Stormspike hounds wove in and out among the tree roots, narrow, sharklike heads questing and sniffing. Starlight gleamed on muzzles smeared with blood and spittle. Niku'a went among them, nipping, snarling, until at last the whole pack crouched or lay in the snow around Ingen Jegger, red tongues lolling.

The Queen's Huntsman calmly looked over his strange congregation, then picked his snarling, dog-faced helm from the ground.

"Too long have you been roaming free," he hissed, "harrying the forest fringes, stealing babies like kennel cubs, running down foolish travelers for the joy of the chase. Now your master has come back. Now you must do what you were bred to do." The milky eyes followed him as he moved to his horse, which waited with supernatural patience beneath the hemlock. "But this time *I* will lead, not you. It is a strange chase, and Ingen alone has been taught the scent." He pulled himself up into the saddle. "Run silently." He lowered the helmet onto his head, so that hound looked at hounds. "We take death to the Queen's enemies."

A low growling rose from the dogs as they rose and came together, sliding against one another, snapping at each other's faces and tails in fierce anticipation. Ingen spurred his horse forward, then turned. "Follow!" he cried. "Follow to death and blood!"

He passed swiftly from the clearing. The pack ran after, voiceless now, silent and white as snowfall.

Huddled deep in his cloak, Isgrimnur sat in the bow of the small boat and watched stubby Sinetris rowing and sniffling. The duke wore a fixed expression of grim preoccupation, in part because he found the boatman's company extremely unrewarding, but mostly because he himself hated boats, especially small boats like the one on which he was now trapped. Sinetris had spoken truthfully about one thing, anyway: this was no time to be on the water. A great storm was flailing the entire length of the coast. The choppy water of Firannos Bay constantly threatened to swamp them, and Sinetris had not stopped moaning since their hull had first touched the water a week before, some thirty leagues northward.

The duke had to admit that Sinetris was a talented boatman, if only in the defense of his own life. The Nabban-man had handled his craft well under terrible conditions. If only he would stop sniveling! Isgrimnur was no happier about the conditions for their journey than Sinetris was, but he would be damned to the blackest circle of Hell before he made a fool out of himself by showing it.

"How far to Kwanitupul?" he shouted over the noise of wind and waves.

"Half a day, master monk," Sinetris called back, eyes red and streaming. "We will stop soon to sleep, then we can be there by midday tomorrow."

"Sleep!" Sigrimnur roared. "Are you mad!? It is not even dark yet! Besides, you will only try to sneak away again, and this time I will not be so merciful. If you cease your self-pitying nonsense and work, you can sleep in a bed tonight!"

"Please, holy brother!" Sinetris almost shrieked. "Do not force me to row in darkness! We will run onto the rocks. Our only beds will be down among the kilpa!"

"Don't hand that superstitious nonsense to me. I'm paying you well and I am in a hurry. If you are too weak or sore, let me take those paddles for a while."

The oarsman, wet and cold, still managed a convincing look of wounded pride. "You! You would have us under the water in a moment! No, you cruel monk, if Sinetris must die, let it be with his oars in his hand, as befits a Firannos boatman. If Sinetris must be torn from his home and the bosom of his family and sacrificed to the whims of a monster in the robes of a priest, if he must die . . . let it be as a guild-man!"

Isgrimnur groaned. "Let it be with his mouth closed, for a change. And keep paddling."

"Rowing," Sinetris replied frostily, then burst into tears once more.

It was past midnight when the first stilt-houses of Kwanitupul came into view. Sinetris, whose complaining had faded at last to a low, self-pitying murmur, nosed the boat into the great network of canals. Isgrimnur, who had briefly fallen asleep, rubbed his eyes and craned his head, looking around. Kwanitupul's ramshackle warehouses and inns were all dusted with a thin coating of snow.

If I doubted that the world had gone topsy-turvy, Isgrimnur thought bemusedly, *here is all the proof I need: a Rimmersman taking a leaky boat to sea in a storm, and snow in the southland—in high summer. Can any doubt the world has run mad?*

Madness. He remembered the hideous death of the lector and felt his stomach gurgle. Madness—or something else? It was a strange coincidence that Pryrates and Benigaris should both be in the house of Mother Church on such a dreadful night. Only a stroke of rare luck had brought Isgrimnur to Dinivan in time to hear the priest's last words, and perhaps to salvage something from this grim pass.

He had escaped from the Sancellan Aedonitis only moments before Benigaris, Duke of Nabban, had ordered his guardsmen to bar all doors. Isgrimnur could not have afforded capture—even if he had not been immediately recognized, his story would not have held up long. Hlafmansa Eve, the night of the lector's murder, had been a bad night to be an unfamiliar guest at the Sancellan.

"Do you know of a place here called *Pelippa's Bowl*?" he asked aloud. "I think it is an inn or a hostel."

"I have never heard of the place, master monk," Sinetris said gravely. "It sounds like a low establishment, one in which Sinetris would not be seen." Now that they had reached the relatively still waters of the canals, the boatman had reassumed much of his dignity. Isgrimnur decided he liked him better when he sniveled.

"By the Tree, we will never find it at night. Take me to some inn you know, then. I must get something under my belt."

Sinetris steered the little craft down a series of crisscrossing canals to the city's tavern district. Things seemed quite lively here despite the late hour, the boardwalks lined with garish cloth lanterns that swung in the wind, the alleyways full of drunken revelers.

"This is a fine inn, holy brother," Sinetris said as they glided to a stop at the dock stairs of a well-lit establishment. "There is wine to be had, and food." Sinetris, feeling bold now that their journey had ended safely, gave Isgrimnur a chummy, gap-toothed smile. "And women, too." His smile grew uncertain as he surveyed Isgrimnur's face. "—Or boys, if that is more to your liking."

The duke forced a great hiss of air between his teeth. He reached into his cloak and pulled out a gold Imperator, then placed it gently on the rowing bench beside Sinetris' skinny leg. Isgrimnur next moved to the bottommost stair. "There is your thievish payment, as I promised. Now, I have a suggestion for how you might spend *your* evening."

Sinetris looked up warily. "Yes?"

Isgrimnur drew down his eyebrows in a horrible frown. "Spend it doing your very best to make sure that I do not see you again. Because if I do," he lifted his hairy fist, "I will roll your eyeballs around in your pointy head. Understood?"

Sinetris dropped his oar-blades and backed water hastily, so that Isgrimnur had to quickly swing his other foot up onto the stairs. "So this is how you monks treat Sinetris after all his favors!?" the boatman said indignantly, puffing up his thin chest like a courting pigeon. "No wonder the church is in bad repute! You . . . bearded barbarian!" He splashed off into the darkened canal.

Isgrimnur laughed harshly, then stumped up the stairs to the inn.

★   ★   ★

After several fitful nights in the grasslands—nights in which he had been forced to keep a careful watch on the treacherous Sinetris, who had several times tried to slip away and leave Isgrimnur standed on the bleak, wind-swept coast of Firannos Bay—the Duke of Elvirtshalla took his sleep in full measure. He remained in bed until the sun was high in the sky, then broke his fast with a manly portion of bread and honey accompanied by a stoup of ale. It was nearly noontide before he obtained directions to *Pelippa's Bowl* from the innkeeper and was out on the rainy canals once more. His boatman this time was a Wrannaman, who despite the bitter wind wore only a loincloth and a broad-brimmed hat with a red, drizzle-soaked feather drooping from the band. The boatman's sullen silence was a pleasant change from the ceaseless carping of Sinetris. Isgrimnur settled back to fondle his new-sprouted beard and enjoy the sodden sights of Kwanitupul, a city he had not visited for many years.

The storm had obviously cast a pall over the trading city. Unless things had changed greatly since his last sojourn, there should be many more boats out on the water at midday, many more folk wandering Kwanitupul's exotic byways. Those who were about seemed to be hurrying to their destinations. Even the ritual cries of greeting and challenge that rang between canal boats seemed unusually muted. Like insects, the residents seemed chilled almost to immobility by the snow that melted in patches on their wooden walkways, and the wind-borne sleet that stung exposed limbs and filled the canals with circular ripples.

Here and there among the sparse crowds Isgrimnur saw small gather-ings of Fire Dancers, the religious maniacs who had gained their notoriety by self-immolation. They had become a familiar sight to the duke since he had first reached Nabban. These wild-eyed penitents, uncaring of the cold, stood on the walkways near busy canal intersections and shouted the praises of their dark master, the Storm King. Isgrimnur wondered where they had heard that name. He had never heard it spoken south of the Frostmarch before, even in a children's bogey-story. It was no coinci-dence, he knew, but he could not help musing on whether these robed lunatics were the pawns of someone like Pyrates or true visionaries. If the latter was the case, then the end they foresaw might be real.

Isgrimnur shuddered at this thought and made the sign of the Tree on his breast. Black times, these were. For all their shouting, though, the Fire Dancers did not seem to be engaging in their familiar trick of setting themselves aflame. The duke smiled sourly. Perhaps it was a little too damp today.

The boatman stopped at last before an unprepossessing structure in the warehouse district, far from the centers of commerce. When Isgrimnur had paid him, the little dark man reached up with his gaff hook and pulled down the rope ladder from the dock. The duke was scarcely halfway up the swinging ladder before the boatman had turned around and was coasting out of sight down a side-canal.

Huffing and cursing his fat belly, Isgrimnur at last made his way up onto the more trustworthy footing of the dock. He rapped at the weather-worn door, then waited a long time in the freezing rain without answer, growing increasingly cross. At last the door swung open, revealing a frowning woman of middle age.

"I don't know where the half-wit is," she told Isgrimnur as though he had asked. "It's not enough that I have to do every other lick of work here, but now I have to answer the door as well."

For a moment the duke was so taken aback that he almost apologized. He struggled with his impulse toward chivalry. "I want a room," he said at last.

"Well, come in, then," the woman said doubtfully, opening the door wider. Beyond lay a makeshift boathouse that stank of tar and old fish. A couple of hulls were laid out like casualties of battle. In the corner, a brown arm protruded from a huddle of blankets. For a moment Isgrimnur thought it was a corpse that had been carelessly thrown into the doorway; when the arm moved, pulling the blankets closer, he realized that it was only someone sleeping. He had a sudden premonition that he might not find the accommodations here up to the best standards, but he forced the thought down.

You're getting fussy, old man, he chided himself. *On the battlefield, you've slept in mud and blood and the nests of biting flies.*

He had a mission, he reminded himself. His own comfort was secondary.

"By the way," he called after the innkeeper, whose brisk steps had taken her almost the entire length of the dooryard, "I'm looking for someone." Suddenly he could not recall the name Dinivan had told him. He stopped, running his fingers through his damp beard, then remembered. "Tiamak. I'm looking for Tiamak."

When the woman turned, her sour expression had been supplanted by a look of greedy pleasure. *"You?"* she said. "You're the one with the gold?" She opened her arms wide as though to embrace him. Despite the dozen cubits that separated them, the duke took a step backward, repelled. The bundle of blankets in the corner began to wiggle like a nest of piglets, then fell away. A small and very thin Wrannaman sat up, eyes still half-closed from sleep.

"I am Tiamak," he said, trying to stifle a yawn. As he surveyed Isgrimnur, the marsh-man's face seemed to show disappointment, as though he had expected something better. The duke felt his annoyance returning. Were all these people mad? Who did they think he was, or expect him to be?

"I bring you tidings," Isgrimnur said stiffly, uncertain of how to proceed. "But we should talk in private."

"I will show you to your room," the woman said hastily, "the finest in the house, and the little brown gentleman—another honored guest—can join you there."

Isgrimnur had just turned back to Tiamak, who seemed to be dressing awkwardly beneath the blankets, when the inside door of the inn thumped open and a horde of children barged through, whooping like Thrithings-men at war. They were pursued by a tall, white-haired old man, who grinned from ear to ear as he pretended to stalk them. They fled him with shrieks of delight, and crashed through the door leading out to the dock. Before he could pursue them any further the landlady stepped before him, fists on hips.

"Damn you for a simple ass, Ceallio, you are here to answer the door!" The old man, though considerably taller, cowered before her as though expecting a blow. "I know you are addled-pated, but you are not deaf! Did you not hear someone knocking at the door?"

The old man moaned wordlessly. The landlady turned from him in disgust. "He's as stupid as a stone," she began, then broke off, staring, as Isgrimnur dropped to his knees.

The duke felt the world tilt, as though giant hands had lifted it. It took long moments before he could speak, moments in which the landlady, the little Wrannaman, and the old doorkeeper looked at him with varying degrees of uneasy fascination. When Isgrimnur spoke, it was to the old man.

"My lord Camaris," he said, and felt his voice catch in his throat. The world *had* gone mad: now the dead lived again. "Merciful Elysia, Camaris, do you not remember me? I am Isgrimnur! We fought for Prester John together—we were friends! Ah, God, you live! How can that be?"

He reached his hand out to the old man, who took it as a child might take something shiny or colorful offered by a stranger. The old man's grip was callused, with a great strength that could be felt even as his hand lay flaccidly in Isgrimnur's own. His handsome face showed only smiling incomprehension.

"What are you saying?" the landlady said crossly. "That's old Ceallio, the doorkeeper. Been here for years. He's a simpleton."

"Camaris . . ." Isgrimnur breathed as he pressed the old man's hand to his cheek, wetting it with tears. He could scarcely speak, "Oh, my good lord, you live."

28

Sparks

Despite the unceasing loveliness of Jao é-Tunukai'i, or perhaps because of it, Simon was bored. He was also unutterably lonely.

His imprisonment was a strange thing: the Sithi did not hinder him, but other than Jiriki and Aditu, they continued to show no interest in him, either. Like a queen's lapdog, he was well fed and well cared for, allowed to roam wherever he could go, but only because the outside world was beyond his reach. Like a prize pet, he amused his masters, but was not taken seriously. When he spoke to them, they responded politely in Simon's own Westerling speech, but among themselves they spoke the liquid Sithi tongue. Only a few recognizable words ever reached his ear, but whole rivers of incomprehensible talk flowed around him. The suspicion that they might be discussing him in their private conversations infuriated him. The possibility that they might not, that they might never think of him except when in his presence, was somehow even worse: it made him feel insubstantial as a ghost.

Since his interview with Amerasu, the days had begun to flit past even more rapidly. As he lay in his blankets one night, he realized he could no longer say for certain how long he had been among the Sithi. Aditu, when asked, claimed not to remember. Simon took the same question to Jiriki, who fixed him with a look of great pity and asked whether he truly wished to count the days. Chilled by the implication, Simon demanded the truth. Jiriki told him that a little over a month had passed.

That had been some days ago.

The nights were the most difficult. In his nest of blankets in Jiriki's house, or roaming the soft, damp grass beneath strange stars, Simon tormented himself with impossible plans for escape, plans that even he knew were as impractical as they were desperate. He became more and more morose. He knew Jiriki was worried for him, and even Aditu's quicksilver laugh seemed forced. Simon knew that he was speaking constantly of his misery, but could not hide it—moreover, he did not *want* to hide it. Whose fault was it that he was trapped here?

They had saved his life, of course. Would it truly have been better to die by freezing or slow starvation, he chided himself, rather than living as a pampered, if restricted, guest in the most wonderful city in Osten Ard? But even though such ingratitude might be shameful, he still could not reconcile himself to his blissful prison.

Every day was much the same. He wandered through the forest alone, or threw stones into the countless streams and rivers, and thought of his friends. In the sheltering summer of Jao é-Tinukai'i, it was hard to imagine how they must all be suffering in the dreadful winter outside. Where was Binabik? Miriamele? Prince Josua? Did they even live? Had they fallen beneath the black storm, or did they still struggle?

Growing ever more frantic, he begged Jiriki to let him speak to Amerasu again, to plead for her help in setting him free, but Jiriki declined.

"It is not my place to instruct First Grandmother. She will act in her own time, when she has thought carefully. I am sorry, Seoman, but these matters are too important to hurry."

"Hurry!" Simon raged. "By the time anyone does anything in this place, I will be dead!"

But Jiriki, although visibly saddened, remained adamant.

Balked at every turn, Simon's anxiousness began to turn to anger. The reserved Sithi came to seem smug and self-righteous beyond enduring. While Simon's friends were fighting and dying, engaged in a dreadful losing battle with the Storm King as well as with Elias, these foolish creatures wandered through their sunlit forest singing and contemplating the trees. And who was the Storm King, anyway, but a Sithi!? No wonder that his fellows were keeping Simon prisoned while the world outside withered before Ineluki's cold wrath.

So the days spun by, each more and more like its predecessor, each increasing Simon's disaffection. He ceased taking his evening meal with Jiriki, preferring a more solitary appreciation of the songs of crickets and nightingales. Resentful of Aditu's playfulness, he began to avoid her. He was sick of being teased and fondled. He meant no more to her, he knew, than the lapdog did to the queen. He would have no more. If he must be a prisoner, he would act like one.

Jiriki found him sitting in a copse of larch trees, sullen and prickly as a hedgehog. The bees were mumbling in the clover and the sun streamed down through the needles, crosshatching the ground with slivers of light. Simon was chewing on a piece of bark.

"Seoman," the prince said, "may I speak to you?"

Simon frowned. He had learned that Sithi, unlike mortals, would actually go away if permission was not given. Jiriki's folk had a deep respect for privacy.

"I suppose so," Simon said at last.

"I would like you to come with me," Jiriki said. "We will go to the Yásira."

Simon felt a quickening of hope, but it was a painful thing. "Why?"

"I do not know. I only know that we are all asked to come, all who live in Jao é-Tinukai'i. Since you live here now, I think it fitting that you come."

Simon's hopes sank. "They did not ask for me." For a moment he had envisioned how it would be: Shima'onari and Likimeya apologizing for their mistake, sending him back to his own kind bearing presents, laden as well with the wisdom to help Josua and the others. Another mooncalf daydream—hadn't he grown out of them yet? "I don't want to go," he said at last.

Jiriki squatted beside him, poised as gracefully as a hunting bird upon a branch. "I wish that you would, Seoman," he said at last. "I cannot force you and I will not plead, but Amerasu will be there. It is rare indeed for her to ask to speak to our people, except when it is the Day of Year-Dancing."

Simon felt his interest quicken. Perhaps Amerasu was going to speak on his behalf, order them to let him go! But if that was the case, why hadn't he been asked to come?

He feigned indifference. Whatever else occurred, he was steadily learning Sithi ways. "There you go about Year-Dancing again, Jiriki," he said. "But you have never told me what it means. I saw the Year-Dancing grove, you know."

Jiriki appeared to be suppressing a smile. "Not very closely, I think. But come, Seoman, you are playing a game. Some other time I will tell you what I can of the responsibilities of our family's house, but now I must go. You, too, if you plan to accompany me."

Simon tossed the piece of chewed-upon bark over his shoulder. "I'll go if I can sit near the door. And if I don't have to speak."

"You can sit wherever you please, Snowlock. You are a prisoner, perhaps, but an honored one. My people are trying to make your time here endurable. As to the rest, I have no say over what you may be asked. Come, you are almost grown, manchild. Do not be afraid to stand for yourself."

Simon frowned, considering. "Lead on, then," he said.

They stopped before the doorway of the great living tent. The butterflies were agitated, fluttering their spangled wings so that shifting patterns colored shadow rippled across the face of the Yásira like wind through a field of wheat. The papery rustle of their gentle commingling filled the whole glen. Suddenly unwilling to proceed through the door, Simon pulled back, shaking himself free of Jiriki's companionable arm.

"I don't want to hear anything bad," he said. There was a cold heaviness in the pit of his stomach, the same as he had felt when he expected punishment from Rachel or the Master of Scullions. "I don't want to be shouted at."

Jiriki looked at him quizzically. "No one will shout, Seoman. That is not our way, we Zida'ya. This may be nothing to do with you at all."

Simon shook his head, embarrassed. "Sorry. Of course." He took a deep breath and shrugged nervously, then waited until Jiriki gently took his arm once more and steered him toward the Yásira's rose-entwined doorway. A thousand thousand butterfly wings hissed like a dry wind as Simon and his companion stepped through into the vast bowl of multi-hued light.

Likimeya and Shima'onari, as before, were seated at the center of the room on low couches near the jutting finger-stone. Amerasu sat between them on a higher couch, the hood of her pale gray robe thrown back. Her snowy white hair, unbound, spread in a soft cloud upon her shoulders. She wore a sash of bright blue around her slender waist, but no other ornamentation or jewelry.

As Simon stared, her eyes passed briefly across his. If he hoped for a helpful smile or a reassuring nod, he was disappointed: her gaze slid by as though he were just one unexceptional tree in a great forest. His heart sank. If any ideas remained about Amerasu's being concerned with moon-calf Simon's fate, he decided, it was time to put them away.

Beside Amerasu, on a pedestal of dull gray rock, stood a curious object: a disk of some pale icy substance, mounted on a broad stand of dark and shiny witchwood wrought with twining Sithi carvings. Simon thought it a table-mirror—he had heard that some great ladies possessed them—but, oddly, it did not seem to reflect. The disk's edges were sharp as knives, like a sugar-sweet that had been sucked to near-transparency. Its color was the frosty near-white of a winter moon, but other, deeper hues seemed to move sleepily within it. A wide, shallow bowl of the same translucent substance lay before the stone disk, nestled in the carved stand.

Simon could not stare at the thing too long. The changing colors disturbed him: in some strange manner, the shifting stone reminded him of the gray sword Sorrow, and that was a memory he did not wish reawakened. He turned his head away and looked slowly around the great chamber.

As Jiriki had suggested, all the residents of Jao é-Tinukai'i seemed to have come to the Yásira this afternoon. Dressed in their emphatically colorful manner, plumed like rare birds, still the golden-eyed Sithi seemed unusually reserved, even by the standards of a retiring folk. Many eyes had turned toward Simon and Jiriki upon their entrance, but no one gaze had lingered long: the attention of all assembled seemed fixed on the three figures at the center of the vast tree-chamber. Glad of the anonymity, Simon chose a place on the outskirts of the silent crowd for Jiriki and himself to sit. He did not see Aditu anywhere, but he knew she would be hard to pick out in the midst of such an array.

For a long time there was no movement or speech, although it seemed to Simon that there were hidden currents moving just beneath his own understanding, subtle communications shared by everyone in the room but him. Still, he was not so insensitive that he failed to perceive the tension of the quiet Sithi, the clear sense of uneasy anticipation. There was a sharpness to the air, as before a lightning storm.

He had begun to wonder if they would go on this way all afternoon, like a group of cat-rivals gathered on a wall, silently staring each other down, when at last Shima'onari rose and began to speak. This time, the master of Jao é-Tinukai'i did not bother with Simon's own Westerling tongue, but used the musical Sithi speech. He spoke for some while, accompanying his soliloquy with graceful hand gestures, the sleeves of his pale yellow robe fluttering as he emphasized his words. To Simon, it was only confusion piled atop incomprehensibility.

"My father speaks of Amerasu and asks us to listen to her," Jiriki whispered, translating. Simon was dubious. Shima'onari seemed to have spoken a very long time just to say that. He glanced around the Yásira at the somber, cat-eyed faces. Whatever Jiriki's father was saying, he had the undivided and almost frighteningly complete attention of his people.

When Shima'onari concluded, Likimeya rose, and all eyes then turned to her. She, too, spoke for a long time in the language of the Zida'ya.

"She says Amerasu is very wise," explained Jiriki. Simon frowned.

When Likimeya finished a great, gentle sigh arose, as though all assembled had released their breath at once. Simon let out his own quiet sigh, one of relief: as the incomprehensible babble of Sithi-tongue went on and on, he had been finding it harder and harder to concentrate. Even the butterflies were moving restlessly above, the colorful sun-patterns made by their wings swimming back and forth across the great chamber.

At last Amerasu stood. She seemed much less frail than she had in her house. Simon had thought her then like a martyred saint, but now he saw in her a touch of the angelic, a power that smoldered low but which could burst out into pure white light. Her long hair moved in a breeze that might have come from the careful movement of a million wings.

"I see that the mortal child is here," she said, "so I will speak in a way that he can understand, as much of what I say came from him. He has a right to hear."

Several Sithi turned their heads to gaze impassively at Simon. Caught by surprise, he dropped his chin and looked down at his chest until they had turned away once more.

"In fact," Amerasu continued, "strange as this may sound, it is possible that some of the things I must say are better suited to the languages of the Sudhoda'ya. The mortals have always lived beneath one kind of darkness or another. That is among the reasons we named them 'sunset-children' when they first came to Osten Ard." She paused. "The manchildren, the mortals, have many ideas of what happens after they die, and wrangle about who is right and who is wrong. These disagreements often come to bloodshed, as if they wished to dispatch messengers who could discover the answer to their dispute. Such messengers, as far as I know of mortal philosophy, never return to give their brethren the taste of truth they yearn for.

"But among the mortal peoples there are stories that say that some *do* return as bodiless spirits, although they bring no answers with them. These spirits, these ghosts, are mute reminders of that shadow of death. Those who encounter such unhomed spirits call themselves 'haunted.' " Amerasu took a breath; her immense composure seemed to slip. It was a moment before she resumed. "That is a word we Zida'ya do not have, but perhaps we should."

The silence, but for the murmur of delicate wings, was absolute.

"We fled out of the Uttermost East, thinking to escape that Unbeing that overwhelmed our Garden-land. That story is known to all but the mortal boy—even those of our children born after the Flight from Asu'a take it in with their mother's milk—and so it will not be told again here.

"When we reached this new land, we thought we had escaped that shadow. But a piece of it came with us. That stain, that shadow, is part of us—just as the mortal men and women of Osten Ard cannot escape the shadow of their own dying.

"We are an old people. We do not fight the unfightable. That is why we fled Venyha Do'sae, rather than be unmade in a fruitless struggle. But the curse of our race is not that we refuse to throw down our lives in purposeless defiance of the great shadow, but that we instead clasp the shadow to ourselves and hug it tightly, gleefully, nursing it as we would a child.

"We brought the shadow with us. Perhaps no living, reasoning thing can be without such shadow, but we Zida'ya—despite our lives, beside which the spans of mortals are like fireflies—still we cannot ignore that shadow that is death. We cannot ignore the knowledge of Unbeing. Instead, we carry it with us like a brooding secret.

"The mortals must die, and they are frightened by that. We who were once of the Garden must also die, although our span is vastly greater, but we each embrace our death from the moment we first open our eyes, making it an insoluble part of us. We yearn for its complete embrace, even as the centuries roll by, while around us the death-fearing mortals breed and drop like mice. We make our death the core of our being, our private and innermost friend, letting life spin past as we enjoy Unbeing's grave company.

"We would not give Ruyan Vé's children the secret of our near-immortality, though they were stock of the same tree. We denied eternal life to Ruyan's folk, the Tinukeda'ya, even as we clasped Death tighter and tighter to our own bosoms. We are haunted, my children. The mortal word is the only correct one. We are haunted."

He did not understand most of what First Grandmother said, but Amerasu's voice worked on Simon like the scolding of a loving parent. He felt small and unimportant, but reassured that the voice was there and that it spoke to him. The Sithi around him maintained their careful impassivity.

"Then the ship-men came," Amerasu said, her voice deepening, "and were not content to live and die within the walls of Osten Ard as the mortal mice before them had been. They were not satisfied with the morsels we tossed to them. We Zida'ya could have stopped their depredations before they became great, but instead we grieved over the loss of beauty while secretly rejoicing. *Our death was coming!*—a glorious and final ending that would make the shadows real. My husband Iyu'unigato was one such. His gentle, poetic heart loved death more than it ever loved his wife or the sons of his loins."

For the first time a quiet whisper began to travel through the assembly, an uneasy murmur scarcely louder than the rustle of the butterflies overhead. Amerasu smiled sadly.

"It is hard to hear such things," she said, "but this is a time when truth must be spoken. Of all the Zida'ya, only one truly did not yearn for quiet oblivion. He was my son Ineluki, and he *burned*. I do not mean the manner of his dying—that may be seen as a cruel irony, or as a fated inevitability. No, Ineluki burned with life, and his light dispelled the shadows—at least some of them.

"All know what happened. All know that Ineluki slew his gentle father, that he was then unmade at the last, bringing Asu'a to destruction as he struggled to save himself and all his folk from oblivion. But his fires were so fierce that he could not go peacefully into the shadows beyond life. I curse him for what he did to my husband and his people and himself, but my mother's heart is still proud. By the Ships that brought us, he burned then and he burns still! *Ineluki will not die!*"

Amerasu lifted a hand as a fresh spatter of whispering rolled through the Yásira. "Peace, children, peace!" she cried, "First Grandmother has not herself embraced that shadow. I do not praise him for what he is now, only for the fierce spirit that no other showed, when such a spirit was the only thing that could save us from ourselves. And he did save us, for his resistance and even his madness gave others the will to flee here, to the house of our exile." She lowered her hand. "No, my son embraced hatred. It kept him from dying a true death, but it was a flame even hotter than his own, and it has consumed him. There is nothing left of the bright blaze that was my son." Her eyes were hooded. "Almost nothing."

When she did not speak for a while, Shima'onari rose as if to go to her, saying something quietly in the Sithi tongue. Amerasu shook her head. "No, grandson, let me speak." A touch of anger entered her voice. "This is all I have left, but if I am not heard, a darkness will descend that will be unlike the loving death which we sing to in our dreams. It will be worse than the Unbeing that drove us out of our Garden beyond the sea."

Shima'onari, looking curiously shaken, sat down beside stone-eyed Likimeya.

"Ineluki has changed," Amerasu resumed. "He has become something the world has not seen before, a smoldering ember of despair and hatred, surviving only to redress those things which long ago were injustices and mistakes and tragic underestimations, but now are simply facts. Like ourselves, Ineluki dwells in the realm of *what was*. But unlike his living kin, Ineluki is not content to wallow in memories of the past. He lives, or exists—here is a place the mortal language is too inexact—to see the present state of the world obliterated and the injustices made right, but his only window is anger. His justice will be cruel, his methods even more horrible."

She moved to stand beside the object on the stone pedestal, letting her slim fingers rest gently on the disk's rim. Simon feared that she would cut herself, and felt an abnormal horror at the idea of seeing blood on Amerasu's thin, golden skin.

"I have long known that Ineluki had returned, as have all of you. Unlike some, though, I have not pushed it from my mind, or rolled it over and over in my thoughts only to enjoy the pain of it, as one prods a bruise or sore spot. I have wondered, I have thought, and I have spoken with those few who could help me, trying to understand what might be growing in the shadows of my son's mind. The last of those who brought me knowledge was the mortal boy Seoman—although he did not realize, and still does not, half of what I gleaned from him."

Simon again felt eyes upon him, but his own were helplessly fixed to Amerasu's luminous face, framed in the great white cloud of her hair.

"That is just as well," she said. "The manchild has been fate-battered and chance-led in many curious ways, but he is no spell-wielder or great hero. He has fulfilled his responsibilities admirably, but needs no more heaped upon his young shoulders. But what I learned from him has, I think, taught me the true shape of Ineluki's plan." She took a deep breath, summoning strength. "*It is terrible.* I could tell you, but words may not suffice. I am the eldest of this tribe; I am Amerasu the Ship-Born. Still there would be some who would secretly doubt, and others who would continue to turn their faces away. Many of you would prefer to live with the beauty of imagined shadows instead of the ugly blackness at the core of *this* shadow—of the shadow that my son spreads over us all.

"So I will show you what *I* have seen, then *you* will see, too. If we can still turn our heads away, my children, at least we cannot continue to pretend. We may keep out the winter for a while, but at last it will engulf us, too." Her voice suddenly rose, plaintive but powerful. "If we are running joyfully into the arms of death, let us at least admit that is what we do! Let us for this once see ourselves plainly, even at the ending of things."

Amerasu let her gaze drop, as though great weariness or sorrow had overtaken her. There was a moment of silence, then just as a few quiet conversations had begun, she lifted her face to them once more and placed her hand on the pale moon-disk.

"This is the Mist Lamp, brought by my mother Senditu out of Tumet'ai as the creeping hoarfrost swallowed that city. As with the scales of the Greater Worm, as with the Speakfire, the singing Shard, and the Pool in great Asu'a, it is a door to the Road of Dreams. It has shown me many things. Now it is time to share those visions."

Amerasu reached down, lightly touching the bowl before the stone disk. A blue-white flame sprang up and hovered wickless above the bowl's pale rim. The disk began to gleam with a secretive light. Then, even as it grew brighter, the entire chamber of the Yásira started to darken, until it seemed to Simon that the afternoon had truly withered away and the moon had fallen from the sky to hang there before him.

"These days, the dream-lands have drawn nearer to our own," Amerasu said, "just as Ineluki's winter has surrounded and worn away the summer." Her voice, though clear, seemed but a whisper. "The dream-lands are troubled, and there will be moments when it is difficult to stay upon the road, so please lend me your thoughts and quiet assistance. The day is long passed when the daughters of Jenjiyana could speak as effortlessly through the Witnesses as from ear to ear." She waved a hand over the disk and the room grew darker still. The tender scraping of butterfly wings increased, as though the creatures felt change in the air.

The disk glowed. A bluish stain like fog crept across its face; when it passed, the Mist Lamp had turned black. In that blackness a scattering of icy stars appeared and a pale shape began to grow, sprouting up from the base of the Lamp's disk. It was a mountain, white and sharp as a tusk, bleak as bone.

"Nakkiga," Amerasu said from the darkness. "The mountain the mortals call Stormspike. The home of Utuk'ku, who hides her agedness behind a silver mask, unwilling to admit that the shadow of death can touch her, too. She fears Unbeing more than any other of our race, though she is the eldest who still lives—the last of the Gardenborn." Amerasu laughed quietly. "Yes, my great-grandmother is very vain." For a moment there was a flash of metal, but the Mist Lamp blurred and the mountain reappeared. "I can feel her," Amerasu said. "Like a spider, she waits. No fire of justice burns within her as it burns in Ineluki, however mad he has become. She wishes only to destroy all who remember how she was humbled in the dim, dim past when our peoples broke asunder. She gave my son's raging spirit a home; together they have fed each other's hatred. Now they are ready to do what they have plotted for so many centuries. Look!"

The Mist Lamp throbbed. The white mountain loomed closer, steaming beneath the cold black skies. Then, suddenly, it began to fade back into darkness. A few moments later it was gone, leaving only sable emptiness.

A long interval passed. Simon, who had been hanging on the Sitha woman's every word, felt suddenly adrift. The crackling tension in the air was back, stronger than ever.

"Oh!" Amerasu gasped, startled.

All around Simon the Sithi were shifting, murmuring, as questioning turned to uneasiness and the seeds of fear began to grow inside them. A gleam of silver appeared in the center of the Mist Lamp, then spread outward like oil on a pond, filling the darkened silhouette. The silver smeared and ran until it became a face, a woman's face, unmoving but for pale eyes that peered from the darkened slits.

Simon watched the silver mask helplessly, his eyes smarting as they filled with frightened tears. He could not look away. She was so old and strong . . . so strong . . .

"It has been many turns of the year, Amerasu no'e-Sa'onserei." The Norn Queen's voice was surprisingly melodious, but the sweetness could not entirely hide the vast corruption beneath. *"It has been long, granddaughter. Are you ashamed of your northern kin, that you have not invited us back among you before?"*

"You mock me, Utuk'ku Seyt-Hamakha." There was a quaver in Amerasu's voice, a frightening note of dismay. "All know the reasons for your exile and the separation of our families."

"You always loved righteousness, little Amerasu." The scorn in the Norn Queen's voice made Simon feel as though a fever ran through him. *"But the righteous soon become meddlers, and so it has always been with your long-reaching clan. You would not scourge the mortals from the land, which might have saved all. And even after they have destroyed the Gardenborn, you cannot leave the mortals be."* Utuk'ku's breath hissed in and out. *"Ah. I see, there is one among you even now!"*

Simon's heart seemed to grow, pushing up into his throat until he could scarcely breathe. Those terrible eyes staring at him—why didn't Amerasu make her go away?! He wanted to shout, to run, but could not. The Sithi-folk around him seemed equally nerveless, struck to stone.

"You oversimplify, grandmother," Amerasu said at last. "When do you not simply lie."

Utuk'ku laughed, and the sound was something that could set stones to weeping.

"Fool!" she cried. *"I oversimplify? You have overreached. You have long*

concerned yourself with the doings of mortals, but you have missed the most important things. That will prove your death!"

"I know what you plan!" Amerasu said. "You may have taken from me what remains of my son, but even through death, I have discerned his mind. I have seen . . ."

"Enough!" Utuk'ku's angry cry blew through the Yásira, a chill gust of wind that bent the grass and set the butterflies to panicky fluttering. *"Enough. You have spoken your last and condemned yourself. It is death!"*

Terrifyingly, Amerasu began to quiver in the dim light, struggling against some invisible restraint, her eyes wide, her mouth moving without sound.

"And you will not interfere further—any of you!" The Norn Queen's voice was rising to a dreadful pitch. *"The false peace is over! Over! Nakkiga renounces you all!"*

All around the Yásira the Sithi were shouting with amazement and anger. Likemeya rushed forward to the darkened figure of Amerasu, even as Utuk'ku's face shimmered and vanished from the Mist Lamp. The Witness fell dark for a moment, but only a moment. A tiny spot of red kindled in the Lamp's center, a small spark which grew steadily until it was a rippling blaze that outlined the startled features of Jiriki's parents and mute Amerasu with scarlet light. Two dark holes opened in the flame, lightless eyes in the face of fire. Simon felt himself seized in a grip of frozen horror, clutched so tight by it that his muscles quivered. Chill dread beat outward from that wavering face, as heat would rise from an ordinary fire. Amerasu stopped struggling, becoming as still as if she had turned to stone.

Another blackness gaped in the billowing flame, beneath the empty eyes. Bloodless laughter issued forth. Sickened, Simon struggled desperately to get away—he had seen this horror-mask before.

The Red Hand! He meant it to be a shout, but fear choked his words into helpless, whistling breath.

Likimeya stepped forward, her husband beside her, helping to shield Amerasu. She raised her arms before the Mist Lamp and the fiery thing that surged within it. A kind of silvery glow surrounded her. "Go back to your shriveled mistress and dead master, Corrupted One," she cried. "You are not one of us any more."

The flame-thing laughed again. *"No. We are more, far more! The Red Hand and its master have grown strong. All of creation must fall beneath the Storm King's shadow. Those who betrayed us will squeak and chitter in that darkness!"*

"You have no power here!" Shima'onari cried, grasping his wife's upraised hand. The glow around the two of them intensified, until the fog of silvery moonlight had grown to encompass the fiery face as well. "This place is beyond you! Go back to your cold mountain and black emptiness!"

"You do not understand!" the thing exulted. *"We, of all who ever lived, have returned from Unbeing. We have grown strong!* **Grown strong!***"*

Even as the hollow voice echoed through the Yásira, overwhelming the Sithi-folk's cries of rage and alarm, the thing in the Mist Lamp suddenly billowed *outward*, expanding into a vast pillar of flame, its shapeless head flung back in a thundering cry. It spread its blazing arms wide, as though to grasp all before it in a crushing, burning embrace.

As the sun-hot fires leaped up, the butterflies clinging to the silken threads overhead began to puff into flame. A million of them seemed to spring into the air at once, a great cloud of fire and smoking wings. Burning, they flew through the air like cinders, careening into the shouting Sithi, crumbling as they struck the trunk of the great ash tree. The Yásira was in chaos, plunged in a blackness shot with spinning, whirling sparks.

The towering thing at the room's center laughed and blazed, but gave no light. It seemed instead to suck all brightness into its own interior, so that it fattened and grew taller still. A wild, writhing knot of bodies leaped around it, the heads and waving arms of clamoring Sithi-folk silhouetted against the red blaze.

Simon looked around in panic. Jiriki was gone.

Another sound was now rising through the chaos, swelling until it equaled the terrible mirth of the Red Hand creature. It was the raw-throated baying of a hunting pack.

A horde of pale shapes came flooding into the Yásira. White hounds were suddenly everywhere, their slit eyes reflecting the hellish light of the thing at the chamber's center, their howling red mouths snapping and barking.

"Ruakha, ruakha Zida'yei!" Simon heard Jiriki shouting somewhere nearby. *"T'si e-isi'ha as-Shao Irigú!"*

Simon moaned, searching desperately for some weapon. A lithe white shape vaulted past him, carrying something in its dripping mouth.

Jingizu.

A memory forced itself into Simon's head. As though the blaze without had kindled a blaze within, a burning tongue of remembrance leaped up inside him: the black depths beneath the Hayholt, a dream of tragedy and ghostly fire.

Jingizu. The heart of all Sorrow.

The tempest of disorder rose and grew wilder, a thousand throats wailing in the spark-flurrying darkness, a broil of flailing limbs and terrified eyes and the maddening voices of the Stormspike pack. Simon tried to stand, then quickly threw himself back to the ground. The scrambling Sithi had found their bows: arrows were flying through the smoky air, visible only as streaks of light.

A hound stumbled toward Simon and sagged to the ground at his feet, a blue-fletched arrow through its neck. Revolted, Simon crawled away from the corpse, feeling the grass and the parchment ashes of butterflies between his fingers. His hand closed upon a rock, which he lifted and clutched. He crept forward like a blind mole toward where the heat and noise were greatest, driven by nothing he could describe, helplessly reliving something he might have experienced in a dream, a vision of spectral figures that ran in fearful panic while their home died in flames.

A huge beast, the largest hound Simon had ever seen, had driven Shima'onari back toward the trunk of the great ash tree, forcing the lord of the Sithi up against the blackened and smoldering bark. Shima'onari's robe was smoking. Weaponless, Jiriki's father held the dog's massive head in his bare hands, struggling to keep the clashing jaws from his face. Strange lights flickered around them, blue and glaring red.

Near where his father struggled, Jiriki and several others had surrounded the bellowing fire-creature. The prince was a small figure standing before the beast of the Red Hand, his witchwood sword Indreju a black tongue of shadow held upraised against the shimmering flames.

Simon lowered his head and crawled forward, still struggling toward the center of the Yásira. The din was deafening. Bodies pushed past him, some of the Sithi racing forward to help Jiriki fight the invader, others running like maddened creatures, their hair and clothes afire.

A sudden blow flung Simon to the turf. One of the dogs was upon him, its corpselike snout thrusting for his throat, blunt claws scraping at his arms as he tried frantically to twist out from under it. He groped unseeing until he found the stone that had slipped from his grasp, then struck at the creature's head. It yelped wetly and dug its teeth into his shirt, gouging his shoulder as it tried to reach his neck. He struck again, struggled to free his weary arm, then brought the stone down once more. The dog went limp and slid down his chest. Simon rolled over and kicked the body away.

A scream abruptly shuddered out, overtopping the tumult, and a wintry wind howled through the Yásira, a freezing gale that seemed to pass right through him. Fanned by that wind, the fiery figure at the center of the chamber grew even larger for a moment, then fell back into itself in a burst of billowing flame. There was a sound like thunder, then Simon felt a great percussive slap against his ears as the creature of the Red Hand vanished in a rain of hissing sparks. Another rush of wind threw Simon and many others flat on the ground as air hurried to fill the space where the blazing thing had been. After that, a strange sort of quiet came down over the Yásira.

Stunned, Simon lay on his back staring upward. The sheen of natural twilight slowly returned, gleaming through the mighty tree whose limbs were now empty of living butterflies, but studded with their blackened remains. Groaning, Simon clambered up onto his shaky legs. All around him the inhabitants of Jao é-Tinukai'i were still milling in shocked disorder. Those Sithi who had found spears and bows were putting an end to the remaining dogs.

Had that terrible scream been the fire-creature's death shriek? Had Jiriki and the others somehow destroyed it? He stared into the cloudy murk in the middle of the chamber, trying to see who it was that stood beside the Mist Lamp. He squinted and took a step forward. Amerasu was there . . . and someone else. Simon felt his heart lurch.

A figure with a helmet made in the image of a snarling dog stood at First Grandmother's shoulder, wreathed in the smoke curling up from the scorched earth. One of this intruder's leather-clad arms was around her waist, clutching her slight, sagging form as closely as it might hold a lover. The other hand slowly lifted the hound-helm free, revealing the tanned mask of Ingen Jegger.

"Niku'a!" he shouted. "*Yinva!* Come to me!" The huntsman's eyes gleamed scarlet, reflecting the smoldering bark of the great tree.

Near the trunk of the ash, the huge white hound rose unsteadily. Its fur was scorched and blackened, its ragged maw all but toothless. Shima'onari remained unmoving on the ground where the beast had crouched, a bloodied arrow clutched in the Sithi-lord's fist. The dog took a step, then fell clumsily and rolled onto its side. Innards gleamed from the opening in its belly as Niku'a's broad chest moved slowly up and down.

The huntsman eye's widened. "You've killed him!" Ingen screamed. "My pride! The best of the kennels!" He carried Amerasu before him as he took a few steps toward the dying hound. First Grandmother's head bobbed limply. "Niku'a!" Ingen hissed, then turned and looked slowly around the Yásira. The Sithi stood unmoving all around, their faces blood-stained and ash-smeared as they silently returned the huntsman's stare.

Ingen Jegger's thin mouth contorted in sorrow. He lifted his eyes to the scorched limbs of the ash tree and the gray sky above. Amerasu was pinned against his chest, her white hair curtaining her face.

"Murder!" he cried, then there was a long moment of silence.

"What do you want from First Grandmother, mortal?"

It was Likemeya who spoke so calmly. Her white dress was smeared with ashes. She had come to kneel beside her fallen husband, and she held his reddened hand in hers. "You have caused enough heartache. Let her go. Leave this place. We will not pursue you."

Ingen stared at her as at some long-forgotten landmark seen after a hard journey. His frown stretched into a ghastly smile and he shook Amerasu's helpless form until her head wobbled. He lifted his hound-helm—the fist that clutched it was crimson-drenched—and waved it in mad joy.

"The forest witch is dead!" he howled. "I have done it! Praise me, mistress, I have done your bidding!" He lifted his other hand to the skies, letting Amerasu slump to the ground like a discarded sack. Blood shone dully on her gray robe and golden hands. The translucent hilt of the crystal dagger stood out from her side. "I am immortal!" cried the Queen's Huntsman.

Simon's choked gasp echoed in the terrible silence.

Ingen Jegger slowly turned. Recognizing Simon, the huntsman curled his mouth in a lipless smile. "You led me to her, boy."

An ash-darkened figure rose from the smoking clutter at Ingen's feet.

"Venyha s'anh!" Jiriki shouted, and drove Indreju squarely into the huntsman's midsection.

Driven backward by the impact of Jiriki's blow, Ingen at last staggered to a halt, bending over the length of the blade which had been wrenched from its owner's hand. He gradually straightened, then coughed. Blood dribbled from his mouth and stained his pale beard, but his smile remained. "The time of the Dawn Children . . . is over," he rasped. There was a humming sound. Suddenly, a half-dozen arrows stood in Ingen's broad trunk, sprouting on all sides like hedgehog quills.

"Murder!"

It was Simon who shouted this time. He leaped to his feet, his heartbeat sounding loud as war-drums in his ears; he felt the whipsong breath of the second volley of arrows as he ran forward toward the huntsman. He swung the heavy stone which he had clutched for so long.

"Seoman! No!" shouted Jiriki.

The huntsman slid to his knees, but remained upright. "Your witch . . . is dead," he panted. He raised a hand toward the approaching Simon. "The sun is setting . . ."

More arrows leaped across the Yásira and Ingen Jegger slowly topped to the ground.

Hatred burst out like a flame in Simon's heart as he stood over the huntsman, and he raised the stone high in the air. Ingen Jegger's face was still frozen in an exultant grin, and for the thinnest moment his pale blue eyes locked with Simon's. An instant later Ingen's face disappeared in a smash of red and the huntsman's body was rolled across the ground by the force of the blow. Simon clambered after him with a wordless cry of rage, all his pent frustration flooding out in a maddening surge.

They've taken everything from me. They laughed at me. Everything.

The fury turned into a kind of wild glee. He felt strength flowing through him. At last! He brought the rock down upon Ingen's head, lifted it and smashed it down again, then over and over uncontrollably until hands pulled him away from the body and he slid down into his own red darkness.

Khendraja'aro brought him to Jiriki. The prince's uncle, as all the other citizens of Jao é-Tunukai'i, was dressed in dark mourning gray. Simon, too, wore pants and shirt of that color, brought to him by a subdued Aditu the day after the burning of the Yásira.

Jiriki was staying in a house not his own, a dwelling of pink, yellow, and pale brown circular tents that Simon thought looked like giant bee-hives. The Sitha-woman who lived there was a healer, Aditu had told him. The healer was taking care that Jiriki's burns were given proper care.

Kehndraja'aro, his face a stiff, heavy mask, left Simon at the house's wind-whipped entranceway and departed without a word. Simon entered as Aditu had directed and found himself in a darkened room lit only by a single dim globe on a wooden stand. Jiriki was propped up in a great bed. His hands lay upon his chest, bandaged with strips of silky cloth. The Sitha's face was shiny with some oily substance, which served only to accentuate his otherworldly appearance. Jiriki's skin was blackened in many places, and his eyebrows and some of his long hair had been scorched away, but Simon was relieved to see that the Prince did not seem badly scarred.

"Seoman," Jiriki said, and showed a trace of smile.

"How are you?" Simon asked shyly. "Are you hurting?"

The prince shook his head. "I do not suffer much, not from these burns, Seoman. In my family we are made of stern stuff—as you may remember from our first meeting." Jiriki looked him up and down. "And how is your own health?"

Simon felt awkward. "I'm well." He paused. "I'm so sorry." Facing the calm figure before him, he was ashamed by his own animality, ashamed to have become a screaming brute before the eyes of all. That memory had weighed heavily on him in the days just passed. "It was all my fault."

Jiriki hastened to raise his hand, then eased it back down, conceding only a small grimace of pain. "No, Seoman, no. You have done nothing for which you should apologize. That was a day of terror, and you have suffered far too many of those."

"It's not that," Simon said miserably. "He followed me! Ingen Jegger said he followed me to find First Grandmother! I led her murderer here."

Jiriki shook his head. "This was planned for some time, Seoman. Believe me, the Red Hand could not lightly send one of their own into the fastness of Jao é-Tunukai'i, even for the few moments it lasted. Ineluki is not yet so strong. That was a well-conceived attack, one long considered. It took a great deal of power from both Utuk'ku and the Storm King to accomplish it.

"Do you think it a coincidence that First Grandmother should be silenced by Utuk'ku just before she could reveal Ineluki's design? That the Red Hand creature should force its way through just then, at a tremendous expense of spell-bought strength? And do you think the huntsman Ingen was just wandering in the wood and suddenly decided to kill Amerasu the Ship-Born? No, I do not think so, either—although it is true that he may have stumbled on your trail before Aditu brought you here. Ingen Jegger was no fool, and it would have been far easier for him to track a mortal than one of us, but he would have found his way into Jao é-Tunukai'i somehow. Who can know how long he waited beyond the Summer Gate once he had found it, waiting for his mistress to set him upon her enemies at just the right moment? It was a war plan, Seoman, precise and more than a little desperate. They must have feared First Grandmother's wisdom very much."

Jiriki lifted his bandaged hand to his face, touching it for a moment to his forehead. "Do not take the blame upon yourself, Seoman. Amerasu's death was ordained in the black pits below Nakkiga—or perhaps even when the Two Families parted at Sesuad'ra, thousands of years ago. We are a race that nurses its hurts a long time in silence. You were not at fault."

"But why!?" Simon wanted to believe Jirki's words, but the horrible sense of loss that had threatened to overwhelm him several times already that morning would not go away.

"Why? Because Amerasu had seen into Ineluki's secret heart—and who would have been better able to do that than she? She had discovered his design at last and was going to reveal it to her people. Now, we may never know—or perhaps we will understand only when Ineluki sees fit to display it in all its inevitability." Weariness seemed to wash through him. "By our Grove, Seoman, we have lost so much! Not only Amerasu's wisdom, which was great, but we have also lost our last link with the Garden. We are truly unhomed." He lifted his eyes to the billowing ceiling, so that his angular face was bathed in pale yellow light. "The Hernystiri had a song of her, you know:

> "*Snow-white breast, lady of the foaming sea,*
> *She is the light that shines by night*
> *Until even the stars are drunken . . .*"

Jiriki took a careful breath to ease his scorched throat. A look of surprising fury contorted his normally placid face. "Even from the place where Ineluki lives, from beyond death—*how could he send a stranger to kill his mother!?*"

"What will we do? How can we fight him?"

"That is not for you to worry about, Seoman Snowlock."

"What do you mean?" Simon restrained his anger. "How can you say that to me? After all we've both seen?"

"I did not mean it in the way it sounded, Seoman." The Sitha smiled in self-mockery. "I have lost even the basest elements of courtesy. Forgive me."

Simon saw that he was actually waiting. "Of course, Jiriki. Forgiven."

"I mean only that we Zida'ya have our own councils to keep. My father

Shima'onari is badly wounded and Likimeya my mother must call the folk together—but not at the Yásira. I think we will never meet in that place again. Did you know, Seoman, that the great tree was burned white as snow? Did you not have a dream once about such a thing?" Jiriki cocked his head, his gaze full of subtle light. "Ah, forgive me again. I wander in thought and forget the important things. Has anyone told you? Likimeya has decreed that you will go."

"Go? Leave Jao é-Tinukai'i?" The rush of joy was accompanied by an unexpected current of regret and anger. "Why now?"

"Because it was Amerasu's last wish. She told my parents before the gathering began. But why do you sound so unsettled? You will go back to your own people. It is for the best, in any case. We Zida'ya must mourn the loss of our eldest, our best. This is no place for mortals, now—and it is what you wanted, is it not? To go back to your folk?"

"But you can't just close yourselves off and turn away! Not this time! Didn't you hear Amerasu? We all have to fight the Storm King! It is cowardice not to!" Her stern, soft face was suddenly before him again, at least in memory. Her magnificently knowing eyes . . .

"Calm yourself, young friend," Jiriki said with a tight, angry smile. "You are full of good intentions, but you do not know enough to speak so forcefully." His expression softened. "Fear not, Seoman. Things are changing. The Hikeda'ya have killed our eldest, struck her down in our own sacred house. They have crossed a line that cannot be recrossed. Perhaps they meant to, but that matters less than the fact that it has happened. That is another reason for you to leave, manchild. There is no place for you in the war councils of the Zida'ya."

"Then you're going to fight?" Simon felt a sudden pinch of hope at his heart.

Jiriki shrugged. "Yes, I think so—but how or when is not for me to say."

"It's all so much," Simon murmured. "So fast."

"You must go, young friend. Aditu will return soon from attending my parents. She will take you to where you can find your folk. It is best done swiftly, since it is not usual for Shima'onari or Likimeya to undo their own Words of Decree. Go. My sister will come to you at my house by the river." Jiriki leaned down and lifted something from the mossy floor. "And do not forget to take your mirror, my friend." He smiled slyly. "You may need to call me again, and I still owe you a life."

Simon took the gleaming thing and slid it into his pocket. He hesitated, then leaned forward and carefully wrapped his arms around Jiriki, trying not to touch his burns as he gently embraced him. The Sithi prince touched Simon's cheek with his cool lips.

"Go in peace, Seoman Snowlock. We will meet again. That is a promise."

"Farewell, Jiriki." He turned and marched swiftly away without looking back. He slowed his pace after he stumbled once in the winding hallway, a long, wind-rippled tunnel the color of sand.

Outside, immersed in a swirl of confused thoughts, Simon suddenly realized that he was feeling a curious chill. Looking up, he saw that the summery skies over Jao é-Tinukai'i had darkened, taking on a more somber hue. The breeze was colder than any he had ever felt there before.

The summer is fading, he thought, and was frightened again. *I don't think they'll ever get it back.*

Suddenly all his petty anger toward the Sithi evaporated and a great, heavy sorrow for them overtook him. Whatever else was here, there was also beauty unseen since the world was young, long preserved against the killing frosts of time. Now the walls were tumbling down before a great, wintery wind. Many exquisite things might be ravaged beyond reclaiming.

He hurried along the riverbank toward Jiriki's house.

The journey out of Jao é-Tinukai'i passed swiftly for Simon, dim and slippery as a dream. Aditu sang in her family's tongue and Simon held her hand tightly as the forest shimmered and changed around them. They walked out of cool grayish-blue skies into the very jaws of winter, which had lain in wait like a stalking beast.

Snow covered the forest floor, a blanket so thick and cold that it was hard for Simon to remember that Jao é-Tinukai'i itself had not been covered, that in that one place winter was still held at bay: here outside the magical circle of the Zida'ya, the Storm King's handiwork was so terribly real. But now, he realized, even that circle had been broken. Blood had been spilled in the very heart of summer.

They walked through the morning and early afternoon, gradually leaving the densest part of the woods and moving toward the forest fringe. Aditu answered Simon's few questions, but neither had the strength for much talk, as though the awful cold had withered the affection that had once flowered between them. As uncomfortable as her presence had often made him, still Simon was saddened, but the world had changed somehow and he had no more strength to struggle. He let the winter world flow over him like a dream, and did not think.

They walked for some hours beside a swift river, following it until they reached a long gentle slope. Before them lay a vast body of water, as gray and mysterious as an alchemist's bowl. A shadowed, tree-covered hill jutted from it like a dark pestle.

"There is your destination, Seoman," Aditu said abruptly. "That is Sesuad'ra."

"The Stone of Farewell?"

Aditu nodded. "The Leavetaking Stone."

The abstraction finally made real, Simon felt as though he were stepping from one dream into another. "But how will I get there? Am I supposed to swim?"

Aditu said nothing, but led him down the slope to where the river rushed into the gray water, spilling across the rocks with a roar. A little distance along the shoreline, out of the way of the river's turbulent inflow, a small, silvery boat bobbed at anchor. "Once every hundred or so winters," she said, "when the rains are particularly fierce, the lands around Sesuad'ra flood—although this is certainly the first time it has ever happened when Reniku the Summer-Lantern was in the sky." She turned away, unwilling to share thoughts written on her face so that even a mortal could understand. "We keep these *hiyanha*—these boats—here and there, so that Sesuad'ra will not be denied to those who wish to visit it."

Simon put his hand on the little boat, feeling the smooth grain of the wood beneath his fingers. A paddle of the same silvery stuff lay in the hull. "And you're sure that's where I go?" he asked, suddenly unwilling to say good-bye.

Aditu nodded. "Yes, Seoman." She shrugged off the bag she had been carrying on her shoulder and handed it to him. "This is for you—no," she corrected herself, "not for you. It is for you to take to your Prince Josua, from Amerasu. She said she believed he would know what to do with it—if not now, then soon."

"Amerasu? She sent this. . . ?"

Aditu put a hand on his cheek. "Not exactly, Seoman. First Grandmother had asked me to take it if your imprisonment did not end. Since you have been released, I give it to you." She stroked his face. "I am glad for your sake that you are free. It pained me to see you so unhappy. It was good to know of you—a rare thing." She leaned forward and kissed him. Despite all that had happened, he still felt a quickening of his heart as her mouth touched his. Her lips were warm and dry and tasted of mint.

Aditu stepped away. "Farewell, Snowlock. I must go back and mourn."

Before he could even lift his hand to wave, she turned and disappeared among the trees. He watched for some moments, looking for some sign of her slender form, but she was gone. He turned and clambered into the small boat and set the sack she had given him down in the hull. It was of good weight, but he was too weary and sore-hearted even to look at what might be inside. He thought it might be peaceful to fall asleep here in the boat, at the edge of the great forest. It would be a blessing to sleep and not wake for a year and a day. Instead, he picked up his paddle and pushed himself out onto the still water.

The afternoon fell away and the deep chill of evening came on. As Simon floated toward the growing shadow of Sesuad'ra, he felt the silence of the winter world envelop him, until he thought he might be the only living, moving thing upon the face of Osten Ard.

For a long time he did not notice that there were torches bobbing before him on the twilit shoreline. When he saw them at last, he was already close enough to hear the voices. His arms were cold and numb. He felt as though he had no more strength left to paddle, but managed to push himself a few last strokes, until a large, splashing shape—Sludig?—waded out from the rocky verge and pulled him into shore. He was lifted from the boat and half-carried up the bank, then surrounded by an army of torchlit, laughing faces. They seemed familiar, but the sensation of dream was upon him again. It was not until he saw the smallest figure that he remembered where he was. He staggered forward and swept Binabik into his arms, crying unashamedly.

"Simon-friend!" Binabik chortled, thumping him on the back with his small hands. "Qinkipa is good! Joyful! This is joyful! In the days since I was coming here I had almost lost my hope to see you."

Simon wept, unable to speak. At last, when he had cried himself dry, he set the little man down. "Binabik," he said, voice raw. "Oh, Binabik. I have seen terrible things."

"Not now, Simon, not now." The troll took his hand firmly. "Come. Come up to the hilltop. Fires have been built there and I am sure there is something cooking. Come."

The little man led him. The crowd of familiar strangers fell in behind, talking and laughing among themselves. The flames of the torches hissed beneath a soft fall of snow, and sparks rose into the sky to drift and fade. Soon one of them began to sing, a good, homely sound. As darkness crept over the drowned valley, the sweet, clear voice rose through the trees and echoed out over the black water.

Appendix

Appendix

PEOPLE

ERKYNLANDERS

Barnabas—Hayholt chapel sexton

Breyugar—Count of the Westfold, Lord Constable of the Hayholt under Elias

Colmund—Camaris' squire, later baron of Rodstanby

Deornoth, Sir—Josua's knight, sometimes called "Prince's Right Hand"

Eahlstan Fiskerne—Fisher King, first Erkynlandish master of Hayholt

Elias—High King, Prester John's eldest son, Josua's brother

Ethelbearn—soldier, Simon's companion on journey from Naglimund

Fengbald—Earl of Falshire

Gamwold—soldier dead from Norn attack in Aldheorte

Godwig—Baron of Cellodshire

Grimmric—soldier, Simon's companion on journey from Naglimund

Guthwulf—Earl of Utanyeat, High King's Hand

Haestan—Naglimund guardsman, Simon's companion

Helfcene, Father—Chancellor of Hayholt

Helmfest—soldier, part of company that escaped Naglimund

Hepzibah—castle chambermaid

Ielda—Falshire woman, Gadrinsett squatter

Inch—foundry-master, once Doctor Morgenes' assistant

Jack Mundwode—mythical forest bandit

Jael—castle chambermaid

Jakob—castle chandler

Jeremias—chandler's boy

John—King John Presbyter, High King

Josua—Prince, John's younger son, lord of Naglimund, called "Lackhand"

Judith—Cook and Kitchen Mistress

Langrian—Hoderundian monk

Leleth—Miriamele's handmaiden

Malachias—one of Miriamele's disguise names
Marya—one of Miriamele's disguise names
Master of Scullions—Simon's Hayholt master
Miriamele, Princess—Elias' only child
Morgenes, Doctor—Scrollbearer, King John's castle doctor, Simon's friend
Osgal—one of Mundwode's mythical band
Ostrael—Naglimund pikeman, son of Firsfram of Runchester
Rachel—Mistress of Chambermaids, called "The Dragon"
Ruben the Bear—castle smith
Sangfugol—Josua's harper
Sarrah—castle chambermaid
Shem Horsegroom—castle groom
Simon—a castle scullion, given name "Seoman" at birth
Strangyeard, Father—Archivist of Naglimund
Towser—jester (original name: Cruinh)

HERNYSTIRI

Arnoran—Hernystiri minstrel
Bagba—Cattle God
Brynioch of the Skies—Sky God
Cadrach-ec-Crannhyr, Brother—monk of indeterminate Order
Craobhan—old knight, advisor to King Lluth
Cuamh Earthdog—Hernystiri god of the earth, patron deity of miners
Eolair—Count of Nad Mullach, emissary of King Lluth
Gealsgiath—ship's captain, called "Old"
Gwythinn—Prince, Lluth's son, Maegwin's half-brother
Hern—Founder of Hernystir
Inahwen—Lluth's third wife
Lluth-ubh-Llythinn—King of Hernystir
Maegwin, Princess—Lluth's daughter, Gwythinn's half-sister
Mircha—Rain Goddess, wife of Brynioch
Mullachi—residents of Eolair's holding, Nad Mullach
Murhagh One-Arm—a god
Rhynn of the Cauldron—a god
Sinnach—Prince, Battle of Ach Samrath war-leader, also at the Knock

RIMMERSMEN

Einskaldir—Rimmersgard chieftain
Elvrit—First Osten Ard king of Rimmersmen

Endë—child at Skodi's
Fingil—King, first master of Hayholt, "Bloody King"
Gutrun—Duchess of Elvritshalla, Isgrumnur's wife, Isorn's mother
Hengfisk—Hoderundian priest
Hjeldin—King, Fingil's son, "Mad King"
Ingen Jegger—Black Rimmersman, master of Norn hounds
Isbeorn—Isgrimnur's father, first Rimmersgard duke under John, also his
    son's pseudonym
Isgrimnur—Duke of Elvritshalla, Gutrun's husband
Isorn—Isgrimnur's and Gutrun's son
Jarnauga—Scrollbearer from Tungoldyr
Nisse—(Nisses) Hjeldin's priest-helper, author of *Du Svardenvyrd*
Skali—Thane of Kaldskryke, called "Sharp-nose"
Skendi—Saint, founder of abbey
Skodi—young Rimmerswoman at Grinsaby
Sludig—young soldier, Simon's companion
Storfot—Thane of Vestvennby
Tonnrud—Thane of Skoggey, Duchess Gutrun's uncle.
Udun—Ancient Sky God

NABBANAI

Anitulles—former Imperator
Antippa, Lady—daughter of Leobardis and Nessalanta
Ardrivis—last Imperator, uncle of Camaris
Aspitis Preves—Earl of Drina and Eadne
Benidrivine—Nabbanai noble house, kingfisher crest
Benigaris—Duke of Nabban, son of Leobardis and Nessalanta
Camaris-sá-Vinitta—brother of Leobardis, friend of Prester John
Clavean—Nabbanai noble house, pelican crest
Claves—former Imperator
Crexis the Goat—former Imperator
Dinivan—Lector Ranessin's secretary
Domitis—Bishop of Saint Sutrin's cathedral in Erchester
Elysia—mother of Usires
Emettin—legendary knight
Fluiren, Sir—famous Johannine knight of disgraced Sulian House
Hylissa—Miriamele's late mother, Elias' wife, Nessalanta's sister
Ingadarine—noble family, albatross house-crest
Larexes III—former Lector of Mother Church
Leobardis—Duke of Nabban, father of Benigaris, Varellan, Antippa
Nessalanta—Duchess of Nabban, Benigaris' mother, Miriamele's aunt
Neylin—Septes' companion

Nuanni (Nuannis)—ancient sea god of Nabban

Pelippa, Saint—noblewoman from Book of Aedon, called "Pelippa of the Island"

Prevan—noble family, osprey house-crest (ocher and black)

Pryrates, Father—priest, alchemist, wizard, Elias' counselor

Ranessin, Lector—(born Oswine of Stanshire, an Erkynlander) Head of Church

Rhiappa—Saint, called "Rhiap" in Erkynland

Rovalles—Septes' companion

Septes—monk from abbey near Lake Myrme

Sulis, Lord—Hayholt's "Heron King" sometimes known as Sulis the Apostate: Nabbanai nobleman, founder of Sulian House, of which Sir Fluiren is best-known descendent

Thures—Aspitis' young page

Tiyagaris—first Imperator

Usires Aedon—Aedonite religion's Son of God

Velligis—Escritor

SITHI

Aditu—daughter of Likimeya and Shima'onari, Jiriki's sister

Amerasu y'Senditu no'e-Sa'onserei—mother of Ineluki and Hakatri, Jiriki's great-grandmother, also known as "Amerasu Ship-Born" and "First Grandmother"

An'nai—Jiriki's lieutenant, hunting companion

Cloud-song—character in Aditu's song

Gardenborn—all those whose roots can be traced to Venyha Do'sae, the "Garden"

Hakatri—Ineluki's elder brother, gravely wounded by dragon Hidohebhi, vanished into West

Ineluki—Prince, now Storm King

Iyu'unigato—Erl-king, Ineluki's father

Jiriki, (i-Sa'onserei)—Prince, son of Shimao'anari and Likimeya

Kendhraja'aro—Jiriki's uncle

Kiushapo—companion of Simon and Jiriki on trip to Urmsheim

Lady Silver Mask and Lord Red Eyes—Skodi's names for Utuk'ku and Ineluki

Lantern-bearer—character in Aditu's song

Likimeya—Queen of the Dawn-Children, Lady of the House of Year-Dancing

Maye'sa—Sitha woman

Mezumiiru—Sithi Sedda (Moon Goddess)

Nenais'u—Sithi woman from An'nai's song, lived in Enki-e-Shao'saye

Rabbit—Jiriki's name for Aditu
Senditu—Amerasu's mother
Shima'onari—King of the Zida'ya, Lord of Jao é-Tunukai'i
Sijandi—companion of Simon and Jiriki on trip to Urmsheim
Sky-singer—character in Aditu's song
Stone-listener—character in Aditu's song
Utuk'ku Seyt-Hamakha—Queen of the Norns, mistress of Nakkiga
Vindaomeyo the Fletcher—ancient Sithi arrow-maker of Tumet'ai
Willow-switch—Aditu's name for Jiriki
Wind-child—character in Aditu's song
Woman-with-a-net—character in Aditu's song (probably Mezumiiru)

QANUC

Binabik—(Binbiniqegabenik) Ookequk's apprentice, Simon's friend
Chukku—legendary troll hero
Kikkasut—king of birds, husband of Sedda
Lingit—legendary son of Sedda, father of Qanuc and men
Makuhkuya—Qanuc avalanche goddess.
Morag Eyeless—Death god
Nunuuika—the Huntress
Ookequk—Singing Man of Mintahoq tribe, Binabik's master
Qangolik—the Spirit Caller
Qinkipa of the Snows—snow and cold goddess
Sedda—moon goddess, wife of Kikkasut
Sisqi—(Sisqinanamook) youngest daughter of Herder and Huntress, Binabik's betrothed
Snenneq—herd-chief of Lower Chugik, part of Sisqi's party
Uammannaq—the Herder
Yana—legendary daughter of Sedda, mother of Sithi

THRITHINGS-FOLK

Blehmunt—chieftain Fikolmij killed to become March-thane
Clan Mehrdon—Vorzheva's clan (Stallion Clan)
Fikolmij—Vorzheva's father, March-thane of Clan Mehrdon and all the High Thrithings
Hotvig—High Thrithings randwarder
Hyara—Vorzheva's young sister
Kunret—High Thrithings-man
Ozhbern—High Thrithings-man

The Four-Footed—Thrithings clan-oath (refers to the Stallion)
The Grass Thunderer—Thrithings clan-oath (refers to the Stallion)
Utvart—Thrithings-man who wished to wed Vorzheva
Vorzheva—Josua's companion, daughter of a Thrithings-chief

WRANNAMEN

He Who Always Steps on Sand—Wran god
He Who Bends the Trees—Wran weather god
Older Mogahib—Wrannman elder
Roahog—potter, Wrannaman elder
She Who Birthed Mankind—goddess
She Who Waits to Take All Back—Wran death goddess
They Who Breathe Darkness—Wran gods
They Who Watch and Shape—Wran gods
Tiamak—scholar, correspondent of Morgenes
Tugumak—Tiamak's father

PERDRUINESE

Alespo—Streáwe's servant
Ceallio—door-keeper at inn called *Pelippa's Bowl*
Charystra—Xorastra's niece, innkeeper of *Pelippa's Bowl*
Lenti—Streáwe's servant, also known as "Avi Stetto"
Middastri—trader, friend of Tiamak
Sinetris—boatman living on coast above Wran
Streáwe, Count—Lord of Ansis Pelippé and all Perdruin
Tallistro, Sir—Johannine knight of Great Table
Xorastra—proprietress of *Pelippa's Bowl*

OTHERS

Gan Itai—Niskie, kilpa-singer on *Eadne Cloud*
Honsa—a Hyrka girl, one of Skodi's children
Imai-an—a dwarrow
Lightless Ones—dwellers in Stormspike
Ruyan Vé—also known as Ruyan the Navigator, led Tinukeda'ya (and
    others) to Osten Ard
Sho-vennae—a dwarrow

Vren—Hyrka boy
Yis-fidri—a dwarrow, Yis-hadra's husband, keeper of Pattern Hall
Yis-hadra—a dwarrow, Yis-fidri's wife, keeper of Pattern Hall

PLACES

Abaingeat—Hernystiri trading port, on Barraillean River at coast
Aldheorte—large forest covering much of Central Osten Ard
Anitullean Road—main road into Nabban from east, through Commeis Valley
Ansis Pelippé—capital and largest city of Perdruin
Asu'a the Eastward-Looking—Sithi name for Hayholt
Bacea-sá-Repra—harbor town on northern coast of Nabban, in Bay of Emettin; means "River-mouth."
Banipha-sha-zé—the Pattern Hall in Mezutu'a
Baraillean—river on border of Hernystir and Erkynland; called "Greenwade" in Erkynland
Bay of Emettin—bay north of Nabban
Bay of Firannos—bay south of Nabban, location of "Southern Islands"
Bellidan—Nabannai town on Anitullean Road, in Commeis Valley
Blue Mud Lake—Lake at eastern base of Trollfells, summer home of Qanuc
Cellodshire—Erkynlandish barony west of Gleniwent
Chidsik Ub Lingit—Qanuc's "House of the Ancestor," on Mintahoq in Yiqanuc
Commeis Valley—Opening to Nabban
Crannhyr—walled city on Hernystiri coast
Da'ai Chikiza—"Tree of the Singing Winds," abandoned Sithi city on east side of Wealdhelm, in Aldheorte
Dillathi—hilly region of Hernystir, southwest of Hernysadharc
Drina—former barony of Devasalles, given to Aspitis Preves by Benigaris
Enki-e-Shao'saye—Sithi "Summer-City" east of Aldheorte, long-ruined
Feathered Eel—tavern on Vinitta
Feluwelt—Thrithings name for part of northern meadowlands in shadow of Aldheorte
Gadrinsett—squatter town near juncture of Stefflod and Ymstrecca, settled by refugees from Erkynland
Garden that is Vanished—Venyha Do'sae
Gate of Rains—entrance to Jao é-Tinukai'i
Granis Sacrana—town in Nabban's Commeis valley

Gratuvask—Rimmersgard river that runs by Elvritshalla

Grenamman—southern island off tip of Nabban

Grinsaby—town in White Waste north of Aldheorte

Harborstone—a rocky promontory in Perdruin's Ansis Pelippé

Hasu Vale—valley on Erkynland's eastern borders

Hewenshire—northern Erkynlandish town west of Naglimund

Hikehikayo—abandoned dwarrow city beneath Rimmersgard's Vestivegg Mountains, also one of Sithi Nine Cities

Huelheim—mythical land of the dead from old Rimmersgard religion

Jao é-Tinukai'i—Boat on [the] Ocean [of] Trees", only still-thriving Sithi settlement, in Aldheorte

Jhiná-T'senei—one of Sithi Nine Cities, now beneath ocean

Kementari—one of Sithi Nine Cities, apparently on or near Warinsten

Khandia—mythical ancient empire in far south

Kwanitupul—large city on edge of Wran

Lake Clodu—Nabbanai lake, scene of Battle of the Lakelands, Thrithings War

Lake Eadne—Nabbanai lake, part of fiefdom of Prevan House

Lake Myrme—Nabbanai lake

Little Nose—also known as "Yamok," mountain in Yiqanuc where Binabik's parents died

Mezutu'a—dwarrow-occupied city beneath Hernystir's Grianspog Mountains, one of Sithi Nine Cities

Pelippa's Bowl—inn at Kwanitupul

Naarved—Rimmersgard city

Nakkiga—"Mask of Tears," ruined Norn city beside Stormspike, also rebuilt Norn city inside mountain. Old version was one of the Nine Cities

Ogohak Chasm—deep place on Mintahoq where criminals are execcuted

Old Tumet'ai Road—road that runs south across White Waste from ancient site of Tumet'ai

Pattern Hall—dwarrow place of maps and charts recorded on stone

Pelippa's Bowl—inn at Kwanitupul

Place of Echoes—sacred spot on Mintahoq

Red Dolphin, The—tavern in Ansis Pellipé

Re Suri'eni—Sithi name for river running through Shisae'ron

Sancellan Aedonitis—palace of Lector and chief place of Aedonite Church

Sancellan Mahistrevis—former Imperial palace, now palace of Nabban's duke

Sancelline Hill—largest hill in Nabban, site of both Sancellans

Sesuad'ra—Stone of Farewell, site of the parting of Sithi and Norn.

Shao Irigú—Sithi name for Summer Gate

Shisae'ron—Sithi name for southwestern realm of Aldheorte forest

Site of Witness—arena in Mezutu'a where Shard stands

Skoggey—Rimmersgard freehold, home of Thane Tonnrud

Sovebek—abandoned town in White Waste, east of St. Skendi's monastery

Sta Mirore—central mountain of Perdruin, also called "Streáwe's Steeple"

Stefflod—river running beside and within Aldheorte's border, joins with the Ymstrecca

Stormspike—mountain home of Norns, "Sturmrspeik" to Rimmersmen, also called "Nakkiga"

Summer Gate—an entrance to Jao é-Tinukai'i, also called "Shao Irigú"

Teligure—grape-growing town in northern Nabban

Tumet'ai—northern Sithi city, buried under ice east of Yiqanuc, one of the Nine Cities

Umstrejha—Thrithings name for Ymstrecca

Urmsheim—dragon-mountain north of White Waste

Utanyeat—earldom in northwestern Erkynland

Venyha Do'sae—The Garden, legendary home of the Zida'ya (Sithi), Hikeda'ya (Norns), and Tinukeda'ya (dwarrows and Niskies)

Vihyuyaq—Qanuc name for Stormspike

Village Grove—Tiamak's home village in Wran

Vinitta—southern island, birthplace of Camaris and Benidrivine House

Warinsten—island off coast of Erkynland, birthplace of King John

Way of the Fountains—scenic spot in city of Nabban

White Way—road along northern edge of Aldheorte Forest, in White Waste

Wulfholt—Guthwulf's freehold in Utanyeat

Yijarjuk—Qanuc name for Urmsheim

Yásira—Sithi meeting-place in Jao é-Tinukai'i

Ymstrecca—west-east river through Erk. and High Thrithings

Zae-y'miritha, Catacombs of—caverns apparently built or modified by dwarrows

CREATURES

Atarin—Camaris' horse

Bukken—Rimmersgard name for diggers; also called "Boghanik" (Qanuc)

Crab-foot—one of Tiamak's pigeons

Diggers—small, manlike subterranean creatures

Ghants—unpleasant, chitinous, seemingly sentient Wran fauna

Giants—large, shaggy, manlike creatures

Hidohebhi—Black Worm, mother of Shuraka and Igjarjuk, slain by Ineluki; also called "Drochnathair" (Hernystiri)

Homefinder—Simon's mare
Honey-lover—one of Tiamak's pigeons
Hunën—Rimmersgard name for giants
Igjarjuk—Ice-worm of Urmsheim
Ink-daub—one of Tiamak's pigeons
Khaerukama'o the Golden—dragon, father of Hidohebhi
Kilpa—manlike marine creatures
Niku'a—Ingen Jegger's lead hound
Qantaqa—Binabik's wolf companion
Red-eye—one of Tiamak's pigeons
Rim—plow-horse
Shurakai—Fire-drake slain beneath Hayholt, whose bones are Dragonbone Chair
So-fast—one of Tiamak's pigeons
Spitfly—small and unpleasant marsh insect
Stormspike Pack—Norn hunting dogs
Vildalix—Deornoth's horse, from Fikolmij
Vinyafod—Josua's horse, from Fikolmij

THINGS

Ballad of Round-Heeled Moirah, The—song of questionable taste sung by Sangfugol and Father Strangyeard
Battle of Huhinka Valley—battle between trolls and Rimmersmen
Battle of the Lakelands—pivotal battle of Thrithings War, fought at Lake Clodu
Boar and Spears—emblem of Guthwulf of Utanyeat
Bright-Nail—sword of Prester John, containing nail from the Tree and finger bone of Saint Eahlstan Fiskerne
Children of Hern—dwarrow name for Hernystiri
Cintis-piece—Nabbanai coin—one hundredth of a gold Imperator
Citril—sour, aromatic root for chewing
Conqueror—dicing game, popular with soldiers
Conqueror Star, The—a book of occult fact, in Nabbanai: "Sa Asdridan Condiquilles"
Crook—star (possibly same as Sithi's "Luyasa's Staff")
Day of Weighing-Out—Aedonite day of final justice and end of the mortal world
Days of Fire—possibly very ancient era of Osten Ard (obscure reference by Geloë)

Du Svardenvyrd—near-mythical prophetical book by Nisses

Eadne Cloud—Aspitis Preves' ship

Elysia Chapel—famous chapel in Saint Sutrin's church in Erchester

En Semblis Aedonitis—famous religious book about the philosophical underpinnings of Aedonite religion and life of Usires

Fifty Families—Nabbanai noble houses

Great Table—King John's assemblage of knights and heroes

House of Year-Dancing—Westerling translation of Jiriki's family name

Hunt-wine—Qanuc liquor (for special occasions, and mostly for women only)

Ice House—Qanuc holy spot, where rituals are performed to insure coming of Spring

Ilenite—a costly, shimmery metal

Indreju—Jiriki's witchwood sword

Kangkang—Qanuc liquor

Kraile—Sithi name for "sunfruits"

Kvalnir—Isgrimnur's sword

Lamp—star (possibly same as Sithi's Reniku)

Leavetaking Stone—Hernystiri song about the Stone of Farewell

Loon, Otter—Wrannamen names for stars

Luyasa's Staff—Sithi name for line of three stars in the sky's northeast quadrant in early Yuven-month

Lutegrass—a long grass

Mansa Connoyis—"prayer of joining": wedding prayer

Mezumiiru's Net—star cluster; to Qanuc: Sedda's Blanket

Minneyar—iron sword of King Fingil, inherited through line of Elvrit

Minog—edible plant with wide leaves, native to Wran

Mist Lamp—a Witness from Tumet' ai

Mockfoil—a flowering herb

Naidel—Josua's sword

Navigator's Children—Tinukeda'ya's name for themselves

Oinduth—Hern's black spear

Pillar and Tree—emblem of Mother Church

Pool—apparently the Witness in old Asu'a

Quickweed—a spice

Reniku, the Summer-Lantern—Sithi name for star that signals ending of summer

Rhynn's Cauldron—Hernystiri battle-summoner

Rite of Quickening—Qanuc ritual performed at Ice House to insure coming of Spring

River-apple—marsh fruit

Sand-palm—marsh tree

Shard—the Witness in Mezutu'a

Shent—Sithi game, reportedly brought from Venyha Do'sae

Silverwood—a wood favored by Sithi builders

Singing Harp—the Witness in Nakkiga, in Great Well

Six Songs of Respectful Request—a Sithi ritual

Sorrow—sword of iron and witchwood smithied by Ineluki, gift to Elias. To Sithi: "Jingizu"

Sotfengsel—Elvrit's famous ship, buried at Skipphavven

Speakfire—the Witness in Hikehikayo

Starblooms—small white flowers

Thorn—star-sword of Camaris

Ti-tuno—famed Sithi horn

Traveler's Reward—popular brand of ale

Tree—the Execution Tree, on which Usires was hung upside down before temple of Yuvenis in Nabban, now sacred symbol of Aedonite religion

Wind Festival—Wrannaman celebration

Winter Lastday—day in Yiqanuc when Rite of Quickening is performed

Yellowroot—a common herb used for tea in Wran (and elsewhere in south)

Knuckle Bones—Binabik's auguring tools. Patterns include:

 Wingless Bird

 Fish-Spear

 The Shadowed Path

 Torch at the Cave-Mouth

 Balking Ram

 Clouds in the Pass

 The Black Crevice

 Unwrapped Dart

 Circle of Stones

Holidays

 Feyever 2—Candlemansa

 Marris 25—Elysiamansa

 Avrel 1—All Fool's Day

 Avrel 30—Stoning Night

 Maia 1—Belthainn Day

 Yuven 23—Midsummer's Eve

 Tiyagar 15—Saint Sutrin's Day

 Anitul 1—Hlafmansa

 Septander 29—Saint Granis' Day

 Octander 30—Harrows Eve

 Novander 1—Soul's Day

 Decander 21—Saint Tunath's Day

 Decander 24—Aedonmansa

Months

Jonever, Feyever, Marris, Avrel, Maia, Yuven, Tiyagar, Anitul, Septander, Octander, Novander, Decander

Days of the Week

Sunday, Moonday, Tiasday, Udunsday, Drorsday, Frayday, Satrinsday

A GUIDE TO PRONUNCIATION

ERKYNLANDISH

Erkynlandish names are divided into two types, Old Erkynlandish (O.E.) and Warinstenner. Those names which are based on types from Prester John's native island of Warinsten (mostly the names of castle servants or John's immediate family) have been represented as variants on Biblical names (Elias—Elijah, Ebekah—Rebecca, etc.) Old Erkynlandish names should be pronounced like modern English, except as follows:

a—always *ah,* as in "father"
ae—*ay* of "say"
c—k as in "keen"
e—*ai* as in "air," except at the end of names, when it is also sounded, but with an *eh* or *uh* sound, i.e., Hruse— "Rooz-uh"
ea—sounds as *a* in "mark," except at beginning of word or name, where it has the same value as *ae*
g—always hard *g,* as in "glad"
h—hard *h* of "help"
i—short *i* of "in"
j—hard *j* of "jaw"
o—long but soft *o,* as in "orb"
u—*oo* sound of "wood," never *yoo* as in "music"

HERNYSTIRI

The Hernystiri names and words can be pronounced in largely the same way as the O.E., with a few exceptions:

th—always the *th* in "other," never as in "thing"
ch—a guttural, as in Scottish "loch"
y—pronounce *yr* like "beer," *ye* like "spy"
h—unvoiced except at beginning of word or after *t* or *c*
e—*ay* as in "ray"
ll—same as single *l*: Lluth—Luth

RIMMERSPAKK

Names and words in Rimmerspakk differ from O.E. pronunciation in the following:

j—pronounced *y*: Jarnauga—Yarnauga; Hjeldin—Hyeldin (*H* nearly silent here)
ei—long *i* as in "crime"
ë—*ee*, as in "sweet"
ö—*oo*, as in "coop"
au—*ow*, as in "cow"

NABBANAI

The Nabbanai language holds basically to the rules of a romance language, i.e., the vowels are pronounced "ah-eh-ih-oh-ooh," the consonants are all sounded, etc. There are some exceptions.

i—most names take emphasis on second to last syllable: Ben-i-GAR-is. When this syllable has an *i*, it is sounded long (Ardrivis: Ar-DRY-vis) unless it comes before a double consonant (Antippa: An-TIHP-pa)
e—at end of name, *es* is sounded long: Gelles—Gel-leez
y—is pronounced as a long *i*, as in "mild"

QANUC

Troll-language is considerably different than the other human languages. There are three hard "k" sounds, signified by: *c, q,* and *k*. The only difference intelligible to most non-Qanuc is a slight clucking sound on the *q,* but it is not to be encouraged in beginners. For our purposes, all three will sound with the *k* of "keep." Also, the Qanuc *u* is pronounced *uh,* as in "bug." Other interpretations are up to the reader, but he or she will not go far wrong pronouncing phonetically.

SITHI

Even more than the language of Yiqanuc, the language of the Zida'ya is virtually unpronounceable by untrained tongues, and so is easiest rendered phonetically, since the chance of any of us being judged by experts is slight (but not nonexistent, as Binabik learned). These rules may be applied, however.

i—when the first vowel, pronounced *ih,* as in "clip." When later in word, especially at end, pronounced *ee,* as in "fleet": Jiriki—Jih-REE-kee

ai—pronounced like long *i,* as in "time"

' (apostrophe)—represents a clicking sound, and should not be voiced by mortal readers.

EXCEPTIONAL NAMES

Geloë—Her origins are unknown, and so is the source of her name. It is pronounced "Juh-LO-ee" or "Juh-LOY." Both are correct.

Ingen Jegger—He is a Black Rimmersman, and the "J" in Jegger is sounded, just as in "jump."

Miriamele—Although born in the Erkynlandish court, hers is a Nabbanai name that developed a strange pronunciation—perhaps due to some family influence or confusion of her dual heritage—and sounds as "Mih-ree-uh-MEL."

Vorzheva—A Thrithings-woman, her name is pronounced "Vor-SHAY-va," with the *zh* sounding harshly, like the Hungarian *zs.*

WORDS AND PHRASES

HERNYSTIRI

Domhaini—"dwarrows"
Goirach—"mad" or "wild"

Isgbahta—"fishing boat"
Sithi—"Peaceful Ones"

NABBANAI

Duos Onenpondensis, Feata Vorum Lexeran!—"God All-Powerful, let this be Your law!"
Duos wulstei—"God willing"
En Semblis Aedonitis—"In the likeness of the Aedon"
Escritor—"Writer": one of a group of advisors to lector
Lector—"Speaker": head of Church
Sa Asdridan Condiquilles—"The Conqueror Star"
Veir Maynis—"Great Green," the ocean

PERDRUINESE

Avi stetto—"I have a knife."
Ohé, vo stetto—"Yes, he has a knife."

QANUC

Aia—"back" (Hinik Aia = get back)
Boghanik—"diggers" (Bukken)
Chash—"true" or "correct"
Chok—"run"
Crookhok—"Rimmersman"
Croohokuq—plural of Croohok—"Rimmersmen"
Guyop—"Thank you"
Hinik—"go" or "get away"
Mosoq—"find"
Muqang—"enough"
Nihut—"attack"
Ninit—"come"
Sosa—"come" (stronger than "Ninit")
Ummu—"now"
Utku—"lowlanders"

RIMMERSPAKK

Dverning—"dwarrow"
Gjal es, künden!—roughly "Leave it alone, children!"
Haja—"yes"
Halad, künde!—"Stop, child!"
Kundë-mannë—"man-child"

Rimmersmannë—"Rimmersman"
Vaer—"beware"
Vjer sommen marroven—"We are friends"

SITHI (AND NORN)

Ai, Nakkiga, o'do 'tke stazho—(Norn) "Ah, Nakkiga, I've failed you"
Asu'a—"Looking eastward"
Hiyanha—"pilgrimage boats"
Hikeda'ya—"Children of Cloud": Norns
Hikeda'yei—second-person plural of "Hikeda'ya"—"You Norns!"
Hikka—"Bearer"
Isi-isi'ye-a Sudhoda'ya—"It is indeed a mortal"
J'asu pra-peroihin!—"shame of my house!"
Ras—term of respect: "sir" or "noble sir"
Ruakha—"dying"
S'hue—roughly "lord"
Ske'i—"stop"
Staja Ame—"White Arrow"
Sudhoda'ya—"Sunset-children": Mortals
Venyha s'anh!—"By the Garden!"
Yinva—(Norn) "come"
Zida'ya—"Children of Dawn": Sithi